BLOOD ON
THE SHAMROCK

To Michael —
For all you do keeping
the spirit of Ireland
alive in the heart of
so many. Your stories are
an inspiration.
Cathal Liam.

Also by Cathal Liam

Consumed In Freedom's Flame:
A Novel of Ireland's Struggle for Freedom 1916–1921

Forever Green: Ireland Now & Again

BLOOD ON
THE SHAMROCK

A Novel of Ireland's Civil War 1916–1921

CATHAL LIAM

St. Pádraic Press
Cincinnati, Ohio

Though inspired by the lives of historical figures and by the actual events surrounding Ireland's Civil War, 1921-1924, this dramatic reconstruction is a work of fiction. The invented characters are meant to complement the historical ones. The story's narrative is intended to portray the thoughts, feelings and behaviours of those who lived during that conflict.

Seán Keating's painting, *Men of the West* (copyright © 1921), is used with the permission of the Crawford Municipal Art Gallery, Cork City, Ireland & its curator Peter Murray. Selected verses from the poem "September Song" by William Boniface (copyright © 2001) are used with his approval. Lyrics to "Mt. Joy Prison" (copyright ©1995) by Rory Makem/Red Biddy Records are used with Mr. Makem's permission. ("Mt. Joy Prison" appeared on a 1995 CD entitled "On the Rocks" by The Makem Brothers.) Lyrics to "Dark Horse On The Wind" (copyright © c. 1966) by Liam Weldon (1933-1995)/Mulligan Records are used with his wife Nellie Weldon's permission. ("Dark Horse on the Wind" appeared on a 1999 CD entitled "Dark Horse on the Wind" by Liam Weldon.)

Please note: A mea culpa for any missing síneadh fada notations that were inadvertently omitted during manuscript preparation. I also share the blame for any 'typos' with the 'little people.' The text was free of those bloody annoyances when it went to press.

Printed in the United States of America

Cover and text design and production by Bookwrights
Front cover: *Men of the West* by Seán Keating (1889-1977)
Back cover: Michael Collins memorial statue, Clonakilty, Ireland (dedicated 22 August 2002 & photograph by Cathal Liam)

First American Edition, June, 2006
10 9 8 7 6 5 4 3 2 1

International Standard Book Number: 0-9704155-2-4
Library of Congress Card Number: 2002109623

Published by
St. Pádraic Press
P.O. Box 43351
Cincinnati, Ohio 45243-0351

For further inquiries: www.cathalliam.com

In remembrance of Turlough Breathnach, a Pearsean friend;
Dick Early, a son of Ireland; & Tim Richardson, a Tipperary
& Galway gentleman,

and dedicated to

Ireland, united and free…

lest we forget.

CONTENTS

MAP OF IRELAND

(Circa 1921–1923)

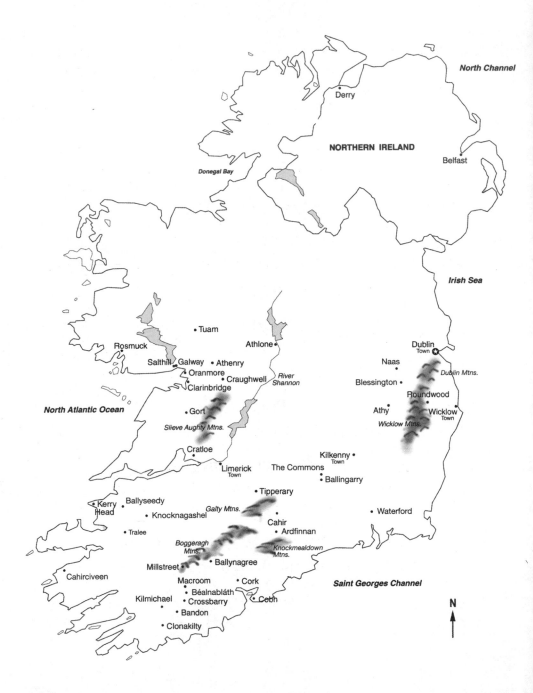

A WORD TO THE READER

BLOOD ON THE SHAMROCK resumes the chronicle of Aran Roe O'Neill, a fictional Irishman, and his determined comrades, who continue Ireland's ongoing struggle for independence and self-government. This time, however, the foe is not so much England as it is their fellow Irish.

The tragedy of Easter, 1916 lies behind them. Spurred on by the euphoria born of London's willingness to negotiate a settlement ending the War of Independence (1919–1921), Ireland finally senses it stands on the brink of triumph: autonomy from British rule. But almost overnight, the green hills of Éireann turn red again—blood red—as the bitter dregs of Anglo-Irish politics erupt into unholy Civil War, the repercussions of which are destined to sully the dream of Irish unity for years to come.

Alas, under such an ominous cloud, this saga rejoins Aran, Michael Collins, Gabriel and Sarah Anne McCracken, Richard 'Shadow' Doyle, Liam Mellowes and others. Together, they endeavour to sort out the mountainous obstacles confronting Ireland: the fate of a nation and its people hangs in the balance.

Like its predecessor, CONSUMED IN FREEDOM'S FLAME, this story, a dramatic reconstruction of the embryonic emergence of Saorstát Éireann, blends historical fact and fanciful fiction told from an Irish point of view. Once more, it was my desire to honestly depict the actual events and the human drama overshadowing Ireland after its War-of-Independence days, while I again portray Britain's long and often unwelcome intrusion into Irish life.

Tragically, however, the vitriolic particulars of this uncivilised time result in a poisonous shadow being cast over the Emerald Isle: one not easily forgotten or expunged. Again, Ireland is forced to sacrifice its boldest and best for the cause of liberty.

❧

In my mind the 1916 Easter Rebellion was a watershed occurrence. It was Ireland's single most historically significant and dramatically important event of the 20th century. Though initially seen as a disastrous defeat for the cause of liberty, it soon sparked a national drive for autonomy. Stubbornly, the Irish people renew their centuries-old fight for freedom from colonial oppression. But tragically, the Irish Civil War, which followed the War of Independence by only a few months, quickly becomes Ireland's most socially destructive yet politically momentous episode of the past one hundred years.

Over the last eleven years, my every day, at least in part, has been devoted to thinking, reading, talking or writing about the men and women of who lived and died during these revolutionary times, 1916–1923. Many of those individuals were historical figures who played some role in the struggle of casting aside the yoke of its foreign ruler while they faced down the long road toward self-government. But if you read *Consumed In Freedom's Flame: A Novel of Ireland's Struggle for Freedom 1916-1921*, you know that some of the people I write about are fictional. They're figments of my imagination who possess some of the qualities and characteristics attributed to real Irishmen and women living three or four generations ago. To me, these invented characters represent a composite of what the everyday citizen might have thought, felt or experienced eight or nine decades ago. As you might expect, some of these imaginary figures came to life, at least in my mind and maybe in yours. I think about Aran, Brigid, Gay and Shadow as if they were as real as Michael Collins, Éamon de Valera or Lloyd George. If this makes me crazy, so be it. Fantasy can sometimes be a lovely resting place when the troubles of the world seem too much to bear.

In many ways, *Consumed In Freedom's Flame* was an easier book to write than *Blood On The Shamrock*. The dividing line between the characters was sharper and more easily defined. From an Irish point of view, the 'good guys and the bad guys' were readily identifiable. It was Patrick Pearse, Michael Collins and Aran Roe O'Neill versus the British government and its army, the Black and Tans and Major George Henry Hawkins. In this new novel, the line separating the protagonists and the antagonists is suddenly blurred and distorted. Few of the characters were all 'anything.' Men who'd once been close friends and comrades now became reluctant adversaries. Choices that had once been easily decided suddenly became difficult and heart-wrenching. Human emotions dispelled the cool logic of former days.

Another major difference between the two books is the level of adventure and excitement. *Consumed...* opened with the 1916 Easter Rebellion. Clashes continued almost non-stop until they finally ended with the signing of the Truce between Ireland and Britain. Most readers seemed to enjoy the action and the possibility of good overcoming evil.

This sequel is different in many ways. With the hostilities on hold, at least temporarily, the action shifts from a war of bullets to a war of words. Compromise and conciliation become the issue. Thus, from 11 July 1921 to 27 June 1922, the times change. The action is marked by political confrontations rather than military ones. This isn't to say there aren't several physical encounters to feed the reader's interest and pique his/her curiosity.

Eventually, bargaining between the Irish pro- and anti-Treaty sides collapses with internecine warfare the violent and deadly outcome. Aran Roe O'Neill and his friends are thrown back into the thick of it. This volatile shifting from military conflict to political disagreement and back to armed confrontation reflects the times and my desire to portray them accurately.

For generation after generation, Ireland was reluctant to talk about and confront the issues that grew out of the Civil War. Those times and events were so contentious, heart-breaking and embittering that it was thought better to ignore them than relive them. History books often set aside those events, not wanting to probe or re-examine them in depth. Many schools concluded their teaching of Irish history with the study of Irish War of Independence, choosing to go no further. The subject of the Treaty and the ensuing Civil War was not mentioned or discussed in polite circles.

Unfortunately, the issues and events surrounding this period remained, festering just below the surface. Part of the responsibility for this unwillingness to deal with the acidic residue of these times could be ascribed to geography, population and the continued existence of a partitioned country. Ireland is a diminutive land mass with a small, often insular population. Thus, the conflicts created by the December, 1921 Anglo-Irish agreement and the ensuing national mêlée have tended to become magnified in the eyes of many. But the inability to resolve the issue of Northern Ireland, to see partition ended, and to achieve nationwide unity remains a constant reminder to all of the failures of past and present politicians, both Irish and English. That acrimony remains palpable today.

The former physician and Minister for Health (1948–1951) Dr. Noel Browne once stated, "...As a young political in Leinster House [Dáil Éireann, 1948], I recall my shock at the white-hot hate with which that terrible episode [the Irish Civil War] had marked their lives. The trigger words were '77', 'Ballyseedy', 'Dick and Joe' [Richard Barrett & Joseph McKelvey], and above all 'the Treaty' and 'damn good bargain'. The raised tiers of the Dáil chamber would become filled with shouting, gesticulating, clamouring, suddenly angry men."[1]

Even in 2006, the Irish Civil War is not a subject to be taken lightly. Besides its many subtle twists and turns, its history is convoluted, filled with strong emotional overtones. That may be why so many historical fiction writers have shied away from it. With the exception of Seán O'Casey (1924), Liam O'Flaherty (1925), Walter Macken (1966), David Martin (1981), Thomas Flanagan (1994), Roddy Doyle (1999) and Morgan Llywelyn (2001), I know of no other authors who've chosen to tackle the topic.

I also note that the list of historians who've dealt with the subject is not as extensive as might be imagined. Despite the clinical overtones of some history books, human emotion always seems to find its way onto those pages devoted to the study of the Irish Civil War.

One other dilemma authors of historical fiction face is how much of their writing should be devoted to fact and how much

1. Helen Litton. *The Irish Civil War: An Illustrated History.* Dublin: Wolfhound Press, Ltd., 1995, 132, 134.

to fancy. Some choose to call it historical fact-sion. It's an issue for me as well. But unlike some, I'm constantly trying to decide what history to leave out rather than what to include. I sometimes wonder if I've selected the right medium to express my love for Ireland, its people and history. I'm always afraid my fondness for historical detail will drown out the human interplay among my characters, real or imagined.

People often ask me how much of my writing is fact and how much of it is fiction. It's hard to be exact, but I usually answer about two-thirds fact to one-third fiction. You, the reader, however, will have to decide for yourself. I only hope my balance is the right one for you.

Finally, my purpose in writing *Blood On The Shamrock* is much the same as it was for the first volume. History to me is meant to inspire the living and to honour the dead. I've never intended it to be an instrument for reopening old wounds or prolonging any sense of hatred or bitterness. It's simply an attempt to explore another page or two of Irish history; to open the door of understanding a crack; and to whet the reader's appetite, hoping further inquiry and exploration might ensue.

Thank you for joining me on this road of discovery.

Cathal Liam
Cincinnati, Ohio
Spring, 2006

ACKNOWLEDGEMENTS

This book wouldn't have seen the light of day if it weren't for the generosity of many. My thanks pale in comparison to the kindness and assistance others have shown me, helping give this book substance and life. Without your support, the hours I've spent hunched over the keyboard would've been more aimless than they were. To each of you I owe a debt of gratitude.

To William Boniface – for your kindness in permitting me to use several verses from your poignant poem *September Song*…

To Gabriel Cooley – for your camaraderie & willingness to share a laugh, a pint and a song…

To Jim Cooney – for your friendship & love of books, especially Irish ones…

To Kevin Donleavy – for your comradeship, never-ending devotion to editing detail & the cause of Ireland…

To John Fitzgerald – for your loyalty & unabashed enthusiasm for distributing my books…

To Tony Gee – for your loyalty & keen interest in reading the manuscript…

To Dr. Ray Hebert – for your support of my writing & championing Ireland's cause…

To Rory Makem & the Makem Brothers – for your music, your singing & especially for your haunting words to the song *Mt. Joy Prison*…

To Father Francis Miller – for your friendship & thoughtful counsel…

To Peter Murray – for graciously giving me permission to use Seán Keating's painting *Men of the South* on the book's cover…

To Ray O'Hanlon – for your kindness & weekly wealth of informative reporting in *The Irish Echo*…

To May & Tom Richardson – for your generous gifts of Irish hospitality, friendship & a willingness to answer all my pesky queries…

To Father Patrick Twohig – for your writing, your historical curiosity & devotion to God and country…

To Nellie Weldon – for giving me permission to use Liam's words from his powerful song *Dark Horse On The Wind*...

To Dr. Tim White – for your kindness, confidence & academic brilliance...

To Tim Pat Coogan, T. Ryle Dwyer, Michael Hopkinson, Robert Kee, James Mackay & Frank Pakenham – for your extensive writings & exhaustive study of 20th-century Irish history...

To all the B&B owners, publicans & other passers-by I've encountered along the way – for your willingness to put up with my incessant curiosity...

To the many others who've helped me with this project over the past five years. To you I owe my thanks and heartfelt gratitude...

...and to two inspiring friends...John 'the Walker' Melton – who puts in his six miles every day regardless of weather & keeps the ties to the past alive & Jim 'Lamar' Wendell – whose determination to greet each day with a smile & a golf club in his hands sets the standard for others to attain...

❈

To Marcia Fairbanks: an editor supreme. She's also a friend at the other end of the telephone or computer connection who works harder than I do, sculpturing the maze of words I write into something more intelligible. My thanks don't do your efforts justice. www.carefulreader.com

To Mayapriya Long: an artist who turns words, sentences and paragraphs into pages and book covers for people to read, to learn from and to enjoy. Your artful mastery of book design and construction knows no limits. My thanks for all you do. www.bookwrights.com

To my wife, Mary Ann: my loving thanks especially to you for putting up with all my madness, my annoying ways, my stacks of books and papers and my irritability. I know without you, my life would be an empty void.

"The dust of some in Irish earth,
Among their own they rest.
And the same land that gave them birth,
Has caught them to her breast.

And we will pray that from their clay,
Full many a race may start.
Of true men, like you, men,
To act as brave a part."

1798 Memorial
Ballina, Co. Mayo
(Unveiled by Maud Gonne McBride, 1899)

❧

"They rose in dark and evil days
To right their native land;
They kindled here a living blaze
That nothing shall withstand.

Alas! That might can vanquish right
They fell and passed away;
But true men, like you men,
Are plenty here today."

To the memory of the men of 1798
Liberty Square, Thurles, Co. Tipperary

CAST OF CHARACTERS

(in order of appearance by chapter)

HISTORICAL

Front Cover:

Seán Keating (1889–1977) – artist; born in Limerick; studied drawing & art in Limerick, Dublin & London; taught at the Metropolitan School of Art, Dublin; through his art he documented Ireland's struggle for independence (front cover: *Men of the West*)[2], the beauty & simplicity of rural life in the Aran Islands, Ireland's 20th-century industrial emergence with the building of the Shannon Scheme hydroelectric plant at Ardnacrusha, Co. Clare, 1926–1929 & his prizewinning work, *The Race of the Gael* (1939); president, Royal Hibernian Academy of Art, 1949–1962

Prologue:
-1-

General Michael James Collins [Mick; the Big Fellow; the Corkman; Míceal; the Chairman] (1890–1922) – Irish revolutionary; Irish military & political leader; staff officer (captain) and aide-de-camp to Joseph Mary Plunkett, General Post Office, Easter Week, 1916; arrested by British authorities & interned, Wales, 1916; released, December, 1916; Secretary, Irish National Aid & Volunteers' Dependents' Fund, 1917; Head-Centre, Irish Republican Brotherhood (IRB), 1917-; Director of Organisation & Director of Intelligence, Irish Volunteers, 1917-; Sinn Féin Member of Parliament (MP), 1918-; Sinn Féin Teachta Dála (TD) & Dáil Minister of Finance, 1919-; Acting Dáil President, 1920;

---

2. *Men of the South*, painted in 1921, depicts members of a North Cork IRA Battalion flying column waiting to ambush a passing British military vehicle. Following the end of the Anglo-Irish War of Independence, 11 July 1921, Keating had members of the battalion visit his Dublin studio where he sketched & photographed them in preparation for completing this painting.

Vice-Chairman, Irish Delegation, Anglo-Irish Peace Talks, 1921; signatory, Anglo-Irish Treaty, 1921; Chairman of Ireland's Provisional Government (PG), 1922; Commander-in-Chief, National Army, 1922; at 31 yrs. shot & killed in an ambush, 22 August 1922; buried, Glasnevin Cemetery, Dublin

M. B. Corry – National Army; Collins's military convoy motor car driver, Béalnabláth, 1922

Major-General Emmet Dalton (1898–1978) – National Army; former major in British Army during First War; member of Collins's contingent, Anglo-Irish Treaty talks, London, 1921; Commandant, Eastern Command, National Army, 1922-; Commander, Cork military area, 1922-; member, Collins's military convoy, Béalnabláth, 1922

Lieutenant John Joseph Smith – National Army; military convoy motorcycle scout, Béalnabláth, 1922

Seán O'Connell – National Army; member of Collins's military convoy, Béalnabláth, 1922

Commandant-General Liam Mellows [Lee] (1895–1922) – Irish revolutionary; member, Irish Republican Brotherhood; Irish Volunteer (IV) organiser in west of Ireland; mobilised c.1,000 IVs, Co. Galway, Easter Week, 1916; avoided arrest & fled to USA, 1916; recognised leader of '1916 Exiles' in USA, 1916–1921; substitute member, Irish delegation, Paris Peace Conference, 1919; assisted Éamon de Valera on tour of USA, 1919–1920; returned to Ireland, 1921; Irish Republican Army (IRA) Director of Purchases, 1921; IRA Quartermaster General, 1921–1922 (buried, Glasnevin Cemetery, Dublin)

John 'Jock' McPeak – National Army; member of military convoy & Slieve na mBán machine gunner, Béalnabláth, 1922

Patrick Henry Pearse [Pat] (1879–1916) – Irish revolutionary; educational innovator; Gaelic scholar, writer & poet; editor, Gaelic newspaper, *An Claidbeamb Soluis*; headmaster, St. Enda's school, Ranelagh & Rathfarnham, Dublin, 1908–1916; member, IRB; member, IRB Supreme Council & its secret Military Council, 1914–1916; Ireland's (Provisional Government) first president, 1916; Commander-in-Chief, Irish forces, 1916; co-author & signatory, Proclamation of the Irish Republic, 1916; at 36 yrs., arrested & court-martialled by British authorities; executed, 3 May 1916; buried, Arbour Hill Cemetery, Dublin

Kevin Barry – medical student; member, IRA; executed by British authorities, 1 November 1920

James Connolly (1868–1916) – Irish revolutionary, socialist; labour leader; organiser, Irish Citizen Army, 1913; member, IRB Military Council, 1916; co-author & signatory, Proclamation of the Irish Republic, 1916; Commandant-General, Dublin Brigade, Easter Rebellion, 1916; at 47 yrs., arrested & court-martialled by British authorities; executed, 12 May 1916; buried, Arbour Hill Cemetery, Dublin

Michael O'Rahilly ['The O'Rahilly'] (1875–1916) – Irish nationalist patriot; born Michael Joseph Rahilly; he changed his name to 'The O'Rahilly' in 1911 (the title 'The' signified his leadership as head of the clan O'Rahilly & the added 'O' renounced the earlier Anglicization of the family name); founder-member, Irish Volunteers, 1913; killed in action leading an IRA squad out of General Post Office, Easter Friday evening, 1916

-2-

Father Timothy Murphy – priest & curate living in a presbytery, Cloughduv, West Cork, 1922-

Liam Deasy – member, Irish Volunteers, 1917-; adjutant, West Cork Brigade, 1919–1921; commandant-general of anti-Treaty forces, West Cork; ordered the organising of an ambush of Collins's military convoy, Béalnabláth, 22 August 1922

Colonial Secretary Winston Churchill [the Butcher of Gallipoli] (1874–1965) – British First Lord of the Admiralty, 1911–1916; Minister of Munitions, 1917–1919; Secretary of State for War & Secretary of State of Air, 1919–1921; Secretary of State for the Colonies, 1921–1922; member, British team, Anglo-Irish Peace Talks, London, 1921; signatory, Anglo-Irish Peace Treaty, 1921 (later British prime minister, 1940–1945 & 1951–1955)

William Cosgrave [Bill] (1880–1965) – GPO veteran, Easter Week, 1916; Sinn Féin MP, 1917-; TD & Minister for Local

Government, Dáil Éireann, 1919-; Minister for Local Government, Dáil & PG, 1922; acting chairman of Provisional Government, 1922-

Florrie O'Donoghue – participated in Easter-Week Rebellion, Co. Cork, 1916; adjutant & intelligence officer, Cork #1 Brigade; took active role in War of Independence, 1919–1921; division adjutant, 1st Southern Division, 1921; member of Munster IRB Supreme Council; declared his neutrality & took active role in trying to prevent Civil War, 1922-

Arthur Griffith [Art] (1871–1922) – Irish nationalist & political leader; newspaper editor; founder of Sinn Féin political party, 1905; Sinn Féin PM, 1918-; TD & Minister for Foreign Affairs, Dáil Éireann, 1919–1921; Irish leader, Anglo-Irish Peace Talks, London, 1921; signatory, Anglo-Irish Treaty, 1921; elected president, Dáil Éireann, 1922; at 51 yrs., died suddenly of a cerebral haemorrhage on 12 August 1922 & buried, Glasnevin Cemetery, Dublin

Richard Mulcahy [Dick] (1886–1971) – Vice-Commandant, 5th Irish Volunteer Battalion, Dublin Brigade, Easter Week, 1916; arrested & interned, Frongoch, Wales, 1916–1917; IRA Chief of Staff, 1917–1922; TD, Dáil Éireann, 1919-; Minister for Defence, Dáil Éireann, 1922-

J. J. 'Ginger' O'Connell – Commandant, Irish Volunteers, 1913-; IRA Director of Training, 1920–1921; Assistant Chief of Staff, 1921–1922; Commandant, the Curragh, 1922-

Seán Mac Eoin [the Blacksmith of Ballinalee] – battalion commandant, IRA, 1919-; TD, Dáil Éireann, 1919-; brigade vice-commandant, IRA, 1921-; Commandant, Western Command, 1922- (War of Independence hero & close friend of Michael Collins)

Kitty Kiernan (1892–1945) – family owned hotel & other retail businesses in Granard, Co. Longford; love interest & fiancée (9 October 1921) of Michael Collins

Part I:

-3-

Prime Minister David Lloyd George [the Welshman; the Welsh Wizard] (1863–1945) – British politician; British Prime Minister (liberal), 1916–1922 of its coalition government; Britain's representative, Versailles Peace Conference, 1919; leader, British team, Anglo-Irish Peace Talks, London, 1921; signatory, Anglo-Irish Peace Treaty, 1921

Major John 'Foxie Jack' MacBride (1865–1916) – veteran of 2nd Boar War campaign, 1899–1902; married Maude Gonne, 1903; officer, 2nd Battalion, Irish Volunteers, Dublin Brigade, stationed at Jacob's Biscuit Factory during Easter Week, 1916; arrested & court-martialled by British authorities; executed, 5 May 1916; buried, Arbour Hill Cemetery, Dublin (son, Seán Mc-Bride: Irish revolutionary, politician, lawyer & founder-member, Amnesty International, 1961- & won Nobel Peace Prize, 1974)

Éamon de Valera [Dev; the President; the Chief; the Long Fellow; the 'Long Hoor'] (1882–1975) – Irish Republican, politician; teacher, 1904-; member, Gaelic League, 1908-; member & officer, IV, 1913-, Commandant, 3rd Irish Volunteer Battalion, Dublin Brigade, Easter Week, 1916; arrested, court-martialled & sentenced to death, May, 1916; sentence commuted to life imprisonment, 1916; released from British prison under general amnesty, June, 1917; elected Sinn Féin PM, 1917; chosen Sinn Féin & Irish Volunteers presidents, 1917; rearrested by British authorities, 1918; escaped Lincoln Prison, 1919; travelled to USA promoting Dáil loan & recognition of Irish Republic, 1919-1920; elected TD, Dáil Éireann, 1919-; returned to Ireland, December, 1920; Chairman, Irish Truce negotiations, July, 1921; elected President, Irish Republic, August, 1921; elected Ireland's political leader, 1932–1948, 1951–1954, 1957–1959; elected Ireland's 3rd president, 1959–1973; at 92 yrs., died in his bed on 29 August 1975 & buried, Glasnevin Cemetery, Dublin

Austin Stack – doctrinaire Republican; member, IRB, 1908-; commandant, Irish Volunteers, 1916; IRA Deputy Chief of

Staff, 1917-; Sinn Féin MP, 1918-; TD, Dáil Éireann, 1919; Dáil Executive & Minister for Home Affairs, 1919-

Robert Childers Barton (1881–1975) – Sinn Féin MP, 1918-; member, Dáil Executive & Minister for Economic Affairs, 1921-; member, Irish Treaty delegation, London, 1921; signatory, Anglo-Irish Treaty, 1921 (Erskine Childers cousin)

Erskine Childers – doctrinaire Republican; sailed his yacht *Asgard* into Howth Harbour (Dublin) in July, 1914 with rifles purchased from Germany to assist arming the Irish Volunteers; elected, Sinn Féin TD, Dáil Éireann, 1921; chief secretary to Irish delegation, Anglo-Irish Peace Talks, London, 1921; Minister for Propaganda (acting), anti-Treaty, 1922 (he was a cousin of Robert Barton & in 1973, his son, also named Erskine, became Ireland's 4th President, succeeding Éamon de Valera)

(Count) George Noble Plunkett – (Count – Papal honour); Sinn Féin MP, 1917; father of Joseph Mary, George & Jack Plunkett: all Easter, 1916 participants

-4-

Tom Cullen [Cú; the Wicklow man] – principal assistant in Michael Collins's Intelligence Section; worked closely with Liam Tobin, Frank Thornton & Ben Barrett, 1919; frequently served as Collins's driver & bodyguard after War of Independence, 1921-

Liam Tobin – Deputy Director of Michael Collins's intelligence network headquartered at #5 Crow Street, Dublin, 1919; a frequent Collins bodyguard, 1921-

Frank Thornton – member of Michael Collins's intelligence network, 1919-; a frequent Collins bodyguard, 1921-

Dan Breen – Irish revolutionary & politician; IRA officer from Co. Tipperary; helped lead Soloheadbeg (Co. Tipperary) ambush on 19 January 1919 that unofficially marked the beginning of the War of Independence; took part in the Knocklong rail station ambush that freed Seán Hogan, 1919; saw frequent action & wounded several times, 1919–1921; Sinn Féin TD, Dáil Éireann, 1919-

Seán Treacy – Irish revolutionary; IRA officer from Co. Tipperary; participant in Soloheadbeg ambush, 21 January 1919; took part in the Knocklong rail station ambush that freed Seán Hogan, 1919; saw frequent action & was arrested, imprisoned & wounded during period 1916–1920; killed in action in Talbot Street, Dublin, 14 October 1920

William Smith O'Brien (1803–1864) – Irish revolutionary, politician & Young Islander; served as Irish MP, 1825–1848; though a Protestant & pro-unionist, he supported Catholic emancipation; later sided with Daniel O'Connell's anti-union Repeal Association, 1843–1846; disillusioned with O'Connell's anti-violence stance, he joined the Young Islanders, 1846; led hapless revolt in Ballingarry, Co. Tipperary, July, 1948; arrested, tried & sentenced to death but conviction commuted to penal servitude, 1848; served five years in Van Diemen's Land (Tasmania), 1849–1854; eventually pardon & returned to Ireland in 1856 but abandoned the political life

Mrs. Margaret McCormack – Widow & mother of seven children whose house & diminutive plot of land (cabbage patch) became the innocent centre of an ill-conceived Rebellion between the Young Islanders & Irish Constabulary, 29 July 1848

Thomas Francis Meagher (1823–1867) – Irish revolutionary & soldier; supported O'Connell's anti-union Repeal Association, 1843–1846; grew to favour physical-force tactics to achieve Irish 'home rule' & broke with O'Connell, earning for himself the nickname of 'Meagher of the Sword;' 1846; founder-member, Young Islanders, 1846; travelled to France to study revolutionary events, 1848; returned to Ireland with 'new' Irish flag modelled after the French tri-colour, 1848; took part in the Rebellion of 1848, Ballingarry, Ireland; arrested, tried but death sentence commuted to penal servitude in Van Diemen's Land, 1848–1852; escaped & fled to America, 1852-; became American citizen, organised Irish Brigade & fought with the Union Army in the Civil War, 1861–1965; became governor of Montana territory, 1865–1867

-5-

Dr. Edward Fannin – member of the Royal Army Medical Corps stationed in Malta for most of First War; had house in Dublin on Rutland Square

Tom Clarke (1858–1916) – Irish revolutionary; a Fenian & sometimes referred to as the 'Father of the 1916 Revolution' at 59 years of age; member, IRB; member IRB Supreme Council & its secret Military Council; first signatory of the Proclamation of the Irish Republic, 1916; member, General Headquarters (GHQ), Dublin Brigade, in General Post Office (GPO) during Easter Week, 1916; arrested & court-martialled by British authorities; executed, 3 May 1916; buried, Arbour Hill Cemetery, Dublin (married to Kathleen Clarke)

Seán MacDiarmada (1883–1916) – Irish revolutionary; member, Gaelic League, c. 1902-; organiser, Dungannon Clubs, 1905-; member, Belfast IRB, 1906-; member, Belfast IRB Supreme Council, 1906-; member & organiser, Sinn Féin, 1907-; manager, *Irish Freedom*, a monthly IRB journal, 1910-; crippled by poliomyelitis, 1912-; member, Provisional Committee of the IV, Dublin, 1913-; member, Supreme Council & its secret Military Council, Dublin, 1915-; signatory of the Proclamation of the Irish Republic, 1916; member, GHQ in GPO during Easter Week, 1916; arrested & court-martialled by British authorities; executed, 12 May 1916; buried, Arbour Hill Cemetery, Dublin

Charles Stewart Parnell [the Uncrowned King of Ireland] (1846–1891) – Anglo-Irish aristocrat, landlord & politician; political leader of the Irish Parliamentary Party (IPP), British House of Commons, 1880s; argued for land reform, Home Rule and Irish independence; 1st president, national Land League; caused IPP to split over his marriage to divorced woman, Katherine 'Kitty' O'Shea; died suddenly at age 45 on 6 October, 1891; honoured with the mythical title 'Ireland's Uncrowned King'; buried, Glasnevin Cemetery, Dublin

Liam Lynch – IRA officer & commander, Cork No. 2 Brigade during the War of Independence, 1919–1921; member, Supreme Council, IRB; Chief of Staff, anti-Treaty, IRA, 1922-;

Commandant, 1st Southern Division, anti-Treaty IRA, 1922-; issued 'Order of Frightfulness,' 27 November 1922

Major Arthur Ernest Percival – British officer; assigned to 1st Essex Regiment, Kinsale; possessed a strong hatred for IRA personnel & noted for his cruel treatment of prisoners

Tom Hales – IRA officer from Co. Cork; saw action in War of Independence; arrested, tortured & sentenced to prison, Pentonville, England, 1920; commandant, 3rd Cork Brigade, 1921-; acting on Liam Deasy's orders, organised the ambush of Collins's military convoy, Béalnabláth, 22 August 1922 (brother of Seán Hales)

Pat Harte – IRA officer from Co. Cork; saw action in War of Independence, 1919–1921; arrested, tortured & committed to mental hospital, 1920

'The Squad' or Twelve Apostles – a group of handpicked intelligence men who Michael Collins used to enforce *his* rule of law in Dublin during the War of Independence, 1919–1921; often employed to assassinate British intelligence agents & Dublin Metropolitan Police (DMP) who arrogantly harassed IRA personnel; served as body guards for Collins after the Truce, 1921-

James Larkin [Big Jim] – Dublin labour leader & organiser; founder, Irish Transportation & General Workers Union, 1909; led its membership against their employers in the Dublin Lock-Out, 1913; in 1914, left Ireland & sailed for the United States to raise funds for his labour union

Thomas MacDonagh (1878–1916) – poet, educator & Irish revolutionary; helped Patrick Pearse found & was first teacher, St. Enda's School at Cullenswood House, Ranelagh, Dublin, 1908-; remained on staff & became assistant headmaster when St. Enda's moved to Rathfarnham, Dublin, 1910-; edited *Irish Review* & help found Irish Theatre, Dublin; member, IV, 1913-; Director of Training, IV, 1914-; member, IRB & member of its secret Military Council, 1915; signatory of the Proclamation of the Irish Republic, 1916; commandant, 2nd Irish Volunteer Battalion, Dublin Brigade, Easter Week, 1916; arrested & court-martialled by British authorities; executed, 3 May 1916; buried, Arbour Hill Cemetery, Dublin

James Fintan Lalor (1807–1849) – Irish revolutionary; member, Young Islanders, 1846; argued for Irish land reform in the 1840s; advocated 'Irish land for the Irish people'

-6-

Tom & Jim Walsh; Willie Ronan – three of the seven Irish Volunteers who defended Clanwilliam House adjacent to Mount Street Bridge during Easter Week, 1916

Margaret Pearse (née Brady) (c.1856–1932) – mother of Margaret, Patrick (Pat), William (Willie) & Mary Bridget, later Gaelicized to Brigid (Mrs. Pearse's husband, James Pearse, died in September, 1900)

Margaret & Mary Brigid Pearse – daughters of James & Margaret Pearse; oldest & youngest sisters of Patrick & Willie Pearse

William Pearse [Willie] (1881–1916) – artist & educator; brother of Patrick Pearse; learned sculpting from his father & studied art in Dublin & Paris; taught art & drawing, St. Enda's School, 1908–1916; member, IV, 1913–1916; 'acting' headmaster in his brother's absence, St. Enda's School, 1914–1916; held rank of captain on GHQ staff, GPO, Easter Week, 1916; arrested & court-martialled by British authorities; executed, 4 May 1916; buried, Arbour Hill Cemetery, Dublin

Joseph MacDonagh – brother of Thomas MacDonagh; took over the running of St. Enda's School after executions of Patrick Pearse, Willie Pearse & Thomas MacDonagh, 1916-

William Woodbyrne – former owner of the Hermitage which the Pearse brothers renamed St. Enda's School, 1910

Josephine Plunkett (née Cranny) – married Count George Noble Plunkett in 1883; mother of seven Plunkett children: Philomena (Mimi), Joseph Mary, Moya, Geraldine, George, Josephine (Fiona) and John (Jack)

Kathleen Clarke (née Daly) (c.1878–1972) – married Tom Clarke in New York, 1901; mother of three sons: John Daly (Daly), Tom & Emmet; miscarried a fourth child in summer, 1916; her husband Tom, executed on 3 May 1916, had no knowledge of her last pregnancy; Kathleen's brother Edward 'Ned' Daly was also executed by British authorities on 4 May 1916 (Ned was commandant of the 1st Irish Volunteer Battalion, Dublin Brigade, stationed near the Four Courts, Easter Week, 1916)

Joe McGuinness – Irish Parliamentary Party (IPP) member of British Parliament; imprisoned after Easter Week; against his wishes, he was nominated by Sinn Féin for a British House of Commons seat in 1917; Michael Collins help organise his campaign using the slogan, "Put him in (to parliament) to get him out (of prison)"; arrested in 'German Plot' charade, 1918; member of 1st Dáil, 1919-

Thomas Ashe – Commandant, 5th Irish Volunteer Battalion, Dublin Brigade, stationed at Ashbourne, north Co. Dublin during Easter Week, 1916; arrested 1916 & interned in England until June, 1917; re-arrested in August, 1917 for seditious speechmaking; began hunger strike on 20 September in Brixton Prison, England; died in jail after being forcibly tube-fed, 25 September 1917; buried, Glasnevin Cemetery, Dublin

John Redmond (1856–1918) – Irish politician; member, Irish Parliamentary Party (IPP), British Parliament from 1881–1918; a devoted follower of Parnell; led pro-Parnellite minority after IPP split, 1891-; strong supporter of Ireland's participation in First War, 1914-; the 1916 Easter Rebellion shattered his pro-British policies; died unexpectedly on 6 March 1918

Harry Boland – close friend of Michael Collins; member of Sinn Féin executive, 1917; helped Collins free de Valera from Lincoln prison in 1919; travelled to Amerikay to help heal rift between Dev and Irish-America, 1919–1920

William Wallace (1270–1305) – medieval knight who rallied the drive for Scottish independence in the late 13th century; when finally captured, he was taken to London & executed

Rob Roy MacGregor (1671–1734) – outlaw & leader of the MacGregor clan; championed the cause of the underclass in The Trossachs, a rugged & beautiful region in central Scotland

-7-

Ernest Shackleton (1874–1922) – Irish-born British explorer famous for his 1907–1908 Nimrod Expedition to Antarctica; on another voyage (1914–1916) while commanding the ship *Endurance*, he & his crew of 27 men became ice bound & were forced to abandon ship; after many hardships, Shackleton eventually led his entire crew to safety, surviving an 800-mile frigid ocean voyage in a makeshift craft; again at sea in 1922, he unexpectedly died of a heart attack; at his wife's request he was buried on Grytviken, an island in the South Atlantic

Cathal Brugha – doctrinaire Republican; Vice-Commandant, 4th Irish Volunteer Battalion, Dublin Brigade, Easter Week, 1916 & badly wounded during the fighting; key leader of Sinn Féin and Irish Volunteer organisations, 1917–1919; Dáil Éireann TD & acting president of 1st Dáil in de Valera's absence, 1919; Dáil Minister for Defence, 1919–1921

Joe Leonard – Squad member & London bodyguard during Anglo-Irish Peace Talks, 1921Tom Jones – Assistant Secretary to the British Cabinet; Secretary to the British negotiating team, Anglo-Irish Peace Talks, London, 1921

Diarmuid O'Hegarty – Irish publicity director & assistant secretary to Erskine Childers, Anglo-Irish Peace Talks, London, 1921

Éamonn Broy [Ned] – one of Michael Collins's Dublin Castle police spies during War of Independence, 1919–1921; acted as one of Collins's secretaries during Anglo-Irish Peace Talks, London, 1921

Joe Dolan – squad member, 1919–1921; London bodyguard during Anglo-Irish Peace Talks, 1921

Joe Guilfoyle – member of Collins & Tobin's Intelligence Section, 1919–1921; London bodyguard during Anglo-Irish Peace Talks, 1921

-8-

Fíonan Lynch – Irish Volunteer, 1913-; fought in 1916 Easter Rebellion; imprisoned numerous times for offences against the Crown, 1916–1919; with Austin Stack and Thomas Ashe, led Mountjoy Jail hunger-strike, 1917; official secretary, Anglo-Irish Peace Talks, London, 1921; Minister for Education, PG, 1922-

George Gavin Duffy – lawyer & constitutional law authority; prepared the unsuccessful defence of his friend & 1916 Easter Rebellion leader Roger Casement, 1916; TD, Dáil Éireann, 1919-; Irish government representative to both Paris & Rome, 1919–1920; member, Anglo-Irish Peace Talks, London, 1921; signatory, Anglo-Irish Treaty, 1921; Minister for Foreign Affairs, 1922-

Sir Charles Gavin Duffy (1816–1903) – self-educated journalist & devoted nationalist; founder & editor of the Nation, a weekly newspaper, 1842–1855; broke with O'Connell & joined the Young Irelanders, 1846; lobbied for Irish land reform, 1849–1855; emigrated to Australia, 1855; became Prime Minister of Victoria, 1871–1880; knighted for his colonial service, 1873; buried in Dublin's Glasnevin Cemetery, 1903

Éamon Duggan (1874–1936) – lawyer; Sinn Féin supporter, 1914-; fought in the 1916 Easter Rebellion; TD member, Dáil Éireann, 1919-; served briefly as IRA Director of Intelligence, 1917; member, Anglo-Irish Peace Talks, London, 1921; signatory, Anglo-Irish Treaty, 1921; Minister for Home Affairs, Dáil & PG, 1922-

John Chartres – barrister; Chief of Intelligence Section for British War Office Armaments Output Committee, 1914–1915; became sympathetic to Irish struggle & Sinn Féin's efforts while posted to Dublin, 1916; gained notoriety for indexing & reorganising The Times (London) reference library; assisted IRA in arms procurement; gathered intelligence for IRA during War of Independence, 1919–1921; assistant secretary to Erskine Childers, Anglo-Irish Peace Talks, 1921

Sir Austen Chamberlain – former Chancellor of the Exchequer, 1919–1921; leader of British parliament's Conservative membership; member of British team, Anglo-Irish Peace Talks, 1921, signatory, Anglo-Irish Peace Treaty, 1921

Moya & Crompton Llewelyn Davies – Moya, born (1881) into a Fenian family in Blackrock, Dublin; married Crompton, a successful lawyer & confidant of David Lloyd George, thirteen years her senior; she returned from London to Dublin & took an active part in the War of Independence by passing intelligence information on to Michael Collins; she was an active writer all her life

Lady Hazel & Sir John Lavery – John, born in Belfast (1856), was a successful and fashionable portrait painter & married Hazel, thirty-one years his junior; Hazel Lavery, an extremely beautiful woman, often posed for him; her famous face graced Irish bank notes from the late 1920s to 1970 (she was the personification of the Irish cailín Cathleen Ni Houlihan); John Lavery painted both Collins & Griffith's portraits while they were in London during the Anglo-Irish Peace Talks, autumn, 1921; he also painted Michael as he lay in the mortuary at Dublin's St. Vincent's Hospital, August, 1922 (he entitled the painting: Michael Collins, Love of Ireland)

Sir James Craig (1871–1940) – Belfast-born politician; served in the Anglo-Boer War, 1900–1901; a Presbyterian, Orangeman & Ulster businessman; lieutenant of Ulster leader Edward Carson, 1910–1918; British MP; strongly favoured the Ulster connection with Britain & opposed ending partition; founded the Ulster Special Constabulary using many former Ulster Volunteer Force (UVF) personnel, 1920-; became Northern Ireland's first Prime Minister, 1921-

Field Marshall Sir Henry Wilson – staunch, lifelong anti-nationalist & pro-unionist adherent; Director of Military Operations at London War Office, 1910–1915; lent his official military support to British military mutiny, The Curragh, Ireland, 1914; British representative to Allied Supreme War Council, 1917–1918; Chief British Military Advisor to the Paris Peace Conference, 1919; special security advisor to Sir James Craig, Northern Ireland, 1922-

General Sir Nevil Macready – former Commissioner of the Metropolitan Police, London; Commander-in-Chief of British Forces, Ireland, 1921-

Sir Edward Carson (1854–1935) – politician & lawyer; defended & won the case brought by the Marquess of Queensberry against Oscar Wilde, 1895; leader of Irish Unionism, 1910–1921; led the cause of Ulster unionism against Irish Home Rule & played a key role in the establishment of Ulster Volunteer Force (UVF), the signing of the Ulster covenant, the Larne gun-running affair & the establishment of the Provisional government of Ulster, 1912–1916; as the forerunner to British partition act of 1920, negotiated with David Lloyd George & John Redmond for the exclusion of Ireland's six north-eastern counties through the end of the First War, 1918; feeling deceived by southern unionists, he withdrew from politics in 1922

-9-

Robert Lewis Stevenson (1850–1894) – Scottish-born novelist, poet and travel writer; many of his works are noted for their psychological depth & have continued to be read & enjoyed long after his death

Daniel O'Connell [the Liberator] (1775–1847) – barrister & political leader; one of Ireland's greatest modern political figures; founded the Catholic Association for Irish Catholic emancipation in 1823; his successful efforts to have Irish Catholics finally seated in the British Parliament earned him the title 'the Liberator', 1828; unfortunately, his Repeal Association movement, begun in 1840, failed to reverse the 1801 Act of Union; near the end of his life, his nationalist 'Young' Ireland followers, who disagreed with his conservative 'Old' Ireland political strategies, broke away from his Repeal Association, 1846; inspired by the French Revolution of February, 1848, the Young Irelanders, who advocated the use of force, staged an abortive revolt in Co. Tipperary, 29 July 1848; buried, Glasnevin Cemetery, Dublin (a 168-foot round tower, the tallest in Ireland, marks his grave)

Michael Davitt (1846–1906) – Irish nationalist, agrarian organiser & journalist; born in Ireland but moved to England with his family at an early age; lost an arm in a Lancashire milling accident at age eleven; joined the IRB at nineteen & was imprisoned for arms trafficking; back in Ireland, he organised peasant farmers against landlord abuses; employed boycotting tactics; as the 'Land War' hotted up, he helped found the Irish National Land League with Parnell as its head; elected to British parliament as MP, 1895–1899; buried in home village, Straide, Co. Mayo

Jonathan Swift (1667–1745) – eighteenth-century Irish poet, writer, political satirist, humanitarian, theologian & Dean of St. Patrick's Cathedral, Dublin

John O'Leary (1830–1907) – Irish nationalist, Fenian & writer; editor of the Fenian newspaper Irish People; imprisoned for both his Young Ireland and Fenian activities, he was later exiled; though disagreeing with later nineteenth-century nationalist movements, he remained the personification of Irish Republicanism; spent much of his last years writing & was a great influence on W. B. Yeats; with O'Leary's death, Yeats wrote, "Romantic Ireland's dead and gone, it's with O'Leary in the grave."

Lord Birkenhead [Frederick Edwin Smith] – lawyer & British Conservative Party statesman, 1906-; worked to secure the conviction & later execution (3 August 1916) of Sir Roger Casement, the last member of the Easter Rebellion leaders to die at the hands of the British authorities; member, British team, Anglo-Irish Peace Talks, London, 1921; signatory, Anglo-Irish Treaty, 1921

Kevin O'Higgins – Sinn Féin MP & imprisoned by British authorities for anti-conscription speech, 1918; appointed Assistant Minister for Local Government, 1919–1922; Minister for Economic Affairs, Dáil & PG, 1922

Piaras Béaslaí – journalist, poet and playwright; Vice-Commandant to Ned Daly's 1st Irish Volunteer Battalion, Dublin Brigade with HQ near the Four Courts, Easter Week, 1916; imprisoned several times by British authorities; elected Sinn Féin MP, 1918; served as liaison officer between Department of Publicity & IRA HQ, 1919-; editor of An t-Oglach (The Volunteer)

Part II:

-10-

Sam Maguire [the London man] (1879–1927) – Irish revolutionary; born near village of Dunmanway, Co. Cork; British civil servant, 1899–1921; leading member of Gaelic Athletic Association (GAA), Gaelic League & IRB in London, 1907–1921; befriended Michael Collins & enrolled him in London branch of the IRB, 1909; IRB Director of Intelligence (London) & helped smuggle weapons to IRA in Ireland; died of tuberculosis; honoured by GAA with its All-Ireland Gaelic Football Championship cup named for him, 1928-)

Seán Moylan – IRA commander, 1918-; active during War of Independence, 1919-1921

Tom Barry (1897–1980) – enlisted in British Army, 1915; saw active duty in Middle East, Italy & France, 1915–1919; IRA intelligence & training officer, West Cork Brigade, 1920; OC, Brigade Flying Column, 1920; active participant, War of Independence, 1920–1921; led attacks against British forces at Kilmichael (28 November 1921) & Crossbarry (19 March 1922), Co. Cork; Vice-Commandant & Training Officer, 1st Southern Division, 1921; anti-Treaty IRA, 1922-; supported demand for Army Convention, 1922

Eoin MacNeill (1867–1945) – Irish scholar & politician; professor of early Irish history, University College Dublin, 1908-; helped organise Irish Volunteers & became its Chief of Staff, 1913–1916; opposed Easter Rebellion but was arrested & interred by British authorities, 1916; released in 1917 & elected Sinn Féin MP, 1918; Dáil TD, 1919-; served as Dáil speaker during the Anglo-Irish Treaty debates, 1921–1922; Minister without Portfolio, Provisional Government, 1922

Seán T. O'Kelly (1882–1966) – Irish revolutionary & politician; member of Gaelic League & IRB, 1898; founder-member, Sinn Féin, 1905; aide-de-camp to Patrick Pearse, GHQ, GPO, Easter Week, 1916; arrested, deported, interred & released by

British authorities, 1916 elected Sinn Féin MP, 1918 & Dáil TD, 1919–1945; as first Dáil Ceann Comhairle, attended Paris Peace Conference, 1919; as friend of Éamon de Valera, he opposed the Treaty (elected 2nd President of Ireland, 1945–1959)

Terence 'Terry' MacSwiney – Irish revolutionary, politician & writer; founded, Cork Celtic Literary Society, 1908; member, Gaelic League & Irish Volunteers; 2nd-in-command to Tomás MacCurtain, Co. Cork, Easter Week, 1916; imprisoned 1916–1917; Sinn Féin TD, Dáil Éireann, 1919; Lord Mayor, Cork City, 1920; arrested by British authorities & transported to Brixton Prison, London, 12 August 1920; died, 25 October 1920 after 74 days on hunger strike

Tomás MacCurtain – Irish nationalist & politician; Easter-Week participant, Co. Cork, 1916; arrested, transported & interred in Wales, 1916; Irish Volunteer leader, Co. Cork, 1917-; elected Sinn Féin Councillor & later Lord Mayor of Cork City, Co. Cork, 1919–1920; active in eliminating corruption in local government, 1920; shot dead in the his home in the presence of his wife, 20 March 1920; coroner's jury returned a verdict of guilty against various British authorities (likely murdered by first group of Black & Tans in Ireland)

Countess Constance Markievicz (née Gore-Booth) (1868–1927) – Irish revolutionary & socialist; joined Inghinidhe na hÉireann (Women of Ireland), Sinn Féin and co-founded Fianna Éireann (Irish warriors, a nationalist 'boy scout' organisation) in 1909; as an officer in James Connolly's Irish Citizen Army, she fought in the Easter Rebellion, 1916; arrested, court-martialled & sentenced to death by British authorities, 1916 (sentenced commuted to penal servitude for life); deported, interred & later released by the British authorities, 1916–1917; president of Cumann na mBán, 1916–1917; first woman elected to the British House of Commons, 1918; elected Sinn Fein TD, 1918; appointed, Minister for Labour, 1st Dáil, 1919-

-11-

Lord Edmund Bernard FitzAlan-Howard, 1st Viceroy FitzAlan of Derwent (1855–1947) – British Conservative party politician; last British Lord Lieutenant of Ireland & first Catholic to occupy that position; replaced Field Marshall Lord French, 1921; served one-and-a-half years until the position was eliminated & replaced by a Governor-General with the founding of the Irish Free State, 1922

Gearóid O'Sullivan – GPO veteran of Easter Week Rebellion, 1916; Sinn Féin TD, 1919-; Adjutant-General & member of IRA Dublin Brigade staff, War of Independence, 1919–1921; elected to IRB Supreme Council, 1921-; pro-Treaty, 1922-

Eoin O'Duffy – member, IRA, 1917; elected Ulster member, IRB Supreme Council, 1917; Sinn Féin TD, 1919-; IRA Brigade Commander & member, GHQ staff, War of Independence, 1919–1921; suffered several periods of imprisonment by British authorities; general & IRA Deputy Chief of Staff, 1921-; pro-Treaty, 1922-; Chief of Staff, National Army, 1922-

Eddie – long-time employee of the Gresham Hotel, Dublin

Patrick J. Hogan – Sinn Féin TD, 1919-; Dáil Minister for Agriculture, 1922-

Joe McGrath – Sinn Féin TD, 1919-; Dáil Minister for Labour, 1922-

Major-General Sir Hugh Tudor (1871–1965) – British junior officer, 2nd Boar War, 1899–1902 & senior officer, First War, 1914–1918; appointed by Winston Churchill to command the reconstituted Irish police force, 1920; styling himself as 'Chief of Police,' he restored flagging RIC numbers & moral but did little to improve discipline; under his command the Black & Tans and Auxies had a virtual free hand to do as they pleased with little fear of any consequences befalling them

Seán Connolly – actor & captain, Irish Citizen Army, 1916; commanded an Easter-Week squadron that occupied City Hall & attacked Dublin Castle, 1916; he was killed in action on Easter Monday, 1916 (most likely the first Irish rebel to be killed during the Easter Rebellion)

Joe O'Reilly – a close associate of Michael Collins; they met in London (pre-Easter, 1916) & he followed Collins to Dublin, 1916; a GPO veteran, he was arrested & interned with Collins

& others after the Easter Rebellion collapsed, 1916; remained a devoted accomplice until Collins's death in 1922

-12-

Rory O'Connor (b. 1883) – Irish revolutionary; conspired with Patrick Pearse & others to mislead Eoin MacNeill regarding the need to initially follow through with the Easter Rebellion plans (O'Connor produced a document showing the authorities planned to arrest Sinn Féin & nationalist leaders just prior to the Rebellion's outbreak); wounded during Easter Week, 1916; resigned in protest from the IRB when it failed to abandon its policy of secrecy; IRA Director of Engineering, 1918-; led IRA offensive in England, 1919; War of Independence veteran, 1919–1921; anti-Treaty IRA, 1922-; signatory of demand for Army Convention, 11 January 1922

Oscar Traynor – Easter-Week participant, 1916; arrested & imprisoned, 1916–1917; War of Independence veteran, 1919–1921; O/C Dublin Brigade, 1921-; anti-Treaty IRA, 1922-; signatory of demand for Army Convention, 11 January 1922

William Ewart Gladstone (1809–1898) – British (liberal) Prime Minister, 1880–1885, 1886, 1892–1894; promoted (unsuccessfully) the 1st & 2nd Irish Home Rule bills in the House of Commons, 1886 & 1893

Ernie O'Malley – Irish revolutionary, writer & artist; Easter-Week participant, 1916; Irish Volunteer organiser throughout country, 1917-; active participant, War of Independence, 1919–1921; member, HQ staff, South Tipperary Brigade, 1920; imprisoned & escaped, Kilmainham Jail, 1921; Commander, 2nd Southern Division, 1921-; anti-Treaty IRA, 1922-; supported demand for Army Convention, 1922

-13-

Michael Staines – Staff Officer, GHQ, GPO Irish Volunteers, 1916; one of James Connolly's stretcher bearers during GPO evacuation on Easter Friday, 1916; member, Supreme

Council, IRB, 1917-; Sinn Féin TD, 1919-; arrested by British authorities, December, 1920 & released, July, 1921; pro-Treaty, 1922-; directed Belfast Boycott, 1922; appointed Civil Guard Commissioner, February, 1922-

Michael Brennan – Irish Volunteer organiser in Co. Clare, 1914–1916; member, IRB Supreme Council, Munster, 1914-; arrested & imprisoned by British authorities for Easter Rebellion activities in the west of Ireland, 1916; active member of IRA during War of Independence, 1919–1921; arrested several times, 1917–1921; pro-Treaty, 1922-; O/C 1st Western Division, 1921-

Seamus Robinson – Irish revolutionary; Irish Volunteer & participated in Dublin street fighting during Easter Week, 1916; led the Soloheadbeg ambush, 1919; took part in the Knocklong rail station ambush that freed Seán Hogan, 1919; wounded in action during Tan War & one of its many heroes, 1919–1921; O/C 3rd Tipperary Brigade &, 1919–1921; anti-Treaty IRA, 1922-

-14-

Liam Devlin – publican & owner of Devlin's Pub, situated on the south side of Rutland Square, just opposite the Rotunda Hospital; he'd returned from Scotland after the Easter Rebellion, 1916 & because of his earlier involvement with Sinn Féin, was introduced to Michael Collins through an IRB connection; Liam & his wife offered Collins the use of their pub as an office, meeting place and lodging whenever he chose; Collins often availed himself of their hospitality

Katharine O'Shea (née Wood) (1845–1921) – born in Essex, England, she married Captain O'Shea in 1867 (2 children); besides supporting Charles Stewart Parnell's parliamentary efforts, she also had a lengthy affair with him (3 children); divorced her husband (November, 1890) & married Parnell (June, 1891); he died unexpectedly four months later

Captain William Henry O'Shea (1840–1905) – Irish politician; husband of Katharine 'Kitty' O'Shea; he also supported

Charles Stewart Parnell's parliamentary efforts until his wife's affair drove him to divorcing her; he cited Parnell as co-respondent & blamed him for ruining his personal & political reputation; Captain O'Shea was granted a divorce, November, 1890

Lord Frederick Cavendish – appointed Chief Secretary to Ireland by the British government, 1882; murdered in Dublin's Phoenix Park only hours after arriving to assume his office by a group of Republican radicals called 'the Invincibles'

Thomas H. Burke – appointed Lord Cavendish's Under-Secretary to Ireland by the British government, 1882; was murdered along with Cavendish only hours after arriving in Dublin to assume his new post

James Carey – informant who divulged the names of 'the Invincibles' who had murdered Cavendish & Burke, 1882; Carey was himself murdered by Pat O'Donnell while fleeing Ireland aboard ship to South Africa; 'twas there that Carey hoped to begin a new life with his family

Pat O'Donnell – murdered James Carey & was later hanged for his crime

Sir Roger Casement (1864–1916) – Irish nationalist & British civil servant; member, British colonial service; gained fame for his exposure of atrocities committed against local workers in Belgian Congo and later in Peru; knighted by King George V for these efforts, 1911; member of Irish Volunteers, 1913; travelled to Germany to enlist support for an projected Irish rebellion, 1914–1916; upon his return to Ireland during Easter Week, he was arrested by British authorities, 1916; deported to England, tried, convicted & later hanged in Pentonville Prison, London, 3 August 1916 (he was the 16th & last of the 1916 leaders to be executed); in 1965, his remains were returned to Ireland where he was given a state funeral & reinterred in Glasnevin Cemetery, Dublin

Field Marshall Lord John French (1852–1925) – British soldier & politician; had a distinguished military career (1866–1916); oversaw the suppression of the 1916 Easter Rebellion & was appointed Lord Lieutenant-General & Governor General of Ireland, 1918–1921

Captain Hardy – British Army intelligence agent; partici-pated in the formation of the Ulster Volunteer Force (UVF) in Northern Ireland, 1913; liaison officer between Dublin Castle & Special Intelligence Office, Scotland Yard during the Tan War; involved in the interrogation of Dick McKee, Peadar Clancy & Conor Clune, 21 November 1920

Head Constable Igoe – member, Royal Irish Constabulary, Co. Mayo; headed a group of plain-clothes RIC men from various parts of Ireland whose job it was to patrol the streets of Dublin looking for wanted IRA men from the provinces who were in town on GHQ business during the War of Independence, 1919–1921; after the Truce, he apparently moved his base of operations to the Six Counties where he was reported to have murdered several Sinn Féin activists in Newry, Co. Down

Dick McKee – commandant, Dublin Brigade, 1918–1920; member of GHQ staff of the Irish Volunteers; arrested in Vaughan's Hotel by British authorities, 20 November 1920; taken to Dublin Castle, he was tortured & murdered the following evening in reprisal for Michael Collins's men killing fourteen & wounding six British intelligence agents earlier that day (21 November 1920 was soon to be nicknamed 'Bloody Sunday' for Collins's actions)

Peadar Clancy – Vice-Commandant, Dublin Brigade; a close associate of Michael Collins & active during the War of Independence; arrested with Dick McKee in Vaughan's Hotel by British authorities, 20 November 1920; taken to Dublin Castle, tortured & murdered the following evening in reprisal for Collins's 'Blood Sunday' attacks

Conor Clune – Gaelic-scholar student from Co. Clare who happened to be staying at Vaughan's Hotel on the night of 20 November 1920; arrested in error by British authorities along with McKee & Clancy; taken to Dublin Castle, tortured & murdered the following evening in reprisal for Collins's 'Blood Sunday' attacks

Seán Hegarty – IRA Army Executive member, anti-Treaty, 1922

Frank Aiken – IRA Officer, 1918–1919; Vice-Commandant, Newry Brigade, 1920; O/C, 4ᵗʰ Northern Division, 1921-; initially neutral in conflict over terms of the Treaty, 1922; later, member, anti-Treaty IRA, 1922-

Darrell Figgis – writer; arrested by British authorities & imprisoned, May-December, 1916; Sinn Féin national secretary, 1917-; re-arrested & deported, 1918–1919; editor of *The Republic*, 1919-; pro-Treaty, 1922-; elected Sinn Féin TD, 1922-; Deputy Chairman of Constitution Committee, 1922

Part III:

-15-

Reginald Dunne & Joseph O'Sullivan – anti-Treaty IRA, 1922; together they were apprehended & implicated in the murder of Sir Henry Wilson, 22 June 1922

Joe McKelvey – Fianna Éireann organiser; defended the nationalist minority during the Belfast pogroms, 1920; O/C, 3ʳᵈ Northern Division, IRA, 1921-; member, anti-Treaty IRA, 1922; member, Four Courts garrison, 1922

Dick Barrett – teacher & part-time IRA officer during War of Independence, 1919–1921; helped raise funds to support comrades who were on the run; arrested & imprisoned by British authorities after Crossbarry ambush, March, 1921; member, anti-Treaty IRA, 1922; member, Four Courts garrison, 1922

Maurice Twomey – IRA officer, War of Independence, 1919–1921; Fermoy Battalion, 1919–1920; adjutant & IO, Cork #2 Brigade, 1920-; general staff officer, anti-Treaty IRA, 1922-

Dan O'Leary – Anti-Treaty IRA, 1922-

Leo Henderson – directed Belfast Boycott for anti-Treaty IRA, 1922; arrested by Free State troops in Dublin, June, 1922 & imprisoned in Mountjoy

Tom Ennis – commandant, 2ⁿᵈ Battalion, Dublin Brigade, 1920; wounded in Custom House raid, May, 1921; officer, National Army; O/C, 2ⁿᵈ Eastern Division, 1922-; issued surrender order to anti-Treaty IRA in Four Courts, 28 June 1922; oversaw Sackville Street offensive, late June-early July, 1922

-16-

Joseph Cashman (1881–1969) – photo-journalist & non-combatant; socialist & early follower of James Larkin; chronicled many of the events surrounding the 1916 Rebellion, the War of Independence & Irish Civil War; photographer for the *Freeman's Journal* until it ceased publication in 1923 (many of his photographic plates were destroyed in the newspaper-office fire set by the IRA after the Army Convention in March, 1922)

P. S. O'Hegarty – writer & non-combatant; active in Gaelic League & other nationalist organisations during his youth; civil servant, London, 1902–1913; pro-Treaty, 1922-; Secretary of the Department for Posts & Telegraphs, Free State government, 1922-; founded the Irish Bookshop in Dawson Street, Dublin

Mike Sheehan – officer, anti-Treaty, IRA, 1922-; commandant & quartermaster for a South Tipperary battalion, 1922-; helped lead the unsuccessful defence of Waterford, July, 1922

Stanley Bishop – pro-Treaty & National Army officer, 1922-; helped lead the successful three-pronged attack on Blessington, Co. Wicklow, July, 1922

Seán Lemass (1899–1971) – Irish revolutionary & politician; Irish Volunteer who fought in GPO during Easter Rebellion, 1916; played active role as IV in War of Independence, 1919-; acting as one of Michael Collins's agents who, along with the help of two others, killed Captain Baggelly, Lower Baggott Street, 21 November 1920 (Bloody Sunday); arrested in December, 1920 by British authorities & interned until after the Treaty was signed, 1921; anti-Treaty IRA officer, 1922-; member of Four Courts garrison, April, 1922; surrendered but escaped Dublin, 30 June 1922; saw action south of Dublin, July, 1922; became Director of Communications, IRA, July, 1922- (his brother, Noel, also anti-Treaty IRA, was arrested by Free State forces, 3 July 1923 & allegedly murdered by pro-Treaty CID; Noel's body was found in the Dublin Mountains, 12 October 1923) (Seán helped co-found Éamon de Valera's new political party, Fianna Fáil, in 1926 & was elected Taoiseach or Prime Minister of Ireland, 1959–1965)

John T. Prout – served in United States Army during First

War; pro-Treaty & National Army officer, 1922-; O/C, 2nd Southern Division, July, 1922-; using artillery, his forces moved through Leinster to Waterford & into Co. Tipperary, July-August, 1922; established his HQ in Clonmel, Co. Tipperary, 1922–1923

-17-

Desmond FitzGerald – member, GHQ garrison GPO, Easter Week, 1916; arrested & interred by British authorities, 1916–1917; rearrested, 1918; elected Sinn Féin TD, 1918; liaison officer between Sinn Féin & GHQ, 1919–1921; arrested & imprisoned for a third time, March-July, 1921; non-Cabinet level Minister for Propaganda, August-December, 1921; pro-Treaty non-combatant, 1922-; government Publicity Director, January, 1922- (because of his marvellous eye for capturing history in the making & his superb sense of the dramatic, there is a large surviving collection of photographs taken at his behest, chronicling Ireland's Civil War)

Seán Hegarty – anti-Treaty IRA, 1922-; member of the 16-man IRA Army Executive, March, 1922

Johnny Collins – Michael Collins's oldest brother who lived next door to the original family home, Woodfield, hard by Sam's Cross & near Clonakilty, Co. Cork

Thomas Davis (1814–1845) – Irish nationalists & poet; called to the bar, 1838; joined Daniel O'Connell's Repeal (of the Union) Association, 1840; co-founder of Young Ireland & the nationalist newspaper, the *Nation*, 1842-; his prose & verse captured the national imagination & inspired many with his vision of an Ireland free & able to follow its own destiny

Joseph Sweeney – member, GPO GHQ garrison, Easter Week, 1916; elected Sinn Féin TD, 1918; commandant, West Donegal Brigade, 1919-; youngest member, 1st Dáil, 1919–1921; O/C, 1st Northern Division, 1921-; pro-Treaty IRA, 1922-

-18-

Albert Power (1883–1945) – Irish sculptor; born & lived entire life in Dublin; studied at the Metropolitan School of Art under Oliver Sheppard; won numerous prizes during his lifetime; many of his sculptors are still on public display in museums & in outdoor parks throughout Ireland

Andrew Bonar Law (1858–1923) – Ulster unionist politician, 1900–1923; born in Canada but made his fortune in Scotland trading in iron; elected leader, British Conservative Party, 1911; entered coalition government, 1915; when the Conservative Party withdrew its support of Lloyd George's coalition government, he became British Prime Minister, October, 1922; as a strong supporter of Ulster, he favoured partition; seven months later (May, 1923), he was forced to retire, suffering to throat cancer; he died later that year in London

James Fisher, Peter Cassidy, John Gaffney & Richard Twohig – members, anti-Treaty IRA, 1922; the first men (of a total of 77) to be executed by the Free State government during the Irish Civil War, 17 November 1922

Seán Hales – Commandant, 1st Battalion, 3rd Cork Brigade, 1919-; elected Sinn Féin TD, 1918-; a flying column commander, 1921; led the left section of Tom Barry's IRA attack at Crossbarry against British forces & Auxilliary Cadets, 19 March 1921; pro-Treaty IRA, 1922; major general & O/C, Bandon garrison, 1922; assassinated by anti-Treaty IRA, Dublin, 7 December 1922

Pádraig Ó Máille – resisted arrest, 'German plot' round-up, May, 1918; elected Sinn Féin TD, 1918-; on the run but attended first session, 1st Dáil Éireann, Dublin, 21 January 1919; pro-Treaty, 1922-; deputy speaker of the 3rd Dáil, 1922-; wounded in assassination attempt by anti-Treaty IRA, 7 December 1922

Part IV:

-19-

Leslie Barry (née Price) – married Tom Barry, 22 August 1921

Timothy Michael Healy (1855–1931) – Irish politician noted for his wit & biting political oratory; initially a supporter of Charles Stewart Parnell, he turned against the Irish political leader during the O'Shea-divorce affair, 1890; he became the outspoken leader of the anti-Parnell wing of the Irish Parliamentary Party, 1890-; quarrelling frequently with its leadership, he was expelled from the IPP, 1902 but retained his MP seat in Westminster; a critic of John Redmond's pro-British First War backing (1914–1916), he found favour with the ideals of Sinn Féin after 1916; appointed first Free State Governor-General, 1922–1927; retired from politics, 1927

Seán McGarry – president, IRB, 1917; arrested on several occasions & often imprisoned by British authorities, 1916–1919; escaped Lewes Jail with de Valera, 1919; IRA commandant during War of Independence, 1919–1921; elected, Sinn Féin TD; pro-Treaty IRA, 1922-; his home was burned by anti-Treatyites & his 7-year-old son died as a result of it, December, 1922

Bill Quirke, Seán O'Meara & Seán Hayes – anti-Treaty Republicans who accompanied Liam Lynch on his fateful trek across the Knockmealdown Mountains, 10 April 1923

Seán Hyde – Dublin IRA Volunteer intelligence officer, 1920–1921; anti-Treaty IRA, 1922-; member, IRA Army Executive, 1922-; accompanied Liam Lynch on his fateful trek across the Knockmealdown Mountains, 10 April 1923

-20-

Michael Fitzgerald – member, Irish Volunteers, Fermoy Company, 1st Battalion, 1918-; vice-commandant, Cork 2nd Brigade; member, brigade flying column, 1920; captured by British authorities, 7 September 1920; went on hunger strike, Cork City jail & died 17 October 1920 (close friend of Liam Lynch)

J. R. Fisher – Northern Ireland's representative to the Boundary Commission & close, personal friend of Sir James Craig; he was appointed by the British government when Northern Ireland Prime Minister Craig refused to nominate someone, 1924-

Honourable Mr. Justice Richard Feetham – member, South African Supreme Court; the official British commissioner (representative) & chairman of the Boundary Commission, 1924-

Douglas Hyde (1860–1949) – Irish Scholar; 1st president of the Gaelic League, 1893-; served one seven-year term as Ireland's 1st president, 1938–1945

-21-

Seán McBride (1904–1998) – Irish revolutionary, politician, lawyer & son of Maude Gonne (1865–1953) & Major John Mc-Bride; member, Irish Volunteers & saw active service in the War of Independence, 1919–1921; anti-Treaty IRA, 1922-; maintained membership in IRA; imprisoned, lived life on the run, moved to Paris & worked as a journalist, 1922–1936; returned to Ireland & became IRA Chief of Staff, 1936; called to the bar & resigned IRA membership, 1937; with the new 1937 Constitution in place, maintained Ireland could accomplish its national objectives via political means, 1937-; founded Clann na Poblachta, 1946; joined first inter-party (coalition) government as Minister for External Affairs, 1948-; founding-member, Amnesty International, 1961-; in 1974 awarded the Nobel Peace for Prize; in 1977 received the Lenin Peace Prize & in 1978 the American Medal for Justice; buried, Republican Plot, Glasnevin Cemetery, Dublin

Epilogue:

-22-

Liam Weldon (1933–1995) – balladeer, political activist, community worker & volunteer, husband & father; born & raised in the Liberties, a inter-city Dublin neighbourhood; he first learned his 'music' as a young boy from the 'travelling people'[3]; with his father's death & six siblings at home, Liam left school at 14 to work; at 22, he married Nellie; between work, mending guitars & making mandolins, he began singing in clubs, pubs & wherever; with his wife Nellie, Liam ran gigs & clubs around Dublin; as the 50th anniversary of the 1916 Easter Rebellion neared, his song, "Dark Horse On The Wind" criticised the broken promises made by Irish politicians in light of the social

---

3. Ireland's displaced, itinerant people who have their origins dating back to the 'Penal Times' of the 1700s. Thrown out of their homes & off their land by the English authorities, these Irish were forced to take to the roads, often in wagons or caravans. Many took up the profession of making or repairing pots & pans, hence the nickname 'tinker' or 'tinsmith' became a common moniker.

failures exemplified by Ireland's high levels of emigration & poverty experienced throughout in the 1930s, 1940s, 1950s & 1960s; in later years, his music challenged the compliancy of middle-class Ireland; his wife of forty years still lives in their family home in Ballyfermot, a Dublin suburb.

FICTIONAL

Prologue:

-1-

Major Aran Roe O'Neill [the Irish Rebel; the Rebel; the Gortman] – Irish Volunteer & member, IRA 1916-; member, Flying Gaels, 1918- (a fictionalised flying column organised by Michael Collins, Liam Mellowes, Richard 'Shadow' Doyle & himself during the War of Independence); member, National Army, 1922-

Thomas Coogan – 1916-Dublin friend of Arthur Griffith whom Aran met while on the run from British authorities soon after the 1916 Easter Rebellion ended; gave Aran a new .45 Colt revolver he'd recently bought in Amerikay

Captain Gabriel McCracken [Gay; Gabby, the Irish-American] – Irish-American; Irish Volunteer & member, IRA, 1917-; member, Flying Gaels, 1918-; married Áine Grogan, spring, 1920; father of Mary Margaret Brigid McCracken; member, National Army, 1922-

Neill Morrison, Tom & Séamus McDonald, Sonny Lucey, Brian Cody, Dónal O'Grady, Shay Keller, Conor Makem, Rory Sheehan & David Palmerston – National Army troopers, 1922-

Major Richard 'Shadow' Doyle [the Limerick man; the baker] – veteran, 2nd Boer War, 1899–1902; member, Irish Volunteer, 1913-; IRA battalion commander, 1916-; member, Flying Gaels, 1918-; owns a bakery in Limerick & a mill in Cahir; father of three young daughters

Captain Danny Kelly – Irish Volunteer & member, IRA, 1916-; member, Flying Gaels, 1918-

Sarah Anne McCracken [Annie] – Irish-American; sister of Gabriel McCracken; IRA courier, 1919–1921; engaged to marry Aran Roe O'Neill

Turlough Molloy – Irish-American; member, Irish Volunteer & IRA, 1917–1920; member, Flying Gaels, 1918–1920; killed during War of Independence skirmish, June, 1920

Áine McCracken (née Grogan) – sister of Pat Grogan; married Gabriel McCracken in spring of 1920; mother of Mary Margaret Brigid McCracken

Mary Margaret Brigid McCracken – daughter of Gabriel & Áine McCracken, born 31 January 1921

Brigid Eileen O'Mahony – love-interest of Aran, 1916; killed in sectarian encounter near Athy, Co. Kildare, May, 1916

Helen Doyle – married to Shadow Doyle; mother of three daughters; killed in War of Independence ambush, near her Limerick home, February, 1921

Part I:

-3-

Major George Henry Hawkins – British army & Black & Tan officer with whom Aran battled during the War of Independence; killed by Gabriel at Shadow's safe-house near Limerick Town, spring, 1921

Duncan Stewart MacGregor [the Nayler] – transplanted Scotsman, Republican & friend of Aran Roe O'Neill, 1921-; though living in Ireland most of his life, he retains a great love & loyalty for his family's Scottish heritage; resides with his father on a small farm near Athy

Gran O'Mahony – Brigid Eileen O'Mahony's fraternal grandmother who raised her from infancy

Mrs. O'Neill – Aran Roe O'Neill's mother

-4-

Peter & Niamh McCracken – Father McCracken's youngest brother; Gabriel & Sarah Anne McCracken's uncle & aunt; the couple lives & owns a pub, the Black Rose, in Cahir, Co. Tipperary

Father & Mother McCracken – Gabriel & Sarah Anne McCracken's parents; they live & farm in Manassas, Virginia & have two other sons: Lawrence (Larry) & Dominic (Dom) who live & farm with them

John McCracken – Father McCracken's oldest brother

Connie Crowe – Friend of Michael Collins from Co. Tipperary

Captain James Madden – officer, British Essex Regiment, stationed in Ireland

-5-

Martin Richardson [Marty] – medical student; met Aran at St. Enda's school in spring, 1916; helped Aran escape from British authorities after Easter Week, 1916; graduated from Harvard University, 1921

Fergal & Nuala Richardson – Martin's barrister father & his mother

Mary Elizabeth Richardson – Martin's younger sister

Nanna Richardson – Martin's grandmother

-6-

Robin Hood – a 11th–13th century English folk hero who represented freedom & nature; he supposedly robbed the rich to aid the poor; his legendary tales might have been inspired by the life of Robyn Hod, who was possibly born in Nottinghamshire

-7-

Mr. MacGregor – Duncan Stewart MacGregor's father

Hannah O'Mahony – Brigid's sister, two years her senior; who moved to Amerikay in 1911 to worked for a wealthy Irish-American family living near Baltimore; after Brigid's death, returned to Athy to oversee the rearing of her three younger siblings & to manage the family-farm household along with her aging grandmother, Gran O'Mahoney

Colonel Edward Allyn Hawkins [Eddy; Black Eddy] – brother of Major George Henry Hawkins, two years his junior

Annie, Mary & Rory O'Mahony – Brigid & Hannah's younger siblings aged 11, 13 & 16 (autumn, 1921); they're also Gran's three youngest grandchildren

Peter Ryan & family – tenant farmer & his family who lease land from the O'Mahonys; together the two families share some of the farm work

-8-

Lawrence (Larry) & Dominic (Dom) McCracken – Gabriel & Sarah Anne's oldest & youngest brothers; both living with their parents on the family farm near Manassas, Virginia

Part II:

-11-

Liam McCullers – member, IRA & Flying Gaels from Galway Town, 1920-; his father was murdered by an Auxie; took part with Aran & Gabriel in Bloody Sunday assassinations, 21 November 1920; pro-Treaty IRA, 1922-

-12-

Pat Grogan – Áine (née Grogan) McCracken's older brother; member, Irish Volunteers & IRA, 1917–1921; member, Flying Gaels, 1918-; pro-Treaty IRA, 1922-

Caoimhín Donleavy, Nick Robinson, Jimmy Carroll, Frank O'Leary & Christopher McKee – members, Irish Volunteers & IRA, 1917–1921; members, Flying Gaels, 1918-; pro-Treaty IRA, 1922-

Part III:

-18-

Patrick Michael O'Neill – son of Sarah Anne & Aran Roe O'Neill

Part IV:

-19-

Thomas Creegan – blacksmith in the village of Ardfinnan, Co. Tipperary

-20-

Father Francis – parish priest from the village of Cahir
Anna Coogan – wife of Thomas Coogan; an acquaintance of Aran's whom he'd met in Dublin while on the run from British authorities after Easter Week, 1916

-21-

Malachy McBride – husband of Marty's sister, Mary Elizabeth Richardson McBride
Fiona Aisling O'Neill – daughter of Sarah Anne & Aran Roe O'Neill

PROLOGUE

Memories keep alive the heart;
death only comes when we remember
no more...

The Declaration of Arbroath

"For, as long as but a hundred of us remain alive, never will we on any conditions be brought under English rule. It is in truth not for glory, nor riches, nor honours that we are fighting, but for freedom—for that alone, which no honest man gives up but with life itself."

Abbot, Bernard de Linton, Chancellor of Scotland

6 April 1320

❧

The Proclamation of POBLACHT NA H ÉIREANN

"We declare the right of the people of Ireland to the ownership of Ireland, and to the unfettered control of the Irish destinies, to be sovereign and indefeasible. The long usurpation of that right by a foreign people and government has not extinguished the right, nor can it ever be extinguished except by the destruction of the Irish people."

Signed on Behalf of the Provisional Government.
Thomas J. Clarke.
Seán MacDiarmada.
Thomas MacDonagh.
P. H. Pearse.
Éamonn Ceannt.
James Connolly.
Joseph Plunkett.

April, 1916

I

*"...every kingdom divided against itself
is brought to desolation; and every city or house
divided against itself shall not stand."*

Matthew 12:25

TUESDAY EVENING, 22 AUGUST 1922

*T*he military convoy wound its way along the narrow Bandon-
to-Crookstown road. Led by a motorcycle, three other vehicles
followed at measured intervals: a Crossley tender, an open Leyland
Thomas-Eight touring car and a Rolls Royce 'Whippet' armoured
car dubbed the Slieve na mBán.

The uncovered lorry transported twelve well-armed Irish
National Army soldiers. The Leyland held four military men
while the Slieve carried an additional five. Strung out in single
file, the procession's mechanised sound disturbed the tranquillity
of the rural West Cork countryside.

The brass clock on the Leyland's dash had just gone ten of
eight. It had been a long day, frustrating at times. Ireland's newly
self-appointed, Provisional Government Army Commander-
in-Chief General Michael Collins dozed in the rear seat of his
fine-looking vehicle. The charismatic, shrewd yet sometimes
impetuous Corkman, still the country's unofficial political leader,
was suffering the effects of gastric ulcers and a weeklong head

3

cold. With chin tucked into his chest and eyes closed, the Big Fellow nodded off. His handsome, powerfully built body appeared constricted in the auto's limited seating space. Up front, M. B. Corry, Collins's substitute driver, sat behind the wheel, operating the forty-horsepower motor car that sported a modified lightweight racing chassis.

Sitting almost sideways next to Corry, his right leg bent beneath his left, was Major Aran Roe O'Neill, fondly nicknamed the Irish Rebel by his close friends. Sans peaked cap, his tousled light-brown, curly hair waved unrestrained as the hoodless auto motored toward its evening destination: Macroom then back to Cork City. The tall, athletic-looking, twenty-three-year-old soldier's coal-black eyes darted anxiously from side to side. Aran steadfastly refused fatigue's seductive call. He was on duty. Lives might well depend on his ability to respond at a moment's notice. Like the others in General Collins's party though, he felt drained of energy. Dark half-moons marked the skin beneath his eyes. He longed for sleep, telling himself: *Once in the bed, I won't rise 'till noon tomorrow.*

Stretching, this seventh son of a seventh son from Gort, a village in western County Galway, arched his back. He tried lessening the growing ache he felt from leaning against the vehicle's side door. As Aran shifted his weight, he glanced back over his right shoulder at his friend and C-in-C seated diagonally behind him.

Collins's large frame, half upright, half sprawled in the Leyland's leather rear seat, infringed on the car's fourth occupant, Major-General Emmet Dalton. The moustached, angular-faced, trim-figured commander of the military area surrounding Cork City was but another of Collins's travelling companions and bodyguards assembled for today's tour of West Cork. Their friendship stretched back over three years to the days when Emmet was Director of Training for the burgeoning Irish Republican Army's General Headquarters staff in Dublin during the recently concluded War of Independence.

In deference to his commander's need for rest, the lanky Dalton gave Collins the extra room Mick's legs demanded.

Turning back, Aran again focused his eyes on the road ahead, searching for anything out of the ordinary. Though they were travelling through Collins's own home county, this was now 'enemy' territory. Many of their *former* comrades-in-arms, commonly referred to as Republicans, anti-Treatyites, anti-Treaty IRA, Irregulars or simply bands had it in for Michael and his lot, branded Free Staters, Staters, pro-Treatyites or pro-Treaty IRA. Some of this latter faction also belonged to the newly formed Provisional National Army or Irish Army for short. The Republicans blamed Collins, titular leader of the newly created Irish Free State, for bargaining with the British and finally reaching a debatable accord with their age-old foe. They believed Mick had sold out Ireland's yearning for a united, thirty-two county Republic, settling for the present-day status quo: twenty-six Free State counties. That agreement left the six remaining counties still under British rule.

Suddenly, Aran Roe's sixth sense alerted him things were not quite right. With his left hand, he hastily pulled his dependable Colt .45 from its hip holster. It was the very one Thomas Coogan had given him in Dublin during Easter Week, 1916. As Aran ran his right hand along its cold, comforting steel surface, he smiled. Nodding with satisfaction, the Gortman patted his trusty American revolver, thinking: *Sure, if anyone tries something out here, they'll have this to deal with.* Deftly, he slipped the weapon back into its leather holder. Momentarily diverting his eyes from the undergrowth lining the isolated roadway, Aran anxiously glanced back again. He marvelled at how relaxed Michael seemed, despite the ominous presence of continual danger. Prior to leaving Dublin's Portobello Barracks on Sunday last, the thirty-one-year-old Collins had repeatedly stated, "*Nobody* would shoot *me* in my own country. Sure, they'd *never* attack me there."

As the linnet flies, they were only a handful of miles away from Woodfield, Mick's birthplace, but that fact offered no great comfort to the Gortman. Through personal experience, Aran knew Mick Collins was a rock of a man, usually in control of his thoughts and emotions; that is until he chose to vent his passion at someone or something. But did the Irregulars care about all that? Weren't they pursuing their own agenda void of Mick's leadership these days?

The Irish Rebel knew the Big Fellow thought he was finally on the verge of bringing Ireland's two-month-old civil war to a *just* end, not just a military one. That's what this cross country journey was all about. Through his own determined force of character, Collins had both sides talking to one another once again: the Free Staters and the Republicans. A tentative agreement might be struck as early as tomorrow, certainly by week's end. Aran smiled to himself, marvelling at the way his friend commanded the respect of the differing parties. Despite the current conflict's many political complexities, Aran often struggled in his own mind to understand why the fighting had broken out in the first place. It all seemed so senseless, Irishmen fighting Irishmen. He couldn't help but think: *A house divided against itself…*

The Gortman's thoughts were suddenly interrupted. Out of the corner of his eye, he caught the glint of metal from the crest of a grassy ridge that ran parallel to their road.

Keeping one eye on the suspicious site, he turned and shouted above the reverberations of the convoy, "Something on the hill behind us…on the right, sirs."

Instinctively, Aran Roe reached under the folds of his unbuttoned greatcoat. There beneath his dark green, roll-neck, serge tunic, safely squirrelled away in its compact shoulder holster, was the German Luger automatic he had grown to prise. Smuggled aboard the Brazilian steamship by America's Clan na Gael in the spring of 1916, as he and the others first made their way to the United States, it had saved his life on more than one occasion. Feeling its comforting presence, he thought: *Ah, my friends, if it's a fight you want, sure…*

His thoughts were suddenly interrupted by the appearance of Lieutenant John Smith, the procession's motorcycle point scout. The young officer, hunched over his bike's handlebars, came flying back around an S-bend toward them. As the man raced down along the rutted dirt road, his frantic cries cut through the evening's air, now growing heavy in a light mist. "Mine in the roadway! Mine in the roadway…just up ahead."

Swinging around the braking Crossley, he sat up in his saddle and began waving an arm in the air. Unaware of the possible danger lurking on the neighbouring ridge, he shouted to the occupants of the Leyland, "Barricade up ahead. Mine, Mine..."

Aran, briefly confused, didn't know which way to focus his attention: hillside or straight on, but the ping of a bullet, glancing off the bonnet of the Leyland, quickly helped make up his mind. Their motor car was taking fire from the flanking hilltop off to their right.

"Bloody hell," cursed Aran out loud. Looking at Collins, he announced, "Irregulars firing down at us, sir."

Moments later, numerous rounds began hitting the roadway around them. Though several hundred yards away, the Irish Rebel could now see three men with rifles...no maybe it was four...all firing in their direction.

At the sound of the first ricocheting projectile and Aran's oath, Collins was wide awake. Sitting bolt upright, he grabbed the back of Corry's seat, and pulled himself to his feet in the open car. Dalton, a battle-hardened soldier who had served three years in the British Army as an officer in the First War, grabbed Michael's arm. "Mick, don't be a bloody fool. Get down...take cover."

Taking his friend's advice, the Big Fellow, muttering under his breath, sat down.

Well accustomed to giving orders under fire, Emmet leaned forward. He barked into the driver's ear, "Put your bleedin' boot down, Corry. Get us out of here...*fast*! Drive like hell. *Drive!*" Abruptly, the car leaped forward.

It had travelled only a short distance, however, when Collins suddenly intervened. Bellowing above the danger, he shouted, "Stop! Stop! We'll fight them! We'll fight 'em here!"

Obeying his Commander-in-Chief, Corry braked sharply, pitching everyone forward. Aran's head banged into the windscreen. Dalton nearly toppled over into the front seat. Momentarily dazed, Aran thought he saw Collins, rifle in hand, bound from the car and disappear from view.

Shaking off the effects of the blow, Aran swung around. Opening the now stopped Leyland's side door, he tumbled out onto the roadway. Following the Gortman's lead, Dalton did likewise. Being careful, they kept the auto between them and the men firing down at them from the ridge beyond.

Corry too, clutching a rifle, made a hurried exit from the motor car. Keeping low and using the undergrowth as cover, the driver ran forward up the road in the direction of the Crossley tender, disappearing around a bend.

Crouched alongside the Leyland, General Dalton and Major O'Neill quickly realised the safety of their present position was lost. They were now under attack from *both* sides of the roadway. Missiles whizzed at them from all directions. They were caught in a deadly crossfire. Moments later, a bullet shattered the auto's windscreen. Another lodged itself in the motor car's door, just inches above their heads. Instantly, both men flattened out on the ground, seeking the limited protection of a low mud bank bordering the road. Fear and anger coloured their faces.

❧

In the meantime, Smith, still on his motorcycle, swung around and roared back up the road. Quickly overtaking the stopped Crossley, he slowed, shouting instructions to the driver, "Keep it slow…follow me!"

As Smith neared the spot where he'd first spotted the cables to a road mine, and where a disabled brewer's dray had been left across the road forming a crude Republican barricade, he was hit in the neck by an Irregular's bullet. Knocked off his bike, the scout rolled toward the edge of the road, seeking the protection of some overgrown foliage.

On his back, Smith performed a hurried examination of his wound. Realising he was just nicked, the scout scrambled up onto his hands and knees. Staying low, the young officer waved for the approaching Crossley to halt. The driver did as he was ordered.

❧

With the tender stopped, the vehicle's other front-seat oc-cupant, sporting a new Thompson machine gun, leaped to the ground. Moments later, as Smith scurried like a frightened ani-mal toward the lorry's sheltering frame, the motorcyclist heard the unmistakable voice of Captain Gabriel McCracken, barking out orders to his fellow troopers. In terse, forceful but composed directives the Irish-American ordered, "You, Neill...Neill Mor-rison...get down out of there from behind that wheel. The two McDonalds...Tommy and Seamus...you two set up the Lewis gun and cover our arses. The rest of yis...out of the lorry. Quick now, before someone gets killed."

Pointing a finger, Gabby ordered, "O'Connell, Sonny Lucey and you Neill...plus two more...Cody and O'Grady, spread out. Work your way back down the road, and give those lads in the Leyland some cover. From the sounds of it, Collins and the others may be in trouble. Seán, you're in charge of them."

Except for the two McDonalds, who were readying the ma-chine gun for action, the lorry emptied quickly.

"Shay, Conor and Rory...over here...you're with me."

"And me, sir? What about me?"

Gabby looked up. One last man was scrambling down out of the lorry.

"Ah, yes. Palmer is it?"

"Not quite, sir," answered the trooper, now crouching defen-sively on one knee in the roadway.

Impatiently, Gabriel took a step in his direction. "Well...?"

"It's Palmerston, sir. Sergeant David Palmerston...at your service, sir."

This man appeared to be in his early thirties, well groomed and fit. The soldier handled himself well, no doubt from years of military service. Since they had left Dublin, however, Gay had noticed the man preferred to keep to himself rather than mixing with the others.

The Irish-American officer hesitated. He disliked the trooper's ingratiating manner, plus the man's accent grated on his nerves. This new recruit was English. Like others, both former officers and enlisted men, he'd been demobbed from the British Army in Dublin earlier in the year. Instead of returning home to face possible unemployment, he'd enlisted in the nascent Provisional Government Army which was hungry for recruits. Once Ireland's foe, today Palmerston and his crowd were in the employ of the new Free State. Needless to say, this conundrum was reviled by many for both historic as well as personal reasons.

With annoyance, Gay said, "Right...Palmerston, you catch up with Seán's squad. Off you go now, on the double."

Hurriedly turning his attention to those left around the lorry, he made a mental note to speak to Michael and Aran about all the 'outsiders' who'd come over lately. He'd been meaning to do so for some time, but had kept his thoughts on the long finger. In his mind, their presence in Ireland's military just didn't sit well with him.

With a sense of urgency clearly audible in his voice, Mc-Cracken hurriedly addressed the motorcycle scout, "Are ye up to scratch, lieutenant?"

Before Smith could answer, he probed further, "J. J., any fight in ya left?"

Touching the bandage Neill Morrison had just wrapped his neck with, the man nodded.

"Right so. We can use an extra gun."

Looking directly at the wounded soldier, Gabriel said, "Ready to push off?"

Again, Smith nodded.

"Then fall in behind me."

With a sweeping wave of his hand, the Irish-American officer told his diminutive force, "Bugger it! Let's give those dodgy lads out there a taste of their own medicine."

Crouching low, Captain McCracken moved away from the security of the lorry. Looking back over his shoulder, he ordered, "Smith and the rest of yis keep your arses down...stay ten paces apart. Remember, no talking and don't fire until I give the order."

Cautiously, the makeshift squad ran single file up the road in the direction of the downed motorcycle. They were under the scant protection of some long grass, leafy bushes and willowy saplings that bordered a small stream to their left.

Like Dalton, Gabriel McCracken was an experienced combatant: not a trenched, barb-wired, poison gas-filled European war combatant like his superior, but a veteran Irish guerrilla fighter. He had met Aran during the summer of 1916. The Gortman and three other Irish rebels, Liam Mellowes, Richard 'Shadow' Doyle and Danny Kelly, had fled Ireland, seeking the safety of Amerikay, after the failed Easter Rebellion. By sheer coincidence or Fate's design, the McCracken family, who farmed near the village and Civil War battlefield of Manassas, Virginia, offered sanctuary to two of the rebels: the wounded Aran and his older Irish travelling companion, Shadow.

As time played itself out, a strong bond grew between the McCrackens and their two Irish visitors. It became so fervent that in the spring of 1917, when the four exiled revolutionaries finally headed back to Ireland, Gabriel, his twenty-one-year-old sister Sarah Anne, and his friend Turlough Molloy decided to join them. They wanted to be a part of what Liam Mellowes called his 'little Irish-rebel outfit.'

Stooped and moving with care, Gabby, the thirty-six-year-old National Army man, who'd become as Irish as the Irish over the past five years, headed up along the verge of the road. Owing to the stress of the moment, his usual smile was absent, but the twinkle in his eyes was still there. It would take more than a few renegade shots to frighten that away.

Gay's good-looking, slender frame was crowned with wavy brown hair, a thinly pointed nose and finely etched lips. Even with danger lurking about, he moved with poise despite the nagging discomfort of sensitive ribs, a War of Independence souvenir. Gripping the Thompson[1] with his left hand, its butt almost kissing the ground, he pressed forward. In his right hand, a Webley & Scott .455 Mark 1 automatic pistol stabbed the air.

Gabriel McCracken felt his face flush, burning with the excitement of it all. Being under fire again both frightened and

---

1. The Thompson machine gun was first imported into Ireland in May, 1921. Tom Barry. *Guerilla Days In Ireland*. Dublin, 1993, 193.

invigorated this Irish-American. Thoughts of his wife Áine and their baby daughter Mary Margaret flashed through his head. These were quickly followed by his own sense of duty for safeguarding his C-in-C, and for keeping himself and those under his charge alive.

Desperately, Gay scanned the undergrowth to his left, searching for an easy way across the Noneen stream and its marshy banks.

Appraising the moment, he thought: *Thanks be to God, we don't seem to be in danger from those eejits behind us. They seem more intent on attacking the motor car and Slieve than my lot.*

Abruptly, though, things changed. Scattered rounds began whistling through the undergrowth around Gabby and his men. More were ploughing into the roadway up ahead. From the sound of things, they were taking fire from the other side of the Noneen as well as from the hilltop just off to their right. The reverberations sounded like a mixture of Lee-Enfields, revolvers and a Thompson machine gun.

As if in answer to an unspoken prayer, Gabriel suddenly spotted an opening in the vegetation. There, off to the left, was a little stone bridge spanning the stream. On the opposite side, a narrow brown track, with a grassy ribbon running through its centre, disappeared up a small hill. To the left, an elevated boreen headed back down along the tributary.

Moving swiftly, the five men crossed the bridge unharmed and fanned out. Warily, they moved up the hillside, taking cover behind trees and bits of an old stone wall that once marked the breast of the hill. Safely out of view of the hillside snipers opposite them, Gay's men strained to see who'd fired at the convoy from the boreen below. Hearing the occasional rifle crack up ahead, the soldiers made ready to meet the enemy. Hoping for the element of surprise, they prepared to counter-attack if the Irregulars failed to surrender.

❧

Under command of their leader, the six lorry foot-soldiers had spread out along the main thoroughfare. Cautiously, O'Connell and his men began moving back toward the Leyland. Along the way they encountered Corry, the auto's driver. He'd sought sanctuary in an eroded gully along the roadside. Seán ordered him to fall in behind the others.

As the soldiers guardedly proceeded, some fired up the hill to their left while others launched an attack at the rifle cracks coming from their right. Both sides of the Noneen's banks, however, were lined with small trees and bushes, making it difficult for the National Army men to see their antagonists.

While all this was happening, the armoured car reversed, taking up a firing position some fifty or sixty yards behind the Leyland. The gunner in the Slieve na mBan, John 'Jock' McPeak, opened fire with his water-cooled Vickers machine gun. He enfiladed three hundred yards of ground opposite him and down to his left, toward a second small bridge, marking the southern end of the boreen.

That was enough for the Irregulars positioned there. Quickly, they began beating a hasty retreat westward across farm fields. Moments later, however, McPeak's gun jammed. Sensing a rebalancing of firepower, several of the anti-Treaty men slipped back toward the lower end of the dirt track. Using the bridge's stone uprights for cover, they resumed their attack on the Free Staters still cornered in the roadway.

In the meantime, Aran's fleeting impression had been correct. Michael Collins had indeed jumped from the car after commanding it to stop. Running low, the Corkman moved north, in the direction of the tender. Taking up a prone position along the edge of the road, he fired his Lee-Enfield rifle at the hill-men.

It was the first time in his storied military career Collins had *ever* fired a weapon at the 'enemy.' Not once had he done so during Easter Week, 1916 or throughout the violence of the following years. In the recently ended two-year-plus War of Independence, the Big Fellow had operated from behind the scenes. Sure, he'd issued many orders resulting in the wounding or death of others, but he'd *never* pulled a trigger in the heat of battle.

Quickly coming to the realisation the enemy was firing at his Free State soldiery from differing directions, Michael stood up and ran back toward the Leyland. With the Crossley tender and its slowly advancing reinforcements behind him, Collins sprinted down the road past Aran and Emmet's position alongside the touring car. On he went, like a man possessed. Finally, he took up a new position well south of the Slieve na mBan. Rather than lying prone on the ground or stopping to use the metal monster for cover, he remained standing, totally unprotected.

As if the heady intoxication of the moment had clouded his judgement, he cried out to his army comrades, "Come on, lads. There they are by the bridge. Let's give 'em a taste of their own medicine."

With poise and courage, the Big Fellow began firing at the men near the second bridge, while bullets danced dangerously around him.

❧

Aran and General Dalton were still pinned down. By lying next to the margin of the road, the auto shielded them from the men on the hill, while a diminutive mud bank and ample undergrowth hid their exact position from those along the raised boreen behind them. Neither Free Staters nor Republicans had clear shots at each other. It was a stand-off. The Irregulars had no desire to show themselves or take any unnecessary chances that might result in personal injury or death. Squeezing off the occasional round to keep the Free Staters at bay, the feuding conflict continued.

❧

Thankfully, the hostilities began to abate as dark slowly descended over the thirty-minute encounter. No one to Aran or Emmet's knowledge had been killed or injured. That was proving commonplace during these early Civil War encounters. It seemed the former comrades-in-arms simply preferred flaunting any military advantages gained at the expense of the other. The battlefield wounds inflicted were, generally, more psychological than mortal. Recently though, Aran wondered when this surrealistic face-off might change.

❧

It was during this momentary lull in the action that Aran and Emmet heard running footsteps approaching their position. Both men looked up to see Collins sprint by their sheltering car. He was heading toward the Slieve.

With his voice full of emotion, Emmet yelled out, "Bloody hell!

Get your feckin' arse down, Michael," but in all the excitement, his words went unheard or unheeded.

Aran's stomach turned. A frightening, angry knot tightened inside him. He knew he had to do something. His beloved friend and commander was in grave danger.

Without need of prompting, dreadful memories flashed through the Irish Rebel's head. Following the collapse of the Easter Rebellion in 1916, he'd been unable to come to the aid of his hero and mentor Patrick Pearse. He often thought: *If only I'd stayed by his side, things might have turned out differently.*

Then he was in Amerikay when Brigid Eileen tragically died, an act of drunken, sectarian savagery. Sure, her murder still haunted him: *If only I hadn't left Ireland...*

There were also the memories of Turlough Molloy, Kevin Barry and Shadow's wife Helen. In his mind he knew he wasn't responsible for their deaths, but his heart frequently ached over those painful tragedies. He often countered this distress with: *Didn't they die for Ireland?* But usually that response didn't quell his torment. The realities of the human cost of war continually resurface. It nagged at him: *Was it worth it all? Isn't there another way?*

It was during such moments of anguish that Aran would remember Pearse's last words to him. They were standing together, inside the General Post Office on that Easter Friday. Their Dublin Rebellion headquarters was ablaze, collapsing around them. James Connolly's occupying forces were abandoning the building, carrying their wounded commandant out on a makeshift stretcher.

In the hurried confusion of the evacuation effort, the Irish Rebel noticed Ireland's new president standing off to one side. He went up to his mentor and headmaster, tears filling his eyes. But Pearse only smiled. His voice was strong and resilient, as he spoke to his beloved student, "Aran, we have lit such a flame that from this day forth, it shall never be put out. It will burn from mountain top to mountain top…from stony field to stony field…from Dublin Town to the smallest hamlet in Ireland.

"God bless and protect you, Aran. You are the hope of a new Ireland. We here have passed our torch of hope and freedom to you. Guard it and care for it well. I know it is safe in your strong hands."

Aran remembered giving Pearse his promise to do so just before he left the GPO under 'The O'Rahilly's' command.

But now, the troubles of the past few months, compounded by the recent years of fighting, only magnified the struggle in his mind between balancing the cost of human life against Ireland's dream of independence and self-government. Today, its asking price mandated more anguish, more sacrifice and more death, as the new Provisional Government's veneer of overseeing a divided Ireland was wearing thin.

Bit by bit, this 'cause for Ireland' was consuming Aran and his countrymen and women. Its repugnant demands were tearing at his nation's soul like rats stealing each others' scraps. This present-day eruption, with its seemingly unquenchable thirst for aggression and, what could only be imagined as far-reaching consequences, threatened to destroy the country's very core. The thought of all this, this blood on the Éireann's shamrock, made the Gortman sick…sick and angry.

Harbouring the weighty sensations of confusion, pain and,

more recently, bubbling anger, the Irish Rebel sprang to his feet. He didn't want the past repeating itself...not here...not again. The Big Fellow was Ireland's hope. Nothing must happen to him. Certainly not if he had any say in the matter.

With fire in his eyes and throwing caution aside, Aran dashed down the road after Michael, firing his .45 and Luger automatic for cover. The distance between the Leyland and the Slieve was about fifty yards. His C-in-C was another thirty or so yards beyond that. Running past the armoured car, Aran, in disbelief, saw General Collins go down.

The rest of the encounter played itself out like a dream. Later, Emmet told him he'd let out a horrendous scream. At first, the Major-General thought his youthful counterpart had been hit. But no, the Gortman kept going.

Moments later, however, Aran Roe was on the ground too, kneeling beside the fallen body of Michael Collins. With weapons aside, he cradled the bleeding head of his leader in his hands.

Forgetting the recent months of bitter dissention and divisive antagonism between former comrades, the Irish Rebel cried out, demanding, "Help! Help! I need help! Somebody! Anybody! Michael Collins has been hit."

The firing stopped, but no answering voice was heard nor any movement seen. The only sounds Aran heard were his own heaving breath and pounding heart. For a split second he wondered: *Where the hell's Emmet?*

Abruptly, he returned his attention to his fallen friend. There appeared to be a gaping wound at the back of Mick's head. Blood and cerebral matter had spilled out onto Aran's uniform. Because of all the reddened matted hair, he couldn't be sure where the wound was: maybe behind his right ear? Frantically, he grabbed at a handkerchief from his coat pocket. In hopes of arresting the bleeding, the Gortman pressed it to Michael's head.

Gasping with emotion, Aran cried, "For the love of God, Míceal...please, please open your eyes...say something. Oh, Míceal, Míceal, don't be afraid, the Lord and I are with you."

Firmly holding the now blood-soaked cloth to Collins's head, the Irish Rebel leaned over. Lovingly he touched his forehead to the Corkman's cheek. Then out of despair, he whispered, "Please, oh heavenly Lord, don't let Míceal die. I love him so. What will I do without him? What will *Ireland* do?"

Now, sitting bolt upright on his knees, the Rebel spoke directly to Michael. At first Aran's voice was strident, almost commanding, but as he continued, it softened, trailing off. "NO! NO! DON'T GO, Michael. *We can't*...survive...without you... don't go...don't... go...Michael..."

But as the seconds passed and Michael failed to respond, Aran's anguish mounted. Calling on Ireland's patron saint, he implored, "For the love of St. Patrick, Mick...open your eyes. Sure, 'tis *only* you who can save *us* from all this bloody madness."

With fear suddenly erupting inside him, Aran Roe again pleaded, "Oh, dear Lord, don't let him die. With all of your power and goodness, please save him...let him live. "

In his next breath, however, overwhelmed by the utter helplessness of the situation, he silently began chastising himself. Desperately, he reasoned: *If only I can still my trembling hands, maybe I'll be able to stop the bleeding...*

But with tears cascading down his face, all Aran could do was cradle his beloved commander's bloodied head, rocking him gently from side to side.

Whispering softly, he said, "Sure I know Thy will be done, but not today, please God, not Michael...no, not today."

Closing his eyes, hoping momentarily to escape the hideousness enveloping him, Aran unexpectedly beheld a vision, a woman dressed all in white, moving toward him. The image floated gracefully though the air, beckoning. He tried, straining to recognise the apparition's shrouded face. Was it a banshee...? *Brigid...?*

❧

Emmet had heard the call for help, but hesitated. Rather than recklessly dashing out in response to Aran's cry, he paused. His military training instincts seemingly had kicked in, overruling what his heart was telling him. Hastily, he reconnoitred the situation from his limited vantage point behind the Leyland. All appeared quiet.

Suddenly, his emotions took over. Realising the catastrophe that was possibly unfolding, and ignoring the likelihood of hidden dangers, the major-general dashed out from behind the safety of the motor car. Keeping low and zigzagging as he went, Emmet Dalton raced toward the downed figures in the roadway.

Less than a step away from the two men, he also fell to his knees, uttering, "Oh my God…no, no! Please, Mary and Joseph, save him. Save Michael in this his hour of need."

As if sensing their presence and responding to their pleas, Mick slowly opened his eyes. With the faintest hint of a smile on his lips, he whispered, "Aran…Emmet…" A moment later, Michael Collins, one of Ireland's greatest military leaders and political masterminds, took his last breath, closing his eyes forever.

Thus it came to pass, that there, on a dusty bit of Irish road, God chose to reach down and take Michael home…home for eternity.

❧

…and so tragically, on that narrow stretch of road, running through the entrance of a subtle, meandering ravine, hard by the River Bride and the little Noneen, both flowing through and around lush Irish fields, at a place called Béalnabláth in the heart of County Cork, the shortest and most significant military engagement in Ireland's storied history was played out. As Father Patrick Twohig later wrote, "The action was neither battle nor ambush. The fighting 'became general' as the expression is. A running skirmish is what it turned out to be."[2]

---

2. Patrick J. Twohig. *The Dark Secret of Béalnabláth.* Ballincollig, Ireland, 1991, 159.

2

*"Greater love hath no man than this, that a man
lay down his life for his friends."*

John 15:13

The morning had dawned sunny and bright. Aran Roe O'Neill
remembered their military convoy departing Cork City's military
headquarters, the Imperial Hotel, at six o'clock sharp. Michael had
planned on meeting several area Republicans during the day. He
wanted to discuss the ground rules for ending the conflict.

Aran vividly recalled that the local IRA leadership had promised them safe passage, and that the word had been spread to
'stand down.' That was the reason they were motoring through
this Republican back garden with such an unusually small military escort.

Despite all the assurances from their former comrades-
in-arms, travelling through West Cork was still dangerous. The
anti-Treatyites, as a general precaution against pro-Treaty, Irish
Army forces attacking them, had trenched many area roads or
barricaded them with felled trees. This made movement from one
place to another often difficult or impossible. The rebels had also

blown up many rail and road bridges. Additionally, motorway links were frequently mined at strategic spots, while roving bands of well-armed men served as lookouts and ambush parties.

Today, War-of-Independence guerrilla tactics were being employed, not against the evacuating British army, but against their own Irish countrymen. Despite the fact the Irregulars were often disorganised and their leadership habitually in disagreement about how to prosecute the war, the rebels were determined to persevere and overcome the obstacles thrown their way by Collins and his newly organised army.

❧

All Aran could think was: *Oh Lord, what have we done?* He was dazed and his eyes wouldn't focus. His head seemed detached from his body. He was numb…all human sensations switched off. Bewildered by the events of the last few moments, the Gortman was unable to move. His world had changed in just a handful of seconds…changed utterly, but this time no terrible beauty would be born…only death. It was too dreamlike to believe, but the evidence was there, stretched out before him. On that dusty bit of Irish road lay the lifeless form of Ireland's greatest modern military and political leader, General Michael Collins: his dear friend.

Kneeling opposite the Irish Rebel was Major-General Emmet Dalton, bent over their C-in-C, feeling for a pulse. Shocked and confused as well, he slowly looked up at Aran. With tears in his eyes, he shook his head, "He's gone, Aran. He's gone."

Rocking back on his heels, Dalton was also too stunned to say any more. Both men just stared down at the lifeless body of the Big Fellow lying between them.

As the seconds ticked by, the once vital remains of the man who had often been credited with 'winning the war,' Ireland's War of Independence with Britain, began to change as death and night slowly enveloped them. Michael's flushed cheeks, a residue of battle excitement, gradually lost their rosy hue. As Aran and his superior looked on in disbelief, Collins's ruddy complexion seemed to fade, leaving only a ghostly ashen remainder on the roadway.

After what seemed an eternity, Aran gently lowered Michael's head to the ground. As he uncoiled from his kneeling position, the Gortman's stiff legs cried out. Once on his feet, however, the Irish Rebel could feel his bodily senses returning. But the knot in the pit of his stomach had returned; that strange old feeling of his was back. It seemed to wash over him like an incoming tide.

Under close inspection, blood and brain matter were evident on the upper part of Mick's uniform, while dirt and mud stained his sleeves and trouser legs. The fingers of his right hand were red, no doubt the result of instinctively touching his head after he'd been hit. In his left hand, Michael still clutched the wooden stock of his new Lee-Enfield Mark 5 rifle, recently supplied to the National Army by Britain.

Michael's peaked military cap was missing, knocked off by the impact of the bullet or bullets that had claimed his life. The Gortman looked for it, but it lay unnoticed some yards away, along the edge of the road.

By now, several of the men housed inside the armoured car had clamoured out of their vehicle. Also joining Aran and Emmet in the roadway were Seán O'Connell and four of his men.

It was before these witnesses that Aran quietly uttered the Act of Contrition. Michael had died defending his beliefs, fighting for Ireland on Irish soil with his beloved Cork hills surrounding him. Unlike another of Ireland's past heroes, 17th-century, exiled patriot Patrick Sarsfield, who died fighting for France in Belgium, Michael had not taken his last breath on foreign soil. Be it a small consolation, but Sarsfield's famous dying words, "Oh, that this were for Ireland," wouldn't be Michael's epithet. "He died for Ireland on his native soil," would seem more fitting.

The major-general, now on his feet as well, had also regained his composure. Noticing that all eyes had shifted from Collins's still form to himself, Emmet realised the troopers were awaiting their orders. Abruptly, his voice came to life.

"Who's in charge of your group O'Connell?"

"I am, sir."

"How many in your command?"

"Six plus meself, sir."

"Fine. Set up a perimeter...up and down the roadway here. Provide us with some cover, though from the sounds of things, I doubt if there will be anymore gunfire tonight."

"As you wish, sir."

With that, Seán set about the task of assigning his small force to positions along the road between their present location to just up beyond the Leyland. "Keep a sharp lookout in all directions. Rifles at the ready men, and don't make a muck of it," he ordered.

As Emmet and Aran quietly conversed, deciding on what to do next, Captain McCracken's voice could be heard from the opposite side of the Noneen. "All clear on this side of the creek. Permission to come across, sir?"

Emmet glanced back down at Collins then answered in a crisp, clear voice, "Permission granted, but we have a casualty."

From his position on the eastern side of the stream, Aran could hear Gabriel ordering his squad to fall in.

Without waiting for Emmet's approval, Aran ran back up the road and climbed atop the armoured car. From this vantage point, he could just make out the stone bridge in the fading light.

Shouting, he directed his friend. "Gay, head downstream. There's a bridge across the water just south of where you are."

Aran jumped off the Slieve and sprinted back past Michael's body toward the bridge.

As Gabriel came into view, Aran called out, "Gay, leave one of your men at each end of the bridge...just in case, and for God's sake, hurry."

Gabriel dashed across the stone overpass followed closely by J. J. Smith and Conor Makem. Shay Keller and Rory Sheehan stayed back as ordered.

As the Irish-American came to a stop alongside his friend, Aran blurted out, "Michael's dead, Gay. He was hit in the head...just up the road here."

"Oh, Mother of God, not Michael!" Gay exclaimed. "What in the hell's going to happen now?"

"It's too soon to answer that, my friend, but I'm afraid the entire country might explode, if we are not careful."

"Where is he? I want to see him."

Aran turned. The two men, followed closely by Smith and Makem, headed back up the roadway to where a blanket from the armoured car now covered the outline of Michael Collins.

Gabriel knelt down on one knee. Slowly he pulled the blanket away covering Michael's face. Upon seeing Mick's blood-covered head, Gay let out a moan of disbelieve and anguish. His shoulders shook as his soft sobs filled the evening's silence.

No one spoke for what seemed the longest time.

❧

Abruptly, Emmet's voice broke the mourning. His tone and words told all he'd assumed command. "Sure, it's time we got the hell out of here. Some of you carry General Collins to the Slieve. We'll transport him up to the Leyland on it."

"By the way, where's Corry?"

"He's back up the road, sir," replied O'Connell.

"Have him make sure the motor car is in running order. We'll need to find a priest and then get directions to Cork City once we're away from here."

Standing beside his superior, Aran interjected, "Just a moment, Emmet. Before we move Michael, I'd like to bandage his head."

Dalton nodded his approval.

With that, Aran shouted up to the men still inside the Slieve, "Where's that first aid kit yis carry?"

Moments later, the Gortman was again kneeling over the body of his friend. Gently, he wrapped a linen bandaging cloth around the Corkman's head. He was careful not to cover the dead man's eyes. Aran wasn't quite sure why he had done that so. Maybe in his heart he hoped Michael might suddenly spring to life, proving the entire episode was nothing but a bad dream.

❅

At last, Michael's body was hoisted up onto the armoured car's metal decking and driven back to the waiting touring car.

In the fading light Dalton could see Corry hovering over the Leyland Eight. His head and shoulders were tucked under the auto's raised bonnet.

"Please God, tell us you can get this thing running, Corry."

"Yes, General Dalton. I think she'll be fine."

With that, Corry lowered the bonnet and slid in behind the wheel. He turned the ignition key and the powerful engine sprang to life.

Looking over at the major-general, Corry nodded. "See, she's as good as ever, sir."

"Fine. Everyone back to their vehicles," directed Dalton. But before obeying their new commanding officer, each man filed past the body of Michael Collins, which had been placed in the back seat of the Leyland. As if to satisfy some personal need, in turn, they reached down, touching the Corkman's body. Most whispered a short prayer, then hurriedly made the sign of the cross before moving away from the motor car.

❅

Positioned to afford the C-in-C the utmost dignity, Aran Roe O'Neill cradled Michael's bandaged head in his lap. The auto's woollen travel rug had been carefully draped over the Corkman's chest and legs.

At Emmet's command, the four-vehicle convoy closed ranks and headed north toward Crookstown: Smith and his motorcycle first, followed by the Leyland, the Crossley and the armoured car, each an orderly fifteen yards apart.

❅

The last vestiges of twilight were settling over the West Cork hills and its lush countryside when the procession stopped a man, presumably a local resident, walking along the road. The convoy had just passed the Béalnabláth crossroads, and was a little more than a mile north of the skirmish site. Dalton, now seated next to Corry, asked where they might find the nearest priest and the best way to Cork City.

The man, noticing Collins in the back seat, asked if your one was ill. "None of your business," snapped Dalton. "Now, answer my queries so."

Having received the requested directions, the convoy made for Cloughduv, which was just east of Crookstown. After several mistaken turns and time-consuming backtracking, the convoy finally found the curate's house.

Responding to Emmet's cry of, "Hello the house," from the roadway, a priest finally emerged, carrying an oil lamp. With his free hand, the man clutched at a coat covering his holy attire.

Remaining in the auto, Emmet introduced himself to the man. Dalton then stated that one of the soldiers in his party had been killed. "Would you be kind enough, Father, to say a few words for the man's departed soul?"

Father Timothy Murphy, not realising who the dead man was, said another Act of Contrition. Several other prayers were offered up after which the priest concluded his blessing with the sign of the cross.

Instead of waiting, however, for the clergyman to return from the presbytery with his Holy anointing oils, Dalton ordered the convoy to move off.

When Aran asked him why they'd left so abruptly, he simply replied, "It's late and getting more so. Sure, I know all of us are cold and hungry. Besides, we're sitting targets for any trigger-happy eejit wanting to make a name for himself."

❧

In the meantime, despite the poor light, the passer-by, who Dalton had stopped for directions near the crossroads, had recognised Collins in the back seat. Immediately after the convoy disappeared from sight, he hurried back to Long's Pub at Béalnabláth Cross.

Entering the door of the dimly lit public house, he excitedly announced, "Sure, yis will never guess who I saw dead in the rear seat of that touring car that just passed by…it was Michael Collins himself. Yes indeed, the Big Fellow, shot through the head as sure as I'm standing here."

People stared at the newcomer, but no one said a word. Several, however, did bow their heads.

As the region was a rebel hotbed, there were several Irregulars seated at a corner table. These men were well aware that an ambush had been organised after Collins and his party were spotted in the area earlier that morning. Though these three IRA men had not taken part in the surprise attack, the scheme was known to most local residents.

By sheer coincidence, officers from several battalion and brigade units of the anti-Treaty IRA's 1st Southern Division had been summoned to Murray's farmhouse for a meeting that day. It was some of the men from this gathering, under the leadership of Commandant Liam Deasy, who had been called upon to lay a trap for Collins's convoy. It was thought the travelling party might be forced to return that way later in the day, as many of the neighbouring roads had been rendered impassable by other fellow rebels.

After a brief conference, one of the Irregulars slipped out the pub's back door. He hurriedly ran up the hill to Murray's farmhouse, located at the end of the laneway that ran directly behind Long's, with the news.

Later, Deasy described his reaction to the news of Collins's death:

"…many of us left Murray's with heavy hearts. To those of us who had known Michael Collins personally…our sorrow was deep and lasting. We parted without discussion of any kind…each of us all too conscious of the tragedy and the loneliness that only time could heal."[1]

---

1. Liam Deasy. *Brother Against Brother*. Dublin, 1998, 80.

❦

The journey to Cork City should have taken the convoy less than an hour. In reality, it took them almost five. In the inky blackness, the grief-stricken party became lost on narrow, unfamiliar and poorly signposted roads.

Out of mounting frustration, the caravan tried crossing several farm fields in a desperate attempt to reach the main Cork road. Unfortunately, both the Slieve na mBan and the Leyland Eight became stuck in the mud and had to be left behind until morning. Fortunately, though, the Crossley tender did manage to free itself with the added traction gained from troopers spreading blankets, greatcoats and tree branches along its path. That, combined with the pushing and pulling by exhausted soldiers, turned the short journey into a long, ghastly nightmare.

It was almost two in the morning when the lorry, overcrowded with wet, mucky men and bearing the body of General Michael Collins finally arrived into Cork City.

During this epic trek of only nineteen miles, it was Aran Roe O'Neill who'd assumed the responsibility of minding Michael. He directed blanket-touting, soldier-porters to be careful as they carried the Corkman across muddy fields, through patches of barbed nettles and over low stone walls. He patiently stood watch over the body, waiting in the pitch-blackness for the Crossley to be finally freed from its muddy entrapment.

During that five-hour-long adventure, Aran had time to think back over the days and hours leading up to Michael's death.

❦

After months of fruitless talks, Civil War fighting suddenly broke out in Dublin Town in the early morning hours of 28 June, just seven weeks ago. By the 5 July, most anti-Treaty elements had fled the city or were captured.

The next task facing Provisional-Government Chairman Michael Collins and his executive was to retake the parts of the country controlled by Irregular forces. Initially, these anti-Treaty bands held the advantage, outnumbering the Irish Army approximately 13,000 to 9,000. The rebels also possessed the majority of the war's initial armaments. But by the middle of July, this National Army weapons deficit had been overcome, thanks in great measure to large shipments of military equipment from Britain. It was clear to Aran and the pro-Treaty leadership that Winston Churchill, the Empire's Colonial Secretary, and the British cabinet were determined to see the new Provisional Irish Government succeed. Westminster also wanted the recently ratified Anglo-Irish Treaty fully implemented.

On 12 July, Michael decided to take military matters into his own hands. He temporarily transferred his authority as head of state to William Cosgrave, Dáil Éireann Minister for Local Government, and assumed the title of Commander-in-Chief of the new Provisional Irish Army. He planned to personally direct the war effort, judiciously ridding the country of its rebellious foe in short order.

By 12 August, the last major population centre, Cork City, had capitulated, under the exceptional leadership of Emmet Dalton. Irregular bands fled the city in advance of the National Army troopers who'd surprised their opposition by sailing into Cork harbour instead of attacking overland. The city fell without a fight.

As a military strategy, sea landings are one of the most difficult and dangerous manoeuvres to execute, but Dalton pulled it off brilliantly. It was later reported that the major-general had succeeded "by breaking all the rules of common sense and navigation and military science."[2]

All that remained now was overpowering the rebel IRA guerrilla columns that had taken safe harbour in the hills, mainly in counties Cork and Kerry.

That was one of the reasons why Michael had motored west. He wanted to bring the conflict to a quick end. He also wanted to inspect Irish Army installations, assess troop strength and scrutinize the extent of damage the war had caused the civilian

---

2. James Mackay. *Michael Collins: A Life*. Edinburgh, Scotland, 1996, 274.

population. The morale of both the Irish people and its military were important to Mick. Finally, the Corkman wanted to treat with the Irregular's leadership via several 'neutral' go-betweens. One such person was Florrie O'Donoghue.

Florrie, a former IRA leader during the War of Independence, had declared his neutrality after Civil War hostilities broke out. His past credentials cemented his position as a mediator between the two sides. Collins first met with O'Donoghue at Macroom's Victoria Hotel late in the afternoon on the 21st. He also planned to confer again with Florrie sometime during the early evening hours of the 22nd, after his day's inspection tour had been completed. With any luck, a truce and an end to the fighting might be forthcoming, almost immediately.

In his own mind, Aran reminisced how Michael and he had often discussed the reasons fuelling the war. Despite the recent turn of events that saw the Republicans revert to their previously successful War-of-Independence campaign of opportunistic hit and run, raid and ambush tactics, there was one element now missing: they didn't have the support and help of the Irish citizenry behind them.

Aran Roe was living testimony that without the aid and comfort of Éireann's dedicated folk, the celebrated War of Independence would have been a failure. During those desperate days of 1919–1921, Ireland's determined fighting force couldn't have withstood the English 'Strangers' brutal assaults and duplicitous treachery without the support and collaboration of Ireland's sympathetic citizenry. Most assuredly, the country would have succumbed to the combined weight of the British army, the Black & Tans and the Auxiliary Cadets if the rebels had been on their own.

Waiting in the dark for the lorry to be freed, with Michael's Lee-Enfield now slung over his shoulder, the Gortman remembered how Mick was quick to point out that one of the other key elements sparking the present-day internecine conflict was the inability of most anti-Treaty leaders to change their thinking from a military-engagement mentality to one centred on political-economic principles.

Aran knew it was because of Arthur Griffith's political views and the wise influence of others that Michael and his Provisional Government ministers understood the need for adjusting old courses of action while embracing new ones. The rebels' obsession with carrying on an armed conflict against the National Army as a means of forcing the British government to renegotiate the Anglo-Irish Treaty was on the Big Fellow's mind. Privately, Michael predicted that the Irregulars were destined to fail in structuring a new peace that satisfied their narrow demands. As each day passed, it became clearer that the anti-Treatyites would have to compromise their principles or die fighting. But now after the events of yesterday, Aran wasn't sure what would happen. Would the Cosgrave government have the strength and wisdom to stand up to the leadership of the anti-Treatyites? Sadly, the Irish Rebel doubted it.

❧

At last, after hours of delay, the convoy finally headed off down the main Cork road. With everyone but J. J. Smith crammed onto the lorry, Aran Roe directed Michael's body be placed across the knees of four seated soldiers and held securely in place on their laps. *Thanks be to God*, Aran thought, *we'll finally be in town in less than thirty minutes.*

Sadly, Aran remembered how their Tuesday, early-morning convoy travelled this same road on their way to Macroom. Thankfully there'd been only one annoying delay.

Upon reaching the peaceful West Cork market town, General Collins dropped off some much needed military supplies for his Irish Army forces stationed at Macroom Castle. Then it was on to Bandon, Clonakilty, Rosscarbery and Skibbereen.

Later that afternoon, the procession planned on retracing its steps back to Cork City with a short stopover at Michael's family home, Woodfield, hard by Sam's Cross, three and a half miles west of Clonakilty.

Unfortunately, the back roads from Macroom to Bandon were

like a rabbit's warren, a crisscrossing maze of secluded dirt tracks usually only travelled by locals. Thus, when their convoy was forced to stop for directions to Bandon at Long's Pub at the Béalnabláth Cross, Michael must have been spotted by an Irregular sentry. Immediately, his presence would have been made known to the area's IRA leadership. No doubt, it was they who'd organised the ambush, in clear violation of the safe-passage promise. The rebel forces guessed correctly that the Collins's convoy might return through Béalnabláth Cross later in the day.

❧

Strangely enough, when the convoy did arrive into Cork City early Wednesday morning, Emmet Dalton and his bedraggled party were directed by the local Civic Guards to the British military hospital, Shanakiel, still staffed by British personnel instead of the local civilian one, Bon Secour. After discovering the mix-up, however, Dalton was too tired to correct the mistake.

As Emmet, Gabriel and Aran waited to be interviewed by the attending physician, a kindly attendant brought the three men hot tea and biscuits. Wrapping their chilled hands around the mugs of steaming liquid, Aran broke the exhausted silence. Sadly shaking his head, he said, "This tragedy of Michael's death will affect many...ours and the lives of countless others. If I'm any judge of it, the people of Ireland will mourn and curse his loss for years to come. I fear Mick's dream, our dream of Irish freedom, might well collapse...it may even die. In case you haven't guessed, this bloody war of ours could easily intensify. Once those opposed to the Treaty find out what happened down here last evening, they'll pull out all the stops to press their advantage."

"You're right, Aran," answered Emmet. The major-general's high forehead was creased with worry and dirt stains marked his face. "With the Big Fellow gone who's going to fill his void? Sure, I don't have much faith in the present Dublin administration. With the exception of Mulcahy, I don't much trust the rest of that lot."

Gabriel countered, "Richard Mulcahy's no politician, Emmet. A good military man yes, but he'll never fill Michael's shoes."

"What about Ginger O'Connell or Seán Mac Eoin? They're both good men," said Aran.

"But they're military men like Mulcahy," said Gabriel.

"That's the trouble, Gay, there's no one really qualified to take his place," said Dalton.

"Jaysus, Emmet, that's a hell of a no-confidence vote," said Aran, "but I think you may be right."

The three fell silent for a moment. Finally the Gortman, looking around the waiting room to be sure they were alone, continued in a low voice, "Sure, maybe I shouldn't be saying this, but I agree with Emmet. I'm afraid the cabinet would rather see the anti-Treaty leadership crushed than negotiated with. Mick's death may be just the opportunity they've been waiting for to even the score. Who can forget all the bitter recriminations that spewed forth during the Treaty debates?"

"What about all those hard feelings that were stirred up over the Army Convention issue and the Four Courts business?" added Gabriel.

Then, with a hint of his old familiar smile lighting up his face, Gay joked, "Ye can't say the Irish don't know how to hold a grudge."

"Ah, bugger off ye Yankee," teased Emmet.

"No, seriously," said Aran, "with Michael's fair-minded respect for our former comrades a thing of the past now, I'm afraid Dublin just doesn't have the gift or desire to bring this conflict to a reasonable and just conclusion. They'll make a balls of it, just you mark my words."

Aran continued, "Then there is the question of whether the British government will support the Provisional leadership with Mick out of the picture? Without the Big Fellow's hand in things, they just might decide to reassert their military and political presence here in Ireland."

His two companions could see Aran was growing more and more troubled. The Gortman's jaw was now clenched and his eyes flashed with anger.

Emmet reached out and touched the Irish Rebel's shoulder.

Before he could utter a soothing word, Aran went on, "Emmet, Gay, hear me out. If Dublin does make a mess of it, Ireland will pay dearly before it's all over…she'll pay with her own blood…and maybe even ours. Just look will yis, Mick already has."

"We'd all better be keeping our opinions to ourselves about this from now on or somebody will be after gunning for us next," cautioned Emmet. There was a ring of ominous truth in his warning.

They all nodded grimly. Gay's light-hearted comment about holding grudges of a moment ago had been forgotten…or had it?

"And just in case yis have forgotten," continued the Gortman, changing the subject, "do you know what yesterday was?"

Blank stares were his only answer.

"The 22nd was to be Mick and Kitty's wedding day. Don't ye remember?"

"Bloody hell!" said Gay. "Sure, with all that's been going on these past two weeks, my mind's been nothing but sixes and sevens."

"Ah, not to bother," said Aran. "Michael was the same. If you remember rightly, he was the one who'd postponed the date until after returning to Dublin. He wanted to sort out this fighting business first."

"Speaking of sorting things out," said Emmet, "I must send word to Dublin as soon as I get back to the Imperial. Since there's no direct line to GHQ, the telegram will have to go via cable to New York then to London and finally on to Dublin. I'm guessing the rest of the world will know about the Big Fellow before the Irish papers ever get wind of it."

Knowing frowns crossed the three men's faces.

"Oh, one more thing, Emmet. After we've had a chance to recover from all this and see to it that Michael has a proper funeral, Gay and I'd like to take a closer look into the circumstances surrounding his death."

"Aye," nodded Gabriel.

"I was thinking along those lines meself," replied the major-general. "Instead of duplicating our efforts, why don't you two have a go at the convoy party. You're from Dublin and the escort was staffed from there. In the meantime, I'll use my contacts in the Cork area to see what I can discover about the ambush from this end. Sound right to yis?"

"Good," answered Gabriel. "Both Aran Roe and meself have our doubts about the *accidental* nature of last evening's attack. It all worked out too neatly for the other side if you ask me."

Fighting exhaustion, the Gortman added, "With Michael being the only one killed, it seems more like an assassination plot or just plain murder."

With that, Aran put his mug down on a nearby table. Fighting back more tears, he pulled on his overcoat. In a husky voice, he said, "Let's go Gay. Can you give the doctor what he needs, Emmet?"

"Off wit yis. We'll talk more over breakfast later this morning."

As the two soldiers headed down the hallway to leave, they heard a woman's voice calling, "Major-General…Major-General Dalton, is it?" A staff nurse was paging Emmet. "Sir, the doctor will see you now."

Pausing before the examination room door, the one through which Michael had been taken upon their arrival, Aran said, "Gay, I'd like to stop in and say goodbye to Mick once more."

"Take your time. I'll pay my respects again in the morning."

The Gortman, with a lump in his throat, pushed through the swing doors. Behind a ring of drawn white curtains lay General Collins. Still dressed in his military jacket, Michael lay on a hospital trolley. A white sheet covered two-thirds of his body. Someone had replaced Aran's blood-soaked bandages with clean ones. The C-in-C's hands were folded across his front. The Corkman's face was ashen white… expressionless…eyes closed in death.

Aran thought: *Oh Michael, I can't believe you're gone.*

Pausing a moment, he said a silent prayer for Michael's departed soul: *Our Father, who art in heaven, hallowed be thy name; thy kingdom come; thy will be done on earth as it is in heaven.*

Blessed be you forever dear Father and blessed be your faithful servant Michael Collins. As you well know, he loved Ireland and its proud, noble people for whom he willingly died, giving his all to the end. Yesterday you took him from us. Now, please welcome him into your heavenly home. Find him an exalted seat beside your other saints and martyrs, who also gave their lives for your earthly children. And in your mercy, dear Father, help save us from the lion's mouth that today seeks to destroy this holy land...the land that Mick loved so. Please Lord, in your mercy, bring us the peace, justice and unity that he and so many others have dreamed of and longed for down through the ages.

And dear God, very selfishly, please bless me. Give me a bit of Mick's strength and understanding that I might help see his work finished. In this world that's gone mad, grant me the wisdom to know what's right and the courage to see it through.

I ask this all in your name, dear Father, for Michael's sake and for the cause of Éireann go brách. Amen.

Blessing himself, he slowly walked up to the side of the gurney. Bending down, he kissed his beloved mentor on his bandaged forehead. Then, in a soft voice he whispered, "Thank you dear God for the gift of this man, Michael Collins, and for the time we shared. Sure, the good Lord must've loved you so Mick to have taken you this early. I don't know what I'm going to do without you. I miss you so already. Through all the good times and bad, you were there: my guide, my inspiration, my source of strength...the rock I could always depend on. Now, like Pearse and the others, you lie here in the cold arms of death, but know you'll always be my hero. Oh Mick, may the good Lord mind you and bless you in His mercy. In your absence, may our Father in heaven see fit to give me just some of your great strength, wisdom and courage. God bless you, Michael...now and forever."

Standing up, Aran reached into one of the pockets of his great-coat. He pulled out his rosary and a small hand-carved, wooden cross Sarah Anne had given him as a good luck talisman. The Gortman lovingly wound the rosary around his friend's clasped hands and placed the cross between Michael's right thumb and forefinger.

With his warm hands encircling Mick's cold hands, he murmured, "Greater love hath no man than this...may God bless you in His mercy, Míceal."

As he turned to leave, Aran was suddenly enveloped in a pool of cold air. It was as if someone had left a door open on a midwinter's night. But this was August. Startled by the strange occurrence, he was abruptly gripped by yet another unexplained sensation. It felt as if a heavy yoke had suddenly been placed on his shoulders. His legs felt weak. For a moment, the Irish Rebel thought he was going to collapse under this mysterious burden. Somehow though, he managed to stay upright by staggering backwards and catching hold of Michael's trolley. Trembling, Aran felt an icy chill pass through him. Seconds later, the frightening feelings vanished as quickly as they had come, leaving him feeling dazed and shaken. His face felt flushed, but when he touched his cheek, it was cold and clammy.

Stunned, he quickly looked around the room. With not a sound to be heard and seeing no one, Aran turned and looked down at the figure on the cart. "Míceal?" he whispered...

PART I

"For, if there is hardness in the land and in the life of the people, there is no meanness in it. They look out over wide spaces; God's world is before their imagination; the past and the future of Ireland are in their daily thought. There is grace and kindliness in their homes, and they give hospitality as their forefathers gave it in the days of their chieftainship in the land. There is wisdom in them that should be shaping the mind of their generation; bravery and freedom are in their spirit, and unyielding pride. They are of the nobility of Ireland, the clans who, because they would not surrender their faith and nationhood, were cast out by the conqueror into the wilderness."

Dorothy Macardle

JULY, 1921–DECEMBER, 1921

"It is in the brightness of the morning air that hope and history walk toward us across the meadows, radiant as a girl in her first beauty."

Thomas Flanagan

3

*"Life springs from death; and from the graves of
patriot men and women spring living nations."*

Patrick Henry Pearse

*T*he Dublin-Galway train pulled out from the Marysborough
rail station. Aran waved through the carriage window to his two
friends left standing on the platform. Richard 'Shadow' Doyle and
Gabriel McCracken had a thirty-minute wait for their connecting
train that would carry them on to Limerick Junction and their
homes: Shadow to neighbouring Limerick Town and Gay further
on to Cahir in County Tipperary.

His heart filled with mixed emotions, the Irish Rebel tried
to find a comfortable position, but the wooden-backed bench he
occupied successfully resisted his best efforts. He was leaving a
hard way of life and good friends behind, but he was going home
to his family and the woman he loved.

Ever on the lookout, thanks to five years on the run, Aran
kept one eye on the handful of other passengers in his car while
deciding if he could relax and doze off or not. From his vantage

point in the last row of seats, he had a clear view of the entire carriage.

The excitement of the past twenty-four hours was ebbing. His last-night's meeting with Michael Collins and the Big Fellow's announcement that he wished to play an active role in the up-coming Anglo-Irish peace negotiations surprised Aran. Usually Mick preferred to stay in the background, a strategy that served him well for the last four-plus years. Collins had moved freely around Dublin Town during the height of the just-concluded War of Independence, slipping undetected through Britain's probing tentacles despite the hefty reward posted for his arrest. His decision to now travel to London and negotiate on behalf of the Irish government flew in the face of Mick's habit of wanting to remain anonymous. Superstitious or not, Aran feared this new tactic might bode ill for Mick and for Ireland.

Knowing the Corkman as he did, Aran guessed there were several motivations behind Collins's sudden desire to surface as a public figure.

Who else knew Ireland's fighting strengths and weaknesses better than Michael? Certainly not Ireland's self-appointed president Éamon de Valera. Dev had been in Amerikay for most of the past two years. He had been out of harm's way and absent from the day-to-day rigors of leading a war-ravaged populace.

Who was better qualified than Michael to delineate the litany of crimes, atrocities and fraudulent schemes perpetrated by British authorities on Ireland in the name of Éireann's best interests? Nobody.

Who else understood the country's financial history and current state of affairs more than its Minister of Finance, Michael Collins? No one.

And what other yoke had his finger on the pulse of Ireland's clandestine intelligence network better than the Corkman himself, the Head Centre of Ireland's secret Irish Republican Brotherhood? Once again, only Michael.

Yes, Aran imagined there was no one in Ireland better qualified to prosecute Ireland's case before Westminster's leadership and the court of public opinion than Michael Collins himself.

Besides hadn't he earned the right to do so? Already people were quietly saying, "It's Michael Collins who won the Tan War[1] for Ireland."

Aran also knew Mick's arrogant self was just waiting for the opportunity to lord little Ireland's military and civic successes over 'the mightiest empire in the world' which today was headed by two powerful, egotistical men: Primer Minister David Lloyd George and Colonial Secretary Winston Churchill.

Other thoughts, this time tactical ones, danced through Aran's head, each keeping time with the train's swaying motion. What military advantage would be lost if the underground Irish Republican Army stepped forward and showed its hand? The Irish Rebel knew Collins was worried. What if the IRA's network of sub rosa guerrilla fighters and supporters were identified? Sure, their ability to re-engage the British would be greatly compromised. With its limited number of combatants and meagre weapon stores exposed to public scrutiny, the cat would be out of the bag. Certainly, Ireland would be vulnerable to any enemy aggression, if hostilities with Britain were to break out again.

Personal worries gnawed at Aran as well. Would he have trouble adjusting to civilian life? Though living on the run was difficult and dangerous, he had become one of them: a revolutionary, a guerrilla insurgent, a Republican freedom fighter. He'd tasted the terror and survived. He'd endured the fear of betrayal, of capture and of death. He'd known the cold, the damp, the sleepless nights, the constant chill of wet clothing, the gnawing

---

1. The Black & Tans were Britain's 'special' policemen in Ireland. In 1919, the effectiveness of the Royal Irish Constabulary had been greatly reduced by the aggressive actions of the IRA. With a general breakdown of civil authority throughout the country, British officials, largely under the direction of Winston Churchill, began recruiting former enlisted military personnel to serve as policemen in Ireland. Because of a shortage of uniforms, they were forced to wear RIC dark bottle-green tunics & British military khaki trousers. Nicknamed the Black & Tans after a pack of hunting hounds, their harsh methods & hateful reprisals earned them an odious reputation that lives on even today. They began arriving in Ireland in March, 1920. Their charge was to make Ireland a living hell for its rebel Army. Eventually, about 9,000 Tans served in Ireland between 1920 & the end of the Anglo-Irish War of Independence.

hunger for a proper meal, the longing for peace and normality. Yes, he'd become one of the 'hard men,' taking pride in his ability to survive the adversities of war and the absence of peace. What challenges would now fill that void? Farming? Marriage to Sarah Anne? Raising a family? What about his friendships with Michael, Shadow and Gabriel? How would they fit into this new life? He had many misgivings; many issues to sort out.

These feelings were all overshadowed by the emotional rush he'd experienced just a couple of hours ago when he raised Michael's Irish tricolour on top of Dublin's General Post Office building. Thoughts of his friend and teacher Patrick Pearse; of Easter Week, 1916; of all the people he'd known who'd fought and sacrificed so much for the dream: the dream that he and others had christened 'for the cause of liberty.' The slow encroaching realisation that the 'troubles' might finally be over was almost more than he could bear. Tears welled up behind his closed eyes.

Just moments ago he'd said goodbye to his two dear friends, Shadow and Gay. Together the three of them had crowded a lifetime of living into the last five years. Shadow had helped whisk him off to Amerikay, no doubt saving his life after the near-fatal ambush along the River Shannon in the spring of 1916. Later, the Limerick baker had spent that summer in Virginia nursing him back to health, with the help of the McCracken family of course. Then there were the months they had spent alone in the cabin up in the Allegheny Mountains above Petersburg, West Virginia. Closing his eyes, he could still see Shadow's amused expression, as the Limerick man saved his hide from a nasty encounter with that wild boar.

Today was Richard Doyle's forty-first birthday or was it his forty-second? At the station in Marysborough, the Irish Rebel surprised him with a handsome bone-inlaid, folding pocket knife. It sported a variety of cutting blades, a leather awl and a special gadget for opening tins. Shadow's delight with the present was evident: a radiant smile illuminated his tanned face as he examined the gift.

After the usual round of goodbyes and handshakes, the older man unexpectedly pulled Aran to his breast. The powerfully built baker and freedom fighter give him a gentle, loving bear hug.

"Bless you, Aran," whispered Doyle in his friend's ear. "Many thanks for the knife. Sure, it will be a constant reminder of our friendship, as if I needed one."

Returning the embrace, Aran answered, "God bless you too, Shadow. Have a wonderful birthday and many happy returns so."

With tears welling up in his eyes, Aran Roe turned and re-boarded the train for the West.

With few exceptions, Shadow hadn't changed much in the five years Aran had known him. Irishmen are good that way: their faces don't show their age as others might. But the years had not been kind to Shadow. Besides his rapidly thinning, grey curly hair and well lived-in lined face, Richard harboured a broken heart. It had been over a year since his wife Helen had been gunned down by that bastard of a man, Major George Henry Hawkins. It had been a military operation gone very wrong, and the sting of it would never go away…not for Shadow, his family, Aran, Gay and the rest of them.

Shaking his head, as if to banish old ghosts, Aran mused about Richard's well-deserved moniker, 'Shadow.' First earned in 1899, during the 2nd South-African Boer War, nineteen-year-old junior staff officer Doyle was a key behind-the-scenes organiser. He assisted in the formation of a small Irish pro-Boer Brigade under the command of now famous, 1916 martyr Major John 'Foxie Jack' MacBride. Years later, Shadow put those same special talents to use again, organising and training Irish volunteers in the west of Ireland during the run-up to the Easter Rebellion. That's when he'd met Liam Mellowes and his sidekick Danny Kelly. Today, those three men had become close friends with General Mellowes serving as Shadow's commanding officer.

Smiling to himself, Aran couldn't help but recall some of the good times and harrowing adventures he'd had with them, as together they battled it out with the bloody Sassenach.

Unexpectedly, Aran's thoughts were interrupted. A young man of considerable size passed into his carriage from the adjoining car. Despite the abundant selection of vacant seats, the man chose to slide onto the neighbouring empty bench directly across from the Irish Rebel. The two men now sat facing one another with only inches separating their knees.

Immediately, the slouching Gortman tensed, sitting bolt upright. Unconsciously, he pressed his right elbow to his side. The feel of his holstered Colt .45 comforted his sudden wariness.

"Sorry. Do ye mind if I sit here across from ye?"

A bit annoyed by the intrusion into his privacy, Aran lied, "Ah sure and why not?"

"I couldn't help but notice you and the other two back there on the platform in Marysborough."

With that remark, Aran felt his emotions flame anew. His suspicious mind flashed: *What in hell's name was this man about? Maybe he's some kind of a quisling. If so, he was taking a very bold approach.*

He thought: *Sure, your one wasn't Irish born; not with that accent on him.*

"Are you certain I'm not disturbing ye?"

"No, you're grand. Not a bother so."

"Ta."

Again, the big man queried Aran. "I'm guessing they're friends of yours. Waiting for the next train…maybe to Cork City?"

"Aye," lied Aran again.

Shifting the conversation from himself, Aran said, "I know you're from somewhere?"

"Athy."

Again, the Gortman tensed.

"Athy?" he queried out loud while thoughts of Brigid, her siblings, Gran, the O'Mahony farm came rushing at him from all directions.

Of all the places in Ireland to be from, why had he said 'Athy?' Was it just a coincidence? Or was he someone sent here to ferret him out? But why take such a direct approach? Aran wasn't sure, but he bloody well was going to be on his toes until he'd solved the riddle.

"Sure, for the last twenty-five years or so. Before that, me family moved around. Belfast mostly, then a few months in Trim. Originally, we are from Scotland. Perthshire…one of the grandest and most beautiful spots in the entire world."

A broad smile now illuminated the man's face. His tousled red hair and piercing green eyes caught and held Aran's attention.

The newcomer continued, but this time there was a disparaging edge to his voice, "It's where the Highlands and Lowlands meet, but bloody well impossible to make a decent living unless you own a sizeable bit of land, if its farming you fancy."

Nodding, Aran extended his right hand, "Aran Roe O'Neill. Sure, then I don't have to tell you about scratching for a living. We Irish have been doing that for centuries."

Shaking hands, the man said, "Duncan…Duncan Stewart MacGregor. Sounds like we're both blessed with noble names. Our parents must have been of like minds."

Aran smiled and relaxed his guard a bit.

"Must be so."

The stranger was older and bigger than Aran. Middle thirties he guessed and well over six feet in height…maybe weighing seventeen or eighteen stones. His rounded face was ruddy, testifying to an outdoor life. The man's hands were large and powerful, roughened by manual labour he guessed. His clothing was clean, but well mended. *Another poor, thrifty Scotsman,* mused Aran to himself.

"Heading to or from home?" the newcomer asked.

"A little of both," said Aran, thinking: *Too many questions; personal ones at that.*

Aran shifted his weight. Leaning his left shoulder against the window, he looked out at the passing scenery. *Maybe your one will get the hint to respect my silence.*

A moment later, the calm of the carriage was interrupted by the boisterous singing of three uniformed British soldiers. It was clear from their swagger and slurred words they had been drinking: a day on the tiles no doubt.

Aran thought: *Celebrating the end of the conflict in their own way? Well, as long as they kept it under control.*

The Gortman's eyes followed the three as they made their way towards the other end of the rail car. An unexpected lurch of the train, however, sent two of the soldiers crashing onto an empty bench. The third, hanging on to the overhead luggage rack for support, roared his amusement at his sprawled compatriots.

Staggering to their feet, the downed men broke into song again. Something about, "God save the king, riding on a paddy's arse."

Aran was about to head down the aisle to interrupt their annoying revelry, but Duncan beat him to it. The Scots-Irishman was three steps ahead of him.

Aran heard the man's soft rolling tongue announce, "Now laddies, we've all had just about enough of your antics. Tuck into you seats and be still wit yis."

Empowered by the drink and blinded by the alcohol, one of soldiers took a lazy swing at Duncan's head, but that was the end of it.

The Scotsman fended off the attack with his left forearm while at the same moment, delivering a powerful blow with his right fist to the man's stomach.

The soldier collapsed onto the floor, spewing a foul, black liquid from his mouth.

"Why you bloody bastard…" came the cry from one of the other two men.

"Ah, if ye know wha's good for you, sit down and say na more."

As if on cue, the two grudgingly sat down.

Duncan grabbed the back of the downed man's jacket collar and propped him up on an adjacent bench. The man moaned and slumped against the window, holding his midsection.

Raising his voice so all in the car could hear him, Duncan said, "Pardon this embarrassment, ladies and gentlemen. I fear these clownish upstarts have had a wee too much of the drink."

Turning, the big man and Aran returned to their seats.

"Jaysus, Duncan, fair play to yourself. Did you ever give those three a fright. No love for his majesty's finest, eh?"

"Nay, not me."

Duncan continued, "For a time my da was a nail maker in Belfast. Sure, because of me size and boxing skills, I picked up the nickname of 'Nayler' along the way. Guess I haven't lost me touch."

Twenty-five minutes later, as the train pulled into Athlone's railway station, the three humbled soldiers couldn't get off the train fast enough.

From the window, Aran and Duncan shared a bit of a laugh at the dishevelled trio, weaving their way across the platform and through the revolving metal gate leading to the stairs and street below.

※

Pulling the sheet over his head, Aran tried to ignore the early September sunshine streaming through the open window. He'd heard someone, probably his mother, enter the room and open the curtains.

Ignoring the not too subtle morning wake-up call, Aran feigned sleep. Breathing through his mouth, he hoped his soft gurgling sounds would convince the intruder to leave him alone, at least for a little while longer.

The bedroom soon returned to its former state, except for his mock snoring. Lulling himself into believing his acting skills had won the day, the Irish Rebel relaxed, welcoming the slowly returning intoxication of sleep.

The next thing Aran knew, he was fighting for his life. A crushing weight pinned him to the bed as a pillow pressed to his face blotted out all light and air.

His mind raced. This certainly was not his mother or father playing a trick on him, nor was it one of his brothers. They just didn't do that sort of thing. As he struggled to free himself from the interloper, the only name to flash through his head was *Collins*, but bloody hell, he was all the way across the country in Dublin.

With legs caught up in the sheet, Aran concentrated on using his left hand to dislodge his attacker, who was now sitting squarely on his chest, knees pressing forcefully against his ribs.

"Hold him still now. It's a piece of ear I want," ordered the one balanced above Aran's thrashing body.

Suddenly, more hands were restraining him. His left arm was now securely pinned to the bed.

Twisting his head first to the left then to the right, Aran tried gasping for air, but precious little was his reward. This was serious. He felt panic overtaking him. He opened his mouth to scream, but a muffled sound was all he heard in return for his effort.

Maybe if I lie still they'll think I've passed out, reasoned the Gortman. *What other choice do I have?*

"Jaysus, Michael, do you think we've killed him?"

"Ah sure, this bleedin' Jackeen is up to one of his tricks. It would take more than the two of us to get the best of your man here."

The two men slid off their victim, laughing. Seated on the polished, boarded floor, their backs propped up against the side of the bed, peals of glee filled the room.

But the light-hearted moment was over as quickly as it had begun.

Free of his muggers, Aran pulled his trusty Luger from under his pillow. With his right arm, he locked it around the nearest neck rising above the mattress.

With his forearm pushing against the man's wind pipe, he pressed the weapon to the man's temple, shouting, "You bloody sods. Do yis have nothing else better to do than scare the living shyte out of me...me who's supposed to be your friend...your comrade?"

Still shaking from the encounter, Aran said in a more controlled voice, "You're both lucky you're not meeting your maker this very moment."

Wiping the tears from his eyes, Gabriel McCracken said, "Ah, we're just havin' a bit of craic with ya. Can't you take the joke of it, Aran?"

"A joke yes, but not when me life's on the line."

Michael Collins reached up and pulled Aran's arm from his neck. "We're just testing ye, Rebel."

"Afraid I might have gone soft are yis?"

"Something like that, old stock."

Both the Big Fella and Gay McCracken scrambled to their feet.

"Now, that's enough horse play for the three of yis this morning. You'll pull the house down around me ears if you keep that up sure." Aran's mother was standing in the doorway, arms akimbo. Her words had the ring of authority to them.

"Sorry to disturb you so. Forgive us, Mrs. O'Neill. We meant no harm. We're only paying our respect to this lazy lump here. It's well after eight in the morning, and himself still sleeping. What kind of soldier of Ireland are ye keeping here?"

Mrs. O'Neill smiled and nodded. "Sure, with friends like you looking after him, he's no need of enemies, that's clear. Now if you're finished with your tom foolin', the kettle's on in the kitchen. I'll have some breakfast for yis in ten minutes." That said, Aran's mother turned and headed down the hall, chuckling as she went.

With the Luger safely tucked away, Aran pulled on his trousers. Snapping his braces into place, he said, "Didn't you hear what ma said? Off with yis. Can't a man wash up and dress in private? 'Tis after that I want to know why I'm so lucky as to have been this rudely awakened by two such infamous scoundrels."

Left alone, Aran thought: *They're right. I must be getting soft. A year ago I might well be a dead man now sure enough.*

❧

Since arriving back home to the family farm just outside the village of Gort, Aran Roe O'Neill had enjoyed a break from the danger of guerrilla warfare and the stress of life on the run. The intoxicating feeling of not having to look over your shoulder constantly or wondering where the nearest avenue of escape might lie was a welcomed relief indeed.

But like other Volunteers he'd talked to that summer, readjustment to civilian life wasn't easy. Many were bewildered by the suddenness of the Truce and bothered by the uncertainty of the peace. Some were frequently tormented by a gnawing feeling of indecision about what direction they should take with their lives. Aran understood their quandaries and sympathised with them.

This respite from active duty was not without its military obligations. Orders from GHQ in Dublin kept local Volunteer commanders busy. General Richard Mulcahy, IRA Chief of Staff, insisted local units continue training and drilling while recruiting efforts were increased. As a result, Irish Army ranks rose dramatically. At the time of the truce in July, 1921 there was an estimated 3,000 active IRA men in the field. Four months later, the ranks had swollen to over 72,000.[2]

Seasoned veterans of the Tan War strongly disliked these new recruits and often labelled them 'Trucileers.' Many of the new enlistees carried on as if they'd won the war, but in reality they'd never served a day or fired a shot. To make matters worse, some of these new soldiers were in point of fact unemployed, demobbed members of the British Army. Looking for adventure and the price of a pint, they enlisted in Ireland's burgeoning military force.

Despite this increased manpower and the stepped-up importation of guns from England, military resources were still not of sufficient quantity to promote Ireland's volunteer force into becoming a full-pledged National Army. Uniforms, weapons, vehicles and experienced military personnel were still in short supply. Additionally, the relationships between the civilian population and the growing ranks of the IRA had become strained. During the War of Independence years, the local populace often did all it could and more to help support their men in the field. But as the realities of peacetime spread, the people grew hostile to soldiers seizing their private property for 'official' IRA use.

A ground-swell of public sentiment quickly arose favouring maintaining the peace and treating with the British. Irish church officials and members of the local press also began exerting pressure on military and political leaders to seek conciliation and compromise regarding matters of national importance.[3]

Between short stints of military duty with the Flying Gaels, Aran thoroughly enjoyed helping his family gather in the summer's corn. He pitched in with his father to haul sods of sun-dried turf back home from the nearby bog. But the highlights of the summer were his two visits to see Sarah Anne and Gabriel's new family down in Cahir. The bicycle rides gave him time to clear his head and think about the future.

On his second visit in early September, Sarah and he chose the date for their long-intended wedding, 28 December, the day after his birthday, was their choice. Aran loved Annie and she

2. Michael Hopkinson. *Green Against Green: The Irish Civil War*. Dublin, 1988, 16.
3. Ibid., 14-15.

him. She was all he could ever want in a woman. She was a loving, caring and intelligent woman with a wise and gentle heart. In addition to all her feminine allures, she was a determined and hardworking woman. Sarah Anne would make a wonderful mother to their children, if they were so lucky, and her loyalty to Aran and the cause of Ireland was unwavering.

Two of the qualities Aran admired in her most were her strong-mindedness and willingness to stand up for what she believed in. Hadn't she proved that to Mick Collins himself and the others over the past months? Hadn't she risked danger, arrest, deportation, even death on more than one occasion? There was no doubt about it. Annie had stepped up and done her bit for Ireland.

Her risk-taking behaviour was something special. It elevated her status in Aran's mind. So often women occupied a more traditional, gentler place in Irish households: a position somewhat below that of God and man. But when the door was closed and all said and done, it was usually the woman who made the important decisions about running the household, caring for the children and minding the family matters. At the close of day, if truth be known, it was the man who usually had to answer to 'herself.' But Sarah was different. Whether publicly or in private, she'd stand up and be counted, damning what the gossips might say about her. Indeed, she was her own person.

Despite all his 'liberal' thinking, love and admiration for Annie's resolve, Aran still held doubts about *his* ability to be a good husband and father. The vicissitudes of war had changed him…embittered him…causing him to distrust and query things in ways that often left him feeling uncertain about the genuine goodness of life's promise. Rather than his hopes and fears being quieted by this recent time of tranquillity, the Gortman was filled with doubts. In what should've been a time of happiness and joyful anticipating, he was repeatedly gripped with a sense of emptiness and sadness. Reflecting on his short life, Aran couldn't help but focus on the fact that war had stolen his youth and innocence. It had robbed him of carefree days growing up on the farm with his family around him. It had taken the much anticipated challenge of school days and boyhood games away, replacing them with fear, death and untold hardships. Even with this late-summer, peaceful respite at home with friends and family, much had changed. Sure, there was a new sense of political and economic optimism with talks now under way between the two governments. Yes, Ireland seemed on the verge of a new tomorrow…a tomorrow he'd helped bring about. But despite all those positives, there was still this palpable feeling of loss that he couldn't shake. An underlying air of tension and uncertainty spun around in his head. Today things were different and not always for the best. The fighting had taken its toll. Too many good people were now dead; too many of the old ways altered…never to be reclaimed. That old feeling in the pit of his stomach kept churning over and over. No matter what, Aran felt vulnerable and alone.

The Irish Rebel talked to Sarah Anne about his worries and fears. She understood the wellspring of his doubts and cherished him all the more for them. Her faith in their love for each other offered her quiet consolation. She felt she understood Aran. Sarah reassured him that her certainty in the strength of their devotion to each other would endure all. She knew this in her heart of hearts. Her assertions comforted Aran. They helped ease his apprehensions, or at least some of them.

Besides Annie's reassurance, the Gortman took solace in the powerful words of his friend, Patrick Pearse. During quiet moments of reflection, he often recalled his mentor's inspiring words spoken at O'Donovan Rossa's graveside ceremony. He'd close his eyes and imagine himself walking with Pearse through the grounds of St. Enda's. In his mind the words flooded back: *Life springs from death; and from the graves of patriot men and women spring living nations.*

❧

On the political front, Aran had learned of Éamon de Valera's journey to London the day after the Truce was agreed to. Once again, the 'Long Hoor,' as Mick often called him in private, chose to ignore Collins's counsel. Dev thought he knew better. Instead he let political rivalries and petty jealousies cloud his judgement. It had happened before. The IRA's attack on Dublin's Custom House, against the Big Fellow's best judgement, had been a political and propaganda success, but a civic and military failure.[4] It had pointed out to the world that Britain's armed campaign in Ireland was not succeeding, but at what cost? Six Republican Volunteers were killed, a dozen more were seriously wounded and nearly one hundred others arrested. Additionally, irreplaceable documents and records were destroyed in the fighting. The largest Irish Army operation against the Sassenach since Easter Week, 1916 was, in the final analysis, a disaster. If the country had fought as de Valera wished, their now hard fought victory, as today's stand-off was believed to be by many, would never have come to pass. At least not in the minds of Aran and Michael as they reviewed matters back in Dublin on that July evening, the day before the Truce took effect on the 11th.

It was clear to the two of them that Michael was the key man to accompany Dev and an Irish delegation scheduled to depart for London in two days' time. Its mission would be to parley with members of the British government regarding the establishment of conferencing ground rules prior to the formal staging of Treaty negotiations. Instead, de Valera excluded Collins, who was Minister for Finance as well as the IRA's Director of Organisation and Intelligence plus president of the IRB. In lieu of the Big Fellow, the Dáil president favoured three other members of his Irish cabinet: Arthur Griffith, Minister for Foreign Affairs and vice-president of Dáil Éireann; Austin Stack, Minister for Home Affairs; Robert Barton, Minister for Economic Affairs

---

4. Upon returning to Ireland in December, 1920 from his twenty-month fund raising & Irish political-promotion tour of America, Éamon de Valera differed with Michael Collins about how the war should be prosecuted. Collins favoured a limited guerrilla campaign while de Valera wanted to stage large impressive monthly attacks on key British targets in Ireland. He thought this approach would gain greater world media attention & increase the likelihood of sympathetic American support. As a result, on 25 May 1921 Dev ordered the IRA to attack the Dublin Custom House.

plus Erskine Childers, acting Minister for Publicity and editor of the *Irish Bulletin*. In addition, de Valera selected TD Count George Noble Plunkett, father of executed 1916 leader Joseph Mary Plunkett, and four others for the London mission.

❧

Washed and dressed, Aran joined the others in his family's kitchen.

Besides Michael and Gabriel, there was a third man seated at the table: Tom Cullen, a Wicklow man, who was acting as Michael's driver and bodyguard on this journey to the West. The rest of the O'Neill family had eaten and were out the door. Aran's father and two of his brothers were headed into Gort. His grandfather was out feeding the hens in the haggard, and his sister was away at school in Galway.

With plates of steaming food set on the table, Mrs. O'Neill politely excused herself saying, "Alright boys, I'll leave you to it. Peckish or no, tuck in there and have yourselves something to eat and a good talk. I know Aran's been dying to hear about what's been going on in Dublin since he left."

"Ah, ye've outdone yourself again, Mrs. O'Neill," said Gabriel. "Everything looks lovely. Thanks a million."

Aran gave his mother a squeeze. "Come sit awhile at the table and listen to this blackguard's bloody Jackeen tales."

"Ah sure, that's all yis want…another fly on the wall. With all that Michael's up to, I'll leave you to yourselves in private."

Nodding their thanks, the four men sat down at the table. After exchanging the day's pleasantries and Aran's news of his pending marriage, Collins launched into a summary of the late summer's political happenings.

"Yis should have seen him," said Collins. "That Long Hoor was certainly in his element. Talking out of both sides of his mouth at once was he. On the one hand he didn't want me going over to treat with the Sassenach, saying if hostilities were to break out again, I'd be needed in Ireland to reorganise things and resume the fight. Then in the next breath, he'd go on about how he wanted to protect me hide from all those bloody English newspaper photographers."

"Afraid the English would see you for what you are," teased Aran.

"Just a simple Paddy with mud on your Wellingtons, no?" chimed in Gabriel.

Collins waived a fork in jest at his two friends. "The two of yis should know better than most the common clay of which I'm made. Bring me into the spotlight of a London conference and quickly the glamour of your legendary Michael Collins will be gone forever."[5]

Not skipping a beat, the Corkman continued, "If you remember rightly, Dev wanted me over in Amerikay immediately after he returned himself Christmas last. Not a word then about protecting my handsome mug from all the Yankee press that would be free to click away as I stepped off the ship."

"It didn't suit his fancy to have you around interfering while he was trying to reassert his presence here after being away from home for a year and a half," said Aran.

"Spot on, my rebel friend," answered Collins.

Shaking his head in disbelief, Gay said, "Bloody hell, it doesn't take a mastermind to see through that disguise?"

"Sometimes I wonder if that Long Hoor isn't a few shillins' short of a pound when it comes to understanding his fellow Irish…especially those he considers his rivals," said Mick, cleaning up the last of his plate.

---

5. T. Ryle Dwyer. *Michael Collins and the Treaty: His Differences with de Valera.* Cork, Ireland, 1988, 46.

4

*"Now limestone walls are all that's left of times of
pain and failure; this country yields the secret of
the beauty that it holds..."*

"The Green Among the Gold"
by Rosalind & Steve Barnes

Monday morning, 12 September 1921

For the longest time, Sarah Anne McCracken stood in the door-way of the Black Rose, her adopted family's pub in Cahir. There was the usual weekday morning activity on the village's cobbled main street. Children walked along the top of the square, past the Black Rose and its neighbour, the Glengall Arms Hotel. In groups of twos and threes, they headed up toward the Market House and Church Street on their way to classes at the National School. Along the way, the youngsters dodged black-skirted, shawl-draped women scurrying home with their early market day purchases. Down at the bottom of Castle Street, at the lay-by, the bus to Cashel was taking on passengers.

The motor car driven by IRA man Tom Cullen had long since disappeared from sight. Besides the love of her life and husband-to-be Aran Roe O'Neill, it also carried her brother Gabriel and Ireland's political and military mastermind Michael Collins. The four men were heading for Kilkenny then on to Dublin. But before he'd left, Aran confided in her that Michael and the rest of them would likely be heading for London soon. Treaty talks between Great Britain and Ireland seemed imminent.

Cahir, Annie's home since arriving in Ireland in May, 1917 was a rural, farming village situated on the banks of the River Suir in the heart of County Tipperary's Golden Vale. Despite being surrounded by rich farmland, much of the local economy depended upon a thriving milling industry begun by a handful of 19th-century Quaker families. Aran's dear friend, Richard 'Shadow' Doyle leased one such mill. His family had operated it for several generations.

It was near here that Ireland's great High King Brian Ború had established a 'royal' residence in the 10th century. Three hundred years later, the invading Anglo-Normans picked Cahir as the site for one of their great fortified castles. Its stone walls and the river provided a defensive barrier against any marauding bands of displaced Irish dissidents wishing to reclaim their native land from the usurper.

Today, the split-level, tree-dotted town square with its memorial fountain was surrounded by shops and houses. A new-found prosperity was beginning to take hold after the political and economic troubles of the last century. There was even talk of doing up the decaying castle in hopes of attracting more curious visitors to the town.

Now, in her twenty-fifth year, Sarah Anne was even more attractive today than when Aran first met her on her parents' Virginia farm in the summer of 1916. Living in Ireland obviously agreed with this striking woman. The statuesque brunette's flashing blue eyes lit up her face while her feminine figure turned many a head. Whether at work in the pub or out for a stroll, she carried herself with an effortless grace that wordlessly demonstrated to others a natural sense of self-confidence.

She'd been the talk of the village ever since she and her brother had arrived four years ago. Eligible bachelors and even older men paused as she passed them on the footpath. It was easy to guess what they were thinking, but Sarah Anne let it be known to one and all she was well spoken for...she had her heart set on marrying Aran Roe O'Neill.

Closing the door behind her, Sarah Anne returned to the McCracken family's ground-floor kitchen at the rear of the pub. Her Uncle Peter and Aunt Niamh were there, lingering over cups of tea. Also at the table was Gabriel's wife Áine. She was using a spoon, helping Mary Margaret finish the last bits of her breakfast. But the child seemed more interested in blowing milk bubbles in her cup than eating.

Tears welled up in Sarah's eyes as she glanced at the four empty chairs still pulled up to the large rectangular oak table. Its sturdy, hand-carved legs and once smooth timber surface were now nicked and scarred from years of use. Repeated cleanings and coats of wax had left the kitchen centrepiece with a rich bronze-coloured veneer.

"They're off so?" asked Uncle Peter.

"Aye," was Sarah's singular response.

"Ah sure, they'll be grand," reassured Aunt Niamh. "Come sit awhile. I've just made a fresh pot of tea and the bread's still warm. No sense in rushing at the day 'till we have to."

"Bless you, Aunt Niamh," said the younger woman, wiping away several tears from her cheek with a clenched fist. Putting on a brave smile, Sarah Anne sat down in the chair Aran had just vacated.

"Ah, you can't be after worrying about those lads all the time, Sarah," said Áine. "They're well able to look after themselves. Armed to the teeth as they are, no one would dare interfere with their comings and goings."

Annie nodded in agreement at Áine's comforting words. But to herself she thought: *Please God you're right, Áine.*

"I know I'm a silly old cod, especially after all they've been through together these past years. But I still can't help it. Aran has so many misgivings about what the future holds, while my brother doesn't seem to have a worry in the world."

Turning her attention from Mary Margaret to Sarah, Áine said, "Ah, give your brother some credit. He's a lot on his mind too."

"Sorry, Áine," said Sarah Anne. "I know he has."

"But I understand what you are saying. That's why I love

him so…trouble seems to roll off him like water off a slopping slate tile. He knows we're all here for him. Besides, the bloody Englander's days in Ireland are numbered. At least that's what Michael says. Sure, and if the Big Fellow believes that, that's good enough for me," said Áine.

"Trouble always finds those who go looking for it, Sarah," said Aunt Niamh. "Life's too short for that. Please God, the good Lord will look after our boys. And why shouldn't He? They're after trying to settle matters with the Sassenach once and for all…trying to finish the work of thousands before them. Sure Ireland's due for a bit of good luck, wouldn't you say?"

Annie just nodded.

"Sarah Anne," piped up Uncle Peter, changing the subject, "have you decided to write your mother and father? It's about time they paid us a visit. Your wedding's the perfect excuse."

"Aran and I want the two of them to come. How many years has it been for Father, Uncle Peter…almost forty now?"

"Well, the four of them left in '82. That broke my father's heart. Three sons and his only daughter…gone. All he could hope for was they were heading for greener pastures…and don't forget, Sarah, your father left just a step ahead of the authorities. 'Twas his seditious, anti-British behaviours that forced him to leave so.

"Their leaving left me alone here…alone to mind my parents and work the farm back in Clare. Sadly, me father never recovered from their going. He died with a broken heart seven years later, leaving everything to my oldest brother John…your one who was off in Amerikay with his siblings."

"Ah, Peter, you're just bringing up yesterday's ghosts," said Niamh.

"Sure, and it's doing no harm," said Peter. "Besides, I doubt Sarah Anne's heard my version from her father."

Sarah just smiled and winked at her aunt. "Ah go on Uncle Peter. I'll stop you, if you're repeating yourself."

"Well, as ye might have guessed, John came back in '89 after Father's death. He'd inherited the farm…'twas his birth right sure.

"Mother died less than a year later. She never could adjust to living on her own. Those were hard times for me. With both of them gone from me, I finally decided to head off on my own. Some folks thought I should've stayed on, but I was no farmer. Besides, John was well able to run things himself. So I left...headed down here on a lark.

"Thanks be to God, my luck changed straight away. I began working in one of the mills and was wise enough to save up a few bob...enough to finally take over the lease to this place. That was my second real break. The third was marrying the beautiful Niamh here."

"Ah, be off with ye. You're nothing but an old blatherer, Peter McCracken." Niamh's cheeks were suddenly flushed with embarrassment.

"Sure, it's true, Niamh Murphy McCracken, and don't you deny it."

Ignoring her husband's flattery, Niamh pushed back from the table and stood up. Beginning to clear away the dishes, she gently chided her husband by whispering to the other two, "Sarah, Áine, he'll be at this table all day with his stories, if you let him. You both know that for a cert."

The two younger women laughed as did Uncle Peter, but he was not to be denied. Looking at Sarah, he continued, "With John back home in Clare and my brother Thomas dead, shot to death in a poker game in Virginia, your father decided to stay on in Amerikay. I think it was your mother, born over there, who insisted on it. She maintained their future seemed so much brighter in Manassas than back in oul Ireland. What's more, there was always the question of whether the authorities would allow your father back into this country. He was the real rebel of our lot."

Finishing his cup of tea, Peter continued, "Well, you know the rest, Annie. Your mother and father made a real success of it in Amerikay...pillars of the community and all that, you might say. Today, you and your brothers are a living testament to your parents' hard work...not to mention your father's loyalty to the dream of Irish freedom."

"We've been very lucky," said Sarah. "I only hope Aran and I will be so as well."

"Sure and why not?" said Áine.

"Oh, I don't know. The times seem so uncertain."

"Today is less troublesome than the days were when your father left home," said Uncle Peter. "The English have always tried to keep the Irish under their heel. But, please God, with the Tans gone and the fighting over, the worst is behind us now. With Collins and his crowd calling the shots, we'll all be the better off."

"But Uncle Peter, from what Aran says, it's not going to be that simple. Éamon de Valera and Michael don't see eye to eye on many things…many important things. Our troubles may not have ended yet."

"Oh, Sarah," said Áine, "things have a way of sorting themselves out. Have a bit of faith, will ye."

"You're probably right, Áine," answered Sarah Anne. "For the sake of us all, I hope you're right."

After dabbing at her mouth with her serviette, Sarah pushed back from the table. "Sure, it's past time I went to work. The bedrooms upstairs need to be tidied up and the bed linen changed. Then sure the lounge out front needs a good going over and there's the restocking to do as well."

"Be there in a tick to give you and Niamh a hand," said Áine, getting up from the table. "I'll just run Mary Margaret home and be back in five minutes."

Though making no signs of rising, Peter, looking directly at his wife, offered, "Don't forget, be sure and leave me the restocking to do."

As she continued clearing the table, Niamh smiled to herself. With a knowing expression, she watched Peter pour the last of the tea into his cup. *Ah, he's such a good man despite his faults.*

Tying on her pinny and leaving the kitchen to her aunt and uncle, Sarah Anne headed up the back stairs to the family's sitting room and first-floor bedrooms. Despite all that Áine had said at the kitchen table, a lingering doubt still filled her heart.

❀

Later that afternoon, Sarah Anne posted a letter to her parents and two other brothers in Amerikay, inviting them to Ireland and her wedding.

In spite of being elated at the prospects of her family coming to visit, she was haunted by Michael's words, spoken to her privately during a quiet moment last evening.

Michael, Aran and Tom had just returned from their Clonmel meeting. She was polishing some glasses behind the bar when the Big Fellow sat down on a stool and said, "Sarah, do you mind if we had a word?"

Surprised but flattered, she replied and nodded, "No. Let's go over to that corner table. We'll have some privacy there."

Once at the table, Michael said, "Sarah Anne, the worst is not yet over. Aran senses it as I do. I'm not sure what's going to happen, but if I need your help again, can I count on you?"

She remembered the chill that ran down her spine as she looked the Big Fellow in the eye. Her mind raced. She'd only a moment to reply. Michael wanted an answer. Gabriel and Áine had just come into the bar and were moving toward them from across the room. No time to think or ask questions.

Her answer still reverberated inside her: *For you, Michael, and for Ireland, yes, but most of all, I will for Aran.*

❀

Michael Collins was in his element. Instead of being cooped up in a Dublin office, he was out touring, 'talking to the country' as he liked to say. His little travelling party had left the O'Neill farm outside of Gort on Saturday last. An overnight in Limerick and then it was on to Cahir. Sunday evening they'd motored over to Clonmel to meet with more of the Brotherhood. As Head Centre of the IRB, Collins wanted to test the pulse of those down the country regarding their thoughts about possible Treaty terms with London.

At the end of each session Collins reminded his comrades

that while the military of both nations were making future plans, generally speaking, the Irish people seemed oblivious to the potentially perilous situation that lay ahead. The Big Fellow told each group that as he travelled around the country, talking to the ordinary folks as well as other IRB men, there seemed to be a general feeling of euphoria everywhere. Ireland seemed to be savouring the sudden improvement in people's lives since the Truce came into effect in July.[1] [2]

❧

Now on this Monday morning, with a good night's sleep behind him and his stomach full of Niamh McCracken's breakfast, the Big Fellow was in great form. Dressed in a three-piece suit, freshly laundered shirt, polished high-topped shoes and carrying a dark-brown leather briefcase, the Corkman looked more like a successful businessman than a ruthless guerrilla organiser. To top matters off, Mick had grown a small moustache over the summer. It was nothing flamboyant…just something to cover the gap between his nose and upper lip.

When asked about it, Collins replied, "Adds a bit of style and sophistication, don't ye think?"

With their cases stowed in the auto's boot, the four revolutionaries and their hosts lingered in the back garden of the McCracken pub, enjoying the sunny morning with its smell of autumn leaves in the air.

Peter had named the pub the Black Rose after one of the town's timeless legends. The front facade of the two-storied, stone and mortared building was covered with two prolific rose bushes…Dog roses to be specific, one growing on either side of the front entrance. Over time, their thorny stems and multitoothed leaflets had blanketed the entire face of the building.

---

1. Mackay, op. cit., 208.

2. The Truce began at twelve noon on 11 July. On that date, both sides agreed to stop all troop movements, military maneuvers, displays of force, troop reinforcement & supplying as well as all spying activities. The Truce could be terminated by either side with a seventy-two-hour notice.

Roses are a popular Irish garden flora and the Dog rose is the most common. Its substantial upright, arching stems are well suited for arbours and for growing up along the sides of stone walls and buildings. Their highly scented flowers are beautiful to see and they fill the mid-summer's air with a heavenly bouquet.

These particular rose bushes had adorned the front wall of the recently leased McCracken pub for generations. In fact, as the story goes, when the great famine of the last century struck County Tipperary in 1845, the vines continued to flourish but bore no blooms or fruit in 1846. Then in 1847 they bloomed again. But instead of their soft pink, fragrant blossoms, the rose bushes produced a darkish, almost black flower that exuded an unpleasant, pungent odour.

To this day, neither horticultural experts nor local residents could explain that happening. Most attributed it to a vivid imagination or simply exaggerated folklore. But others maintained that it was God's way of showing His sympathy for a downtrodden and starving people. And so it is that the residents of Cahir remember Black '47, not only for its widespread human tragedy, but also for the legend of the black rose.

Mindful of those troubled times and respecting the old village tale, Peter and Niamh decided to name their new establishment the Black Rose. The wooden sign hanging over the front door, with its leafy green vines and single black rose, was a deliberate reminder of the village's past.

❧

With the clock ticking, the morning's outdoor interlude was broken by the sing-song brogue of the Corkman. "Time to go, lads. Say your goodbyes. We must be heading out. Sure I want to be in Kilkenny by noontime."

Turning to shake hands with his host, Collins said, speaking for Tom as well, "Again, Peter, my thanks to you. It was a lovely time we had here. God bless and mind yourselves."

Turning to Aunt Niamh and the two younger women, the Big Fellow tipped his grey trilby, smiled and said, "You're all grand.

With any luck, we'll get through this patch together."

Tom Cullen, standing by the auto, opened the back door for his superior. Moments later, with Collins comfortably seated inside the car, the intelligence man cum bodyguard slid in behind the wheel. Aran and Gabriel lingered a moment longer...time for one last kiss goodbye.

When all four men were finally in the car, the Big Fellow gently ribbed both Aran and Gabriel about their lengthy parting embraces with Sarah Anne and Áine.

"Ah Jaysus, the four of yis are no better than love-starved puppies. You'd think I've nothing better to do than wait around for you and your romancing to end," teased Michael.

Still standing by the motor car, Sarah overheard Mick's taunt.

Smiling down at the Big Fellow though his open window, she said, "Patience, Michael. Your time is coming, if you're lucky enough so."

"Hum," was his only reply.

Impatiently, he leaned forward and tapped Cullen on the shoulder with his finger, "Let's go."

Tom turned the ignition key. The motor of the newly imported Austin 7 sprang to life. It was just off the boat from England. The Irish government had purchased four of them for its official business travel only a month ago. This journey was Collins's first opportunity to give one a go. Happily, it met with his approval. On its first outing, the auto was serving his needs well. He'd already met with IRB leaders in both Limerick and Clonmel. Now, they were off to another powwow in Kilkenny, then home to Dublin and an important meeting of the Dáil executive on Wednesday.

As the vehicle eased out of the pub's rear car park, Aran couldn't help but jab back at the Corkman, "If you weren't such an ugly bowsie, Mick, decent women might have more to do with ye."

The words were barely out of his mouth, and before he could raise a hand in his defence, Michael was on top of him. With his arms pinned to his side, the Gortman was virtually helpless.

Aran had witnessed and been a near-victim to such attacks by Collins before. The Corkman was famous for his 'bit-of-ear' assaults on friends and foe alike. Instead of a bloody nose, a bloody ear was Michael's way of having some fun at the expense of others.

Now, the Irish Rebel could feel his friend's hot breath on his cheek.

"A bowsie am I? Well, we'll just see who the bloody louser is in this car," crowed a gleeful Collins.

"Shyte," uttered Aran.

But before older man could satisfy his revenge with a piece of Aran's ear, he carelessly miscalculated his younger opponent once again.

Seeing his chance, the Irish Rebel suddenly twisted his head sideways. Unexpectedly, he took a nip out of his commander's unprotected left ear lobe.

Recoiling from the painful bite, Michael abruptly freed Aran from his bear-hug hold. Grabbing his own ear, he cried out in surprise, "Bloody hell! You're a divil of a whoor's melt."

"I've me a good teacher," retorted Aran, pushing himself back upright in the Austin's rear seat.

"Jaysus wept!" cursed Collins, famous for his frequent use of colourful words. "Who said his bastard's bark is worse than his bite? Gabby, help. I'm after needing something to stop this bleeding."

With order finally restored and after everyone had had a good laugh, the Austin finally pulled out of the pub's laneway. If anyone had glanced inside the car, they'd have been surprised to see Michael Collins holding a bloodied handkerchief to his wounded ear.

As Cullen turned the corner and drove past the front of the Black Rose, he honked twice at the solitary figure standing in the doorway. Turning to look back through the vehicle's rear window, Aran Roe could see Annie McCracken waving goodbye.

Tom also watched Annie wave through the car's wing mirror. "She's a great one, Aran. You're a lucky man…but I still wonder why on earth she ever left Amerikay for the likes of you."

"I've sometimes wondered that meself," answered Aran.

❧

With Aran and Michael lost in thought in the back seat, Gabriel, seated next to Tom, served as navigator. He'd taken the roads from Cahir to Kilkenny many times and knew them well.

Like Mick and Aran, both men up front were dressed in mufti: shirts, ties, jackets and trousers. They wore tweed caps and, owing to the fine seasonal weather, had stowed their trench coats in the car's boot along with their luggage. Their civilian attire attracted less attention than if they'd worn their uniforms. Though the Truce was holding, British military units had been known to harass high-ranking IRA men in military attire, particularly in Munster and around Dublin. But their innocent appearance belied the fact that they were well armed soldiers. Each man carried one or two handguns on his person, while a small cache of rifles and two Thompson machine guns were safely squirrelled away under the back seat cushions.

As they drove into Cashel along the main road, Gabby gave Tom a short history lesson about the eye-catching, hilltop, ecclesiastical ruins that dominated the rural village at its feet.

"Just think, for over seven centuries that was the seat of the kings of Munster. Then back in 450 AD, St. Patrick himself was supposed to have baptised King Aengus up there. Legend has it that as the high priest concluded the ceremony, he drove his staff into the ground. Unfortunately, Aengus's foot was in the way. Not realising the blow wasn't part of the rite and not wanting to show weakness before his assembled clan, Aengus remained stoic despite the pain and blood of it all."

"Sounds like a load of cobbles to me, Gay."

"You're probably right, but I've been told by a reliable source that the Lord Mayor of Cashel has a bloodied stone in his office. He swears it has Aengus's blood on it…been passed down over the ages…and who's say it isn't."

"I for one, Gay. Jaysus, if you believe that, you're as bad as those who go out after looking for gold at the end of rainbows."

"All right, have your laugh, but it does make a fine story, no?"

"Ah, yes it does. Especially the way you tell it…with such sincerity. For an Irish-Yankee, Gay, you do us proud."

Cullen was too practical a man to entertain such nonsense seriously, but as the Rock of Cashel loomed overhead, he slowed the motor car and had a long look. The massive limestone outcropping with its stone walls, structural remnants and round tower did catch his fancy.

"Press on, Tom. We've no time for sightseeing tours today. I'd like to be in Kilkenny to hear the Angelus ringing and I don't mean the six o'clock one," said Collins from the back seat.

The driver, obeying the order, put his boot down.

※

Michael had first met Tom when he was a captain in the Wicklow Volunteers. They had met at Larkfield, Count Plunkett's Dublin home in the suburb of Kimmage, just prior to the Easter Rebellion. Afterwards, Cullen had joined forces with Liam Tobin and Frank Thornton. Together, the three established themselves as Collins's top agents in Mick's underground Intelligence Section. Working out of offices at #5 Crow Street headed up by Tobin, Tom, Frank and others, they gathered information and ran cover operations for the Big Fellow throughout Dublin during the War of Independence. He played a key role in helping save the life of Dan Breen and Seán Treacy after their tragic Fernside affair in October, 1920. Then, just a month later, Cullen luckily survived interrogation by some of Britain's most feared undercover operatives, the Cairo Gang, at Vaughan's Hotel in Rutland Square. Today, Tom, now in his late twenties, continued on as one of Michael's top intelligence men as well his bodyguard and driver.

Born in County Wicklow, Cullen was as loyal as they came. Dedicated to the cause of Irish freedom, he supported Michael in every possible way. A man of medium height and modest stature,

Tom had a strong nose, sad eyes and rather prominent ears. A good-natured smile usually illuminated his face. Words like 'soft spoken' and 'serious minded' described him well, but he did have a sense of humour and enjoyed some moments of light-hearted fun. Unfortunately, however, many of his colleagues felt sorry for Tom as he was often the butt of Mick's endless baiting.[3] It was one of Mick's worst personality traits and understandably drew the anger of others. But despite everything, Cullen cared deeply for Collins and refused to be put off by his teasing.

Aran had first met Tom, who was serving as GHQ's assistant quartermaster, when Michael called him to Dublin at the end of October, 1920. The Big Fellow had hoped the Irish Rebel might successfully organise a jail break and rescue Kevin Barry. Collins's previous attempt to free the medical student had failed. The British were holding the young man for murder in Mountjoy Jail. The eighteen-year-old had innocently taken part in an IRA raid in Dublin's Church Street. Unfortunately, things went wrong. Three British soldiers were killed and Barry was arrested though he never fired a shot.

Tom and another member of Tobin's team assisted Aran but to no avail. Despite all of the Big Fella's efforts and a concerted international appeal for clemency, the young medical student was hanged on 1 November.

Afterwards, as Tom and Aran briefed Michael and a handful of others about their failed attempt to free Barry, the Irish Rebel decided to honour Tom with the nickname Cú for his bravery and willingness to risk his life to save the teenager from death's rope.

"Jaysus, you should have seem him, Michael. Tom here was up and over the wall and into the blockhouse without a sound or false move. We would've had Barry out, but for the lack of the right key. The warders had moved their captive to an adjoining cell only that day and our key wouldn't open the feckin' lock.

"At that point, we were discovered and bullets began flying. Tom here bravely stood in the open, holding the bloody screws at bay as the rest of us made it back to the top of the wall from

---

3. Tim Pat Coogan. *Michael Collins*. London, 1991, 135.

where we could cover him. Then he scrambled up the rope ladder and down the other side. The entire operation took less than ten minutes.

"Thanks be to God we were in and out without a scratch, but tragically without Kevin in tow."

Collins didn't say a word.

Amid the others' protestations for their collective bravery, Aran continued, "Pearse was a great one for touting the Ulster Cycle exploits of the great mythological warrior Cúchulain. Since Cúchulain is sometime pronounced Cú Cullen, I think it only fitting to fix our friend Tom Cullen here with the nickname Cú for short."

"Ah, get away wit ye, Aran," retorted Tom. "Me exploits are none to compare to that Ulster hero of old."

"You say," argued the Rebel. "If the shoe fits, wear it, Tom… and do so proudly."

"Bloody hell," roared Collins. "Sure, I didn't ask for two of my best friends to be at each other's throats over a feckin' name.

"Aran's right, Tom, the moniker fits. Wear it proudly. Now, I'll hear no more of it, understood? We've more important business to attend too."

And so it came to pass, that in Aran's mind at least, Tom Cullen became Cú…Cú Cullen.

After the meeting about the failed attempt to free Kevin Barry broke up, Collins asked Aran to stay on in Dublin. Plans were being formulated to destroy London's spy network in Dublin. Michael wanted Aran's help.

A week later Gabriel joined Aran in Dublin and together Tom Cullen, Gay and Aran spent some time together. They became friends. Tom even invited the two of them to his upcoming wedding. But as things turned out, Aran and Gabby thought it wiser to stay in their safe house in the Galty Mountains rather than risk a dangerous cross-country journey in Ireland's dicey December weather.

❧

Outside of Cashel, the Austin motor car left the main Dublin road and headed northeast toward the villages of Dually and Ballinure. Traffic was almost nonexistent except for the occasional farmer's horse and cart. The four country men enjoyed the rural landscape with its patchwork of fields and groves of trees.

Aran, gazing out the rear window of the auto, remembered reading that once Ireland was almost entirely forested with trees, mostly oaks. So dense was the vegetation that waterways offered the only practical avenues of travel. Those were in the days before the English cleared vast tracts of confiscated land for their planting and grazing pleasure. Then beginning with the Tudor's reign in the 16th century, Ireland became England's plantation. Irish grain, meat and farm-grown products fed its island neighbour, while a growing shipbuilding, furniture and building boom demanded a steady supply of Irish timber. Today, the rape of the land was over, but the great forests of yesterday were gone forever.

The Irish Rebel could almost hear his grandfather's voice in his ear as the car bounced along the rutted road: *Aye…'tis the great Irish oak tree that built the Empire. The ships, the great houses, charcoal for iron smelting, barrels for whiskey…sure the list goes on and on…and Aran, don't forget the little people so. It's from the oak trees' acorn that the leprechauns make their wee pipes for smoking.*

Aran almost laughed out loud. His grandfather was wise and well schooled in the history and folklore of Ireland. Pearse would have enjoyed his company.

Michael was dozing next to Aran. The gently rocking Austin was conducive to nodding off. Up front, Gay was going on about the similarities between American and Irish farming. Tom Cullen would pass the occasional comment, but spent most of his time repeating uh-huhs and dodging pot holes.

❧

As the weather in Ireland is apt to do, it changed. The sunny, blue sky of the morning gradually gave way to dark clouds, patchy rain and drizzle.

Suddenly, Collins was awake.

"Gay, are we near Ballingarry?"

"Not far...maybe five miles or so, Mick," replied Gabriel.

Before anyone could ask why, Michael said, "Good. Head for it, Tom. There's somebody I want to see."

The gently rolling countryside soon gave way to the Slieveardagh Hills with their uneven sloping terrain. Suddenly, the legend of the Black Rose and Ireland's famine years flashed through Aran's head.

"As ye well know lads, seventy-five years ago, the bloody hunger was all around us," observed the Rebel, studying the countryside through the Austin's window.

No one responded.

Welcoming the deafening silence, Aran Roe closed his eyes. In his mind the lush green of Tipperary turned stony grey as he pictured the rocky ground and weathered hills of County Galway, not far from his family's farm. The poignant words of his grandfather flooded his consciousness: *Now limestone walls are all that's left of times of pain and failure. Sure, this country yields the secret of the beauty that it holds...*

"Sure, it blanketed most of Munster and Connacht, Aran," answered Tom, unexpectedly interrupting the Gortman's reverie. "That's no secret. Those were terrible times indeed."

Hesitating but a moment, Aran thoughtfully responded, "Aye Cú, but did you know it was very near here, despite those troubles, that William Smith O'Brien and the Young Islanders[4] rose up in support of the land they loved? They risked all, striking bravely for Irish independence during that blighted summer of 1848."

Having piqued his travelling companions' interest, Aran continued. "As a consequence of the 1798 Rebellion, Ireland was unioned with our island neighbour. We all know that. But fifty

4. Originally followers of Daniel O'Connell's Repeal (of the Union) Association, they were cultural nationalists who supported non-sectarian education. In July, 1846, a group of men grew impatient with their leader's distaste of violence, except in extreme cases. Calling themselves the Young Islanders, they broke away from O'Connell's leadership & formed their own association.

years later, revolutionaries just like us sought to break that bond. Earlier that fateful year, with death, disease, starvation and the tragedies of emigration rife, Smith warned Britain's parliament that if she didn't dissolve the Union, Ireland would strike for its independence."

Gabby turned in his seat to catch Aran's eye. "The Rebellion of '48...sure, my father often referred to it as one of Ireland's bloodless, non-violent revolts...just like the one in 1867. Wouldn't you agree, Aran?"

"Yes and no, Gay," answered the Gortman. "Yes, because the fighting was restricted to really one day, July 29th, and was limited to the area immediately surrounding us now, Ballingarry. But no it wasn't bloodless. Two of the Young Islanders or maybe it was two of their supporters were killed and a number of others were wounded...no one knows the exact numbers for sure."[5]

"Didn't Smith O'Brien go up to some widow's cottage window and treat with the peelers who were illegally occupying the place? With the force of numbers on his side, didn't he demand their surrender?" asked Tom.

"That's right, Tom," said the Big Fellow, taking a real interest in the conversation. "The widow, a Mrs. McCormack, I believe, had left her five children, all under the age of ten, at home by themselves while she nipped out to run an errand or something. Upon returning, the widow woman found her home surrounded by a hundred or so Islanders and her cottage occupied by two score or more constabulary.

"Fearing for her children's lives and the safety of her home, she convinced O'Brien to try and negotiate a peaceful resolution with the ensconced soldiers.

"It was while O'Brien was at one of the cottage windows, offering his hand and trying to convince the authorities to surrender and vacate the premises, for the sake of the children, that the fighting erupted."

"That's right, Michael," said Aran. "Someone outside in the crowd was supposed to have yelled, 'Slash away, boys. Slaughter

---

5. Robert Kee. *The Green Flag, Vol. I*. London, 1989, 284-285.

the lot of them,' or words to that effect. At any rate, stones were thrown and shots were fired."

"You can bet the rozzers did most of the firing. When did our crowd ever have the advantage?" said Gay.

"Ah, shyte," said Mick, "that wouldn't have been fair, would it? We're just Irish so."

Ignoring the Corkman's sarcasm, Tom said, "I've always thought O'Brien was lucky he wasn't killed...and more of his followers too."

Aran leaned forward in his seat. "Well, yis all know what happened. The Rebellion, if you can call it that, sputtered and failed. In reality, I think the Islanders' skirmish was more a flight from authority to avoid arrest than it was a fight for Irish freedom. But to this day, many folks naively chalk up O'Brien's actions as simply retaliation for Britain's callous response to the troubles surrounding Black '47.[6]

"Ah, the Battle of the Cabbage Patch," said Tom.

"That's it," answered Aran, "the widow's cabbage patch. Soon after, most of the rebels were rounded up, tried, convicted and transported...Tasmania, I think it was."

Aran paused for a moment's reflection and then continued, "Sure, the Young Irelanders' uprising may have failed as a revolution, but it didn't disappoint as an educational or propaganda tool for future generations. Those Irish rebels left Éireann with an enduring and inspiring legacy of poems, prose and myth."

❧

As the motor car entered Ballingarry, Collins interrupted, "Pull up there, Tom, in front of the forge. I want ya to come with me. We won't be long. Aran and Gay, you stay here and scout around. Keep a sharp lookout just in case."

Pulling on their overcoats they'd retrieved from the car's boot, Aran and Gay stretched their legs on the tarmacadam road. The

---

6. Black '47 was the nickname for the deadly & destructive potato-blight famine that swept through parts of Ireland during the years 1845-1849, with 1847 being possibly the worst year of the five.

village of Ballingarry was barely more than a crossroads: a half a dozen, well-kept houses with tidy front flower gardens; a draper's shop; a grocery cum post office cum pub; a second public house; an ironmongery; and, of course, the blacksmith's establishment into which Collins and Cullen had disappeared.

For centuries in Ireland, the village farrier was closely associated with revolution. With his hands, he fashioned pikes for battle and, with his ear to the ground, he was a reliable conduit for information. His professional services were valued and required by both friend and foe. With a keen eye and a quick wit, the blacksmith was in a position to know most of what was happening in the village.

"A soft day surely, thanks be to God," said Aran to a passing stranger.

"Aye, and God save you," came the reply.

The man continued on his way without looking back.

"A cup of tea would go down nicely right now. What ya think, Aran? Maybe we could talk the Big Fella into one?"

No sooner were the words out of Gabriel's mouth than Collins and Cullen came hurrying toward them from around the side of the forge.

"Into the car, lads," ordered the Corkman.

With all back inside, Cullen wheeled the Austin around and made a sharp left at the t-junction across from the draper's shop.

"Straight on…it's only a short drive up the road," barked Collins.

"What's up?" queried Aran.

"We may have stumbled onto something," said Collins.

"Something?" repeated Gabby.

"Just before we arrived into Ballingarry back there, a lorry load of Auxies[7] wheeled through the village on their way up to The Commons. Apparently, there's been a running war of words between the local constabulary and some area residents over the

7. With violence in Ireland continuing to escalate after 1919, the British government enlisted the further aid of demobbed British military officers. These Auxilliary Cadets or Auxies were posted to Ireland beginning in September, 1920. They wore either RIC uniforms or British army dress without insignia or rank. Their signature was a Glengarry cap & drawn pistols.

flying of the Irish flag," explained Tom. "Mick thinks we ought go up and offer our help. Sounds like the Sassenach are throwing their weight around in violation of the Truce. "

"Kick some feckin' arses if need be," muttered Michael.

As if on cue, both Aran and Gabriel reached under their jackets and pulled out their weapons. After a quick check to make sure all was ready, they slid them back into place.

"Now, now lads...yis just be careful how you use those," cautioned Michael.

As their motor car raced over a low hill, its occupants could see a small cluster of buildings a mile or so up ahead.

Thoughts of 1848 flashed through Aran's mind: *The Commons. Huh. Wasn't it the day before the storied cabbage patch affair that one of the Young Irelanders, Thomas Francis Meagher, raised the first Irish tricolour? Inspired by the French flag he was...yes, I think so. What were his words...something like "...the white in the centre signifies a lasting truce between the Orange and the Green...?" Ah, Jaysus wept....*

All of a sudden, out of the corner of his eye, Aran noticed a small sign along the side of the road. From the speeding motor car, he had but a second to read its words: 'The Widow McCormack's cottage, 200 yards' with an arrow at the bottom pointing off to the right.

Bloody hell: thought Aran. *1921...the second siege of the Cabbage Patch.*

As they drew near the tiny village and its crossroads, Collins cautioned, "Slow down, Tom. We don't want to attract any unnecessary attention."

Aran could hear the tension in the Big Fellow's voice. Sure he knew his friend was not afraid of a fight, but he also knew Mick hadn't tasted the throws of battle like Gabby and he had.

"Park back here, Tom. Gabby and you take the right side of

They travelled around Ireland in motorised packs murdering & destroying anything that suited their fancy. Often referred to simply as 'Tans,' they were even more hated & feared than the actual Black & Tans. Over 2,000 were eventually stationed in Ireland during the later stages of the War of Independence.

the road and stay behind us. Aran and I'll go up the left side. Remember…keep your weapons out of sight, unless you have to use them."

"Lookin' for anyone or anything special?" asked Aran.

"There might be an old man, low sized with wavy white hair and a beard. He's an old friend of mine. His name is Connie…Connie Crowe. Tough as nails and afraid of nobody he is," said Mick.

As the two walked up toward the crossroads, a crowd was gathering…maybe twenty or thirty people…mostly farmers. There were men of all ages plus a smattering of older women in their long black dresses with white oversmocks. Several dogs were barking and weaving their way in and out of the tangle of legs. Children were conspicuous by their absence.

Studying the situation, Aran reasoned: *These folks must know something is up or why else wouldn't there be younguns around? They must be expecting some kind of trouble…*

Parked in the middle of the narrow road to their side of the intersection was a British lorry. An Auxilliary Cadet dressed in boots, leather gaiters, black trench coat, white scarf tied around his neck and signature Glengarry cap was standing up on one of the lorry's wooden benches. Two holstered service revolvers were strapped to his hips.

Just like a damn cowboy, thought Aran.

Circled around the lorry, forming an armed guard, were a dozen or so Auxilliary Cadets. Some wore regular British military uniforms while the others had on their more traditional overcoats, belted at the waist, and Glengarries. They stood at attention, facing the loosely gathered knot of farm folk. Each held his rifle in both hands, angled across his chest.

Aran glanced over his shoulder. Gabby and Tom were about ten paces behind and to the right. Both had their hands jammed in their coat pockets. The Rebel knew Gay's held his Webley & Scott automatic.

The Gortman wisely resisted the urge to pull his Luger from its shoulder holster. He reasoned: *That's all we need…flash a gun and the fireworks'll begin.*

At the centre of the commotion was a flag pole with the Irish tricolour halfway up, or was it halfway down? Aran couldn't be sure.

Suddenly, above the crowd's low murmur came a strident Irish voice. "Bugger off ye boyo. This flag's been flying here since before you were born, and it will go on long after you're gone. Now, unhand me."

Immediately, Aran Roe recognised the rebellious man: low sized...wavy white hair...beard. It was Michael's friend, Connie Crowe. He'd the flag pole rope in one hand and was holding off an Auxie with the other.

All at once, the gathering hushed and then a voice cried out, "It's Michael Collins...The Big Fellow himself is coming up the road so."

"Where?" asked another.

"Down there...just beyond the lorry."

"Jesus, Mary and Joseph," said a third.

"Where he'd come from?" questioned a woman.

"I can't believe me eyes," responded someone else.

By now, all attention had turned from the flag pole to the figure of Michael Collins striding up the road.

As he moved forward, the sightseers parted like the Red Sea had for Moses.

"Connie...nice seein' ye again. What seems to be the trouble?"

"Ah, it's these bloody lousers. They're after telling us we can't fly the flag at The Commons. 'Tis been so since Meagher first ran it up in '48. You tell 'em Mick."

"Who's the officer in charge here," snapped Collins.

Silence.

Again, Collins ordered, "Who's in charge?"

"I am," said the man from the back of the lorry. "Captain James Madden, Essex Regiment."

"You're a long way from home, captain. Didn't like the accommodation in Bandon?"

"Been reassigned...Beggars' Bush in Dublin."

"Well, I suggest you load up your men and be on your way.

In case you've forgotten, there's a Truce in place between our governments for two months now. You're after not to be out flexing your muscles in the countryside any longer. But just to be on the safe side, my men have your bloody lot surrounded…and if you haven't noticed, they're itching to have a go at yis. So be a good man and off you go."

Defiantly, Collins stood facing the captain still astride the lorry some twenty yards away. The Big Fellow's legs were spread apart as if he was standing on the deck of a rolling ship. His chin was jutting forward and his eyes flashed with anger. Additionally, Michael's jacket was unbuttoned and his thumbs were now wedged down inside his waistcoat pockets.

The captain turned his attention from Collins and slowly glanced around the intersection.

All he could see were capped heads and upturned leathery faces. The crowd wore a determined expression.

The officer looked back down at Collins.

Aran could feel the apprehension mounting.

More silence.

Suddenly and without provocation, the Auxie, who was being restrained by the old man, drew one of his revolvers and shot the defiant gentleman through the head.

Amid a chorus of stunned gasps, the white-haired man sagged to the ground. His eyes were fixed on Michael.

A moment later, a second then a third shot rang out. *Pop! Pop!*

In what seemed like less than a heartbeat, the Auxie, who'd murdered Connie, was on the ground, sprawled atop the dead Irishman. Blood ran from both heads as the Irish standard they'd been arguing over fluttered softly to earth.

Ducking sideways, Aran firmly pushed Michael Collins back into the protection of the bystanders. His still smoking automatic now pointed at the chest of the nearest Tan.

A moment later, a fourth pistol shot broke the stunned silence. *Bang!*

With a gasp of pain, the lorry captain pitched forward, tumbling over the slatted side of his vehicle. The officer's lifeless body thudded onto the pavement. Thump! His legs twitched twice then a third time before they were still forever.

Brashly, Gabriel's voice boomed over the horrified gathering. "Brits, drop your weapons or you'll be next. *NOW*!"

No one moved.

Gabriel fired another shot into the air.

"Drop them. I *mean it*! You're surrounded."

Slowly at first, then in a cascade of sound, the solders dropped their rifles and unbuckled their holsters. The clatter of their military hardware reverberated through the stunned audience as the weapons hit the ground.

Gay's gamble had paid off. Leaderless, the enemy lacked the will to press the attack.

"That's it! Now, back up into the lorry," ordered Gabby. *"MOVE!"*

Up scrambled the soldiers, void of their weapons.

Eager Irish hands reached out, collecting the discarded arms.

The two dead soldiers were quickly hoisted up into the back of the lorry.

Gay shouted one last order, "Now, you bloody sods, drive like the very divil is after you. Get your feckin' cowering selves the hell out of here."

Moments later, the lorry roared to life and raced down the road toward Ballingarry.

The horrified throng didn't know whether to cry or cheer.

Michael quickly regained his composure. Before ordering his comrades back into their car, he made sure Connie's body would be well looked after.

"I'll be back for the funeral," said Collins.

He quickly scribbled an address on a slip of paper and handed it to one of the concerned onlookers.

"Just give me a day's notice. Connie was a friend...a grand man and a proud Irishman."

With the onlookers scattering for home and the Irish flag flying from its accustomed pole, the Austin turned east and faced for Kilkenny.

❧

Silence wrapped itself around the four stunned revolutionaries for several miles.

Aran nerves were frayed and he had that old unmistakable sinking feeling in the pit of his stomach. Every time he took a life, a little bit of him died too. Sure he'd killed before, over the last five years, but never at such close range. This time he even remembered hearing the dying Auxie gasp as he took his last breath. *What compelled him to shoot poor defenceless Connie like that? The old man was doing no harm…just standing up for what he believed in so. That eejit Auxie deserved the same…maybe even worse.*

Aran didn't remember pulling out his handgun and shooting the bastard or even pushing Collins for that matter. Just instinct he guessed. But sure he remembered standing there in front of what seemed like the entire British Army with just his Luger in hand. *Bloody hell! That could've been a real disaster. Sheer foolishness. Must've been a better way to settle matters with those bastards than killing in retaliation? But that's all in the past…too late now. Thanks be to God for Gay's quick thinking…sure he took the wind out of their sails, or maybe we both did? Who knows? I'm just damn glad we all made it through alive…one more time.*

Collins's voice finally broke the silence. "Sweet Heart of Jaysus.

What was that all about? Gunfight at the OK Corral or something? Out of the feckin' blue, I've lost me a friend and Ireland a brave man. We could've all been wiped out. The two of yis were bloody lucky to pull that one off. Quick thinking or just dumb luck? I don't know or want to know what in the hell you were thinking, but thanks all the same. You certainly left that Auxie lot with something to mull over for a good while, I'm betting.

"Sure, de Valera and Lloyd George will be hotter than hell when this news reaches them. All I can say is…they'd better get use to it."

5

"He shall not hear the bittern cry
In the wild sky, where he is lain,
Nor voices of the sweet birds
Above the wailing of the rain."

Francis Ledwidge

MONDAY NIGHT, 12 SEPTEMBER 1921

ichael Collins and his party pulled into Dublin just before
midnight. They'd been on the road from Cahir's Black Rose most
of the day and half the night. Collectively, the four men were dog
tired and in a foul mood.

Collins was upset…roaring mad about the senseless death
of his friend Connie Crowe. The following day he fired off letters to the Dáil cabinet and Churchill about the incident at The
Commons. Mick warned the English that such violations of the
Truce would not be tolerated. The retaliatory shooting of the
undisciplined Auxie and his irresponsible commander, a certain
Captain Madden of the Essex Regiment, were justified actions in
lieu of Ireland's outrage and intolerance toward Britain's breaches
of the peace agreement. Further defiance of their country's mutual
understandings would be dealt with most harshly.

The Corkman concluded his letter to the Secretary of State

for the Colonies with another rebuke regarding the outrages and criminal behaviour of one Major A. E. Percival, 1st Essex Regiment stationed in Kinsale, South Cork. Percival was directly responsible for the beating and torture of two IRA officers, Tom Hales and Pat Harte, in July, 1920 and the burning of Michael's family home, Woodfield, at Sam's Cross in West Cork nine months later. Michael again demanded the British military authorities take responsibility for Percival's uncontrolled and vengeful behaviour.

What he didn't tell Churchill in his letter was that he'd tried unsuccessfully to have Percival assassinated by members of his Squad on several occasions, both in Cork and afterwards in England.[1]

The following week, the Dáil secretary received a curt response to the Big Fellow's letter. It simply stated that the Colonial Office would look into the matters raised in Minister Collins's grievance.

After learning of the correspondence and its contents, Collins guessed nothing more would be forthcoming from London regarding either matter.

Tuesday night had turned into Wednesday morning. Aran Roe O'Neill said good night to his two friends, Gay and Tom Cullen. Gabriel had accepted Cú's kind offer of a bed for the second night in a row.

Leaving them to make their own way home, he headed up the street to his room in Dublin's Vaughan's Hotel. It was his second late night in succession. He'd meant to be back by eleven o'clock, but his watch now told him it was well after one. It was a short walk from Conway's Pub at #70 Great Britain Street, just a few yards off of Sackville Street, to his lodgings at #29 Rutland Square. Each step, however, was filled with memories.

Ah bloody hell, the Irish Rebel thought: *I must be up at the crack of dawn…even earlier. Collins is expecting me at his office in Harcourt Street at 7 o'clock in the morning…sharp. I'll be damned*

1. Coogan, op. cit., 147.

lucky to get four hours of sleep tonight…too much good company and too many good pints.

Almost wishing he'd shown a bit more restraint and had called it a night earlier, Aran glanced to his left at the doorway of #44 as he passed. The terrace house's brass plate by the entrance read: Ancient Order of Hibernians. He knew the house well. The leadership of the Irish Volunteers occasionally convened there in the old days. Hadn't he even attended some of their meetings with a few of his St. Enda's classmates? But it was his forced retreat into that building in April, 1916 that would forever stick in his mind. Running for his life from a British military patrol, he briefly availed himself of its protection after Pearse's surrender on that fateful Easter Saturday.

Without warning, the remembrance of that momentous struggle reverberated through his head: *1916! My God! Sure, that was a lifetime ago.*

He glanced across the street at the fencing surrounding the Rotunda Hospital. Just opposite him, on the far side of the square, he could see a light shining in the window of #3, Dr. Fannin's house. Aran speculated: *Maybe the good doctor is home from his military medical travels.*

Instantly, the Gortman's thoughts turned to his gun battle with the two attacking British soldiers and to his two captives trapped in the house's hallway: *Jesus, Mary and Joseph, I was lucky to get out of there alive! I wonder if any of them did as well.*

Feeling much older than his years, the Gortman faced for the top of the street. *Mother of God, I'll be lucky to get out of this life with my health and sense of humour intact, or maybe all that's just not in the cards, you maudlin ole cod you…*

Just before he pulled open the hotel's front door, Aran swung around and looked back at the square. Just off to his left, across the street, and situated at the top of the quadrangle was #25, the headquarters of the Gaelic League.

Wasn't it there that Ireland's 20th-century revolt had its beginning? he thought.

"Bloody well it was," he proudly said to the night air.

Remembering the stories he'd heard, the Rebel stood motionless: *Sure, it was inside that innocuous-looking, red-brick building that Clarke, MacDiarmada and Pearse first met and began their scheming.*

The history of it all flooded his mind: *Aye, that was in September, 1914 and those three sons of Ireland had revolution on their minds.*

It was as if he was reading again from some old newspaper account. Britain had entered Europe's escalating conflict that August. Soon after, a handful of Irish revolutionaries began thinking that with any luck, the old Fenian dream of England's difficulty being Ireland's opportunity might be at hand.

Aran knew their reasoning: *Weren't the forces coming to bear that might allow Ireland to strike for its long-denied independence from its island neighbour? Mightn't the time be ripe for putting aside old yearnings and for taking action?*

Diagonally opposite from where the Gortman had halted, hidden behind the façade of the Rotunda Hospital, stood the imposing statue of Ireland's uncrowned king, Charles Stewart Parnell. A few steps further along Great Britain Street at #75A had been Tom Clarke's modest little newsagent shop.

In their own way and in their own times, both men hungered for Irish independence. Though they were from opposite ends of the political and social spectrum, Parnell and Clarke shared a common longing: Éireann's freedom. But now, both were dead…both buried in Irish soil…both with their dreams still unfulfilled.

Aran fantasised: *Would Ireland's past rebels approve of today's goings on? Ireland was closer to gaining its independence than ever before, but it wasn't copper-fastened yet. There was much to do and much that could go wrong. Hadn't men like Parnell, Clarke and the others passed the torch of liberty to the next generation…his and Gay's and Michael's? But now the burden of yesterday's unfinished work rested on their shoulders. Ah sure, it's always a long road that knows no turning…*

Nodding to the night desk clerk, Aran headed for the stairs and his first-floor room, but the wooden steps and narrow hallway flooring resented being disturbed. They squeaked and groaned under the weight of his boots. *Just like the old days,* he reflected. *That's one of the reasons why Collins and his friends had picked this place to stay in the pre-truce days...it had its own built-in alarm system. The bloody Tans and peelers didn't have much of a chance catching men-on-the-run unawares with all the old boards complaining so.*

Resisting the urge to undress and change into his night clothes, Aran Roe simply fell into bed. Pulling a blanket over him, he reminisced: *Some old habits are hard to break. There's many a night I slept with me clothes on before the Truce and I managed to survive. One more night won't do me any harm. Sure, and if Mick is right, I'm guessing there'll be a few more nights like this in the days to come.*

❧

With a hurried splash and a change of shirts, Aran was out the door. It had been an unusually warm autumn. Everywhere you turned, people were complaining about the heat and close weather, but this Wednesday had dawned cool and damp.

The lone occupant seated in Vaughan's lobby looked up from his newspaper as the Gortman hurried toward the front door. "Soft day," he said, and then added, "but the flowers will like it if it doesn't chill up."

"Sure, we're due for a few like this," replied Aran, pushing the door open.

It was a good twenty-minute walk to #6 Harcourt Street... down Sackville Street, past the GPO, over O'Connell's Bridge, through College Green and by Trinity then up the length of Grafton Street. Finally, it was along the western side of Stephen's Green before he'd arrive into Sinn Féin's headquarters. Mick would be waiting for him in his second floor office.

Aran's head was a bit sore from the copious number of pints consumed the night before. To make matters worse, his stomach growled at him as well.

Despite these handicaps, he set a brisk pace past Parnell's statue, reasoning: *I'll die of the hunger if I don't get something to eat.*

Maybe if there isn't too much of a queue at Bewley's in Westmoreland Street, I'll stop in for a quick tea and a bun. Just the thought of substance helped ease his discomfort.

❧

Aran had been in Dublin for two weeks…most of it on his own. For a good bit of it, time had weighed heavily on his hands. After the first few days, Gabriel decided to travel back to Cahir. The pending journey to London, as a member of Collins's travelling party, was still a week or more away. Aran didn't begrudge Gay wanting to spend a few extra days with Áine and Mary Margaret. The recently married couple were looking for a small house or cottage to let. Living with his parents-in-law was not Gay's idea of an ideal arrangement. Both he and Áine wanted a place of their own.

Between hours of sentimental wanderings though Dublin, Aran made the reacquaintance of an old school friend, spent time with Cú Cullen and, of course, saw a good deal of Michael. The Gortman was proving to be one of the Big Fella's favourite sounding boards. In light of the current state of affairs, there was much to discuss.

But certainly one of the highlights of this Dublin stay was the unexpected arrival of his great friend Shadow Doyle. The baker cum miller cum military leader cum widower-father of three had spent three days in the capital conferring with Collins, Liam Mellowes, Richard Mulcahy, Liam Lynch and others about military preparations in case the Truce should collapse. Aran himself sat in on some of those meetings, but it was the evenings and out-of-town excursion to Athy with his old mentor that was memorable for more reasons than one.

❧

Looking back, it was on the 15th, his first Thursday back in Dublin, that Aran had an unexpected surprise. Returning to Vaughan's just after five in the evening, the desk clerk handed him a note left at the desk earlier in the day. It was from Martin Richardson, a friend from his St. Enda's school days.

The message read:

A, I've just returned. After reading newspaper accounts regarding MC's travels, I'd hoped to find you in Dublin too. After asking around, I discovered himself often stayed here at Vaughan's, so I chanced an inquiry. Success. If you're not too busy, stop in for tea this evening…say about half six, if that suits. If not, please call into the house tomorrow anytime.

The carefully folded paper was signed: MR, Drumcondra, 15 September.

To say Martin Richardson was just a former classmate was an understatement. In the days following the Easter Rebellion's collapse, Marty from Drumcondra, a northern suburb of Dublin, had engineered the scheme freeing Aran from British custody. It was a daring plot requiring planning, luck and a great measure of bravery.

Martin's parents, Fergal and Nuala, had moved to Dublin in 1895 from County Tipperary. That was two years before Marty was born. Quickly, Mr. Richardson established himself as a successful barrister-at-law, often arguing cases in the stately Four Courts building on the Quays. In point of fact, however, the majority of his practice was spent defending the less fortunate against their wealthier and more powerful Dublin employers and overlords. These altruistic pursuits earned him a popular reputation among the working class, but limited his economic advancement.

Additionally, Marty's father's friendships with Arthur Griffith, Jim Larkin and James Connolly often resulted in his da being 'brought in for questioning' by the authorities when political or labour turmoil disturbed the balance of power in Dublin. The events surrounding Big Jim's 1913 lockout were classic examples. During that ill-fated summer and autumn, it seemed that his father spent more nights in Dublin Castle or at the Brunswick Street police barracks than he did at home.

The Richardsons resided in an unpretentious Victorian terrace house on the Carlingford Road. In the shadow of his doting parents' influence, Marty grew up with a younger sister Mary Elizabeth, two years his junior, and his storytelling grandmother, who everyone called Nanna. Though this was considered small for a Catholic family of their day, it suited Marty just fine.

While they lived comfortably, the Richardsons were by no means wealthy. Many of Fergal's clients were financially unable to afford even his modest fees. If someone in the family ever complained about the scarcity of money in the house, Mr. Richardson would simply smile and say, "'Tis God's work that needs doing. Sure if this country's ever going to raise itself up, it'll be on the backs of the working people."

But despite his family's modest financial circumstances, necessitating Professor Pearse waiving some of St. Enda's tuition requirements for admission, Marty was more fortunate than most of his generation. Inexcusably, large numbers of Dubliners were forced to grow up in poverty and squalor that had become a perennial way of life in much of Dublin.

As Aran clearly remembered, Marty was stockily built, soft-spoken but possessed the athletic grace of a centre half-back. Because of his quiet, unassuming ways and his bookish interests, many of his classmates underestimated him, but not Pearse. The older man frequently praised Martin for his thoughtful analysis of problems and critical thinking skills. Any careful observer could easily find many similarities between the master and his pupil.

"Martin," Pearse was heard to say on more than one occasion, "you're going to make a fine doctor one day."

Wishing to further develop their son's curious mind, his interest in medicine and his love of ancient Ireland was motive enough for his parents enrolling him in Patrick Pearse's newly established, bilingual, private boy's school in 1910. It was Headmaster Pearse's growing reputation as an innovative teacher, Gaelic scholar, poet and writer that had attracted the notice and respect of Dublin's learned set.

St. Enda's school *was* unique. It cultivated a learning environment that allowed for each student's individual differences and special talents to flourish. This was far removed from the traditional 'grind of the Intermediate Examination system.' Proudly, in the school's brochure, Professor Pearse stated, "The educational goal of St. Enda's will be...not at all the cramming of boys with a view to success at examinations, but rather the eliciting of the individual bents and traits of each."[2]

Pearse spoke of school as a 'child-republic,' operating independently of the prevailing traditional educational system. He believed his Irish school to be different from others. "What I mean by an Irish school is a school that takes Ireland for granted. You need not praise the Irish language...simply speak it; you need not denounce English games...play Irish ones."[3]

In addition to fostering this sense of individualism, Pearse wished to impart a deepened appreciation of Ireland's Celtic past in the hearts and minds of his pupils. He hoped St. Enda's would become a cauldron of intellectual ferment that would spark a national Irish political and cultural revolution. Furthermore, this Sinn Féin ideologist and romantic separatist believed in the principles of Celtic masculinity. He employed the use of Gaelic games and military drills "to inculcate the physical virtues associated with the ancient Gaels and which (would be needed) to defend the Irish nation."[4]

❦

It had just gone six o'clock. The Angelus was ringing throughout Dublin. No need for a hard bicycle ride to the Richardson house. There was plenty of time before he was expected.

Heading up Dorset Street toward the Drumcondra Road, the Irish Rebel called to mind his own first days at St. Enda's and his initial meeting with Marty.

It was early March, 1916. He was only seventeen. As a new

---

2. Pat Cooke. *Scéal Scoil Éanna: The Story of an Educational Adventure.* Dublin: Office of Public Works, 1986, 12.
3. Ibid., 36-37.
4. Timothy J. White. "Book Review, Pearse's Patriots: St. Enda's and the Cult of Boyhood." *Celtic Studies Association Newsletter* 22.2 (2005):3.

arrival in the lecture hall, all his classmates' eyes were fixed on him. He remembered his cheeks feeling hot: burning with excitement and anticipation. But he recalled his one overriding emotion, self-confidence. He knew he could handle himself in almost any situation, and with Pearse's freshly uttered words of encouragement ringing in his ears, he was not afraid.

Everyone was in his seat. Then without warning, the classroom door burst open. In bustled Thomas MacDonagh, arms filled with books and pages of notes. His black lecture gown fanned out behind him, buoyed up by his breezy arrival.

With no word of introduction, he began lecturing...something about peasantry and landlordism in the 19th century.

When he'd finished, he asked, "Any queries?"

No one said a word for the longest time.

Aran could remember slowly rising to his feet. He could hear a low murmur emanating from those seated around him.

In a steady voice, the newcomer questioned, "Why hadn't the ideas of nationhood and land reform, championed by Fintan Lalor and others in the 1840s, been seriously debated prior to the 1801 Act of Union?"

Reflecting on that moment over five years ago, Aran Roe smiled: *Why you cheeky troublemaker. Were you trying to provoke the lads or test MacDonagh? Maybe both?*

Chuckling to himself, he recalled the electricity of the moment. *No, that wasn't it...I just wanted to prompt a discussion... see what the others thought.*

Again silence.

Finally, MacDonagh, standing by the podium, nodded his head. "Aran, you've anticipated my next lecture by a week, but from the tone of your voice, I guess the idea of land reform is a subject dear to your heart. Come by and see me tomorrow. We can have a bit of a chat about it."

Aran nodded and sat down.

Now, while bicycling over the Royal Canal, the Irish Rebel fondly replayed MacDonagh's next words over again inside his head. He could almost hear the Tipperary man speaking. "Gentlemen, just in case you haven't met Mr. Pearse's newest pupil, this is Aran Roe O'Neill. He comes to us from near Gort in County Galway. His people are farmers."

Walking over to where Aran sat, the teacher continued, "From his question you can see he takes his Irish history seriously…as we all do…yes, as we all do. It's a pleasure to have you at St. Enda's, Aran."

With that, Thomas MacDonagh, clutching his lecture notes and books, walked out of the room as the Gortman's classmates rapped their pens on their desks in welcome.

It was later the same day that Martin Richardson literally ran into him on the school's playing pitch. It happened during hurling training. The two strangers were after a rolling sliotar. As they neared the ball with their sticks at the ready, Aran Roe gave Martin a hip. The Dublin man went flying as the newcomer scooped up the sliotar with his hurley and raced on down the pitch.

After practice, Aran remembered approaching Martin and introducing himself. Apologising for the collision, he shook Marty's hand.

That was the beginning of a relationship which was destined to blossom into a real friendship.

❧

Martin answered his knock. The recent Harvard University graduate stood several inches taller than Aran remembered. Gone was the podgy face and pale skin. In its place was a lean, suntanned and robust-looking young man, a year older than himself.

"Jaysus, are ye ever a sight for sore eyes," exclaimed Aran. "Sure it looks like Amerikay suited you just fine."

The two shook hands warmly.

Keeping a hold of Aran's hand, he pulled his old classmate into the hallway, saying, "Come through…come through. So glad the hotel gave you me note and you were able to make it this evening. Tea will be ready soon. But first, come in and meet my parents and have something to wet your whistle, as they say in Amerikay."

Marty continued, talking over his shoulder as they went. "Ah, it was a grand four and a half years. I miss Boston already, but not like I missed Dublin. Ireland's me home. I can never get enough of this place, old stock."

"Sure, that's the way it was with me too," answered Aran, replying to the back of his friend's head.

Marty opened the sitting-room door and ushered him in.

"This is my mother who you know well from that Easter business."

Aran smiled and shook her extended hand.

My goodness, Marty's mother is certainly showing her years. The woman's shoulders were beginning to stoop and there were numerous lines radiating from around her eyes and mouth.

Ah, don't be so critical, Aran. She's certainly had her share of troubles…all the stress and worry of a lifetime caring about her family. Sure, her husband's been in the thick of it most of his life, and then there's Marty…under the gun at Jacob's with MacDonagh during Easter Week, risking his life to spring me along the Quays and lately off in Amerikay…gone for over four years. It's been no easy lot for her so.

"Hello, Aran. I trust you and your family are all well."

"Thank you, Mrs. Richardson," said the Gortman, nodding his head. "Yes, everyone's quite well indeed."

Marty continued, "…and Aran, this is my father, Fergal Richardson, whom you've never met."

A tall man with greying hair crossed the room in three strides. "Well, this is a pleasure. I've heard your good name mentioned in this house often. You've been here two…three time before, I believe. Seems I was always away. The Sassenach are a demanding lot as you well know. But with what you and your comrades have managed to pull off, please God those days are soon over."

Shaking the barrister's hand, Aran sputtered, "You give me too much credit, sir. It's one Michael Collins you should be addressing."

"Oh, I have and he tells me it's men like you that this country owes a real debt of thanks…sacrificing so much for the cause of our liberty."

Marty broke the momentarily awkward silence. "Enough of that, please Da. Sure the both of yis know something about giving."

Turning to his friend, he said, "What would you like, Aran? A bit of Jameson? Sure, we'll all have a drop before tea."

❧

Pedalling back to Vaughan's that evening, Aran struggled with his emotions. With a full stomach and an alcohol-induced light head, he ignored the steady rain that soaked him to the skin in just minutes.

Not wishing to be a bother, he'd rejected the Richardsons' kind offer of a bed for the night. With a wave of his hand, he'd dismissed their hospitality, insisting the ride back to the city would be good for what ailed him.

"Nothing like a little Irish rain to wash away the cobwebs and set me thinkin' straight," he'd said to them. "If the Irish people only knew of all the behind-the-scene word games going on between Dublin and London over possible Treaty talks, they'd all be going for a walk around the block or down the lane in it."

Pulling on a light jacket and donning his soft black Cronje hat, Aran smiled at the Richardsons. Shaking hands all around, he said, "Not to worry. I'll be grand. Besides, these clothes of mine could do with a good washing. If Sarah Anne were here, sure she would be after me on that score."

❧

Fifteen minutes into the ride home, Aran wished he hadn't been so cavalier about refusing the Richardsons' offer to stay the night. He was wet and chilled to the bone.

The rain was coming down harder than ever. The flashes of lightning and rumbles of thunder that had been some distance way were now growing nearer by the minute.

From overhead, street lamps cast evenly spaced pools of light that punctuated the blackened water-filled street. He seemed to be the only occupant of this usually busy thoroughfare.

Hunching low over his handlebars, Aran swore out loud, "Bloody hell, 'tis a night fit for neither man nor beast."

With the words hardly out of his mouth, a bolt of lightning illuminated the road directly in front of him. For an instant, night became day. Aran wasn't sure whether it was the lightning strike or the thunder clap an instant later or maybe both, but he flinched, almost losing his balance on the bike.

A few moments later, somewhere off to his right, another collision of the elements caused a tree limb to hit the ground. The crash of the falling branch and the shattering of glass more than startled him.

Cannon to the right of me, cannon to the left of me...'tis the charge of the Light Brigade all over again...time to seek cover or I'll be the next one skewered.

Wheeling left, the Gortman turned into Gardiner Street and sought the protection of a public house two doors down.

The dimly lit place was a throw-back to a secluded shebeen he'd once visited near the village of Corofin back home. A few rough tables were scattered about. Straight-backed, hand-woven súgán chairs dotted the room. A coal fire glowed at the far end of the narrow room where two men were hunched over some card game.

Aran noted that neither player bothered to look up when he entered the establishment.

The bar itself was a wide wooden plank laid over three evenly spaced, roughly hewn barrels. Half a dozen stools offered seated comfort for customers, but tonight there were only two. The aroma of stale tobacco smoke and sour beer filled the air.

At least it's dry air, thought Aran to himself.

The barman left his elbows and stood up. Aran's entry apparently interrupted his conversation with the two shapeless forms seated at the bar. Dressed in tweed caps and wearing full-length overcoats, the two customers turned and eyed the newcomer.

"God save all here," said Aran.

"God save you kindly," came a mumbled reply from the end of the bar.

"It's a dirty night to be out," said Aran, shaking the water off his black brimmer.

"...'tis that and more," answered the barman, who appeared to be in his forties, rail thin and with a ruddy complexion.

The ride and rain storm had stolen away any lasting effects of the evening's earlier libations. Trembling from the cold and damp, Aran ordered a whiskey.

Only a few bottles lined the wall behind the bar. The usual selection of strong drink was on the top shelf while unopened bottles of Guinness Extra Stout filled the lower one.

"What's your pleasure, young man," asked the barman.

"Paddy's will do nicely," replied Aran.

A glass with a finger's worth of whiskey in it and a small ceramic pitcher of water soon appeared before the Gortman.

Aran dug into his pocket. Producing a sixpence, he placed it on the bar next to his drink. It was promptly removed, replaced by several smaller coins.

Silence returned to the room. Fresh clouds of smoke wreathed the card players. The two at the end of the bar lit up as well. One of them turned to Aran, offering him a cigarette, but he declined.

Jaysus, Gay wouldn't say no to such generosity, mused Aran.

Softly, the barman broke the quiet, "Going far?"

"Aungier Street," lied Aran. *You can never be too careful*, he reasoned.

"Near Jacob's?"

"Not far."

With that, the barman launched into a history of how his father worked at the biscuit company for years prior to himself spending time there too.

"I was even out in '16...hold up there inside it I was...the entire week."

Aran nodded.

"Yes indeed, Commandant MacDonagh, may he rest in peace, was one of the finest men I've ever known."

Aran sat up straighter on his stool. He studied the man's face more closely.

"Ever hear of him?" the barman asked.

"I think so," lied Aran again.

"Here, let me show you something I saved from the newspaper."

With that, the barman pulled a carefully folded but tattered newspaper clipping from his wallet.

Handing it to the Irish Rebel, he reverently said, "Have a read of this." The man's eyes glowed with affection.

Because the light in the pub was poor and paper creased in several places, he'd a difficult time reading some of the typed words. It was a poem by Francis Ledwidge, who'd just recently died. The tribute was simply entitled *Thomas MacDonagh*. The first few lines read:

He shall not hear the bittern cry
In the wild sky, where he is lain...

After reading the poem's three verses, Aran looked up and handed the clipping back to the barman.

"You're a lucky man to have known one so great. Ireland needs more like him."

"That she does, young man. That she does."

Even in the dim light, Aran could see that the man had a determined look on his face. Standing almost at attention, he said in a clear voice, "God save Ireland."

Aran acknowledged the man's conviction with a smile and a nod. Standing up, he said, "Sounds like the weather's improving. It's getting late. I must be on my way. Thanks very much for your hospitality."

"It was my pleasure. Come by any time. Slán leat."

"Slán," answered Aran.

The Rebel was out the door and back onto his bike. *Ah, it's good to know that the green fire still burns brightly, even in little places like that. Pearse would be pleased. So would MacDonagh. Please God, I hope we'll all be able to keep it alive.*

❧

It had been on 20 September, five days after his evening with the Richardsons that Aran Roe was rudely awakened by a knocking at his hotel room's door.

Pulling himself up on his elbows, he called out in a sleepy voice, "For Jaysus sake, who's there?"

No answer.

The Gortman glanced over at his pocket watch lying on the little wooden table next to his bed. It read 9.50.

Nine fifty in the morning! Mother of God, I've slept half the day away.

A dim grey light filtered into the room through a thinly veiled yellowed lace window curtain. He'd meant to have a lie-in this morning, but not one this late.

Again, the Rebel called out, "Who is it? What do you want?"

Instead of an answering voice, the knocking commenced again, more insistently than ever,

"Enough. Enough," he cried. "I'm coming, you bloody waster."

Abruptly, the pounding stopped.

Why won't that blighter identify himself? I know he heard me answer his indignant summons. Better be on the lookout...just in case.

Aran threw off the bed covers, pulled his Colt .45 out from under his pillow and, in bare feet, padded across the wooden floor toward the door.

Standing with his back to the wall next to the door, he carefully turned the key in the lock with the thumb and forefinger of his right hand. In his left, the revolver was aimed, head high, at the door...its hammer cocked...ready for action.

"Once more, I say, who's there. Identify yourself."

"It's me, you lazy arse. Now out of the bed and open this door."

"My God, Shadow...is that you?"

In a heartbeat, the little drama was over. The visitor was a friend, not a foe.

Lowering his weapon, Aran threw open the door.

Standing there before him, in all of his cheerful glory, was his dear friend, Richard 'Shadow' Doyle. His powerful, low-sized frame filled the doorway. His now greying curly hair was almost totally obscured by the cap he wore, pulled down low over his forehead. Just the remains of a few curls fell out from under the hat. They hung down over the top of his ears, giving the older man a tousled look.

He could stand a haircut. Sure, life without Helen must be hell for him, but what a great surprise.

"You bloody scoundrel, I almost shot you through the door. What in world are you doing here? How'd you find me so? Why didn't you let me know you were coming?"

Without a word of reply to Aran's volley of queries, the visitor stepped into the sparsely furnished rented room.

For the first time ever, Aran noticed that Shadow's broad shoulders were beginning to round, but his comrade's broad smile was ever present. It lit up the little room like a beam of sunlight.

Suddenly, without warning, the forty-one-year-old man reached out and pulled his protégé toward him.

The embrace lasted for only a moment, but it was heartfelt. They both knew that.

Pushing back, Shadow said, "Is that the way you welcome a friend?" The veteran guerrilla fighter was nodding at the revolver still in Aran's hand.

Defensively, Aran sputtered, "But how was I to know?"

"Rightly so," came the reply.

Now standing at arm's length, Shadow said, "Here, let me have a good look at you. Ah sure, I see two months back home appears to have done ye no harm. A little soft around the edges, though, I suspect."

"Get out of it. Not at all. I'll have you know that I'm in fine form…never better. But what about yourself? As lumpy as one of your loaves of bread under that jacket, I imagine."

"Lumpy me arse. Now, pull on some trousers and a shirt. I'm dying for one of those grand Dublin fries."

❄

The scattered remains of breakfast marked their corner table at Devlin's pub, just down the way from Vaughan's. Satiated, the two men leaned back against the wooden partitions of their facing benches, while they enjoyed a second mug of hot tea.

"Jaysus, Aran, this is some life you lead...getting paid for sleeping late and doing nothing."

"Doing nothing? I'll have you know I earn me four and ten a week," said Aran. "Mick has me doing all kinds of jobs for him, plus I seem to be his only sounding board when Kitty's not around. But that aside, how'd you find out about me being on Mick's payroll?"

"Sure, you know nothing is sacred when it comes to keeping a secret in Ireland. Beside, himself told me he was thinking about it before we left Dublin last July. I just took a guess."

"Sure, then I suppose you know. Ever since the Truce came into being, Michael's been making some subtle changes, with the approval of the cabinet of course. As the Dáil's Minister for Finance he's some latitude...so a week ago, he added me to his payroll as a 'special' member of his Squad."

"So Collins has taken pity on ye, has he?" teased Shadow.

"Ah sure, that's easy for you to say...you with a thriving bakery and milling business under your wing. But don't you agree, it's past time the Irish government recognises that we have and still are providing this country with a valuable service. You can volunteer for national duty only so long.

"Shadow, you know what it's been like for these past three plus years. Living hand to mouth off the land and being minded by the goodness of the Irish people...never having so much as a penny in your pocket...life on the run...sleeping rough...you realise you can't go on like that forever...not with mouths to feed and clothes to put on your family's back...much less a farm or business to look after."

Shadow smiled, nodding his acknowledgement.

"...and oh, by the way, speaking of families and all, Sarah Anne and I are planning to marry at the end of December."

More smiles and nods from Shadow's side of the table.

The Irish Rebel continued, "...and Shadow, I've been meaning to ask you...I want you to stand up with me...be my best man and all. Will ya?"

Shadow hesitated for only a moment. "Nothing would make me prouder, my young friend. It'll be an honour."

"I knew I could count on you. It's the 28th...December 28th...the day after my twenty-third birthday. It'll be in Cahir... and oh, guess what...the McCracken clan from Virginia might come...at least they've been invited. Sure, it'll be a wee bit different than me 18th...the one we spent together up in the mountains in Amerikay. You remember, don't you?"

Shadow smiled again...even broader this time, but his eyes had a far-away look about them.

"Look here, old stock, I've been blathering on about myself and I haven't heard a word of your news. How are the girls and your bakery doing? How are you holding up without Helen, God rest her soul?"

6

*"You sowed the seeds of freedom in your
daughters and your sons."*

"The Seeds of Freedom" by Tommy Sands

FRIDAY MORNING, 23 SEPTEMBER 1921

No sleeping late this morning. In fact it was Aran who was waiting in Vaughan's lobby for Shadow when the Limerick man, in Dublin for the past three days, finally put in his appearance. The clock on the wall had just gone seven.

"You push even harder than Mick does," said Shadow, shaking the younger man's hand.

"Sure, sure...sleep well, you ol' cod?" teased Aran.

"Well enough, but I'm not used to keeping all these unsociable hours like you young bucks are. A night on the tiles with Michael and his friends can seriously shorten one's life, if it becomes a regular habit so."

Nodding agreement with Shadow, Aran answered, "Why'd you think I called it an early evening? I've partaken in enough of those affairs to know when to say goodnight."

Richard Doyle had finished his business in Dublin. But instead of heading for home straight away, he was taking a few extra days to spend with his young comrade, Aran Roe O'Neill.

Shadow's bakery lorry, a 1914 Pagefield with a three-ton chassis, was parked just outside Vaughan's front door. It was the same vehicle Aran and Gabriel had hitched a ride in two years ago when they were stopped at a British roadblock on their way from Limerick to Cahir.

Seeing the old flatbed vehicle by the curb jolted Aran's memory. Looking down at the two ugly, misshapen fingers of his right hand, he vividly recalled his encounter with the then Captain Hawkins. Badly beaten by the enraged, out-of-control officer, Gabby and he were lucky to have escaped alive, considering the captain's wrath. Thanks to a sympathetic RIC constable and the help of a passing stranger, the two Irish volunteers were able to flee Tipperary Town for the safety of the Galty Mountains.

Thankfully, their interrogation injuries healed. Gabriel's shoulder mended perfectly, but his ribs still bothered him whenever he physically exerted himself. Happily, Fate had smiled on the transplanted Irish-American. As a bonus to surviving that horrific night, Gay met and later married Áine Grogan.

As for himself, his right hand was almost as good as new, despite its ugly appearance. On occasions, however, his crushed ring and little fingers become painfully swollen. That bother, coupled with the early onset of arthritis in the injured hand, never permitted Aran the luxury of forgetting his short-lived incarceration at the Tipperary RIC barracks.

Noticing that Aran was gazing down at his right hand, Shadow remarked, "Thoughts of Hawkins running through your head, eh?"

"Yes," answered Aran, "but it's hard to imagine you're even able to say that bastard's name after what happened to Helen."

For an instant, Shadow stared down toward the Rotunda Hospital, fighting back his emotions.

Several seconds passed. Only the sounds of the city waking up were audible to their ears.

Then with his lips pursed, the older man slowly turned to Aran. Softly, but in a firm voice he said, "I know what you are thinking, my friend. Sure, the name George Henry Hawkins, may he rest in hell, is not welcomed in my heart or home. But as they say, time does heal most wounds. In the place of my hatred for that despicable man, I've chosen to remember the love Helen and I once shared. Seeing our three girls growing up and blossoming helps keep her memory alive in me heart."

Pausing for a moment, as if to gather his composure, Shadow continued, "Then there's the love I have for this country. I want to see her finally free of the Stranger's bloody grasp. So together, you and I and people like Michael and others continue to press on for the cause of Ireland...for the cause of the Republic."

Shadow looked Aran straight in the eye. He studied his young friend's face for several seconds before speaking again. "Aran, I've much goodness in my life...a lovely family and a successful business, but it's people like you and our friendship that adds that extra sense of richness to it all. I won't let the bitterness of yesterday eat away at me. You've learned that lesson too, have you not?"

"Aye, Shadow...at least I tell myself I have. I'm so lucky to've met Sarah Anne...someone like me to share my life with. We love each other very much, but I must admit, ole stock, I've moments when memories of Brigid come flooding back."

"Ah, that's only natural. Don't punish yourself over that," replied Shadow. "You'd no control over what happened to her. Unfortunately, 'twas not like that for me."

"Oh, Shadow, what happened to Helen could've happened to either of us...on many occasions...and for that matter still could. Helen's death was simply a terrible accident."

"Sure, I know that."

Putting his arm around Shadow's shoulder, Aran said, "It's good to talk to you about our troubles. We've more in common than most people ever realise."

Grabbing the Irish Rebel by the arm and pushing him toward the lorry, Shadow smiled, saying, "Now, before we end up shedding tears on this bleedin' footpath and makin' a spectacle of ourselves, time's a wastin' and me stomach's crying to be fed."

❧

With another of Devlin's hardy breakfasts under their belts, they drove across town with Shadow behind the lorry's wheel. They headed for #5 Mespil Road, bordering on the banks of the Grand Canal. As they passed over Mount Street Bridge, the two guerrilla soldiers blessed themselves. In their own way, their simple act honoured the memory of 1916 and the rebel fighters of the 3rd Dublin Battalion. For without the bravery of those seven men of "C" company, who single-handedly held off an advancing column of British Sherwood Foresters for over three hours, the failed Easter Rebellion would have ended without a single taste of victory.

Turning to Shadow, Aran said, "I've often wondered what ever happened to Tom Walsh. The last I saw of him he was headed for the Wicklow coast with his comrade Willie Ronan…that's after our shoot-out with the RIC in Roundwood."

"Well, with the grace of God, he's grand…just like we are," answered Shadow.

"Sure, I hope so. I know Willie's all right, but I still think about Tom. Imagine it…seeing your brother shot down before your very eyes. After all they'd been through, Jim's death would be a tough one to get over."

The baker's vehicle turned right at Haddington Road, passed St. Mary's Church and crossed Baggot Street into Mespil Road. A minute later, the lorry pulled to stop in the little alleyway behind #5.

"Let's make this quick," directed Shadow. "I don't want to attract any unnecessary attention."

Standing before the building's back door, Aran dug around in his jacket pocket, finally producing a well-worn key. He hadn't been back to this address, one of Michael's so-called safe-houses, since Sarah Anne's narrow gun-running escape from British authorities at Kingstown Harbour. That had been just before the Truce was announced a little over two months ago.

The memory of that close call made him shudder: *If she'd been arrested or killed, I don't know what…*

"Do ye have the right key?" asked Shadow in a low voice. Aran could hear the anxiousness in his query.

Before he had time to respond, the lock clicked open and they were inside.

"Where is it?" asked Aran.

"Mick said the stuff would be under the floorboards of the cabinet beneath the steps."

The Gortman quickly walked across the sparsely furnished room toward the stairs. Seeing the narrow door built into the wall below the steps, he pulled a wooden peg from its latch and swung the door open.

"Do ye have any matches Shadow? It's as dark as night in here."

"Right so," answered Shadow, handing his companion a pocket-sized box of wooden matches.

Holding a lighted match in one hand, Aran fumbled for and then pulled up on a small medal ring indented in the cabinet's flooring.

"Got it. Shyte! Wait a minute, I have to light another match."

Five minutes later the two men were staring at a great cache of weapons. There were twenty-two new Lee-Enfield Cavalry carbines, the ones specifically designed for use by the Irish Royal Constabulary. These bold-action rifles sported a magazine holding eight .303 rounds. In addition there were half a dozen Webley & Scott revolvers. They were the newest models with six-inch barrels and a six-round cylinder. There were also three German 9mm Parabellum pistols and one Thompson machine gun with a 20-round box fitted to fire a standard .45 calibre shell. All were lightly oiled and wrapped in sacking to protect them from corrosive sea air. Finally, there were six small wooden crates packed with various sizes of ammunition.

"Jaysus wept," murmured Aran, "you'd think we're after going to take on the might of the British Army."

"Well, if things don't resolve themselves between our two sides soon, that just might be the case," answered Shadow.

"You're right. Sure, Michael's not taking any chances is he? With the IRA drilling and reorganising all over the country, he's making damn sure we'll put on a good show for those limeys, if need be."

After rewrapping the uncovered weapons, Aran stood up and said, "As I mentioned to you when you first arrived back into town, I've some real concerns about all this business. We need to have a good talk about it this morning."

❧

After all the booty was safely stowed away in the recently enlarged hidden compartment under the floorboards of Shadow's lorry, Aran announced he wanted to make one more stop before they headed out of town.

"Shadow, I haven't seen Mrs. Pearse in over four years. I was hoping we might catch her in. She's someone I'd like you to meet, and besides, I'm curious to know how the school's getting on."

Twenty-five minutes later, the two drove up the Hermitage's gravelled drive. Before them stood the impressive home of Patrick Pearse's school...the one he'd had called St. Enda's after the patron saint of the Aran Islands.[1]

Fortunately for them, Mrs. Pearse was home. After organising tea and biscuits for her two guests, she proudly brought them up-to-date on the school's status.

"As ye know, Aran, after the Rebellion was squelched, the British stationed a squad of soldiers here at the school. Though the school was closed to students, the authorities allowed Margaret, Mary Brigid and me to stay on living here. You see, by doing so, I was determined that the memory of Patrick and William, God save them both, should not die."

Turning to Shadow, she continued, "So, Mr. Doyle, in the autumn of '16, I reopened St. Enda's at Cullenswood House[2] in Ranelagh. Under the able leadership of Tom MacDonagh's

---

1. St. Enda (died c. 530 AD) was a legendary Celtic warrior who later converted to the priesthood. His brother-in-law, the King of Cashel, gave him land on the Aran Islands where Enda founded several monasteries including Killeany on the island of Inishmore. With St. Finnian of Clonard, he is known as the father of Irish monasticism.

2. Cullenswood House was the home to Pearse's first school. Also called St. Enda's, it was not an ideal location for his avant-garde educational experiment.

brother Joseph, whom I'd appointed headmaster, things began returning to normal...well almost."

Sipping her tea between words, she continued, "Then two years ago, Joe, the staff and I decided to move the school back here, where it really belongs."

After refilling her guests' cups, Mrs. Pearse sat down and picked up the threads of her story. "When Pat signed the lease for this place in 1910, he must have been clairvoyant. He'd asked the owner, a Mr. William Woodbyrne, to include a clause in the agreement stating that he could purchase this entire property, house and all, for £6,500 sometime before the first of July, 1920.

"Well, can you imagine it? As the date approached, I knew it would be impossible to borrow that amount of money, especially since the school was hardly making ends meet. But the good Lord must've been looking after us. Thanks be to God, a campaign was undertaken in Amerikay...you remember Aran, Pat went there, back in the spring of '14, to raise funds for the school."

While she paused to pour herself another cup of tea, Margaret Pearse, Mrs. Pearse's forty-three-year-old daughter, walked into the room, introduced herself and took a seat next to her mother on the couch.

"As I was saying," said Mrs. Pearse, smiling at her eldest daughter, "a drive was started over there to raise money for me to buy the lease off of Mr. Woodbyrne."

Aran knew what was coming, but didn't say a word.

Being the Victorian woman that she was, Mrs. Pearse tried hard to restrain her delight, but her satisfaction was evident. "As sure as I'm sitting here, Pat must've been looking over my shoulder. For believe it or not, the money *was* raised and just in time. Finally, December last, I signed the last of the papers...the Hermitage is ours free and clear."

At the time Ranelagh was a bourgeoning suburb so Pearse continued looking for a more suitable location. From 1908 to 1910, Cullenswood was home to St. Enda of Aran. In 1910, Pearse discovered & leased the Hermitage. With its imposing 18th-century Palladian-style building, its spacious grounds & peaceful surroundings, away from the noisy distractions of Dublin, the Hermitage fulfilled his desire of replicating the pastoral surroundings of the early Irish scholars who valued solitude & meditation.

She softly patted her daughter's hand. "Can you image it...me...elected to the 1ˢᵗ Dáil in '19 and now the Pearse family is the owner of this grand place. Both Pat and Willie would be so proud...and with Joe MacDonagh's continued help, St. Enda's School will continue fulfilling Pat and Willie's dreams."

As Margaret Pearse looked on smiling, both Aran and Shadow could see her mother's face radiate with pride.

❧

Back in the lorry again, the two friends headed southwest toward Naas and beyond to their day's final destination, Athy.

"I'm glad we took the time to stop," said Aran. "She's a good woman and it was wonderful to see the old place again. I'm glad you were up for stopping. So many memories...the spirit of Pearse and MacDonagh still haunts the place...please God, may it never die."

❧

For awhile they rode on in silence, lost in their own thoughts.

Finally, after coming into Naas, Shadow spoke up. "Aran, there were some things you wanted to talk about...about Michael and this business between Dev and London."

"Yes, but I really don't know where to start."

"Maybe from the beginning my young friend. Mick doesn't talk much about his former days or about the Chief with me so."

"Well, as you know, I first met Michael in the General Post Office building during Easter Week. He was posted there by Pearse as aide-de-camp to Joe Plunkett. Did you ever know him?"

"Never met him, but sure I've heard his name. He was the one who was married in Kilmainham just hours before he was shot. Besides being one of the signatories of the Proclamation, didn't he help map out the military plan for the Rebellion?"

"That's right. You see, Mick hooked up with the Plunketts

in January of '16 upon his return from England. Prior to coming home, he'd spent ten years living in London, working for their post office system. He was just a young man when he first went over.

"Back in Dublin, he did the Count's books for him at Lark-field in Kimmage, the Plunkett family home. He also worked for a Dublin accountancy firm...on Dawson Street I think, but...uh...uh-h-h...its name escapes me at the moment."

"It's no matter, but I seem to remember hearing that Larkfield was a hotbed of subversive activity just before the Rebellion broke out," interjected Shadow.

"It was...military planning, munitions factory, safe-house for returning Irishmen wanting to avoid British conscription and more. As you say, ole stock, a real beehive of sedition.

"Michael once told me the Count used to go around saying, 'You sow the seeds of freedom in your daughters and your sons,' and he should have known. The man and his wife Josephine had seven children: four daughters and three sons.

"During Easter Week, the Big Fella mostly looked after Joe Plunkett, who, as you'll recall, was deathly sick from tuberculosis. But despite those responsibilities, Mick did make his presence known in other ways. I remember him helping secure the building on Easter Monday and fighting the roaring fires that engulfed the GPO on Friday.

"After the surrender, he was rounded up with some of the others and taken to Richmond Barracks. That's where our paths crossed again. Michael and I, along with thirty or so other men, spent a few hours packed into a tiny cubicle of a room there. My God was that ever an awful night."

"Sure, I remember. Over three thousand, mostly all men, many with nothing to do with the Rebellion, were arrested in the days after the fighting ended. About half that many were eventually interned... shipped over to England and wherever without trial. Of course that's not counting the ones the blighters executed, God rest their brave Irish souls."

"What did you expect, Shadow? We'd wounded the Sassenach's pride...put a dent in her armour...they had to show us who was boss, didn't they?"

"Sure, it's the same old story over and over again. Rise up and be knocked down twice as hard...Jaysus, you'd think we Paddies would learn our lesson," derided Shadow.

"Do I detect a hint of bitterness in your reproach?" teased Aran.

"Bloody hell..."

"All right...back to my story. I managed to slip out of the limey's bloody clutches, but Mick didn't. He spent six months in Frongoch[3] before being released at the end of December.

"'Twas then that Tom Clarke's widow, Kathleen, set him up as Secretary to the Irish National Aid Fund. Backed by both public conscription here at home and from American Clan na nGael[4] money, the fund assisted dependents of those killed or jailed for their Easter-Week activities.

"That was a real turning point for Mick. His reputation for organisation, record keeping and financial management plus his studious attention to detail began opening eyes. This, combined with his growing notoriety for being a hard-nosed tough guy devoted to Ireland's cause, began pushing him into the limelight.

"Through his various fund activities, Michael established contacts with sympathetic Republicans throughout the thirty-two counties. This work, in addition to his burgeoning, behind-the-scenes political activities on behalf of Sinn Féin, helped elect Joe McGuinness, Count Plunkett, Arthur Griffith and Dev to Parliament. Of course, those men all ran on the premise that if elected, they wouldn't take their seats in London."

"So you might say that both Mick and Dev had their start in politics with Sinn Féin back in '17."

"Aye, but de Valera beat Michael to the punch as far as being thought of as a military mastermind. Because of his 3rd

---

3. Frongoch Internment Camp in north Wales, near the village of Bala, was a former Welsh whisky distillery. It had been converted to a German prisoner-of-war facility at the outbreak of the First War. After the Easter Rebellion, the German occupants were shipped out & replaced by Irish internees, who began arriving in early June. The Irish prisoners had been temporarily held in various British prisons during May.

4. Clan na nGael was an American nationalist organisation founded in 1867. It had strong appeal among working-class Irish-Americans & helped fund the Easter Rebellion. John Devoy was one of its key leaders.

Irish Volunteer Battalion's success during Easter Week, and by virtue of the fact that in autumn 1917, he was the only surviving Easter commander after Tom Ashe's death, many thought Dev the most likely candidate to lead Ireland's renewed drive for independence. That October, the Long Hoor, as Mick likes to refer to him now, won election as both Sinn Féin party and Irish Volunteer presidents.

"But despite his growing reputation, Mick was still a bit player back then, despite his recent elevation to Head Centre of the Irish Republican Brotherhood[5] with Ashe's death. Because of its clandestine nature, few were aware of his IRB promotion.

"Later that October, our friend was chosen to be Director of Organisation for the Irish Volunteers. Using his IRB and Fund connections, Michael immediately began using his new office for the development of a highly sophisticated spy and underground intelligence network. As we both know, that paid huge dividends over the last two years.

"Things really came to a head a few months later. Lloyd George made two major blunders in the spring of 1918. At that time, the war in Europe was dragging on and on. British public opinion had turned decidedly anti-war and anti-government. Hoping finally to crush Germany with more men on the ground, the Welsh Wizard decided to impose conscription in Ireland. The move backfired. Ireland rose up against the idea of sending more men to feed Britain's war machine. Any Irish support for England's war effort vanished almost overnight. The conservative Irish Parliamentary Party withdrew its elected members from Westminster in protest. Despite the IPP's walkout, support

---

5. The Irish Republican Brotherhood, originally the Irish Revolutionary Brotherhood, was a militant, secret, oath-bound society pledged to the overthrow of British rule in Ireland. Its motto was 'England's difficulty is Ireland's opportunity.' Founded in 1858, it was influenced by the United Irishmen of the 1790s & the Young Islanders of the 1840s. Its members were often called Fenians after the legendary 3rd-century Celtic-hero Fionn mac Cumhaill (Finn MacCool). In actuality, the Fenians were the name of the IRB's American offshoot, but gradually it became popularized in Ireland. The leaders of the Easter Rebellion were members of its Supreme Council & newly formed Military Council. Traditionally, the Head Centre of the Supreme Council of the IRB was thought of as the President of the (mythical) Irish Republic.

for Redmond's national party quickly deteriorated. The bulk of Irish political sympathy turned to favour Sinn Féin almost overnight.

"Then to make matters even worse for his government, Lloyd George and his cronies concocted some trumped-up charge of Irish collusion with Germany. As a result, he had most of the Sinn Féin's leadership arrested...locked up in English jails for the next ten months."

Shadow interrupted, "Wasn't that the infamous German Plot conspiracy, no?"

"Right," answered Aran. "That move, on top of the conscription threat, quickly eliminated any British sympathies Ireland might've felt for her bedevilling neighbour. In reality, those two decisions actually made matters worse for Mother England."

"As I remember things, Aran, Collins had wind of the arrests beforehand. One of his Castle touts or someone let the cat out of the bag. Didn't he warn Dev and the cabinet to go into hiding?"

"He did, Shadow. But de Valera thought the political backlash from such an outrageous act would favour Ireland's cause and turn public opinion against London."

"It didn't, did it?"

"No, not really. Instead of broadcasting Ireland's plight to the world, the arrests simply removed its most rational voices from the stage of public opinion. With the exception of Mick and a few of his friends, who heeded the advance warning, the British authorities deported the bulk of Sinn Féin's top officials.

"The results were predictable. With Dev and Sinn Féin's moderate administration out of circulation, a more militant leadership arose within what was left of Ireland's leading political and military people.

"You know the rest, Shadow. Michael stepped up to the table and began reorganising the IRA. His close friend Harry Boland did the same for Sinn Féin's political wing."

With pride in his voice, Richard Doyle said, "That's when Mick began putting the squeeze on the RIC and the Sassenach's spies. He declared war on the feckin' Tans and began a guerrilla campaign that will go down in history. But what about Dev and Michael?"

"During those early years, they didn't know each other very well, but sure Mick respected Dev. You remember...I even helped Michael spring de Valera from Lincoln Jail early that February in '19.

"Three months later de Valera decided Ireland's best hope for achieving its ends was by seeking international recognition for its cause, while tapping the purse strings of Amerikay. So for the next year and a half, Dev and his entourage were in the USA while Mick ran the show from here."

"But things changed, didn't they?" said Shadow.

"In a big way. Just imagine, Michael...prosecuting the war with his guerrilla tactics and getting the best of what the British could throw at us."

Half jokingly, half seriously, the Rebel added a bit of drama to the conversation. "There he was...Michael Collins, the man of mystery and intrigue...rallying the Irish people against the evil empire...a legend in the making so."

"Ah sure, if he could only hear you now, Mick would box your ears," warned Shadow with smile.

"It's about time someone else had a piece of *his* ear," laughed Aran.

In a more serious vein, the Gortman continued, "Well, the next thing you know, Dev is back on the scene...feathers ruffled...his campaign for Irish recognition in tatters. The Irish-American leadership across the Atlantic took umbrage at his attempts to dictate to them. Though he raised a good bit of money, his political goals hadn't been realised."

Shadow didn't say a word. He just nodded his head.

"Oh yes," continued Aran, "another issue festering just below the surface was the way Dev chose to present himself, especially to his fellow Irish sympathisers in Amerikay. Thinking that his elected title of Priomh Aire might be misunderstood or wasn't quite grand enough, Dev began calling himself 'the President of Ireland.'"

Aran chuckled out loud. "We're not so big on titles over here, as you know Shadow. I guess Dev felt like he had to dress up his office like the old spinster at a dance…with plenty of paint and powder."

Avoiding any unnecessary barbs, the Limerick man said, "Sure then, there was that business of the Custom House raid."

"I promise you," replied Aran, "that entire episode enraged Michael. Just think: a major battle for journalistic exposure that compromised the lives of so many of our Irish Volunteers. It was a military disaster that flew in the face of our limited talent and meagre resources.

"Thanks be to God, the Tan War lasted only six more weeks. I fear we'd still be arguing over Dev's shift in tactics if it hadn't.

"Oh, one more thing, Shadow. With Dev back home and Mick putting the pressure on the enemy, London began sending out peace feelers. Ireland countered and so was born this battle of wits about Dominion status and an Irish Republic that hasn't been settled to this day."

"You're right, Aran, it hasn't. We talked about it this week. I'm afraid it has the makings of our undoing," said Shadow.

"Could easily, my friend, could easily. Nobody really knows where the other stands…certainly the English don't understand us…they've never tried. On the one hand, we often have a hard time understanding ourselves. For instance, there's Dev, now a true hardliner, making all those restrained statements to Lloyd George. While all their polite political bantering is going on, London has the distinct impression that Michael is the divil incarnate, ready to jump down their throats with both feet. In actual point of fact, the Corkman would be a much more reasonable official to deal with than de Valera ever is. In my mind, it's all going to end up in a lot more than a war of words."

❧

The bakery lorry pulled to a stop in Emily Square alongside the Leinster Arms hotel, Athy's only hostelry of any size. The old 18th-century market house at the bottom of the plaza stood empty, quietly waiting for tomorrow's bustle of buying and selling. Market day was still a major event in this rural town. Besides its economic importance to local farmers and retailers, the festive gathering was the social highlight of the week for most of its residents.

The town had been named after the 2ⁿᵈ-century Irish chieftain, Ae, who was killed by a rival at a nearby ford along the Barrow River, which flowed through the centre of Athy today. The modern history of the town dated from the 12ᵗʰ century when it first became an Anglo-Norman settlement. Gradually, the village grew into an important military outpost along the southern boundary of the English Pale.[6] It received its first town charter in the 1500s, and with the regional completion of the Grand Canal in the early 1790s, Athy became an important commercial hub halfway between Kildare and Carlow towns.

Aran was well acquainted with Athy. His familiarity stemmed not from its historical past, but from personal experience. It had been the home of Brigid Eileen O'Mahony, his first love.

After the Rebellion, he'd accidentally met Brigid and her small family while fleeing Dublin and certain arrest by the British authorities. The O'Mahonys had offered him sanctuary while on his trek home, alone and on foot, to County Galway.

※

"Aran, now that we're here, are you certain you want to be?" Shadow's face had a quizzical look about it. Between mouthfuls of a rasher buttie and swigs of beer, the Limerick man studied his companion's face.

---

6. The English Pale, a term first used in 1495, describing the area radiating from Dublin that the Anglo-Irish (English) authorities could control & protect from hostile Irish tribes who lived 'Beyond the Pale.' Today, the area would likely include the counties Dublin, Meath, Kildare & Louth. The word 'pale' refers to 'paling' or picket (pointed) fencing & was first used by Sir Edward Poynings, England's deputy lieutenant in Ireland during the late-15ᵗʰ century. In reality, there was no 'wall' separating the two groups. Rather, it was more of a shifting frontier of administrative, political, cultural & military jurisdiction. Depending on who held the balance of power at the time, the Anglo-Irish or the Irish, the Pale expanded or contracted. The division between the two groups became more blurred with the advancing Tudor conquest of Ireland in the mid-16ᵗʰ century.

"Of course…just me being my ole sentimental self, I guess." Aran's voice sounded a little defensive, as he wiped the last bits of a bacon-and-cabbage lunch from the corner of his mouth with his serviette.

"I've a special place in me heart for the O'Mahonys. I came back here to visit after returning from Amerikay in '17 and then again just before Christmas December last. Gay was with me then and I told them all about Sarah Anne and me. Now I'd like you to meet Brigid's little family. They're such grand people. Besides, I've told them all about you and our time together in Amerikay."

"A pack of lies, no doubt. Jaysus, you've probably built me up into something I'm not."

"Yeah, yeah…nothing less than the second coming of Cúchulain, you ole cod. What do ya think? Afraid I might've described you as a demented old troll or something worse?"

"All right wit' ya…so I'd that coming," grinned Shadow.

Thankfully, the two of them were sitting by themselves at a corner table next to the window. If anyone had overheard their conversation, surely they'd have thought: *Just a couple of country bumpkins halfway around the bend no doubt.*

The pub cum dining room was empty…too late for any lunch crowd and too early for the after-work drinkers. Shadow had picked a table by the window for a good reason. He wanted to keep an eye on the lorry. The old guerrilla fighter was a bit concerned about leaving it and all its contents unattended. Even in this quiet little town, you could never be too careful.

Beside the weapons they'd hidden away beneath the bed of the lorry, Shadow had made several purchases in Dublin. There were two crates of assorted milling bits and pieces, a small used wood-burning cooker, still in fine condition, for his own use and large oaken table for the shop. But the major purchase was a new 1920 Beardmore Precision motorcycle. Build by F. E. Baker Ltd. in Birmingham and shipped into Dublin, the cycle sported a special spring suspension, a petrol tank made from two steel pressings welded together to form part of the frame and a recently improved dual braking system.

Aran and he had tried it out for the first time on the streets of Dublin last evening and both agreed it was a beauty. Though tied down and covered with a tarpaulin, its presence might prove too tempting for some dodgy person.

Since the end of the First War, inflationary prices were the order of the day, plus money and petrol was generally in short supply. Together, these facts placed financial pressures on many people. As a result, motorcycles had become an important means of economic transportation. Though the £75 he paid for it seemed dear, Shadow felt it was a wise investment.

Needless to say, Aran was a bit envious of his friend. Besides expressing words of awe, he glibly asked, "What are you going to do when it rains, Shadow...dress up like Lawrence of Arabia in your oilskins?"

※

The two men were relaxing after their meal, enjoying the last swallows of the beers, when Shadow sprung to his feet. "Be back in a tick," was all he said.

No one had entered the dining area of the pub since they'd sat down. The Gortman was alone except for the barman who was busy reading a newspaper. Looking out the window, Aran was only in position to see the bonnet of the lorry. All seemed quiet on the square.

Suddenly, the Gortman was aware of voices from outside... someone was shouting. Aran looked out the window again. Still all appeared normal. An instant later, however, something or someone crashed against the outside of the hotel, very near to where he sat.

"Bloody hell," mumbled Aran. He was on his feet and heading for the door.

Once outside, Aran could see a small crowd gathering at the bottom of the square. Someone called out, "I'll get the constable."

Rounding the side of the Leinster Arms, Emily Square and the lorry came into his full view. The Irish Rebel couldn't believe his eyes. Two young toughs in their late teens had the tarp off the cycle and were hacking away at its restraining ropes. Its canvas cover lay on the ground. Another man, with a revolver in his hand, had Richard Doyle backed up against the side of the hotel. He was only slightly older than the two up on the lorry's decking. Another man, maybe in his early twenties, was on his arse, slumped up against the hotel, almost at Shadow's feet.

Good ole Shadow. Looks like you've delivered the first blow, smiled Aran. *That's one for the good guys.*

The Gortman's next thought was to go for the Luger holstered under his jacket, but his hand stopped before he drew his weapon.

Emerging from around the front end of the lorry was a fifth then a sixth man. Both were wearing scarves tied around their faces. Only their eyes and a bit of their foreheads were visible between the make-shift masks and their caps.

The first one held a Webley-Fosbery automatic revolver.

Haven't seen many of those around, puzzled Aran. *We don't use them and I don't think the British army does either...found them wanting early on in the First War.*

The sixth interloper held a two-barrelled, pump-action shotgun.

If that guy is any good with that thing, he'll squeeze off three or four shots before I can pull out my automatic.

Suddenly, Aran realised what was happening: *Jaysus wept, this is a bloody set-up. We must've been followed. Maybe they know about the hidden arms...*

"You all right, Shadow?" shouted the Irish Rebel to his friend.

"Ah shyte, never better," came the reply. "How about doing something yourself...I knocked one on his arse."

Jaysus, Mary and Joseph...what a time for a joke, thought Aran.

The Gortman took a step forward.

"One more like that and you can kiss this world goodbye." It was the shotgun man speaking.

An English voice. Well, I'll be damned. Demobbed Tan or Auxie? British intelligence in mufti?

"I beg your pardon, sir. You have my friend and me at a bit of a disadvantage," replied Aran to the shotgun-wielding son-of-a-bitch.

"As it should be. Now, shut up and get your hands in the air."

Complying, Aran thought: *From the sound of it, this one's used to giving orders.*

The Rebel glanced over at Shadow. The Limerick man nodded and shrugged his shoulders.

Not much the two of us can do at this point. Maybe the constable or some townspeople will come to our rescue.

At this point, Aran was willing to trade the Beardmore for their lives. There'd be time for retaliation later.

"You two...get that motorcycle off the lorry...make it quick...

then splash this around...we're going to have a bit of a bonfire."

My God, he's not going to fire the lorry...not here in the square...not with all our hidden hardware onboard...Mí eal will have our hides for sure...

No sooner were the words out of his mouth, than the English-one bent down and hoisted up a large container of petrol, handing it to one of the lads on the lorry.

No one in the growing assembly of onlookers said a word, but several astonished gasps were audible. Looks of surprise and horror dotted most faces.

Aran mumbled under his breath, "Cowards, the lot of yis. If you're not going to do anything, why are yis standin' there like you do? Don't you know somebody might be shot or killed?"

As if expressing his contempt, the Gortman turned to confront the bandits again, shunning the impotent onlookers.

As the two on top struggled to free then lower the cycle, Aran felt a growing sense of anger racing through his body.

Trying to control his surging emotions, the Irish Rebel riveted his eyes on the bandit group's apparent leader.

About my height, but he must weigh at least twenty stone, guessed Aran.

But the moment didn't lend itself to logical thinking. There was no denying it. The thought of what this gang of bandits was planning made his blood boil.

One of these days our paths will cross again. Sure, that'll be the day when the boot is on the other foot, you fat bastard...

Not wishing to antagonise the shotgun man any further with his hateful staring, the Gortman glanced over at his comrade. Shadow looked angry too.

Maybe I've conceded the motorcycle too soon, thought Aran. *Shadow looks angry enough to take on the lot of them...best be on my toes in case he decides to make a move.*

All of a sudden, confusion began to dampen his wrath. *Would Shadow dare risk everything for a £75 bike? No...*

Hoping his Limerick friend wouldn't try anything foolish, at least for the moment, Aran turned his attention back to the ringleader. The man's pulled-up scarf and lowered cap certainly added an ominous sense of foreboding to the moment.

Sure, that's something an Auxie would do to hide his cowardly mug, reasoned Aran.

Almost wishing the man might be goaded into reacting, the Rebel daringly tried to catch and hold the Englishman's attention: *Sure, smallish eyes for someone your size...sinister...evil-looking...maybe even defiant...hateful...yes, indeed hateful...*

The Englishman took a step in Aran's direction.

That's it, you bastard...react...lose you cool composure...make a mistake and you're dead.

The Gortman continued to stare at the lead bandit.

Light on your feet, eh...confident...athletic despite your size... well groomed too... ironed shirt...neatly pressed suit...you're no ordinary highway man, are ya? A man of good breeding and taste no doubt, you gobshyte.

Deciding he'd better concentrate on getting a grip on his erratic emotions, Aran shifted his attention back to the little drama slowly playing itself out before him. Shadow still hadn't made a move.

Better wait a bit longer. If they torch the wagon, the burst of flames will buy me a moment's time...that's when I'll hit the deck and start firing.

❧

It seemed like an hour had passed since he'd first encountered this bizarre scene, but in fact it had been only a couple of minutes.

Hoping to elicit some help from the now twenty or thirty onlookers, Aran shouted out to the Englishman, "This nonsense of yours has gone far enough. Release my friend there and put an end to this silly game. Your joke's gone on too long."

"You must be the one who's joking," came the reply.

Suddenly, Aran's attention shifted. A new voice rang out from across the square...a Scottish one. "Whoa there me laddies. 'Tis enough of this foolishness indeed. Me boys and I have the drop on yis. On the ground with your weapons...NOW."

Aran was pleasantly dumbfounded. Standing there as proud as you please, not more than thirty yards away with a revolver in one hand and a claymore in the other, was none other than Duncan Stewart MacGregor, the Nayler himself, dressed in full kit: shirt, kilt, sash, sporran, knee socks, flashes...the whole lot.

As the Scotsman's command of "NOW" echoed around the square, a half a dozen other well-armed men stepped forward from around the plaza. The lorry and its little drama were cornered, this time by friendly forces.

Mother of God, thought Aran. *What's he like? William Wallace, Rob Roy MacGregor or maybe just plain ole Robin Hood...but sure it's nice to have friends at a time like this.*

"Sir," said Aran lowering his hands, "I believe the tables have turned."

The leader with the shotgun quickly glanced around. The motorcycle was now on the footpath, steadied by one of the two lads. The other one was still standing in the back of the lorry, gripping the petrol container. Now, almost comically with the tables turned, the bandit holding the Webley automatic looked panic stricken.

Looking for a place to hide, you bloody bugger, thought Aran.

"The jig's up, you blighters," crowed Shadow. Coolly, he reached over and twisted the revolver out of his captor's hand.

"Not so fast," exclaimed the Englishman, turning his attention to the Nayler. "Looks to me like it's a stand-off. We'll back off and no one will be hurt."

Aran looked at Shadow, at the Englishman and then at the Nayler. "What do ye think, Duncan? Fight or let them run?"

"Ye know me, Aran. I've never said no to a good fight. But in this case, your one's right. Too many innocent ones might be hurt."

Suddenly, Shadow's voice filled the square. Pointing his confiscated revolver at the man still seated on the pavement, "On your feet, you bloody eejit. You all have thirty seconds then I'm startin' firing." Everyone could hear the angry reverberations in his voice.

In response to the baker's demand, the Englishman yelled, "Tommy, we're done here. Bring the car around."

Slowly, the shotgun-wielding bandit began backing off toward the bottom of the square.

Taking his lead, the others pulled back too.

Moments later, a Benz sedan roared into the square from the back side of the market house.

"In you go, lads," ordered the Englishman.

Seconds later, the car reversed and spun around. Facing to the east, it raced off, past the old barracks building and out of town.

7

*"Whenever I wanted to know what the Irish
people wanted, I had only to examine my own
heart and it told me straight off what the
Irish people wanted."*

Eamon de Valera

*W*ith relief and a broad smile etched upon his face, Aran Roe O'Neill stepped forward with his hand extended to the kilted man.

"Hail Mary full of grace, 'tis a miracle you showed up when you did. Just where in the bloody hell did you and your lads come from? Out of thin air was it?"

Ignoring the Gortman's queries, the Scotsman replied, "Ah Aran, a bonnie good day to ya. Welcome to Athy, but who's surprisin' who here?"

As the two men warmly shook hands, the curious bystanders began dispersing with Duncan's encouragement, "Ah sure, it was just a little misunderstanding. 'Twas nothing at all, so be on your way and God bless you for it."

Both knew, however, that most of the evening's conversations in Athy would centre on what'd just taken place in the square: a residue of the Tan War no doubt, or at least so it appeared.

With the public to-do ended, the jovial Scotsman seemed genuinely delighted to renew Aran's acquaintance. "Looked like yis could've used a little help, so the lord mayor asked me to drop by with me welcoming committee. Lads, this is an acquaintance of mine, Aran O'Neill."

Duncan's accomplices crowded around, each offering his hello.

"Thanks a million for your good timing, lads. I doubt if we could've held them off much longer," quipped Aran.

"Uh-huh," replied Duncan, flashing a quick smile in Aran's direction.

Turning his attention to Shadow, the Scotsman said, "...and this is your companion, no doubt? If I remember rightly, you were on the platform at Marysborough...connecting on to Cork City back in July was it?"

Richard Doyle looked puzzled, but shook the hand offered to him.

"That's right," said Aran, giving Shadow a knowing look. "This is my friend Richard Doyle, but most call him Shadow. Shadow this is Duncan...Duncan Stewart MacGregor...a proud son of Gregor and of Scotland...more recently from Belfast and now Athy. This is 'the Nayler' and his merry band of men. Did I get all that right?"

"Ah, ye did that. You have a good memory, Aran, but if yis don't mind me asking, what in the world are you doin' here in Athy...the two of yis and this lorry here?"

Lowering his voice a notch, Aran said, "Sure, it's a long story. I'll fill you in...but not here in the middle of the square so."

The ginger-haired Scotsman nodded his understanding.

Turning his attention to Shadow, Duncan said, "Shadow, is it? That's an unusual name, but tell me, if I may be so bold to inquire, why the lettering on the lorry's door says 'Doyle's Bakery, Henry Street, Limerick' and not Cork City?"

Aran interrupted before Shadow could reply, "All in good time, Duncan, but would ye mind giving us a hand with this motorcycle?"

❧

Twenty minutes later, Shadow, Aran and Duncan, with the Beardmore and the Scotsman's bicycle in back, drove into the MacGregor farmyard. The thatched, stone cottage with its several additions and two outbuildings was just south of Athy on the main road to Kilkea.

"Here we are. Welcome to our bit of home," chirped Duncan. "Aside from the fact that Ernest Shackleton was born just down the road from here in Kilkea House, the neighbours have nothing better to talk about than what the two Scots are doing on their bit of land."

"The two Scots?" asked Shadow.

"Aye. Me father and I raise a few cattle and grow some corn on the land we lease here. Most of the work, however, falls on these shoulders. As you'll soon see, me Da is getting' up in years. Mother died three winters ago, God rest her soul. After that, my younger brother moved back to Edinburgh. Me two sisters, both now married, are livin' in England at the present."

During the short journey to the MacGregor farm, Duncan explained that he and his mates had just happened to be passing through Athy on their way home from an IRA training exercise out along the River Barrow.

"We've been busy this summer, just in case, you understand. Me and the lads are part of the 1st West Kildare Battalion. Been out for two days and were just returning to town, collecting our bicycles, when we happened upon you two in the square. All I can say is you're damn lucky we did. From what I gathered, things were about to go from bad to worst."

"I can't tell you how grateful we are," repeated Shadow for the third time.

"Not only were they going to make off with Shadow's new motorcycle, Duncan, but can you believe it, they were threatening to set fire to our lorry...right there in the town centre," recounted Aran. "By the way, do you have any idea who those feckin' blighters were?"

"Sorry…never saw them before in me life," answered Duncan.

The Scotsman turned to Shadow with a questioning look on his face, but Richard Doyle just pressed his lips together. The baker shook his head no, saying nothing.

Peering around Duncan's broad form, wedged between the two Irishmen in the front seat of the lorry, Aran asked, "Do you think we were followed from Dublin, Shadow?"

"I'm not really sure." The Limerick man paused for a moment before continuing. "Sure with our stop in Rathfarnham to visit your old school, I somehow doubt it, and there wasn't much traffic on the road after we left Naas. If we were being followed, you'd think I might've noticed."

"But you're not one hundred percent sure?"

"No, not entirely. Sure I wasn't givin' any real thought to being followed though. If you remember rightly, we were talking a good bit."

"Well, the important thing is it's a done thing, Mr. Doyle."

Duncan turned his head in Aran's direction, "What'd ya guess they were after…just the cycle?"

"I wish I knew," said Aran, "but I like to think I'll know that English one with the shotgun, if I ever come across him again. What about you, Shadow?"

Again, the Limerick man said nothing.

Changing the subject, the Scotsman asked, "Aran, what were yis doing in Athy anyway?"

The Gortman caught Shadow's nod: an unspoken order to tread lightly.

In as few words as possible, the Irish Rebel explained that the two of them had been in Dublin…Shadow buying some needed equipment for the bakery and himself visiting old school friends. On their way back west, they'd decided to stop off in Athy. He wanted to call into a family living nearby.

"Maybe I know them. What's their name?"

"The O'Mahonys. They've a farm just west of town."

"Any relation to the woman who was killed in a riding accident some years back?" asked Duncan.

"That's right. A terrible mishap it was," answered Aran, being careful to control his emotions.

"It was the talk of the town for months," said Duncan. "Seems as if a bloody rozzer and some limeys decided to give the lady a scare... chased her out of town they did. Apparently, the woman's horse tripped. She fell and was killed.

"As I remember it, the authorities ruled it was an unfortunate accident, but who'll ever know. The RIC and the military higher-up probably swept the real truth under the rug."

"No doubt," replied Aran.

"Did you know the woman well?" asked Duncan.

"Just met her once," answered Aran, "but I've known the family for several years."

Shadow came to Aran's rescue, "So you'd like to know about my nickname, eh? Well, fair's fair, I'd like to know about yours too."

"Not much to say. Me father use to be a nail maker in Belfast...that coupled with the fact I'm handy with me fists...sure the name Nayler just seemed to fit...and yourself?"

Sparing most of the details, Shadow briefly described his involvement in the Boer War with the Irish Brigade, back around the turn of the century.

Still uncertain about Duncan's exact loyalties, the Limerick man decided not to go into any detail about Aran or his present-day IRA involvement. *No sense in rushing things*, thought the baker cum battalion commander. *If he's spends any time with us, he'll find out soon enough what we're about...think I'll just keep those surprises for later.*

Pushing aside old memories, Aran spoke up. "Earlier, Duncan, you asked, 'Was it Cork or Limerick?' If you recollect rightly, you were the one who guessed my friend here was waiting for the train to Cork. On the spur of the moment, I decided I'd go along wit' ya. If you think about it, I didn't have the faintest idea who you were at the time."

"You're right, Aran. Many a cause has been lost because of a slip of the tongue."

"No hard feelings?" asked Aran.

"None at all," answered Duncan. "So, who *do* we have here today?"

Shadow piped up, "A grateful baker from Limerick and a lucky farmer's son from County Galway."

Deciding to keep his silence, the Scotsman thought: *Fair enough...there's plenty of time for knowing more later.*

❧

Aran and Shadow kindly accepted Duncan and his father's hospitality to stay the night.

"Sure we've plenty of beds in this old cottage, and besides, yis never tasted me own beef stew with veg straight from the garden," insisted Mr. MacGregor.

With the lorry safely out of sight in the barn, the four men whiled away the evening, enjoying the delights of a home-cooked meal and the taste of good Irish whiskey.

Duncan, who seemed to be in great form that night, raised his glass more than once to toast his two guests, "Here's tae us, wha's like us...God bless us one and all."

After the meal and the wash up, the foursome adjourned to the cosy sitting room. Beside a warm turf fire, they listened to Duncan's father regale his guests with stories of the proud Mac-Gregor clan and of Rob Roy himself; of Bonnie Prince Charlie and the tragedies of Culloden; of a family's life in transplanted Belfast and later here in County Kildare.

❧

At mid-morning the following day, after promising to keep in touch, Aran and Shadow bid the two MacGregors goodbye. Shadow planned to drive straight home after their visit with the O'Mahonys and Aran would take the train back to Dublin. The Rebel would inform Michael of the aborted Athy hijacking and his reacquaintance with Duncan. Both Shadow and he felt that the Scotsman might become a useful member of their organisation's future plans.

❧

Aran hadn't told Gran or Hannah O'Mahony of his possible arrival. He thought it better just to drop in, spending what time as seemed appropriate. *Surely, someone will be home and the others wouldn't be far behind.*

Driving back toward Athy, the Irish Rebel couldn't contain his curiosity any longer. "Shadow, you know something that you're not telling me and I want to know what it is."

"What in the world makes you think that, my young friend?"

"It's just the way you've been acting since yesterday's trouble in the square...you're too tight lipped and overly serious. Sure I can understand your wanting to be careful around strangers, but not with me. What's up?"

"You're right, Aran. I was going to let Michael tell you, but maybe this is as good a time as any. Mick's men in London have uncovered some new information about that blighter, George Henry Hawkins. It appears that the major had a brother, two years younger...a certain Colonel Edward Allyn Hawkins. Apparently, he's known to his friends as Eddy or Black Eddy...that's according to whom you talk to though."

"Wait a minute, Shadow. Are you saying that that murdering-bastard-of-a-man Hawkins has a brother, who from the sound of it is as bad or even worse than the bloody murderer himself?"

"Afraid so...at least if we can rely on Michael's intelligence sources that is."

The Gortman was thunderstruck. Exhaling loudly, he threw his head back in disbelief, banging it loudly against the rear window of the lorry's cab. "Holy Mary, Mother of God," uttered Aran. "I suppose you're now going to tell me that he's coming over here to avenge his brother's death?"

"Uh-huh," replied Shadow softly, glancing over at his friend.

"What'd ya mean, 'Uh-huh?'" retorted Aran.

"Just that. Michael's informant tells him that Eddy's been makin' inquiries about the Flying Gaels, about Liam Mellowes, even about the Big Fellow himself. He's been talking to demobbed Auxies and Tans who served over here…ones who've relocated back home in England. It seems he wants revenge for his brother's death…family honour and all that shyte."

The Rebel couldn't believe his ears. A thousand thoughts flashed through his head. Major Hawkins, the trained assassin who'd been involved in so many cruel and senseless acts: the mysterious business regarding Brigid's death, the murders of Turlough Molloy and Shadow's wife Helen, the beating he'd meted out to Gay and himself and who knows what else.

He looked over at Shadow. The Limerick baker seemed rather composed in light of the information he'd just relayed. On the other hand, the Gortman's face felt flushed, hot with anger and tinged with the gnawing reality of fear. Aran's tongue told him his mouth had gone dry and he could feel his heart pounding.

What if that bastard's brother comes after Sarah Anne or Áine…after Shadow or Gay or Lee or even Míceal? Sure, and then why wouldn't he come after me? Bloody hell, this is more than just war…it's personal isn't it. All right, Eddy or whatever your bloody name is, let's have a go at it…this is one fight I'm not backing away from.

Lost in thought, Aran stared out the lorry's window at vine-covered stone walls. Hedgerows of green-leafed rhododendron and red-tipped fuchsia appeared and disappeared from his view. The passing scenery seemed to have a hypnotic effect, relaxing his churning stomach and tormented mind.

Gradually returning to a more composed state, Aran shifted his attention back to his friend. "Jaysus, Shadow. It's one thing to go out and battle the enemy on even terms, but it's a different matter all together contemplating someone murdering the ones you love."

"You're right. We're just going to have to sharpen our wits and warn everyone else to do the same."

Suddenly, Aran sat bolt upright. "Shadow, do you think yesterday had anything to do with Hawkins?"

"Don't know."

"There was that Englishman...the one wielding the shotgun...do you think that could have been Hawkins, dangling us on a string?"

"It's crossed my mind, but I don't know how he could've found us out and organised things as they did."

"Yeah...probably not...but your one with the scarf over his gob...I wonder if that could've been Hawkins...a colonel you say. A colonel of what? Mother of God, anything's possible, isn't it?"

"Yep."

That old, familiar haunting, gnawing feeling at the core of his being suddenly sprang to life again. It had come and gone during his War of Independence days. It had even made its presence known to him in the years before. Like some sixth sense, this imagined ghostly spectre was a source of mysterious revelation as well as a herald of pending doom.

❧

"Aran, Aran is that you? Quick, everybody, Aran's come calling."

Mary, now almost thirteen and the spitting image of Brigid, was the first one out the door. It was almost as if she'd been sitting by it in anticipation, waiting for their motor's arrival.

Moments later, eleven-year-old Annie was standing in the doorway, "Gran, guess who's here...it's Aran and he's brought someone with him...another man."

"Gran says you're both to come in this minute," relayed Annie to the lorry in a loud voice.

The next Aran knew both O'Mahony girls were running across the front garden toward him. He braced himself for their onslaught, but he needn't have. Whether suddenly remembering their manners or unexpectedly embarrassed about showing affection in front of a stranger, they both stopped a few steps short of Aran.

"Whoa," said the Gortman in surprise, "no hugs for an ole friend?"

That was all the encouragement they needed. Two steps later, Aran was squeezing the two as they hugged his waist.

"I can't believe me eyes. The both of yis are growing up so fast. Come, let go a minute…here, meet a friend of mine. His name's Shadow and he has three girls of his own…just about your ages."

After coyly shaking the Limerick man's hand, they grabbed Aran by his jacket pockets and pulled him toward the front door.

"Come on, Aran. Gran is waiting inside to see you," said Annie.

As they neared the house, Mary tugged at Aran's sleeve and whispered, "Gran's not feeling so well lately, but hardly a day goes by without our mentioning your name. She'll be so glad to see you."

❧

Annie was the first to hear the horses and wagon pull into the farmyard. Rushing out of the house, she proudly announced, "He's here."

"Who's here?" came the reply.

"It's Aran…he's come to visit and what's more, he's brought Shadow with him."

"Shadow…what do ya mean…a shadow?"

"Come, see for yourself."

Moments later Rory O'Mahony stepped into the kitchen through the back door. Aran was on his feet, ready to greet the young man's arrival.

With Brigid's death five years ago, Rory had gradually begun assuming more and more of the responsibility for running the family farm. Today, at six-feet-one there was no doubt that he was in charge. Broad shoulders, tanned face, wavy reddish-brown hair and a strong, rough-textured grip, Rory was a man…and a handsome one at that.

Grinning from ear to ear, Aran exclaimed, "Rory, you're a sight for sore eyes! Over sixteen and all grown up, I'd say."

"Aran Roe O'Neill, this is indeed a real surprise."

Suddenly, the two men were embracing. Their eyes sparkled with the pooling of emotional tears that couldn't be constrained.

"Here, let me have a look at ye, Rory. My God…and just a few years ago you were such a wee lad, minding the sheep and running errands for your family. Now today, you're the one who's giving the orders."

Glancing over at Shadow and then back at the young man, Aran said, "Rory, come meet a friend of mind. Rory O'Mahony, this is Richard 'Shadow' Doyle. Shadow meet Rory, the one who I've told you so much about."

The two shook hands. "Mr. Doyle, it's a real pleasure sure. Aran's told us all about you, your nickname, your adventures together in Amerikay and then back home with the Flying Gaels…"

"Ah son, you embarrass me. But as you've already discovered sure, your friend here is a great one for telling stories…why I don't know…must be the Irish in him."

Squeezing the baker's arm and nodding his head, the Rebel interrupted, "…and look who's just coming in the door…"

In a flash, the Gortman empted Hannah's arms of parcels and had her spinning around on the kitchen flags.

❧

There was so much to talk about and catching up to do that Aran and Shadow accepted the family's invitation to stay the night.

Gran's health was beginning to fail but her eyes still twinkled with delight at Aran's presence. She doted on her two guests as if they were her own kin.

Hannah had assumed the full responsibility of running the family household. Peter Ryan and his family still helped Rory and the girls with the big yearly jobs of calving, sheep shearing, planting and harvesting, but in reality today, the O'Mahonys helped them just as much with their big chores.

Now twenty-eight, she was the fancy of several local farmers.

Quietly on the side, however, she told Aran she'd her heart set on a young man who ran his father's draper's shop in town.

Aran caught everyone up-to-date on Sarah Anne and their wedding plans. He relayed news of Gabriel and Áine while Shadow proudly talked about his three girls.

During their stay, Rory took the two older men out around the farm. He pointed out the changes he'd made and sought out their opinions on future improvements.

Gran cut some flowers from the back garden and all went to visit Brigid's grave. She squeezed Aran's hand, letting him know that his pending wedding met with her approval. She didn't begrudge him a wife and, hopefully, a family.

After their evening tea, they adjourned to the back porch and relaxed in the súgán chairs. While Hannah, Gran and the two girls finished up the dishes, Rory talked about his interest in joining the local IRA unit. He wanted Aran and Shadow to put in a good word for him. The young man reminded the Gortman that Aran's father had fiddled with his birth date back when he was underage.

The Gortman said he'd think about it. He told Rory he might speak to an IRA acquaintance who lived nearby, but he shouldn't let his hopes run too high. He reminded the sixteen-year-old that his family and the Ryans depended on his help here on the farm. In his heart, though, the Rebel knew his logic was likely to be ignored, especially if the fighting was to break out again.

Privately, Aran reflected: *Sure, I don't want him to get mixed up in any of the troubles. I just wish he wasn't so damn eager. Lord knows he needs to stay where he is and mind the little ones and his grandmother.*

❧

Aran and Shadow left the O'Mahony farm early the next morning. They were headed for the Marysborough rail station where the Gortman would be dropped off in time to catch a train back to Dublin. Shadow would then head for Limerick and home. There'd be a lorry to unload, Michael's little armoury to secret away, work to catch up on and tea with his daughters.

For the first month or so after Helen's death, her mother had moved down from Sixmilebridge to help Shadow mind her grand-children. In early April, he'd hired a nanny cum housekeeper. The Limerick man wanted to keep his little family together despite the huge void Helen's absence created in their lives.

❧

There were two other people waiting for the Dublin train at the Marysborough rail station. The quiet of the late-September morning was disturbed only by the singing of a lark from a nearby elm tree. The colourful signs of approaching winter were visible everywhere in the reds, oranges and yellows of changing leaves. The musty scent of freshly ploughed earth filled the air. Aran imagined his father and brothers back home readying the ground for another crop of spring corn.

The thought of farming and married life with Sarah Anne called out to him. He longed for the peace and comfort of a rural Irish home, untouched by the violence and bitterness of war. If Ireland can just safely navigate this last bit of rough water in her political evolution, maybe just maybe he'd be able to enjoy the fruits of his past five-year military labours.

Off in the distance, Aran heard the whistle of the approach-ing Dublin train. He was looking forward to meeting Marty and Cú at Croke Park. Together the three of them had tickets for the All-Ireland between Dublin and Galway that afternoon. But the Gaelic football match and time with his friends were only temporary diversions.

His morning exchange with Shadow had been worrisome. Methodically, he kept replaying their talk over and over in his head. But no matter how thoughtfully he mulled things over, Ireland's future still seemed so uncertain.

Finally on board the train, Aran intentionally sat by himself in the last carriage, trying once more to mentally replay his con-versation with Shadow...

"Jaysus, you're a lucky man, Aran, to have such good people saying a prayer for you each day. Sure it's more than most have."

"Yes, I know, Shadow. Gran, Hannah and the three younger ones are very special. They're like a second family…just like you are. The lot of yis plus Sarah Anne and Michael add such meaning and goodness to my life."

"Speaking of Michael, Aran, we both know how good he's been to us. He treats you like a son and me a brother. But that's not the side everyone sees of Mick. He can switch on and off like an electric light. You and I marvel at his courage in the face of adversity, his keen military mind, his ability to rally the Irish people around him for the cause of liberty, his charisma and his force of character. These are the traits his close friends and colleagues admire in him."

Aran nodded his head in acknowledgement of Shadow's words.

The Limerick man continued, "But Michael has a darker side as we well know. His contradictory nature sometimes infuriates others, especially those who don't agree with him. They view Mick as some kind of an egotistical bastard bent on having his own way, regardless of what they might think. You've seen it drive a wedge between himself and Cathal Brugha, Austin Stack…

Aran finished Shadow's sentence, "…and now it's Dev who's turned against him."

"Yes, I'm beginning to think so, Aran."

"But Shadow, I think Dev's a chip off the same block: arrogant, opinionated, thinks he knows what's best for Ireland and its people.

"Just last week, Michael told me about one of Dev's infamous pronouncements. The cabinet was discussing making a final offer to treat with the English. Dev was going on about how the Irish people deserved the right to decide their future. Mick said, 'Are you speaking for them or yourself, Eamon?' In reply, Dev said something to the effect, 'Whenever I want to know what the Irish people want, I have only to examine my own heart and it tells me straight off what the Irish people want.' Can you imagine that, Shadow?"

Aran shifted in his train seat, just as he had during their remembered conversation in the lorry. He'd wanted to see the Limerick man's face as he responded.

"As president, I believe Dev does speak for the country, but I admit, my young friend, that he can be as hard to read as Mick is at times. For instance, this business of whether we should hold out for an Irish Republic or settle for some sort of dominion status is as clear to me as it is perplexing to others.

"Aran, for the past five-plus years the both of us have been fighting for a Republic: a land free and unfettered from any foreign dictates. Now, finally, we're on the verge of sitting down to hammer out a Treaty with the Sassenach. If we settle for anything less, it'll be a betrayal of Ireland's cause…a denial of what so many have lived, sacrificed and died for. Wouldn't you agree?"

Aran turned uncomfortably in his seat.

"On the surface, Shadow, I believe you're right. Taking that position says, 'I'd rather go on fighting, even die, than concede anything to the Brits.' But Mick says absolutes aren't always attainable, and I'm beginning to see the wisdom of that position. Don't forget, the London diplomats have to save face. They need to be seen as reasonable men, willing to give a little but not surrender everything. If they granted us our Irish Republic, the shock waves of that decision just might bring down their house of colonial cards."

Richard Doyle looked at Aran and frowned. "You're not compromising our dream of a Republic, are you?"

"Shadow, you know Dev's just playing their game. On the one hand he's the spokesperson for doctrinaire Republicans like us but, on the other, he must appear moderate to the Westminster crowd. Instead of demanding a Republic, which, as you know Lloyd George rejected out of hand during their July talks, Dev is simply blowing smoke in their eyes. As I see it, he's playing the middle road for the moment by simply insisting that the Irish people have a right to determine for themselves their own form of government.[1] He wants to see what the Englanders have to offer before he plays his next card.

"Sure I know it's hard to disagree with the idea of self-determination, but it could turn out to be a double-edged sword. What happens, Shadow, if the Irish people choose dominion status over the Republic?"

1. Dwyer, op. cit., 30.

Shadow shook his head. "That depends, Aran. If Dominion Home Rule means complete control of our own destiny, then I don't see any real difference. But sure I can't imagine the Welsh Wizard and his cabinet granting that. They'll attach some conditions to dominion status that just might prove too difficult for Ireland to accept."

"Well, the obvious difference between us and the other Dominions is geographic, isn't it?" said Aran. "We're on their doorstep while Canada and Australia are halfway around the world."

"That right," answered the Limerick man. "The fact that we're only a few miles from British soil is the rub. In the end, I'm sure, they'll want some form of military concession...naval bases...their boots on our soil...something. Then there's always the matter of economics... money. You know, trade concessions and the like. Finally, there's the big question of Ulster...the Six Counties...will they be part of the package...in or out? Will Ulster be given a choice to join us or be told what to do?"

"If Dev wants the twenty-six to choose, sure he must be willing to offer the six the same," said the Gortman. "If the North is coerced into joining us, there'll certainly be civil war and nobody wants that.

"Personally, I think the issue of northern self-determination is done and dusted. It's only a matter if it's accomplished county by county or the six as a whole. If they decide county by county, Tyrone and Fermanagh would probably join us...maybe even Derry. But if it's all or none, my guess is they'll vote to stay outside," said Aran.

"Bloody hell," muttered Shadow. "We just can't let that happen...but what choice do we have? Our negotiating team is going to have a tough row to hoe, but with Dev's leadership, I know he won't let us down."

"I hope you're right, Shadow, but I'm afraid words not deeds might be our downfall."

"Have a little faith, my friend. I was talking with Dev two days ago. He said, 'If the status of a Dominion is offered to me,

I will use all our machinery to get the Irish people to accept it.'"[2]

Shifting in his seat again, and turning his attention to the rails ahead, Aran thought to himself: *Well, we'll just see what the Long Hoor does.*

❧

The football match was exciting. Dublin won 0-6 to Galway's 0-4. But despite Galway losing, it proved to be a beautiful autumn afternoon. The stands were full of GAA supporters, waving county banners and cheering for their side. It was thrilling to be a part of such an emotional event, as some thirty thousand Irishmen and women celebrated one of their ancient Irish sports. It was the first All-Ireland Aran had witnessed. He marvelled at the skill and determination of the players and the sense of community felt by the spectators. He only hoped the Irish people would be as united in their desire for independence, in whatever form it takes, as they were about their enthusiasm for the match on the pitch.

Later that evening Marty and Tom Cullen met Aran for a few drinks at Conway's pub at the bottom of Rutland Square. They regaled Marty with stories about the Tan War. Between pints of beer, the three young men shared their opinions about the possible pending treaty negotiations with England. Of course, Marty insisted on relating how he'd freed Aran from the grasp of the Red Coats[3] after Easter Week.

Later, in response to Cú's inquiry about his going to Amerikay for his university education, Marty was happy to oblige.

---

2. Ibid., 38.

3. The term 'Red Coat' was first used to describe an English infantry soldier in 1645. Oliver Cromwell dressed the soldiers of his New Model Army in red coats. This was England's first 'national' army. Previously, the crown had relied on local yeomanry for its defence. British soldiers continued wearing red tunics until c. 1899. During the 2nd Boer War (1899-1902), Boer sharpshooters became so adept at targeting British soldiers in their signature red coats that the army switched to khaki. Today, the British Army continues to wear red coats for some of its ceremonial dress. As a result, the term 'Red Coat' may still be used to refer to a British soldier just as a British sailor is sometimes called a 'Limey,' though no one sucks on limes today to ward off scurvy.

"I returned to St. Enda's, now moved from Rathfarnham to Cullenswood House in Ranelagh, in the autumn of '16 to complete my secondary education.

"In the spring of 1917, with the country still in the post-Rebellion grip of heightened British military control, my parents sent me off to Amerikay and Harvard University.

"I left Ireland about the same time Aran was returning home...like ships passing in the night we were."

"Sure, what a life ye led. Cú and I fighting off the might of the British Army and ye sweet talkin' all those Boston girls," taunted Aran.

"Ah, he's only having ye on. Pay him no matter," said Tom in Marty's defence. "Go on with your story."

"Ta," smiled Marty. "After arriving, I spent two months living in New York with friends of my parents. My father called it my adjustment period to living in Amerikay. My mother simply referred to it as a paid holiday.

"Later, I moved to Cambridge, enrolled in summer school and began working on my BS. I needed to take some prerequisite science courses that weren't offered at St. Enda's.

"Well, to make a long story short, four years later here I am...degree in hand with a major in the sciences and premed."

Tom wondered, "Marty, in all that time you never came home?"

"No. Too expensive, plus with the war in Europe winding down and the one here hotting up, my parents preferred I stay where I was."

"Makes sense," said Cú. "What's next?"

"I'm going to stay in Dublin, take a course or two and work at the Mater Hospital. If everything goes according to plan, I'll go back to medical school at Harvard next autumn. I've already been accepted into their medical school."

Abruptly changing the subject, Marty smiled and said, "Before then, however, we've a wedding to go to in Cahir."

"Anyone we know?" teased Tom.

"Ah, just some country lad who's dying to tie the knot," retorted Marty.

❧

The morning after the Sunday football final dawned grey but mild. The pints and late-night comradery had left Aran with a sore head. As he peddled across town, he thought: *If I can just make it to Bewley's, I might survive another one of Mick's early morning meetings.*

With his shirt damp from sweat and his tie straightened, Aran Roe O'Neill walked through the front door of #6 Harcourt Street, Sinn Féin headquarters. He was only a couple of minutes late.

"He's waiting for you upstairs," said the receptionist.

The Gortman took the stairs two at a time.

The door to Michael's office was closed.

He paused a moment to catch his breath then knocked.

"Come."

The Big Fellow was seated behind a desk neatly piled with stacks of paper. Wearing a white shirt, tie, waistcoat and brown tweed suit, Collins could've been your family banker or an international corporate executive. He certainly didn't fit the image of an unbending Republican who'd recently put the British in an awkward position…would they bargain with the man who won Ireland's War of Independence or not?[4]

"Late, eh. Sure I haven't much time for ye today, Aran. Sorry for that, but I do have some news. The Long Hoor is about to announce we're going over to treat with Lloyd George and his murder gang."

By now, Collins was on his feet, swiping at a lock of brown curly hair that had fallen onto his forehead.

Aran could see the fire in his eyes and heard the edge in his voice.

"That feckin' Dev has me going over with Arthur and a handful of others. Bloody suicide if you ask me. But he knows I'm a soldier…a soldier of Ireland, and I'll go…following the President's orders despite what my best judgement tells me."

---

4. On the face of things, Michael Collins & his crowd were Sinn Féiners, yet they only supported its policies to a point. They agreed with Arthur Griffith's philosophy of abstention & self-sufficiency, but they didn't adhere to his ideas of non-violence & recognition of the British Crown. Coogan, op. cit., 65.

Aran's inner voice stirred: *Jaysus, Mary and Joseph...surely a moment of truth. Míceal's going over to be a part of something that very well might change the course of Ireland's history.*

"Do you hear me, son?"

"Aye, Michael. What can I do?"

"I'll get to that in a minute."

Collins moved to a window overlooking Harcourt Street.

"Come over here...see that flag flying...the tricolour... Connie Crowe died for it...you recall so."

The Gortman nodded.

"A lot of other good men and women have too. Remember McBride's dying words at Kilmainham?"

"Mind the flag."

"That's right...'mind the flag.' That's what we all have to do, Aran...you and I and thousands of others, if we're ever going to see this land of ours free."

The Corkman put one hand on his young protégé's shoulder. "If Dev sends us over with instructions to hold out for a Republic, there's no point in going. We can never hope to bring that back...we can never deliver all that Ireland wants and deserves...but maybe, just maybe, cooler heads will prevail and something can be worked out...only time will tell.

"Just imagine it, Aran, what that conceited Hoor told me the other day. He said he wanted Arthur and meself to head up the negotiating team but that he's staying at home. He said something about keeping his finger on the pulse of the people. I say shyte to that. I told him he was our best man to head things up, but no, he's staying back. Jaysus, you'd think he was the Holy Ghost or something."

Collins released the Rebel from his grasp. Returning to his desk, the Big Fellow said, "In the meantime, Aran, we'll go to London and talk peace...what choice do we have? But mind you, in the back of my head I'll be preparing for war.

"Now, when I said 'we,' I mean you...the both of us. It will take ten days, maybe a fortnight, to finalise everything. As soon as possible, I want you to go home, visit your family, see Sarah

Anne, but I want you and Gabriel back here no later than the 5th or 6th. We'll have time then to make our final plans. "

❧

Aran Roe O'Neill and Gabriel McCracken arrived into Kingsbridge rail station a little after one on Thursday afternoon, the 6th. The streets along the quays were still wet from a recent rain shower, but as they climbed aboard a tram bound for O'Connell's Bridge, blue sky shone overhead.

Peter McCracken had driven Gabriel and Aran from Cahir to the Limerick Junction rail station earlier that morning. During the ride the publican expressed his excitement and anticipation shared by most of the country about the pending London negotiations scheduled to begin in five days' time.

Ever since the announcement a week ago, speculation ran rampant. What would the delegation bring back to the Irish people? Independence? A Republic? Dominion status like Canada and Australia enjoys? In or out of the British Commonwealth?

Other queries piqued Ireland's curiosity. Why wasn't de Valera part of the negotiating team? What's this business about External Association the President was proposing? If no settlement is reached, will the troubles begin anew?

But the general atmosphere was positive. "Not to worry," the people repeated, "Sure, whatever is decided, Collins and Griffith won't let us down."

Glancing over at his two passengers, Peter asked, "You two certainly have the Big Fella's ear, what's this scheme of Dev's regarding External Association?"

Aran and Gabby just looked at each other. Neither spoke. Finally, Gabriel gave the Gortman an elbow. "Aran, you have a go at it, will ya?"

He began hesitantly, "I'm not all that clear about the details, but as I understand it, it's Dev's way of getting around London's insistence that there'll be no talk of her granting us full independence or our Republic."

"Sounds like politics to me," said Peter.

"Ah, I think it's more than that," replied Aran. "Dev wants Britain to acknowledge our independence regarding our own internal affairs. What's more, he wants equal footing with other British Commonwealth countries…a kind of mini League of Nations.

"There's also something in his proposal that paints the difference between reciprocal and common citizenship, but I'm not very clear about that. All I know is that we'd be Irish citizens and they'd be British ones. Both will have equal rights in the other's country, as well as in their own, of course."

Gabriel sighed, "Sure, I don't envy our team going over. They'll have their hands full trying to sort out all the subtle nuances and political chicanery the Welsh Wizard and his lot have up their sleeves."

"Ah, ye of little faith," retorted Aran. "Just remember the coup Mick pulled off in springin' Seán Mac Eoin. He'd the bloody Sassenach eating out of his hand so."

"Never heard that story," said Peter. "What happened?"

"Sure, you must remember? Back in March, three months before the Truce was announced, Mac Eoin was pulled off a train on his way home from Dublin. Jailed and sentenced to death, he was refused a pardon when the other arrested Dáil deputies were finally freed a month or so ago. The damn lousers were going to do the Blacksmith of Ballinalee in…set an example and all that. Well, as you can imagine Michael was enraged that his friend wasn't released. In a shrewd countermove, Mick, without Dev's knowledge or approval, released a statement to the press stating that any British peace overture *must* be considered by the *entire* Dáil. That put the London crowd in a fix. Pressured by the press and public opinion for a settlement to the Irish question, Lloyd George had little choice. Michael's bluff worked. Commandant Mac Eoin was released the following day and the rest ye know…so sure we're off to Downing Street next week."

"I take back what I just said," smiled Gay. "Maybe our side won't have to eat humble pie after all."

❧

The break at home had recharged Aran's energies. Labouring outside along with his father and brothers was hard but satisfying work. The sweet smells of harvest time and the pungent aromas of freshly tilled fields told him this was where he belonged. For a brief interlude, his need for keeping an eye peeled for danger wasn't necessary. Happily, he'd laid aside his fears and guns for the feel of a single-board plough and the sound of the slash hook cutting a clean swath through tall grass.

But the realities of the day couldn't be cast aside that easily. He'd seen the announcement and follow-up story in the newspaper. Friday's headlines announced the news to all Ireland: Griffith and Collins to head Irish team…talks begin in London on 11 October.

The lead paragraph carried Ireland's reply to Britain's formal invitation: Dáil Éireann, the freely elected Parliament of the Irish people, does hereby agree to send a delegation of its representatives to treat with His Majesty's Government. The express purpose of this conference will be to ascertain how the association of Ireland with the community of nations known as the British Empire may best be reconciled with Irish national aspirations.[5]

So Míceal was right. He is going over without Dev. The honeymoon's over…time to strap on the guns again, just in case.

※

Two days later, after Sunday Holy Mass, the Irish Rebel repacked his case. His brother drove him down to Cahir for a reunion with the McCracken clan and Sarah Anne.

While he was there a letter arrived from Amerikay. Father and Mother McCracken along with son Larry planned to arrive into Queenstown Harbour in early December. Of course Sarah Anne and Gabby were ecstatic about the news and so was Aran. The three planned on staying five weeks. They'd visit some of

---

5. Robert Kee. *The Green Flag: Volume III Ourselves Alone.* London, 1972, 148.

Father's old friends and favourite haunts and, of course, be part of the wedding. Unfortunately, out of necessity, Dominic was staying behind to mind the farm.

Lost in all the excitement of the McCrackens' anticipated arrival and the pending wedding, Sarah Anne's news that she'd joined the local branch of Cumann na mBan[6] was almost overlooked. Aran, however, made a point of discussing it with her. She promised not to undertake any more risky assignments without telling him first. As her sincerity seemed so genuine, the Gortman decided to drop the matter, at least for the moment.

❧

During the four years Annie had lived in Cahir, Aran and she had been intimate on only a handful of occasions. The night before Gay and he were to leave for Dublin was one of them. Afterwards, he quietly tiptoed back to his upstairs room in the Black Rose. His body tingled as he savoured her passionate touch. Soon they'd be married and this innocent deception of theirs would be a thing of the past. Aran Roe longed for the comforts and pleasures of hearth and home and freedom: the inviting aromas of home-cooked meals, the quiet moments of after-work relaxation before a fire with pipe in hand, the sound of children laughing…all safe in the knowledge that the Sassenach wouldn't be knocking at the door with a warrant for his arrest.

As the Irish Rebel curled up under his warm, quilted duvet, thoughts of Sarah Anne's urgency aroused him again. He remembered her…moving in the darkness like a shadow over

---

6. Cumann na mBán: a woman's auxiliary founded on 5 April 1914 to champion Ireland's cause for liberty & to support the arming of the Irish Volunteers in defence of their country. It played an important role in the 1916 Easter Rebellion. By 1921, there were approximately one thousand branches nationwide as the women actively participated in the War of Independence. Besides carrying messages, smuggling weapons, caring for the sick & wounded, feeding & providing safe- houses for men on the run, some women took part in ongoing military operations. Their badge, a rifle intertwined with the organisation's initials, signified its militarism & commitment to Irish freedom.

him…leaning down and kissing his hungry lips…hearing her excited breath whispering love's passion in his ear.

Later, as he rose to leave her bed, she quietly murmured, "The next time…there'll be snow on the ground and we'll be as one…"

❧

The Big Fellow had sent word to Gabriel at the family pub in Cahir that they were to be at #22 Mary Street, Dublin no later than two o'clock on the 6th.

Knocking on the brick building's nondescript door a full fifteen minutes before the appointed hour, the two men where surprised to see Michael Collins poking his head out of an upper story window.

"Jaysus, yis took your own sweet time getting here," roared an impatient voice.

Then in a softer more welcoming tone, he called down, "No need to knock…the door's unlocked. Haven't you heard…I'm not on the bloody Limey's wanted list anymore?"

Never one to tout patience as one of his virtues, the Big Fellow was standing at the head of the stairs as they climbed the steps. Instead of another vitriolic volley of words, the Corkman was all smiles and handshakes.

Maybe a touch of guilty conscience for berating two of your best friends, thought Aran. Then he shook his head with a smile, refuting any such thought.

"Good to see you two. I trust your time home was enjoyable so."

Then quickly turning on his heels, Michael headed for an open door down the hallway. Over his shoulder, he called back saying, "Now it's time we all went to work. Come on and meet the others."

Gathered in the small, almost barren room were half a dozen men. Heading the list of apparently invited dignitaries was General Emmet Dalton, dressed in mufti. Next to him sat Seán Mac Eoin, the very man they'd talked about earlier in the day. Both men nodded as Aran and Gay entered the temporary office. Leaning against the back wall was Liam Tobin, who politely tipped his hat to them. Behind them, standing just inside the door and armed with a Thompson machine gun, was Frank Thornton. Aran noted his stern face and thought he was certainly taking the job of sergeant-at-arms literally. From across the room, Joe Dolan flashed a smile in their direction. Finally, on his feet with his hand outstretched was Tom Cullen.

I'm glad he's in on this one, thought Aran.

In a reassuring voice Cú whispered, "How ya keeping?"

Before the Gortman or Gay could answer, he added, "Don't worry, we all just arrived here ourselves."

Both the two newcomers nodded their acknowledgement at his reassurance.

Without any formalities, Collins called the meeting to order by rapping his knuckles on the desk. Clearing his throat, the Big Fellow looked around the room. From the jut of his determined jaw and flashing eyes Aran could see that Mick was all business. This was no afternoon social gathering.

Standing tall and facing his audience, the Corkman paused momentarily. With a skill born of practice, Michael swept back an annoying lock that had fallen onto his forehead.

"Gentlemen, this is it. 'Tis a new war we are about to engage in. It's not a war of battlefields and bullets but a war of words and political opportunity. But make no mistake, the dangers are just as great as the ones we faced together in the Tan War. The future of Ireland depends on us doing our jobs…and doing them well. With the exception of Eoin here, yis are all going over to London with me. We leave on the weekend. Guilfoyle, Leonard and Ned Broy are already there. They're working with Fíonan Lynch and some of our London boys to ready things for our arrival."

Heads nodded as Collins studied the room, catching each man's eye in turn.

"As you might have heard, Arthur is going to be heading the team. I respect and admire his judgement, but the weight of the last two years has taken its toll…he's no longer a young man. But despite everything, he's still keen on championing Ireland's cause. Art's our foreign affairs man.

"I'll be going over as deputy leader of the delegation. Despite my image as a son-of-a-bitch hardliner, my brief will actually be to oversee financial matters and monetary reimbursements. Rumour has it the feckin' London bureaucrats want us to help pay their bleedin' war debt. Fat chance of that I say. In fact, the way I calculate things, they owe us about four billion pounds...and that's just since the Act of Union."[7]

Everyone in the room laughed.

Aran thought: *That's it Míceal, give 'em hell.*

"The third member of the delegation is Robert Barton. I'd like to think we can count on Bob, but don't be surprised if he sides with the Long Hoor. Dev's put him on for propaganda purposes... wealthy land owner and member of the present-day 'Protestant ascendancy.' He should stand up well to the likes of the English aristocratic set. Economic and agricultural trade are his main responsibilities."

Michael paused and took another swipe at the annoying lock of hair that refused to stay put.

Now, pacing back and forth before his loyal followers, he continued, "Messrs George Gavin Duffy and Éamon Duggan, members of the bar, have been included on the team too. I only know a little about the two of them, but I believe Duggan's in our camp. He was out in '16 and did some IRA intelligence work after that.

"As you might know, Duffy's father was none other than the eminent Sir Charles Gavin Duffy, the famous Young Islander. If any of that nationalism rubbed off, we'll be grand. He's one of our two constitutional law experts going over."

---

7. Following the Rebellion of 1798, Ireland's parliament, composed almost entirely of Anglo-Irish aristocrats, voted to divest itself of its legislative authority. Consequently, all future governmental decisions would be relegated to the parliament in Westminster. Their 1800 capitulation came into effect on 1 January 1801. As a result, Ireland became a part of (or was unioned with) Great Britain. Together with Wales (1536) & Scotland (1707), Ireland became the fourth member of this governmental entity. Thus, the red saltire of St. Patrick was added to the white saltire of St. Andrew & red cross of St. George, forming a new British Union Jack flag.

Pausing a moment, Collins asked if there were any questions.

No one said a word.

Picking up the threads of his narrative, Collins continued, "The Long Hoor's appointed Erskine Childers of *Asgard* fame to be the Chief Secretary. Personally, I believe he's been assigned to keep an eye on us...to be a conduit from our lips to Dev's ear. Be careful what you say around him. Consider him a spy in our midst.

"Diarmuid O'Hegarty will serve as our delegation's publicity director and assistant to Childers while John Chartres, a loyal Sinn Féin member and constitutional lawyer, will work with Diarmuid."

Looking off into space, the Big Fellow paused for a moment, seemingly lost in thought.

With his attention back on the men before him, he added, "Oh yes...one more thing...while we're in London, we'll have our own Irish typing and household staff with us. Sure you can never be too careful."

Once again the Big Fella studied the faces of all those in the room. Without a word, he nodded his head in affirmation of their silent attention and sat down.

Next, Emmet Dalton took the floor. He detailed the specifics of their departure plans. A contingent of Collins's men would leave from Dublin's North Wall quay in two days' time. They would be accompanying Griffith and the others, as the main body of the delegation headed over to England.

Michael and his remaining entourage would leave from Kingstown on Sunday evening. After their docking in Holyhead, the group would board a train for its Monday-morning arrival at London's Euston Station. The Big Fellow wanted to avoid the notoriety planned for Griffith's Saturday-evening London arrival. Instead, he preferred to slip quietly into town, settling down in his rented quarters before the start of the talks on Tuesday morning.

Just before the meeting broke up, Michael rose to add another comment. "I think you all know my position in this matter. I am going over against my better judgement and, I dare say, the judgement of a good few knowledgeable friends. But I am going…going as a soldier under orders. But, my friends, don't be after kidding yourselves. If the Irish people expect our delegation to deliver a Republic, we just as well might not go…there'll be no Republic. Lloyd George made that very clear to Dev and the cabinet earlier this summer."

The Corkman's eyes flashed as he threw his shoulders back in defiance. "But each of you know that down through the years and the decades and yes, even the centuries, the Irish struggle has always been about freedom—freedom from English occupation, from English interference, from English domination, not for freedom with any particular label attached to it. That's what we're going over for and together, we won't stop fighting until we finally succeed."

❦

Later that same evening, Michael Collins and Tom Cullen slipped in through the back door and took seats in a snug at the rear of Devlin's. The two joined Aran and Gabriel who'd arrived earlier.

After Cú returned from the bar with a round of drinks, the Corkman filled in the two recent returnees with the latest news. He described how the Dáil had sanctioned the appointment of the five nominated delegates, giving each full plenipotentiary power. They were charged with negotiating and even concluding a treaty or treaties of settlement between Ireland and Britain. But Dev, never one to let power slip too far from his fingers, reminded the Irish parliament that they still reserved the right to accept or reject any Treaty signed in London, if it didn't meet with their approval.

With an empty glass before him, Collins continued, "Then I'll be damned if the Long Hoor didn't go behind the assembly's back and have the cabinet issue another set of orders…secret instructions."

Aran and Gabriel leaned forward as Collins lowered his voice.

"Our delegation was told we had to keep the cabinet informed of any and all development. Additionally, we were directed that we must furnish the cabinet with a copy of any draft Treaty under consideration and await their instructions before signing."

"Can you imagine the cheek of them!" exclaimed Gay. "Going over the heads of the Dáil...sounds like Dev's doing."

"...and this is the crowd that refused to go over and do the dirty work themselves,"[8] said the Rebel, shaking his head in disgust.

"What a bloody mess," said Tom. "If the job isn't difficult enough, Dev and his people keep throwing spanners into the works."

---

8. In October, 1921 the Dáil cabinet or executive was composed of seven members or ministers: de Valera, (President), Griffith (Foreign Affairs), Collins (Finance), Barton (Economic Affairs), Brugha (Defence), Stack (Home Affairs) & Cosgrave (Local Government). Cosgrave was not asked to be a delegate. Brugha & Stack flatly refused to be part of the negotiating team. The President also refused to serve & gave several reasons for this decision: as President, he said he was the symbol of the Republic and, therefore, perceived by others to be a doctrinaire republican; knowing the delegation would have to compromise, he felt he was the best person to stay home & unite Ireland in case the war hotted up again; de Valera also thought by staying in Dublin he could control other leading hardliners, e.g., Brugha & Stack; finally, if the treaty negotiations reached a stalemate, he could join the delegation in London and, hopefully, tip the balance in favour of Ireland's side. In appointing Griffith & Collins, the cabinet chose two of its moderate members. De Valera reasoned that moderates, as opposed to extremists like Brugha & Stack, might entice Lloyd George to be more generous in his Irish treaty concessions. By having Barton, also a moderate, on the team, de Valera felt he'd be a check on Griffith & Collins while remaining loyal to him and his wishes. Prior to the final selection of delegates, Cosgrave made a last appeal for de Valera to be included on the Irish team. His motion was moved, seconded and put to a vote. Griffith, Collins & Cosgrave voted in favour of the motion. Brugha, Stack & Barton voted against it. De Valera, as President, broke the deadlock. He voted not to go.

[Author's personal note: I realise there're two, three and sometimes four sides to every story, so here's mine. As a plenipotentiary, Collins must have felt he was being fitted for a straight jacket. On the one hand de Valera and half of the cabinet placed him in an impossible position. In Collins's own words, "...we could never hope to bring back all that Ireland wanted and deserved to have." Yet Michael knew someone had to go, so who bet-

"Shyte...," uttered Aran under his breath, "...as if trying to achieve the impossible isn't enough. Sure, we're after having to deal with England's shrewdest and most experienced political devils, all surrounded by their worldly trappings of power and prestige. Lord God Almighty, just imagine, having Lloyd George, Churchill and the rest of that crowd parading ya around #10. It would be like trying to break a wild stallion inside a walled garden...boxed in and with no place to run."

---

ter than himself to speak for Ireland. The distrust between Collins and de Valera continued to grow in the weeks leading up to 11 October. But despite Dev's chicanery, Collins seemed to conceal his misgivings. One moment the President was forcing him into an untenable situation and the next he's offering him support. Historian T. Ryle Dwyer observed, quoting de Valera, "... (We, the cabinet,) are asking them (the plenipotentiaries) to secure by negotiations what we are totally unable to secure by force of arms."

The fact that de Valera did not take part in the London negiotiations was, I feel, a turning point in Irish history. Most historians agree that he should have gone, as he was considered Ireland's most experienced and capable politico. I concur, but feel Dev selfishly refused because he didn't want his name linked with pending disaster. Though thought of as Ireland's ablest diplomat, his failures in America (1920) to enlist Democratic and Republican Party support for Ireland's cause and for his alienation of Irish-America's leadership did not speak well of his skills. Furthermore, de Valera failed to seriously consider Northern Ireland's new Unionist leader James Craig's offer (1921) to discuss Irish North-South differences under the Council of Ireland clauses contained in the 1920 Government of Ireland Act that partitioned the country. By rebuffing Craig, the President missed a golden opportunity to begin bringing their two sides together. Ultimately, this error in judgement made it more difficult for the British government to resolve unionist-nationalist differences during the Treaty Talks. I also think de Valera was hedging his bets. If the talks were unsuccessful in delivering all that Ireland sought, which was very likely, his name (as Collins's was later) would be linked to that failure. Such a catastrophe might have destroyed his fledging political career, as the Irish populists might have turned their backs on him. Finally, I think de Valera's overinflated ego led him to believe that no matter what happened in London, his power of personality and exaggerated image of self could right any sinking ship. Because of his haughty arrogance, Ireland *was* plunged into a deadly Civil War which *was* then followed by years of national malaise. It is only with the recent emergence of the Celtic Tiger that Ireland has begun eradicating the stain of Dev's political myopia.]

Chuckling out loud, Gabriel interrupted, "That reminds me of a story I overheard at the Black Rose the other night. There were these two men talking at the bar. One asks the other about the origin of the expression 'the sun never sets on the British Empire.' Without missing a beat, the other replied, 'Ah sure, it's God given. You see, He can't trust 'em with the lights out.'"

After a good laugh, they all ordered another round.

8

*"England's policy in the past has been to treat
Ireland as a conquered and subject country. If
there is a change in the policy of subordinating
Ireland to English interests, then there appears to
be [the] possibility of peace."*

Arthur Griffith

WEDNESDAY MORNING, 19 OCTOBER 1921

The Irish delegation had been in London just over a week. The main body of the Dublin negotiating contingent had arrived into Euston rail station on Saturday evening, the 8th. An unexpected surprise awaited them. Hundreds of eager Irish supporters lined the streets, cheering on the emissaries who were there to confer with some of the crown's ablest representatives. With the first plenary session scheduled for eleven o'clock on Tuesday morning, the 11th, the Irishmen had ample time to settle into their rented Victorian house at #22 Hans Place.

Much to the crowd's disappointment, though, the eagerly anticipated celebrity figure of Michael Collins was nowhere to be seen. The de facto leader of the Irish plenipotentiaries, and his handpicked party slipped quietly into town two days later, on Monday morning, October 10th. Besides detesting public notoriety, the Big Fellow had proposed to his sweetheart Kitty Kiernan the day before. They talked about marrying the following August. The date of the 22nd was discussed.

Tom Jones, the British Cabinet Secretary, had rented the Collins party a fine three-story, bricked, terraced house at #15 Cadogan Gardens, near Sloan Square. The quiet residential street made security's job easier. Michael was venturing into the very belly of the beast. Sure, the ever-calculating mastermind was not going to take any foolish chances without proper backup.

Aran remembered the Big Fellow's first-day reaction to their newly rented digs.

"By God, our Irish lads here in London have done some fine work getting everything ready for us. This place is just what I had in mind," exclaimed the Corkman.

Indeed, Michael was genuinely pleased with their comfortable accommodation after returning from a quick inspection of its many rooms.

Making a sweeping gesture with his right arm, the Corkman said, "All of this is hard to imagine, no? Sure, just a few months ago Lloyd George and his lot would be after having my guts for garters. They'd have loved to stick me in the bloody tower...now they're footing the bill for all of this. Just imagine..."

Aran Roe O'Neill joined the Big Fellow in his amazement. "Yes, 'tis hard to fathom. With what some say was a £10,000 price tag on your head, yesterday the Sassenach would have done anything to put you behind bars in Brixton Prison. Today here we are enjoying their royal hospitality. Maybe you are after winning the war, Mick, and we just don't realise it."

"Jaysus, Aran," interjected Liam Tobin, Collins's head of intelligence, "you paint a rosy picture. After the cock-up job Dev did on his return from Amerikay, we're all lucky to be alive and in one piece."

"Liam's right, Aran," replied Mick's public relations man Diarmuid O'Hegarty. "De Valera's thrown more than one spanner into the works since Christmas last. First, there was his insane jealousy of Michael here followed closely by his insatiable desire for control. Sure, he nearly undid all the good we'd realised over the last two years."

Collins just smiled, but he knew the assessments were spot on.

Rolling up his sleeves, Michael took charge. "Enough of this carry-on. It's time we went to work. Liam, be a good man and close those draperies. Someone turn up the lamps. It's time we got organised."

❧

Attending early-morning Mass at Brompton Oratory of St. Philip Neri was something Collins insisted on including in his daily routine. Built in 1884, the ornate, Italian Baroque-style church in the London suburb of South Kensington was a short drive from their rented lodging.

Arriving a few minutes before nine o'clock on the 19th, the Irishmen's two motor cars pulled to a stop at the curb in front of the impressive Catholic Church. Collins, accompanied by his security force, strode quickly into the building's quiet, candlelit interior. Stopping before the green, Connemara-marbled side chapel dedicated to St. Patrick, Michael crossed himself and said a short prayer.

As his comrades moved off down the centre aisle, Gabriel McCracken, Éamonn 'Ned' Broy, a former Dublin Castle detective once employed by the British authorities, and Joe Dolan, a member of Michael's elite assassination team founded in the summer of '19, stayed behind covering the church entrance. They acted as the Big Fella's rear guard.

On this particular Wednesday morning, the Irish Rebel and Liam Tobin walked ahead followed by Mick and Joe Guilfoyle, another member of Tobin's Intelligence Section. Bringing up the back was Michael's dear Dublin friend General Emmet Dalton and Captain Tom Cullen, another first-rate intelligence officer cum body guard.

Prior to the group's arrival in England, the ever-calculating Collins leaving no stone unturned, had Dalton purchase a light aircraft from a sympathetic Canadian businessman.[1] Joe Leonard, a second Squad ally, was assigned the task of making sure the plane was ready to take off at a moment's notice from Croydon's small airport just north of London.

Surrounded by his trusted comrades, Collins and his party took part in the thirty-minute Mass. Aran and Liam occupied the pew ahead of Mick and Joe while Emmet and Cú sat directly behind their leader.

The huge church was almost empty. A few old women with their scarf-covered, white heads dotted the dimly lit nave. A handful of black-draped nuns sat together near the church's alter railing. Other worshippers sat by themselves or in little knots of twos and threes. A number of what might be described as students or tourists wandered the side aisles examining the statuary and artwork or simply paused to pray.

Waiting to receive the Eucharist at the communion rail, Aran said a prayer for Pearse's departed soul. He often prayed that his hero and mentor was at peace in God's Kingdom and that his dream of Irish freedom still bloomed in Éireann's heart: *You sowed the seeds of freedom in your daughters and your sons, Patrick Henry Pearse. Please God, by the body and blood of your earthly Son and by the power of the Holy Ghost, may I've the chance to see your dream for Ireland come true.*

With the Mass over, the knot of Republican revolutionaries-turned-Irish diplomats retraced their steps back up the aisle. Ned Broy and Joe Dolan, the party's drivers, were out the door, headed for their vehicles. Gabby stood just outside the church, keeping an eye on the pedestrians and the vehicular traffic passing by on busy Brompton Road.

Just as Collins and his men emerged into the grey light of a London morning, they heard the squeal of tyres. A black salon

---

1. The fact that Collins arrived in London with such a large retinue of security personnel all but eliminated any possibility of his anonymity. It also precluded his former intelligence agents of ever resuming their former undercover positions should war resume. The purchase of an 'escape' aircraft seemed to indicate that the likelihood of such an eventuality was rated a strong possibility. Coogan, op. cit., 234.

motor car wheeled out of Egerton Terrace and headed down the main thoroughfare toward the Oratory.

Gabriel was the first to sense danger. Pulling out the Thompson gun he'd concealed from under his trench coat, the Irish-American sprinted for the cover of a car parked along the curb. As he dashed, Gay shouted, "Look out! This may be trouble."

No sooner were the words out of his mouth than the footpath in front of the church was alive with machine gun fire. The sound of bullets whistled and whined as they ricocheted above the now prone transplanted rebel.

Aran could hear the unmistakable barking from Gay's weapon as his comrade showered the speeding car with bullets of his own. Besides offering Gabriel cover, the parked vehicles in front of the church prevented the assassins from having a clear shot at their intended targets.

Thinking the danger had passed, Aran jumped to his feet. Sprinting toward their lead vehicle, he shouted, "Ned, crank it up. Let's catch those bloody bastards."

Cú Cullen was right on the Rebel's heels.

By now Broy had the back door open and the motor racing.

Aran dove in first, closely followed by the intelligence man.

As Ned popped the clutch, the vehicle quickly lurched forward, throwing the two backseat passengers off balance. Moments later, however, they were ready for action.

Leaning out the left-hand rear window, the Gortman with Luger in hand, shouted, "Did you get a look at them, Ned? How many?"

"Three, I think...two in the back plus the driver. Wearing hoods they were, but there might have been a fourth. They were by me so fast."

"Only one shooter?" queried Aran above the roar of the engine.

"I think," answered Ned.

Hanging out the right rear window of their pursuing vehicle, Cullen shouted, "Any chance of catching them in this traffic?"

"They're just up ahead…the boxy-looking black one. See it weaving?"

"I see them, but don't dare risk a shot from back here," snapped a frustrated Aran.

"Is the boot down, Ned?" bellowed the intelligence man.

"Don't dare go any faster in this traffic, Cú. Sorry."

"Yeah, I know. Those bloody lousers are as good as gone."

❧

Back at the Oratory, Collins and his crowd had escaped harm. Several of the other churchgoers, however, weren't as lucky. One elderly gentleman had received a superficial wound to the side of his head, while a sobbing, bewildered woman clutched her left arm. Blood oozed from between her fingers.

By the time Ned's vehicle had returned to the scene of the ambush, they could see Collins, Tobin and Guilfoyle seated in the back of their other car. Joe Dolan was behind the wheel. Emmet and Gabriel were on the footpath talking to the police. Moments later an ambulance arrived and the two wounded victims were taken away.

As Broy pulled along side Dolan's car, Collins motioned to them. From inside the sedan, the Big Fellow caught their attention. Pointing behind him, he silently mouthed the words: *Cadogan Gardens.*

❧

The first plenary session began promptly at eleven o'clock on the morning of 11 October. Excited crowds of onlookers cheered on both contingents as they arrived at #10 Downing Street.

One account reported: "Lloyd George opened in grave yet friendly tones, saying, 'England was anxious to make peace, but there were limitations beyond which she could not go.'"[2]

"Arthur Griffith replied in his cold, impassive style, each word

2. Frank Pakenham. *Peace By Ordeal*. London, 1992, 121.

dropping like a stone, 'England's policy in the past has been to treat Ireland as a conquered and subject country. If there is a change in the policy of subordinating Ireland to English interest, then there appears to be [the] possibility of peace.'"3

The next two weeks passed uneventfully, except of course for the shoot-out in front of Brompton's Oratory on the 18th.

Regarding that incident, Collins and his party of intelligence agents were unable to turn up any leads as to who was responsible. After his near-tragic Athy encounter and his conversation with Shadow, Aran again brought up the matter of Eddy Hawkins and his possible vendetta, but Collins dismissed it as pure rubbish. But despite the Big Fellow's cavalier attitude regarding the entire affair, Aran, Gabriel and the other body guards were in a state of heightened alert.

❧

The Irish Rebel, Gay, Cú and Liam Tobin usually took turns driving Collins to and from the plenary sessions. One would drive and the other two would bide their time in an anteroom, waiting for Mick to emerge from his meeting. Occasionally he'd call for one of them to collect a certain document or some papers from Hans Place or Cadogan Gardens and bring them to the conference room.

Not privy to the sessions themselves, the Gortman learned of their substance second hand. Collins was good about keeping his handlers informed of the conference's progress.

Specific areas of discussion at the first seven plenary sessions included trade, finances, Ulster's partition, coastal defences and naval ports, dominion status, allegiance to the British Crown, the idea of External Association, Truce infractions and the establishment of a north-east Boundary Commission.

Michael took an active role in each topic while his fellow plenipotentiaries usually restricted themselves to their areas of expertise. Mick was particularly strident in his demands for

---

3. Ibid.

reparation being paid to Connie Crowe's family for his senseless death. The Big Fellow also introduced the idea of a Boundary Commission to help resolve the partition issue.

Earlier that summer, de Valera assured Lloyd George that Ireland had no intention of coercing Ulster's six north-eastern counties into joining them. He'd hoped reason and economic pressure would resolve their differences instead of using force. Lloyd George agreed wholeheartedly with this tactic. During the fourth plenary session on the 14th, the Welshman stated, "But we promise you to stand aside and any efforts to induce Ulster to unite with the rest of Ireland will have our benevolent neutrality."[4]

Later that day, Arthur Griffith expressed his delight with Britain's apparent endorsement of Collins's Boundary Commission idea. "…if the majority of the North-East are not to be coerced they in turn must not coerce others."[5]

On the 24th, Griffith and Collins quietly suggested to Lloyd George that they'd be interested in breaking away from the plenary-session format and use a more intimate sub-conference arrangement to carry on their talks.

The Welshman jumped at the idea. Both he and the two Irish leaders wished to streamline the talk's process and limit the number of delegates who were seated around the plenary table. The British had nine men representing their interests and the Irish had seven. Additionally, Lloyd George disliked two of his team's members while Childers was detested by Griffith and distrusted by Collins. The Big Fellow had described Childers's council and opinions as being "…like farmland under water–dead."[6]

Soon after the talks began, Collins discovered that Childers's reports back to the cabinet in Dublin included not only a running account of their daily negiotiations but included his own biased observations. In Michael's own words, they were "…masterpieces of half-statements, painting a picture far from the true state of things."[7]

---

4. Ibid., 130.
5. Ibid.
6. Kee, op. cit., 155.
7. Dwyer, op. cit., 67.

The first two weeks of talks had been a testing period. The members sized up one another, stated their positions, exchanged points of view, but no important decisions were made. By discontinuing the general sessions, the talks became more pointed, less time consuming and more direct. Often Griffith, Collins, Lloyd George and Chamberlain met as a foursome. Occasionally, it was simply the two governments talking one to one. Over the next weeks, there were twenty-four such informal sub-conference rounds. It was from these meetings that the core of the Peace Treaty emerged.

❧

Collins was in a dither. He was anxious not to miss the late afternoon train to Holyhead and his return to Dublin for the weekend.

While waiting for his last sub-conference notes to be typed by the secretarial staff, Michael was busy sorting through a stack of important documents he'd need for his weekend meetings. Besides a Saturday afternoon briefing with the Dáil cabinet during which he and Arthur were scheduled to attend, Michael was also meeting with the Supreme Council of the IRB. As its president, he'd met with them twice after the London talks had begun, both during Dublin weekend visits. In addition to these two usually lengthy meetings, the Big Fellow planned to meet with Richard Mulcahy, IRA Chief of Staff, and General Seán Mac Eoin. He wanted a full report on the current state of the army: its enlistments, preparedness and general ongoing training. Collins wanted to be sure, if hostilities were to break out again, Ireland would be as ready as possible to meet force with force. Finally, he was dining with his fiancé Kitty Kiernan in one of the Gresham Hotel's private suites on Saturday evening.

Usually, Collins travelled with six or seven bodyguards in addition to John Chartres. Griffith usually joined him on the weekend journeys home. This time, however, his party was smaller than usual. Besides the head of the Irish team, Aran, Gabriel, Liam Tobin and Tom Cullen would be their aides.

In separate automobiles, Ned Broy and Emmet Dalton drove the Irish party to Euston Station. The six men boarded the train that connected with the Dublin overnight mail boat with only minutes to spare.

After locating their compartments in one of the train's first class carriages, Collins, Gabby and Tobin headed for the dining car to enjoy a drink or two followed by supper. Arthur, Aran and Cú stayed behind. They wanted to relax and, hopefully, nap for an hour or two.

When the Corkman and the others returned two hours later, Art, Aran and Cú walked down for their evening meal.

After arriving at Holyhead, both Collins and Griffith fell asleep in the departure lounge. Though the benches were hard, that didn't seem to bother the two negotiators.

Michael had been keeping late hours and, as a consequence, so had his body guards. The Big Fellow was a celebrity in London and many of his off hours were filled socializing. Society hostesses fell over each other inviting him to dinners and the like. All seemed to find him devastatingly handsome and quite debonair.[8]

Four of his dear friends, occupying much of his time, were Moya and Crompton Llewelyn Davies and Lady Hazel and Sir John Lavery. Both were prominent, wealthy families who had homes in Dublin as well as in London. Rumours circulated that Michael had had a sexual relationship with both women, but it was mostly hearsay. The Corkman ignored the rumour mongers, discounting their gossip as petty jealously, while he continued to enjoy his friends' warm London hospitality.

Last night had been no exception with Collins arriving at the Davies posh home at half seven for dinner. Both Aran and Gay fought sleep as they waited for the lengthy meal to conclude.

After having their tea in the kitchen, the two friends played cards and read in a small waiting room just off the main parlour. They wagered as to what time Michael would call them for the drive back to their rented digs. Aran guessed half eleven. Gabriel

8. Mackay, op. cit., 218.

said it would be after one. Gay was right. Finally, they heard Mick's booming, cheerful voice bidding his hosts 'good night' at ten minutes after one.

"Jaysus, Gay, I don't know how he keeps up with the hours he does. The three of us were out the door and to early Mass this…I mean yesterday morning…before seven."

"That's why they call him the Big Fellow," joked Gay.

❧

The mail boat was late loading and taking on fuel. It was after three in the morning when the lights of Holyhead finally disappeared from sight. Arthur Griffith was in his tiny below-deck compartment. Outranking Tom, Liam Tobin claimed the upper bunk while Cú stood watch by the companionway just outside the head delegate's door.

With several hours of restful sleep, first on the train and then in the ship-terminal building, Collins wasn't sleepy. Together the Corkman, Aran and Gay walked the top deck. It was surprisingly mild for an early November night on the Irish Sea. Despite the dozen or so dim emergency and safety lights strategically situated around the ship, it was a dark night. Thousands of stars dotted a moonless sky.

With his two companions, Michael talked about the merits of continuing the Ulster-goods boycott…the one the Dáil had officially declared at end of May, but, in fact, had been selectively initiated by some county councils as early as March, 1920.

"Sure, it's putting the squeeze on 'em, but it's hurting our economy too," said Michael. "Catholics in the North are still being thrown out of their jobs, maybe even more than ever, while England just increases her shipments to and from Belfast."

"…and don't forget, Michael, there's the matter of the increased violence in the Six Counties. I'd call it a sectarian pogrom, if you ask me…and it seems to be getting worse," said Gabriel. "The bastards up there are putting the pressure on our nationalist communities…afraid our successes down here might influence London to drop their north-east Ulster claim."

"Seems to me, if there's any delay in bringing along the six-counties and uniting Ireland, Craig and his lot will want to do away with the RIC and establish their own police force. In the meantime, the decision to create and then arm the Specials[9] was a predictable cock-up. Can you imagine the fecklessness of it, giving guns to that crowd? Wilson and Macready should be tarred and feathered." Aran's voice had an edge of defiance mixed with sarcasm.

"Don't forget, we're to blame too," replied Collins. "Sure our people in the North have been under the gun, so to speak, ever since the Irish chieftains fled their homelands after the Battle of Kinsale back in 1601. Displaced, murdered and subjugated, the Irish Ulsterites have had to endure the wrath of the transplanted, mostly Protestant, land grabbers ever since."

"Now Michael, you don't have to lecture me on the plight of Ulster. In case you've forgotten, I'm an O'Neill so," interrupted Aran.

"No offence intended, my friend. I was just trying to point out that being Irish in Ulster has always been difficult, especially these last ten years. Ever since the talk that Irish Home Rule might become reality, the Unionists have been very protective of what they think is theirs."

Collins paused to lean against the ship's railing. "Sure, I haven't made matters easier for the folks up there either. We've been secretly shipping guns to the North for some time now...you know that. Ever since Carson brought all those weapons into Larne back in '14, his Ulster Volunteer Force has been itching for a fight. So to safeguard our own interests, we've been sending our lads weapons to protect themselves."

---

9. In late 1920, a special police force, the Ulster Special Constabulary, was created. Many of its membership were recruited from the ranks of Edward Carson's former Ulster Volunteer Force. The constabulary was divided into three groups: the c. 3,500 'A' Specials were full-time members; the c. 16,000 'B' Specials were part-time members; the c. 1,000 'C' Specials were a reserve force called into service only in emergencies. From 1920 to the early 1990s, when the Specials were finally disbanded, the 'B' Specials earned themselves the reputation of being vicious, sectarian vigilantes, enforcing their own brand of unionist/loyalist justice in nationalist/republican communities throughout Northern Ireland.

Resuming their walk, Gabriel said, "Sure, you're damn if you do and damn if you don't. Arming Nationalists just means the Unionist leadership continues arming and inflaming their side."

Before Michael or Aran could reply, a shot rang out, pinging off the ship's railing just in front of them.

"Bloody hell," cried Collins. "Are we under attack here?"

POW...a second gunshot exploded. Its bullet ploughed into Aran's right arm.

The Irish Rebel let out a yell, crying, "For fuck sake, I'm hit."

Grabbing his right arm, the Gortman threw himself to the deck. Keeping his wits about him, he rolled toward a companionway about ten feet off to his right.

Both Collins and McCracken spun around and made for a metal partition, jutting out from the ship's main superstructure onto the wooden promenade.

Two more projectiles smashed into the walkway where they'd just been standing.

"Are you all right, Aran?" cried Gabby, concern clearly audible in his voice.

Silence.

This time it was Michael's turn, "Aran, where are ya, son?"

More silence.

"Son-of-a-bitch," cursed the Corkman under his breath. "Maybe he's really hurt."

"Please God he's not," responded Gabriel.

More silence.

At least he's not moaning or crying out in pain, reasoned Gabriel.

"Michael, are ye armed?" whispered Gabriel.

"Feckin' right I am," came his commander's low but indignant reply.

"Good. Stay out of sight right here and cover my back. I'm going to work me way around to the far side of this tub. I can't imagine those shots went unheard. So for God's sake, mind yourself. Wouldn't want any of the crew gunned down by mistake or someone shooting at you again."

"Bloody hell, I'm no eejit. Just because you were out killing Tans while I sat in an office pulling strings doesn't mean I can't take care of business."

"Sorry. Didn't mean to insult your abilities...just looking after your hide, old stock."

"I know that. Now, get the hell out of here. I'll be grand, but you be damn careful yourself. I'm not of a mind to be after driving down to Cahir with bad news," mumbled Michael under his breath.

"Me either," replied Gay.

Crouching low, Gabriel headed aft. With his Webley & Scott revolver primed for action, the Irish-American darted between wooden benches, suspended lifeboats and metal supports marking the deck.

From up above, in the direction of the bridge, Collins saw a shaft of light pierce the darkness.

"Anyone down there?"

No response.

"I say, is there anyone down on the deck?"

More silence.

After a few moments, the light switched off.

Fucking hell, thought Collins. *This is a bloody mess. Maybe Aran was right about that louser Hawkins.*

Two, three then five minutes passed...just the sound of the ship burrowing its way through the placid Irish Sea.

Suddenly, the peaceful night air was punctuated by the sound of gun fire. POW, POW, POW...Collins couldn't count the number of rounds exploding, there were so many and so close together.

Jaysus wept, this is serious. I'm going to have to find some better cover right now.

Suddenly, the cry of a man's voice pierced the inky blackness. It was a blood-curdling shriek cut off in mid scream.

That didn't sound like Aran or Gay's voice. At least, please God, I hope it wasn't, thought the Corkman.

Pausing a moment to consider his options, the Big Fellow was suddenly aware of footsteps coming in his direction from the bow of the ship...unhurried but steady, they drew nearer.

Pulling back further into the shadow of the ship's superstructure, the Corkman waited, gun at the ready.

"Michael, are you there?"

It was Gay's voice.

Exhaling, Collins exclaimed, "Jaysus, Mary and Joseph, what's going on? It sounded like the GPO on Easter Week all over again."

Still on edge, Michael cautiously stepped out into the dim light of the walkway.

"This way...follow me. See what we have," ordered Gabriel.

"We? Don't tell me...it's Churchill, disguised as a renegade seaman on board keeping an eye on me?" joked the Big Fella. He was obviously relieved the drama of the moment had passed.

As the two men made their way forward, Collins demanded, "Gay, just what'en the hell's going on. Is Aran all right?"

"You'll see."

Rounding the bow of the ship, Gabriel began scrambling up a ladder affixed to the side of the superstructure.

With Collins on his heels, the two made their way up onto a small deck, a dozen feet or so above the ship's main walkway. There was Aran, arm wrapped in a bloody towel. With him was Tom Cullen. Both smiled when they saw their friends appear.

From up above, the ship's captain was visible, leaning over the bridge wing, looking down at them. At the same time, two others, bathed in a spotlight and dressed in nautical attire, were making their way toward them on metal steps fastened to the outside of the ship's bridge.

❧

Michael, Gabriel and Cú were comfortably seated around the captain's mess table. Mugs of steaming hot tea and a plate of Jacob's biscuits decorated its surface. Griffith and Tobin were nowhere to be seen. Apparently, they'd slept through the entire episode.

The ship's master, seated at the head of the table, busied himself, making notes in his log. His second in command, at the other end of the table, studied Collins. He watched in awe at every move the famous Irishman made.

Aran sat in a chair off to one side of the others. The ship's purser who was standing next to him smiled and remarked, "There...almost as good as new, young man."

He'd just finished attending to the Irish Rebel's wounded arm. The prognosis was good: only a flesh wound, minimal bleeding, no apparent bone or nerve damage, see a doctor as soon as possible after you arrive into Dublin.

"You're lucky," commented the purser to the Gortman. "Sorry, I can't say as much for the other two."

Collins took a swallow of whiskey from the small glass beside his mug and said, "Gabriel, why don't you fill the captain in on what went on out there."

"Not much to say, Mick."

Turning to face the head of the table, he began, "Aran, that's Aran Roe O'Neill with the arm over there, Michael Collins, you know who he is, and meself, Gabriel McCracken, were stretching our legs and catching a breath of fresh air up on deck...I'd say it was about half three."

Looking for more tea, Gay nodded in the direction of the steward.

"From out of the dark, someone began shooting at us. Mr. O'Neill was hit in the arm and crawled off toward the protection of a nearby companionway. At the same time, Mr. Collins and I ran for cover behind a bulkhead partition."

Adding some milk and a scoop of sugar to his tea, the Irish-American continued. "Mr. Collins stayed back, guarding the starboard walkway. I moved around the ship's stern, taking up a position on the port decking. That's when I ran into Mr. Cullen here and our wounded comrade. Seems Mr. O'Neill had gone below and located Mr. Cullen. After wrapping his arm in some towelling from Mr. Collins's quarters, they came up onto the deck very near where I was positioned."

Gabriel looked at both Aran and Cú for story confirmation. Both nodded in agreement.

"We waited a minute or so, trying to discover the source of the assault. Presently, we heard voices. Determining they were about to commence their attack again and, in the process, foolishly exposing themselves to our position, we opened fire. Unfortunately, the light was poor. In trying to disable them, they were mortally wounded."

Finally, Gay said, "I wish we could've taken them alive. I'd liked to know who they are and what they thought they were about."

"That's it, Captain," concluded the Big Fellow. "Need any more for your report?"

"No...no, Mr. Collins...that'll do it. I'll turn their bodies over to the RIC in Kingstown. If there is anything else, they'll know where they can reach you. I'm just thankful to God above, you four made it through with only that one scratch."

Rising, the captain said, "The four of yis are welcome to spend the rest of the night in here. Those two benches over there pull out into make-shift bunks. There's more tea, biscuits and the fixins' for a sandwich in the press. Just make yourselves at home...it's an honour to have you on board."

Before he returned to the bridge, the captain stuck out his hand to the Big Fellow. "Good luck, Mr. Collins, with your business in London. Like the rest of Ireland, I'm counting on you to bring us through."

"We're doing our damnedest," replied the Corkman.

Finally alone with his comrades in the mess, Collins turned to Gay, "When we're away from here, I want to know what really happened up there on that deck."

Gabriel smiled and saluted, "Aye, aye, captain."

9

"The very title of the agreement which the del-
egates brought back from London —'Articles of
Agreement for a Treaty Between Great Britain
and Ireland' —announced a new era in Irish
history, a change as fundamental in its way as
that brought about by the arrival of the Norman
barons seven centuries before. The use of the word
'Treaty' conferred a status Ireland had never
before seen granted."

Robert Kee

Thursday evening, 1 December 1921

*A*ran Roe O'Neill's sixth sense told him things were coming to a head. He could feel the tension in the air. Collins was not his usual self, nor were the other delegates. After two months of being thrown together in close proximity, the Gortman had an understanding of what made each plenipotentiary tick. Their ways and moods certainly reflected their individual personalities. As for Michael, he was more withdrawn and less jocular than usual.

Prudently, he'd taken the Holyhead-crossing attack seriously, as opposed to the Brompton Oratory incident. The Big Fellow had alerted his spy networks on both sides of the Irish Sea to find out what they could. They were ordered to report back directly to him.

Looking back on that sleepless crossing more than a month ago, Aran remembered the mail boat being met at Kingstown by several IRB men early that morning. After a short motor car ride into Dublin, Gabriel and he were dropped off at the Mater Hospital on Eccles Street to have his injury looked after. Sure, the purser had been correct in his diagnosis: the bullet hadn't done any real damage.

With the gunshot wound cleaned, dressed and his arm fitted with a temporary sling, the Rebel recalled walking back to Rutland Square for breakfast with Gabby. Together, they'd discussed the shipboard incident in detail. A pattern of violent, personal assaults was rearing its ugly head, giving more and more weight to Shadow's earlier warning about Eddy Hawkins. Taken in isolation, the first incident in Athy could be discounted as nothing more than happenstance. Combined with the London church shooting, they might be regarded as simply coincidence. But the three lumped together...well, a pattern was emerging.

Aran couldn't be sure if anyone in his circle of friends was specifically being targeted. All he knew was that he'd been the only one of them involved in each attack.

Looking back over time, the Gortman certainly had had a number of run-ins with your one, Major George Henry Hawkins. Gabriel was certainly living testimony to that. They'd been together on each occasion: the RIC barrack's raid in Craughwell back in June, 1919; their tortured interrogation in Tipperary Town a few weeks later; the mountainside fire-fight above Ballynagree in the Boggeraghs that following summer; and finally, the shoot-out at Shadow's safe-house just outside Limerick Town earlier this year.

Thoughts of that last encounter had shaken Aran to the quick. How could such a simple plan for testing the loyalty of one of their IRA comrades go so terribly wrong? Though Gay finally put an end to the major's murdering ways on that soft, grey afternoon, Shadow's wife, an innocent victim of accident, had been tragically killed. It was a burden the Gortman would take to his grave.

Michael, Lee Mellowes, Shadow, Gabriel and a small group of handpicked Flying Gaels had all played a part in the planning and execution of that ambush. That is, after the IRA Executive had authorised the man's execution.

Despite his dastardly and often cowardly tactics, Hawkins's likely involvement in Brigid's death had tipped the scales in favour of his planned elimination in Aran's mind.

Now, it seemed as if Hawkins's brother might be behind this recent series of attacks, but who was he after? Gabriel and himself? Sure, that was possible, maybe even expected in light of everything. Shadow? That didn't seem likely. He was only indirectly involved in Eddy's brother's death. Michael? He was even more removed from the action than Shadow.

The more Aran thought about things and discussed them with Gabriel, the more likely he reasoned they weren't personal attacks at all. Rather, they were attempts, isolated or otherwise, to destroy Ireland's chances of ending partition and fulfilling her dream of freedom and independence from British rule. The most plausible culprits would be disgruntled unionists from the north-east. Fanatically loyal yobs bent on retaining British rule in at least one part of Ireland.

One thing, however, troubled Aran. There was that cryptic slip of paper found on one of the dead mail-boat assassins.

The Big Fellow, Cú, Gay and he all agreed they'd never laid eyes on the two before. Michael even had Arthur and Liam view the bodies. No luck there either.

The two dead men looked like they were in their twenties. Each was of average height and weight with no distinguishing marks or features. One was even what you might call 'good looking.' Their pockets were empty except for the mysterious note, two packets of Woodbines, a box of pocket matches and a small bag of 9mm shells. No identification. No labels in their clothing. There was nothing in the way of a clue to tell who they were or what their true intentions might have been. Granted they'd only a brief time to search the bodies, but both Gay and he felt confident they'd not missed anything.

The slip of paper they'd found in one of the predator's shirt pockets was a small torn-off piece of some rather ordinary-looking stationery. In its centre was a simple inch-round, circular black spot. Above it, printed in black ink, were the words M-I-C-H-A-E-L C-O-L-L-I-N-S.

Who in the hell knew what that meant? Was it the name of their intended victim or simply a warning to be left behind on their prey, be he alive or dead?

All Aran could remember about the image of a 'black spot' was from his reading Robert Lewis Stevenson's *Treasure Island* years ago. Something about "...if they tip me the black spot, it's me old sea chest they're after..." But that didn't make any sense. Neither did the vague connection with rose bushes and their black spot disease. The Gortman briefly thought of and then dismissed any link with the McCrackens' pub in Cahir, the Black Rose. Finally, there were the traffic calming signs being posted along hazardous sections of roadway in both England and Ireland, large black spots that warned approaching drivers of dangerous patches where serious accidents had occurred in the past.

The only other possible association the Gortman could think of between the image of a 'black spot' and Hawkins was his brother's odd nickname, Black Eddy, but that seemed unlikely.

Aran and Gabriel puzzled over all the little bits and pieces surrounding the mystery. Together, they agreed to discuss things with Mick on their return journey to London that following evening. They would encourage the Big Fellow to alert his Dublin and London contacts, hoping they might ferret out information regarding the mail boat attack.

❧

Collins called Aran, his bullet-wounded arm long since healed, Gabriel and Cú into the little room he'd been using for an office at Cadogan Gardens. It was after ten in the evening. A cold December wind rattled the windows.

After filling each man's glass with two fingers of Jameson, the Big Fellow walked over and poked at the small coal fire burning in the grate.

Turning, he smiled at his three comrades. Despite his vain

attempt to appear upbeat, Michael looked tired and dejected. Even to the casual observer, the stress of the last two months was clearly visible on his face. Aran had noticed its gradual progression and had done his best to offer Mick daily encouragement. Lately though, Michael seemed to ignore even his friend's support, preferring to keep to himself.

"Well lads," Collins began, "the work here is nearly done. A lot of the boys back home are going to be disappointed. Sure, I can only imagine what their reaction will be to the agreement we'll bring back."

"Bollocks, Mick," countered Tom. "'Tis just the beginning...it's not the end. We've taken everything the Sassenach has thrown at us...the Tans, the Auxies, their reign of terror. We came through it all. If they won't give us what we want and deserve, we'll have another go until it's ours."

"That's the trouble, Tom. We succeeded in the past because we stuck together. This time I'm afraid it won't be that easy. Division not unity will be our downfall unless the Long Hoor and the others do an about face."

Collins walked across the room. He pulled back a curtain and gazed out the window.

With his back to his audience, he said. "I think our team's done a good job of standing up to Lloyd George and his lot. The problem is we've had one hand tied behind our back since the very beginning. Our bargaining position's been too weak and theirs too strong."

Turning to face his three loyal comrades, he continued, "We knew this going in. Sure, I've managed to live with it, knowing if we held on together, Ireland could weather this storm. Our history tells us others in the past have done so. Daniel O'Connell did...Michael Davitt did...and Parnell did...or at least to some degree they did."

"And we will too," encouraged Gabriel.

"Ah well, time will only tell, won't it, Gay," answered Michael.

The Corkman moved to a chair and sat down.

"As you know, Childers's been sending daily reports back

to the cabinet, coloured as they might be by his narrow bias. More directly, I've been back to Dublin almost every weekend, updating Dev and our IRB lads. Furthermore, there's been no shortage of letters exchanged and information shared between Arthur, Dev and the rest."

"No one can fault you on that account, Michael," said Aran. "In fact, we're all going over again tomorrow evening, aren't we?"

"Aye, we are that," answered Collins. "But the sad fact of it is the team's made a grave mistake. Instead of focusing our energies on getting Ulster back in the fold, much of our discussions have focused on the issue of our allegiance to the crown."[1]

"But that's what the doctrinaire Republicans wanted. Break on Ulster but not on the crown. Hasn't that been their mantra all along?" said Gay.

"Yes, to a great extent it was," answered the Big Fellow. "But the vocal minority isn't the voice of the silent majority. I believe the bulk of Irishmen and women see things differently. They're more interested in practical issues…the ones affecting everyday life…rather than matters marked by subtle political differences having broad international implications."

Aran nodded his head slowly. During the past two months, his thinking had undergone changes. He'd come to realise that certain words and labels had become more important than the actual benefits that sprang from them. Words like 'Republic' and 'independence' had become so intertwined that some believed you couldn't have one without the other. If a 'Republic' wasn't achievable, then it was back to the battlefield until it was. Compromise was a forbidden word.

If de Valera's idea of 'External Association' wasn't conceded by the British, no amount of 'Dominion status' would be welcomed in exchange, even if the dividends were comparable.

---

1. Allegiance to the British crown was an all encompassing term. Besides defining Ireland's future relationship (association) with Great Britain, British national security was a key component. England was concerned with defending herself from enemy attack, if another war should break out. This insecurity was magnified with a potentially 'independent' Ireland off her western shore. Thus, in return for Dominion status, Britain demanded defence concessions, i.e. so called 'Treaty ports' with nearby aviation facilities for its naval base protection.

Gradually, sometimes even painfully, the Gortman had abandoned the idea of an Irish Republic as being the end-all. After listening to Collins and the others discuss matters, he'd come to realise that the word 'Republic' was in fact a symbolic representation of the actual freedom Ireland sought for herself. The Irish Republic, once a means to achieving broad ends, had become a narrow end itself. Aran understood that it wasn't the form of government that mattered as much as it was the freedom from foreign interference in Ireland's affairs that made the real difference.

This was not an easy realisation considering he'd fought side-by-side with men whom he feared no longer shared his point of view.

Arthur Griffith was never a revolutionary. He'd never espoused violence in achieving his constitutional ideal of dual monarchy. Griffith's political philosophy tolerated owing allegiance to a foreign monarch, even an English one, as long as that ruler had no say in Irish affairs. His concept of freedom was based on self-rule. Irish self-sufficiency would be a driving force, not isolation from the rest of the world as the words 'Sinn Féin' were often thought to mean.

Pearse and Collins were both doctrinaire Republicans at one time in their lives. Originally, Aran's teacher had been a supporter of Irish Home Rule, relying on government and the political process to achieve peaceful ends. But with England's decision to postpone its implementation until the First War was won, the Dublin educator changed. He'd become a militant physical-force adherent more interested in redemptive sacrifice than political process.

The Corkman had changed too. As Mick grew into manhood, he'd become a hard-line Republican. Embracing that vague yet powerful and compelling word 'Republicanism,' he'd sought to uphold the rule of law by demonstrating to the British that the consequences of their use of violence would not be tolerated in Ireland. But recently, his thinking had undergone a metamorphosis. Instead of physical force, he now sought political process via negotiations with Ireland's age-old foe. Hopefully, compromise would render the justice and freedom that guns and violence had failed to deliver.

Aran now wondered if men like Shadow, Liam Mellowes, Danny Kelly and others would join Michael in making the transition from gunman to politician. Would they help Ireland achieve its dream of freedom as she struggled to throw off the shackles of tyranny?

The question the delegates were struggling with was how much must be conceded to the British in order for them to obtain a just result for Ireland. The majority of Irish nationalists back home wanted national unity and greater independence while the minority hardliners, seeking a fabled Irish Republic, were bogged down in the peripheral issues of an oath of allegiance to the king and recognition of the crown. Even such revered men as Jonathan Swift and John O'Leary were not blinded by fanciful delusions. Unlike de Valera, Brugha and Stack, Aran remembered that even they were prepared to swear allegiance to a monarch, knowing that the vow didn't constitute grounds for royal intervention.

Michael had driven that point home after returning to London from one of his Dublin cabinet weekend visits. He caustically spoke of the differences between those with their heads in the clouds and those with their feet on the ground. In a word, Michael was voicing the…

Suddenly, Aran was aware of the Corkman's presence. The Big Fellow was standing over him looking down.

"Day dreaming or are my words putting you to sleep?" demanded Collins of his protégé.

Looking up, the Rebel saw Mick smiling at him.

"Sorry, sir. Just reflecting on something you'd said…about Dev and his lot."

Pushing a lock of his hair back into place with a sweep of his hand, Michael put his other on the Gortman's shoulder, "We not only have the English to contend with, but the boys back in Dublin make it doubly hard, no?"

Returning to his chair, Michael resumed his analysis saying, "As you know, lads, British public opinion has been working against us as well. Caring little about the disposition of Ulster while ever mindful of our lack of loyalty to their crown, the British military establishment seems willing to resume the war if we don't agree to settle. This throws the diehards of both nations up against one another again. The only saving grace will be world public opinion and the power of the British press. I sincerely doubt the English would risk military retaliation, especially if our counter offer is a reasonable one."

"What about Dev's idea of External Association?" asked Tom.

"No deal," said Collins. "Just like the notion of their granting us a Republic or recognising our autonomy, External Association, with its independence component, was a non-starter from the beginning. Limited Dominion status within the community of nations known as the British Empire is our only alternative. Either that or renew the fighting."

Michael rose from his chair. Addressing the fire, he added a shovelful of coal to its dying embers.

After refilling his glass, he passed the bottle to his friends.

"Gentleman, with a few minor details yet to be worked out, the British government is offering us what I choose to call Saorstát Éireann...something they're calling the Irish Free State. We'll have the same status as the other dominions except in the areas of trade and defence. Lloyd George is insisting on free trade and four naval ports. There are some other minor details, the biggest of which is the oath of allegiance to the Irish Free State and its yet-to-be-written constitution.

"That's all fine, but when you add adherence to the Community of Nations known as the British Empire along with loyalty to the king as head of state and the empire, problems arise. Just ask Childers."

The Corkman stood up. "Unfortunately, I think the oath could be the deal breaker. I'm betting the Long Hoor and his cronies, especially Cathal, will find it too hard to swallow."

As he headed for the door, Michael turned to his friends saying, "Food for thought, no? Now off wit' yas. We'll talk some more tomorrow."

❧

The entire delegation and all ancillary personnel returned to Dublin on the 2nd for weekend talks. Copies of the proposed draft Treaty were given to the cabinet for review.

When it became obvious that Griffith and Collins had done most of the negotiating, Cathal Brugha became incensed. He said that the British had handpicked 'their own men.' Arthur took umbrage at the remark and demanded an apology. Brugha refused.

Collins, coming to the aid of his colleague said, "Cathal, if you don't like what we have for you, get another five to take our place."

Thus, the tone of the day was set.

The President, avoiding personal attacks, rejected the document. To him the oath was unacceptable. He also didn't like it that north-east Ulster could vote itself out of the Free State in a month.[2] This is the same man who only weeks before had said, "If the status of Dominion is offered me, I will use all our machinery to get the Irish people to accept it."[3]

---

2. A clause in the proposed Treaty initially included the Six-County government as part of the Free State with the condition that within a month of the Treaty's ratification, by both Dublin & London, it could vote itself out of the thirty-two counties, restoring its partitioned status as determined by the 1920 Government of Ireland Act. If that were to happen, and all knew it would, a Boundary Commission would then be appointed to redraw the border between the two bodies based on the wishes of the citizenry. The English government led the Irish delegation to believe that Counties Tyrone and Fermanagh plus Derry City & parts of Armagh & Down would opt to rejoin the Free State while only small sections of Donegal, Cavan & Monaghan would choose to come into the northern Irish satellite. (Of course, Lloyd George led the Ulster leaders to believe just the opposite.) As history notes, border changes proved to be a pipe dream. Nevertheless, at the time, it seemed logical. The Free State projected that the remaining sections of the north-east would prove to be both politically & economically unviable. Thus, the Six Counties would eventually be forced to join the other twenty-six, finally reuniting Ireland.

3. The British offered de Valera Dominion status exclusive of the partitioned counties during their initial, informal summer talks in 1921. Dev made two counter demands: first, Dominion status inclusive of the six north-east counties; later, Dominion status with total independence for the southern twenty-six

During the lunch break, Michael, Aran, Gabby and Cú Cullen taxied across town to meet with the IRB's Supreme Council. Earlier in the morning Mick had sent over a draft copy for his comrades to study.

The discussion lasted forty-five minutes. The Council was in general agreement with the proposed document, but also had some misgivings regarding the oath of allegiance. They gave Mick a revised oath proposal for him to study and discuss with his fellow delegates. As imagined, the IRB men were not happy with the Ulster clause and defence concessions as outlined in the draft.

After taking careful notes, the Corkman gathered up his papers and headed back to Mansion House. The cabinet was scheduled to resume its discussions at three o'clock.

On their return taxi journey, Michael asked Tom to remain behind in Dublin when the rest of them departed for London on Sunday evening.

"Tom, I want you here to ready things for my return. I don't think we'll be over there much longer."

Cú's only reply was a loyal, "Yes, sir…as you wish, Mick."

The Dáil cabinet meeting didn't break up until after eight that evening. With the members anxious to leave, there was some confusion as to who was to do what next. Several things were clear, however. The delegates were to return to London and continue bargaining with the British. The oath was the major topic of dissatisfaction.[4] Everyone except Griffith agreed it must be reworked or, if not, rejected. The seven cabinet men also thought the trade and defences clauses must be revised.

---

counties. Both rejoinders were rejected out of hand by Lloyd George. Kee, op. cit., 147.

4. "The chief mistake the Irish delegation made was to allow the two all-important issues of the Crown & Ulster to become confused. They did not sufficiently single out Ulster as the issue on which to challenge the British. This was largely because, though the unity of Ireland was more important than the issue of allegiance to most Irish citizens, the issue of allegiance was of equal importance to the minority of Republican dogmatists whom the delegates also represented." Kee, op. cit., 150.

As the meeting dragged on, Bob Barton again argued that de Valera should accompany the team back to London. Once more, Dev refused, stating that if he were to do so, the English might interpret his presence as a sign of weakness. Éamon thought the Irish could squeeze out a few more concessions from the other side, but with him present, it might not be possible.[5]

Just the before the cabinet meeting finally ended, Arthur Griffith affirmed that he wouldn't break on the issue of the crown. "When the last compromise has been achieved, I plan on signing the document. I'll then bring it back to the Dáil...they're the proper body to decide if we go to war or not."

Cathal Brugha retorted, "If you do that, you'll tear this country from top to bottom."

Considering Brugha's remark, Griffith paused, then replied, "I suppose you're right, Cathal. I'll tell you what...I'll go back and not sign. What I'll do is I'll bring it back to Dublin...to the Dáil and to the Irish people, if necessary."

Michael ended the evening on a rather ominous note. When asked about his intentions of signing or not, the Big Fellow said, "I will not agree to anything which threatens to plunge the people of Ireland into a war not without their authority. Still less do I agree to being dictated to by those not embroiled in these negotiations. If they are not in agreement with the steps which we are taking, and hope to take, why then did they themselves not consider their own presence...in London?"[6]

❄

As Collins and his party boarded the mail boat to Holyhead on Sunday evening, 4 December, he told them to pack up everything when they arrived back in London. His exact words were, "We won't be staying much longer."

5. In point of fact, de Valera had no authority to represent Ireland at this point. He'd not been appointed by the Dáil to the negotiating team as a plenipotentiary.
6. Dwyer, op. cit., 88-89.

Reflecting on the five months since the Truce had been agreed to, Aran Roe felt he'd aged years. He'd also observed changes in the Corkman as well. Not just the ordinary changes brought on by lack of sleep or exposure to stress, but more fundamental changes of thought and attitude.

Was he mirroring Michael...certainly, to a degree. There was no doubt the Big Fellow influenced his thinking. Mick's ability to analyze a problem, consider the alternatives, compromising if necessary, and plot out a course of action was remarkable. He admired the courage and force of character the Big Fellow displayed as he confidently made difficult decisions. Michael's decisiveness was only reinforced by the loyalty and respect shown to him by his friends.

Being with Michael in London had been a life-changing experience for Aran. From the innocent, naïve boy of seventeen, who'd first arrived in Dublin to attend Pearse's school, to the maturing yet idealistic guerrilla fighter, inspired by dreams of freeing Ireland from the grip of the Sassenach stranger, to the present. Now, just days before his twenty-third birthday and his marriage to Sarah Anne, the Gortman felt he'd gained an understanding and insight into the ways of the world. Instead of accepting things at face value, he'd learn to question the motives of others, to look below the surface for underlying causes and to critically examine his own thinking and behaviour.

He'd been lucky to have such kind, wise and understanding teachers. In addition to his family, the Irish Rebel had benefited from three remarkable mentors: first Pearse, then Shadow and now Collins.

Aran had also witnessed the Big Fellow maturing. Mick had moved beyond his unquestioning, doctrinaire beliefs to adopt a more critically astute, insightful political perspective. The Rebel remembered reading a letter Michael had written to a fellow Republican back in the spring. In it he'd stated he was standing for an Irish Republic without any qualifications, but three months ago, Collins told another that an Irish Republic means Irish freedom.[7]

---

7. Dwyer, op. cit., 51.

Recently, the Corkman had spoken to him of his desire to invite the north-east Unionists to join the rest of Ireland in forming a new government...a government that would provide for the ambitions of all. Michael maintained that the southern counties could afford to be generous in their offer of unification. Repeatedly, Michael had told him, "We can afford to give them even more than justice."[8]

❈

The Irish delegation huddled at Hans Place on Monday, the 5th. The distrust between the delegates that had been brewing for two months seemed to overflow. They argued among themselves as they reviewed the substance of their weekend Dublin cabinet talks.

Regarding the revision of the oath, Barton thought the President had suggested recognising the King as the 'Head of the Association' while Childers's notes stated 'King of the Associated States.' It was a subtle difference sure, but enough to drive another wedge between men of differing minds.

Their debate continued. Should they resubmit Dev's proposal for External Association in lieu of Britain's offer of limited Dominion status? Collins erupted at this suggestion, stating to do so would be a waste of time. In fact he went so far as to say, "Ireland's problem is not with London, but lies back in Dublin."

That afternoon, Griffith, Collins and Barton met with Lloyd George, Chamberlain, Birkenhead and Churchill at #10 in a final attempt to iron out their differences.

Michael took the offensive, demanding an answer to Craig's stance about assenting to the unity of Ireland. He maintained Ireland's position had always been based on its association with the British Commonwealth of Nations and was contingent on the unity of Ireland. Unless the Six County Prime Minister agreed to an all-Ireland Parliament, their delegation would not sign any treaty.

Lloyd George became agitated. He said the Irish were going

---

8. Ibid., 52.

back on their word not to break on the Ulster issue. Furthermore he said Mr. Griffith had promised so just several weeks earlier.

The Prime Minister dramatically rifled through a stack of papers on the table before him and produced a memorandum, signed by Arthur. The Welsh Wizard pushed the document toward the three Irishmen.

"In the past, you have always accused us of breaking faith. Now, do you think it's your turn to renege on your promise or do you pledge to keep your word?"

Lloyd George's challenge and the signed document caught the Irish negotiators by surprise. Griffith had forgotten the paper's existence. Thinking it a minor matter, he'd even failed to inform the others of it.

The substance of the letter assigned a Boundary Commission the responsibility of fixing north-east Ulster's border, if a negotiated agreement regarding an All-Ireland parliament could not be reached. Lloyd George said that such a condition would pressurise Craig, who had earlier suggested that Ulster become a separate Dominion. This side agreement would also demonstrate that London and Dublin were in agreement on the Ulster issue. Unfortunately, Griffith's signing could also be interpreted as his, and thus Dublin's, acknowledgement and acceptance of Ulster's partition.

Griffith, ever the gentleman that he was, said he'd honour his word. He'd break on the Ulster issue, but that it wasn't right for his team members to concede the point.

The discussion gradually moved on to other areas of concern. Collins had offered several minor changes to the proposed Treaty that morning and the British delegates now accepted them. One detailed revisiting the defence-clause issue in two years' time with the thought of Ireland taking some responsibility for her coastal security then. The English negotiators also accepted Collins's revised oath with only a few minor changes.[9] Finally, if the Irish

---

9. "I...do solemnly swear true faith and allegiance to the Constitution of the Irish Free State as by law established, and that I will be faithful to H. M. King George V, his heirs and successors by law, in virtue of the common citizenship of Ireland and Great Britain and her adherence to and membership of the group of nations forming the British Commonwealth of Nations." Pakenham, op. cit., 288.

would give on a couple of minor points, the British would drop their claim for free trade between the two parties and grant Ireland fiscal autonomy. This was an important concession to Michael. He'd now have a free hand in raising money at home and abroad, funds that would be needed to finance Ireland's new government.

All this while, Aran and Gay were in the anteroom, overhearing everything that was being discussed. Looking through the keyhole, the Gortman suddenly saw the Welsh Wizard jump to his feet.

"Gentleman," the Prime Minister called out in a loud voice, "my delegation is prepared to sign this document and sign it today."

Lloyd George looked at the three Irishmen seated around the table and demanded, "Are you prepared to do the same?"

The abruptness of the command caught the Irishmen off guard.

"Furthermore," Lloyd George said, picking up two envelopes that were lying on the table, "I have before me two envelopes. I must communicate with Sir James Craig tonight. A courier waits to take your reply via train to Holyhead and then by ship to Belfast."

Aran could see Michael gripping the arms of his chair. The knuckles of his hands were white.

"One envelop contains the Articles of Agreement agreed to by our two governments. In the other, a letter stating that the Irish representatives refused the oath of allegiance and refused to come into the Empire.

"If I send this second one, it's war and war within three days. The decision rests with you. Craig must have your answer by ten o'clock tonight. You have until then and no later to decide whether your country remains at peace or is catapulted back into war."[10]

As Michael walked out of the conference room, Aran and Gay had never seen such an expression of controlled anger and bottled up rage in their friend's face before.

---

10. Dwyer, op. cit., 97-98.

All Mick muttered was, "Hans Place...now!"

❧

No one suggested they ring Dublin on the telephone and ask for advice. That flew in the face of their 'private' cabinet instructions to which they'd all agreed to back in October. It also was at variance to Arthur Griffith's decision not to sign the proposed Treaty given only two days before.

Sometime around half five, the Irish delegates sat down around the large table in the Hans Place dining room. Seated behind them, forming an outer perimeter, were all the other members of the team excluding the secretarial and household staff.

The debated raged on and on. Griffith's signing was a given. Michael said he would sign. He told the gathering that he feared the worst if the IRA was forced to resume the fight. He also pointed out his ability to run an effective intelligence operation would be greatly compromised. His face and the identity of his key men were now known to all. They'd be marked men. Furthermore, he told his fellow negotiators that at the height of the War of Independence there were only two thousand Volunteers in the field.[11] The Corkman turned to look back at both Aran and Gabriel.

"Two of those two thousand are seated in this room. Do you wish to send these men out to be slaughtered...along with the rest?"

That was enough for Duggan. He confirmed his intentions of signing as well.

After a whispered conversation, Barton and Childers, the two cousins, excused themselves and left the room. Minutes later they returned. Barton said he would sign too.

When Bob Barton agreed to sign, Duffy made it unanimous.

---

11. "The IRA was growing in strength & influence; at the time of the Truce, it has been 3,000 strong, but by November 1921 it had 72,000 members. The new troops were referred to, rather contemptuously, a 'Trucileers,' keen to have the name of IRA membership without having actually done any fighting." Helen Litton. *The Irish Civil War: An Illustrated History*. Dublin, 1995, 39.

By now it was nearly two in the morning, almost four hours after Lloyd George's ultimatum.

Straightening their ties, buttoning their waistcoats and donning their jackets, the exhausted and frustrated plenipotentiaries, accompanied by their body guards, drove back to #10. At ten minutes past two o'clock, in the early morning hours of 6 December 1921, both parties signed the agreement.

On their way back to Cadogan Gardens, Collins spoke freely to Aran and Gay. "Unquestionably, the alternative to the Treaty, sooner or later, is war. To me it would be a criminal act to refuse to allow the Irish nation to give its opinion as to whether it will accept this settlement or resume hostilities."[12]

From behind the wheel, Aran said, "'Tis right the Irish people make the final decision."

Together, the three friends speculated as to the percentage of the population that would support the agreement. Collins said fifty-five to sixty percent of all concerned would. Gay thought the number would be even higher.

Aran, refusing to give a number, said, "The critical difference will be made up by Dev. If he supports it, it'll be a landslide. If not, and I suppose he won't, we'll have a fight on our hands. Brugha was no doubt right when he said it could split the country from top to bottom."

As they pulled up in front of #15 Cadogan Gardens, Collins said before they exited the motor car, "Aran...Gay, just think, think what have I got for Ireland...something which she has wanted these past seven hundred years. Will anyone be satisfied at the bargain? Will anyone? I tell you this, early this morning I signed my death warrant. I thought at the time how odd, how ridiculous...a bullet may just as well have done the job five years ago. Those signatures are the first real step for Ireland. If people will only remember that...the first real step."[13]

❧

---

12. Dwyer, op. cit., 102.
13. Ibid., 103-104.

Cú Cullen was standing on the Kingstown quay as the mail boat from Holyhead pulled into its slip. It was a cold, blustery Thursday morning in Ireland, but the country was alive with the news of the Treaty signing. Tom was joined by a welcoming honour guard put together by Mick's IRB supporters. It was, however, a disappointing welcome compared to the send-off they'd received at Euston Station last evening. Hundreds of Irishmen and women had greeted Arthur Griffith, Michael and their aides as the contingent headed for the train. The Big Fellow was even hoisted onto the shoulders of some enthusiastic individuals, alarming his guards who feared for the Corkman's safety.

Art, Michael, Aran, and Gay, surrounded by Liam Tobin, Joe Dolan, Joe Guilfoyle, Joe Leonard and Ned Broy were in the first group of passengers off the ship. Ever since the incident on the mail boat a few weeks back, Michael had insisted on greater security vigilance. Though his body guards were ready for action, there'd been no further trouble.

Griffith and Collins's arrival back on Irish soil marked a seminal moment in Ireland's history and a significant milestone in the Big Fellow's life. Michael and the other delegates had accomplished in two months what Ireland had struggled and fought for down through the centuries: basic freedom from English interference in its national and day-to-day affairs. Their achievement exceeded the aspirations held by most Irish nationalists just a decade ago when Ireland's third Home Rule bill was introduced in the House of Commons.

As the two delegates and their party emerged onto the ship's decking, a bystander cried out in a clear voice, "God bless ya, Michael." Another shouted, "Éireann go brách!"

As for Collins himself, his evolution from diehard Republican extremist to moderate political statesman was equally as impressive. From idealist to realist, he'd grown and matured as a man. Now, he was on the verge of leading Ireland into a new age of hope, prosperity and world importance. No longer would Éireann be Britain's pawn, subjected to her every whim and fancy. The only 'if' in the equation was, would Michael's fellow Republican comrades, the ones he'd associated with and commanded during the war years, continue to follow his lead?

Stepping off the gangplank, Mick called out to Cú, who was first to greet him, "Tom...Tom, what are our own fellows saying?"

"What's good enough for you is good enough for them," was Cullen's encouraging reply.[14]

After tipping his hat to a few bystanders, the moustached Collins stepped into a waiting motor car. Aran, Gay, Liam and Cú were on his heels.

As they pulled away from the quay, Tom said, "Word has it Dev's in a state...supposedly vacillating between raging anger and irritable depression. Rumour has it he's demanded Griffith, Barton and your cabinet resignations."

"The feckin' bastard," muttered Collins.

"Thanks be to God, Mick, but you're off the hook. Bill Cosgrave's come to the rescue. Apparently, he's persuaded the omnipotent one to wait until you've all had a chance to defend your actions in person."

"When's that?"

"This morning...at ten...in just over an hour," answered Cú.

"I knew he wouldn't embrace the document, that selfish son-of-a bitch. It didn't have his personal stamp of approval on it so he wants to reject it. Sure, we'll just see what the Irish people think. He'd his chance to go over and bargain with the Welsh Wizard, but no. He knew it would come down to this...Dominion status. That's what was on the table when we went over and that's what we brought back."

"Mick, be careful. I sure he's going to try and drive a wedge between you and the people," guessed Aran.

"Let him try," said Gay. "He'll have a fight on his hands if he does."

�֎

The cabinet meeting began a few minutes after ten. Besides the seven cabinet ministers, Childers, O'Hegarty and Kevin

---

14. Margery Forester. *Michael Collins: The Lost Leader.* Dublin, 1989, 260.

O'Higgins were in attendance. Several other ministerial subordinates were in the room so Michael had Aran and Gay sit in as silent observers.

The President rose and spoke first. Quivering with rage, he demanded to know why the delegates hadn't consulted him before signing, as they'd promised.[15]

Accusations flew around the table. Had they signed under duress? Griffith said he hadn't, as he'd agreed to sign prior to Lloyd George's ultimatum.

Barton felt he'd been under pressure to sign…psychological pressure. He said Lloyd George's threat of war if all members of their team didn't sign and sign that evening had pushed him over the brink.

"I didn't want Irish blood on my hands," said Barton. "The man refused us the opportunity to refer back here. Besides, weren't we vested with plenipotentiary powers?"

Collins maintained that if he was pressurised, it was simply because the cards were stacked that way…the realities of the offer on the table versus the prospects of plunging the country back into war. To do otherwise would have been foolish and irrational.

Rising to his feet, the Big Fellow said, "We are not descended from fearful men, and we will not be driven by fear into the unknown."

Pausing, Michael looked around the room, catching the eye of each man at the table. In a passionate voice he continued, "The very title of the agreement which we brought back from London announces a new era in Irish history, a change as fundamental in its way as that brought about by the arrival of the Norman barons seven centuries before. The use of the word 'Treaty' confers a status Ireland has never before seen granted."[16]

Brugha and Stack looked at Dev as if to say, *"Is it so?"*

Before he sat down, the Corkman addressed de Valera directly, "Mr. President, as we continue our discussion today and, I suppose, in the days ahead, please remember one thing: we must not confuse dissent with disloyalty."

---

15. Mackay, op. cit., 228.
16. Kee, op. cit., 152.

Again, looking around the table, Mick added, "...and please God, I beseech all of you not to forget...each one of us has fought for Ireland in the past...let us not resort to fighting among ourselves in the future."

The cabinet recessed for lunch.

Ninety minutes later the meeting resumed.

They talked and argued for hours. Bob Barton even blamed de Valera for the mess they were in. He accused the President of dithering and refusing to join the negotiating team.

De Valera blamed Griffith for signing and not keeping his Saturday-last word that he wouldn't sign.

Aran and Gay were shocked and amazed that the leaders of their country could behave with such venom and pettiness. It was an ugly display.

Finally, a vote was taken. The cabinet approved the Treaty by the narrowest of margins: Griffith, Collins, Barton and Cosgrave voting in favour...de Valera, Brugha and Stack voting against.

The meeting ended with O'Higgins, who didn't have a vote, making an eloquent plea for unity. He stated that though he didn't like the terms of the document, it had been signed and approved by the cabinet. It was now time to face the Dáil and the country. We must give Ireland a chance to accept or reject the Treaty on its own merits.

After listening to the cabinet quibble among themselves, it was apparent to Aran and Gabriel that de Valera and his supporters were caught in a trap...a trap between the London-signed agreement and the mythology surrounding the dream of an Irish Republic. There was also the overriding fear that if the Treaty, granting limited Dominion status, wasn't ratified by the Irish legislature, the Sassenach military would return with a vengeance. No doubt they'd do what the Tans and Auxies had failed to achieve. This time they wouldn't rest until they'd broken the people's spirit with their renewed brand of terror, fear, torture and death. Sure, the Irish people could only take so much before they were forced to bow down to the Stranger's whip-hand.

❧

Two days later the Supreme Council of the IRB met to consider the Treaty. As Head-Centre, Michael Collins presided. After a full discussion of the document, the Republican Council voted to endorse it. It did stipulate, however, that its Dáil membership was free to vote their conscience when the legislature convened to consider the matter. The only dissenting vote was cast by Liam Lynch. He regretted doing so but stated that his disapproval wouldn't impair his relationship with the Big Fellow.

His parting words had a haunting ring to them. "Thank God all parties can agree to differ."[17]

❧

During Michael Collins's two-month stay in London, Winston Churchill and Sir Henry Wilson, with their mutual disdain for Ireland, weren't hesitant letting him know that contingency plans were in the works. If the Irish government reneged on the proposed settlement, they'd ship an additional 100,000 British soldiers to Ireland. Furthermore, £100 million had already been set aside to finance this new, massive military effort, calculated to bring Ireland to its knees in just weeks. Finally, if this imperial effort was somehow slowed, the British Navy would be called upon to blockade key Irish ports, effectively halting the flow of goods to and from their island neighbour.

"You'll not escape our efforts this time, Mr. Collins," they warned.

Michael almost laughed out loud when he told Aran of their latest threat.

"Bluff and bluster, the two of them are," snarled the Corkman.

"Embarrassed they are that little Ireland held their colonial might to a stand-off," quipped Aran.

"Aye," said Michael. "Sure the world knows they're the stronger party. By holding them off as we did, we gained for ourselves a large measure of self-respect and a rare Irish victory to boot."

"But Michael," cautioned the Rebel, "we mustn't let that go

17. Dwyer, op. cit., 111.

to our heads. We know they're the stronger force. By treating with us, ye might think we're equals, but we're not. Churchill and Wilson were just letting you know they'll drop the other foot anytime they want."

"Of course you're right, my friend. It's just another of their cat and mouse games. They'll slap you in the face with one hand, and when you don't buckle under, they'll offer you a sweet with the other. If you reject that kindness, they'll seem justified in slapping you twice as hard the next time."

"Sure," said Aran, finishing the Big Fellow's thought. "They always maintain the high moral ground. Public opinion often sides with the aggressor, thinking the ungrateful victim deserves nothing more."

❧

Wednesday, 14 December, dawned dull and rainy.

"Sure, it wouldn't be Ireland if the sun shone all the time," joked Michael, as Aran Roe O'Neill, Gabriel McCracken and the Big Fellow dashed up the steps of University College Dublin on Earlsfort Terrace. The Dáil's much anticipated Treaty deliberation was minutes from beginning.

Gay and he had reserved seats on the bench just behind Michael's.

"I'm not asking for sunshine all the time, Mick," insisted Gay. "Just half the time would be grand."

"Uh-huh," mumbled Collins, his mind suddenly on other things.

Walking into the meeting hall, Aran noted how packed-out it was. Normally, such a conclave would've met in Mansion House, just up the way on Dawson Street, but because of a scheduled Christmas Fair, the Dáil had to find other accommodation.

The world press, represented by over a hundred reporters, was seated behind the Dáil's Ceann Comhairle. Seated to the Speaker's left were de Valera, Brugha and Stack. Diagonally across from the President and his men sat the five plenipotentiaries. The remaining Dáil membership found seats facing the assembly's Speaker while members of the public were positioned behind them. Finally, ancillary members of the Treaty's delegation party sat just behind the plenipotentiaries.

With such an arrangement, it was apparent to any keen observer that the imagined split in the Dáil's leadership over the Treaty had become reality. Clearly, the signing of that document had already divided Ireland. Could Civil War be far behind? Would Irish blood be spilled again on its mountainsides and valleys, even in its finest hour?

After the roll call, De Valera was first to speak. He began in Irish but quickly reverted to English. He said he'd like to continue in Irish, but knowing some members of the assembly weren't conversant in Gaelic, he'd speak English.[18]

With the eloquence of a diplomat, the President thanked the negotiating team for their efforts. Correctly, he noted that the team had acted properly. As Dáil plenipotentiaries, they'd the authority to sign any agreement they deemed proper and in Ireland's best interest.

"However," he chided the five men before him, "you failed in your pledge to the executive. You didn't submit the final draft for cabinet approval before signing."

This was the first time the world had learned of the cabinet's secret instructions to its delegation.

Looking directly at Griffith and Collins, he continued by reading the four paragraphs of clandestine orders.

"Now, regardless of whether you should've signed or not, we aren't here to debate that. We're here to consider the merits of the document you've brought before us and nothing more."

Leaning over, Aran whispered in Gabby's ear, "That lets Dev off the hook for his bloody, arrogant underhanded directives."

Gabriel nodded in agreement.

Ignoring the audience's surprised reaction to the secret-order revelation, the President asked the Speaker for an adjournment.

---

18. Later, de Valera admitted he himself didn't have a good command of Irish and that's why he decided to proceed in English. Ibid., 112-113.

He wished the cabinet to retire to executive session to discuss the differences between the plenipotentiaries and the cabinet more fully.

Leaning forward, Aran mumbled to the Corkman, "He wants to exclude the TDs, the public and the press from hearing him air his dirty laundry."

In the next moment, Collins was on his feet.

"Ceann Comhairle, if you please. If the President doesn't wish to make an issue of our signing, he shouldn't have brought it up. Mr. Griffith and the team didn't sign a Treaty. We signed an understanding that we now bring before ye. It's entitled 'Articles Of Agreement For A Treaty…' It is not a Treaty. It will only become such when this body and Britain's House of Commons ratify it so."[19]

"That's why we're here," interrupted de Valera.

"Is it?" queried Collins.

Before the President had a chance to respond, the Big Fellow continued, "Then tell me sir, why weren't the original Dáil instructions read into the record along with the cabinet's private ones?"

"They weren't?"

"No, they weren't. So if I may Ceann Comhairle…"

Michael read out the Dáil's original plenipotentiary directives, detailing their authorisation *to conclude* an agreement with Britain.

De Valera interrupted again. "Since the instructions clearly state 'to conclude,' isn't that what you've done?"

Arthur Griffith took the floor. "Though we had the right to bind this assembly to an agreement, we didn't. Neither did the British delegation bind their legislature. Both delegations' signatures imply referral not acceptance. The Dáil and the House of Commons *must* formally approve the agreement."

As Griffith took his seat, Michael rose again.

"Mr. Speaker, Mr. Griffith's words speak for all of us on our team. We have *not* acted outside of our authority. Furthermore, I take umbrage with those individuals who've chosen to call me 'a traitor' for doing my sworn duty."

---

19. Ibid., 114.

De Valera challenged Michael to name names.

"I'm a bigger man than that," answered the Corkman. "But if there is anyone here who wishes to challenge me, let him address me here, in public, or later, in private."

After several more exchanges, the assembly was adjourned so the cabinet could convene in private.

It was then that the President's motives for doing so became clear. He'd prepared an alternative document, hoping it would replace the London agreement. Dev further asked the executive to keep this proposal private, not disclosing its existence to anyone.

Dubbed Document No. 2 by Michael, it was almost a duplicate of the London-signed agreement. The partition clause remained, with only minor modifications. Predictably, the oath of allegiance was missing. Interestingly enough, the word 'Republic' wasn't used, but for the purposes of association it stated that Ireland *would* recognise His Britannic Majesty as head of their Association.[20]

In reality, Dev's alternative was nothing more than a restatement of his External Association proposal that had been voted down by London on each occasion it was presented.

Michael's reaction to it was one of utter amazement. He felt the differences between it and the original agreement were so slight that it wasn't worth taking a chance and risking the advent of war. Dev agreed to a point, but countered, maintaining that the differences were so minor that Britain wouldn't gamble on provoking a war with Ireland.

The private session ended with Document No. 2 being rejected.

The public consensus was clear. Piaras Béaslaí spoke for many when he said, "There is no alternative to ratification of the Treaty but war. Document No. 2 is no alternative if we must die. Men have died to the cry of 'Up the Republic', but I cannot imagine they would die for the cry of 'Up External Association.'"[21]

---

20. Litton, op. cit., 24.
21. Ibid., 27.

In the week that followed, thoughtful discussion was interspersed with heated accusations. Finally, with the debate still unresolved, the Dáil adjourned on a hopeful note for the Christmas recess on the 22nd.

Late in the afternoon, the President, apparently tired and haggard, rose from his bench. Looking pale but managing to smile, he said to the assembly, "There is a definite constitutional way of resolving our differences."[22]

That's wonderful, you Long Hoor, thought Collins, *but who in the bloody hell's going to find it?*

As the members stood, the Ceann Comhairle announced the Dáil would reconvene on 3 January.

Bidding adieu to their Dublin comrades, Aran and Gabriel headed west for a reunion with the Father, Mother and Larry McCracken, a Christmas homecoming followed closely by Aran and Sarah Anne's wedding.

❧

Sarah Anne, Áine and Larry McCracken met the two of them at the rail station at Limerick Junction. With their side arms out of sight and spirits high, Aran and Gabriel walked through the front door of the Black Rose. Father McCracken hadn't aged a day in the four-plus years since they'd left Virginia. Gay's mother looked grand as well. The only one of new arrivals to show his age was Larry. His curly black hair, now streaked with grey, was cut much shorter than Aran remembered. His lightly tanned skin still reflected a deeply rooted Celtic-Mediterranean connection. With twinkling brown eyes, Larry's good-natured and optimistic self-confidence brightened any room he entered.

Gay's father was just as Aran remembered, tallish but with slightly stooped shoulders from years of manual labour. The elder McCracken was overjoyed to be reunited with his son, daughter and Aran. The strength of the old man was still apparent when first he shook Aran's hand then gave the Irish Rebel a bear hug.

The welcoming reunion's excited chatter soon settled down.

---

22. Pakenham, op. cit., 266.

Everyone moved to Peter and Niamh's kitchen. Bottles of beer, glasses of whiskey and cups of tea were soon in evidence. Niamh and Mother McCracken made sandwiches as old and new stories made the round.

Gabriel, with little Mary on his knee, sat between his brother and father. While everyone was being entertained with Gay's account of their London and Dáil adventures, Aran and Annie slipped out of the room. After a few moments of passionate embracing, they headed out doors for a walk. There was much to talk about and last-minute plans to go over.

❧

On Christmas Eve, Aran and Sarah arrived into the O'Neill home. This was his first real Christmas at home, free from the threat of arrest, in six years.

Discounting last summer and the recent week in September, the Gortman had spent precious few days in the comfort of his family's home. As expected, another great reunion followed. His parents, grandfather, brothers and sister welcomed the wayfaring warrior with warmth and affection.

It had been two years since Aran had first introduced Annie to everyone. Again, she was welcomed with open arms.

Talk of London, the Treaty, old Christmas stories and the pending wedding, now less than a week away, filled the evening hours and the following day.

After Holy Christmas Mass, everyone returned to the farmhouse for dinner. It was a feast like none before. One of Aran's brothers had butchered and cleaned a goose. In addition to the fowl, a huge roast had been prepared along with several different kinds of potatoes, gravy, veg and freshly baked bread. Pots of tea and bottles of porter added to the festivities. Finally, a huge trifle and glasses of Irish whiskey topped off the gala.

After the wash-up, the O'Neills and Sarah Anne gathered around a roaring fire in the family sitting room. Grandchildren played with the gifts that had been opened the night before. Some of the men took their ease with pipefuls of tobacco before the fire. Aran's oldest brother brought out his guitar and led those willing in song.

The following day, St. Stephen's Day, Aran, his father and three brothers spent the morning walking the land and inspecting the animals. That afternoon Aran and Sarah went calling on several of the O'Neills' neighbours.

Later that evening after tea, they bid everyone goodbye and drove back to Cahir in Uncle Peter's car. Tomorrow was Aran's twenty-third birthday. A small celebration was planned and, of course, the wedding in two days time.

❧

The marriage was scheduled for eleven o'clock in the morning at St. Mary's Church. Noted for its fine lantern tower and pipe organ, the impressive building possessed a handsome chancel supported by two immense columns of polished Aberdeen granite.

For the past two nights, Aran had been banished to Gay and Áine's newly rented cottage on the edge of town. It was bad luck for the groom to lay his eyes on the bride prior to the ceremony. Sarah Anne was taking no chances. They'd said their goodbyes with a kiss and a wave on the night of Aran's birthday.

Though the church was only two blocks from the pub, Peter had arranged for five coaches to transport the wedding party. The first trap was reserved for Annie and her parents. In the second were Aran's parents, his grandfather, sister and two of his six brothers. The third transported Gabriel, Áine, Larry, Uncle Peter and Aunt Niamh. In the fourth, the one Aran dubbed 'The Revolutionary Run-about' was the Big Fellow himself. Accompanying him were Cú Cullen, Liam Tobin, Emmet Dalton and Danny Kelly. Finally, in the last coach sat the proud Aran Roe O'Neill, wearing a blindfold just in case. It was Gay's idea. More of your tomfoolery than superstition complained the Rebel to his friend. Joining Aran was his school friend Marty Richardson, Nayler MacGregor, in full kit mind you, and his best man, the baker and guerrilla fighter, Richard 'Shadow' Doyle.

With the ceremony concluded, the wedding party paraded

back to the Black Rose. This time Aran and Sarah Anne rode with Shadow and

Áine, Annie's matron of honour. They were followed by both sets of proud parents with the others riding behind. The forty or so church celebrants walked along after the last coach.

The pub was cleaned and polished to the nines. Food and drink filled the bar and surrounding tables. A fiddler, uillean piper plus a box and bodhran player supplied the music. As custom dictated, Aran and Sarah had the first dance but were not permitted to sing. That would be bad luck.

Aran joked that indeed it would be bad luck if he started singing. "I'd drive 'em all out of the place with a ringing in their ears that wouldn't stop for a week."

At least one member of each family in the village was expected to stop in and pay their respects. Not to do so would be regarded as a slight not easily forgotten. Besides, no one wanted to miss out on the merriment, not to mention all the wonderful food and drink.

One person who did miss the festivities was Liam Mellowes. Aran had hoped he would come, but at the last minute Lee sent a note expressing his regrets at being unable to attend. Besides wishing the new couple congratulations and all the best, he asked to be remembered to Father and Mother McCracken.

Just as night was falling, the strawboys put in their appearance. Disguised in old, oversized clothes and with their faces blacked with burnt cork or soot, the six neighbourhood young men waited at the door to be invited in by the bride's father. Once inside, the leader headed straight for Annie. He wished her much happiness and good luck, and then he asked her to dance. Soon they were joined by three other soppers and their chosen partners. Led by a strawboy fiddler, the eight of them danced a reel while the other guests clapped and tapped their feet.

The festivities lasted far into the night. Knots of people gathered around Michael, asking him questions about the Treaty debates and would there be war if it wasn't approved. Ever the consummate gentleman and politician, the Big Fellow tried to reassure them that Ireland would not let them down. He stated in no uncertain terms that the Treaty was not an end, but just a beginning. It was a step forward in the long and difficult process of freeing Ireland.

PART II

"Toward the path of blood…"

JANUARY, 1922 – JUNE, 1922

SEPTEMBER SONG

by William Boniface

The Torch of Liberty is burning bright,
And freedom quickens as an upheld light,
But dark the smoke and sad the lonely flight
That dims the day for minds that worship might.

Such minds avoid the light of lucid day.
When thought is free, it scares them clean away.
They run to battle, cower in the fray
Lest they find peace, put down arms and play.

For peace of mind requires that one trust,
Obey the rules by "want to" not by "must",
Heed laws' intent, let judgement limit lust,
Raise welcome's arms, not sharpened arms that thrust.

The Torch of Liberty is burning bright,
And freedom quickens as an upheld light
Through dark and smoke, and sad the lonely fight
That dims the day for minds that worship might.

10

"I wouldn't want you [Mrs. Kathleen Clarke] *to vote for it. All I ask is that if it is passed, you give us the chance to work it."*

Michael Collins

Aran Roe O'Neill and his new wife Sarah Anne O'Neill said nothing. They just smiled at one another as their hands touched across the table. From the kitchen, they could hear Áine Mc-Cracken in the sitting room talking to little Mary Margaret, now eleven months old. The child was precocious for her age. Taking her first steps two weeks before Christmas, the wee one's curiosity was unquenchable. She already had a vocabulary of a dozen or more words and a smile that would melt your heart. Ma-Ma, as the toddler called her mother, had her hands full.

They could hear Áine trying to explain to Mary Margaret where her father was going, but the child just kept repeating, "Da-Da bye-bye."

Seemingly pleased with herself, she kept repeating the same two words over and over, as Áine patiently answered, "Yes, Mary Margaret, Da-Da and Aran are going bye-bye."

Though the 2nd of January was a holiday in Ireland, Aran and Gay were leaving for Dublin that afternoon. Uncle Peter would drive them to Limerick Junction in time to catch the three o'clock train.

The wedding and all the festivities were over but their wonder remained. Sure, it was all any young couple could've ever asked. For three days the pub was filled with a constant stream of well-wishers. Many good friends stopped by to reminisce and talk of tomorrow. There'd been a never-ending banquet of food and drink. Aran thought he must have put up nearly a half stone. The waistband of his trousers never felt so snug and he had to let his belt out a notch.

All the Dublin crowd plus Duncan had been booked into the Glengall Arms Hotel next door to the Black Rose. At this time of year, the place was almost empty. Michael actually preferred it that way...a little peace and quiet after all the celebrating and questions. It also made the security issue more manageable for the boys.

Peter and Niamh had made arrangements for Shadow to spend his two nights upstairs above the pub with the rest of the McCracken clan. As Niamh said, "We're busting at the seams but isn't it grand so."

Gabriel and Áine were happy to convert their newly rented cottage into the 'wedding suite,' as Gay jokingly called it. That was fine with the new couple. It was a wonderful retreat from all the comings and goings at the pub. Áine had filled the kitchen cupboard with good things to eat and she'd even decorated each of the cosy rooms with evergreen boughs and dried flowers. Gabriel had made sure the wood box was filled with a dozen well-seasoned logs and an ample supply of turf was stacked neatly under the eaves beside the front door.

The McCrackens' rented cottage was a picture of comfort. Built of natural materials, stone, wood and thatch, it was a fitting tribute to the architectural ingenuity of Irish craftsmen. The picturesque dwelling blended in with the natural beauty of its rural surroundings. Located on a hectare of open ground, surrounded by a low stone wall, the property was just off Old

Church Street and hard by the main road for Clonmel Town. Not far from Cahir's village centre, it was less than a half mile walk to the Black Rose public house.

As for the church, Old St. Mary's probably dated from the 15th century. It had been the medieval parish church of Cahir for decennia. The structure had undergone many alterations over the years but hadn't been used for the last one hundred or so. Its surrounding cemetery, however, still witnessed the occasional burial.

Earlier in the summer, Áine's father had learned that the newly renovated cottage would be available for letting in the autumn. He immediately spoke with the owner and paid the first three-months' rent. Imagine their surprise when the Grogans handed them the keys.

After thanking his parents-in-law, Gabby couldn't resist adding, "Trying to get rid of us, are yis?"

The exterior of the one-hundred-year-old cottage was built of native, unplastered, whitewashed Irish limestone. Its walls were three feet thick. During its initial construction, the hipped roof had been framed in wood, then covered with scraw and finally thatched. Just recently, it had undergone only its third thatching.

The original compacted mud floor was today covered with handsomely polished, limestone slabs. Three two-over-two windows had been fitted into both the front and back walls of the structure, allowing east-west light to shine into each of its three rooms.

The freshly painted half door opened into a small lobby with its partitioned jamb-way protecting the fireplace from unwelcome drafts.

To the left of the entrance was the kitchen, a new addition built on at the end of the last century. Besides the large wooden dining table and its odd assortment of chairs, the room was rimmed with a sink, work counters, a wood-burning cooking stove, a large wood box and a floor-to-ceiling cupboard. This massive piece of furniture with its lower half containing shuttered shelves and sliding drawers served as storage space for food items and everyday kitchen utensils. On top of the cupboard was a dresser with its shelving and plate rails for holding dishes, bowls, cups and saucers. Another feature of the room was the small hand pump installed just over the sink. It conveniently allowed fresh running water to be piped in from the underground cistern located in the back garden.

The old gable wall, now dividing the kitchen from the sitting room, had been opened in the centre during the recent renovation. The gap's finished stonework created a massive fireplace, warming and helping illuminate both rooms. On the kitchen side, a swinging metal crane still held the blackened cooking pot that today looked as old as the cottage itself. Finally, as was customary, a large slab of bacon hung in the chimney shaft for easy accessibility and additional smoke curing.

Súgán chairs plus several cushioned benches filled a homey sitting room. A tall bookshelf, overflowing with books, lined the wall opposite the fireplace. Additionally, another dresser, for displaying the 'Sunday china,' a writing desk and two side tables dotted the parlour. Paraffin lamps, Mary's cot plus a large, reed-woven basket containing dried sods of turf completed the room's furnishings. A picture of the Sacred Heart and several other framed photographs decorated the walls.

At the lower end of the cottage was the third room. Slightly smaller than the other two, it contained a double bed with metal frame, an armoire for hanging clothes and two end tables, each with an oil lamp. A crucifix hung on the wall above the bed.

The last touch of the cottage's interior design was a hand-woven St. Brigid's cross made of reed. It was fastened to the wall just above the freshly painted, yellow front door while a small Holy-water font hung at eye level just beside the entrance way.

Finally, the outhouse was at the end of the walk out back. Conveniently close on a cold winter's night.

Sarah Anne loved all the personal touches Áine had added to make the cottage seem so comfortable and homey for her family of three.

As Annie relaxed in the comfort of Áine's cottage, she longed for a place of their own...somewhere Aran and she could call their own and, hopefully, begin raising a family. But dreams of such wedded bliss were on hold...indefinitely. Her husband was off to serve his country again...this time, thank God, it was only Dublin, but that was as good as being a thousand miles away.

The Big Fellow had apologised to Sarah on the evening of their wedding. He agreed the timing was poor, but things were beyond his control. The Dáil was scheduled to resume its debate on whether to accept or reject the Treaty on the 3rd.

That conversation had been five days ago. Now, in less than two hours, Aran was leaving. Together with Gabriel, the two would be standing by, ready to answer the call of their friend and military commander, Michael Collins.

It was not as if Sarah Anne hadn't grown used to Aran being away. Months of being on the run during the Tan War followed by his recent three-month stint in London and Dublin, should've prepared her for the life of a soldier's wife. Sure it had. But now things were different. Instead of his juggling time between active duty, his own family and her, the wedding changed everything. She was now his responsibility. Didn't she have a right to expect him home every evening? Home to begin building a new life with her and not off on some bloody adventure risking his life for God only knew what?

Michael's coming to the wedding was an honour. When he walked into the church and later the pub, you could feel his magnetic presence resonating among the guests. Annie remembered the whispers and wide-eyed stares of those in the pub after the Mass.

She hadn't seen the Corkman for several months. Despite all the pressure he was under, Michael looked grand. Rested, smiling and always ready with a laugh...he seemed his old self. The Christmas break from the debates had done him a world of good.

Unfortunately, the Big Fellow's charisma couldn't erase the memory of the last job he'd asked her to undertake. It almost cost her dearly. Annie vividly recalled delivering Michael's cryptic message to his old friend Sam Maguire in London. But the return trip proved to be a disaster. It was a harrowing experience, but thanks to Aran and her brother's quick thinking, they'd saved the day.

Sarah Anne wondered if the beautiful crystal bowl he'd given them as a wedding gift wasn't partly an apology for his other present: a promotion for Aran.

Indeed that was a surprise and one she welcomed with grave reservations. In a private ceremony in Peter and Niamh's kitchen, Michael announced Aran's promotion from captain to major in front of their two families. At the same time, he'd also upgraded Gabriel from lieutenant to captain. Everyone applauded and offered their congratulations…everyone but Sarah Anne and Áine. Looking at each other, they both knew what the other was thinking…*where would all this lead?*

Sarah O'Neill couldn't help but wonder: *What new demands will Michael and the IRA make on these two now that they're higher ranking officers and unquestionably loyal Irishmen?*

Despite their wives' misgivings, both Aran and Gay were thrilled with the advancement. Besides a few more shillings in their weekly pay packets, Aran was being made OC of the soon-to-be organised 2nd Battalion of the Dublin Guards. Gabriel would be his Vice O/C and they'd have a largely free hand in recruiting and training the four hundred or so men who'd eventually make up the unit.

Sure, on the eve of his departure, Sarah realised Aran's advancement was a reward for his brave and loyal service to Michael and Ireland, but she also feared for his safety. Wouldn't he just be a bigger target for some trigger-happy, bog-trotting amadán?

When Aran, Gabriel, Áine and herself had a quiet moment alone with Michael on the day after the wedding, the Corkman wasn't very optimistic about the Treaty's likelihood for success.

"If the Dáil rejects the agreement, the country faces going to war again, unless de Valera pulls off the unimaginable and convinces the English to agree to his Document No. 2. The other scenario, and the more likely in my opinion, has the assembly and later the country agreeing to the Treaty which would effectively split the IRA and the people into two camps: those for and those against it."

The Big Fellow's celebratory smile had now disappeared. A worried look cast its gloomy presence over his face.

"If a split does occur, God only knows where it'll lead. War with England? War with Ulster? Civil War among our own right here at home? In any event, the drums of defiance and hatred are beating louder and louder. Unfortunately, regardless of what happens, we're all bound as bloody hell to be right in the middle of it."

❧

"Thanks be to God, the three o'clock was late or we'd be walking to Dublin right now," exclaimed Gabriel.

Aran shared his sigh of relief, as the two of them threw their cases up onto the overhead luggage rack and took their seats.

"'Twouldn't have been any way to begin a new job," muttered Aran out loud. "Sure, Michael would've had our guts for garters if we'd been a day late arriving back into Dublin, wedding or no."

"Bloody well he'd," acknowledged Gay. "But we're all right now. No need to worry. Let's go down and have a cup of tea and a bite to eat. I'm starved so."

"Starved, you old gaffer. Sure its food and drink you've had non-stop for the past week...but a cup of tea does sound good. Let's go."

The two men found a quiet table at the far end of the dining carriage. After they'd placed their order, the conversation turned to the business at hand: the Treaty.

"Michael's been keeping close track of the country's reaction to the Treaty and its debate. Do you know what he's found, Gay?"

"No, but I can guess. The people are sick and tired of war. They want peace and as much independence from Britain as we can squeeze out of 'em."

"Exactly," answered Aran. "Both the British and Irish press plus a great many County Councils are backing the Treaty."[1] [2]

1. Dwyer, op.cit., 128.

2. "A total of 328 statutory public declared themselves by 5 Januway [1922] in favour of the Treaty's terms, only five declared against." hopkinson, op. cit., 35.

"To my knowledge, only the *Cork Examiner* has come out against it," replied Gay. "Uncle Peter told me he'd read that the editor feels the mounting tide in favour of the London agreement is drowning out all opposition, regardless of how narrow-minded it might be."

"That's one I wish we had on our side. You know what an important part 'Rebel Cork' played in the War of Independence. Men like Tom Barry, Liam Lynch, Seán Moylan and Liam Deasy carry a lot of weight. I'd hate to see them turn against us."

"If you ask me, Aran, I think the heart of the problem is not so much with the agreement itself, but that it's not Dev's agreement. We both know he said he was willing to compromise last summer, however, what Mick and the others brought back wasn't *his* compromise."

"I agree, but somehow Dev's original willingness to concede ground on sovereignty instead of the north-east was lost in the rush trying to appease the doctrinaire Republicans. In casting his lot with the hardliners, he's alienated the majority of the Irish people."

"Don't you think he's lost control of *both* sides now? The voice of the ordinary person is lining up against him. To make matters worse, his ability to keep a bridle on Cathal and the others isn't working either. He's just isolating himself more and more and I think he knows it. He's running scared."

"Sure, and that's probably the reasoning behind his championing Document No. 2. In his heart of hearts, I believe he actually supports the Treaty. No doubt he thinks it's workable and that it just might deliver a Republic…but only in time. Time, however, isn't on his side. So in his mind, No. 2 was an attempt to take the best of what Michael brought back, something he knew the British championed. To it he added a few of his own touches. With some of his bits in the mix plus the backing of the Dáil and the Irish people, maybe just maybe the English would buy off on it…"

"…or at least go back to the negotiating table with himself now in charge?" countered Gay, finishing Aran's thought.

"That would be better than a feckin' war," mumbled the Rebel.

The tea and Gay's bacon buttie arrived at the table. A minute or two of thoughtful reflection ensued.

Carefully refilling his tea cup in the swaying carriage, Aran interrupted the train's rhythmic sounds.

"Gay, in point of fact, I think Dev's idea of External Association is a good one. Unfortunately, with London's political climate being what it is, it's a non-starter...no backing from the Tory's side. If Lloyd George didn't have to put up with his bloody conservative coalition's sectarian malice, Dev's model might just prove to be a winner... something the other Commonwealth partners could find attractive as well. Just imagine...Ireland being the pace setter, championing Australia, New Zealand, South Africa and Canada's drive for full independence while still preserving our mutually advantageous ties. The new Commonwealth...our own little League of Nations."

"But that brings up a thorny issue, Aran. Our longing for a Republic *and* full independence has become so intertwined that to envision one without the other is impossible, at least in the minds of some. I think that's at the heart of it, too. The Treaty doesn't say 'Republic.' So without that, how can we be free and independent? Cathal says we can't and no amount of reasoning will convince him otherwise. It's either all or nothing in his mind."

"Unfortunately," said Aran, shaking his head, "he can't see there's a middle ground. As Michael says, 'Some now and more later.'"

"I think all of this caught Dev by surprise," said Gabriel. "He thought he could control the hardliners and bring along the doubters... that's why he said he stayed back in Dublin instead of going over to London."

"Right, but now it's all coming to naught. His strategy of maintaining unity among the ranks has failed..."

"...and there's going to be shyte to pay by everyone," retorted the Irish-American.

❧

Back in their seats, the two friends talked of the wedding and of finding something more permanent in the way of living accommodation in Dublin. Staying at Vaughan's was fine for the short term, but if they're going to be posted to the city, it wouldn't do. Besides, their wives wanted to move to Dublin once the battalion was organised. Being apart from each other for months on end wasn't anyone's idea of married life.

Rocked in the comfort of the train's gentle pulsing, Aran closed his eyes. Though married less than a week, he could sense the compelling effect of Annie's undeniable love for him and for their mutual desire to share a life together.

He felt a new sense of wholeness and peace with the world. A subtle but palpable feeling of renewed self-confidence had taken hold of him, filling him with a strange sensation of completeness and even invincibility.

It excited him to know that he was capable of love. Sure, he was still learning how to express it, but Sarah Anne was a good teacher. During the last six years he devoted most of his life to making war and staying alive. But now with the possibilities of peace in Ireland and with the advent of his marriage, Aran wanted to turn his attention to being a husband, a provider and, hopefully, a father. In doing so, the old bonds of friendship and love for Ireland wouldn't need to be forsaken. Michael, Shadow, Gay and the others would still be a part of his life…Sarah Anne's and his life now. And as for Ireland, though centuries old, she too was in her infancy. Together, please God, they'd all grow and, hopefully, prosper together.

Slowly, his thoughts turned again to the wedding. They nourished him as he crossed his arms over his chest. The jumper he was wearing, Annie's Christmas present to him, warmed him as if the two of them were lying together in the bed. Last week had been special: being back in his boyhood home again with his family around, Christmas Day with its Mass and grand feast, his twenty-third birthday, the wedding with family and friends, retreating to Gay and Áine's 'wedding suite,' so many wonderful memories. Days and nights of living rough on-the-run seemed to melt away and were forgotten.

Though they had been exhausted from the celebration and the lateness of the hour, Annie and he held each other in their arms that night. Quietly, they talked of yesterday and tomorrow. Then, overcome with the realisation of their wedding bond, their hands touched in ways unknown before. Responding to their mutual caresses, they came together as one.

❧

The train stopped at Marysborough to discharge and take on passengers. Aran and Gabriel stepped off their carriage to breathe some fresh air and stretch their legs. With the peace firmly entrenched, they'd both talked of not carrying their handguns, but the memories of 'the black spot' and other recent attacks changed their minds. At least for the present, carrying arms was an ongoing fact of life.

Back aboard the train, the talk of pending war again crept into their conversation. Plans for organising their new unit and who they'd like to have serve in its leadership positions dominated their discussion. Suddenly, they both came to the same realisation. Didn't their choice of personnel depend on whether there was unity or division among the ranks? Some of the names they'd thrown out might elect to cast their lot with the 'other' side.

Gabriel summed it up best. "Jaysus, Aran, that's something I'd rather not think about…at least for now."

Aran nodded his agreement.

❧

No one envisioned the Dáil Treaty debates dragging on as it had. No one imagined the bitter vindictiveness of the charges and counter-charges with which its members assaulted one another. No one ever dreamed that the greatest political victory in Irish history would end in argument and dissension. It was worse than anyone's most evil nightmare.

The malevolence spread like a poisonous cloud, infecting all who came in contact with it. Germinated first in the Dáil's cabinet, it had spread, out of control, enveloping the entire countryside.

In their arrogance and narrow-mindedness to control things, the Dáil, led by its president Éamon de Valera, first turned its vindictiveness inward on itself. Divided into two camps, its own internal partitioning gradually became obvious to the entire country. Dev, backed by Cathal Brugha and Austin Stack, faced off against the Collins contingent of Arthur Griffith and William Cosgrave. The seventh member, Robert Barton, vacillated back and forth between the two halves.

Aran and Gabriel were not the only two to recognise the cabinet's disunity: Dev and his followers clearly lacked faith in, or maybe it was suspicion of, Michael and his supporters. This absence of confidence in their own handpicked London delegation only festered and finally bubbled forth during the debates. That absence of fraternity and presence of partisanship further exacerbated the division within the executive.

The Gortman maintained it was jealousy that drove Dev, Cathal and Austin to differ with Michael. But whether it was personal or professional, it really didn't matter…it was there. You would've had to be blind to miss it.

❧

Later that evening, as Aran and Gay huddled over their evening meal and a pint at Conway's, their talk of Ireland's current state of affairs continued, dominating the conversation.

Picking up the threads of an earlier exchange, Gabriel said, "Whatever the source of the cabinet's divide, it's spread to the Dáil and is creeping out into the countryside, enveloping the people with its own poisonous tentacles. People are beginning to take sides, witness the newspaper editorials and council endorsements. Unfortunately for Dev's supporters, his lack of leadership plus his slow and confused response to the pluses and minuses of the Treaty are driving public opinion to favour it. If he'd been better prepared, maybe he could have turned people away from the document in a positive way. In doing so, Dev might have united

Ireland in such a way that England would've been forced to step back and renegotiate."

"Maybe," answered Aran, "but you're forgetting one important thing. Remember Dev saying, 'in a democracy, there are ways to resolve our differences' or something like that?"

"Yes."

"Well, the way things have been run these past few months, I'd be hard-pressed to call Ireland a democracy."

"What do you mean, Aran?"

"If you remember rightly, back in July and August, when Dev was exchanging letters and proposals with Lloyd George, the Dáil didn't convene to discuss things. No, the cabinet handled everything. Finally, Dev did call the assembly together to approve one of his London replies…and it was a good thing they did, because Dev had already sent his answer six days before."[3]

"Sure, I knew they weren't in session often, but I didn't realise things were that bad."

"I didn't either until Michael brought it to my attention last week."

The Gortman continued, "Gay, you must remember that Dáil membership was more a function of Sinn Féin's leadership picking who they wanted rather than the electorate nominating their representatives. Sure, the people voted for a candidate, but with Sinn Féin holding most of the power, who'd be elected had already been decided. The entire process discouraged divergent thinking and independent views from being heard. Power rested in the hands of a few, mostly Dev's cabinet, and decisions were made with little debate. Dissent was usually unheard of, according to Michael."[4]

"But Aran, those choices are now coming back to bite them. They've selected diehards loyal to the 'The Republic' and it's that crowd that's voicing their objections to the Treaty."

"Ironic, isn't it?" responded the Gortman.

---

3. Dwyer, op.cit., 42.
4. Ibid.

Motioning to the barman to start another round, Aran leaned over the table in Gay's direction. In a hushed voice, the Gortman said, "Mick told me something interesting…something Béaslaí let slip before the team ever departed for London. Annoyed at Dev for his high-handedness, Piaras said to Mick, '…nothing could well be less democratic in practice than the government which we recognise as the government of the Irish Republic.'"[5]

"That all fits, doesn't it?" said Gay. "Dev's been running things his own way for a good while now. As long as he's in control, all's grand. But throw a spanner in the works, and he has no democratic process to fall back on…just argument, innuendo and, in Cathal's case, venom and intimidation."

"It's a sad state of affairs, isn't it, Gay? The dogmatic character of Irish Republicanism is ill-suited for the give-and-take of parliamentary assemblies."[6]

❧

The weather had turned cold. A biting wind, an English wind blew from the east as Michael's entourage, including Aran and Gay, hurried up the steps of University College Dublin and into the warmth of the academic building.

At the onset of the debates, prior to the Christmas recess, Arthur Griffith had formally moved for the Dáil to ratify the Treaty. He'd proudly stated, "By that Treaty I am going to stand."[7]

Eoin MacNeill, the Dáil's Speaker, seconded the motion saying, "I take this course because I know I am doing it in the interests of my country, which I love."[8]

Unfortunately, the following days were not marked with reasoned or intelligent discourse, but were filled with long-winded speeches and emotional dialogue. MacNeill often had trouble controlling the deputies and was beset by interruptions.[9] From

---

5. Ibid.
6. Hopkinson, op. cit., 38.
7. Mackay, op. cit., 231.
8. Ibid.
9. "During thirteen days of public & private, he (de Valera) interrupted the proceedings more than 250 times." Dwyer, op. cit., 112.

their beginning, the debates were characterised more for their personal attacks on Collins than they were about discussing the merits of the Treaty. But Michael controlled his notorious temper and emerged as a skilful politician and polished debater, in the eyes of most at least.

In stark contrast to Mick, "the Long Fellow was shown up as a political pygmy, a poisoned dwarf who had no compunction about sacrificing his country on the altar of his own pigheadedness."[10]

This behaviour on the part of the Chief, coupled with his 7 December scathing press release denouncing the Treaty, only further succeeded in dividing the country. By toying with the nation's emotions as he did, Dev continued pushing Ireland closer and closer to civil unrest and possibly even war.

❈

Upon their return to Dublin from their Christmas holidays, Aran and Gay learned of several attempts to move the debates along in a more constructive manner.

A group of Labourites made two constructive suggestions. First, in accord with the terms of the Treaty, the Dáil should first appoint a provisional governing body. This committee should proceed to formulate a constitution post haste. Secondly, as this governing document would be of and by the Irish people, not something originating from London, the offending oath of allegiance could be eliminated, thus removing one of the major objections to the agreement.

In another attempt to resolve Treaty differences, Seán T. O'Kelly called members of both sides together. After discussing the matter, they proposed that Dev abstain from voting against the Treaty in the interests of national unity. In return, he'd retain his Dáil presidency and also be recognised as president of the new provisional body.

Upon learning of these schemes that both Griffith and Collins agreed to, de Valera flatly refused to accept either. Instead,

10. Mackay, op. cit., 230.

he offered a revision of his Document No. 2 that he dubbed Document No. 3.

Arthur Griffith was so angered by de Valera's bull-headedness, that he released his copy of No. 2 to the press. When the full text of it was published, Dev lost even more credibility with his extremist sidekicks and further bewildered the general public. They couldn't see much difference between No. 2 and the original Treaty and wondered what all the fuss was about.[11]

Some of the strongest Dàil Treaty opposition came from its women membership. Unlike the men, many of whom had seen active service against the Black and Tans as well as the Auxies, the women hadn't. Granted, Ireland's women had made many important contributions. They'd seen loved ones killed, homes burned and lives destroyed, but they'd seldom experienced the rigours of actual combat. Perhaps because of their lack of front-line experience or possibly spurred on by a festering distain for the Sassenach, the reality of some women was distorted, creating an aura of illusion. By masking the potential horrors needed to deliver Ireland's ultimate dream, Dáil women continued to cling to the fantasy of the mythical 'Irish Republic.'[12] Their ranks included Mrs. Margaret Pearse, mother of executed Patrick and Willie; Mrs. Kathleen Clarke, widow of Tom and sister of executed Ned Daly; Miss Mary MacSwiney, sister of dead hunger-striker Terence MacSwiney; and Mrs. O'Callaghan, widow of the murdered Lord Mayor of Limerick.[13]

On the evening prior to the vote being taken, Michael and Aran called into see Mrs. Clarke. She welcomed them, but the reception was cool. After serving tea, the trio spent a few minutes chatting. Finally, Kathleen asked Michael why they'd come.

The Big Fellow talked about the Treaty and how he felt it represented progress on Ireland's road to full independence. Not

---

11. Coogan, op. cit., 303.
12. Dáil women were not the only victims of this illusion. Many in Ireland, both men & women, seemed unaware or chose to ignore the great sacrifices that would be required by all if the Treaty was rejected & the war with Britain was renewed.
13. keep, op. cit., 157.

the freedom Tom and Ned had died for, but it was more than Ireland had ever been granted in the past.

The Corkman went on to say that she certainly realised that the IRA could never have achieved a military victory over the colonial imperialists, but when the British military begins leaving Ireland, soon after the Treaty's been ratified, it will be proof positive that our national liberties are finally being established with great certainty.

Aran thought that Mrs. Clarke didn't appear convinced.

In a final attempt to appeal to her Irish loyalty, Michael almost pleaded, "If you can't bring yourself to vote for it, all I ask is that if it is passed, you give us the chance to work it."

Mrs. Clarke, the wife of one of Ireland's greatest revolutionaries, chose not to reply. Instead, she stood up, shook her guests' hands and bid them both a "good night."

❦

The day had finally come, Saturday, 7 January. The issue of whether to ratify the Treaty or not had arrived. An air of expectancy filled the debate hall. Michael and Gay were optimistic. Aran wasn't. He felt no matter which way the votes were cast, Ireland would be the loser. Mick tried to buoy up his spirit.

"Look here, my young friend, you now have a lovely wife, a new command and Ireland is facing a bright tomorrow...have a little faith, lad."

"Please God, Michael, you're right."

Throughout the day, the threat of Civil War lurked behind the unspoken warnings of most of the speech-makers. Others talked of a romantic and idealised Ireland, trying to appeal to the noble, sentimental interests of their fellow deputies.

Late in the afternoon, Liam Mellowes rose to address the assembly.

Both Aran and Gay inched forward in their seats. They hadn't talked to or seen Liam in months, but they both held him in high esteem. Aran's heart filled with admiration and respect for this wise and brave Republican commander.

This was the same man Aran had first met in Shadow's safe-house outside Limerick after the collapse of the Easter Rebellion. It was Mellowes who, with the help of Shadow and Danny Kelly, had saved his life by smuggling him aboard a Brazilian steamship bound for Amerikay. It was through Liam's connections with Clan na Gael that the foursome found safe lodging on United States soil. Without Lee's intercession, he wouldn't have developed his close relationship with Shadow and wouldn't have met the McCrackens. Now Sarah Anne was his wife and Gabriel his close friend and fellow comrade. Then two years later, after they'd all returned to Ireland, it was Liam and Michael who'd masterminded the funding and organising of their special guerrilla column, the Flying Gaels. Yes, Liam Mellowes was one of his heroes.

Wearing a three-piece suit and his signature leather gaiters, Liam stood before Ireland's assembly. Carefully, he adjusted his pince-nez glasses. Beginning slowly, his measured words gradually turned into an impassioned plea.

"We would rather have this country poor and indigent, we would rather have the people of Ireland eking out a poor existence on the soil, as long as they possessed their souls, their minds and their honour."[14]

His head spinning, Aran slumped back in his seat as Mellowes sat down. He wanted to agree with his former commander, but couldn't.

Cathal Brugha was the last one to speak before the voting commenced.

Aran watched Michael, seated on the bench directly in front of him, tense. The Irish Rebel leaned forward and gave his friend a reassuring pat on the shoulder. The Big Fellow cocked his head to one side in acknowledgement.

Leaning over in Gay's direction, Aran whispered, "The bloody louser, this could be a feckin' slanging-match."

Cathal's comments began as a deliberate argument calling for the rejection of the Treaty. But as the minutes passed, his speech

---

14. Litton, op.cit., 28

evolved into more of an embittered verbal assault against Michael. He finished his attack with three accusatory queries: What was Michael Collins's real position in the army? What actual military action had Michael Collins seen? Had Michael Collins ever fired a shot at Ireland's enemy?"

A deathly silence fell over the assembly hall.

Pausing to let the impact of his words sink in, Cathal then continued, "If you won't respond, let me answer those embarrassing questions for you. To begin with Mr. Collins was only a minor, low-level member of Headquarters Staff..."

Arthur Griffith sprang to his feet, shouting, "Let me repeat it again, Cathal...Michael Collins *was* the man who won the war. Not you, not the President, no one else but himself...Mr. Michael Collins."

Turning to face the other deputies, Art continued, "He was the man whose matchless energy, whose indomitable will, carried Ireland through the terrible crisis; and though I have not now, and never had, an ambition about either political affairs or history, if my name is to go down in history, I want it to be associated with the name of Michael Collins."[15]

Another member stood, shouting, "Hear, hear."

A second voice proclaimed, "...and so he did."

Then stridently from the back of the room came, "Mr. Minister of Defence, I believe we've heard enough."

However, someone else cried out, "Let him finish."

But Cathal was finished. He sat down.

Speaker O'Neill called for a ten-minute adjournment.

Michael walked over and shook Art Griffith's hand. The two spoke quietly for several moments.

Gabriel turned to Aran, "That does it...Brugha's outburst just copper-fastened the Treaty's approval. Anyone still on the fence must see that Michael's arguments were sounder, more reasoned and far better grounded than that emotional tripe Brugha just finished spouting."

"...and another thing, Gay," said Aran, "no doubt that disturbing outburst clearly exposes the bitterness and jealousy that's

---

15. Mackay, op. cit., 240

been going on behind everyone's back for lo these many months. Brugha's shown the Long Hoor's side of the cabinet for what it is…a group of petty and vicious men incapable of leading this country out from under its chains of bondage."

Again standing behind his desk, the Ceann Comhairle called the assembly to order. One by one, in alphabetical order by constituencies, Diarmuid O'Hegarty read the roll. The TD's charge was to respond, 'Is toil' or 'Ni toil' to the question of whether the Treaty should be ratified or not.

In a calm clear voice, O'Hegarty called, "Armagh."

Armagh was the first constituency on the list. Michael Collins, its representative, slowly rose to his feet. Standing tall with his shoulders squared and his fine jaw set, the Big Fellow voted in an unmistakably passionate voice, "Is Toil."

The polling continued. As the deputies voted, people strained to hear each reply. Some made mental notes. Others marked the 'yeas' and 'nays' on pieces of paper.

Finally, with the voting concluded, Eoin MacNeill read out the results, "Sixty-four in favour of ratifying the Treaty; fifty-seven against it. Mr. Griffith's motion is carried."

Moments later, the President rose, telling everyone he was resigning his position as leader of Dáil Éireann.

Michael was on his feet in an instant. In an emotional outpouring, he protested Dev's action. He stated his loyalty and devotion to the President and pleaded with him to reconsider. But the poignant moment was shattered by Mrs. Mary MacSwiney. She cried out, "The betrayal of this glorious nation."[16]

Reverently, Éamon de Valera asked O'Neill if he could make one final statement.

With approval granted, the President began, "I would like my last word here to be this: we have had a glorious record for four years; it has been four years of magnificent discipline in our nation. The world is looking at us now…."

In tears, de Valera sat down, unable to continue.

The Minister of Defence Cathal Brugha came to his Pres-

---

16. Ibid., 241.

ident's aid. Rising to speak, apocryphally he promised, "So far as I am concerned, I will see, at any rate, that discipline is kept in the army."[17]

The Ceann Comhairle adjourned the Dáil.

❃

Though there was no great outpouring of emotion from within the assembly hall, word of the vote had leaked to the outside. Several hundred delighted onlookers enthusiastically greeted the deputies as they emerged from the college. This earnest reception and vocal affirmation seemed to buoy up the spirits of the TDs as they and Ireland prepared to face the birth of a new nation.

❃

The Deputies reconvened two days later, but the bitterness spawned by the Treaty debate hadn't subsided. In fact, it had grown worse. Any hope of reasoned dialogue was soon cast aside as heartfelt suggestions were belittled and ignored. Members seemed to relish engaging in the art of personal attack. A crescendo of chaos and violence threatened to descend on the delegates.

Aran thought the disgraceful scene, playing itself out before him, must have been analogous to the College-Green days of 1800, when the Irish parliament chose to dissolve its own assembly. Treachery, bribery and personal assassination had been the order of the day back then. Now something equalling that climactic event was happening again.

The drama continued as de Valera rose to formally tender his resignation. Again, the Big Fellow objected, suggesting instead they establish a joint committee of pro- and anti-Treaty representatives to try and mend the Dáil's differences.

But before the motion could be discussed, members rose to denounce it, saying they didn't want the Republic tainted or weakened by compromise in any way.

17. Ibid.

Once again Kathleen Clarke stood and called for the immediate re-election of de Valera. Liam Mellowes seconded the motion. But others, including the Corkman, objected. Michael stated that the Dáil had voted. It was now time to move on to other issues.

Again Michael's suggestion was ignored. In its place came more petty wrangling.

The Big Fellow looked at Art Griffith. The senior man angrily shook his head in disbelief.

Turning to Aran and his sidekick, Michael muttered, "Bloody, fecken' eejits."

Neither could object.

Amid the mounting brouhaha, one of the deputies reminded those listening that any delay in following through on enacting the terms of the Treaty might result in the British authorities postponing their planned withdrawal from Ireland.

As a counter to this warning, Austin Stack loudly objected, stating, "He was a Republican…someone who stood for the Irish Republic and its president Éamon de Valera."

In a counter move, another TD reminded the assembly that Document No. 2 was not a Republican manifesto in word or in meaning.

To this, Michael, angry and impatient, blurted out, "No tactics! Let's be honest. I propose an amendment: that this House ask Mr. Griffith to form a Provisional Executive."[18]

After a short recess, the members voted fifty-eight for and sixty against re-electing Dev as their president.

Just before the Dáil adjourned for the day, de Valera, showing a glimpse of his former political savoir faire, announced to his pro-Treaty rivals, "We will be there with you against any outside enemy at any price."[19]

Events of the last few days reached a second climax on the 10th. Things quickly ground to a halt over what Griffith should and would do as President of Dáil Éireann, if he was elected.

With all eyes on the fifty-year-old political chief, he proudly

18. Ibid., 242
19. Ibid.

and unequivocally stated, "Let nobody have the slightest misunderstanding about where I stand. I am in favour of this Treaty. I want this Treaty put into operation. I want the Provisional Government set up. I want the Republic to remain in being until the time when the people can have a Free State election, and give their vote."[20]

Once more on her feet, the outspoken Mary MacSwiney asked Mr. Griffith not to combine the office of Dáil president with leader of the Provisional Government, as if the new position might taint the older one.

Receiving no satisfaction, she declared, "I tell you here, there can be no union between the representatives of the Irish Republic and the so-called Free State."[21]

Aran and Gabby whispered to each other as the hall broke into a low buzz of conversation. But the lull lasted for less than a minute.

Michael was on his feet again, calling for the question as to whether Griffith should be voted in as president, replacing Dev.

Éamon de Valera took umbrage at this demand. Stridently, he said, "As a protest against the election as President of the Irish Republic of the Chairman of the Delegation, who is bound by the Treaty conditions to set up a State which is to subvert the Republic, and who, in the interim period, instead of using the office as it should be used to support the Republic will, of necessity, have to be taking action which will tend to its destruction. I, while this vote is being taken, as one, am going to leave the House."[22]

Aran couldn't believe his eyes. As the former president made his exit, several dozen of his followers stood and walked out after him.

Michael, pushing back an unruly lock of hair that had fallen onto his forehead, roared with anger, "Deserters all! We will now call on the Irish people to rally to us. Deserters all."

---

20. Ibid.
21. Mackay, op. cit., 243.
22. Ibid.

One of the men leaving with Dev turned and cried back, "Up the Republic!"

Standing, with his arm outstretched and finger pointing, Michael retorted, "Deserters all to the Irish nation in her hour of trial."

"Oath-breakers and cowards," screamed Countess Markievicz, walking out behind de Valera.

"Foreigners! Americans! English!" shouted an enraged Collins, his face red and his jaw set in defiance.

"Lloyd Georgeites!" she yelled, turning her back on the remaining deputies.

Amid such chaos and confusion, William Cosgrave's calm voice could be heard saying, "Now, Sir, will you put the question."

Thus, in the heat of verbal abuse, angry feelings, desertion and betrayed loyalties, Arthur Griffith was elected President of Dáil Éireann. Sixty-one of the one hundred twenty-one original TDs remained in the hall, each voting for the question.[23]

Under such an horrific state of affairs, the 2nd Irish legislative assembly of the 20th century adjourned.[24]

---

23. [Author's note: I have chosen to take selected parts of this last dramatic exchange between pro-Treaty & anti-Treaty deputies from James Mackay's account of the Treaty debate's final day. He captures the essence of the dialogue & for this I am grateful.]

24. Collins's derogatory references to foreigners, Americans & English were directed toward Markievicz, born in England & married to a Polish aristocrat; de Valera, born in the United States; & Childers, born in England. The other disparaging references are self evident.

II

Lord FitzAlan, British Lord-Lieutenant in Ireland, on the hand-over of Dublin Castle to the Irish Provisional Government on 16 January 1922:
"You're seven minutes late, Mr. Collins."
Michael Collins, Irish Provisional Government Chairman:
"We've been waiting 700 years. You can have the seven minutes."

WEDNESDAY MORNING, 11 JANUARY 1922

*D*espite his ill-temperedness, proclivity for hard language and ironclad determination to deliver Ireland the freedom she so long deserved, Michael Collins was a sensitive man. Kind of heart and easily moved to tears, Mick's emotional complexities endeared him to his close friends. One minute he'd be roaring mad, shouting out a string of obscenities, and in the next, you'd be on the receiving end of one of his heartfelt 'bear hugs.'

Aran attributed these sudden mood shifts to the immense pressure his friend was under, not to some troubling psychological disorder. Instead of keeping his emotions bottled up inside him, Michael was quick to release the mounting strain. This venting allowed him to focus more fully on the important business at hand and political matters demanding his attention.

It was now thirty-six hours after the blow-up in the Dáil. As the Gortman waited for Gabriel to join him in the lobby of Vaughan's, he didn't envy Michael's position, caught between feuding factions as he was. How many balls could any one person continue juggling before disaster struck? Besides keeping the British cabinet satisfied, the Irish government was proceeding on pace with its Treaty obligations. Suddenly, there was this Sinn Féin political divide to deal with. Additionally, the Big Fellow feared a potential IRA break-up. Then, what about the IRB? On which side would they fall? Of course, there was also the overriding issue of the Irish people…how would they react to this recent news? Would they back the Big Fellow and Arthur Griffith or side with Éamon de Valera?

On that fateful Monday evening, Michael had called a few of his intimates together for evening tea. In a small, private dining room, his loyal following including Dick Mulcahy, Gearóid O'Sullivan and Eoin O'Duffy gathered to discuss Dev's walk-out. Mick also wanted their suggestions regarding the formation of his Provisional government's executive.

Aran was one of the last to arrive. Eddie was on hand to greet him. The older man had been a waiter at the Gresham for donkey's years. Mick had even brought him over to London to butler at #15 Cadogan Gardens. Having him around had made the delegation feel more at home. Besides being an accomplished server, the man was just great craic to be with.

On seeing the Rebel enter, Michael motioned him over to where he was seated at a linen-covered dining table.

"Aran, do me a big favour. Find an envelope at the desk and post this letter across the street at the GPO. It's to Kitty. If you hurry, it should go out this evening."

In the hotel lobby, the Gortman found embossed stationery supplies. He carefully addressed the envelope as he'd done so often in the past: Miss Kitty Kiernan, Greville Arms, Granard, Co. Longford.

Without intending to read its words, he glanced at the single page of writing. Michael's hand was difficult to read, but Aran had had lots of practice. The Big Fellow's pain jumped out at him.

"I'm absolutely fagged out and worn out and everything, but I send you this note to give my little remembrance of you. If you knew how the other side is 'killing' me God help me. We had to beat them again today. Please come up as soon as you can..."[1]

Aran stopped reading and carefully folded the letter. Slipping it into the addressed envelope, he hurried across Sackville Street to the General Post Office. After pushing the communiqué through the mail slot, the Gortman paused on top of the low steps under the portico. Closing his eyes, he could almost see Pearse standing beside one of the building's tall pillars reading the Easter-Week Proclamation. Saying a prayer for his fallen teacher, Aran made the Sign of the Cross and hastily returned to the Gresham.

❧

Wednesday-morning breakfast with Gay at Devlin's had given the two of them a chance to discuss the events of Monday evening and Tuesday. Just as he felt he was experiencing a personal renewal with his marriage to Sarah Anne, so too was Ireland reawaking from its demoralising seven hundred fifty-year-old epoch of bondage. The big difference was his rebirth was welcomed and pleasurable, while Ireland's outlook didn't seem as bright.

With Art Griffith elected as Dáil president, taking over the post formerly held by Dev, and Michael's selection as Chairman of the newly formed caretaker body, two new executives had to be chosen.

Both men made their choices quickly. Griffith, head of Dáil Éireann, tapped George Gavan Duffy to replace himself as Minister for Foreign Affairs. He also called on Éamon Duggan (Home Affairs), William Cosgrave (Local Government), Kevin O'Higgins (Economic Affairs) and Dick Mulcahy (Defence) to assist him. Finally, the new President rounded out his team by retaining Michael as his Minister for Finance. Thus, four of the five plenipotentiaries who'd signed the Treaty were part of the

---

1. León Ó Broin, ed. *In Great Haste: The Letters of Michael Collins and Kitty Kiernan.* Dublin, 1996, 102.

new Dáil executive. The only one missing, Bob Barton, the fifth signatory, had walked out with de Valera yesterday afternoon.

The charge of the 2nd Dáil was to keep Ireland's government functioning until such time as the Treaty's new Irish Free State government was ready to assume full control of the country's affairs. Before that was possible, however, a constitution had to be written and approved by both the British government and the Irish people. A Free State assembly election, forming the 3rd Dáil Éireann, would complete the transition from old to new.

Aran and Gay both knew Michael had carved out an ambitious agenda for himself. They didn't envy him, but would do all they could to help the Big Fellow. Besides retaining his position as Dáil Minister for Finance and tackling the new post of Ireland's Provisional Government Chairman, Mick wanted to be its spokesperson, too. Who else was better suited to give interviews to the media and tour the country, speaking on behalf of the new government? His new position would also necessitate his periodic travel to London. He'd be required to update the British cabinet in general and Churchill in particular on Ireland's Treaty-compliance progress. Furthermore, his IRB responsibilities needed attention in addition to the important work of keeping part or all of the IRA military-leadership from mutinying.

As a result of the Monday evening meeting, Michael told Aran of his cabinet choices on Tuesday morning. The Big Fella added that he was planning a meeting with his new team later that afternoon.

The formal announcement of Michael's executive wouldn't take place for a few days. First the 2nd Dáil had to meet and properly ratify the Treaty. After that, it must officially authorise the creation of a care-taker Provisional Government. This temporary body would be invested with the responsibility of bridging the gap between Britain's administrative machinery that ran Ireland's day-to-day affairs in the past and the formation of the Free State government, the one created by terms of the new Anglo-Irish accord. A year would be set aside for this change over to occur, at which time the Provisional administration would be replaced by the new government of Saorstát Éireann. The old Dáil would also cease to exist, officially transferring its authority to the Dáil of the new Irish Free State.

❧

Digging into their eggs and rashers, Aran and Gay glanced around the pub, making sure their privacy was protected.

"Just imagine it! Michael Collins out promoting the likes of the British government while trying to set aside the dream of an Irish Republic. What a bloody mess! As if Mick didn't have enough to deal with breathing life into the Treaty demands, Dev's absence and possible active resistance will make it three times more difficult."

"But sure as hell, Gay, you could see it coming, couldn't ya?"

"Unfortunately, yes," answered the Irish-American, taking a gulp of his tea. "After that divisive statement he issued to the press, implying his immediate opposition to the Treaty...all that before Art, Mick and the others ever had a chance to defend their action to the cabinet or the Dáil much less the Irish people."

"As we'd guessed, Gay, Dev knew something like this might happen...a Treaty giving some, but not all of what Ireland wanted. He knew the hard-liners would oppose any compromise and there'd be hell to pay because of it. Rather than face up to the challenge and use his influence in support of the agreement, Dev took the easy way out."

"Yeah, he showed his true colours, didn't he...the gutless, two-faced bastard. Staying home, giving everyone the impression he was backing the London delegation, when in fact he was biding his time, waiting to see which way the chips fell...

"...and when the predictable became reality, he chose to side with minority doctrinaires...spouting some shyte about the majority didn't have the right to err."

Pausing for a moment to butter a slice of bread, Gabriel continued, "I know it's too late now, but I just wonder what would've happened if Mick had refused to go over?"

"Who knows if there even would've been a conference? But

if there had been, I suspect the outcome would've been much the same. On the other hand, if Dev had gone instead of Michael, I'd imagine we'd have been back at war again, maybe for the last month."

"Unless a miracle happens, I'm guessing we'll be again soon enough. This time, however, it won't be the Red Coats in our sights. It'll be Irishmen, our own comrades and kin, fighting one another."

"Gabriel, get out of it! I can't even think of such thoughts. The possibility of an army split-up is too horrific to contemplate, but if anyone can bring the sides together, it's Michael. People will listen to him...they respect him so."

"But Aran, you heard them in the debate...whipped into a frenzy they were, spewing venom without thought or rationale. Dev, Cathal, Lee, the Countess and don't forget Mrs. Clarke... Jaysus, what would Pearse have said?"

"I'm not sure, but I'd like to think his sense of history and his level-headed thinking would have won the day."

"Even after what happened in '16?"

"Please God, one sacrifice was enough...Ireland doesn't need any more blood on its shamrock...especially its own blood."

Finishing their breakfast, Gabriel added, "One more thing, Aran. Don't you think Mick was a bit disingenuous when he said he won't be responsible for returning Ireland to war without the approval of the Irish people? Sure, he didn't take that position two years ago when he declared war on the RIC and the bloody Tans?"

"I think that was just his way of signalling to others he's changed...from revolutionary militant to more moderate politician.

"During the Christmas recess, Mick was out talking to the people, TDs and the like, explaining his take on the Treaty...some political arm twisting if you like. But sure as hell, Dev was out there too...having a go at some of the same folks. The big difference was that Michael appealed to reason and national interests while the Long Hoor browbeat them with innuendo and threats of treason if they didn't side with him.

"Gay, in many ways Dev reminds me of a spoiled child. If you won't play by his rules, he'll take his toy and go home."

Glancing around the pub, Aran continued, "I remember when the Big Fellow and I were locked up in Richmond Barracks after the Rebellion. Mick was critical of Pearse for being too idealistic and not practical enough. Well, maybe the Corkman had been too idealistic himself for a long time…thinking that might would right wrong. Now, in the last few months, we both have seen him change. He's laid down the sword and is taking up diplomacy as his way of winning this war."

"Sure, there's no doubt the Big Fellow's a different person. Unfortunately, Dev, Cathal and Lee Mellowes don't share that opinion.

They seem stuck in their old ways so…motivated by yesterday's thinking."

"And that's the personal pain of it all, Gay. To know that men, fine men like Lee, haven't made Mick's transition. Times are changing and changing fast. Dev and his lot are going to be caught on the wrong side."

"But what about Shadow?"

"Oh, Gay…the possibility of losing Lee Mellowes is tough enough, but not Shadow. I'm just afraid he's going to side with Dev and the others. As soon as I can, I'm going down and have a talk with him. Of all the ones, we can't lose him."

❧

A reddish winter's sun rose over the Dublin Mountains on Saturday, 14 January. Sarah Anne kissed Aran on the forehead as the Irish Rebel resisted her urgings.

She'd been after him for ten minutes to get up, clean his teeth and wash his face before dressing for the day. It was an important day: Dáil ratification of the Treaty and the establishment of Michael's Provisional Government. But Monday next would be even bigger: Britain would finally be turning over Dublin Castle to Irish authority.

In 1204, King John, of Magna Charta fame, ordered construction begun on what was soon to be an imposing military fortress. Gradually, however, with the country's pacification and subjugation virtually a fait accompli during the 16th and 17th centuries, the massive structure became the administrative centre of English then British rule in Ireland.

More recently, however, its hallowed halls again rang with tortured cries of Irish Republicans as they had the last breath of life beat out of them. The infamous British excuse of 'he died while trying to escape' wasn't very believable when a badly bruised, beaten and mutilated body was finally turned over for burial to horrified family members. Oftentimes the number of stab wounds and bullet holes in the corpse defied counting.

Annie's unannounced arrival into Dublin Town on Wednesday evening caught Aran by delighted surprise. He was about to leave his room to have supper with Gay when she knocked at the door. Growing impatient, she'd taken matters into her own hands and had come to the city, looking for lodging, or at least that was what she'd said. But from the gleam in her eyes, Aran suspected she had ulterior motives. It didn't matter though, they were back together again and that was all that counted.

After recovering from the initial shock, Aran could see Sarah peering over his shoulder. Suddenly, he felt a bit embarrassed.

From her startled reaction at the sight of his Spartan digs, he immediately realised this was no place for her.

"Never mind," she said, throwing her arms around his neck, "we'll just make do…at least for a few more days…until we find something more suitable for us."

Between fittings for a new uniform and showing Sarah around Dublin the next two days flew by.

❀

On Saturday, seated in the front row of the visitor's gallery at Mansion House, Sarah Anne, Gabriel and Aran watched the 2nd Dáil formally ratify the Treaty. The next official act of business, in accordance with the terms of that Anglo-Irish accord, was to approve the formation of a Provisional Government. To no one's surprise, Michael Collins was chosen as its chairman.

With his nomination made official, the Big Fellow grinned over at them as he rose to take his oath of office. His three friends led the house in applause when the formality was concluded.

With everyone back in their seats, Michael publicly announced his new cabinet. Several of the men he'd picked were also members of Griffith's Dáil executive: Duggan (Home Affairs), Cosgrave (Local Government), O'Higgins (Economic Affairs), Fíonan Lynch (Education), Pat Hogan (Agriculture), Joe McGrath (Labour), Eoin MacNeill (Minister without Portfolio) and finally, he named himself as Minister for Finance.[2]

With his new cabinet in place and everything arranged for Monday's hand-over, Michael, accompanied by his Cadogan Place comrades plus Sarah Anne, walked the two short blocks to The Bailey at #2 Duke Street. The Corkman had arranged a celebratory luncheon at the legendary public house to mark the occasion. After the meal and numerous stories, some retold for the umpteenth time, Mick slipped a shiny new key into Aran's hand. The attached tag read #5 Mespil Road.

"I know yis are looking for a place in town. With everything out in the open now, I've no longer any use for it as a safe-house. When I returned to town after your wedding, I asked a few of the boys to brighten up the place and bring in some new furnishings…it even has hot and cold running water now. It's yours as long as you want it. You can move in this afternoon if you like. I know Vaughan's isn't very well suited for a young married couple."

Aran Roe was flabbergasted. He rose in protest, but the Corkman just smiled.

Squeezing Aran's arm, Michael whispered into his ear, "Sure if Sarah Anne wasn't here, I'd be after a piece of your ear, you bloody old bog-trotter."

Unable to speak, Aran gave the Big Fellow one of his own patented bear hugs.

"Thank you, Michael. God bless you for all your kindness to us."

"I don't have much choice in the matter. There're so many

2. Coogan, op. cit., 310.

after me arse now, I have to have one or two of you yokes on my side," joked the Corkman in reply.

❧

The two of them were thrilled.

"It's a dream come true," Sarah kept saying.

During the taxi ride from Vaughan's to Mespil Road, Aran couldn't help but remember his previous visits to the house overlooking the Grand Canal. Back in May of '17, immediately following his return to Dublin from Amerikay, they'd all regrouped there: Michael, Liam Mellowes, Danny Kelly, Shadow, Sarah Anne, Gay, Turlough and himself. It was there they'd divided up the 'equipment' that Clan na Gael and the IRB had smuggled into Ireland aboard their freighter from the States. Now, Sarah Anne and he were married and Turlough Molloy was dead. What's more, the loyalty that had so tightly bound Liam's original little band together was threatening to dissolve.

Aran's second visit was on the eve of Bloody Sunday, 21 November 1920. Gabby, Liam McCullers and he had spent the night there prior to executing one of a dozen or so British spies who'd all met their end on that fateful morning.

Later the following summer, Shadow, Gay and he'd spent a few nights at the Mespil Road address. Thoughts of Sarah's narrow escape crowded out the pleasurable memories of his comrades' discussions, just prior to the announcement of the Truce on 11 July.

Finally, only a few months ago, Shadow and he'd made a hurried visit to collect some rifles, handguns and even a Thompson that Michael had secreted away under the stairs. "Something for the lads down your way," the Corkman had said to them.

The Irish Rebel had one more overriding memory of the Mespil Road place. It was there that he'd given to his close friends, the ones he'd spent time with in Amerikay, the small, metallic, Easter-lily badges he'd had made in New York City prior to his return to Ireland.

Closing his eyes in the taxi, that moment came to life as if it was happening now for the first time.

The words he'd said even flooded back: *May these badges remind you of the ideals of Easter, 1916. May they serve as symbols of our trusted friendship for one another and as tokens of our commitment to the common cause that binds us all together...and to Ireland.*

❧

Michael had underplayed his gift to Aran and Sarah Anne. Number 5 had been lovingly redone...each room was freshly painted. The cosy parlour had been completely refurnished. Several new overstuffed chairs, a comfortable couch and a large rug now covered the floor. Additionally, a bookcase and several tables, each with a paraffin lamp, decorated the room. It was all two newly-weds could've asked for. Even a fire had been laid and the coal scuttle was full.

A dining room, well-equipped kitchen and small bathroom completed the ground floor plan. At the top of the stairs was a narrow hallway with two bedrooms, one at either end.

Unable to resist, the Gortman pulled open the narrow door built into the wall below the steps. There in the floor of the storage space was the concealed compartment from which Shadow and he had removed Michael's little armoury just a few months earlier.

The accommodation wasn't quite as homey as Gay and Áine's cottage, but Aran and Annie were thrilled with it. Walking from room to room, she kept repeating over and over, "Beyond my wildest dreams, Aran, beyond my wildest dreams."

The Gortman was thunderstruck as well. It was a lovely surprise and only a short walk to Beggars' Bush Barracks: down Mespil, past Baggot Street Bridge and along Haddington Road. The barracks was only a block from historic Mount Street Bridge of Easter-Week fame.

❧

The British had already cleared out of the small, stone-walled facility earlier in the week and IRA GHQ moved in right behind them. The installation of the Irish colours at Beggars' Bush was overseen by General Richard Mulcahy, newly appointed Minister for Defence and General Eoin O'Duffy. The next day, O'Duffy and General Emmet Dalton took the British hand-over of Portobello Barracks, not far from Harold's Cross, a southern suburb of Dublin.

Immediately following the exit of Britain's high command in Dublin, Mick set up an office for himself at Beggars' Bush. It was directly opposite the main gate house on the eastern side of the parade ground. Four doors down the hall from him, the Big Fellow had reserved a modest two-office suite for Aran and Gabriel, the new Dublin Guards 2nd Battalion's commander and vice-commander.

The next morning the two friends stood at attention. They proudly saluted the tri-colour as it was hoisted up the flag-staff just outside the barrack's main building. Dressed in their new dark-green, Irish Army uniforms, Aran fought back tears. No words could express how overjoyed he was to see that green, white and orange banner waving in the breeze…so many had died to see this moment come true. Millions had given their all for the cause of Ireland and freedom from British rule. Now, on 15 January 1922, it was becoming a reality. Aran could only bow his head and stand for several long moments thanking God.

Roused from his prayer of thanksgiving by a military band playing *The Soldier's Song*, Aran wished: *If only Pearse could be here to see this day.*

With the ceremony concluded, Gabby and he walked out of Beggars' Bush and headed back up Haddington Road to St. Mary's Church. There, Sarah Anne would be waiting for them in time for Sunday-morning Mass.

❧

Aran Roe O'Neill knocked on Michael's office door Monday morning.

"Come," the Big Fellow's replied.

"Aran, I'm glad it's yourself. I'd like you to meet Liam Deasy.

Liam's the O/C of the 3rd Cork Brigade. He was raised in Kilmac-simon Quay near Bandon...that's not far from Woodfield, my family's home."

"It's a pleasure so. I've heard your name mentioned in good company before," said Aran, shaking the man's hand.

You've come to my attention as well. Congratulations on your marriage. Michael here has been telling me all about it."

With time being a precious commodity today, Michael re-turned to the business at hand, "Aran, we've been talking about the Treaty and the matter of peace without full freedom."

As he spoke, the Corkman motioned Aran toward a chair.

The Rebel nodded his thanks.

"Liam was reminding me of the fact that since the first Sinn Féin by-elections in 1917, the Irish people have never been unduly influenced by election results."

"That's right, Mick," said Liam. "Our mission was to con-tinue the Fenian policy, to rouse the country and to strive for its freedom."[3]

"Sure, that was our charge," acknowledged the Big Fellow.

Liam continued, "From the time we were children, we knew 'the voice of the people' as expressed by the Irish Parliamentary Party at Westminster was a spent force. Slowly, Ireland came to realise that nationhood would never be won by talk only. It had to be fought for, no matter what the cost. Once this was accepted, the people enthusiastically took the cause to heart."[4]

"...and we couldn't have accomplished what we did without their support," interrupted Collins. "But Liam, do you think it's right and just to subject the people to continued war when, in fact, we've peace knocking on our door? Just look around you. Some of the colonial bastards have left already and more are scheduled to ship-out in the coming days."

Liam didn't answer Michael's query. Instead he said, "Speak-ing for myself and others, it's our desire to hold the anti-Treaty forces together in the hope that a Constitution will emerge which

---

3. Liam Deasy. *Brother Against Brother.* Cork, Ireland, 1998, 43.
4. Ibid.

will leave all free to subscribe to it without the stigma of an oath to a foreign king."[5]

"That's my intention too, Liam. I've just appointed a Constitutional Committee and the first meeting is scheduled for next week, the 25th. I'm going to chair it. It'll be a true democratic constitution. It won't contain the legalities of the past but the practicalities of the future. I want it to be short, simple and easy to alter as the final stages of complete freedom are achieved. It's my intention to omit everything mentioned in the Treaty including the oath. Our new constitution must be one which will guarantee our equality of status not only within the British Empire but amongst all the nations of the world."[6]

Nodding his head in agreement, Liam stood up. He thanked Michael for his time and offered him his hand. "I trust we'll have a chance to talk again in the near future."

"Please God," answered the Big Fellow. "All the best, Liam."

Turning, he shook Aran's hand and wished the Rebel good luck with his new command.

Nodding once more to Michael, Deasy turned and headed out the door.

After he'd left the room, Michael said to Aran, "That'll be just the first of many. But as long as we're still talking to one another, there's hope we can keep this divide from escalating out of control."

The Corkman paused. He turned and stared out the window as Liam Deasy walked past the guard house and out through the gate.

With his back still turned to Aran, he said, "Do you know who last had this office?"

Without waiting for an answer, he replied, "General Hugh Tudor, the feckin' lout responsible for heading up the Tans, Auxie, British Intelligence and Secret Service over here."

Aran let out a low whistle. "Jaysus wept, if these walls could only talk…"

---

5. Ibid., 40.
6. Coogan, op. cit., 312.

Turning back to his desk, Michael added "…and if they could, they'd run red with the blood of brave Irishmen and women battered to death by his feckless thugs, sure they would.

"Now, if I'm going to make it over to the Castle by two, I must hurry," said Michael. A note of impatience marked his voice.

"Anything else?"

"Yes, Mick, but this will take just a minute. Do you remember the note you had Sarah Anne take over to Sam in London last spring?"

"Sure. What about it?"

"She told me last night she'd caught a glimpse of your cryptic message…the one in which you said, 'nail up Henry's picture.'"

"Go on."

"I was just wondering if the Henry in your letter might refer to Field Marshall Sir Henry Wilson. If he'd wind you might be after his arse, wouldn't he do his damnedest to stop you before you took action?"

"What are you thinking? Wilson might have something to do with that Black Spot business?"

"It's just a thought. The man certainly has motive, especially with you sticking your nose in his Northern Irish affairs. He also has the means and plenty of opportunity, now that you're a public celebrity."

"It's an interesting theory, Aran. See here, I'll be in London at week's end to confer with Churchill. I'll make time to have a talk with Sam. Want to come along?"

"Absolutely. Would you also add Gabby's name to your iota of body guards and ancillary personnel?

"Consider it done, my friend. Now, if you'll bugger off, I've a few more details to attend to before we 'take the Castle.'"

❧

Members of the new Irish Army stood at ease in 'fours' just below Cork Hill in Dame Street. The impressive domed rotunda of City Hall shone in the afternoon sunlight. The dull overcast of the morning had given way to a blue sky with scattered, fluffy-white cloud, but a bitter wind was blowing through the streets of Dublin. Spectators lining the footpath turned their backs to it, seeking what little protection they could.

Major Aran Roe O'Neill, Captain Gabriel McCracken and fellow officers Tom Cullen, Liam Tobin and Frank Thornton stood behind their military superiors. At the front of the formation milled Generals Seán Mac Eoin, Emmet Dalton, Eoin O'Duffy and Richard Mulcahy. A hundred or so additional troopers filled in the remaining ranks.

Cú Cullen turned to Gay saying, "At least you have to give the feckin' Limeys credit, they're leaving with dignity and proper military protocol."

"Cú, you must be jokin'. Sure, they're great ones for marching and parading up and down main streets, but turn 'em loose in the alley-ways and villages and they're nothing but rabble. Soldiers, Tans, Auxies…they're all the same. They've no regard for Ireland or the Irish people. We're just shyte under their boots. I've no respect for them, their ways or their masters. Its bloody well time they're gone. Who invited them anyway?"

"Colonial imperialism and damned military might that's who," riposted Liam Tobin.

"It's a divil isn't it," said Aran. "They're finally leaving, but look what's left behind…mistrust and division. It's seeds like that that could rend this nation in two if we're not careful. British authority may be leaving, but the residue of 'divide and conquer' remains."

Emmet Dalton, overhearing the talk behind him, turned and joined in the slanging, "Just imagine it, lads, Lloyd George and Churchill must be rubbing their hands together in glee…hoping we'll self-destruct."

"That's all it'll take for them to come marching back in here," offered Frank.

In a mocking voice, Gabby added, "Sure, and if they need an excuse, they'll simply say, 'for Crown, Commonwealth and *our* own good.' Besides, didn't they tell us often enough, 'you're not fit to manage your own affairs.'"

At that moment, a Buick touring car with its hood down,

swept around the soldiers milling about in the street. Seated alone in the back seat was Michael Collins. He was in civilian attire and wearing a grey Trilby hat.

"Atten...tion." It was Mulcahy, shouting out orders.

The Provisional Government chairman saluted the troops as he passed.

"Right shoulder, huh," cried Mulcahy.

"Forward...march."

Four columns of uniformed men paraded past City Hall and up Cork Hill.

As the soldiers made a left turn into the upper Castle yard, Aran noticed a clock on the corner building. It read six minutes past two o'clock.

A bit late we are, mused the Irish Rebel. *Ah well, its Irish time not theirs.*

A few steps further along, the Irish Rebel glanced up toward the dome of the City Hall.

God bless you, Seán Connolly, he murmured to himself.

Aran knew his story. The actor and captain in James Connolly's Citizen Army had led his Easter-Rebellion garrison to this very spot. But while returning enemy fire, he was shot and killed on the building's roof. Some say he was the first Irish casualty of '16.

Passing through the guarded entrance into the gravelled courtyard, the Gortman could see Michael standing at attention facing his approaching men.

When the last soldier had passed through the gates, the Minister for Defence ordered, "Troopers...halt."

"Left face...turn."

"Present...arms."

Aran's column was now the front row, facing the centre of the quadrangle. Three rows of Irish soldiers stretched out to his left and behind him. Dick Mulcahy was to his right.

The Corkman stood alone, perhaps five or six paces in front of his armed detail. Across the Castle yard, facing Collins and his men, were three rows of British soldiers. They were standing at attention with arms sloped and bayonets fixed.

Across the south side of the quadrangle, with their backs to the main building, stood several dozen senior civil servants, each apprehensive about meeting the man who would be their 'boss' from this day forth. This was the same man that the British had made out to be a monster and murderer. Wasn't it his agents and assassins who'd done his bidding…terrorising and supposedly eliminating scores of 'innocent' persons?

A sudden silence fell over the parade ground.

Moments later, one of the Castle doors opened. Lord FitzAlan, Britain's Lord Lieutenant in Ireland, appeared in full military dress uniform: a scabbard sword by his side and chest medals flashing in the bright sunlight.

The man approached Michael and saluted. The Big Fellow held out his hand.

FitzAlan hesitated then shook it.

In a firm voice the British official said, "You're seven minutes late, Mr. Collins."

Michael's reply was clearly audible to Aran and many of the others, "We've been waiting for seven hundred years. You can have the seven minutes."

The Corkman took a step backwards.

FitzAlan, also retreated one pace, turned and walked over to a waiting motor car.

With the auto heading out the gate, a British officer shouted out an order. At quickstep, he ceremoniously marched his men out of the yard, down to the quays and aboard a waiting naval cutter.

With the British military clear of the yard, the Provisional Chairman turned and again saluted his men. But instead of leaving, he walked over and shook the hand of each administrative official. He assured them their positions were safe if they would simply dedicate their efforts to supporting Ireland's new government. The relief on the men's faces was noticeable.

With this personal undertaking completed, Mick instructed Joe O'Reilly to bring the Buick in through the gates.

Again with the Corkman in the rear seat, the motor sped off in the direction of Beggars' Bush.

Richard Mulcahy stepped forward. He reformed his men and together they marched out of the walled fortress. The hand-over of the Castle was complete.

❦

When Aran arrived home later that evening, he had a surprise waiting for him. Sitting in one of the overstuffed chairs before a glowing fire was Larry McCracken.

"Holy Mother of God," exclaimed the Gortman. "This is a nice surprise, but I thought you and your parents sailed from Cobh two days ago."

"They did, but as you can see, I didn't."

"Aran," said Sarah Anne, coming into the room from the kitchen, "Larry wants to stay and join Michael's new army."

"Your jokin' aren't yis?" replied an astonished Aran.

"Not a bit of it," said Sarah. "He's dead serious."

"What in the world did Father and Mother say about all this?"

"They were upset when I broke the news to them on Wednesday last, but by the next day they seemed resigned to the idea," answered the thirty-eight-year-old. "All Father kept saying was that Ireland's finally taking back what she gave up years ago."

"...and the farm, Larry, how will they manage without ye?"

"Dom and the two hired hands we took on last summer should be able to handle the work. Father still likes to help out, but he spends most of his time staying close to the house or fishing. Don't forget, he's up into his sixties. We're not exactly certain what year he is, but as sure as he's Irish, he's not telling anyone. I don't even think Mother knows how old he really is. But one thing's for certain, seeing Sarah Anne and you again put new life in his step. He's so proud of the both of you. You're all he could talk about after you three left for Dublin in '17."

Aran was still in a state of shocked surprise. He remembered Shadow's initial impression of Larry when they'd first met back in the summer of '16: impulsive but hard-working. But Shadow had him pegged exactly right...a chancer with rough hands. That plus the fact he reminded the Limerick man of his old friend Major 'Foxie Jack' McBride tipped the scales in Larry's favour.

Shadow was right. He was a good man. Now he was in Ireland...ready to do his bit for the ould sod. Who in their right mind could turn him away? Not when Ireland needed every good man it could find.

"Jaysus, Larry, have you told Gay about this?"

"Not yet, but as soon as I see him I will."

"He'll be knocked off his feet, I can tell you that," said Aran.

"Ah shyte, it'll do him good. He's getting too set in his ways as it is."

"Now come here and tell me Aran, what about this fighting business? Wherever I've been, people are talking. Do you really think there's going to be war again?"

"With the English...no, I doubt it. With our own lads...maybe... it's still too soon to tell, however, but please God, I hope and pray not."

❧

On Friday evening, the 20th, Aran, Gabby, Cú and Liam Tobin met Michael in Kingstown with just minutes to spare before the mail boat sailed for Holyhead. In Mick's company were Emmet Dalton, Dick Mulcahy, Eoin O'Duffy and Piaras Béaslaí.

The Big Fellow had weekend meetings scheduled with Churchill and Birkenhead at the Colonial Office. The three would be reviewing Britain's strategy for overseeing the introduction and approval of the Irish Free State Bill that would soon be making its way through both houses of the British legislature.

Churchill had also arranged for Michael and Sir James Craig, the Ulster Unionist leader, to meet. It would be an historic event: the first conference between Ireland's two new leaders.

After their initial handshakes at the quay, Gay quipped, "Ah, do yis think we've enough gunmen to keep the lousers at bay?"

Michael, not to be denied, retorted, "We'll scare the livin' shyte out of them. Sure, they haven't a chance. Gay, you take the point and lead the way."

It had been a momentous two weeks: first, the Dáil's Treaty approval then de Valera's resignation and Griffith's election as president. Those actions were immediately followed by Dev and his supporters walking out of the assembly.

Within the past week, the British had handed over two of their Dublin barracks and on Monday last the Castle. Those were monumental events, representing both symbolic as well as practical signs that the Irish people couldn't ignore. In spite of the disparaging words some were saying about the agreement, the Treaty *was* producing tangible, positive results.

Aran knew that some pessimists were beginning to believe that maybe, just maybe, Michael Collins was right.

As the Gortman stepped aboard the mail boat, he thought: *Please God, may the doubters finally see the light. Sure, the Treaty can be a stepping stone to the real independence we've all sought for so long.*

❧

Later that evening, the nine Irishmen huddled in Michael's cramped quarters below deck.

He outlined for them his four major areas of concern. First, there was the need to gain political and administrative control of the new twenty-six-county Free State. Michael saw de Valera as his major obstacle here. Next, were his dealings with the British government over the Treaty's implementation. Third, was the matter of Northern Ireland with its many ramifications: Boundary Commission; the ongoing Dáil boycott; employment, housing and sectarian violence; and the status of Republican prisoners. Finally, his most immediate and pressing concern centred on the IRA. Will they support the new government or not?

Michael summarised the conversation he'd had with Liam Deasy earlier in the week.

"Deasy, speaking for many in the Southern Command,

reminded me that they who'd manned the front line and with greater hopes of success than at any other time in history, felt they could settle for nothing but an Irish Republic."[7]

The Big Fella continued, "Granted that sentiment reflected the war-footing outlook in Cork just prior to the Truce. As you well know, they felt they'd the Stranger on the run. Then came 11 July and everything changed. Sure, the boys thought the ceasefire would only last three or four weeks before more petrol would be poured on the fires of war."

"But things didn't turn out that way, did they?" interrupted Emmet.

"No, they didn't, Emmet," answered Michael. "Despite the terms of the Treaty, Liam believes England is once again at her old game of compromise…a role all too familiar to Irishmen and a role that breeds suspicion rather than hope or trust in the heart of any Republican."[8]

"But Michael," Aran inserted, "any talk of granting complete Irish independence would've sent shock waves through the entire Empire. It would've likely set off a disturbing chain reaction. You can't expect any government to be that generous and stay in business very long."

"That's the rational approach, Aran, but Deasy's more emotional. He feels that by accepting the Welsh Wizard's 'just and righteous settlement of the Irish question,' the PM's torn apart our unity. With it, we'd have been unconquerable. Without it, we're setting ourselves up for defeat."[9]

"Oh, Michael, I don't envy you," bemoaned Piaras. "It's so easy to get caught up in a war of words whose meanings differ with whom-ever you speak: self-determination, independence, freedom, a Republic, limited or full Dominion status. Then of course there's the matter of 'External Association.'"

"Compound all that with certain personal agendas and you're up to your arse in it," said Cú.

---

7. Deasy, op. cit., 21.
8. Ibid., 23.
9. Ibid., 30.

"You wouldn't be after referring to the Long Hoor, would ye, Cú?" quipped Gay.

No one said a word.

❖

Aran and Gay slid into the last snug in the Bunch of Grapes, a fashionable public house in West Kensington not far from Cadogan Gardens and Brompton Oratory.

They'd just ordered a pint from the barman when a medium-sized man in his forties slid in next to Gabby.

In a hushed voice, he said, "O'Neill? McCracken?"

"That's right," answered Aran. "Ye must be Sam...Sam Maguire?"

The Irishman's West Cork accent gave him away before he'd spoken two sentences.

Maguire, born in 1879 in Mallabraca, a townland just north of the village of Dunmanway in County Cork, was the IRB's Director of Intelligence for England. A close personal friend of Michael's, he controlled one of the IRA's major conduits for smuggling weapons from England to Ireland.

After exchanging a few pleasantries, the transplanted Irishman said, "M said you're interested in moving over here."

Aran gave Gay a look.

"I think you must be mistaken, Mr. Maguire. We're quite happy where we are. If on the other hand, you might recall meeting my wife last spring...remember...she delivered a note to you from M."

"Yes," replied Maguire.

"You had her bring back some new 'equipment'...some of Mr. Webley's stuff."

"Hum," answered the IRB man. "Did she have any luck?"

An indignant Aran snapped, "Feckin' right she had some luck. It was all bad...almost cost her her life. Thanks to some fancy driving by himself sitting next to ye, we managed to snatch her from the jaws of the very divil."

"Sorry, lads, I just wanted to be certain I was in the right company. Sure, I heard all about it from M. Thought I could slip them through without any trouble. I trust she's well so. Oh, by the way, congratulations to the both of yis. I heard about your wedding in Athlone."

"Mr. Maguire, enough is enough, interrupted Gay. "We're here on a matter of great interest to M, and really, to all of us."

During their brief exchange, Aran had noticed two men who'd saddled up to the bar shortly after Maguire had joined them in the snug. Every few seconds or so the Rebel glanced over in their direction.

"I see you've a good eye. Relax. They're friends of mine. You can never be too careful. You can understand that."

Aran and Gay both nodded in agreement.

"Now to the business at hand...you're wondering about the reference to 'hanging H's picture'?"

"Uh-huh," answered Gabriel softly.

"Sure, it won't come as any surprise, M ordered him dealt with before the talks began. He thought it would be to our advantage. As a result, I posted two men to do the work, but H is a hard one to get a hold of. Now, with the Treaty signed, I've backed off."

"We can understand that," said the Irish Rebel, "but do you think any word leaked out about your arrangements. We've been having a bit of trouble lately and wondered if your one is out to even the score."

"Funny you should bring that up. Just before Christmas, one of the lads I'd had helping me in the matter earlier turned up dead...fell off the Sloan Square Underground platform. The coppers said it was a tragic accident, but now I'm beginning to wonder meself."

"Thanks, Mr. Maguire. That's all we wanted to know. If you wouldn't mind, keep a sharp eye out for any other news. Let M know if you learn anything. We'd appreciate it."

"You have my word," answered the transplanted Londoner.

With that, Sam Maguire stood up and headed for the back door. His two associates quietly walked out behind him.

Aran and Gabby finished their drinks in thoughtful silence and left by the front door.

12

"If they accepted the Treaty, and if the Volunteers of the future tried to complete the work the Volunteers of the last four years had been attempting, they would have to complete it, not over the bodies of foreign soldiers, but over the dead bodies of their own countrymen. They would have to wade through, perhaps, the blood of some of the members of the Government in order to get Irish freedom."

Éamon de Valera

THURSDAY MORNING, 16 FEBRUARY 1922

*T*he cloudy light of a winter's day greeted Aran Roe O'Neill as he walked up the sloping grade that is Baggot Street Bridge. His travel case wasn't heavy but his heart was.

He longed to be tramping through the hills of Galway or Tipperary, enjoying their many contrasts of colours and geography. With the coming of early spring, the yellow furze and purple heather would be dotting the landscape, providing contrast against the greens and browns of regenerating flora. Adding to the rugged beauty would be outcroppings of grey limestone, spotted with yellowy-black lichen. If he was lucky, he might even catch a glimpse of a stoat darting among the ruined remains of an old stone wall or a hare zigzagging from cover to cover.

But the pleasures of rural Ireland were not on his agenda today. There was business, personal business, to see to. He was off to Limerick to see his dear friend Richard 'Shadow' Doyle.

In the month since the Dáil had approved the Treaty much had transpired. Michael's worry over the IRA splitting was justified. As many members of the assembly were also influential members of the IRA, the Dáil's political split had spilled over, infecting the military. The same could also be said of the IRB with its high concentration of high ranking army men. In fact, nationalist bodies from Dev's former seven-man cabinet, down to the Dáil, to Sinn Féin, to the IRA and IRB and to the Irish people had all split over the Treaty.

Halfway from the bridge to Merrion Square, the Irish Rebel hailed a side car to take him on to Kingsbridge rail station. An unplanned stop at Beggars' Bush had put him behind schedule. His much-anticipated walk across town had to be cut short.

Once in the jaunting car, Aran continued to mull things over in his mind while he bounced along the cobblestoned streets.

There was no doubt about it, he thought: *Historians of the future will say 6 December 1921 was a watershed date in Irish history. The moment our side agreed to sign the Treaty, it sparked a fire no one seems able to control. Now the weeds of bitter disunity are sprung up, strangling the flowers of accord that once bloomed with such promise only a few months ago.*

The handwriting *was* on the wall. Civil War was imminent. Only a miracle could avert it. Panic sometimes grabbed Aran by the throat when he thought about it. He knew that if someone of Michael Collins's stature and ability felt helpless to prevent it, Ireland was doomed. He longed to lock all the belligerents in a room and only let them out after they'd decided to work together for the common good. But that was foolishness and he knew it.

As things stood now, three distinct military groups were emerging. There were those who supported the Treaty and the new government. Their ranks continued to grow as new enlistments signed up daily. But their expanding numbers presented problems: most were inexperienced soldiers with questionable motives.

On the other hand, the anti-Treaty numbers remained more or less static, but they'd a distinct advantage. Their leadership and core membership were made up of seasoned veterans. Most were dedicated guerrilla fighters who'd tasted the rigours of battle during the War of Independence.

There was one ray of hope, however, in this grim scenario. Some of the old hands had taken a more moderate approach. Men like Liam Deasy and Liam Lynch. They were holding out hope that some accord might be reached. If it could be, war might still be averted.

Unfortunately, Aran's good friend and former commander Liam Mellowes was not one of the moderates. He along with Cathal Brugha and others had sided with de Valera.

Liam's words backing the idea of a Republic still rang in his ears. "It is a living tangible thing. Something for which men gave their lives, for which men were hanged, for which men are in gaol, for which people suffered and for which men are still prepared to give their lives."[1]

The invectiveness and bitter recriminations from the Dáil debates had spilled over and had hardened Liam's and his followers' hearts. No amount of reasoning seemed able to dissuade them from their mad desire for war: renewed fighting with England or, if necessary, internecine warfare with their fellow Irishmen. Yesterday's shared sense of IRA comradery and esprit de corps had disappeared almost overnight.

Éamon de Valera had begun to fan these flames of dissent. Now unburdened of his political responsibilities as president, he seemingly felt free to manipulate the passions and uncertainties of the Irish people.

While the Big Fellow was out stumping for Treaty support, Dev was doing just the opposite. In one such speech in Thurles he told his followers, "If they accept the Treaty, and if the Volunteers of the future tried to complete the work the Volunteers of the last four years had been attempting, they would have to complete it, not over the bodies of foreign soldiers, but over the dead bodies of their own countrymen. They would have to wade through,

1. Kee, op. cit., 158.

perhaps, the blood of some of the members of the Government in order to get Irish freedom."[2]

Again, in Carrick-on-Suir, the Long Hoor gave notice to an audience that included several hundred IRA men, "If the Treaty was accepted the fight for freedom would still go on; and the Irish people, instead of fighting foreign soldiers, would have to fight the Irish solders of an Irish Government set up by Irishmen. If the Treaty was not rejected, perhaps it was over the bodies of the young men he saw around him that day that the fight for Irish freedom may be fought."[3]

But the headlines of today's newspaper were enough to curdle the blood of the Irish Rebel: "Dev declares Civil War the only path to independence."

How can that bastard continue to incite the Irish people with his rubbish? Is everyone blind?

As Aran read the account of his speech, dateline Dungarvan, County Waterford, his stomach turned.

"The Treaty…barred the way to independence with the blood of fellow-Irishmen. It was only by Civil War after this that they could get their independence…if you don't fight today, you will have to fight tomorrow, and I say, when you are in a good fighting position, then fight on."[4]

Jaysus wept! Is that a prediction or a threat? How can any man in his right mind say things like that? Please God, Shadow has more sense than to believe that tripe.

The Gortman had reason to fear. He'd heard via the grapevine that Shadow had chosen to side with the anti-Treaty moderates. That surprised him, knowing the Limerick man's friendship with Lee Mellowes and Shadow's dogged Republican beliefs. But it did affirm in his mind the Limerick man's wisdom and savvy about sizing up a situation. If needless conflict and bloodshed could be avoided, especially among former comrades, the Gortman felt confident his old friend would explore every avenue before taking up arms. That was the reason for his trip today to Limerick. It was past time the two of them sat down and talked.

---

2. Tim Pat Coogan. *De Valera: Long Fellow, Long Shadow.* London, 1993, 310.
3. Ibid.
4. Ibid.

❧

Richard 'Shadow' Doyle, the forty-one-year-old baker, was standing on the platform at Limerick Junction when Aran stepped off the train.

They shook hands warmly and Shadow took Aran's case from his hand.

"Jaysus, you're travelling light these days."

"Ah, it's sure I didn't come down here for a fashion parade. But I did bring along three lovely peppermint rods for the girls and some wedding snaps that Sarah Anne put together in a book for ye."

"Any news from Dublin?" queried Shadow.

"None that can't wait until after tea," answered the Irish Rebel.

As the two climbed into Shadow's bakery lorry, the Limerick man paused before turning the key in the ignition.

"Aran, I've been meaning to write, but couldn't find the words."

The Gortman looked over at his dear friend. A serious look had darkened Shadow's face.

"Ever since your wedding, I've been spending more and more time alone in the safe-house."

Aran studied his comrade's face. "You're upset with the recent turn of events?"

Choosing not to reply for a few thoughtful moments, Shadow switched on the motor and headed the lorry north toward Limerick Town.

"That's part of it...a big part of it," he finally said.

"What else is it then?"

"It's a combination of things. Seeing Sarah Anne and you together...happily married now...it breaks me heart all over again about Helen...bejaysus, I miss her so much. Living without her is harder than I ever imagined."

Out of the corner of his eye, Shadow glanced over in Aran's direction.

The Irish Rebel nodded his understanding in return.

With his eyes back on the road, the Limerick man continued, "I also worry about the girls. Who'll take care of them if something happens to me? Sure, I know Helen's mother won't abandon them, but she's getting up in her years..."

Aran had never heard his tough, warrior-friend pour out his heart so.

"...then to top off matters, this fecken' mess over the Treaty is driving me off the rails. One minute I'm in the lorry driving up to Blackrock to wring Dev's bloody neck and in the next it's Mick's I'm after."

"Shadow, I think I know what you're feeling. I too am often thrown into a quandary. It's a confusing matter with old beliefs banging up against new realities, but I just don't have much sympathy for Dev's position. I've seen him and his crowd work their dirty-tricks campaign ever since the Truce, and quite frankly I'm afraid their selfish interests are going to get some of us killed...and for what reason...for no reason at all!"

"But the Treaty...it's the divisive element in the equation."

"Was...is...I'm not so sure," answered Aran. "But one thing I do know is that it wasn't the Treaty so much as *what* we chose to do with it that's been our downfall to date."

"But Aran, I reject the idea of those who are simply boiling it down to a face-off between unyielding Republican principles and more flexible moderate practicality. Dev's not a stupid man. He knew we'd have to compromise. He just wanted to keep his options open as long as possible and squeeze the bloody Sassenach for as much as he could get out of them."

"Sure, I can't blame him for that, but look, his last offer was still second best. Document #2 missed the mark. It left out what was important to both sides, the oath to the Londoners and Ulster to us. Furthermore, Westminster isn't willing to grant us our sovereignty and concede Treaty-port limitations any more than Craig is interested in being part of a united Ireland."[5]

"But, what about the Boundary Commission?" countered Shadow.

"Boundary Commission, me arse! If you ask me, it's another damned British smoke screen. They're not going to concede us

---

5. Pauric Travers. *Éamon De Valera*. Dublin, 1994, 20.

fuck all. It's simply a little political nicety to keep north and south happy for the moment. Mark my words, when the time comes to exercise that part of the Treaty, the Brits will bugger about on their promise."

The two men lapsed into silence, lost in their own thoughts.

With the evening darkening down, the verdant Irish countryside lined with its low, grey limestone walls, took on a fiery reddish-orange glow. A brilliant crimson sunset had momentarily broken through an opening in the heavy overcast of boiling black cloud.

Shifting his weight in the lorry's front seat, Aran took a different approach. "On the positive side of the ledger, Shadow, the Treaty has finally changed our centuries-old relationship with those on the other side of the Irish Sea. Things between England and Ireland will never be the same and for that, all I can say is, 'thanks be to God.'

"Just think, after all we've been through during the Tan War and over the past seven centuries, it's a new beginning…a fresh start. Things are now in our hands, not someone else's. It's our turn to do or die, isn't it?"

The Boer-war veteran didn't answer. He was still absorbed in his own thoughts.

The two drove on to Limerick and north beyond. Nearing Cratloe, Shadow turned off the main artery. A narrow, secondary road led them to a tiny hamlet and his safe-house on the outskirts of the settlement.

As Aran walked into the modest thatched cottage, memories of Liam Mellowes huddled by the fire, Helen's death and Gay gunning down Hawkins all came flooding back to him.

Shadow busied himself lighting several oil lamps and stirring the fire back to life.

A large pot, emitting a wonderful aroma, simmered away on the cooker. Two golden-crusted loaves of bread and a pot of butter sat on a wooden cutting board atop the dining table.

"Stew," answered Shadow in reply to Aran's inquisitive nose.

With the kettle on and several new sods of turf feeding the fire, the two men pulled up chairs. With pipes in hand, they relaxed with a dram of whiskey by the warmth of the hearth.

"You know about the Army Convention business, I suppose?" asked Aran.

"Aye. Lee Mellowes, Liam Lynch, Rory O'Connor, Oscar Traynor and a few others made the demand of Mulcahy soon after he took over from Brugha," answered Shadow.

"That's right. They wanted it held on the 5th, but Dick postponed it until later next month…I think it's scheduled for the 26th."

"That just goes to show you, Aran, things aren't as bad as Dev paints them to be. I don't think we're on the brink of war…at least not yet. Both pro- and anti-Treatyites are still talking to one another. Sure, around the country senior officers from both sides are holding meetings, trying to figure out ways they can cooperate with the new government and with each other."

"I imagine you've been in on some of them yourself?" speculated Aran.

"Yes, a couple, and pretty amiable they were if I do say so. Don't forget, most of us fought side-by-side for over a good few years."

"Ye don't have to remind me. That's what makes me so sick. How can a few words divide such stalwart men?"

Aran put his pipe to one side. Glancing over at his friend with greying, curly hair, he nervously cleared his throat. But before he could say a word Shadow broke the awkward silence. In a gentle voice he asked, "You're wondering where I stand on all this, aren't ye?"

As if the floodgates had opened, Aran turned to face his friend, "Damn it, Shadow. I've heard you're against it. Tell me it isn't so. Mick wants you to come to Dublin and serve with him."

In the lamplight, Shadow could see tears shining in Aran's eyes.

"As you said, it's not an easy choice…and no, you've heard wrong. I'm not committed to one side or the other…at least not yet."

The baker reached out and gave the Gortman's shoulder a squeeze.

"A drop more?" he asked, reaching for the bottle on the floor next to his chair.

"Ta," answered Aran.

"Dev may be preaching division and war, but matters are no longer in his control. He's not the one the IRA leadership is listening to anymore. We're looking to our own men for direction. Sure, some are itching for a fight, but most are taking a wait and see attitude. What happens at the convention will be an important deciding factor. Look, it's still over a month away...a lot of good can happen between now and then. Sure, I've even thought about going to ground and declaring neutrality. Florrie O'Donoghue and others are considering doing the same thing."

"Merciful Jaysus, Shadow, are you serious? Doing that would be a whole lot better than taking up arms against our own kind. Having you in between could be a plus for both sides. Your influence on Lee and the others would be a great help in keeping the lid on, but I guess that means no to Michael's Dublin offer?"

"Yeah, I couldn't turn my back on me friends just like you can't turn yours on me."

Wiping away the tears that had momentarily obscured his vision, Aran said, "That's what Dev doesn't seem to understand. This whole business of lobbying for Civil War is much more about family and friends than it is about political beliefs. We'd the courage and conviction to fight the Sassenach to a standstill. Now they're some who want to throw it all away over a meaningless oath. Parnell didn't have any difficulty in acknowledging loyalty to the crown as he worked for independence, did he?"

Without waiting for an answer, the Gortman continued, "Parnell was more concerned with the bigger picture. Sure, wasn't it 'the Uncrowned King' who sparked the birth of the Home Rule movement? Parnell and Gladstone...the two of them. If it hadn't been for the First War, we probably wouldn't be in this mess. Home Rule was a first step down the road to our independence. It didn't happen. Now, the Treaty offers us another chance. Look, one of Griffith's founding Sinn Féin principles was modelled after the scheme of the Austrian-Hungarian dual monarchy...a shared crown but each country having separate governments."

"Bloody hell, Aran, you sound like a lecturer at UCG," teased Shadow.

Laughing, Aran stood up. He stretched and paid the cooker another visit. Dipping a spoon into the simmering mixture, he exclaimed, "Shadow, this is lovely stuff! Ever thought about a new career?"

"If it tastes as good as you're letting on, I just might," joked the Limerick man, "but then who's going to mind the bakery? You, I suppose?"

Back in his seat before the fire, the Rebel returned to the topic at hand.

"About the Volunteer meeting, Mulcahy was right to push things back as he did. It gives both sides more time to talk, and, besides, it's keeping the lid on. By postponing the Convention and the possibility of an IRA split, he denied Churchill any reason for stopping the troop withdrawals. That's a key trump card in Mick's hand...because of the Treaty, the feckin' Strangers are leaving. Who can contradict that benefit?"

"No doubt about it," replied Shadow, "but it's left the door open for trouble. Now, there are two factions competing for the takeover of those evacuated barracks. That possibility can only further exacerbate any differences."

❧

Over their evening meal, the two friends talked at length about Aran's recent promotion as O/C of the Dublin Guards' 2nd Battalion. Despite his qualms over handling his new responsibilities, the Gortman delighted in reviewing his first organising steps with his wise friend. In much the same way as Collins had on several recent occasions, the Gortman talked about his personal feelings regarding his recent advancement and position. Though he'd only admit it to a precious few others, both Michael and he felt they were in over their heads with worry and responsibility.

Like the Big Fellow, the Gortman knew a lot depended on

his making sound choices and surrounding himself with good people. He'd never been in command of such a sizeable force before and would have to depend on past friendships for help and support.

The Dáil had officially authorised the unit's creation at the end of January. As its commander, his first decision was to appoint Captain Gabriel McCracken as his Vice O/C.

Minister Mulcahy had promised him three hundred to three hundred fifty men by the time the battalion was fully manned. On hearing that news, he remembered looking at Gay in utter bewilderment. The magnitude of the effort required to organise and train such a unit had finally sunk in.

As Aran talked on, Shadow kept nodding his encouragement and offering a word or two of advice here and there when it was appropriate.

The Rebel described how Gay and he'd poured over a rota of possible men to fill the unit's key positions. With Michael's blessing Tom Cullen was tapped to be adjutant. Liam Tobin accepted the position as the unit's intelligence officer as well as one of the battalion's three company commanders.

"Bloody hell," commented Shadow, "you're lucky to have snared such qualified men and good soldiers. But mind you, however, Mick will be after wanting you to share those two with him."

"Hopefully, that won't be a problem. Sure, we're all on the same team, aren't we?" answered the Gortman.

Pouring more tea into their mugs, Aran continued, "You'll be glad to know that Duncan 'the Nayler' MacGregor answered my call to be quartermaster and the second of my three company commanders."

Stirring milk and sugar into his drink, the Gortman exclaimed, "...and Shadow, you'll never guess what happened next. That crafty Nayler brought along twelve of his comrades. They insisted on serving under him. But, there's the kicker, one of those men who marched into Beggars' Bush behind the great kilted one was none other than Rory O'Mahony."

"That doesn't surprise me one bit. He's just taking after

yourself, he is," observed the Limerick man. "I'm betting he'll be a top notch trooper in no time."

"Well, despite what you say, I was still gobsmacked. At first I strongly objected, regretting I'd ever told Nayler of the lad's interest in becoming a Volunteer. But after a few minutes alone with Rory I grudgingly relented. Knowing he might face my opposition, the clever lad had his reasons well rehearsed. His coup de grâce, though, was throwing up to me that I was only seventeen when I marched off to war at Easter, 1916."

Shadow could only smile as Aran tried to hide his delight.

"As you can well imagine, Shadow, later that same evening, I had a bit of a sit-down with the Nayler…"

"…over a few pints I'm guessing," said Shadow.

Ignoring the Limerick baker's astute comment, Aran persisted, "I made the bloody Scotsman swear he's not to let Rory out of his sight. I also made him promise he'd keep the lad out of *every* possible danger."

When Shadow heard this he only shook his head, "Mother of God, the world's gone mad and just think, you're the one doing the driving. How the hell is Duncan going to do that?" asked the baker rhetorically.

Seated back before the fire, Aran went on with his staffing saga. He outlined how the post of battalion engineer fell on the capable shoulders of Pat Grogan, Áine's older brother.

"As you well know, Shadow, he's a veteran IRA man and was a loyal member of the Flying Gaels. Pat's a natural leader and fearless soldier. He's also agreed to head up the battalion's third company."

In a surprise move, Aran described how he asked Martin Richardson, his old schoolmate, if he'd consider becoming the battalion's medical officer.

"As you might imagine, it only took Marty a few seconds to agree," said Aran. "But to ease me own conscience a bit, I asked him if he wouldn't be so kind and gently break the news to his parents. Sure, I don't relish never being welcomed back into his home again."

Smiling at his own foolishness, he said, "Shadow, you should have heard him laugh at my idiocy. He reassured me that I'd nothing to fear. He'd already talked to his parents about doing something like this. He'd even told them that medical school could wait for a year or two, but that Ireland couldn't."

Despite the growing lateness of the hour, the two men talked on, fortified by the reopened whiskey bottle.

"I filled the other key spots with former Flying Gael volunteers. Caoimhín Donleavy gladly accepted the role of transportation officer. Nicholas Robinson consented to work with Pat as assistant engineer. Jimmy Carroll, Frank O'Leary and Christopher McKee agreed to serve as assistant company commanders…and oh yes, Liam McCullers is also coming onboard. He said he'd like to work with Marty as he's developed an interest in medicine recently."

"Jaysus, Gay and you are off to a flying start…fair play to yis both."

"But, Shadow, here's the kicker. Gay's brother, Larry, you remember him, is staying on over here. He's even enlisted. Michael's offered him a commission as a second lieutenant. With his background and work ethic, he going to serve under the Nayler and be assistant quartermaster. What Duncan doesn't know is that Larry will teach him a thing or two. Sure, the both of them will make a great pair I'm betting."

Aran paused and held out his empty glass for more sustenance. Taking a swallow of the sharp, sweet liquid, he said, "Now, for the bad news…I've been saving it for last. Danny Kelly, one of my choices for a top position demurred along with several other of our former Flying Gael comrades. Danny told me that as much as he respected all of us, his loyalty to Lee Mellowes was too strong. If, however, something changed, he'd let Michael or me know.

"It was a hard blow to accept, Shadow, but once again, the bitter division caused by that bloody Treaty has reared its ugly head."

"Just as you said earlier, my young friend, this business is more about friendships than it is about politics."

"Oh Shadow…that's just it…friendship. I'm dreadfully worried. One of my greatest fears is that *we* might end up on opposite sides of an unholy divide."

"Please God, no," replied the Limerick man, "but if something should happen, at least our respect and steadfast friendship will carry us through, no?"

"Don't even say that. It's beyond me how this country of ours, once so unified and determined to overcome all ills, has fallen to pieces. Our solidarity seems to be crumbling by the day...and for what? All over a few worthless, distasteful words in an oath that means nothing to Ireland...nothing to you and nothing to me. If we could somehow just simply just ignore it, it might go away."

"I tend to agree with you," said Shadow. "I think the British would be hard pressed to march back in here over an oath. They might, however, over something more profound...national sovereignty and border violations. That's the stuff wars are fought over."

"Wouldn't that be better than taking up arms against your comrades?"

In answering his own query, Aran said, "Of course it would. But if we only work the Treaty as Michael hopes, the problems surrounding our cry for independence might just disappear too."

"Pretend there are few if any limitations and what's ignored goes away?"

"And why wouldn't they?" answered the Gortman. "If we can show the English a strong, united Ireland that poses no threat to them, she might begin respecting us. That's what Britannia wants...a strong neighbour to her west. We'd be her best insurance against outside intervention."

Aran, now sitting on the edge of his chair, his voice full of anger and resentment, asserted, "...but this feckin' idea of taking up arms against our fellow Irishmen over bowing down to that repugnant King George V and paying homage to *his* government, *his* parliament and *his* military are beyond comprehension. *They're just not worth it.* Ignore the bastards, I say. Truly, they care nothing about us..."

"...but unfortunately, many English and Irish don't see it that way. Their vision has narrowed over the years."

"That's right, Shadow, narrow-mindedness...the disease of the Lilliputians. Where was England's consideration during the summer of '98? That was our self-proclaimed 'Year of Liberty' when, after centuries, a freedom-hungry people rose up, seeking democracy and independence. The colonial bastards answered our cry by putting 30,000 Irishmen to the sword for daring to challenge her imperial might. And back in '47, where was British concern for a famine-starved people? In that time of want, we died beside the road, our teeth stained green from eating the only fare available…grass, while Great Britain continued exporting tonnes of Irish grown foodstuffs. And once again, just four years ago, after thousands of our soldiers had died fighting for the 'rights of small nations' in the mud-filled trenches of France, the House of Commons showed her empathy toward our war-weary people by breaking its Home Rule promise. Instead of giving Ireland a limited measure of independence, she gave us partition and the Black and Tans."

❧

Back on the Friday noon train to Dublin, Aran felt reassured after his evening with Shadow. The Limerick man *was* taking the sensible approach. How could he ever have doubted his friend? As he well knew, Shadow's thoughts and emotions were too well grounded.

However, two things did concern him. He was troubled that Helen's death was still weighing so heavily on Shadow. He had even alluded to feeling depressed and lonely. That mood was not in keeping with the Shadow he'd known for six years. Maybe he'd turned too much of the day-to-day responsibility for running the business over to his staff at the bakery? Then too, as ridiculous as it sounded, maybe he was missing the challenge and excitement of battling the Sassenach? Mourning for Helen and with too much time on his hands, the Limerick man's zest for life seemed to be ebbing.

The Irish Rebel couldn't be sure if his diagnosis was correct regarding his old friend, but he'd certainly have a talk with Michael about it. Maybe the Big Fellow had some undertaking that would pull Shadow out of his lethargy.

Staring out the train's window, Aran thought: *This Treaty business has thrown everything out of kilter. People now doubt each other and themselves. There's a destructive force loose in the land and we'd better put an end to it before it destroys all of us.*

With more than two hours of his journey yet remaining, the Gortman leaned back in his seat and closed his eyes. Final decisions on his unit's training needed to be made this weekend. He'd already called a meeting of his leadership for tomorrow morning to address the matter.

Aran also reminded himself that he and Gay were going to London with Michael over the following weekend. Hopefully, Sam would have some news for them. With no renewed personal attacks by the Black-Spot crowd, the danger they presented had been pushed aside while other more pressing matters took centre stage.

The Gortman knew Michael was under increasing stress from all sides, and there seemed little he could do to help. Besides the continued burden of balancing IRA and British demands, the political pot was boiling too. Recently, the Big Fella faced increased pressure from an unexpected quarter: Arthur Griffith and Bill Cosgrave.

Both men felt a strong, unwavering Provisional government was needed to put an end to the country's unrest and reassure the British that Treaty terms were being met. Unfortunately, these two had begun doubting Michael's ability to carry Ireland's load. They feared the Corkman's apparent lack of decisiveness especially over IRA differences might compromise matters.

Griffith, in particular, felt Civil War was inevitable. He maintained that the anti-Treaty element would not coalesce with the pro-government side. Thus, the sooner this element was defeated or neutralised, the better off Ireland would be. He believed a short, aggressive campaign to end their rebellion would signal to all that the government was on solid footing.

Michael, however, was resisting this pressure to challenge and wage war against his old comrades. After all, Griffith was a non-combatant during the Easter Rebellion and Tan War while Cosgrave had only participated briefly during Easter week. Both men were political, not military leaders. Mick, on the other hand, was new to politics. He'd spent the last six years leading the IRA in war. These were his compatriots and fellow officers. Though granted they'd now chosen to oppose him, Michael had no taste in his mouth for waging war against them. Unfortunately, this sentimental weakness was undermining his ability to govern and was further dividing Ireland.

There was another element in the equation. Neither Griffith nor Cosgrave had much sympathy for the IRB. As Head Centre, Michael still pulled its strings, but again faced a dilemma. Composed mainly of military men, its unity was beginning to crack. The bulk of its secret membership had joined the fight for freedom after '16. Pledged to the establishment of an Irish Republic, they'd fought with distinction. But suddenly the Truce and now the Treaty had changed everything. Despite victory seemingly at hand, the IRB still recognised the need for Republican unity. It feared that with Sinn Féin's division, Ireland's old Irish Parliamentary Party might regain its lost political footing and that would never do.

Though small and of questionable national influence, this underground Republican faction was positioned to possibly unite the disparate parties. But it was proving not to be. Once again, with the contrary leadership of de Valera being felt, Michael and the IRB were losing more ground in their desire to unite the fracturing Republican movement. It was becoming readily apparent that the Long Hoor felt his power of personal magnetism could determine the outcome of the 'revolution' rather than relying on more traditional avenues of influence.[6]

This negative force was further enhanced by some of the old hard-line Republican guard who were opposing Mick's efforts to patch up the differences. Liam Lynch, Liam Mellowes, Ernie O'Malley, Tom Barry and Rory O'Connor were adamantly opposed to any compromise. Their continued intransigence was pushing the military mutiny nearer the point of no return.

Counterbalancing the IRA's push for war were some powerful

---

6. Owen McGee. *The IRB: The Irish Republican Brotherhood from the Land League to Sinn Féin.* Dublin, 2005, 363.

positive forces. The Catholic Church, numerous trade unions, most of the country's newspapers and influential members of the business community wanted to see an end to all conflict. The War of Independence had been particularly disruptive and destructive to the country's economy. With the Treaty and peace on the horizon, financial systems were anticipating a rebound.

Joining these nationalist institutions were the southern unionists who too had suffered greatly during the Tan War. They were interested in supporting the efforts of the Provisional government and eventually the new Irish Free State.

Finally, most of Ireland's civilian population, fed up with the rigors of wartime, longed for peace and the end of conflict. They saw Michael's government offering them that choice. On the other hand, following de Valera's lead seemed to signal a return to yesterday's 'troubles.'[7]

❧

Growing restless in his seat, the Gortman decided to seek out the dining carriage for a cup of tea and something to eat. In another thirty minutes, he could stretch his legs and get a breath of fresh air in Kildare. Then it would be on to Dublin. Annie would have the fire lighted and supper waiting for him at home. He was also anxious to tell her all the details of his visit with Shadow.

❧

The main road into Kildare passed very near the rail platform. Through a scattering of leafless trees and over a low wrought-iron fence, it was clearly visible especially at this time of year. A car park extended just north of the quaint Victorian structure that served as the Kildare station house. The Dublin train usually stopped for only three or four minutes to discharge and board passengers. Mail sacks were also thrown onboard for later sorting at the main GPO.

7. Mackay, op. cit., 247.

As the engine steamed to a stop, Aran noticed an unusually high level of activity on the station platform. Upon disembarking and with his curiosity piqued, he asked the conductor what was going on.

"Don't rightly know, sir," came the reply. "There's been an accident on the rails just beyond the station."

"Accident? What kind of accident?" asked Aran.

"I can't tell you, sir. I've no more information."

Despite his civilian attire, the Gortman decided to investigate.

Leaving the train behind him, Aran could see some activity about three hundred yards up ahead along the tracks.

A dull day and a light mist restricted his vision.

By now, two other men had joined him.

Peering ahead, the Irish Rebel asked, "Any idea what's going on up here?"

"Someone back there said it's a military operation," answered one of the newcomers.

"Clearing some trees that had been felled across the rails, I think," said the other man.

"Was it an accident, do you think?" asked Aran.

"Don't think so. I heard the stationmaster say that some National Army troopers from the 1st Eastern Division were clearing away trees that a group of anti-Treaty soldiers had knocked down," recounted the second man.

"Republicans flexing their muscles and making a show of it, I guess," said the first stranger.

Bloody hell, thought Aran: *Since when have they decided on a campaign of civil disobedience?*

"I was hoping the Treaty would've settled all this, but it seems more and more like there's still trouble ahead," remarked the second man.

"Please God, no," said Aran, reaching under his coat jacket to make sure his Luger automatic was safely holstered in place.

"Looks like they're about finished," said the second man.

"Good, I'm expected in Dublin. Now, I'll be late again," complained the first one.

Ignoring their banter, Aran turned and headed back toward the train. He could see its engine steaming impatiently.

Suddenly, a shrill whistle sounded above the hissing… WHOO, WHOO…WHOO, WHOO…

After retracing his steps, the Rebel noted he was one of the last passengers to board the train. Feeling it pulse and beginning to lurch forward, he reached for the rail car's metal handle, preparing to pull himself up onboard. At that very moment, as he looked down to find the moving metal step with his foot, a bullet, only inches above his head, ripped into the carriage's wooden frame.

Zing…another one shattered the window in the opposite door just over his right shoulder.

The first shot had caught him totally by surprise, but by the time the broken glass from the second bullet was hitting the carriage's metal decking, he was flat on his belly.

With the Luger out and ready for action, he crawled forward into the rail car itself. There were only a handful of passengers seated inside. None acted as though they'd heard the shots or realised there was any danger.

Reholstering his weapon, Aran cautiously stepped back and peered around the opening leading to the outside. The carriage's unfastened door was banging at regular intervals against the outside of the car.

Carefully, he stuck his head outside for a quick look around. Nothing seemed out of place. The platform was empty. The tail light of a motorcycle was fading into the distance on the otherwise empty road.

"HELLO-O-O-O," came and went the salute from one the soldiers who'd helped clear the tracks of the fallen trees. The Gortman counted five…six…no, seven men standing at ease as they watched the train pass by them.

Aran reached out and pulled the door closed. The only audible sound was the train's rhythmic clickety-clack…clickety-clack.

Slumped back in his seat, Aran cursed to himself: *Son-of-a-bitch!*

He didn't know if what just happened was a freak accident, another warning or an assassination attempt gone wrong.

Son-of-a-bitch, he swore again. *One shot, yes that could be an accident or a warning, but not two rounds fired so close to me head and in such rapid succession. That's no accident. So who in the hell's been trailing me today? Wonder if it had anything to do with the rail blockade back there?*

Rather than unnerving him, it just made Aran mad...mad and a little curious about who might be after him.

Did this have any connections with the other attacks? Was it that bloody Black Spot crowd again? One of these days, I'm going to get to the bottom of this business...then we'll see who settles what score.

❧

Deciding not to worry Sarah Anne, Aran said nothing to his wife that evening about the Kildare incident. The next day, however, he gave Michael, Gabby, Cú and Liam Tobin a full report.

Collins was alarmed. "That's it! I want you men to get to the bottom of this feckin' business before someone gets killed," he ordered.

They all nodded in agreement. It was past time.

Besides Aran's news of Shadow's declining the Big Fellow's offer and the mysterious attack in Kildare, the Corkman was agitated.

The pact that he and James Craig had first discussed in London back in January and which they finally concluded just two weeks ago had suddenly collapsed.

After making the formal announcement in Belfast of their agreement's provisos, the Northern prime minister had run into such opposition from his unionist power base that he was forced to withdraw his support of it.

Labelled by the press as the Craig–Collins Pact, it was immediately thought to be a landmark document and Michael's first major political accomplishment since the ratification of the Treaty. Though as yet little had been made of it in public, Mick was proud of his achievement and rightfully so. He'd hoped the Pact would be the first of many successes for his fledgling government.

"The bloody unionists blew it out of the water and never gave Craig a chance to make it work," roared Michael to his Dublin-Guard friends. "It could have worked and worked well. I wonder if Churchill had a hand in its defeat because his name wasn't written all over it."

The five-point pact had called for Ireland's new constitution to guarantee the North's sovereignty. In addition, the Treaty's Boundary Commission scheme was to be abandoned with both Collins and Craig sorting out the border issues together by mutual agreement. In return, Craig promised he'd see to it that the some 10,000 redundant, Catholic shipyard workers who'd lost their jobs would be reinstated. At the same time, Michael agreed to call off the Belfast economic boycott that was begun two years ago. Lastly, the two men had decided to sort out the issue of Republican prisoners who were being held in northern jails. Some of those men were facing execution for their alleged offences.

Though the two leaders were encouraged by London to revisit the terms of the pact and seek some type of accommodation, the rancour facing Craig back home was too great. The agreement that had held so much promise in the beginning ended up in the rubbish bin with both sides accusing the other of breaking faith and failing to keep their word.

Michael's spirits did a reverse the following week. At the Sinn Féin Ard Fheis in Dublin, Michael and Dev were able to concur that the Anglo-Irish Treaty would only be discussed and not voted upon. Despite the strong likelihood that an anti-Treaty majority was present at the convention, the ensuing nationwide vote certainly would have found the bulk of the Irish people endorsing the agreement. Instead, the two men agreed to postpone the scheduled national election for three months during which time the Ard Fheis also would be suspended.

The Long Fellow wanted more time to lobby against the agreement, hoping to influence the 'no' vote. It would also give him more opportunity to consider organising a shadow Republican government to oppose Michael's Provisional one.

Dev's words at the Ard Fheis clearly spelled out his feelings about the Treaty. The Chief urged that Sinn Féin "...put forward and shall support at the coming parliamentary elections only such candidates as shall publicly...pledge themselves not to take an oath of fidelity to, or own allegiance to the British King..."[8]

On the other hand, the Corkman hoped the delay would postpone the mounting threat of a split within the political party which would ultimately lead to a similar divide among the military. Michael's impassioned words foretold of a looming national disaster as he pleaded for party and national unity.

With the additional three-month grace period, Michael had a better chance of having a constitution written that would satisfy both British and Republican demands while at the same time staving off possible Civil War. The move would also assure the continued hand-over of British authority in Ireland to his Provisional Government.[9]

"Michael, how in the world did you get de Valera to agree to something like that?" asked Aran back at Beggars' Bush.

"Sheer political brilliance," bragged the Big Fellow, sticking his thumbs in his waistcoat armholes. "If the Treaty had been put before the convention, Dev's anti-Treaty side would surely have won the day. But at the consequent popular election, they'd have most likely been defeated by the electorate at the polls. Sure, it was a gamble the Long Hoor wasn't willing to take. Instead, I'm wagering that with an extra three months, it'll buy me some time and give us a chance to bring the pro- and anti-Treaty sides back together. Hopefully, it'll keep Sinn Féin and the IRA from splitting as well. I traded off giving Dev his moment of glory at the convention while saving him from certain public defeat at the polls afterwards. He needs more time to rally his forces just as we do. It's chancy, but worth the risk."

---

8. Coogan. *De Valera: Long Fellow, Long Shadow.* op. cit., 306.
9. Ibid.

13

*"He wonders also about himself —that he cannot
learn to forget, but hangs on the past: however far
or fast he runs, that chain runs with him."*

Friedrich Nietzsche

Wednesday afternoon, 22 March 1922

Aran Roe O'Neill glanced over at Gabriel McCracken then
back at the four lines of men trailing along behind them. Leop-
ardstown Race Course was not far off to their right. The village of
Sandyford was just up ahead.

The 2nd Battalion of the Dublin Guards was concluding its
third three-day trek south of town into the Dublin Mountains.
These were the very same hills and valleys he'd trained among
with the Irish Volunteers as a student at St. Enda's in the spring
of 1916.

Now, in less than two hours they all would be back at Beggars'
Bush. The Gortman knew the troopers were looking forward to
their forty-eight-hour passes. There'd be time to wash off the
sweaty grime of the bivouac, relax and enjoy some decent food,
washed down with a few pints of beer.

Aran and his staff officers had outlined a rigorous training
routine for their charges. The usual regime of military drilling had

been augmented with numerous physical training manoeuvres that emphasised competition and unit cooperation. Additionally, the men spent three to four hours a week improving their marksmanship skills at a target range the battalion had built on North Bull Island. The highlight of 'range' days, as they were called, saw the platoon with the best accumulative score ride the four miles back to the barracks in lorries instead of marching home.

Besides digging strategically place protective trenches on the island, the men constructed stone-wall barricades to replicate conditions they might encounter during rural engagements. They also built a dozen simple wooden structures on the deserted island to simulate house-to-house fighting should they be forced to go into battle in populated areas. Finally, the battalion erected a massive earthen backdrop that served as their target range.

But this was only part of the training the soldiers encountered. While on field exercises, they cleared wasteland of trees, brush and stones. They slept rough and cooked over open fires. In addition to the military training and hard physical work, the three companies, each composed of two platoons, learned battlefield tactics by participating in mock manoeuvres in Dublin streets and over mountainous terrain. The Flying Gaels' guerrilla tactics employed during the War of Independence were handed down to the new recruits by their experienced leaders.

In less than a month, all the demanding work and training were paying off. A real sense of unit pride and esprit de corps was developing. With the malcontents falling by the wayside, the remaining men in their new dark-green uniforms had good reason to hold their heads high.

Today, the battalion's original allotment of two hundred ninety-five men totalled just two hundred fifty-nine. A handful had requested transfers, but most of the others decided they weren't cut out for military life. That was fine with Aran and Gay. If men wanted to wear the uniform of the new Irish Army, they'd have to earn it with hard work and dedicated service. In the past, the price to see Ireland free hadn't come cheaply nor would it now.

As an added touch of national pride and connection with the

past, Aran designed a special patch for his battalion. In keeping with the tradition begun with the Flying Gaels, he'd a bright green pike head with the numerals '98' above it sewn onto each man's tunic. Unlike the previous pike head that had been surreptitiously worn on the underside of their flying column's jacket pocket, this insignia was proudly displayed just below the shoulder on the right-hand sleeve of each man's uniform.

❧

As he approached the outskirts of Sandyford, Aran thoughtfully reflected on the events that had transpired since his February visit with Shadow. Matters throughout the country and particularly in Dublin were coming to a head. The initial harmony between the pro- and anti-Treaty armed forces, a residue left over from their earlier fight with the Sassenach, was deteriorating almost daily. The anti-Treaty Republican leadership within the IRA was becoming increasingly belligerent in its demands. In particular, the strident tones of O/C Oscar Traynor, 1st Dublin Brigade commander, were growing more and more confrontational. Supported by four Dublin battalions, his voice of opposition to the Treaty was of great concern to the new Provisional leadership. Despite the annoyance of this Republican element, Michael Collins took comfort in knowing that the majority of active service units in Dublin had declared for the Treaty. Aran suspected this allegiance was more influenced by personal loyalty to Michael than it was to the newly ratified Anglo-Irish agreement.

One of the principal issues resulting in the military's breakup involved finances. With Britain contributing thousands of pounds' worth of equipment and arms to the Provisional government's military for its restructuring, the Republicans were at a decided disadvantage. Though initially holding the upper hand in troop strength and military know-how, they were woefully lacking in weaponry. They couldn't compete with London's generous supply of rifles, artillery, armoured cars and military transport.

Thus, with no funding sources available to them, the Republican soldiery were forced to take matters into their own hands.

In much the same way as the Volunteers had raided RIC barracks and private homes for arms during the Tan War, the anti-Treaty military began raiding banks, post offices and custom offices throughout the country for money to buy weapons and other much needed supplies.

This thievery only added to the growing national unrest initially sparked by the Treaty debate. To further compound matters, there were ever increasing incidents of insulting allegations, shootings and even arrests. In what had begun as a casual drift toward anarchy was now rapidly becoming a flowing tide, threatening to engulf everyone.[1]

As the Dublin Guards passed through the village of Sandyford, Aran ordered the men to close ranks and quickstep through the small settlement. He wanted his government troopers to make a positive impression on the townspeople as well as shorten the journey home.

Beyond Sandyford and with the men back to their normal walking pace, Dundrum was less than a mile and a half ahead. Aran, lulled by the rhythmic cadence of the march, tried shutting out his surroundings as he reflected on other recent developments.

Looking back over the weeks since Michael had formed his Provisional government, isolated incidents of bitter accusation, duplicity and bad blood had become commonplace. He remembered reading an interview Liam Deasy recently gave to the *Cork Examiner*. In it he lamented, "In many cases, petty jealousies, splits, and genuine grievances have contributed in no small way to a looming IRA division and the increased likelihood of Civil War."[2]

Bloody hell, swore the Irish Rebel to himself. *From the moment Mick and the rest of them, pressurized as they were by Lloyd George, relented and signed in London, the country's been on a downhill slide. That action, coupled with Dev's reflexive, irrational decision to condemn the agreement, a document he'd not yet even read, has funnelled us straight toward disaster. Oh, woe was that fateful December day when the seeds of dissent were sown…*

---

1. Deasy, op. cit., 44.
2. Ibid., 56.

Many of those with whom Aran associated blamed the Long Fellow for the country's precipitous fall from unity into dissent. As easy as it would've been to join their chorus, the Gortman pushed himself to be more realistic. Sure, Dev was doing precious little to keep the one army from becoming two, but other forces were at work as well.

As Aran recalled, one reporter had recently noted that de Valera's "...anti-Treaty attitude undoubtedly gave coherence and a political point of focus to anti-Treaty opinion in the country."[3] But despite the former president's behaviour, others must shoulder the blame for the divisiveness that was now loose upon the land. With de Valera's self-induced political isolation, responsibility for the present-day IRA discord rested with its own anti-Treaty leadership. They were the ones, not Dev, who were now the driving force behind the looming Civil War. But because of his defiant anti-Treaty stance coupled with his rabble-rousing rhetoric and frequent references to 'the majority has no right to do wrong,' the former president had become the lightning rod of the anti-Treatyites. His seditious declarations were a constant reminder of just how far Ireland's former political figurehead had sunk.

As the Rebel marched on toward Dundrum, he wondered: *How can any intelligent man continually thumb his nose at the very people who love and revere him? Was he so out of touch? The majority of the people do support the Treaty and he's wrong to say they don't. He's making a big mistake thinking they don't. His demented approach to winning back his lost power and influence is being marginalised by his own mistaken foolishness.*

Suddenly he turned to Gabby, asking, "Gay, what was it that the Archbishop of Cashel recently said about the people and the Treaty?"

Without answering directly, Gabriel teased, "What are ye going on about now? Fighting the war in your head, are ye?"

"No, not quite. I'm just thinking how the Long Hoor isn't giving the people of Ireland any credit for their opinions...two opposing forces on opposite sides of the fence they are."

---

3. Kee, op. cit., 159.

"Ah sure, you're just torturing yourself. Just imagine, what would've happened if Mick, Griffith and the Long Fellow had returned from London with *their* names on the Treaty?"

Without waiting for an answer, Gay continued, "We both know the answer to that one. The opposition to the agreement, at least in the twenty-six counties, would've only been a fraction of what that blighter's stirred up here in the past three months."

"All right! All right! That's probably so, but do you remember what your man said?" insisted Aran.

Pausing a moment to search his memory, Gabriel answered, "The Archbishop said something to the effect that '...the people of Ireland, by a vast majority, are in favour of the Treaty, and in a democratic country the will of the people is the final...something...'"[4]

"That's it...'the final court of appeal,'" said Aran. "Yes...the final court of appeal."

"The trouble is, Aran, Dev will never concede that point, will he?"

Ignoring the query, Major O'Neill turned and shouted back at those behind him, "Look smart now, men. Close ranks and quick step...ho."

❧

Shadow had been right. The business of taking over control of British-evacuated barracks was proving to be a nightmare. Under peaceful conditions it would've been a fairly straightforward proposition, but with tensions stretched to the breaking point and the military coming apart at the seams, it had become problematical.

To compound matters further, the pro-Treaty government was having difficulty establishing control with the scheduled disbanding of the RIC now currently under way. They also faced problems creating a workable judicial court system.

The establishment of a competent civilian police force was of particular concern to Michael. Back in January, on his first

---

4. Hopkinson, op. cit., 35.

visit to London after assuming the chairmanship of the caretaker Provisional government, the two regimes concluded plans for the elimination of the RIC. It would be replaced with a civilian force headed by Commissioner Michael Staines. As before, the Dublin Metropolitan Police would continue serving the capital while the newly formed Civic Guard would have authority throughout the remainder of the twenty-six counties.

Three weeks later on 21 February, the Civic Guard, initially an armed police force, was officially established. But things didn't go smoothly. In many cases, there was public resistance to the hiring of former RIC personnel based on previous history. Taking control of former police barracks was often problematic too because of local political loyalties. Finally, anti-Treaty areas of the country refused to cooperate or recognise the new authority.

With pressure mounting and the British military evacuation projected to be completed by Easter, Michael and his cabinet were growing desperate. Their ambitious scheme of assuming governmental authority over the country was proving problematical.

Both Michael and the British were caught in the middle. The Provisional government needed to put its best foot forward. It was crucial for Mick's administration to stabilise matters and reassure the people they were fit to govern. London, on the other hand, dared not interfere. If they did, it would likely consolidate presently splintered Republican sentiment, further endangering the already fragile Anglo-Irish settlement. As a result, British Army troops and RIC units were ordered to abandon outlying posts and to mass in centralised locations. It was hoped this would speed up their departure and protect the men from possible attack by rogue IRA elements.

Matters only became worse when armed hostilities broke out along the Northern Ireland border. During the first three months of 1922, a succession of serious incidents coupled with sectarian rioting in Belfast alarmed both Dublin and London.

Not surprisingly when nationalists were faced with a common foe, both Treaty and anti-Treaty IRA veterans eagerly joined forces to protect their side's interests. Unfortunately, both 'A' and 'B' Specials did the same in support of their unionist communities.

As expected, armed confrontations soon became a commonplace occurrence. In just a short period of time, these hostilities resulted in over one hundred forty deaths, with more than two-thirds of them Catholics. Almost overnight, nationalist refugees began flooding south, seeking protection from sectarian attacks.

To counter the violence, some British troop withdrawals were slowed and army units were increased along the border. The situation escalated even further when the major responsibility for policing was handed over to the Specials during the transition between RIC reduction and RUC creation in the North. This rash step only further exacerbated matters in the politically and religiously divided Six Counties. Instead of trying to deal with the causes behind the violence, this stopgap measure adopted by the Northern government only dealt with the symptoms of the troubles between its two communities.

In the militarily divided South, the Provisional government was able to establish a unified 'sub rosa' IRA Northern policy which only added fuel to the fire. Weapons were shipped north. In order to avoid understandable British outrage, Michael arranged for newly issued weapons to be distributed to *both* pro- and anti-Treaty IRA units in the twenty-six counties. Their older, untraceable rifles and revolvers were collected then smuggled into the Six Counties. These were used to arm IRA units who were still united in their fight against the British Army and Loyalist gunmen. Additionally, raids and kidnappings were coordinated between IRA leaders on both sides of the border. Gradually though, as matters cooled, hostilities began to decline.

For obvious reasons, the Big Fellow could not accept or acknowledge any responsibility for this border campaign but simply chalked it up to "natural reprisals by indignant comrades of the men detained by the Northern Government."[5]

Despite Michael's best efforts to support the IRA in the North with arms and ammunition, matters were deteriorating elsewhere. Local IRA units, be they pro- or anti-Treaty, began filling the void created by the departing British.

The ill-prepared, fledgling Irish Army, unable to respond in

---

5. Ibid., 80.

an assertive manner to the evacuations, came face-to-face with an equally confused anti-Treaty IRA military force. Despite their distinct edge in troop strength and experienced officers, the Republicans had no coherent plan to exploit their advantage. Events were happening faster than either side could effectively respond to.

Matters soon came to a head in Limerick. On 18 February, British troops began leaving the handful of military barracks in and around the city. Eoin O'Duffy, National Army chief of staff, decided Limerick was too important to leave to anti-Treaty units. If the city on the northern perimeter of Munster should fall to the Irregulars, Irish Army positions in County Clare and further north from the Atlantic to the midlands might become isolated.

As a result, O'Duffy sent in National Army troops to occupy the former British-held barracks scattered around the city. In response, anti-Treaty men from Ernie O'Malley's 2nd Southern Division coupled with Commandant General Tom Barry and some of his supporters marched into the city four days later.

Overnight, Limerick became a powder keg, threatening to explode at any minute. Additional reinforcements from both sides were rushed to the city. Demands and countermands were made. Both sides wanted their opposite numbers to surrender their positions and give up their arms.

In a desperate attempt to prevent an outbreak of war, Michael called the two sides together in Dublin. Liam Lynch and Oscar Traynor representing the anti-Treatyites met with the Chairman, Dick Mulcahy and Eoin O'Duffy. A satisfactory solution to the stand-off was finally concluded.

Several days later, Liam and Oscar drove down to Limerick and met with Ernie, Tom Barry and Michael Brennan, the leader of the pro-Treaty forces in town. Three weeks after the confrontation had begun, the agreement was finally solidified. Pro-Treaty troops were confined to barracks and anti-Treaty soldiers marched out of town, proudly still in possession of their weapons. Thankfully, a major catastrophe had been avoided.

A few days after things had quieted down in Limerick, Aran

discovered that Richard 'Shadow' Doyle had played an important role in the peaceful settlement of the clash. It was through his power of persuasion and personal friendships with the key figures involved that the agreement had been concluded.

Then only last week, the Gortman learned that the Limerick baker had been instrumental in peacefully resolving another conflict, this time in Galway. As Renmore Barracks, on the eastern outskirts of town, was evacuated, two hundred National Army troops took over its control. Almost immediately, they were confronted by an equal number of Irregulars. Violence was threatened. However, instead of calling upon Dublin for assistance, local military commanders were called in, with Shadow being one of them.

Not wishing to fire the first shot, both sides reluctantly backed down from their defiant positions. This time it was the government men who retired, but minus their weapons. Later, Shadow's comments to the press were headlines across the country: "Old friends make reluctant fighters."

But there was one disturbing portion of the report that finally filtered down to Aran about the Galway incident. Reliable sources clearly indicated that his old friend, the Limerick man, had seemingly sided with the Republicans. Afterwards, he'd been overheard sympathising with Liam Lynch and Rory O'Connor's plight.

In discussing the matter with both Sarah Anne and Gabby, Aran wondered if Shadow was leaning away from his moderate stance and planned to side with the Republicans.

❧

The IRA confrontations in Limerick and Galway were repeated in Templemore and Birr. Both the Provisional government and the British were greatly disturbed by what was happening, as both sides clamoured to gain strategic footholds.

Upon learning that Irish Army troops were surrendering arms to Republicans and that vehicles, including an armoured car, had been stolen from under the noses of Collins's forces, Churchill became angry. He refused to continue supplying weapons to government forces until he could be assured they were going to and would remain in proper hands.

Michael's government was irate and embarrassed as well. Griffith pressed for more decisive military action and called for the occupation of all barracks. Dick Mulcahy objected, citing his army's lack of preparation and overall strength to accomplish such a task.[6]

Still trying to establish an army presence, the Minister for Defence faced the usual recruitment, arming and training problems encountered by any new military force. These dilemmas were further compounded by increasingly poor morale, gradually more desertions and frequent failure to meet weekly payroll obligations. Clearly, the new Provisional Army was not ready for any major confrontations with its opposite number.

❧

Exhausted from the three days of training, Aran welcomed the warmth of home and Sarah Anne's love. Her sweet lips and passionate embrace greeted him as he walked in through the door.

Annie seemed over the moon about something. Without waiting for so much as a hello, she pulled him toward the fire and the comfort of the couch. Kneeling beside him on its cushions, Aran felt her trembling with excitement. Gently, she held his face in her hands and kissed him again. This time it was soft and almost delicate.

"My dearest Aran, I've something to tell you. I wasn't sure before, but I am now. I'm pregnant. We're going to have a baby...our baby and what a beautiful one it'll be."

The Gortman couldn't quite grasp the words he was hearing. It was as if Annie was talking to him from the other end of a long tunnel. Her words had a hollow, metallic ring to them. They lacked coherent meaning as they echoed back and forth in his head...a baby...a baby...a baby.

Suddenly, as if someone had switched on a light, he was back

---

6. Ibid., 64.

in the present. His eyes focused; his ears aware of everything.

"Oh my God, Sarah!" he exclaimed. "That's wonderful. Are you sure?"

Sarah Anne, biting her bottom lip and smiling at the same time, just nodded her head in answer to his query.

"Oh, Annie, that's absolutely wonderful. Sure, it's grand."

The Irish Rebel stood up, gathered his wife into his arms and kissed her long and slow and lovingly. Finally, Aran lowered Annie to her feet. Holding her back at arm's length, he filled his eyes with her radiance.

Cautiously, as if he were trying to tempt a timid fawn to feed from his hand, the Gortman reached out and touched Sarah Anne's belly. She smiled and clasped his hand to her with her own.

"Oh Aran," was all she could say as she fell into his arms again.

Later that evening, after the initial wonder and excitement had worn off, he asked when the child was due.

"The doctor said around the middle of November…more than in time for Christmas."

Then, in an excited flow of words, she said, "The next thing we must do is to decide on a name…a girl's and a boy's."

"No need to rush. Let's give it some time. Sure, it's an important decision so," said Aran. "I know we'll have lots of help from everyone…help from those we know and from those we don't."

Annie laughed, "Oh my dear husband, everything's going to be so wonderful…I can hardly wait."

❧

With the Provisional government's ill-preparedness and public embarrassment over the evacuated barracks' debacle continuing, on 16 March, Dáil President Arthur Griffith banned the Army Convention from taking place.

Back in January, the Dáil had authorized O'Duffy, army Chief of Staff, to contact all battalion and brigade commandants. He was asking local commanders to nominate men as representatives from their various units to attend the meeting scheduled for 26 March at Mansion House in Dublin.

Now, at the last minute, the convention was cancelled. Art was afraid the strength of the anti-Treaty side would be too apparent, further weakening the government's position. He was also afraid the Republicans would succeed in striking out on their own and elect a new Army Executive in an attempt to usurp control of the IRA. The meeting then would only facilitate severing the army's ties with Dáil Éireann, the country's duly elected authority. Griffith asserted, "…(that the Dáil was) the sole body in supreme control of the Army and that any effort to set up another body in control would be tantamount to an attempt to establish a Military Dictatorship."[7]

When Aran heard his rationale, the Gortman was convinced that the president was referring to a newspaper interview in which Rory O'Connor, former Director of Engineering of the old IRA and now the recognised leader of the new, breakaway anti-Treaty IRA, had stated in no uncertain terms that there was no government in Ireland that he would pay allegiance to.

When further queried if he and others planned on setting up a military dictatorship, O'Connor replied, "You can take it that way if you like."[8]

One other significant event occurred just prior to the scheduled Army Convention, indicating to Aran and Michael Collins just how far things had deteriorated in the last weeks. Éamon de Valera announced the formation of his own new political party, Cumann na Poblachta, with himself as its self-appointed leader. Its membership was composed almost entirely of anti-Treaty members from the 2nd Dáil.[9]

The handwriting was now on the wall in bold letters. The IRA was irrevocably split. The only remaining hope was to somehow keep both sides of the military from declaring war on each other.

---

7. Ibid., 66-67.
8. Kee, op. cit., 159.
9. Coogan. *Michael Collins.* op. cit., 319.

❦

Despite the ban, the Army Convention went off as scheduled. The Provisional government did nothing to prevent it from taking place, but Minister Richard Mulcahy did state that from this day forward, the breakaway Republican Army would receive no further support from GHQ.

In a counter move, the newly elected IRA leadership publicly stated it wouldn't recognise the authority of the Minister for Defence.

The following day, Monday, the 27th, the *Freeman's Journal* carried a full account of the proceedings under the headline: "233 delegates attend banned Army Convention."

Sitting in Michael's office in Beggars' Bush Barracks with Aran, Gay read aloud some of the meeting highlights as reported in the newspaper.

The Irish-American began with the story's lead paragraph: "The Army Convention held in Mansion House, Dublin, reaffirmed itself as a Republican Army and chose an executive of sixteen members headed by Rory O'Connor. Liam Lynch, Liam Mellowes, Liam Deasy, Seán Moylan and Ernie O'Malley, among others, were elected too."[10]

Between glances at his two friends, Gay continued reading: "In addition to the election of an Executive, an Army Council was selected with Liam Lynch chosen as its Chief of Staff. Additionally, plans for writing a new army constitution were approved."

Michael hammered his fist on his desk. "From the sounds of it you'd think the lads are well organised, but they're not. That convention is nothing more than huff and bluff."

With silence filling the small office, Gay took it as a signal to read on: "Furthermore, it was resolved that the Belfast boycott should be reimposed, that dog-licence money could be collected by the IRA, and that the new Civic Guard should be boycotted in the way that the old RIC had been. Finally, a motion to prevent

---

10. Litton, op.cit., 45. [Two days later, the Freeman's Journal offices were vandalized by some of O'Connor's men and the presses wrecked as a result of its published story about the convention.]

a general election was discussed and widely supported, before being referred to the next executive meeting."[11]

In a companion article on the second page of the paper, another reporter, writing about the resolutions discussed at the Sunday conference, noted, "...(they) included 'the declaration of a dictatorship which would...overthrow the four Governments in Ireland opposed to the Republic – Dáil Éireann, the Provisional Government, the British Government and the Northern (Irish) Government.'"[11]

❧

In what had been an extraordinary month, March ended with two additional noteworthy happenings. The first was to prove most embarrassing to the British government and outraged Michael, while the second continued to put pressure on the Provisional government to continue to work the Treaty despite the difficulties the breakaway IRA military posed.

On 29 March, anti-Treaty units of the 1st Southern Division stormed a British vessel as it was departing Haulbowline Dockyards in Cork Harbour. The following day, the *Cork Examiner* carried a full accounting of the incursion under the headline: "Republican forces capture cargo of arms."

A stream of oaths could be heard coming from Michael's office as he read the report.

"On 29 March, anti-Treaty forces of the 1st Southern Division boarded a British Admiralty vessel, the *Upnor*, as it left Haulbowline, and raided her cargo of arms[12] and ammunition; these were landed at Ballycotton and removed by lorry."[13]

That was enough for Michael. Moments later he was on the telephone to Churchill accusing him of duplicity and aiding the 'enemy.'

---

11. Hopkinson, op. cit. 68.
12. The British War Office estimated that 381 rifles and 700 revolvers were taken in the haul. Coogan. *Michael Collings.* op. cit., 315
13. Litton, op. cit., 45.

The moment he said 'enemy,' the word caught in his throat. It was the first time he ever remembered referring to his former comrades and friends as the 'enemy.' That word had always been reserved for the Sassenach...the Stranger...the English occupier. It had slipped out unexpectedly, this awful reference to his own fellow Irishmen.

Though the Colonial Secretary denied it, Michael doubted Churchill's sincerity. He was convinced this was a clever ploy on the part of the British to destabilise his government. The Big Fellow accused the Englishman of knowing in advance of the ship's cargo and the likelihood that Republicans would try to intercept it.

The Corkman demanded to know why the vessel hadn't been properly escorted and under secure naval protection.

No satisfactory answer was forthcoming.

Later the following day, the Big Fellow met with his cabinet. Speculation ran rampant. Had London somehow conspired with Tom Barry, helping him to pull off the job? Was the British government trying to undermine Ireland's struggling transitional authority? Unless Michael could right things in the next few months, the British might use his failings as an excuse to reoccupy the country. On the other hand, maybe in some demented way, Churchill was trying to strengthen the IRA's rebellious hand and return de Valera to power. The former president, viewed by London to be more decisive than Collins, might be able to restore law and order in Ireland while effectively pushing the sometimes hesitant Corkman from power. England's dirty-trick tactics in Ireland were nothing new. They'd been practiced for aeons.

The Big Fellow was painfully aware that London was unhappy with his inability to enforce the rule of law in Ireland and control the growing unrest that now gripped the country. He'd often been accused, even by Arthur Griffith, his friend, that he lacked the backbone to stand up to his former comrades and put them in their proper place.

The other event that ended the month occurred on the 31st. Unlike Ireland, which was slow in fulfilling all the terms of the Treaty, the British cabinet, under Churchill and Birkenhead's leadership, wasted no time in seeing the Irish Free State Bill approved by both the House of Commons and the House of Lords. It received the Royal assent on the last day of March, 1922.

As one historian writing in a Dublin newspaper noted, "Whether one agrees or disagrees with the terms of the Treaty, it has to be conceded that Churchill's prowess in steering the ratification through his own constitutional and political minefields made a significant contribution to the creation of modern Ireland."[14]

❧

Much to Gabriel's joy Áine and Mary Margaret arrived into Dublin on Sunday, 2 April. Both Uncle Peter and Aunt Niamh drove the two of them up from Cahir.

During the past three months Gay had made several weekend visits to their rented Tipperary cottage, but his being away from them had been a hardship on all three. Just gone two years of age, Mary Margaret was growing and changing quickly and he sorely missed being a part of it.

After looking for just the right flat, Gabby settled for a small ground-floor accommodation on Northumberland Road, just half-a-block east of Haddington Road. It had once been a stately red-brick, Victorian home, but the new landlord had converted the building into three separate flats.

Its cosy, bright sitting room had tall windows, a large fireplace and had been newly furnished. The kitchen was a woman's delight with two cupboards, a large dresser, a modern range and even double sinks. There were two small bedrooms, one for Mary Margaret and one for themselves. The newly renovated bathroom, complete with a flush toilet and hot and cold running water, had the usual sink and bathtub. The hot water was heated by the warmth of the fireplace and conveniently stored in a boiler located in a recessed hallway press. Finally, the back of the house opened out onto a lovely fenced-off garden that'd be perfect for

---

14. Coogan. *Michael Collins*. op. cit., 313.

Mary Margaret to play in and for Áine to grow a few veg and some summer flowers.

It was an ideal location, less than two blocks from Beggars' Bush. Gay teased Aran that he could sleep in an extra fifteen minutes in the morning and still beat him to work.

That evening was the first time the seven of them had been together in months. With the elder McCrackens spending the night with Aran and Sarah Anne, they all enjoyed a wonderful meal and celebrated the news of the coming baby.

The two women fussed over Annie, insisting she take it easy. After repeatedly telling them she was fine and didn't want or need their thoughtful but unnecessary attention, she gave in, letting them finish preparing the meal and later doing the wash up.

Around nine that evening, Michael stopped by to say hello and have a drink. Soon talk turned to the news concerning the Treaty. Mick asked about what was going on in Tipperary.

Peter reported that, as with other areas of the country that had been active during the War of Independence, Cork, Kerry and certainly County Tipperary had gone almost completely anti-Treaty. He pointed out that some of the local old IRA commanders were on the verge of becoming warlords. Men like Tom Barry, Ernie O'Malley, Seamus Robinson and to some extent Seán Moylan had assumed more or less total control of their local areas.

Niamh, with emotion filling her voice, was quick to add she'd recently heard that around home and in southwest Munster there've been numerous clashes and skirmishes, as anti-Treaty elements try seizing barracks, commandeering vehicles and disarming pro-Treaty forces, including the intimidation of Treaty-party sympathisers.[15]

"Niamh's right, Michael," said Peter. "The snipings, shootings and arrests are tearing this country apart. Please God, can't you do something about them?"

Michael just shook his head and sat quietly staring into the fire.

Finally, looking up, he said, "The humiliating fact has been brought home to us that our country is now in a more lawless

---

15. Mackay, op. cit., 253.

and chaotic state than it was during the Black and Tan regime. Could there be a more staggering blow to our national pride, and our fair national hopes?"[16]

❧

With Dev advancing his Republican stance and promoting his own anti-Treaty-party agenda during late March and early April, the Provisional government was dealt another devastating blow in the early morning hours of Good Friday, 14 April.

With the Dáil and the Provisional government preparing to celebrate the sixth anniversary of the 1916 Rebellion, Dublin Town was caught off guard. When dawn broke on the 14th, its citizens awoke to discover that Republican troops had taken possession of the country's judicial and legal centre. The massive, sprawling complex on Inns Quay, bordering the River Liffey, housed not only the law courts but the tax offices and governmental records of the former British administration. Thus, its seizure was a symbolic swipe at the Dáil and the Provisional government as well as the political infrastructure of all Ireland.[17]

In addition to the Four Courts, anti-Treaty IRA men from Oscar Traynor's 1st Dublin Brigade and reinforced by Irregulars from south Tipperary also occupied several other buildings in town including Kilmainham Goal.

Later that morning, Rory O'Connor, the self-proclaimed leader of the anti-Treaty military, issued a statement to the press declaring that the Four Courts was now Republican military headquarters. He was joined by other prominent heroes of the Tan War including Liam Mellowes, Ernie O'Malley, Seán Moylan and Seamus Robinson in stating their defiance of the elected authorities.

Upon hearing the news, Michael immediately huddled with Mulcahy and Griffith. The Dáil president was in favour of issuing an ultimatum demanding the IRA's immediate withdrawal from Dublin. But the Minister for Defence, wanting to avoid an armed

16. Coogan. *Michael Collins.* op. cit., 315.
17. Mackey, op.cit., 254

conflict with what he viewed as a superior force, disagreed. Mick sided with Mulcahy. As he had in the past, the Big Fellow chose not to exert his authority and confront the breakaway anarchists. He hoped time and dialogue might sooth their savage breasts and restore unity to the now-divided military.

After publicly disavowing the Republicans' duplicity and calling on Rory to withdraw his men, the Corkman sent for Aran, Gabriel and Cú Cullen.

✽

Despite the mounting pressure he must have felt, Mick appeared composed as his three loyal comrades entered his office.

Greeting them with a "Lord save us from our so-called friends," Michael motioned them to sit.

Pacing back and forth behind his desk, the Big Fellow studied the floor, trying to control his emotions. Finally his temper got the best of him.

"For fuck sake!" he shouted. "The Long Hoor and the Welsh Wizard are finally getting their revenge. This business of political namby-pamby has got to come to an end. I'm not cut out to be toadying after those nancy London bureaucrats any more than I'm suited to bow down to those bloody warmongers across town."

Back in his chair, the Corkman pushed his hand through a lock of hair that had fallen down onto his forehead.

"That damned Churchill has been on the telephone twice to me this morning. With O'Connor on the bloody loose, it's not as if I don't have other more important things to do than placate that London louser."

The three National Army officers were expecting Mick to call them to arms, but no, he didn't. The Big Fellow wasn't finished venting.

"You should hear that two-faced bastard go on to me. Publicly Churchill applauds me for taking the cautious approach with our Republican crowd, but privately he's wondering why I don't surround the infidels and starve them out. That's the same strategy he was threatening last summer just before the Truce: send in the British Army, some 250,000 strong, and blockade our little island with their navy. Has he no respect for human life?"[18]

"You know the answer to that, Mick," retorted Gay. "Any man who lets the Tans, Auxies and spying quisling touts do his bidding is only out for himself."

Nodding his approval at Gabriel's remark, Aran said, "He'd be a fool to order his troops into the fray. That's just what Rory and his lot want. I know what they're thinking. With British redcoats back in action over here, the IRA would coalesce and the Republicans will have their war…not against us, but against the Limeys."

"That's it," stated Cú. "The Treaty would go down in flames and we'd be back where we were before the Truce was agreed to."

"No doubt," agreed Michael. "So here's what I want you three to do. Aran, send in word you want to meet with Liam. See if you can talk some sense into him."

The Rebel nodded.

"I also want you lads to survey the situation. Just in case I have to make a move, I want to know the lay of the land."

On his feet again, the Big Fellow added, "Oh, by the way, I don't know if you realise this, but Shadow is inside Four Courts with them. I'm not sure what his position is, but from the looks of it, he's joined them."

Aran was greatly disturbed on both accounts. It looked like the belligerents were trying to force Michael's hand. The first gunshots of the year that had been fired were more to frighten and intimidate than to maim or kill. But the Irish Rebel knew things could quickly turn deadly, if this kind of aggressive action persisted. The news, however, that Shadow might've thrown in his lot with the rebels was more than he could bear. He prayed to God that things weren't as they appeared.

---

18. Kee, op. cit., 142.

In response to his request, Aran received a note delivered to Beggars' Bush and signed by Liam Mellowes. In it his old commander said that Gabriel and he were welcome to come in and talk. The message stated they were to appear at six o'clock outside the Chancery Place gates, a side entrance to the Four Courts complex.

Promptly at the appointed hour, they arrived, turned out in their National Army uniforms. They'd parked their military motor car on Wood Quay and had walked across the bridge spanning the Liffey. As they approached the high, wrought-iron fence surrounding the Four Courts, they could see that the entrance gates facing the river were fortified with sandbags and assorted wooden furniture, no doubt hauled out of the building for additional fortification. It reminded Aran of the Easter Week, six years ago, when he'd helped stack mailbags and bookcases against the window openings of the GPO. Around the top of the Four Courts fence barbed wire had been strung as a final reminder that visitors weren't welcome and that the men inside were serious about their intentions.

Lee Mellowes, sporting a new short Lee-Enfield rifle, was waiting for them at the gate. Two sentries unchained the opening and the bespectacled revolutionary ushered them into a small kitchen off one of the complex's main hallways.

Comfortably seated with steaming mugs of tea before them, the three men exchanged pleasantries. Aran told Lee of his pending fatherhood and Gay mentioned that Áine and their baby had recently moved to town.

Lee remarked he'd heard that Larry had decided to stay in Ireland after the wedding. Looking over at Gay, he said, "Chip off the old block, I'd say."

Gabby nodded and Liam added, "Sure, it must have been a difficult decision, especially with your father getting up in years as he is."

Again, Gabriel nodded saying, "Yes, but Dom will be able to manage so."

Though the three men spent five minutes talking of friends, family and old times, the warmth of the past was missing. There was uneasiness in their voices and each spoke as if he were walking on egg shells.

Finally, Lee said, "We all know why you're here. Michael's sent you."

Aran interrupted, "Yes and no. Yes, Michael asked us to come, but that's only half it. We both wanted to come and would have even if we hadn't been asked. You're our friend. Many of those in here with you are our friends and were our comrades, Lee. I even heard Shadow's here too."

Mellowes nodded his head, "Yes, he's here and so is Danny Kelly. By the way, Shadow would like to have a word when we're finished here."

Looking into his friend's eyes, Aran hesitated then said, "Good. I'd like to speak with him too."

Glancing over at Gay, the Rebel changed the subject. "Liam, there must be some way out of this. Sure, nobody wants a confrontation...nobody wants to see this whole thing end in dishonour and bloodshed. Talk to us."

The Republican, dressed in his signature three-piece suit with trade mark leather gaiters, tousled hair and pince-nez eyeglasses, looked too mild-mannered to be a doctrinaire revolutionary. But looks can be deceiving, as they were in this case.

Reaching into an inside pocket of his suit jacket, Liam pulled out a piece of lined foolscap paper.

"I want to read this to the both of yis and then I want you to deliver it to the Big Fellow and to Griffith. It's our peace terms."

Unfolding the single sheet of stationery, Liam, the secretary of the newly formed Army Council, began reading, "#1: Immediate disbandment of the Civic Guard; #2: Dáil Éireann shall pay all of our financial liabilities; #3: Agreement that no elections will be held while the threat of war with Britain still exists."[19]

Listening to Liam read the list of IRA demands, Aran couldn't help but think: *Liam and the others are hard men, unaccustomed to the ways of negotiating, compromise and majority rule. Michael had trained them well. Now, their hard-handed policies of the past*

---

19. Hopkinson, op. cit., 72.

were coming home to haunt them and Ireland. That made it almost impossible for them to take the next step and seek conciliation.

Liam looked up and handed the paper to Aran.

"Aran, also tell Michael that this is most likely the last hope the Dáil and PG has of saving the country from Civil War. Expect no retreat from this end."

All three stood up and shook hands.

"I'll go look for Shadow now...wait here."

Several minutes passed before Aran and Gay heard footsteps moving toward them from the hallway outside. Moments later Richard Doyle came through the doorway. For an instant, the three stood looking at each other. Suddenly, Aran rushed over and threw his arms around his old friend.

Almost shouting, Aran exclaimed, "Bloody hell, this is a divil of a mess we're all in here!"

Gathering his composure, the Irish Rebel released the baker from his grasp. In a more sombre tone he said, "Sorry, Shadow."

"Aran...Gay, I want you to know I'm here out of my loyalty to Liam and the cause of Irish freedom. I'm not convinced they've chosen the right path. We're talking and I'm still trying to make up my mind about what's right. Give me a little time, will yis?"

"Ah Jaysus, Shadow," answered Aran. "Take as much time as you need, but don't forget your loyalty to Michael and us. Believe me, we can all still work things out. It's not too late, but please God, don't do anything rash. I don't know what I'd do if you joined their side."

Taking Shadow by the arm, Gay said, "Come over to the table and have a seat. Let me fix you a cup of tea. I don't suppose you have a drop of something we could add to it, do ya?"

Gabriel's touch of humour was all that was needed to break the tension.

With smiles on their faces, Shadow and Aran sat down as Gay busied himself making the tea.

"Believe me, I've given the matter a lot of thought, especially since your last visit to Limerick, Aran. I keep going back and forth. But no matter how I hypothesize about things, I can't seem to learn to forget. The past hangs on, haunting me, no matter how far or how fast I try running from it. It's like a chain that runs with me...holding me down and pulling me back to God only knows what...yesterday, I guess."

"Ah sure, we Irish are great ones for holding onto our history. Its shadows haunt us wherever we go," said Aran in an understanding voice.

The three men talked of yesterday and tomorrow...personal remembrances and family things. But as the hour grew late, Aran suggested something out of the blue, "Shadow, why don't you come home with me? Sarah Anne would love to see you and besides, she's some news to tell ya."

"You mean about the baby?"

"How'd you know?"

"Ah sure, good news travels fast, and besides, Lee told me when he came down to get me."

"Jaysus, is there no secret that's sacred around here?" joked Gay. "I suppose you also know what I had for breakfast."

"Ah, bugger off, you bloody Yank," teased the Limerick man. "It all just goes to show you that despite everything, we're all still part of one big family."

14

*"...(that there are) rights which a minority may
justly uphold, even by arms,
against a majority."*

Éamon de Valera

TUESDAY EVENING, 25 APRIL 1922

*M*ichael Collins was as angry as a bag of cats. He'd just had
his second brush with death inside a week. The turmoil of the last
several months hadn't lessened one bit, while in the North, things
were growing worse. Anarchy was afoot everywhere you turned.

Éamon de Valera's Easter proclamation, delivered just hours
after the IRA took possession of the Four Courts, further accelerated the downhill spiral. The Long Fellow ended his address with
such rabble-rousing words that Michael, Aran, Gay and many
thousands of pro-Treaty Irish viewed it as treasonous. Standing
before a crowd in Sackville Street,[1] he said, "Young men and

---

1. Dublin's main thoroughfare was originally named Drogheda Street in the 17th
century after its designer, Viscount Henry Moore, Earl of Drogheda. In 1714, a
wealthy banker & property speculator, Luke Gardner purchased the upper half
of the street, redesigning & further developing it. Gardner changed the street's
name to Sackville Street in honour of his friend Lionel Cranfield Sackville,
an 18th-century British Lord Lieutenant posted to Dublin & the 1st Duke of
continued

young women of Ireland, the goal is at last in sight. Steady; all together; forward. Ireland is yours for the taking. Take it."[2]

❧

Not one for porter, Michael called for a whiskey as he sat down at a table in the back room of Liam Devlin's Pub in Rutland Square. With him were Liam Tobin and Cú Cullen. Already seated and having their second round of pints were Gabriel McCracken, his brother Larry, Duncan MacGregor, Pat Grogan and Aran Roe O'Neill.

"The feckin' blighters are at it again," swore the Corkman.

Aran glanced over at Cú, seeking acknowledgement of Mick's utterance.

The Wicklow man just nodded his confirmation.

After downing his whiskey in one swallow, the Chairman uttered, "That little scar-face bastard will think twice before he tries something like that again."

"Tries what?" asked Pat.

"Tries to kill me, that's what," retorted the Big Fellow. "Here Liam, you tell them what happened, I want another drink. Anyone else?"

"Thanks, Mick, we're all grand so," replied Gabriel, speaking for everyone around the table.

With Michael ordering his whiskey through the little window that served their back room, Larry asked impatiently, "So Liam, what happened?"

"On our way over here, the three of us stopped at Vaughan's for a few minutes. Mick wanted a word with someone staying there. I went in with him while Tom here stayed in the car parked out front.

"We weren't inside more than ten minutes. With Mick's business finished, the two of us headed back out the front door.

---

continued

Dorset. Eventually, 'the widest street in Europe' was renamed O'Connell Street in 1924 to honour the man who spearheaded Irish Catholic emancipation in the early 19th century.

2. Dwyer, op. cit., 144-145.

As we stepped onto the footpath, we were suddenly accosted by four men with rifles. Where they'd come from, I haven't a clue. They must've been watching from across the way and moved into position when we went inside."

As Liam described the scene, all Aran could think of was the old business with that Black Spot crowd.

By now, Michael was back at the table, this time with a large whiskey in front of him.

Liam continued, "Before I could draw my service revolver, Mick had his out...pointing it straight at the forehead of the closest man he was.

"Michael ordered your one to drop his weapon. When he didn't, Mick pulled the trigger. Lucky for that son-of-a-bitch it jammed."

"Mother of God," muttered Larry. "What happened next?"

"Faster than ye can finish that pint there, Michael knocked the rifle out of his hands with the barrel of his pistol and shoved the man up against our motor car still sitting at the curb.

"By now, I'd my revolver out. When the other three saw that, they turned tail and ran."

"Jaysus, Mick, you were bloody lucky," said Gay.

"Lucky? They're the lucky ones. I'd had their guts for garters if they'd stayed around any longer."

"What'd you do with the one you'd disarmed?" asked the Nayler. "Tie him to a lamppost?"

"We drove him to where he belongs...Mountjoy," answered the Corkman.

"Did ya know any of them?" asked Aran.

"Never saw them before in me life," answered Michael. "But from the accent off your one, I'd say Ulster...sounded like he was from Belfast."

"That's twice in a week, Mick. Either there's a quisling among our ranks or someone's keeping an eye on ye all the time," said Aran.

"Bollocks!" exclaimed Michael. "Probably the both if you ask me."

On Thursday last, the Big Fella had been down in Cork, addressing a crowd of people. Afterwards, as Michael walked up a street to visit his sister, a lone gunman stepped out from the shadows of a building shouting, "Collins I have you now." But before the man could fire his revolver, General Seán Mac Eoin, Mick's friend who was acting as a body guard, disarmed the interloper. Turning to the Big Fella, Mac Eoin was reported to have said, "Will I shoot him?" To the query Mick replied, "No, let the poor bastard go."[4]

Those were not the first two incidents of Michael coming face-to-face with the unrest that was now infecting the country.

Back in March, the Big Fellow was outraged when a group of armed anti-Treaty men blocked his entry to a Republican cemetery plot outside of Cork City.

Later that day, the Provisional Government Chairman addressed a throng of more than 50,000 people. As one reporter noted, "Shots were continuously being fired into the air throughout the speech. Later as Michael was concluding his remarks, someone shouted, 'Mr. Collins, why don't you go and tell it to Lloyd George and leave Ireland to us, traitor.' Without batting an eye, Collins turned to his attacker. In a confident and controlled voice, he shouted back, 'I'd like all of you here today to apply one simple test. Whoever ends in possession of the battlefield, it's they who've won the war. The British are leaving and would be gone altogether if de Valera and his friends would just allow them to depart.'"[5]

✻

Unrest and violence were blanketing the entire country and Michael seemed helpless to stop it. Much of the lawlessness in the run-up to the occupation of the Four Courts and beyond was due in large measure to ineffective local and national governments. Beside the death and destruction wrought by the War of Independence, its residue of political and social upheaval left much of the country resentful and distrustful of any governmental institution, be it British *or* Irish. Even if the Treaty hadn't been viewed as

---

4. Coogan. *Michael Collins*. op. cit., 316-317.
5. Ibid., 316.

contentious, Ireland's new administration would have faced many of the same problems and experienced much of the same unrest as it currently was. But the void left by its civilian government was being filled, in many cases, by military anarchists.[6]

Matters in Northern Ireland continued to deteriorate. In summarising the situation, one journalist wrote a commentary bearing the headline: "Riots in Belfast continue unchecked."

The story went on to report, "The IRA has stepped up its campaign to sweep away the new (Northern Irish) state and unite the island by force. Current estimates peg Republican strength at 8,000 fighters.[7] With their backs to the wall, suspicious of Britain's intentions and fearing invasion from the South, loyalists have reacted violently."[8]

Many in Michael's government were paying scant attention to the issue of partition. Their worries centred on preventing Civil War in the South. If someone did raise the issue of the border or the Treaty Commission, it was usually in reference to Britain using Belfast as a bridgehead to try and gain control of the entire island once again.

Aran and his fellow officers, because of their close relationship with the Big Fellow, had often sat in on meetings with Mick and Dick Mulcahy. The Minister for Defence candidly hoped that if all the terms of the Treaty could be successfully implemented, it had the capability to unify the country and destroy the Northern Parliament.[9]

---

6. "Compulsory levies continued to be made, post offices were raided for funds, newspaper distribution often interfered with, and the train services frequently disrupted. The government referred in the Dáil to 331 raids on post offices between 23 March and 19 April and 319 attacks on the Great Southern and Western Railway by armed men between 1 March and 22 April." Hopkinson, op. cit., 89-90.

7. The vast majority of IRA men in the North supported the anti-Treaty side, while almost all funds & weapons used by them in the Six Counties were supplied by Collins's Provisional government. Most pro-Treaty politicians were unaware of Collins & Mulcahy's aggressive Northern policy which was aimed at embarrassing & destabilizing Craig's government while at the same time encouraging the search for army unity within their own divided military. Hopkinson, op. cit., p 85.

8. Litton, op. cit., 48.

9. Hopkinson, op. cit., 83.

Michael clearly understood that the situation in the North was not about religion, but rather about power and money. The terms 'Catholic' and 'Protestant' were simply convenient labels to distinguish Nationalist from Unionist; Republicans from Loyalists.

This upheaval in Northern Ireland had its own backlash in the twenty-six counties. IRA elements began taking their venom out on Protestants and Unionists living in the South after an anti-Treaty officer was shot on a Protestant-owned farm in County Cork. Other murders, kidnappings, robberies and burnings followed with the result that Protestant families began leaving the country, heading for the Six Counties or London.[10]

Griffith spoke out strongly against this displacement. As Dáil President he said, "Dáil Éireann…will uphold, to the full extent, the protection of life and property of all classes and sections of the community. It does not know and cannot know, as a National Government, any distinction of class or creed."[11]

With the collapse of the first Craig-Collins Pact, Aran was surprised when Michael told him he was going over to London, again at Churchill's request, to meet with Sir James Craig. The Englishman wanted the two leaders to try and resurrect their earlier short-lived agreement.

On his return to Dublin, Michael reported to his cabinet that he'd agreed to put a halt to IRA activity in the North and to release the captives of cross-border kidnappings. Craig again promised relief for expelled Catholic shipyard workers and agreed to release some political prisoners held in Northern jails. Of equal importance, several committees would be established to deal with policing issues and matters of equal employment.

This second Craig-Collins Pact, designed to lessen friction between Catholic nationalists and Ulster Orangemen again received much favourable press but soon collapsed[12] because it failed to deal with the causes of the troubles: partition and a

---

10. Litton, op. cit., 55.
11. Ibid.
12. The agreement lasted nine days.

Catholic minority population subjected to living under the wing of a Northern Irish Unionist government.

Other factors aided the breakdown as well. The British government was taking a blind eye to Ulster problems for fear of damaging the Treaty agreement while communication between southern institutions and northern minority nationalists was marginal at best. Finally, Dublin's Belfast economic boycott was proving ineffectual. Its furtherance only reinforced Northern Ireland's resolve to maintain its ties with Britain and ignore the rest of Ireland.

❧

Aran and Gabriel's inquiry into who was behind the spate of personal attacks was gradually yielding results.

On their last visit to London with Michael at the end of March, Sam Maguire had some news for them. After much digging through old intelligence communiqués and the shrewd questioning of unsuspecting military personnel, whose tongues had often been loosened by the effects of drink or the allure of sexual favours, the London man had unearthed some interesting information. Surprisingly, a thread of evidence could now be traced as far back as the 1880s.

Apparently some fervent political underlings, with military connections, in Prime Minister William Gladstone's liberal administration had joined forces with several malcontents in the Security Service to establish a secret, underground 'Death Squad' of sorts.

One evening while Michael was having dinner at the Laverys', Aran and Gay found themselves riveted to their seats in the Bunch of Grapes on Brompton Road. Sam had made his usual backdoor entrance, accompanied by his two bodyguards.

With glasses filled, Sam began his report by observing, "A fascinating series of events and coincidences you've turned me on to. I've been trying to make some sense of it all for over a week now."

"Don't spare us any details," urged Aran.

"Yes, by all means, start from the very beginning," begged Gabriel.

"Well," said Sam, "if you remember your history so, it seems it all started with the Land League, Parnell and his relationship with William Gladstone, Kitty O'Shea and her husband Captain William Henry O'Shea back in the early 1880s. I'm sure you know the story."

"Sam, every word now…don't leave anything out," demanded Gabby.

"Very well. As you might recall, the good Captain was elected to Parliament as a Home Rule MP from County Clare in 1880. He'd supported Parnell's drive for leadership of the Irish Parliamentary Party in the House of Commons while ignoring the illicit relationship 'the Uncrowned King' was having with his English-born wife, Katharine."

"For appearances sake, I suppose," inserted Aran.

"That's my guess," answered Sam. "Anyway, both Kitty and the Captain were involved in the Kilmainham Treaty business. She was one of Parnell's go-betweens with Prime Minister Gladstone while her husband actually helped broker the deal."

"Jaysus, you wonder what they talked about at night after they blew out the candle?" kidded Gay.

Aran laughed, "Go on, Sam. Just ignore him, if ye can."

"Back in October, 1881, Parnell and some other Land Leaguers had been locked up in Kilmainham Gaol for supporting tenant farmers who still refused to pay their landlords' rent even after the Land Bill had passed earlier that year.[13] The bill granted Michael Davitt, the Land League's real driving force, and his followers some of their demands but not all. The big issue of land ownership was still unresolved. Parnell, the figurehead-president of the Land League, took a cautious approach while Davitt and his followers continued to press hard for their long-denied reforms. They saw the land movement as a potentially revolutionary force…one that might release Ireland from the grip of its oppressive colonial overlord.

---

13. 1881 Land Bill granted the 3 F's: fixity of tenure, freedom of sale & fair rents. It also set up land courts to establish fair rents between tenants & their landlords.

"Anyway, to make a long story short, Gladstone had Parnell and a handful of others arrested. At this point, we have the O'Sheas trying to help Parnell."

"Meanwhile all hell is breaking loose in the west of Ireland," interrupted Aran. "Coercion of the worst kind rules the land. People are being evicted from their homes…thrown out into the ditches…along the sides of the road. The police and the military are running wild. Land League leaders are being arrested, meetings are broken up and newspaper offices are raided. Violence and intimidation is running amok."

"Ah sure, ye don't have to tell me. My father was there. He's told me the stories," said Gay.

"That's right," affirmed Sam. "After much give and take, Parnell and Gladstone finally reach a compromise. Gladstone releases Parnell and the others in May, 1882. Parnell gives his assurance that all tenants will begin paying their back rents and will stop their boycotting tactics. He also implies that the recalcitrant farmers will denounce their refusals to obey the law. Parnell further agrees to cooperate with Gladstone's party in promoting land reform throughout Ireland. In return, Gladstone promises to introduce legislation establishing institutions of local self-government and seeing to it that landlordism is finally eliminated as the dominant class in Ireland.[14]

"All this had many positive ramifications back home, but the hard-line Land Leaguers like Davitt saw it as a sell-out. This infuriated many of their fellow IRB comrades who were also part of the land movement."

"I don't see how all this connects with the Black Spot business," said Gay.

"I'm just getting to that," answered the London man. "I'm guessing that some political-military friends of the Captain, tired of seeing their man embarrassed by Parnell's affair with his wife and upset over the concessions granted Ireland by Gladstone, decided to take matters into their own hands. They formed a sort of secret cabal.

---

14. Liz Curtis. *The Cause of Ireland: From the United Irishmen to Partition.* Belfast, 1994, 97-110.

"From what one of my undercover operatives was able to discover, they soon began calling themselves the Black Spot Brothers."

"Black Spot?" questioned Aran. "Do you think they picked that name out of thin air or because it was reminiscent of the potato blight that infected Ireland in the 1840s? One of the first signs of the fungus's infestation was black spots on the plants' leaves, you know."

"Your guess is a good as mine, but it makes some sense," replied Sam. "The gang's obvious disdain for Ireland manifested itself in actions designed to weed out the best and boldest; those who might disrupt England's grip on its island neighbour."

"Ah, the muck savages," muttered Gabby. "Ye couldn't even trust 'em with the shirt off your back, could ya?"

Both Aran and Sam nodded, as the London man resumed his story. "Apparently, the Black Spots first reared their ugly heads after the murders of Lord Frederick Cavendish, Britain's Chief Secretary, and Thomas H. Burke, his Under-Secretary, in Phoenix Park during May 1882."

The Gortman turned to Gabby, "Those two were stabbed to death with some sort of surgical knives by an IRB splinter group. They called themselves the Irish National Invincibles or just 'the Invincibles' for short. Their aim was to rid Ireland of despots, especially British ones."

"It was the talk of the land on both sides of the Irish Sea. The papers labelled it 'the Phoenix Park murders,'" said Sam.

"...and Gay, what made the whole affair so sensational, apart from the death of the two British officials, was that it was the first so-called 'political assassinations' anyone could remember. Sure, as you know, there'd been many an armed insurrection and much agrarian violence in Ireland for years, but never one with solely political motives," said the Irish Rebel.

"Ah yes, the dawning of a new day...murder by a new name and the Sassenach bastards are still at it," retorted Gay.

"Sounds like Michael's trained you well," said Sam, eying Gabriel carefully.

"It goes deeper than that," said Aran.

"All right! All right! Enough's enough. Let me get back to my story," said Sam.

"First, another round here, no?" interrupted Gay.

With his two tablemates' glasses empty, the Irish-American was off to the bar for three more pints.

Upon his return, Sam resumed his story. "That was the last of the Invincibles but just the first of your Black Spot crowd. It seems as if someone on the inside talked…a man by the name of James Carey. Five of the Invincibles were hanged in Kilmainham on his evidence.

"As you can imagine, Carey was now a marked man in Ireland. So the authorities gave him a new identity and Carey and his family were shipped out, heading for South Africa they were. But on the journey there, Carey was murdered by a Pat O'Donnell.

"Apparently, O'Donnell was one of the original members of the Black Spot cabal. He was out to avenge the death of the two British government officials. Later, despite all the secret group's efforts to exonerate their comrade, O'Donnell met the hangman himself.

"But that was not quite the end of it. With the group's considerable influence in high places, they did their damnedest to implicate Parnell and the Land League in Cavendish and Burke's murders. In the end, however, it was all to no avail."

"Sam, that was years ago, but what about today?" asked the Gortman.

"I'm getting to that now," said Sam. "Over the last four decades, a small cadre of dedicated men, who've some grudge to bear against Ireland or Irishmen, have carried out assassinations or at least attempted ones both over here and back home. A lot of these attacks were personal ones."

"Like in the tradition of defending Captain O'Shea's honour," added Aran.

"Yes, exactly," said the IRB man.

"Sam, do you mean to say that some of these 'high-placed' men are actually gunmen?" asked Gabriel.

"Yes, in some cases they are, but often they hire out a job to a known criminal or simply apply pressure, 'encouraging' someone, not of their rank but who has a personal motive for revenge, to take some kind of retaliatory action."

"I suppose with their political influence and financial resources, they're able to pay off and protect those directly involved," guessed Aran.

"That's it! Power and money buys a lot of loyalty," observed Gay.

"Yes, indeed," said Sam. "My people have discovered links that might astound you. The plot to discredit Roger Casement after his arrest during Easter Week seems linked to the Black Spot boys. The release of those incriminating diaries impugning Casement's character and exposing his homosexuality were all linked to his efforts to form an Irish Brigade, with the Kaiser's blessings, from Irish prisoners-of-war. Casement wanted the men returned to Ireland so they could take part in the '16 Rebellion."

"I guess their strategy worked. Casement was hanged in London the following August," said Aran. "You remember that, Gay, don't you? Shadow and I were staying with you in Virginia at the time."

Gabby nodded, confirming his remembrance.

"Ah lads, the list goes on and on. Most of it is from recent times as that information is the freshest," said Sam.

"For instance?" asked Aran.

"Michael was put on their 'hit list' after he ordered the assassination of Lord French back in the winter of '19. The mythical £10,000 reward for his arrest or death can now be linked directly to your Black Spot crowd.

"...and Tom MacCurtain's murder...apparently one of the Tans who did that job was on their payroll.

"Oh, and guess what? Two old names have cropped up...Hardy and Igoe...both tied to the Castle and the Special Intelligence Office at Scotland Yard. Apparently they've been on the payroll of MI5 since before '16. With what I've been able to uncover, it looks like they were also under the control or influence, at least to some extent, of the Black Spots. The list those two have tortured and murdered is as long as your arm."

The Gortman interrupted Sam. "Over a year ago, Michael

found out that it was Hardy who was responsible for the torture and deaths of Dick McKee, Peadar Clancy and Conor Clune in Dublin Castle on the night of Bloody Sunday."

"That just confirms my information," said Sam.

"But what about us?" asked Gay.

"It looks like it," answered Sam.

"What do you mean it looks like it?" countered Gay.

"It means with your involvement with Michael and the death of Captain Hawkins, that's enough reason to have your names added to their list. I'm guessing that helps explain the troubles you've encountered lately.

"I can't be certain, of course, but I'm guessing that it's all tied in somehow with Field Marshall Sir Henry Wilson and his friendship with the Hawkins family. The old man, Colonel Hawkins, has all the necessary military pedigree required to put him in touch with the likes of the Black Spots. But today the driving force behind your troubles appears to be his other son Edward or Eddy, as he likes to be called by his friends.

"When you two and the Flying Gaels staged that ambush and killed his brother George, it was enough to tip the scales. God only knows that bloody sod deserved his end, but Eddy and the Black Spots don't see it that way."

That's exactly the same information Shadow passed on to me after he'd heard it from Michael, thought Aran, *but who could have imagined it was so twisted and tied to the past like this? God help us or we'll all be dead soon.*

Sam, interrupted by a swallow of beer from his pint, quickly forged on with his story. "Apparently, Michael's continued support of our boys in the North and Wilson's recently acknowledged role as security advisor to Craig's government have only increased the urgency to settle some old scores.

"Wilson, a long-time acquaintance of the Hawkins family, is somehow tied in with the Black Spots. Sure, and to make matters even worse, it seems likely that Wilson has recently learned of Mick's interest in knocking him off. He's doubled his body guards, anticipating some kind of attack or possible kidnapping."

"That coupled with Hawkins's drive to avenge his brother's death explains a lot," said Gabriel.

"I'll say it does," muttered Aran. "The attack in front of Brompton Oratory, the Athy business with Shadow, the Holyhead mail-boat affair and most recently the two bullets aimed at me head in Kildare...I'm just wondering if Eddy was in on any of those or they were simply incompetent hired guns?"

"Speaking of Eddy, Sam, do you have any idea where he is or what he looks like?" asked Gay.

"No, not really. Your man seems to have dropped out of sight altogether. As for a description, it's all very vague. His only distinguishing feature seems to be his coal black eyes."

"Ah," exclaimed Gay, "hence the nickname Black Eddy, I'm guessing."

"Sounds right to me," agreed Sam.

Aran seemed lost in thought.

"Something on your mind?" queried Gay.

"Un-huh. I was just thinking. Eddy's gone missing just like his feckin' brother did in '16 after Brigid's death. Years ago, Gay, Shadow and I guessed brother George might've been singled out for some specific assignment or special undercover training. Now Sam, with your news of Eddy's disappearance, it wouldn't surprise me one bit that he isn't following the same path."

"Jaysus wept, that son-of-a-bitch could be anywhere," swore Gabriel, waking up to the reality of the moment. "He could be right here in London, taking aim at Mick or the three of us this very minute."

"Sure, he could or maybe he or one of his hirelings is in Ireland, just biding their time, waiting to pick us off over there, Gay. How does that idea suit your fancy?"

"Not very well, I can tell you that, my friend. But one thing's for cert, we've all got to be a lot more careful than we've been, if we expect to see our children grow up so," warned the Irish-American.

Needless to say Michael was enraged when he heard that Wilson might somehow be implicated in the attacks against his friends as well as himself. The Big Fellow was quick to blame the deteriorating conditions in the Six Counties for aggravating things, pushing them almost beyond the point of no return.

The Corkman reminded Aran and Gay that throughout the War of Independence he'd refrained from ordering political killings. He and Seán Mac Eoin had even stopped Cathal Brugha from spearheading an attack on members of the British House of Commons. But this news was stretching his patience.

When Aran reminded him of his note to Sam about 'nailing up Henry's picture' which Sarah Anne has taken over to London during the closing stages of the Tan War, Michael just dismissed it with a wave of his hand.

"Oh, it was nothing. I called that off as soon as the Truce was agreed to," said Michael.

Aran knew Mick was annoyed that he had questioned his word but Aran was bothered as well. The Rebel thought: *Why then had the Corkman risked Sarah's life…all for 'nothing'?*

The Rebel decided not to press the matter. Michael was under enough pressure as it was, walking the narrow line between the breakaway IRA who had the cheek to set up their HQ right under his nose in Dublin. That, coupled with the outrageous sectarian violence in the North, which showed no signs of abating, coupled with London's insistent demands that Mick sort out his Provisional government and get on with Treaty compliance was making life miserable for the Big Fellow. No, Michael had enough to do besides defending an isolated action taken a year ago.

'Tis better to let this sleeping dog lie, thought the Gortman.

Along with all of his everyday demands, the Big Fellow's health was beginning to erode. Mick's stomach had been acting up recently. He was frequently experiencing chronic pain and lately it was growing worse not better. Aran, Gay and Joe O'Reilly were after him to see a doctor but Michael claimed he'd no time. Occasionally, things became so bad that he wasn't able to eat at all. Aran was convinced he was suffering from stomach ulcers, but Michael wouldn't admit anything was seriously wrong with him, even to his closest friends.

To compound matters, the Corkman seemed to be continually suffering from one cold after another, sometimes it was in his head and the next week it had settled in his chest. Mick couldn't seem to shake their effects. Needless to say, these ailments only compounded the misery and stress he was under.

❧

With Churchill and Craig continually ratcheting up the stakes, the Chief, as de Valera's supporters like to call him, wasn't helping matters. The date for the upcoming election was only six weeks away.

Earlier in the year, Mick and Dev had agreed to postpone the election. Now, the 16 June date was quickly approaching. Both Michael and Arthur Griffith continually pressed de Valera about the issue of the election and controlling intimidation at polling places. They sought his assurance that the Irish people would be able to freely exercise their franchise.

In response to their pleas about guaranteeing that the polling locations would be free of IRA threats of violence, the Long Fellow was quoted in the newspapers, saying that, "...there are rights which a minority may justly uphold, even by arms, against the majority."[15]

❧

As Michael continued trying to keep the upper hand on events, the Chief also struggled. Through all these difficult times Michael did manage to maintain control and move forward while Dev continued to backslide, gradually losing support among his Republican following. He'd been completely marginalised by the IRA and his political credibility diminished by his anti-democratic and unconstitutional stance.

The *London Times* stated it succinctly, "Mr. de Valera's wild speeches in the South of Ireland have shocked the whole country. They indicate a rapid change in his attitude for some little

15. Hopkinson, op. cit., 71.

time ago he was protesting that the will of the electors must be respected."[16]

Dev protested these indictments as misrepresentations. He insisted his inflammatory remarks were meant as warnings of possible war, not agitation for civil conflict.

❧

Finally, several little bits of good news helped lift pro-Treaty spirits.

One final post-Treaty IRB meeting was held in Dublin. Members of the Supreme Council and divisional centres gathered to voice their opinions on the Anglo-Irish document. To Michael's disappointment the majority of those in attendance opposed the Treaty, but there was one ray of hope shining through the gloom: the IRB membership decided it would use its influence to try and prevent Civil War. Michael took this as a positive sign.

Soon after, a group of senior IRA officers, representing both sides of the divide, issued a joint statement, seeking army and political unity talks. Their petition began on an ominous note: "(Civil War)...would be the greatest calamity in Irish history and would leave Ireland broken for generations."[17]

It was their proposal that Treaty acceptance be the basis for army unification, a noncontested election and afterwards, the creation of a coalition government.

Top leaders of the old and new armies met at Mansion House. An air of optimism could be felt throughout Dublin. The pro-Treaty side was represented by Seán Mac Eoin, Eoin O'Duffy and Gearóid O'Sullivan while Seán Moylan, Liam Mellowes and Liam Lynch[18] spoke for the anti-Treaty IRA.

Again, the results of several days of talks were bitter-sweet. Both Moylan and Lynch would not and could not accept the Treaty as a basis of army unity and an instrument for furthering

---

16. Ibid.
17. Ibid., 94.
18. Soon after its occupation, Liam Lynch was appointed Chief of Staff of all IRA forces outside the Four Courts.

peace. On the other hand, the three Republicans didn't want to make a complete break with Dublin's GHQ either.

Michael was accustomed to receiving such mixed signals and took their reluctance to sever all relationships as encouraging. He also was quick to point out to Griffith and Mulcahy that there appeared to be little unity within the IRA ranks. Such a division could only be positive, for how could a divided IRA successfully wage war on a united pro-Treaty army and government?

When the Mansion Conference released its concluding statement, the anti-Treaty Executive debunked Lynch and Moylan's hope of maintaining GHQ ties.

Days later Seán Hegarty, a member of the anti-Treaty Executive, was permitted to address the Dáil, despite the fact he was not a TD. It was his opinion that his fellow Republicans had no other choice but to accept the Treaty. He recognised it wouldn't deliver Ireland the Republic she sought, but to reject it would only bring the British back.

Though Liam Mellowes denounced Hegarty's assertion from the IRA HQ in the Four Courts, it did spark the beginnings of a debate in the Dáil. Sean Moylan, appearing to waffle a bit, stated he was hopeful the Treaty might be what Collins had said it was, a stepping stone to a Republic. He further hoped that the new constitution, when completed, would prove his optimism correct.

When Hegarty suggested an army truce, the Chief issued a statement saying to the effect that peace was possible. But when Griffith pressed de Valera to use his influence to change IRA minds, the Long Fellow said, "The Army has taken an independent position in this matter."[19]

With talks between the two sides at a virtual standstill, Frank Aiken, the O/C of the 4th Northern Division who had troops in the Six Counties and had made numerous sorties over the border, visited Dublin. He urged both sides to table their differences in light of the worsening situation within the ranks of the IRA and Catholic minority in the North. He made an impassioned plea stating, "Should the (IRA) split unfortunately become fi-

19. Ibid., 95.

nal, our people in the North are bound to be influenced by the issues in the other counties, and our forces will be divided and disheartened, so that we are bound to succumb to the powers opposed to us."[20]

Based on Aiken's plea, both sides of the army agreed to continue the Northern offensive. But Rory O'Connor was quick to point out that as long as the IRA held the Four Courts, the brunt of the blame for Irish military action in the Six Counties would be focused on them. He speculated that was most likely the reason behind the Provisional government not demanding his men withdraw from their co-opted HQ. When asked about that, Michael carefully sidestepped the question.

As one newspaper reporter discreetly noted, "Although the Northern question provided a major stimulus for unity...it also created tensions between the two sides as each blamed the other for the failure of the offensive."[21]

In a public address given in mid-May, Michael stated that since Ireland was finally rid of most of its British agents, it was now time to consolidate the government's position and strike for unity in Ireland. But the Big Fellow warned that it would be easy for the British to return, especially if the Irish began fighting among themselves.

Unfortunately, the Dáil Peace Committee talks that began so hopefully at the beginning of May collapsed on the 16th.

※

In a stunning development Michael Collins and Éamon de Valera announced a mutual agreement regarding the upcoming June election. Immediately, the newspapers labelled it the Collins-de Valera Pact.

In what appeared to be an important step in keeping the country free of Civil War and in helping maintain a united Northern front, the two men agreed to a united coalition panel of Sinn Féin candidates. Both elements of the party, pro-Treaty

20. Ibid., 96.
21. Ibid.

and anti-Treaty, would be represented according to their existing strength in the Dáil. The agreement had been concluded with the help of their mutual friend Harry Boland.[22]

For every three pro-Treaty nominees on the ballot there would be two anti-Treaty candidates listed. This ratio conformed to the Dáil's current balance of pro-Treaty and anti-Treaty Sinn Féin TDs. It was also agreed that a nine-member coalition Cabinet would be chosen following the election with a proportion of five-to-four favouring of the majority-elected party. Lastly, the newly elected Dáil membership would choose a president as it had in the past, by majority vote, with a Minister for Defence selected by the army.

In its attempt to explain the agreement to the people, a Dublin newspaper wrote, "Under the banner of Sinn Féin, the party to which both [pro-Treaty and anti-Treaty] factions nominally adhere, the pro-Treaty element would nominate sixty-six candidates while the anti-Treaty group would put up fifty-eight. Thus, the voters would still be electing Sinn Féin."[23]

Pressed further on why he felt the need for the Pact, Michael gave the usual answers but added that without the anti-Treatyite's cooperation, he was afraid the IRA would do everything within its power to disrupt the election. Thus, the final results would be eschewed and the Irish people prevented from exercising their right to choose.

The Corkman also knew his government would be unable to protect all polling stations, particularly in those areas dominated by fervent anti-Treaty sentiment. By concluding the Pact, he was more hopeful that the election might be fairly conducted in all constituencies.

With the election structured in this way, the Irish people wouldn't actually be voting for Treaty approval or disapproval. Instead, they'd only be indirectly indicating their preference, according to the professed Treaty bias of the candidate for whom

22. Harry Boland was one of Collins's closest friends who for the last two years had been an aide to de Valera. Presently, Boland was de Valera's private secretary.
23. Mackay, op. cit., 257.

they voted. Tragically and quite illegally, this tactic completely ignored Ireland's smaller parties.[24]

The majority of the population seemed relieved that the matter of Treaty acceptance or rejection had been muted. Unfortunately, they were totally unaware of the Pact's incendiary political undertones.

Arthur Griffith was furious with Michael for making such an agreement. He felt betrayed and manipulated by the Big Fellow's underhanded tactics and did his best to have the Dáil Cabinet reject it.

Sadly, from that day forward he refused to call Michael by his Christian name. The supportive fatherly-son relationship that both men had once enjoyed was suddenly shattered...damaged beyond repair.

Needless to say, Churchill was incensed too. He described the Pact as a disaster that would keep the country from voting its conscience on the Treaty, a requirement of the Anglo-Irish agreement. He pointed out that the Irish people, traditionally a parochial lot, would be more influenced by a particular contestant's personality or local standing than on the candidate's stance regarding the Treaty.

The Colonial Secretary wrote ordering both men to London. Churchill ended his terse letter with the indictment, "Your Government will soon find itself regarded as a tyrannical junta which, having got into office by violence, is seeking to maintain itself by a denial of constitutional rights."[25]

---

24. The non-Sinn Féin nominees standing for election represented the Farmers' Party, the Labour Party, the Southern Unionist Party, the Ratepayers' Party plus a number of independents. Contrary to criticism leveled at Collins for his concluding the Election Pact, Michael insisted that all candidates, regardless of party affiliation, were free to contest the election. He was gambling that many of the non-Sinn Féin candidates, who had all declared for the Treaty, would defeat their anti-Treaty competition, thus adding to the strength of his projected pro-Treaty majority.

25. Ibid., 258.

The announcement of the Collins-de Valera Pact coincided with the release of advance copies of the new constitution. Begun back in January, it had taken over three months of hard work by the Constitutional Committee. Meeting in the Shelbourne Hotel, which faced onto Dublin's St. Stephen's Green, Michael had charged its membership with creating a democratic Irish Free State rather than focusing on Anglo-Irish relations which was at the hub of the Treaty.

The Corkman often attended committee meetings, but left its day-to-day affairs to Darrell Figgis, its paid secretary. In the final analysis, however, the Big Fellow was responsible for drafting the constitution.

Both the British government and dissonant Republicans wanted copies of it prior to the election to ascertain the Provisional government's stance on matters dear to them. London wanted to be sure it conformed to the Treaty's requirements while the IRA wanted to be sure Collins's expressed intentions had been fulfilled.

As printed, the constitution reflected Michael's and Ireland's desire for sovereignty and the elimination of the British Crown in Irish affairs.[26]

Lloyd George and his Cabinet were not surprised at Michael's efforts. "Totally unacceptable," were the Welsh Wizard's words.

Michael, Arthur Griffith and others spent the next three weeks going back and forth between Dublin and London as the document was amended by the British government.

Despite Michael's valiant attempt to infuse the constitution with a Republican flavour, it was not to be.[27]

---

26. Hopkinson, op. cit., 105.
27. "The Irish legislature was to consist of the King & two houses. Parliament was to be summoned & dissolved in the name of the King. His Representative, that is, the Governor General, was to sign any Bill passed by the two Houses, before it could become law. Right of Appeal to the Privy Council from the Irish Supreme Court was included, thus making it a superior court to any in Ireland. Above all, the Oath of Allegiance contained in the Treaty was made mandatory on every member of the Irish Parliament." Coogan. *Michael Collins.* op. cit., 328.

The Prime Minister stated that the draft document, as originally presented, reintroduced the old issue of Ireland's quest for a Republic versus the Treaty's Free State offer. Chamberlain asserted Collins must choose between satisfying de Valera's quarter or the Anglo-Irish agreement as signed back in December.

In reality, Collins and Griffith had little choice.

❧

London's ire inflamed by the Collins-de Valera Pact and the need to revise the new Constitution again halted British troop withdrawals. North-South border positions were reinforced and made ready for war.

Unable to appease Lloyd George and harbouring little hope of avoiding an armed clash, the Big Fellow decided to take matters into his own hands. In a speech in Cork City, two days before the election, Michael repudiated the Pact. He told his audience to vote for the candidate it thought best. The Big Fella went on to say, "The country must have the representatives it wants. You understand fully what you have to do and I call on you to do it."[28]

❧

The new constitution was published on the day of the election, 16 June. It gave the Irish citizenry little or no chance to read it before casting their votes. Most people, however, felt it made little difference. The twenty-six counties were solidly behind the Treaty despite the fact that armed anti-Treaty men intimidated both candidates and voters alike prior to and on election day.[29]

The vote was significant considering the number of non-Sinn Féin votes cast and candidates elected. Ninety-four out of the one hundred twenty-eight TDs elected favoured the Treaty. The

---

28. Kee, op. cit., 164.
29. "Pro-Treaty panel candidates won 239,193 out of the 620,283 votes. Anti-Treaty candidates won 133,864 & non-panel (non-Sinn Féin candidates) 247, 276." Hopkinson, op. cit., 110.

country had given Michael a democratic endorsement to work the Treaty. It also showed the people's desire for a stable government and reflected a level-headed attitude toward continued relations with their island neighbour.

Almost immediately, Rory O'Connor directed a large body of well-armed Republican troops to reinforce the garrison stationed within Four Courts. His aggressive move clearly had the word 'trouble' written all over it.

❧

The following morning, Saturday, the Big Fellow called Aran and Gabriel into his office.

After some congratulatory handshaking, Michael said, "Lads, I'm going to ask you for a personal favour."

"Anything for a bogman like yourself," chirped Gay.

"No, Gay, this is serious stuff. This is not your usual feckin' Saturday-night-at-the-pub-affair request."

"Sorry Mick. Sometimes my twisted sense of humour does me in."

"No, you're all right, Gay. It's me that's been off lately. Here we're all trying to keep things the bloody hell together despite London's hammering away at me with all their 'this and thats.' I feel like a damn puck goat up in his chair…a target for anyone with an axe to grind."

"Jaysus, Mick," offered Aran. "Sure it would be nice if we'd a little cooperation and some understanding from the other crowd. If O'Connor and his lot would only stop beating their war drums long enough to realise they're digging a hole big enough that no one's going to be able to crawl out of."

"A bloody worry they are, Aran, and they're our friends and comrades to boot. Churchill has blood in his eye and wants me to throw them out, but others see the deal I'd struck with the Long Hoor for what it is: a 'war-time' emergency measure trying to buy us a little more time. It was the only way I could see that would allow me to maintain some control of the situation."

"A bargain with the divil so."

"That's right, Gay. The IRA Executive is calling for a meeting with army unity the first item on their agenda. Please God, they decide to pull back and come together."

"Playing for time while we build up our national forces."

"Yes, Aran, but also hoping that time will either bring the two armies together or drive a wedge in theirs that will break the IRA's will to fight."

"I have to give you credit, Michael. It's a gamble...but Jaysus, Mary and Joseph, it's worth it so," said Gabriel.

"Ta," answered the Corkman, "but sure I didn't call yis in here to pat me on the arse. There's a job I want you to do. It's feckin' dangerous but if anyone can pull it off, yis can."

Aran and Gay glanced over at each other.

"I suppose you've read the last invective spewed from Sir Henry Wilson's mouth. He's trying to rub salt in me wounds over the election pact. That muck savage says de Valera has me in his pocket."

Both men, sitting in front of the Mick's desk, wagged their heads in the affirmative.

"That's just one lick too many. The living hell he's putting our people through in the North has gone on long enough. I've tried bargaining with those bastards on more than one occasion. They're grand when they're sitting across the table from ya, but they've no control of their sectarian wags back home. When Craig invited Wilson to take over the business of restoring law and order in Northern Ireland, he got more than he bargained for. Instead of easing tensions, he's done just the opposite. Instead of muffling the Specials, he's given them a free hand. It's time to call that Philistine to account for his sins. His bullying, threats and intimidations must end and end now."

"You want us to go over to London and take him out," said the Gortman.

"Yes. Apparently, from what Sam's told you, he's directly or indirectly ordered our deaths. It's time we returned the favour. I want you to take the Nayler and head over there tonight. Sam knows you're coming, I talked to him on the telephone last night about it."

"What about the battalion?" asked Gay.

"Cullen and Tobin will be fine with it. Depending on what O'Connor's next move is, we may be running out of time and I'll need you back here in case things start hotting up. You may not think I've noticed, but your lads are turning into real soldiers. Do you think they're ready to go?"

"Hard to say. Gay and the others have done a fine job," said Aran. "It's when the shooting starts that we'll know for sure."

"Baptism by fire, they always say, right?"

"Right, Michael," replied Gabby. "That's when we'll all have our mettle tested."

❧

The three Irishmen had been in London for two days. Sam had arranged everything. On Monday afternoon, the four went out into the country, northeast of London. Sam introduced them to a new German Karabiner 98. It was a bolt-action Mauser with a telescope sight. Being heavier than the short Lee-Enfields they typically fired, it took some time getting used to the sniper weapon.

After an hour at a makeshift firing range, it became apparent Aran Roe was the best marksman. That was fine with Gay and Duncan. The Nayler said he'd prefer to be the driver while Gabriel was happy to serve as lookout and backup man.

The plan was fairly straightforward. Two-thirds of the way down the block from Wilson's residence was a house with some interior rooms being painted. Beginning tomorrow morning, Aran and Gay were replacing the regular painting crew. One of Sam's IRB men from Manchester had bought the lads off. While they were stalking Wilson, the real house painters would be off enjoying a three-day, all-expenses-paid holiday in Blackpool. If the job took longer, Sam would have to make other arrangements.

With the family conveniently out of the house on their summer holidays and the real painters on theirs, Aran and Gay would have the run of the place. Duncan would be in a motor car on the next street over. It was a straight shot out the back door of the stake-out house, through the garden and down a connecting alleyway to where the Nayler would be parked.

The car had been rigged with an enlarged boot. The Gortman and Gabriel would jump in and Duncan would take off. Once around the corner, they'd pull down the backseat and conceal themselves in the boot. To the casual passer-by, only the driver would be visible. In the unlikely event that the authorities were to stop the vehicle, all they'd discover would be a lone red-headed Scotsman, dressed in his tam-o'-shanter, shirt, waistcoat and kilt, heading for home. Once in Glasgow they'd backtrack, with the help of some IRB connections. The three men would take the train from Glasgow to Liverpool then a ship back home to Dublin.

On Tuesday morning, dressed as house painters, they began reconnoitring Sir Henry's house from their vantage point down the street. Positioned in a second-story window, Aran had a clear shot at Wilson's front door and steps. Any vehicle collecting or dropping him off wouldn't block his line of fire.

The retired army officer lived in a large Victorian brick home on a quiet, residential street at the corner of Eaton and Belgrave Place, not far from Victoria rail station. When he left military service, Wilson had entered politics, winning election as a Unionist MP for North Down in February, 1922.[30]

"He's been in Belfast for the last week, but supposedly was returning home this evening," reported Sam. "He's usually with three uniformed British soldiers and one plainclothes body guard. Sometimes he travels in a private sedan and on other occasions he takes a taxi. As a general rule, he spends very little time out in the open. The bastard seems afraid of being attacked and well he should."

When Sam inquired if they'd a good description of Wilson, Aran replied, "We've a good idea of what he looks like. Mick showed us several snaps. He's about five-ten, fit-looking, moustache, usually dressed in military attire, carries a walking stick and looks ten years older than his fifty-eight years," rattled off Aran.

---

30. Mackay, op. cit., 260.

"I guess it's the weathered, facial wrinkles that make him appear older than he is," commented Duncan.

"That's him all right," said Sam. "Jaysus, Mick sure picked the right ones for this job."

Aran and Gay waited at the ready all Tuesday. With the long summer day at hand, they hung around until nine o'clock that evening.

They wondered if Duncan wasn't going mad sitting in the parked auto. They also wondered if his presence might not arouse the neighbours' suspicions.

As they were about to leave for their posts on Wednesday morning, Sam arrived with the newspaper. In it he read aloud an article announcing that Wilson would be dedicating a war memorial at the Liverpool Street Station at noon on Thursday, 22 June.

Looking up from the paper, Sam said, "So take a break, lads. No sense wasting your time today. We'll give that bully louser what for tomorrow."

❧

Thursday dawned rainy. But by the time the two Irishmen arrived in their painter's lorry, the sun was peeking out and the day promised to be fair.

At half-ten a taxi pulled up in front of Wilson's home. The front door opened and two uniformed men stepped out. After a quick look around, one of the men turned and motioned to someone in the house. A moment later, Wilson appeared in the doorway, followed by a man dressed in mufti.

As soon as the taxi arrived, Aran had the Mauser, resting on a tabletop two feet from the open window, ready to fire. Gay was on his knees, pretending to paint an adjacent window sill while he scanned the street for signs of life.

"All quiet here, Aran," he whispered.

In less than five seconds it would be over.

"Didn't have a clear shot, Gay," announced the Rebel. "Too many heads in the way. Looks like we'll have to wait until this afternoon."

"Bloody hell," replied Gay. "The real painters are due back tomorrow and then we'll have to come up with something else if we're going to satisfy Mick's order."

"Just keep your fingers crossed, Gay. Maybe we should have a bit of lunch while we wait?"

At quarter-to-two, a pair of black taxis arrived in front of Wilson's door.

"This is it, Aran. Looks like the body guards have split up. Maybe this time you'll have a clear shot at the fucker."

No sooner were Gay's words out of his mouth, than Wilson stepped out of the first taxi followed a step later by the mufti man.

As the Northern politician and security advisor began to ascend the four steps to his front door, Aran fired.

Only one crack was audible from his rifle.

Instantly, Wilson pitched forward, face down on the steps, his walking stick clattering to rest on the footpath behind him.

"That's it, Gay. Let's get the hell out of here before they figure out where the shot came from."

As the two stripped off their painting outerwear, a series of gunshots could be heard.

Looking out the window, Gay exclaimed, "Mother of God, Aran. Look out there will ya!"

In the street below, two men, straddling bicycles, were firing in Wilson's direction. The two body guards who'd alighted from the second taxi lay motionless on the footpath. The one who'd ridden with Wilson was crouched behind the first motor car, firing at the two strangers who were now heading off down the street on their bicycles.

The two Irishmen noticed that one of riders must've been hit. He was riding slumped over his handlebars, but to the man's credit his legs were still pumping.

"Wonder what the hell that's all about?"

"No time to waste, Gay. This place will be crawling with rozzers any minute."

Dressed in ties, shirts and suits, the two Irishmen hurried out through the back garden and down the alleyway.

PART III

"The only thing necessary for the forces of evil to win in the world is for enough good men to do nothing."

Edmund Burke

JUNE, 1922 – DECEMBER, 1922

MT. JOY PRISON

by Rory Makem

To Mountjoy Prison we were taken without trial,
For the freedom of our country.
From Dublin's Four Courts on that evening in July,
We surrendered to the clergy.
Our rebel troops gave fight, but never gave in,
One-hundred and three tens of them were standing in the end.
They pledged their treatment to ourselves and our men,
They will answer to God.

I am Rory O'Connor and from Dublin I came,
By trade I am a cooper.
My comrades follow me, our fate is the same,
On earth we'll be no longer.
Our lives are given so our country shall be free,
For the cost of freedom, the price of liberty.
The Free State condemns us, but our dreams have been set free,
They will answer to God.

I am Liam Mellowes and for Ireland I'll die,
At eight o'clock this morning.
For five long months I have been rotting in my cell,
An hour is my warning.
But, for the cause I am prepared to give my life,
By the blood of countless martyrs that wars have sanctified.
And when their time has come, the devils will be tried,
They will answer to God.

15

*"We have declared for an Irish Republic and will
not live under any other law."*

Liam Lynch

*A*ran Roe O'Neill and Gabriel McCracken arrived back into
Dublin from England on Saturday evening. The front pages of
both English and Irish newspapers continued carrying reports of
Sir Henry Wilson's murder. Initially they reported the brutal assassination was carried out by two 'anti-Treaty' Irishmen with IRA
connections named Reginald Dunne and Joseph O'Sullivan. They'd
been arrested almost immediately by the police who were aided
by an angry mob. They'd stopped the fleeing men only minutes
after the atrocity had been committed. In fact reports indicated
that the arresting policemen probably had saved the shooters' lives
as the enraged crowd had set upon the two with fists, stones and
anything else they could lay their hands on.

The daily publications soon revealed that O'Sullivan had once
served with the British Army in France during the war and had
lost a limb in the fighting. Handicapped by a wooden leg, he'd
fallen off his bicycle and wasn't able to keep up with his partner.

But, instead of fleeing, Dunne turned back in an effort to aid. At that point, the two were surrounded and assaulted. Papers and other personal effects recovered from their lodgings identified the men and tied them to Ireland and the IRA.

On Saturday morning, as Aran, Gay and Duncan waited to sail back to Dublin, Gay noticed a short report on page three in one of the dailies entitled: "Sniper weapon found." The story went on to say that an unnamed family, living on Sir Henry's street, had returned from their summer holidays and found a sniper rifle in an upstairs bedroom. The report further stated that house painters, discovering the weapon under a bed, had set it to one side, thinking nothing of it. Back home Friday evening the husband reported the matter to the local police who promised a full investigation.

With the IRA implicated in the murder, the British prime minister, laying the blame for Wilson's death at the feet of the men inside the Four Courts, fired off a damning letter to Michael in which he stated, "The ambiguous position of the Irish Republican Army can no longer be ignored by the British Government. Still less can Mr. Rory O'Connor be permitted to remain with his followers and his arsenal in open rebellion in the heart of Dublin in possession of the Courts of Justice, organising and sending out from this centre enterprises of murder not only in the area of your Government but also to the six Northern Counties and in Great Britain."[1]

Lloyd George further notified General Macready, Commander-in-Chief of British forces in Ireland, to prepare to attack the Four Courts.

The general, aware that such an act might reunite Ireland's divided army and allow the IRA to concentrate its venom on his depleted forces, stalled. He hoped that Britain's anti-Irish anger might subside, allowing cooler heads to intercede.

The British were not the only ones up in arms. When Dick Mulcahy learned of Wilson's murder, he threatened to resign.

---

1. T.Ryle Dwyer. *Big Fellow, Long Fellow: A Joint Biography of Collins & de Valera.* New York, 1998, 306.

Needless to say, when Michael returned to Dublin from a weekend trip to Cork City, the pot was on the boil and in imminent danger of bubbling over.

In telephone conservation with Churchill on Sunday afternoon, the Minister issued a further warning to Michael. The Londoner said that in the past, the British Cabinet had taken a more passive role in demanding action in light of the Provisional government's weak standing. But since the election, that position had been strengthened immensely. Churchill, however, warned the Big Fellow that if Michael and his government didn't take immediate steps to oust the Four Court interlopers, the British would consider the Treaty violated and would take action that they deemed necessary.

Michael had just hung up the telephone when Aran and Gay walked into his office.

"Let that fucker come over here and do his own bidding," shouted the Big Fellow to no one in particular.

"Let who do what bidding?" asked Aran.

"Churchill, that's who," answered Mick.

"Wilson?" queried Gay.

Michael sank into the chair behind his desk. He looked tired and dejected.

"Aye Gay, Wilson. But before I say another word, I want to thank you two and Duncan. Did ya have any trouble?"

"None," said Aran. "Just as we planned."

"But what's this about the two who the peelers picked up?"

"We're as mystified as you. I'd taken my shot, Wilson was flat out on the footpath and, as we're about to leave, these two men come bicycling down the street. They emptied their pistols into Wilson and his body guards and took off. I'd say there was less than fifteen seconds between my shot and theirs."

"Jaysus wept. That's unbelievable. They must've been shadowing the Limey all day...both waiting for a quiet moment to make their move. Didn't they hear your gunshot or see Wilson drop?"

"It's questionable if they heard the shot. We were down the street a bit. The 'pop' could have been caused by anything...a back fire, a workman, who knows what, but sure as hell they saw the man go down. Maybe they thought he tripped or something, we just don't know."

"Guess they figured they didn't have time to inquire after his health. They simply did what they'd set out to do and ran," said Gabriel.

"I thought the one of them had been hit," offered Aran. "He was bent over his handlebars. But after reading he'd a wooden leg, I guess he was just trying to get his foot situated on the pedal."

"You have to give Dunne great credit for going back and helping his cohort. Not too many men would've done that. I'm sure most would've just kept going," said the Gortman.

"Two brave soldiers doing what they thought best," said Michael. "Tragically, considering the state of things today, I'm certain their lives will be forfeited. More good men lost in the cause of liberty. May God bless their souls."

As if on cue, the three men crossed themselves.

Suddenly rising to his feet, Michael Collins looked across at the two soldiers before him. "Lads, I want this understood. This is the last time we'll ever speak of Wilson's death or make any reference to this entire affair...among ourselves or with anyone else. Is that clear?"

Both Aran and Gay nodded their understanding. No verbal acknowledgement was required.

With the Wilson business behind them, they turned their attention to other matters.

"Have you seen the final election results?" asked Mick. "They were just announced."

"We saw them in one of the London papers yesterday," said Gabriel. "Good news and bad, no?"

"That's right," said Michael. "Yes, we claimed fifty-eight seats to the anti-Treatyites' thirty-six, but, did you realise that combined, Sinn Féin lost thirty seats[2] over the last general election from just a year ago?"

---

2. Sinn Féin pro-Treatyites lost 8 seats in the election while anti-Treatyites lost 22 seats.

"I noticed that," remarked Aran. "Sure, the big winners were the non-Sinn Féin crowd. Combined, they outpolled our side by ten thousand votes. Labour certainly made a very strong showing, taking seventeen of eighteen seats while the Farmers' Party and Independents combined to take another seventeen.[3] Thanks be to God, they all supported the Treaty," observed Aran.

"But on the plus side, Michael, you should be happy knowing the Irish people are solidly behind the Treaty. If the Labour Party had run more candidates, they might've knocked Dev's crowd into third place."

"You're right, Gay," said Mick. "Under the circumstances, I guess we should take comfort in knowing the people do support the Treaty and the Provisional government, at least in the short-term. That's what London is telling me anyhow. 'Mr. Collins, you now have a public mandate, exercise it.'"

"Sure, Michael, with your new Free State governmental sanction, you should be able to step up and run things as you wish, knowing it's what the Irish people want so," said the Rebel.

"I just wish the Long Hoor would see things that way. He's still opposed to peace with social and economic stability as its backbone. If I know that bloody gobshyte at all, he has no intention of accepting the people's vote. If I hadn't worked the deal with the Pact, there would've been no election. I'm certain of that."

"Mick, you were both in a tight spot, Dev in particular," noted Gabriel. "He's a desperate, disenfranchised man who's

---

3. Of the 128 seats contested for the 3rd Dáil, the election produced 58 pro-Treaty Sinn Féin TDs (of which 17 were unopposed), 36 anti-Treaty Sinn Féin TDs (of which 16 were unopposed), 17 Labour Party, 7 Farmers' Party & 10 Independents (of which 4 were unopposed). Among contested seats, 41 of 49 pro-Treaty candidates were successful versus 19 of 41 anti-Treaty challengers. Approximately 60% of the eligible voters cast ballots, of which 78% had voted, indirectly, to support the Treaty. [Two notable anti-Treaty candidates who played important parts in the War of Independence but strongly opposed the Treaty in the Dáil during the debates lost their seats: Mrs. Margaret Pearse, mother of Patrick & Willie Pearse, & Countess Constance Markievicz.]

trying to maintain some control over the situation. He's mad for re-establishing his 'exalted' position within Sinn Féin and within the entire Republican movement as well. I still think he even has hopes of renegotiating or, at the least, modifying the Treaty somehow, but you saw what happened. The Irregulars largely ignored his pledge to conduct a peaceful election."

"Sure, Gay, we know that his people broke both the spirit and the letter of the Pact with their verbal intimidations, armed interventions, house and ballot-box-burning hooliganism."[4]

"But it was the Pact, Mick, which at least kept the Irregulars' bullying tactics and coercion to a minimum."

"Ah, you're right, Aran, but I fear now with Dev's election loss behind them, it'll bring our conflicting political and military issues into sharper focus."

"Just yesterday," said Gay, "Áine heard that O'Connor had summarised Dev's standing within the IRA's HQ. She said it was something to the effect that his Executive was no more ready to stand by de Valera than it was for the Treaty. I guess Rory and his people are feeling the heat too."

"They are that, Gay. The boyos in Whitehall are shelling out the blame for last week onto the Four Courts crowd. Sure, I think the lads inside are feeling as much pressure as I am," answered Michael.

"Good, maybe they'll buckle."

"I doubt it, Aran," said the Corkman. "From all indications, they're preparing to fight.

"When you two were away, they held another IRA convention in town. My informers told me they proposed to give the Brits seventy-two hours notice before they terminated the Truce and took up arms against them again. Thankfully, cooler heads finally prevailed but only by a narrow margin.

"Can you believe it, Cathal Brugha even voted 'no' to their motion. But O'Connor and his hardliners refused to going along

---

4. "The IRA was certainly not wedded to free speech or to free elections; local units allegedly burned out the houses of thirty-seven Dáil candidates long before Collins repudiated the pact." Tom Gavin. *1922: The Birth of Irish Democracy.* Dublin, 1996, 128.

with the 'cowards' as they called them. Together, Rory and his boys voted Lynch out and elected Joe McKelvey, a Tyrone man, as their new Chief of Staff."

"So we're down to the final straw, are we? Either Churchill runs them out or we're forced to do his dirty work. If we wait much longer, I fear they're going to come after us instead...the both of them."

"Afraid so, Aran, and to make matters worse, Arthur is as happy as a dog with two tails over the election results. He now sees we've a democratic mandate to govern. He's tired of this tandem government arrangement with the Dáil and the Provisional administrations operating side by side. He wants to press on and see the elected Free State government installed. In his mind, the Four Courts siege is a stumbling block to that happening, so he's after me as well to go in there and rout the belligerents out. All of this is beginning to drive me crazy."

Michael leaned forward and put his head down on the desk. He rested his forehead in the folds of his arms for several moments.

Aran and Gay stared at Mick but didn't say a word. They knew the terrible pressures their friend was under. Overseeing the transition of all administrative structures as Provisional government chairman was a job big enough for several men. But then when you added on his other responsibilities, it was too much to ask of any one person.

Suddenly, the Big Fellow looked up. "Say, I've an idea. Let's nip across the road for a drink. There a nice little pub just down the way where we can have a quiet drink. Sure, something to drown our troubles with."

"You're on, Mick," said Gay, "but only if you're buying, old stock."

"Ah, bugger off you bloody sod. You're one of the most overpaid soldiers in me army."

The colour was back in the Big Fellow's face and there was even a sudden spring in his step.

"Just give me a minute," said the Rebel. "I'll go over and get a few of the boys to trail along with us...just in case one of the Black Spots bastards is nosing around."

❧

Michael was right, the pub was indeed cosy. Having just reopened for the evening trade, they'd the place all to themselves.

The four soldiers that Aran had co-opted sat at the bar while Michael, Gay and himself chose a snug near the back door.

With whiskey and tea in front of them, the three seemed lost in their own private thoughts.

Staring into his tea, Aran remembered walking in the front door of Mespil Road last night. Sarah Anne was in the kitchen making one of his favourites: bacon and cabbage. A wonderful aroma filled the house and his mouth watered in anticipation.

Upon hearing the front door open and close, she hurried into the sitting room.

After a long, loving embrace, she pulled back, saying, "I read all about it in the papers. Were the two of you involved so?"

Aran paused, remembering his promise to Michael.

"Oh please God, tell me no."

Again her plea was met with silence. Aran was torn between saying nothing and divulging the entire affair.

Annie charged, "How could you've? He was just an old man."

Finally, giving in to her insistence and hoping to put the matter behind them, Aran said, "Old man or no, he was a soldier making war on innocent people. He had to be stopped."

"But he didn't have a fighting chance."

"Sarah Anne, what chance did those thousands of people in the North have? There're over twenty-five thousand Specials running amuck in the Six Counties. Wilson and his kind are not restraining them, they're encouraging them."[5]

Annie studied his face. His pain was evident.

---

5. In Northern Ireland, during the two years between June, 1920 & June, 1922, it was estimated that 428 people had been killed, 1,755 were wounded, 8,750 Catholics were forced from their jobs & 23,000 Catholic families were driven from their homes. Coogan. *Michael Collins.* op. cit., 382.

"Things have changed in the North. With Carson's departure eighteen months ago, there was a ray of hope life would be different with Craig in charge, but it isn't. In fact, things are worse than ever. His Special Powers Bill now permits flogging and anyone found with an unauthorised weapon is a dead man. Things are as bad as they were up there in the 1790s."

"I know some of the Orangemen from the old UVF days have gone mad, but wasn't there another way?"

"God only knows Michael's tried. Two Pacts with Craig are out the window. IRA men have been deployed to help protect nationalist communities and neighbourhoods, but they're out-manned and outgunned.[6]

"Mick did what he thought he had to do: shake up the balance of power. He hopes that with Wilson out of the way, Craig and the others might come to their senses; back off their programme of violence and try working out a peaceful settlement."

"Well, Mick should be happy...he's certainly gotten people's attention. I just wish it'd been some other way."

"Sarah, what's the matter? Going soft on me, are ye?"

"Oh no, my love," sighed Sarah Anne, pulling him into the warmth of her arms again. "I'm just growing weary of all this fighting, bickering and posturing. I worry about you all the time. I want us to see our children happy...for us to grow old together...for peace to finally come to Ireland."

"Hush, hush, dear one," whispered Aran in her ear. "I know this is a bad patch we're going through. But with God's help and Michael's determination, we *will* see it through. I *know* we will."

❧

"Aran, Aran, are ye asleep?"

It was Michael rousing him from his daydream.

"No, I was just thinking how hard all of this has been on Sarah Anne. The political troubles, my being away so much and

---

6. Political historian Tom Garvin states, "In the North, savage Orange pogroms against Catholics and almost equally murderous IRA retaliations went on." Tom Garvin. *1922: The Birth of Irish Democracy.* Dublin, 1996, 126.

her being pregnant as she is, it's not an easy time for any of us sure.

"What about you and Kitty?"

"Ay, don't remind me. We're lucky to find a few hours every week or so. Sure, I realise we're busy with work, but the women just must sit back and worry. I don't know which is worse."

"Well, I for one am glad my wife is at home just up the way," said Gabriel. "She's a great comfort when the day's over. Maybe that's the difference with having an Irish wife instead of an American one. They've grown up living with all that shyte the colonials have dished out in Ireland over the years. Maybe it's embittered them and toughened their skin so."

"Jaysus, I hope not," answered the Gortman.

"Embittered or not, I wanted you to hear this from me," said Michael. "While yis were away, I made a big decision. I've called off the Northern offensive, both for the military as well as my scheme for civilian noncompliance. Together, they've been an all-round feckin' disaster. Instead, I'm instituting a new policy of peaceful obstruction toward Craig's government."

"You mean the offensive is off in favour of a more passive approach?" asked Gay.

"Yes. With the round-up and internment of IRA activists, reports from Belfast are extremely gloomy. The military organisation there is almost destroyed. It's reported that it would be nearly impossible to keep things going as we have in the past. The morale of the men is going down day by day and the spirit of the people is practically dead."[7]

"So you think it's inevitable, don't you," said Aran. "We're going to war then aren't we?"

"I'm afraid so," answered the Big Fellow. "We don't have any options left. This business last week just brought everything to a head."

"In some perverse way, I'm almost glad," said Gay. "It's like finally having an infected tooth pulled. You can leave it in, but

---

7. Ibid.

the pain is too much. However, you're afraid to have it pulled because that pain might be even worse. But after you've had it out and have recovered, you wonder why you didn't have it pulled much earlier.

"All I hope is that it's short and no one's killed."

"Jaysus wept, Gay," retorted Michael, "short yes, but no one gets killed? You're a bigger dreamer than the one sitting next to ya."

❧

Éamon de Valera, still confident he'd be a member of the new 3rd Dáil's government, based on his Election Pact agreement with Michael, played no part in the goings-on at the Four Courts.[8] Instead, he busied himself with political matters. He denounced the election results. He called them, "a triumph for the Imperial methods of pacification."[9]

In an interview reprinted in Sunday's newspaper, the former president reiterated his old saw of "the majority have no right to do wrong." He further elaborated by saying he was "refusing to accept that he had a duty to observe the decision of the majority until it was reversed."[10]

Towards the end of the piece in the paper he proudly reminded his audience that he was not an extremist when he stated, "I have always regarded moderation in everything as the highest human value." But one paragraph later he was warning the Irish people that if they wanted freedom in the future, "they could not put aside the physical force weapon."[11]

From the tone of the article, it seemed that the Long Fellow still held out hope for acceptance of his Document #2. Mick on the other hand knew it was a dead issue. The British were in no mood to renegotiate the Treaty. Dev kept reasserting to the Big

---

8. Since their occupation on Good Friday, the anti-Treaty Republicans were free to come & go from their self-appointed headquarters without interference from National Army forces. Admittance, however, was closely guarded by the IRA militia.
9. Ibid., 306.
10. Ibid., 282.
11. Ibid., 286.

Fellow that the difference between his document and the Treaty was *'only a shadow'* and the British *wouldn't* go to war over the difference.

Michael, who'd spent two months bargaining with the Sassenach, knew otherwise. He maintained that the British *would* go to war even though the difference *wasn't* worth the fight.

There was one big distinction between their two positions. The Corkman would be faced with the responsibility for leading his country into war while Dev wouldn't. Michael refused to take the Long Hoor's bait.

❧

Michael's connection with Rory O'Connor and his men was growing more desperate by the hour. The barring of Liam Lynch from the Four Courts and the locking of its gates to all outsiders only exacerbated matters. Lynch, still the leader of the moderate Republicans, had moved his headquarters to Dublin's Clarence Hotel on the quays. There he surrounded himself with a small staff of supporters including Dick Barrett. Barrett, a Corkman, was a teacher and part-time Vice-Commander of the West Cork Brigade. He'd joined the Four Courts garrison when they'd first taken over the justice complex back in April.

In light of the election defeat and the negative fallout from Wilson's death, the occupying Irregulars needed to make a move if their actions were to carry any weight with their supporters. The talk of their renewed war with Britain had been voted down and their threat of going north to join their comrades fighting in the Six Counties appeared unlikely at best.

In an effort to consolidate their position, the men in the Four Courts held a war council with Lynch and his followers on the evening of the 27th. In the room were Rory O'Connor, Liam Mellowes, Joe McKelvey, Richard 'Shadow' Doyle and a handful of others. Accompanying Lynch were Dick Barrett, Liam Deasy, Maurice Twomey, Éamon de Valera and Dan O'Leary.[12] The men met until after midnight.

───────────────

12. Deasy, op. cit., 45-46.

The upshot of the meeting was that the two disagreeing sides had once more healed their differences. Lynch resumed his role as Chief of Staff of the whole anti-Treaty IRA Army and if Collins and his army wished to take on the belligerents they'd be facing a united front of determined, veteran soldiers.

Lynch's concluding words rang true in the ears of the other Republicans. "We have declared for an Irish Republic and will not live under any other law."

Based on his leaders' decision to reunite in common cause, Dick Barrett decided to rejoin the men occupying the Four Courts while Shadow decided to throw in his lot with Lynch.

It had been a difficult decision for the Limerick man to make. His personal loyalty to Liam Mellowes butted heads with his admiration for Liam Lynch's more moderate Republican stance. Now that the two sides had mended their differences, the choice was an easier one. Still personally supporting Mellowes, the baker found his philosophical position more closely wedded to Lynch's. It was the best of a difficult situation.

As the IRA meeting broke up, Liam Mellowes pulled his friend Shadow aside. Speaking in a quiet but determined voice, Liam said that the Four Courts' men were expecting a Free State attack, possibly as early as tomorrow.

Shadow stared back in disbelief. "Sure, has it all come down to this? The years of struggling to overcome the savage injustices of war and imposed poverty; the years of holding out against the occupying might of an Empire; the years of Irish unity and determination forged upon the anvil of sacrifice? Tell me, Liam, it can't be so…that it all wasn't for naught?"

"Shadow, I'm sorry but it appears it was. Our brothers in arms have become the new imperialist power, threatening to impose their will on their own kind. We *can't* let that happen…we *won't* let that happen."

The two men looked into each other's eyes as if to uncover some unspoken truth that might heal the festering wound. Sadly, none was forthcoming.

The two shook hands.

"God bless you, Liam."

"God bless you too, Richard."

Tears welled up in both men's eyes.

Shadow turned and headed for the street.

A moonless, starless night greeted the Limerick man as he headed east up along the Liffey.

Instead of going straight to the Clarence Hotel though, he made a detour. At a brisk pace, he headed across town to a residence at #5 Mespil Road.

❧

Since his Sunday afternoon meeting with Aran and Gay, Michael had done his best to stall the British authorities who were pressing him even harder to attack the Four Courts. The excuse he offered was a demand that they produce evidence connecting O'Connor's men with Wilson's death. He knew he was on safe ground because there wasn't any.

❧

Twenty-five minutes later, as Shadow crossed Leeson Street Bridge and turned left into Mespil Road, he could see lights on at Aran and Sarah Anne's.

Praying that his two greatest fears hadn't been realised, problems with Annie's pregnancy or that the country was again at war, he knocked.

Moments later, Sarah Anne opened the door. She was in her night dress covered with a dressing gown.

"Oh, Shadow," she cried, "you've heard then?"

"Heard what? Are you and the baby all right?"

"Yes, I'm fine, but it's all just beginning. Aran's upstairs getting ready."

"Getting ready? Ready for what?"

With her voice quivering, Annie said, "Michael's brought in two field guns. Emmet Dalton's collected them…two 18-pounders from the British still at their headquarters in Phoenix Park. Unless Rory surrenders this morning, Michael's going to drive him out."

Sarah Anne, with tears running down her cheeks, slumped into a chair, her face in her hands.

Shadow walked over to comfort her. He patted her trembling shoulders and rubbed her back before pulling up a chair and sitting down across from her.

"Sarah, no one's fired a shot yet. There still may be time. Please God, calmer heads may yet intercede."

"No, no, you don't understand. Those men in the Four Courts won't give in. I just know it."

"Sarah, I just left there. I didn't see any big guns or troopers for that matter."

"They're all hidden, tucked away on the side streets. At four o'clock, Ennis will give the order and men will attack."

"Are you certain? What's happened that I don't know about?"

Before Sarah Anne could answer, Aran appeared on the stairs.

Dressed in his dark-green National Army uniform, the Irish Rebel walked down the remaining steps and over to his old friend as Shadow rose to his feet.

The Gortman held out his hand but then changed his mind. Instead, he wrapped his arms around the greying man's stooped shoulders.

"Shadow, I thought I heard you down here. It's so good to see you and know you're away from that place. Have you come to your senses and decided to join us?"

Shadow wrapped his arms around the younger man's shoulders. As they embraced, the Limerick man could feel the muscles, rippling hard, under the serge fabric of Aran's tunic. This man, who'd been a boy when they'd first met back in '16 and whom he loved like a son, was about to march out and declare war against his own people.

"No, I haven't. I've decided to throw in me lot with Lynch and his men. They're good Republicans with level heads on their shoulders. We'll hold our ground in the hope that Michael will change his mind. Even if Mick drives Rory out of the Four Courts, it won't be too late."

"Somehow I doubt it, Shadow."

"Ah sure, we'll just have to wait and see."

Taking a step back, the baker ran his eyes over the Gortman.

"Jaysus, if Pearse could only see ya now. I wonder what he'd say."

"I wonder that too. But I know he was a proud and determined man who believed in what he did. I only hope he'd have seen the power in the Treaty's ability to bring peace and justice and unity to this land. He once spoke of the battlefield's red-wine. If necessary, may there be little of that spilled tonight, and if so, may it be the last."

"Please God you're right my friend…and what about Annie here?"

"Áine and Sarah Anne will look after each other if Gay and I must be away. What about yourself?"

"It all depends, but Liam's talking about going down to Limerick if things collapse here in Dublin. At the present, we're all holed up in the Clarence."

Glancing at his pocket watch, Aran said, "I must be going. My battalion's staging at Beggars' Bush at half two. Here, walk down with me as far as Baggot Street."

Aran pulled Sarah to her feet and the couple clung fast to each other. Locked in their embrace, Aran wondered if he'd ever see her again.

Quickly dismissing the terrible thought from his head, Aran kissed Annie as they hugged each other once again. Squeezing his wife's hand, he whispered in her ear, "I love you, my dearest wife. Mind yourself and the baby. I'll send word of what's happening as soon as possible."

Throwing his greatcoat over his shoulder and adjusting his peaked military cap, the Irish Rebel grabbed his newly issued Lee-Enfield Mark 5 rifle. He blew Annie a kiss, and with Shadow beside him, they disappeared into the darkness of the night.

❧

As the two men walked the short distance to Baggot Street, Shadow asked, "What's brought all this to such a head?"

"More nonsense than you can believe. But as they say, ''Twas the straw that broke the camel's back.'

"Seems a detail of men from the Four Courts, operating under O'Connor's orders, were out stealing some motor cars from a garage here in town. Apparently, the Irregulars were planning to drive men and arms up to the Six Counties and resume fighting the British.

"Just as the boys were about to drive off in the vehicles, a squad of National Army troopers spotted them. All of them managed to get away except for one. A man named Leo Henderson was arrested and taken to Mountjoy.

"When the anti-Treatyites returned to their HQ to report what had happened, someone in the Four Courts issued a retaliatory order."

"Mother of God," muttered Shadow.

"A short time later, J. J. O'Connell was lifted off a street here in Dublin.

"Seeing as he's one of Mick's top generals and O'Duffy's Deputy Chief of Staff, Michael lost his patience. He ordered Emmet to requisition the field guns, a supply of shells and several Lancia armoured cars from the Sassenach.

"That was at half-ten tonight. At the same time, Mulcahy ordered the men of the 1st Battalion of the Dublin Guards to fall in under the command of Tom Ennis. They should be over around the Four Courts by now. My men and I will be stationed elsewhere. If everything's on schedule, an ultimatum of surrender will be issued to Rory and his crowd in little over an hour."

"Where are you going to be?" asked Shadow.

"Can't really say. You understand though, don't you?" replied Aran.

The darkness hid Shadow's surprised disappointment. Then it suddenly came to him, he was now conversing with 'the enemy.'

"Uh-huh," was all he managed to say in response to Aran's directive.

A few steps later they were at Baggot Street.

"Going back to the Clarence?" asked Aran.

"Yes, and for Christ's sake, keep your bloody head down, will ya?"

"You have my word, Shadow…and you too," answered Aran.

"Good luck," said the Limerick man.

The two men shook hands again. Shadow faced west and headed over the bridge toward the town centre.

With his right hand, the Limerick man reached into his trouser pocket. With a sense of relief, his fingers wrapped around the folding knife Aran had given him for his birthday, just a year ago. It had been his companion ever since…a constant reminder of their friendship. He knew the days ahead would test the metal of their friendship, but he also knew the bond between them was too strong to break.

Aran, leaving his friend to go his own way, continued on northward. Turning onto Northumberland, he stopped to collect Gay. Together, the two walked the last block to Beggars' Bush Barracks.

❧

The Big Fellow was waiting for them in his office. Returning their smart salute, Michael, also dressed in military attire, barked out their orders. "You and your men are to proceed to Sackville Street. There you'll erect barricades blocking off access along its western perimeter. Position them at Bachelors Walk along the quays, at Abbey Street Middle, at Henry Street and at the top of Sackville in front of Devlin's. Your orders are to prevent, by force if necessary, any Irregulars who might be fleeing the Four Courts and attempting to link up with others of their kind presently holed up along the eastern side of Sackville Street. Rumour has it they intend to occupy Sackville from Parnell's statue down to North Earl Street. You'll be eyeball to eyeball with them from just across Sackville Street. Sounds like Easter Week all over again, doesn't it?"

"Yes sir," they both replied.

"Any queries?"

"No sir."

"Dismissed," replied the Corkman. Then in a more subdued tone, he said, "Good luck lads and keep your feckin' arses out of the way of any flying lead."

Aran and Gay, trying to keep from smirking, saluted once more.

❧

Out on the parade ground, some two hundred fifty or so National Army troops stood about at ease. Off to one side were Cú Cullen, Liam Tobin, Nayler MacGregor and Pat Grogan.

Close by Aran spotted Marty and Liam McCullers. Near them were Caoimhín, Nick, Jimmy, Frank and Chris McKee.

Walking over to the Nayler, Aran asked, "Where's Larry?"

"Ah sure, he'll be right along. He's over in the barracks collecting some last-minute gear."

The Rebel passed along Michael's orders to his three company commanders.

"Any questions?" he asked.

They each shook their heads no.

"Spread the word but remember it's important that your defences protect you from men advancing in your direction from the Four Courts as well as any Republican fire that may be directed at you from the far side of Sackville Street. The north-south surrounding buildings should provide some minimum protective cover, but keep alert for the odd chancer who might be trying to pick off you or some of your men from any of the overhead windows."

Suddenly the walled-in barracks came alive with shouts and movement. The three company commanders ordered their men to form up. With the help of their junior officers and NCOs, a quick inspection was conducted. Besides their uniforms and greatcoats, each man had with him a rifle, one or two revolvers, two hundred rounds of ammunition, a canteen of water, rations for three days and a blanket.

At two-forty-five in the morning the 2nd Battalion of the Dublin Guards marched out of Beggars' Bush. The three assistant company commanders quickly took the point on bicycles. Their job was to scout ahead on the odd chance that the Irregulars were planning some kind of surprise ambush.

As the battalion, strung out in double file with ten paces between each man, rounded the corner and headed for town, Larry McCracken fell in behind his brother and Aran. He carried an eight-foot-long flag staff from which a banner was flying. Sewn onto the flag was a replica of the patch Aran had designed, a copy of which each man wore on his tunic sleeve. Clearly visible on the banner's rippling surface was an enlarged pike head with the numerals '98.

Suddenly Duncan was at Aran's shoulder. "Does that meet with your approval, sir? It's a gift from the men to you."

Aran stared at the flag in surprise. "Great stuff, Nayler. Let the men know I approve most wholeheartedly."

"Yes sir," he replied, smiling.

❧

General Ennis's order to surrender was issued at three-forty. With no acknowledgement forthcoming by the four o'clock deadline, the bombardment began at four-fifteen. *The Irish Civil War had begun.*

Ennis had positioned one 18-pounder at the junction of Merchants Quay and Winetavern Street. The gun faced the southeast corner of the justice centre. The other was stationed at the bottom of Footbridge Street to the southwest of the Four Courts. With only the River Liffey separating the attackers from those being attacked, single rounds were fired at fifteen-minute intervals. Each field piece and its firing detail were provided covering fire by a Lancia armoured car equipped with a Lewis machine gun and two gunners.

At two minutes past four, prior to the first round being fired, men from the 1st Battalion of the Dublin Guards rushed forward and occupied a building at the western end of the Four Courts complex. They met with only light opposition.

While this was happening, an additional two unmanned Lancias were driven up against the Four Courts' two main gates. This strategy would prevent the Irregulars from exiting the courtyard in the Rolls-Royce 'Whippet' armoured car they'd captured in Templemore and had parked there some weeks earlier.

So once again, on the morning of 28 June, Dubliners were awakened to the sound of artillery and small arms fire. It had been only six years before that a band of Irish rebel soldiers had occupied selected buildings in the town and declared the dawning of 'an Irish Republic.' Today, some of those same men were taking up the fight again, but this time they weren't trying to oust foreign soldiers, they were attacking one other.

❦

Despite its initial impressive showing, the National Army had problems. The gunners firing the field guns were inexperienced and lacked the necessary training to be truly effective. Innocent civilians and their property were taking a pounding.

The shells for the 18-pounders were the wrong type. They were wire-cutting, high explosive rounds that had little effect on the thick stone walls of the Four Courts. The British would have to send for additional stockpiles from the Carrickfergus arsenal in Northern Ireland.

Neither army had truly made any war plans. The bombardment of the Four Courts caught both sides ill-prepared despite all the bluff and bluster of the preceding months. The one thing it did do, however, was to clarify the situation. The fighting was clearly between men of the Free State and men representing the Republic. The issue was whether the terms of the Treaty would be implemented or not.[13]

Arthur Griffith, Kevin O'Higgins and their political allies quickly applauded Michael's action. So did the British administration in Whitehall. As one newspaper reported the following day,

13. Ibid., 117.

"The decision was a necessary affirmation of the right to govern by democratic authority and the need to stand by the Treaty."[14]

After nine months of political dickering and worthless posturing with Dev, the Brits, Craig and the anti-Treatyites, Michael had had enough.

On the morning of the 28th, he issued a statement to the press, explaining his actions to open fire on the justice centre. In part it read, "The Irregular Forces in the Four Courts continued in their mutinous attitude. They openly defied the newly expressed will of the people."[15]

He further went on to state that the Provisional government had only two real choices, "…either to betray its trust and surrender to the mutineers, or to fulfil its duty and carry out the work entrusted to it by the people."[16]

But by accepting assistance from the British military still stationed in Ireland, the Free State government was treading on thin ice. Regardless of Churchill's persistent demands to 'do something about the Four Courts,' General Macready was reluctant to supply Michael with all the materials needed to effectively neutralise the belligerents. Despite this handicap the Corkman had to be careful not to appear he was just following London's orders. If the anti-Treatyites felt the Free State wasn't acting out of public conviction but simply doing Lloyd George's bidding, the propaganda victory for the Irregulars would be enormous.

❧

After several hours of hard work, Aran's men were well hunkered down behind their stout barricades. Lorry loads of supplies had followed them into town, bringing sandbags, heavy fencing material and cobblestones. Two-sided barricades had been erected as per Michael's orders. Men were assigned to man them while others fanned out as scouts, periodically reporting back to their company commanders. Buildings were broken into to satisfy

---

14. Ibid.
15. Dwyer. *Big Fellow, Long Fellow.* op. cit., 308.
16. Ibid.

the need for equipment storage, sleeping accommodations and a first aid station.

As uncanny as it seemed, Aran set up his HQ inside the recently refurbished GPO. This time, instead of Pearse or Connolly giving the orders, it was Gabriel and he who were issuing the commands.

❧

On 30 June, after more than two full days of shelling, the situation inside the Four Courts became desperate. Fires in the complex's outlying buildings were burning out of control. The wounded urgently needed more medical attention than was currently available to them. The death total was mounting. Outside, Free State troopers had surrounded the entire city block, offering the IRA inside no hope of escape.

At eleven o'clock in the morning, Dublin was suddenly rocked by a massive explosion. The IRA had stored vast amounts of ammunition and explosives in the basement of the main domed building. Whether accidentally ignited by one of the uncontrolled fires or torched on purpose, the dump exploded. The blast scattered centuries of priceless, irreplaceable historical records, stored in the adjacent Records Office, over much of Dublin. The air was filled with scraps of charred paper. Children thought it was snowing in June. Property records, birth, marriage and death certificates, tax statements and countless other historical documents were destroyed…lost forever.[17]

Thirty minutes later a truce was declared. The wounded, members of the women's IRA auxiliary Cumann na mBán, and several Franciscan friars, who'd remained inside to administer last rites, were allowed safe passage out of the Four Courts.

At three o'clock that afternoon, Oscar Traynor, O/C of the 1st Dublin Brigade, was allowed to treat with the men inside the

---

17. Some accused Rory O'Connor, a guardian of the Republic, for touching off the explosion as repayment for the embryonic Free State government's attack against his men inside the Four Courts. Despite all the rumours, no one ever substantiated them.

IRA's HQ. Shortly afterwards, the garrison surrendered. Prior to the Irregulars' marching out of their burning inferno, they destroyed their weapons.[18]

Once outside, the men were directed to line up on Inns Quay. Surrounded by Ennis's Free State troopers, a formal surrender was accepted. The leaders, including Rory O'Connor, Liam Mellowes, Joe McKelvey and Dick Barrett, were loaded into lorries and taken to Mountjoy Jail while others were held in temporary holding areas awaiting transportation to Mountjoy or Kilmainham Gaol. For his efforts in effecting the surrender, Traynor was not held.

Two other notable Republicans had also been captured, Tom Barry and Ernie O'Malley. Barry was eventually taken to Mountjoy but O'Malley escaped his captors almost immediately and fled Dublin.

Observers of the three-day drama couldn't help but recall Easter Week, 1916. In both cases, the insurgents found themselves holed up in buildings in central Dublin. Both groups of rebels, surrounded by hostile armies, were forced to surrender after enduring a withering attack inflicted upon them by a superior force. In the end, both groups of revolutionaries were sent off to jails. This time, however, they weren't transported to English prisons but to Irish ones where most were destined to live out the war.

⁙

With the surrender of the Four Courts, the brunt of the fighting shifted to Sackville Street. On the 29th, anti-Treaty forces, many of them from Traynor's 1st Dublin Brigade stationed outside

---

18. Later, Ernie O'Malley described the final minutes inside the Four Courts as the men destroyed their weapons: "The machine-gunners stripped their guns, jumped on the parts, twisted and battered them; their hands were torn and bleeding but they did not heed, they smashed in a frenzy… The rifles and revolvers were heaped in a large room… Paraffin was slopped around the floor, and then with blinding flashes incendiary grenades were thrown; flames flared on the rifle pyre, licking the butts and the woodwork. We watched for a time, tears of rage in our eyes." Litton, op. cit., 71-72.

the Four Courts, infiltrated the buildings on the northeastern side of street, just as Michael had thought they might.

In 1916, the rebels had occupied both sides of Sackville Street Lower. Now, it was the top quadrant. As during Easter Week, tunnels were opened through the buildings for aid in the rapid deployment of men, equipment and supplies. In this section of town there were several large hotels such as the Hammam and the Gresham plus numerous stores including Cleary's. This area was quickly nicknamed 'the Block.'

Though General Ennis and his troops had done a fine job of maintaining a secure perimeter and keeping O'Connor's men confined to the Four Courts compound, scattered anti-Treaty soldiers had filtered into Dublin. Combined with Traynor's forces they posed a real threat. Soon, Aran and his men were coming under sniper attack and occasionally extended exchanges of machine gun fire.

On the evening of the 29th, the Gortman notified HQ that he needed more reinforcements. General Mulcahy immediately dispatched two companies of men from Ennis's 2nd Eastern Division. Dick also felt the attack on the Four Courts would be successfully concluded soon. When it was, he would immediately issue orders for Tom to reposition his two 18-pounders at the top and bottom of Sackville Street Upper. This would add immensely to Aran's ability to counter the Irregulars' offensive capabilities.

On Friday evening, the 30th, Mulcahy was as good as his word. General Ennis arrived with his two field guns and took charge of positioning them. By now the general's men had gained valuable experience and were more successful in hitting their intended targets, but the problem of limited ammunition stilled dogged Ennis.

Aran's once clean uniform, shiny leather gaiters and boots were now torn, scarred and covered with grime, but his determination to put an end to the street fighting was undiminished. Dodging sniper fire, he dashed from one barricaded street to the next, checking on his men, making sure they were well supplied and conferring with his staff officers.

Back at his GPO HQ, he met with Marty and Liam Mc-Cullers. They were overburdened with wounded men and were in desperate need of more medical supplies. Aran assigned Rory O'Mahony and three other men to act as an ambulance service, driving lorries back and forth from HQ to the Mater Hospital. He also composed and signed a letter, authorising Rory to requisition their much needed medical supplies on behalf of the Free State government.

The Nayler was proving his weight in gold. Twice on Friday and once on Saturday, he led squads of men across Sackville Street to throw petrol bombs into the lower level windows of the besieged buildings. His bravery under fire took Aran's breath away and he said a prayer whenever the kilted-one took off running.

Besides the anguish he felt every time one of his soldiers or an opposing IRA man was hit or fell, it was the pride he felt in working with Gay and Cú that took the edge off things. They were at his side or covering his back wherever he went. Looking out for each other as they did only further cemented the bond of friendship between the three men. He kept reminding them that the fight for Dublin would soon be over and maybe, just maybe, saner heads would prevail. With any luck the Civil War would be over within a week.

❈

With the addition of Ennis's two field guns and several Rolls-Royce 'Whippets' with their mounted Vickers machine guns, 'the Block' was reduced to little more than a huge pile of rubble in less than a week of fighting.

Between the uncontrolled fires and incessant shelling and gunfire, the Irregulars didn't have a chance. With their cover exposed or destroyed and their ammunition in short supply, they fled out the rear exits of 'the Block.' But as soon as they'd made their escape, they were arrested by waiting National Army soldiers in the narrow back laneway that ran behind the buildings. Unceremoniously, they were quickly rounded up and marched off to jail.

By some strange quirk of fate, the Republican leadership who had foolishly congregated in the Gresham Hotel after the Four Courts had fallen managed to slip away undetected during the final days of fighting. Dev, uninjured, made it out to safety in a Red Cross ambulance. Oscar Traynor, Robert Barton, Countess Markievicz and Austin Stack also escaped unscathed. Only Cathal Brugha decided to remain behind and continue waging his own personal war against his enemies.[19]

Finally, during the day on Wednesday, 5 July, a white flag was hoisted above the Hammam Hotel. The last of the insurgents filed out of the back entrance with their hands raised.

At long last, like some gallant sea captain on a sinking ship, Cathal Brugha emerged, a pistol in each hand.

Warning cries and orders to drop his weapons were issued and reissued.

Disregarding the shouted commands, Cathal continued to advance toward the ring of National Army military that formed a semicircular barrier some forty paces away. Raising both revolvers chest high, he appeared ready to fire. But before he could pull either trigger, he was cut down by a hail of Free State bullets.

The 1916 hero of North Dublin Union, who had sustained some two dozen bullet wounds during the Easter Rebellion and had miraculously survived to fight another day, crumpled to the ground mortally wounded. He died in hospital two days later.

Sadly, with his death, a little of Ireland and its cherished dream of freedom died too.

---

19. Coogan. *Michael Collins.* op. cit., 387.

16

"O Churchill dear and did you hear the news
from Dublin town, They've listened to your
good advice and blown the Four Courts down;
And likewise with Sackville Street, the like I've never
seen, And guns (the best) as per request,
and lorries painted green."

Author unknown

THURSDAY MORNING, 6 JULY 1922

*A*ran Roe O'Neill was unexpectedly roused from a sound sleep
by the sound of a little voice in his ear.

"Wake up, Aran. Wake up."

Choosing to ignore the cheery command in the hopes it might
tire and leave him in peace, he remained motionless in the bed
with his eyes closed.

"Momma, he can't hear me."

"Oh, he can hear you all right. He's just hoping you'll go
away. Try tickling his nose."

Several moments passed before Aran was aware of a handful
of tiny fingers tapping out some imaginary rhythm on the tip
of his nose.

Now fully awake, he tried deciding between opening his mouth with a roar and engulfing the child's hand, or simply opening one eye and saying 'boo.'

Not wanting to frighten Mary Margaret, he decided on the latter action but refrained from making any sound.

Cracking open one eye, he found himself staring at the little McCracken who was watching him intently from a distance of less than a foot.

Turning, she exclaimed, "Oh, Momma, he's awake!"

Returning to gaze at the recumbent figure in the bed, the child asked, "Aran, are you awake?"

"Aye, Mary Margaret, I am…thanks to you. Now where's that mother of yours? I've something I want to say to her."

"Momma? Momma? He wants you."

Pushing himself up onto his elbows, Aran looked around the room. Áine was nowhere in sight.

"Sarah Anne. Sarah Anne," he ordered. "Come here this minute."

Falling back into the warmth of the bed, he pulled the duvet up over his head while he strained, listening for Annie's saving footsteps.

Seconds passed but no rescuing sounds could be heard.

Thinking he was playing a game with her, Mary Margaret began pulling the bed covering away from his face.

As the tug-of-war commenced, amid mounting shrieks and giggles, Aran finally realised he was on his own.

Begrudgingly admitting defeat at the hands of this wee child, the Gortman swept Mary Margaret off her feet and rolled her up in the folds of the quilt. While she struggled to liberate herself, he made a dash for his trousers folded over the back of a chair in the room's corner.

Before his godchild could free herself and climb out of the bed, Aran was halfway down the stairs, buttoning his shirt.

"Áine? Áine, you have some difficult explaining to do. Doesn't a man have the right to a lie-in after what I've been through?"

"Ah sure, just preparing you for the pleasures of parenthood, old stock."

It was Gay's unsympathetic voice coming to his wife's rescue from the kitchen.

As he rounded the room's corner, there they all sat, grinning from ear to ear.

"Jaysus wept. The three of you have some kind of a perverted sense of humour," roared Aran. "The least one of yis could do is pour this poor man a cup of tea."

❧

It had been a horrific eight days. Aran thought he'd every right to expect a few extra hours of sleep. Sure he hadn't many in the GPO. No one had. The constant crack of rifles and the burst of machine-gun fire plus the booming of the 18-pounders were enough to keep the dead awake. That incessant racket was only offset by the constant worry of being overrun by some imaginary force, and both were magnified by the perpetual concern for the safety of his soldiers. But the fear of IRA reinforcements encircling his positions never materialised. The attack on the Four Courts had caught the anti-Treaty forces by as much surprise as it had the National Army and the citizens of Dublin.

For the second time in six years, parts of the Irish capital lay in smouldering ruins. As in 1916, the Fire Brigade commanders refused to expose their men to the dangers of flying bullets. Fires that blazed uncontrollably were simply and tragically allowed to burn themselves out.

By 3 July, all isolated IRA strongholds around the town centre had been recaptured. Fighting continued only in the area know as the 'the Block' along the northeastern side of Sackville Street Upper.

Two days later, with the last of the Republican faithful captured, dead or on the run out of town, the shooting stopped. The aftermath revealed millions of pounds of property destroyed with some three hundred Irishmen wounded and over sixty dead.

❧

After breakfast and clad in clean uniforms, Aran and Gabriel bid their wives goodbye and walked the short distance west along the Grand Canal to Portobello Barracks. Michael had moved his offices there on the 3rd. It was far more spacious than the smaller, somewhat confining Beggars' Bush Barracks. The new facility allowed for a larger assemblage of military personnel and equipment in one place. Instead of his staff being housed in various buildings around Dublin, they were now comfortably situated in one central location. Evacuated by the British earlier that spring, Portobello further distanced his HQ from the civilian population and made defence of the large compound less problematic.

The two men entered the main building and followed a paper sign tacked up in the foyer. In neat lettering it simply stated, 'Chairman, Provisional Government.' An arrow pointed down a hallway, off to the left.

Finally, after two further inquiries and being directed by a young corporal to 'please take seats, sirs,' the Big Fellow ushered Aran and Gay into his private inner office.

"By God, you two are to be congratulated…fine job indeed," were the first words out of Michael's mouth.

Motioning them to wait just a moment, the two overheard the Corkman ordering the corporal to organise some tea and biscuits.

Finally, with the door closed behind him, Michael erupted, "For fuck sake, what were those sons-of-bitches thinking?"

Flipping a lock of unruly hair back into place, Michael motioned them to sit. Several comfortable-looking leather chairs were grouped around a low table off to one side of the spacious office. Michael's desk and chair, two book shelves, a wooden filing cabinet, a coat rack and wardrobe had been placed around the room. A large window looked out onto an inner courtyard formed by other wings of the sprawling main building.

In a calmer voice, the Big Fellow exclaimed, "Some digs, eh!"

Aran and Gabriel nodded their approval.

With the three seated around the table, Michael picked up the emotional thread of his previously expletive-filled outburst.

"That feckin' Brugha! As much as we battled it out across the table and in the Dáil, I loved that man. He was the epitome of Irish Republicanism. Courageous to a fault, sure he was, but he never backed down from what he believed to be right for Ireland. Hard-headed so, but he was never afraid to face a foe. He'd the heart of a lion. We lost a giant yesterday when he fell behind the Hammam."

Nodding his agreement, Gay asked, "What's the latest news?"

"Not good. He's again riddled through with bullets. The doctors say he hasn't a chance, God bless his Irish soul."

Silence filled the room only to be interrupted seconds later by the corporal's knock. The tea had arrived.

"Put it on the table," snapped the Corkman. Then in a softer tone he said, "Thank you, corporal. That'll be all."

With the room again to themselves, Aran busied himself pouring the steaming liquid into the three mugs that had been neatly arranged on the tray.

With milk and sugar dispensed, the Gortman looked up. "Mick, you know Cathal was a lot like you."

Putting his tea back down on the table, Michael buried his head in his hands. Between sobs, he blurted out, "Many would not have forgiven—had they been in my place—Cathal Brugha's attack on me in January. Yet I would forgive him anything. Because of his sincerity I would forgive him anything. At worst he was a fanatic—though in what has been a noble cause. At best I number him among the very few who have given their all that this country—now torn by Civil War—should have its freedom. When many of us are forgotten, Cathal Brugha will be remembered."[1]

Regaining his composure, Mick dried his eyes with a handkerchief.

"Mary, Mother of God, sure I'm glad it's you two in here and not someone else. Those tears have been building up ever since I heard he was brought down by a hail of bullets."

With emotion-filled eyes, Aran said, "It was told to me by a soldier who was there that men on both sides shouted out to

---

1. Ibid., 387.

Cathal to surrender. He simply ignored their commands. He must have thought he was invincible ever since '16."

"I heard the same report, Aran. Feckin' eejit! It would take more than ten to equal him," blurted out the Big Fella.

Changing the subject, as if trying to forget the Brugha tragedy, Michael asked if they'd heard the news about Lynch and the others.

"No," replied Gay. "Sure, weren't they among those rounded up after the Four Courts surrender?"

"Let me bring you up to date on the latest."

With a steady hand, Mick picked up his mug and began, "Now, I don't want you leaving here thinkin' I'm blaming Dick Mulcahy in any way, but apparently he and some of his men had arrested the two Liams, Seán Moylan and a handful of others who were hightailing it out of town soon after the attack on the Fours Courts began.[2]

"Seems they were first taken to Wellington Barracks on the South Circular Road. O'Duffy was there and interviewed both Lynch and Deasy. Not knowing that the rift between Lynch and the hardliners had been healed, he quickly sent the lot of them on their way to Kingsbridge. It was his best judgement that Lynch and the others might be able to influence the boys down the country. If they could talk some sense into the others to give up the fight, they just might bring things to a quick end."

"So you're saying that O'Duffy had no idea that the boyos had mended their bridges?" interjected Gay.

Nodding at Aran, he continued, "...and you can bet your arse they weren't about to set the record straight with O'Duffy either."

"All the same," said Aran, "sure we'd be a hell of a lot better off if only he'd held them for a few days...just to be on the safe side."

"Hindsight, my young friend, hindsight," scolded Michael.

"Ah sure, I know, but it might have made things a lot easier down the road.

"Any news about Shadow?" asked the Gortman.

Michael just shook his head no.

---

2. Deasy, op. cit., 48-49.

Moving on, Gabby asked, "What's this we heard about Dev, dressed out in a white coat, fleeing the Hammam in an ambulance?"

"I heard that too," answered Michael. "The part about the ambulance has been confirmed, but the Long Hoor robed in medical attire is apparently only rumour."

"Sure, that wouldn't surprise me one bit. Too bad Cashman wasn't around with his camera. It would've made a great picture on the front page of the *Journal*," said Aran.

"Glad you've your sense of humour back, Aran," said Michael. "But in all seriousness, supposedly Dev's re-enlisted and has taken up the mighty rank of 'private.' But don't hold your breath; I'm betting we've not heard the last of him by a long shot."

"Sure, you're right Mick," said Aran. "He may have lost the respect of men like Lynch and O'Malley for the moment, but taking the back seat is just not his style.

"Speaking of Ernie, Gay and I heard he'd escaped again just like he did from Kilmainham when he was under the watchful eye of British warders last year."

Ah sure, you can't keep a good man down," joked Gay, "but with himself and Lynch on the loose, they'll certainly rally their men."

"Sure they will, Gay, but things will be different this time, whether they realise it now or not. Here, have a read of this."

Michael pushed a copy of the morning's newspaper lying on the table toward them.

It was open to a story entitled: "Fighting ended in Dublin."

The story was written by P. S. O'Hegarty, who, like Michael, had worked as a civil servant in London during the years before the First War. He'd already written several pieces highly critical of de Valera and the IRA split.

"In this editorial, he pulls no punches," said Mick. "Here, Aran, you read what he has to say."

The Rebel began aloud, "The responsibility for...the civil war lies almost altogether on Éamon de Valera."[3]

"Wow," said Aran, "he obviously doesn't see eye to eye with Dev and his bloody tactics."

3. P. S. O'Hegarty. *The Victory of Sinn Féin.* Dublin, 1998, 108.

Glancing over the typeset page, Aran said, "Here...listen to this. '[The Republicans]...beaten in the Dáil, and knowing they would be beaten in the country, placed their reliance on the gun, on forcing the Provisional Government, by the threat of the gun, to withhold putting the Treaty into operation, or to put it into operation shorn of its objectionable features.'"[4]

"Jaysus!" exclaimed Gay. "He doesn't mince words, does he?"

"Wait," said Aran, "there's more. 'The Irregulars, in fact, had speedily realised that they had no popular support, that the Irish people supported the Treaty and the Government established by it, that they themselves were the enemies of the people, and they accepted that position.'"[5]

The Rebel briefly summarised O'Hegarty's words as the author described his presence in the assembly hall back in January when the Dáil had voted not to reinstate Dev as its president.

Looking up again, Aran said, "...and I quote, 'His [de Valera's] demeanour was that of a man taken completely by surprise, and wounded in his tenderest part—his vanity. It was unbelievable, to him, and not to be borne, that he should be beaten in a straight vote in Dáil. It was unbelievable to him, also, that there should be in Ireland a Government without himself as President of it. He was ready to do anything to prevent that, and he went to all lengths to prevent it.'"[6]

The Gortman glanced up at Mick and Gay. "Listen, this is how he ends the column with the Civil War finger of blame again pointing at the Chief. '...[the blame lies with] Mr. de Valera's refusal to accept majority decisions, his appeal to violence, his rejection of democratic procedure, his formation of a Terrorist army, and his failure to control that army. He's the moral force and the voice behind the whole pseudo-Republican-Irregular movement.'"[7]

"I'd hate to see that one standing against us," muttered Gay.

---

4. Ibid., 88.
5. Ibid., 90.
6. Ibid., 110.
7. Ibid., 112.

"With us or against us, that doesn't matter. What matters is right versus wrong," retorted Michael.

"The safety of the nation is the first law and henceforth we shall not rest until we have established the authority of the people of Ireland in every square mile under their [the Irish people's] jurisdiction,"[8] continued the Big Fellow.

"This is it, isn't it, Michael. No more second chances. You're going to take this war to them, aren't you?"

"Yes, Aran, that's what I've decided to do. Just between the three of us, in a few days I'm planning to step down, at least temporarily, as Provisional Government Chairman, and assume command of the National Army."

Aran and Gay just stared at their friend.

"I've given it a lot of thought. Part of it has to do with showing that London crowd I really do mean business. They've been impugning my moral character for some time now and to tell you the truth, I'm feckin' tired of it. And another thing, I'm bloody well tired of the Long Hoor stirring up trouble. If he has Ireland's best interests at heart, he has a funny way of showing it. His fancy dancing and double talk must stop before the blood on the shamrock is knee deep."

By now Michael was on his feet, pacing back and forth like a caged lion.

Pausing a moment before his two comrades, he looked down at them still seated in their chairs. "Well, what do yis think? Can I pull it off or not?"

Jumping up, Aran almost shouted, "Bloody hell, Mick, can you pull it off? You bet your sweet arse you can. That's just what we need...someone who knows what he's doing and has the guts to make it happen."

Now on his feet as well, Gay stretched out a hand in Michael's direction. "I can't tell you how happy I am with your decision. Besides taking you out of the political arena for a bit, it gives you a chance to do what you do best. Remember what Griffith said about you in the Dáil...you're 'the man who won the war.'"

"I take that as a compliment, Gay...as backhanded as it may be."

8. Coogan. *Michael Collins.* op. cit., 386.

"Ah, for fuck sake, Mick, you know what I mean. Politics has never been your game, even though you do it better than most and that includes the Long Hoor. You're too direct and impatient to play the waiting game. You're a man of action; a leader of men."

"Get out of it, Gay, or you'll be having me name up for sainthood before long."

"No, seriously Michael," interrupted Aran, "it's just what this country needs. Someone to inspire them, move them forward and put an end to this Civil War rubbish. Our old friends will take kindly to your move. It should shorten the war by a big margin. You just mark my words."

"Sure as hell, I was hoping you'd see it that way. I should've done this months ago. If I had, maybe last week wouldn't have been necessary."

"Uh-uh," chided Aran. "Don't forget what you just said to me, Michael? About hindsight and all that? But seriously, what's the next move?"

"As you're well aware, most of the Republican forces, staring defeat in the face, headed south and west. They couldn't get out of Dublin fast enough. Somehow courage and conviction lost their way."

"Wait a minute, Michael," interrupted Aran. "I thought we had this discussion six years ago. If only our Easter leaders had been willing to make that same sacrifice…"

"You're right. If we'd run to fight another day maybe things would've been different. But we didn't and today they did. So let's put '16 behind us. The lads are on the run so and now it's our job to go after them. Sure, there'll be a good few more who'll take up arms out of sympathy for the IRA because we dared fire upon them. So be it. But as O'Hegarty points out in his editorial, the people won't be after supporting them as they did during the Tan War. The people are tired of their lives, their work, their everything being disrupted by gangs of gunslingers. Without the support of the country behind them there's no way they can fight a successful guerrilla campaign. Remember lads, just three weeks ago Ireland spoke with a clear and decisive voice. The citizenry are willing to give the Treaty a chance, as imperfect as it may be. Sure I signed that Treaty and I'm going to help see it succeed, even if it's the last thing I do."

❦

The following day, Friday, 7 July, was one of mixed blessings. On the one hand, Dublin rejoiced as the cause of democracy had been upheld.

In a touch of biting sarcasm, one of the local Dublin newspapers featured a cartoon depicting Winston Churchill firing an 18-pounder at the Four Courts with Michael Collins standing by ready to pass him another shell. Over the Big Fellow's shoulder, the figure of the Chief could be seen. He was on the run out of town with the tails of his medical coat blowing in the wind. Below the cartoon were the words:

O Churchill dear and did you hear the news from
    Dublin town,
They've listened to our good advice and blown the Four
    Courts down;
And likewise with Sackville Street, the like I've never seen,
And guns (the best) as per request, and lorries painted
    green.

On a sadder note, Cathal Brugha died in hospital. Though he was given the best medical care possible, his wounds were too serious. The doctors were unable to save him.

His body lay in state at the Mater Hospital. An honour guard of uniformed Cumann na mBán kept vigil over his body while many in Dublin filed past his lifeless form as they paid their final respects.

The 'proud' Cathal Brugha was laid to rest in the Republican Plot at Glasnevin Cemetery. Seán T. O'Kelly was one of the pallbearers.

Despite the national bitterness that was beginning to erupt after only one week of Civil War fighting, Michael Collins refused to be dragged into the mêlée over Brugha's death. He flatly refused to listen to or repeat any personal criticism of the hero of South Dublin Union and the Hammam Hotel.

❄

On Sunday, the 9th, Aran, Gabriel and two companies of men headed south out of Dublin in lorries. Section Commanders Duncan MacGregor and Pat Grogan were in charge of the two groups consisting of ninety men each. Joining them in supporting two-thirds of the battalion were Adjutant Cú Cullen, Medical Officer Marty Richardson and his assistant Liam McCullers, Assistant Engineer Nick Robinson and Section Vice-Commanders Chris McKee and Jimmy Carroll. Transportation Officer Caoimhín Donleavy drove the lead sedan with Aran, Marty and the Nayler inside. Lined up in single file behind them was a convoy of twenty military transports and a Rolls Royce 'Whippet' nicknamed 'The Pikeman.' Bringing up the rear was a second sedan driven by Gay. It held Cú, Pat and brother Larry. Chris and Jimmy rode up front in two of the lorries. They were heading south to reinforce pro-Treaty forces in Blessington, County Wicklow. According to reports, fighting had been going on in the area since the 2nd. From there the battalion was scheduled to head due south with orders to link up with General Prout and help take back Waterford Town.

Just prior to their departure south, Michael Collins issued a directive to the press that hence forth the state's army was to be referred to as either the 'National Army' or the 'Irish Army' and their opposites were to be labelled 'Irregulars' or simply 'bands.' No other references were to be attached to the now divided IRA Army.[9]

Aran knew that was fine for the media outlets, especially those backing the new government's position, but many of the locals living down the country, no doubt, would still refer to the warring factions as pro- or anti-Treatyites. Some used the labels 'Free Staters' or 'Staters' while their opposite numbers were labelled simply 'Republicans' or just 'IRA.'

---

9. Litton, op. cit., 82, 85.

Not knowing what awaited them up ahead, Aran wished he had his full complement of men, but the Big Fellow had ordered Liam Tobin and his company of men to stay back in Dublin. There were still some isolated pockets of IRA resistance scattered around Dublin and Mick wanted Liam involved in the necessary mopping-up operation.

Though a week of inner-city fighting had tested the mettle of his men, Aran knew what awaited them would be entirely different. The Dublin action had been very limited. In town, well constructed barricades and the stone façades of buildings protected his forces. Few of the troops had been exposed to actual combat on open ground and there'd been no hand-to-hand skirmishing whatsoever. His troopers and the likewise barricaded Irregulars had exchanged many rounds of gunfire but the fighting was more akin to target practice than traditional warfare. The decisive elements that led to the IRA's defeat were delivered by the 18-pounders, the armoured cars and the out of control fires. Without those elements on the Free State's side, the siege might still be going on today, if ammunition had held out that is.

Now they were about to face a much more dangerous situation. Casualties would be greater. To date no one in his battalion had been killed though a number had received wounds, three seriously. Aran knew that was all about to change. Both sides would take prisoners as battlefield tactics shifted with the usual ebb and flow of combat.

With Gay's help, he tried to prepare the men, but words and training were no substitute for actual shoot-to-kill, battlefield conditions. Even the dozen or so former British soldiers now in the battalion's ranks and who'd seen action in France were on edge. As one of them said, "It's hard to get used to someone trying to kill you."

The Irish Rebel knew the Irregulars would have the edge, at least initially. Their forces were larger; they held almost all of Munster and most of Connacht plus isolated pockets of Leinster. Many of their troops were experienced guerrilla fighters well versed in fighting under all kinds of conditions. The veteran volunteer army, battling on *their* own soil, would put up one hell of a fight.

On the other hand, the National Army that Aran was a part of held a big edge in weaponry,[10] but was smaller and vastly less experienced than its opponent. Essentially, it was a mercenary force, comprised of men with questionable motives. Already the 2nd Battalion of the Dublin Guards had seen some two dozen men pack up and head home after just one week of action. Aran expected the number of defectors to grow as the fighting continued. But as Michael had pointed out prior to the battalion's departure, the longer the fighting continued in the towns, villages and down the country, the less likely the Irregulars would find support and succour from the civilian population. The Irish people had had their fill of war, both at home during the Tan 'troubles' and abroad in Europe between 1914–1918. "They won't put up with much for long," were the Corkman's exact words.

❧

The Big Fellow speculated that the Irregulars would choose to fight a defensive war, not an offensive one. "It just isn't in their nature," Mick said to his team of intimates at a military planning session in Portobello just the day before Aran and Gabriel's companies headed south.

"Based on what we know of their Tan War strategies, of their limited number of arms and their inadequate transport dilemma, I don't expect them to be taking the initiative and attacking Dublin or any other large towns," said Michael.

"Sure, we've already witnessed some early indications of their battle tactics," noted Liam Tobin. "In trying to deprive us of our ability to respond to their moves, the Irregulars have blown

---

10. London continued to supply the Provisional government with a steady stream of arms while the IRA forces were required to depend on stolen or captured weapons. Additionally, Collins's National Army was the beneficiary of heavy field guns (18-pounders), Lancia & 'Whippet' armoured cars, Vickers machine guns, numerous lorries & millions of rounds of ammunition. "Between 31 January and 26 June 1922, the British government had supplied 11,900 rifles, 79 Lewis machine-guns, 4,200 revolvers & 3,504 grenades." Hopkinson, op. cit., 127.

up some rail lines leading out of Dublin as well as derailing the Blessington tram."

"That's right, Liam," said the Corkman. "They're just shooting themselves in the foot when they do that. Such tactics actually limit *their* mobility not ours. With the amount of transport we've available, the tram line in and out of Blessington is the least of our worries."

Gay, standing in the back of the room, spoke up. "I'd guess we'll see more of the same, just like in the old days: roads trenched, bridges blown and rail lines torn up."

"Damn right," offered Duncan, "but the only time we may see them on the offence is when they choose to raid a police barracks or a military installation for weapons and supplies."

"Sure, they may catch us short-handed at first on that score, but with increased manpower and superior arms, we'll tip that balance in our favour very soon."

"Cú's right there," said Aran. "With our men on the advance, they'll either have to surrender or be pushed into the sea. My real concern, however, is how much of a fight they'll put up in the populated areas. That's when the casualties and civilian damage could certainly mount."

"For that very reason, it's paramount we take the initiative and strike the first blow. Set them back on their heels and turn their faces for home," stated Michael. "The longer we delay in taking the offensive, the more time they'll have to dig in.

"Look lads, their military command at best will be a loosely knit affair, with poor lines of communication. If we pressurise them enough, they'll be after spending more time on the move, trying to keep out of our way than they will in organising effective assault or counterstrike strategies. The trick will be to keep the pressure on and anticipate their next move."

"Michael," said Liam, "sure and don't forget, we've other factors working for us as well. Our intelligence capability is so much greater than theirs. So are our lines of communication. We saw that here last week. No one from outside Dublin came to Rory's rescue. Their occupying 'the Block' only demonstrated another of their weaknesses: lack of sound leadership and good planning.

We caught them with their trousers down and all they could do was turn tail and run."

"And what about the whole business of prisoner detention," noted Gabby. "We'll be able to move our captured men back to secure central locations while they'll be in the same fix we were with Sassenach captives during the Tan days. Men on the run can't be spending time minding prisoners. Sure, it'll be difficult enough for them to look after themselves much less our lads."

"And tell me," asked Pat Grogan, "how are Irregulars going to plead their case to the outside?"

Before anyone could respond, Pat answered to his own query. "They won't be able to. With their nonparticipation in the new Dáil, they'll have no public or political voice to offer up in support of their position. Then, once they've been driven out of the major population centres, they'll have no forum whatsoever, especially when you consider that any sympathetic media channels will be in our hands."

"Poor ole Dev. What'll he do then with no one is listening to his prating?" mocked Gay.

"He'll have to resort to setting up clandestine meetings with members of the international press or smuggling out secretive missives, hoping they'll be read by like-minded souls," teased Cú.

"Sure, that'll really cramp his style," laughed the Nayler.

"Listen lads, on a more serious note," said Aran, standing up to address the meeting. "There's one thing that both sides have in common. I firmly believe that neither of us wants to maim or kill the other. That's a big issue for me and I know it's on the minds of the rest of yis."

Suddenly, the meeting took on a sober tone. "Aran's right," said Michael. "It's a matter we've all wrestled with during these last weeks. Unfortunately, I don't have an answer for you, but for the love of God, each of you be careful and don't take any foolish chances.

"Our initial efforts must be to throw a cordon around Dublin that will keep the Irregulars from returning. Next, the National Army must fan out from the capital and begin advancing toward the enemy where it's weakest here in Leinster. At the same time we must begin reinforcing and holding barracks and strategic buildings in areas that our forces initially occupied when the Red Coats left. Any questions?"

No one spoke.

"Assuming things go according to plan, Emmet Dalton and I have worked out a strategy whereby we'll transport troops by ship around the island, landing at key spots and catching the enemy by surprise. They'll be pinched between our land and sea forces. The only choice we'll give them is to drop their weapons and run or we'll simply kick the living shyte out of the lot of them where they stand."

With the meeting over, the assembled officers stood to leave.

"Oh, one more thing, gentlemen," said Michael, rapping his knuckles on the table to regain their attention. "During these next crucial weeks, I want you to remember one thing. For all you know it may save your life and the lives of your men."

His words stopped his comrades in their tracks.

With all eyes fixed on him, the Big Fellow cynically warned, "We have no Army; we have only an armed mob."[11]

❧

Early reports indicated that men from south Tipperary, led by Mike Sheehan, had moved in and occupied the village of Blessington. Reinforced by some of Oscar Traynor's retreating Dublin 1st Brigade men, it looked like a significant confrontation was brewing.

But it was not to be. National Army forces, in a three-pronged advance, sent the Irregulars running after just a short engagement.

Men from Curragh, from Dublin and up from the coast had overwhelmed the IRA. Despite the government's communication edge, Aran and his two companies of men were surprised to learn that Blessington had fallen to Free State forces on Saturday morning, the day before.

Aran was surprised their advance on Blessington was so uneventful. There were no signs of the enemy or that any fighting

11. Garvin, op. cit., 131.

had taken place. The main Naas-Blessington road hadn't been cut at all.

Just before noon on Sunday, Aran halted the convoy. Taking fifteen men with him on foot, the Irish Rebel moved north and east toward the village. Pat Grogan, accompanied by another group of men, took a more southeasterly course. Their objective was to scout out the immediate area for Irregular forces and, if all went as hoped, they'd converge on Blessington in one hour's time.

As the Gortman worked his way across fields, over stone walls and through stands of birch and white thorn, he had to pinch himself to make sure he wasn't dreaming. Though it had been well over a year since he'd played this game for keeps, it felt like only yesterday. Upon reflection, it seemed he'd lived a lifetime, maybe two, in those twelve months. The sudden thrill of the hunt sent chills running up and down his spine. The pounding of his heart and the knowledge that other men's lives depended on his abilities as a soldier invested him with almost superhuman energy. On more than one occasion he had to caution himself to go slower and use all his senses, if he was going to come through this day unscathed and set an example for the others to follow.

As they approached the outskirts of Blessington, Aran could hear and see an unusual level of activity in the village centre. Irish Army troops had beaten them there. In fact, from the casual demeanour of both civilian and military personnel spotted through his field glasses, he was certain things were well in hand.

Not wishing to disobey his own orders, he instructed his men to lie low while he moved to the south to make contact with Pat and his men.

At five minutes to one, they rendezvoused behind a stone wall, two fields over from the main road into the village.

With their plan of attack agreed upon, Aran rejoined his squad. At fifteen after the hour, the two groups of Dublin Guards advanced, crouching low and in single file, into the village.

Using stone walls and buildings as cover, they moved cautiously. One mistake here could cost someone his life.

Peering around the corner of a building that faced the main

street, Aran could see five transport vehicles and several dozen National Army soldiers milling about. Recognizing an officer he had met at Beggars' Bush earlier that spring, Aran called out his name, "Bishop…Commandant Bishop."

Looking up from the map spread out on the bonnet of the lorry he was standing beside, the man answered, "Who wants to know?"

"Major Aran O'Neill. Over here."

As the man peered in his direction, Aran stepped out from the building's cover and began walking toward the commandant.

"Jaysus Lord, where'd you come from?"

"Lucky for you it's me. You'd have been a goner if I was an Irregular."

Looking a bit chagrined from the upbraid, the officer replied, "Guess so, but thanks be to God you weren't. A group of us took this town yesterday. Arrested over one hundred with another thirty dead or wounded."

"Congratulations," replied Aran.

The Rebel turned and waved at his men to join him. Moments later, Pat and his squad moved up from further down the way.

"Feckin' right, you weren't kidding, were you. Where'd you come from anyhow?"

"I've two companies of men, an armoured car and twenty lorries. We left Dublin this morning and came in via the Naas Road. These men and I walked the last mile or so across country. Never saw a scout or a lookout or anyone. As I said, you're bloody lucky we weren't the other crowd."

"I see what you mean, but I'd heard all the Irregulars had hightailed it south into the mountains and on toward Waterford. We scouted the area around the village yesterday afternoon and found nothing."

"That isn't to say a number of them might not have doubled back to catch ye by surprise. Then there's always the possibility that some stragglers coming down from the north, looking for a meal or a dry place to sleep, could have disturbed your comfort."

"You're right, Major. I won't let this sort of thing happen again."

Changing the subject, Aran asked, "I could go for a nice cup of tea, Bishop. Any suggestions?"

"Just up the way. Let me show you."

Aran sent a detail of four men back to tell Gay it was safe to bring the convoy into the village.

With steaming cups of black tea before them, Pat, Commandant Stanley Bishop and himself exchanged news.

From the officer Aran learned that Ernie O'Malley and Seán Lemass had been in charge of the Irregulars surrounding Blessington. According to Bishop, the two IRA men had escaped from Jameson's Distillery on the 30th after the others in the Four Courts had surrendered. They, along with other prisoners, had been held there until transportation could be arranged to move them across town to Mountjoy.

Much to Aran's surprise and personal disappointment, he also learned that Liam Mellowes had been with the two escapees at the distillery. Unfortunately, his former commander and friend was busy shaving and missed out on the opportunity to make a break for it.[12]

Bishop also informed Pat and himself that the Irregulars, now with Liam Lynch in overall command as Chief of Staff, were planning to establish a line from Limerick to Waterford. It was their intention to hold that line to its south and west, only falling back toward Cork and Kerry if absolutely necessary. Under the direction of Lynch and Deasy's 1st Southern Division coupled with O'Malley's 2nd Southern Division, the leadership and battle strategy of the Irregulars was becoming clearer. They intended to hold their 'Munster Republic' at all costs.

❧

After a short break in Blessington, Aran and Gay decided to press on southward. They knew they'd likely be walking in on the heels of retreating bands of Irregulars, but they'd little choice.

Aran knew they would have to be extremely careful in approaching anyone they encountered. Michael had warned him

12. Eoin Neeson. *The Civil War 1922-23*. Dublin, 1989, 133.

that at this early stage in the fighting not all National Army troops had been issued uniforms. Thus, persons in civilian dress might be just that, civilians, but they could also be National Army troopers or Irregulars. Mufti was not always an indication of a person's political affiliation or military sympathy. To make matters even more confusing, some IRA officers had chosen to wear the same dark green uniforms that pro-Treaty soldiers wore.[13]

Aran's men were among the fortunate. They'd all been issued complete sets of uniforms, new rifles, revolvers, everything. It was a great boost to battalion morale. Aran had thanked Michael for his generosity, but the Big Fellow simply brushed off the appreciation stating it was just the luck of the draw. But Aran knew better. Coupled with Gay's and his leadership and hard work plus Michael's support, his 2nd Battalion men had every reason to hold their heads high.

The Gortman's convoy left Blessington at three in the afternoon. Unfortunately, the weather had turned. Cold rainy showers and breezy conditions greeted the battalion as it passed through Baltinglass and Tullow. Following the River Slaney south they bivouacked along its grassy banks just north of Bunclody on the Wicklow-Wexford border.

Later that evening, the sky cleared and the breeze subsided. Taking all the necessary precautions of organising scouting parties and posting sentries, the men passed a peaceful and restful night.

The following day, Monday, the 10th, the battalion hooked up with Major General John Prout just outside of Enniscorthy. Prout, an Irishman, had served with United States troops in France during the First War. He was a veteran soldier and well used to fighting backed by large numbers of men. Aran and Gay, on the other hand, were experienced guerrilla fighters. Prout remarked this was the best of both worlds.

The Major General was thin, moustached and stood about two inches shorter than Aran. He spoke in a deliberate manner and exuded confidence. From their conversations, he seemed

13. Ibid., 162.

to have a great understanding of troop movements and battle tactics.

Within the past week Michael and Dick Mulcahy had made several major military-assignment decisions. With the entire 2nd Southern Division under his command, General Prout was assigned the south-eastern region of the country. General Seán Mac Eoin was given the Western Command to oversee. Additionally, other postings were announced. General Eoin O'Duffy, Army Chief of Staff assumed the added responsibility as GOC of the east; General Emmet Dalton was put in control of Ireland's southern region; and General J. J. 'Ginger' O'Connell was given command of all Curragh forces.[14]

Aran looked forward to working with Prout as the two teamed up with National Army troops from counties Waterford, Wexford, Kilkenny and the southern half of Tipperary. These men were fighting on familiar ground, but as far as Gay and he were concerned, it was foreign territory.

After careful study of the local roads, it was decided to divide up the men into company size groups and make a slow, careful approach on New Ross situated on the River Barrow. Prout ordered a thorough fine-tooth combing of the entire area. It would literally be a house-to-house search of the entire rural countryside. The General wanted added insurance that when the attack on Waterford began there would be little likelihood that any Irregular force would pose a threat to his rear flank.

The sweep to New Ross took four and a half days. Fortunately, they met with only slight resistance. No fatalities were recorded and Aran's men only sustained two accidental gunshot wounds that needed treating. On the other hand, they did flush out a dozen Irregulars who were immediately placed under arrest.

The combined National Army force, now in excess of six hundred men, found temporary lodging in New Ross. The men spent the next two days resting in their commandeered quarters, cleaning their equipment, relaxing and catching up on sleep. The drinking of alcohol was strictly forbidden under penalty of thirty days confinement.

---

14. Litton, op. cit., 82.

On Monday, Prout's men marched out along the main road to Waterford. Aran and his forces, back in their lorries, followed the next day.

On Tuesday evening Prout's command fanned out over a one-mile area and moved to within a half mile of the town.

Aran volunteered and led an advanced scouting party up to the top of the heights overlooking the River Suir and Waterford on its opposite shore.

Expecting to find a well entrenched anti-Treaty perimeter above the town on their side of the river, the Rebel was surprised. They met with very light resistance, only scattered rifle fire and no enemy entrenchment. There below them, shrouded in the mist and fog of a soft summer's evening, lay the unguarded town of Waterford.

Returning to Prout's line with the good news, the National Army men rushed forward, hoping to surmount the heights and race down the other side and into the city over the cantilevered bridge crossing the Suir.

But plans for the motorised, lightning attack had to be scratched as they disappointedly watched a group of Irregulars raise the span.

With only one 18-pounder field gun in his artillery, Prout decided to begin shelling the town from on high at seven o'clock that evening. The targets were two barracks, Infantry and Cavalry, plus the Ballybricken Jail. All three represented the major strongholds in the town and were heavily invested with anti-Treaty troops, arms and explosives. Because of Prout's positioning above Waterford, the three targets were more or less in a single line at a point of aim some one thousand to twenty-two thousand yards away.

With night darkening down, the second phase of the attack was inaugurated. Aran and Gay commanded a force of approximately one hundred and fifty Dublin Guards. They moved south behind the ridge to a spot about a mile east of Waterford. There they waited for low tide at half eleven.

At the appointed time, the men moved down the overlooking hillside and waded across the tide-shallowed river. At the crossing point, the water was only waist deep, but the slippery, rocky riverbed made the going treacherous. Luckily, the men only had fifty yards of river to navigate.

Safely across and with their weapons dry and ready, they moved into town. Their objective was to stay well clear of Prout's targets: the two barracks and jail. They were also to ignore any lightly guarded outposts and quietly occupy a strong position in the town centre, overlooking the river. Once the bridge was in their control, they'd be in place to give covering fire as the main body of Prout's forces entered the city.

Once in Waterford without a shot being fired, the Dublin Guards proceeded along the quay and broke into a large, deserted warehouse on the waterfront. With fifty well-placed men inside its stout walls, Aran led a second group of fifty behind a low stone retaining wall that commanded a good view of the bridge and the main road leading into the heart of the city. Anyone attempting to stop Prout's men from advancing would be caught in a deadly crossfire.

With two-thirds of their troopers well placed, Gay led the remaining men through back streets forming a protective semi-circular boundary which would offer great protection to the stationary men in the warehouse and along the quay.

All the while, Prout's men kept up a steady barrage with the field gun. Shells were exploding every twenty minutes or so. With the insistent pounding shaking the surrounding buildings, all Aran could think: *If those gunners are any good, the lads holed up in the barracks and jail will be blown to bits before long.*

With the bridge secured, Aran fired off a flare, his signal to the Major General that the waterfront had been seized and he was to advance.

The Dublin Guards on the city-side shore waited anxiously for their anticipated reinforcements, but none were forthcoming.

By now the Irregulars in town were aware of Aran and Gay's presence. Soon the Rebel's men were coming under small arms fire. Between keeping an eye out for Irregulars, the Gortman kept glancing back at the bridge, but still Prout's forces were no where to be seem.

Keeping a low profile, the advance party waited throughout the remainder of the night and into the following morning.

With its limited shell reserves, the 18-pounder had stopped its assault hours ago. Aran and his men began feeling isolated and vulnerable.

Finally, the Irish Rebel decided to send two men back down the river. They were to re-trace their steps and find out what had happened to cause the reinforcements to delay their advance. Aran knew that with their meagre supply of ammunition, his troops would be hard pressed to hold out for much longer.

Finally, at quarter-to-ten in the morning, Aran saw Prout and his forces streaming down the heights toward the bridge. Leading the formation was his battalion's armoured car, 'the Pikeman.' Its ominous advance was punctuated by a blazing Vickers machine gun.

Following along behind came a string of lorries with the last one pulling the 18-pounder. In the wake of the motorised vehicles marched General Prout's remaining men, rifles at the ready.

Aran was more than a bit annoyed over Prout's delay. His anger, however, was quickly assuaged when the Major General explained that their rear flank had been unexpectedly attacked by a large contingent of Irregulars in the early hours of the morning.

Apparently, IRA men from Tipperary and Cork were hoping to catch the National Army troopers in a crossfire, but the shelling of the town and Aran's presence along the quay prevented the bands in Waterford from crossing the river and attacking up the heights.

Prout's men engaged the enemy until mid-morning before the Irregulars decided they'd had enough and withdrew, leaving their wounded and dead behind.

As the Free State Army leader explained to Aran and Gay, the IRA lads were poorly organised but determined. Unfortunately for them, their battle plan was ill advised with both groups of Irregulars asked to fight uphill in the face of overwhelming odds and better armed men.

"We held the high ground and by God, we weren't going to relinquish the advantage," grinned the veteran soldier.

With the added Free State reinforcements now across the river, the Irregulars knew the fight was over. They torched the two barracks prior to retreating. Powerful explosions rocked Waterford as the magazine in Infantry Barracks blew up. A huge cloud of black smoke blanketed the city. The entire scene was reminiscent of the one recently played out in Dublin.

Many of the retreating Irregulars headed west out along the coast. Some however, decided to stay in the jail and fight it out. But as soon as Prout and his men levelled the 18-pounder at the building, they surrendered. The general's men swept in and disarmed the defeated men.

With the city liberated and the Irregular line of occupation in the southeast turned, Aran and his men bid Prout a fond farewell and struck out for Dublin. They planned on travelling 'till dark before stopping. With any luck, the Dublin Guards would be home for tea the next evening.

17

"He [Arthur Griffith] forced England to take her
right hand from Ireland's throat and her left hand
out of Ireland's pocket."

P. S. O'Hegarty

FRIDAY NOON, 21 JULY 1922

*T*he Angelus was ringing in a nearby church as Aran Roe O'Neill walked through the main gate of Portobello Barracks. Though dressed in mufti, his brisk stride and erect posture revealed his military identity. His purposeful look and determined bearing told any careful observer of the human condition this man must be on an important mission.

Despite all exterior appearances, the Gortman's body still ached from the nearly two-week ordeal he'd just experienced. He'd told Sarah Anne as much after getting out of bed this morning. A day or two or three was one thing, but twelve days on the road, living under less than ideal conditions, had taken its toll. Suddenly he felt twice his age. Over his strenuous objections, Sarah insisted on drawing him his second hot bath in less than twelve hours.

"Jaysus don't tell Gay about this or he'll never let me hear the end of it," muttered the Rebel to Annie, as he slipped into the tub's warm, soothing water.

She was right. A leisurely soak was just what he needed.

As he slid down, ducking his head under the water to wet his hair, it suddenly hit him. It was so good to be home again. All the excitement, pressure and military action of the past weeks had dulled his senses to the pleasures of wife and hearth.

Resurfacing and wiping the water from his eyes, he watched Sarah Anne as she carefully brushed her hair in the mirror above the sink, only an arm's length away. Though she was still wearing her night dress, he could see her body was changing. Her breasts were larger, fuller and her belly was rounding outward. He'd heard that pregnant women often radiated a particular glow. This morning was the first time he'd noticed it with Sarah Anne.

She had been asleep when he finally arrived home from the battalion's long trek back to Dublin from Waterford. The clock in St. Mary's steeple was striking one when he passed it on his way from Beggars' Bush to #5 Mespil Road. He was looking forward to the warmth of his wife's arms and to eating a monstrous fry in the morning. Tepid food prepared over an open fire had long ago lost its romantic appeal for him.

As he walked the final block home, Aran was ticking off in his mind all the things he wanted to discuss with Michael. He'd a rather surprising strategy to propose to his new Commander-in-Chief of the National Army.

While Gay and Aran were on the road, word had filtered down that Michael had for the moment resigned his position as Chairman of the Provisional Government and had appointed himself C-in-C. Some had said he'd been forced out, but others insisted it was only a temporary measure until order in the country was restored.

Mick had forewarned his two comrades of this intended action prior to their leaving on the 9th, but he hadn't mentioned anything about an internal cabinet power-grab aimed at out-manoeuvring him with the offer of military leadership in exchange for his mantle of political authority.

❦

On entering Michael's outer office, the same corporal who'd

previously guarded Mick's inner door was on duty again. Jumping to his feet, the young man saluted Aran.

Though in civilian attire, Aran returned the gesture.

"Is he in?" asked Aran.

"Yes, sir, but he's in a meeting right now."

"Who with?"

"Generals Dalton and Mulcahy, sir."

"That's fine. I'll just show myself in."

"But sir, he asked not..."

Before the corporal could finish his sentence, Aran was past him and knocking at the closed door.

"Yes?" boomed the Big Fella's voice.

The Gortman depressed the handle and opened the door.

"Bloody hell, if it isn't the Irish Rebel himself," blurted out the new C-in-C. "By all means, come through."

By now the two generals were on their feet.

Aran walked over and shook their hands, saving Mick's for last.

"Mick was just saying, you've been down in Waterford with Prout. Have any trouble?" asked Emmet.

"None to speak of, sir," replied Aran. "Waterford's generally free of Irregulars and Prout's turned their so-called 'Munster Republic Line of Demarcation.' When Limerick falls, we'll have their two flanks on the run."

"Limerick was taken yesterday," the Minister said, smiling, "with only a nominal fight."

"Congratulations, sirs," said Aran.

"Listen," interrupted Michael, "we can drop all this 'sir' shyte while we're in here. We're all friends so let's get on with it."

Turning back to face Emmet, Aran said, "Blessington had already been sorted by the time we arrived there on Sunday afternoon. Apparently there'd been a brief skirmish on Saturday morning. If the numbers are correct, there were some hundred Irregulars taken prisoner and another thirty or so dead or wounded. I bumped into a Captain Stanley Bishop in the village centre. He seemed to have things under control. Our boys experienced only light casualties."

"That confirms the reports we received earlier," said the

Minister for Defence who was now back in uniform, doubling as Chief of Staff.

Continuing with his informal report, Aran said, "Bishop also reported to me that there'd been engagements in the villages of Brittas, Baltinglass and Kilbride."

Again the three superior officers nodded.

"O'Malley's men?" asked Emmet.

"For the most part," answered Aran, "with some of Oscar's 1st Brigade in the mix as well."

The Gortman glanced over in Michael's direction before continuing, "If yis don't mind me saying so, I've begun to see a rather disturbing pattern developing. Both in Kilbride and again later in Waterford, the Irregulars are leaving their wounded and dead behind when they pull back. As fellow Irishmen, I guess they know we'll take care of them."

"That's just another indication of how poorly prepared and led the bands are," said Michael. "They've bitten off more than they can chew, but you're right Aran, it's a feckin' disgrace all right."

"How did Prout get on in Waterford?" ask Mulcahy. "We heard you and your boys have reason to be proud."

"Thank you, and yes, Prout's a good man. He's well organised, thorough and not afraid to be assertive. His prior military experience is certainly apparent."

"That's nice to hear, but I wish he'd pushed the attack more. I heard he didn't go after the retreating Irregulars when they headed back toward Tipperary," said Dalton.

"In the man's defence," Aran offered, "sure, he'd lost some of his advantage when we left. You also realise, of course, that he's operating under a bit of a handicap. He currently has only one 18-pounder at his disposal and precious few artillery shells for it."

"I'm taking care of that right now," said Michael. "We've dispatched him your third company of men, Aran, along with another big gun as well as additional supplies and ammunition."

"Did you send Liam along in charge of the company?"

"No, Aran. I've something else in mind for him. Liam's going to hook up with Emmet here when he heads for Cork City. I've promoted him to general and he'll be reporting directly to Emmet.[1] He seems pleased with the advancement," said Michael.

"What's going to happen to my 2nd Battalion?"

"We'll talk about that later, after I'm finished here," replied the Big Fellow.

The Gortman quietly excused himself. "I hear Gay's voice in the outer office. No need to rush on my account. Finish your meeting. I'll just be outside, Michael."

Standing at attention, Aran gave a sharp salute and left, closing the door behind him.

※

Thirty minutes later, Aran and Gay were enjoying a glass of whiskey around Michael Collins's office table.

"We heard about your announcement, Mick. Congratulations. Again, I think it's a great move on your part, but is there any truth to the rumours that a conspiracy in your cabinet pushed you out?"

"Not a feckin' one, Gay," retorted Michael, obviously annoyed at Gabby's cheek for even mentioning it. "Here, read this and tell me what *you* think."

Mick thrust several sheets of paper into Gabriel's hand and pointed to the appropriate paragraph.

Reciting aloud from the minutes of PG cabinet meeting dated 12 July, Gay read, "Mr. Collins announced that he had arranged to take up duty as Commander-in-Chief of the Army and would not be able to act in his Ministerial capacity until further notice."[2]

"Now, old thing, does that sound like I've been pushed out?"

Answering his own query before Gabby could speak, the Corkman said, puffing out his chest, "From that you can clearly see I'm the one giving orders, not taking them. The cabinet is still beholden to me; they serve at my pleasure."

1. Coogan. *Michael Collins.* op. cit., 394.
2. Ibid., 392.

"You're right, Michael. Please forgive Gay's brashness. We're just wondering and concerned about ya, that's all. Sure, you know how manipulative some politicians can suddenly become if they catch a whiff of power. I'm just glad you're still calling the shots. That's the way it should be so," replied Aran.

"I appreciate you saying that, but as you both damn well know, I can look after meself."

"No offence intended," apologised Gabriel.

"None taken, you bloody Yank. Someday, when you're deserving enough, I may even call you an Irishman," snapped Michael.

"Deserving? Why there isn't a more loyal man in your ranks, with the possible exception of the Rebel here. You should be minding your tongue before you speak to me like that, *Mr. Collins.*"

Gay could hardly keep the grin off his face.

"All right, you two. Enough's enough. Sure there are other things more important to talk about than spending the afternoon baiting each other," Aran quipped.

"You're right, but do me a favour, tell your friend sitting there to mind his ears. You never know when I'll decide to have a go at one of them."

Gabby stood up and pretended to take a swing at the Big Fellow himself.

With a grin on his face as wide as the River Shannon, Michael held up both hands, "Just coddin' ya, Gay, but don't say I didn't warn you."

With the twinkle suddenly gone from his eyes, the Big Fellow returned to the matters at hand. "On the day I resigned my chairmanship, I also announced the establishment of a Provisional Government War Council of Three. Have ya heard of it?"

Both Aran and Gay shook their heads.

"With the war looking like it's going to be more than just an overnight affair, I've decided to shift gears. With action spreading to the provinces, things will only grow worse until I can put my hands around them. The Council of Three is a move in that direction. With my assuming command of the army, Mulcahy's consented to taking over O'Duffy's old job as Chief of Staff so Eoin can concentrate his energies on his new military command in the southwest. Besides accepting the post of COS, Dick's keeping his old portfolio as Minister for Defence. With the three of us focusing our energies on the budding uprising, I'm confident we can put an end to it before the heart of Ireland is torn to shreds."

"We've already witnessed some of that 'shredding,'" Aran said.

"Mick, it may be already too late. Surely you're not forgetting all the political intrigue and personal animosities levelled at so many over the last nine months, are ye?" asked Gabriel.

"No, how could I? But you're right, I guess I was thinking of more recent events," replied the Corkman. "Dublin's still in a turmoil over the Four Courts and Sackville Street fighting."

Aran, nodding his head, replied, "And well they should."

"Now, added to all that, you two have had a bit of a glimpse of what the country's thinking. Sure, I'm guessing the people are bracing for more of the old 'troubles' and hating every minute of what's to come."

"It's that and more, Michael," answered Aran. "Yes, the people are angry their lives are going to be disturbed again. They've every right to be, don't ya think, but things are unravelling for all of us right here in Dublin.

"Arthur's been giving you the cold shoulder ever since that Election-Pact business. Now, Liam Mellowes and the others, our trusted old comrades from not so long ago, are behind bars in Mountjoy."

Aran finished his glass and winced as the whiskey burned the back of his throat.

"That's only the beginning. As difficult as it is to believe, I'm almost certain Shadow has joined the Irregulars. And speaking of the Irregulars, truly fine men like Liam Lynch, Ernie O'Malley, Liam Deasy and Tom Barry, just to mention a few, have turned against us. Now, Cathal Brugha, the essence of Ireland's Republican spirit, is dead. What a feckin' mess this is turning out to be!"

"Jaysus," said Mick, "I can see all of this is really wearing on ya. Sure, it *is* a feckin' mess. Now you know how I've been feeling for months with the weight of the world on me shoulders day in and day out."

The three old friends silently exchanged helpless looks.

"Well, by God, I for one am not going to let this get me down," exclaimed Gabriel, "and I'm not going to let it drag the two of yis or this country down either. Mick, I'm counting on you, Aran's counting on you and so are the Irish people. We're here to help, so let's get to it."

"I'm trying, Gay, I'm trying, and with all the decisions I've made in the last few days, we should be able to right the ship."

No sooner had he uttered those hopeful words than Michael's demeanour changed. He was on his feet. A look of determination suddenly replaced his previously dejected air.

Confidently pounding a fist into the palm of his hand, the Big Fellow announced, "Give me a month and I'll have this dirty business cleared up. You just mark my words, lads."

With the mood of despondency broken, Aran breathed a sigh of relief.

"Who's taking over for you as Chairman? Griffith or Cosgrave?"

"Cosgrave," answered Michael. "Arthur's worn to bits by all that's been going on. His nerves are shot. He needs a break. I've urged him to check into a nursing home for some much needed rest. But knowing the man as I do, I've my doubts he'll take the time off work to do that.

"But enough about me, I want to hear what you've learned. I understand you've a proposal for me to consider."

"Yes, we do," said Aran, "but first, let me preface my remarks with an observation or two. Gay and I have noticed that the old, more informal organization of the Volunteers isn't lending itself to the more structured ways of running a large army. Guerrilla fighters and regular soldiers are two different breeds. We were more self-reliant and determined. The troopers of today seem indifferent to the cause they signed up for. Three meals a day and a weekly pay packet; that's what seems to drive them. Just look at the numbers. After their six-month enlistments are up, they're gone."

"Sure, some don't even stay around that long," added Gay.

"Our 'Trucileer Army' has melted away to almost nothing. Once over seventy thousand, today we're lucky if we've ten thousand among our ranks," said Aran.

"The good thing is," said Gay, "the Irregulars aren't much better off, despite their fighting for their own separatist ideals. Though I'd guess they outnumber us, at least initially, their lack of command structure, communication and arms will no doubt level the pitch. Also, I'm betting with Lynch, Deasy and O'Malley on the loose, their independent-mindedness will only help to decentralise the Irregular forces. I don't see it uniting them."

The Big Fellow stopped his pacing and rejoined Aran and Gay around the table.

"One other thing, Michael, you shouldn't ignore. The IRA Executive doesn't have you behind it any longer. With the Long Hoor taking the back seat, you're the country's leader and inspirational focus, at least for most of the population. What you say and do influence so many. You're the best advert Ireland has for what's right and just."

Michael dipped his head. Aran knew the Big Fellow was embarrassed despite the accuracy of Gay's words.

Wanting to save Michael from having to address Gabby's comments, Aran asked, "Mick, any good news on the enlistment score?"

Glancing up and looking relieved, Michael answered, "Some, Aran. Since the first of the month, I've authorised funds for an additional twenty thousand new recruits. In the past two weeks, our ranks have increased by over five thousand. With the added enrolment and a big influx of British arms, things are looking up."[3]

"What about training?"

"As much as I hate to admit it, Mulcahy and O'Duffy have had to resort to hiring ex-British officers to fill that void. With the exception of your 2nd Battalion and a few other units, our soldiers are woefully under trained. With former First War soldiers swelling our ranks, however, their experience should begin paying

---

3. Hopkinson, op. cit., 136.

off. But until each man is trained, equipped and in uniform, it's going to be an ongoing problem.

"Sure, Aran, this pressure for delivering a properly trained and armed fighting force is just one of my problems," said Michael. "Besides Emmet and the others badgering me for more men and equipment, the setting up of a new CID department in Oriel House hasn't gone smoothly.[4] Some of the lads who served for me on 'the Squad' are objecting to the new structure. I hate to ask you this, but I'm afraid I'm going to have to pull Cú from your ranks. I want him to try to sort things out. Sorry, lads."

Aran glanced over at Gabriel before he spoke. "I guess this is as good a time as any. With Tobin reassigned to Emmet's Southern Division and now with Cú going over as an IO at Oriel House, we'd like to suggest you eliminate the 2nd Battalion of the Dublin Guards all together. Reassign the men to other units and allow us to create a special central command flying column."

Michael leaned forward in his chair. "Go on."

"Gay and I have given it a lot of thought. It would be similar to the old Flying Gaels column Liam Mellowes, Shadow and you set up in the winter of 1918–1919."

Eagerly, Gabriel added, "From the look of things, the National Army will take back most or all of the major towns in the south and west in the next month or so. Despite our lack of personnel strength and training, the Irregulars are not putting up much of a fight. With our rapid troop deployment and artillery capabilities, they're just no match for us.

"Aran and I figure they'll soon be forced to retreat into the hills of Tipperary, Cork and Kerry and wage the kind of war they're good at: a guerrilla one. Large armies of men will be at a disadvantage just as the Sassenach were. We'll have to adjust to ferreting them out or we'll never get the upper hand."

Michael studied their faces intently.

"I suppose you want to take the cream of the crop with you."

"Yes, Michael, you've read our minds," Gay said.

The Big Fellow smiled. "Wasn't hard to do. Go on."

---

4. Ibid., 138.

Aran continued, "Once we're organised, we'd probably move our base of operation out of Dublin…closer to where the action is centred. Initially, we'd take fifteen or twenty of the 2nd Battalion lads with us. If we need more later on, we'd recruit our own men. What'd ya think?"

"Sure, it doesn't surprise me one bit. Yis are having as much trouble as the rest of us are in adjusting to the army's new demands. But with the Limeys coming in with their First War experience, it makes sense.

"Let me give it some thought. I'll talk to Dick, Eoin, Emmet and Seán Mac Eoin about it. Right now, you both deserve a couple of days off. Keep your men busy here. I'm going off on a short inspection tour of the southeast. I want to see for myself how things are in south Munster. I'll let you know about the column when I get back."

※

Not wanting any grass to grow under their feet, Aran and Gay went to work formalising their plans to reconstitute the Flying Gaels. With Liam Tobin and Tom Cullen scratched off their list by necessity, they'd happily settle for the likes of their remaining officer corps including the Nayler, Pat Grogan, Caoimhín Donleavy, Nick Robinson, Jimmy Carroll, Frank O'Leary and Chris McKee.

Aran wanted Marty and Larry to be included and didn't feel Michael would voice any strong objection to their being part of the column. Both men had taken to military life and would add several valuable skills to the new unit. Besides Marty's valuable medical talents, he'd become an excellent marksman. In a rather perverse display of humour, Marty often said, "I'm good at supplying my own patients."

With Marty onboard, he'd insist on including Liam McCullers. Together the two were more than capable of taking care of most medical emergencies.

Larry would be another great addition to the column. Energetic, resourceful and a fearless warrior, he and Duncan had become fast friends. With those two around, Aran knew Rory O'Mahony would be well looked after.

Besides the old guard whom they'd known for more than three years, Gabriel was quick to add his own favourites to their rapidly growing rota. From the ranks of men in their command he added Neill Morrison, a Kerry man; the brothers Tom and Séamus McDonald, whose Scottish ancestry endeared them to Duncan; Conor Makem, an Ulsterman; and Dónal O'Grady from Mayo or maybe it was Sligo, Gabby wasn't sure.

Sitting back, the Gortman and Gay were pleased with their personnel choices. The next thing to decide was which barracks they'd use for their HQ and how much training they'd need to plan for before the column could be activated.

As the Civil War intensified, the Provisional Government was faced with the growing issue of prisoners and what to do with them. Without any initial, formalised policy, the first captives were temporarily confined in jails or housed in military barracks. Many of those were soon released, however, if they pledged not take up arms against the Free State government again. But as the number of prisoners continued to rise and with many Irregulars going back on their promise, other arrangements were required. Soon the Curragh Camp was organised to accommodate up to twelve thousand prisoners. Kilmainham Gaol in Dublin was also turned into a military jail.[5]

Michael returned from his inspection tour of the southeast on the 25th. He promised Aran and Gay an answer to their request by week's end. "First," he said, "I have to deal with several pressing matters."

One of those issues dealt with the mounting pressure being exerted on Mulcahy and himself by his civilian Provisional Gov-

---

5. Ibid., 139.

ernment. In particular, both Cosgrave and O'Higgins were becoming impatient over the lack of information they were receiving on the military's war effort. Initial media reports were critical of the National Army. As a result, the government's civilian leadership began demanding increased press censorship, and an active programme of pro-government and military propaganda was launched. Desmond FitzGerald received instructions to amplify his efforts in an attempt to glamorise the successes of the Free State army. Soon carefully staged photographs of smiling army troopers and triumphant military confrontations were splashed across the pages of national and international newspapers.

❧

With the war suddenly erupting all around the country, the swearing in of the 3rd Dáil, scheduled to meet in August, was postponed until September. That was fine with Michael. The delay represented one less security worry for the Big Fellow and the National Army to deal with. It also helped forestall any political pressure generated by its assembly that he might have to face.

❧

While Michael and Dick Mulcahy were coping with the difficulties of prosecuting a war they loathed but were forced to fight, Éamon de Valera had moved south from Dublin to Clonmel where the Republicans had set up their GHQ. He was now in the unenviable position of being the political leader of a cause that had no use for politics.[6]

The bombardment of the Four Courts had convinced Lynch he'd been right to think that he was the best man to lead Ireland's Republican cause against the pro-Treatyites. Though many of his close disciples tried to convince him that terminating hostilities was the most plausible course of action, he demurred. Liam would hear nothing of seeking terms with Ireland's new government. True to his word, he'd once promised Rory O'Connor

6. Coogan. *De Valera.* op. cit., 327.

and their sixteen-man Executive, "I have pledged to support the Four Courts' garrison and all that you stand for. If attacked, I'll fight to the death, if necessary, to uphold our mutually-held convictions."[7]

But for once the Chief proved to be the realist. He quickly realised that the Free State, with its support of the Irish people and the British government, would likely emerge victorious. This forced Dev to assume two postures, not unlike the roles he'd played during the Treaty negotiation last year. To his IRA militant supporters, he needed to appear to be one of them, while secretly he knew only a peaceful track had any hope of success.

By the middle of July, de Valera had given up his subservient position of private and had become Adjutant to Seán Moylan, IRA Director of Operations.

As one reporter facetiously observed, "...most of Moylan's operations consisted of retreats not advances."[8]

❧

As July came to an end, Michael was faced with another personal crisis. His dear friend Harry Boland, who had taken the Republican side, was lying low in the Grand Hotel in Skerries, a seaside resort north of Dublin. On the evening of the 31st, while preparing to retire for the night, a group of National Army soldiers surprised him.

Unarmed, and with his usual brashness, he tried to escape. But in all the confusion and excitement surrounding Harry's arrest, an inexperienced soldier shot him.

Others say of that night that Harry had no chance of escaping. The hallway and stairs were full of troops. So while insisting on being taken to the arresting squad's commander, he was shot in the stomach.

Regardless of the circumstances, Harry was very seriously wounded. After several hours' delay, he was transported back to Dublin and on to Portobello Barracks.

---

7. Deasy, op. cit., 73.
8. Coogan. *De Valera*. op. cit., 328-329.

With no adequate medical personnel on hand, he was finally driven to St. Vincent's Hospital. But it was all for naught. He'd been mortally wounded and there was nothing the doctors could do to save his life. He died three days later on the 2nd.[9] [10]

Michael was beside himself with grief when he heard the news of Harry's death. Suddenly, the bitter taste of Civil War was forgotten as the Corkman's mind was flooded with the sweet memories of their fun-loving times together.

Overcome with emotion, Mick decided to visit Harry, still lying in the hospital mortuary. As he approached St. Vincent's, however, the Corkman suddenly changed his mind and walked on. The following day he wrote Kitty saying:

> Last night I passed Vincent's Hospital and saw a small crowd outside. My mind went into him lying dead there and I thought of the times together, and whatever good there is in any wish of mine, he certainly had it. Although the gap of 8 or 9 months was not forgotten – of course no one can ever forget it – I only thought of him with the friendship of the days of 1918 and 1919. They tell me that the last thing he said to his sister Kathleen, before he was operated on, was 'Have they got Mick Collins yet?' I don't believe it so far as I'm concerned and, if he did say it, there is nonecessity to believe it. I'd send a wreath but I suppose they'd return it torn up.[11]

As per Harry's request, his sister had him buried in Glasnevin Cemetery in the Republican plot next to Cathal Brugha.

❧

Three days after Harry's death, Michael visited Aran and Gay at Beggars' Bush Barracks.

Both men could tell Michael was again suffering from one

---

9. Mackay, op. cit., 272.
10. Coogan. *Michael Collins*. op. cit., 388.
11. Ó Broin, op. cit., 219.

of his persistent head colds. Despite his ill health, Michael put up a cheery front.

"Good news," he announced, after the three had exchanged hand shakes. Glancing around the Spartan-looking office, the Big Fellow sat down in one of the straight-backed, wooden chairs positioned in front of Aran's desk. "It's all set. The Cabinet's approved your idea of setting up the Flying Gaels on my specific recommendation. They've allocated a small fund to finance your operation. Nothing large I warn you, but enough to put fifteen or twenty men in the field with equipment and military transport. Work up your final details. Submit them through the proper channels and I'll approve them. I'd suggest you be ready to move out after we return from our inspection in the southwest. I want to leave on the 9th or 10th. I'm putting you two in charge of organising all the convoy details including guards and vehicles."

The Gortman and Gabriel could hardly contain their glee at the news.

"Michael...sir...eh...uh...thank you. You won't regret it. We'll make you proud." Still on their feet, the two snapped to attention and saluted.

"Cut out all that feckin' nonsense with me. Remember, you're now guerrilla fighters again. None of this military protocol shyte. It's ties, jackets, caps and gaiters and blow their bloody arses off if they don't lay down their weapons and surrender. You understand?"

"Jaysus wept," swore Aran, "you drive a hard bargain, but I suppose you still want reports, in duplicate, each week."

"For fuck sake, in triplicate from the likes of yis. Sure, I'll keep you so smothered in paperwork you won't have time to get yourselves into trouble."

Aran and Gay grinned at each other, but said nothing.

Gay wanted to ask if that was the kind of war Michael was running, but he managed to hold his tongue.

"Speaking of paperwork," continued the Corkman, "I've just completed a memorandum for the cabinet. The military situation is looking very positive. With the exception of Dundalk, Clonmel, Kilmallock, Tralee and Cork City, all the major towns are in Free State hands. Kilmallock and Tralee should surrender this weekend. Emmet's set to sail on Monday with a flotilla of three ships, a thousand men, an armoured car and an 18-pounder. Both Clonmel and Cork should be in National Army control in ten days' time…two weeks if we meet with some stiff resistance. As soon as he's wrapped up Cork, I want to head down there.

"With some of the old IRA leaders like Seán Hegarty and Florrie O'Donoghue taking a neutral stance in the war, there's a good chance I can work out a deal and bring this bloody nonsense to a quick end. I also want to visit my brother Johnny and a few old friends. It's been a long time since I was home."

"Michael, I'm not sure it's such a good idea for you to be running around down there, at least just yet."

"Ah, for fuck sake, Aran, they wouldn't shoot me in me own country now, would they?"

The Irish Rebel and his Irish-American sidekick didn't answer, but they wanted to say, "Hell yes they would, if they'd a chance."

❦

After the fall of Dublin and Michael ascending to C-in-C of the National Army, Ireland witnessed some hard fighting. As the days wore on, however, it became apparent that the Free State Army had gained the upper hand militarily, while the Irregulars showed more and more of an inclination not to fight.

Back in Dublin, Aran's 2nd Battalion was disbanded. Its soldiers were dispersed and absorbed by other units. Aran, Gay and the others who were going to make up the lion's share of the flying column prepared themselves for the move. Initially, they planned on occupying an old deserted RIC police barracks in the village of Ardfinnan on the River Suir.

Duncan, Pat and some of the other lads were already down there fixing up the place. It was centrally located and not far from Fermoy, Mallow and Cork City. Conveniently for Aran and Gay, it was only a few miles to Cahir in County Tipperary. Sarah Anne and Áine were planning to move back down home by the end of the month. If the war dragged on, the column would be well positioned to spend time tooth-combing the mountains of West Cork and Kerry for isolated pockets of Irregulars. With their HQ in Ardfinnan, they'd be able to respond to most any situation in a matter of a day or less.

Michael, Aran, Gay and their convoy were in Tralee on 12 August. For the last two days they'd been on an inspection tour of Tipperary, Limerick and Kerry. With the day's assessment of troops and facilities in Tralee completed, Michael and his travelling party returned to their hotel only to learn that Arthur Griffith had died that morning in a private Dublin nursing home. He'd suffered a cerebral haemorrhage while bending over to tie his shoelaces as he finished dressing for breakfast. As the message from acting Free State government Chairman Bill Cosgrave said, "Though he was only fifty-one, the worries and anxieties of the past two years had taken a terrible toll on him. The hard bargaining with the British and all the travelling back and forth during the Treaty negotiations had broken his health. Finally the eruption of the Civil War was a blow from which he never recovered."[12]

The Collins entourage left Tralee the following morning for a hurried return to Dublin. Prior to departing Michael had met with several reporters. When asked if he would comment on his friendship and association with Arthur Griffith, the Big Fellow said, "There seems to be a malignant fate dogging the fortune of Ireland, for at every critical period in her story the man whom the country trusts and follows is taken from her. It was so with Thomas Davis and Parnell, and now with Arthur Griffith.

"Only those who have worked with him know what Arthur Griffith has done for Ireland; only they can realise how he has spent himself in his country's cause. I've no shadow of doubt that the President's untimely death had been hastened by mental anguish as a result of the Civil War."[13]

12. Mackay, op. cit., 275.
13. Dwyer. *Big Fellow, Long Fellow.* op. cit., 321.

❊

During the days surrounding Griffith's death, Aran began keeping a mental log of the ups and downs that dogged the Big Fellow. Two issues took centre stage: the Civil War and Northern Ireland.

As far as the war was concerned, Michael's memorandum to the Cabinet on 5 August painted a rosy picture. The Big Fellow's prediction that the other remaining towns not in Free State control would be soon had come true. Kilmallock fell that same day followed by Tralee on the 6th. Clonmel surrendered on the 10th. On the day of Griffith's death, Emmet Dalton sent word to Michael that Cork City had capitulated without a fight. Dundalk would be in National Army hands by the 15th.

The successes, however, didn't come painlessly. Casualty figures were mounting. The old strategy of 'shoot to miss and hope they retire' had changed. More often than not now, it was 'shoot to kill and hope you don't miss.'

The Free State government's patience and policy of moderation was at the breaking point. If the war was going to end quickly, its frequent mollycoddling approach must end. Michael had stepped over the line when he issued a directive stating, "Any man caught looting or destroying should be shot on sight."[14]

Aran doubted that such a harsh policy directive would be uniformly carried out, but it did signify a newer 'get-tough' course of action.

The Corkman was particularly disturbed after attending a Requiem Mass at Portobello Barracks for nine National Army troopers killed in action in Kerry. He wrote to Kitty telling her, "We have had a hard few days here – the scenes at the Mass yesterday [7 August] were really heartbreaking. The poor women weeping and almost shrieking (some of them) for their dead sons. Sisters and one wife were there too, and a few small children. It makes one feel I tell you."[15]

In Dublin, Michael, as well as members of his cabinet, had to

---

14. Ibid., 320.
15. Ó Broin, op. cit., 221.

be continually vigilant. Though most Irregulars had been arrested or had fled town, occasionally IRA snipers would take pot-shots at government officials or military figures.

Just prior to leaving on their inspection tour, Aran had hand-delivered some documents to Minister O'Higgins in Government Buildings on Merrion Square. Upon inquiring about his health, O'Higgins astonished Aran with a personal assessment of the current situation.

"Aran, you might be surprised to know that the Provisional Government is now forced to live as well as work here. There are too many people gunning for us out on the streets. Why just the other night, I went up to the roof for a cigarette and a breath of air. Sure I hadn't been there more than two minutes when a sniper's bullet nearly took me head off."

From the look in the Minister's eyes, the Gortman knew he wasn't slaggin' him.

With a sympathetic listener before him, O'Higgins continued, "If you were to ask me to describe the state of the government today, I'd say we're simply eight young men standing amidst the ruins of one administration [the 2nd Dáil Éireann] with the foundation of another [Saorstát Éireann] not yet laid, and with wild men screaming through the keyhole!"[16]

Besides the war, the issue of Northern Ireland continued to pray on the Big Fellow's mind. Aran knew that from the mixed signals Mick was continually giving off.

The lives of Reggie Dunne and Joseph O'Sullivan preyed on Michael's mind. On 18 July the two had been tried and convicted in London's Old Bailey for murdering Sir Henry Wilson, Northern Ireland's security advisor. They'd been sentenced to hang in London's Wandsworth Prison on 16 August. Mick urged Cosgrave to intercede on behalf of the Provisional and Dáil governments.

The mercy that the Big Fellow sought didn't materialise. As Arthur Griffith was being buried in Dublin on the 16th, Dunne and O'Sullivan were executed, meeting their Maker at the end of an English rope.

---

16. Coogan, op. cit., 398.

With the Civil War necessarily occupying his full attention, Michael was forced to put the matter of partition and the Six Counties on the long finger.

On a recent occasion the Big Fellow had told a reporter, "My attitude towards Ulster, which is the attitude of all of us in the government, is not understood. There can be no question of forcing Ulster into union with the twenty-six counties. I am absolutely against coercion of that kind. If Ulster is to join us it must be voluntarily. Union is our final goal; that is all."[17]

Two days later at a gathering of Northern IRA leaders which both Aran and Gay attended, Michael assertively stated, in what to Aran seemed like a contradictory position, "With this Civil War on my hands, I cannot give you men the help I wish to give and mean to give. I now propose to call off hostilities in the North and to use the political arm against Craig so long as it is of use. If that fails, the Treaty can go to hell and we will start again."[18]

❧

The Big Fellow called Aran and Gay to his office in Portobello the day after they'd returned from Tralee.

Looking fatigued and complaining of stomach pain, Michael still greeted his two visitors with a smile. "Glass of milk," he offered, pointing to his on the desk, "or a nice cup of tea?"

"Tea would do nicely," replied Aran.

Immediately, the corporal was summoned and the order given.

"First, I want to thank you both for seeing to my travel this week. I never have to worry about details when you two are in charge."

Both Aran and Gay smiled at their military leader and friend as they accepted Michael's offer to be seated.

"Arthur's funeral is to be in two days time, the 16th. We leave again on the 20th. With Cork in our control, I want to finish our inspection tour and meet with Emmet. I've also some other business to attend to as well."

---

17. Dwyer, op. cit., 319.
18. Ibid., 320.

"Michael," Aran said, holding up both hands as a sign of opposition, "won't you reconsider? Give it another week or two. From what I understand, West Cork is crawling with Irregulars."

"Ah shyte, Aran, don't believe everything you hear. We're going and that's that."

The Irish Rebel reluctantly lowered his hands.

"Since you two are going with me, we'll have to delay your move to Ardfinnan. I want you around until at least after the new Dáil meets on the 9th. That all right wit yas?"

"Fine," answered Aran. "We'll just put everything on hold until mid-September."

Gabby nodded his concurrence.

"Oh, one more thing," said the Gortman. "With Sarah Anne and Áine leaving soon, we want to invite you for one last get-together at #5. Nothing fancy. Just a few friends and some good food. Annie said she won't take no for an answer."

Michael smiled. "Sure I know what that means, but if my stomach is still acting up like it is today, all I'll be having is me curds and whey."

"Ah, you'll be grand by tomorrow. Aran will take care of the details and you just leave the worrying to me," offered Gabriel.

"Sure, if it were only that simple." Michael smiled.

The Big Fellow stood up and walked over to his desk. Flipping through his diary, he said, "How's the 17th suit?"

"Perfect," answered Aran. "Say around seven that evening?"

The two watched Michael scribble in his book before returning to the table.

With the three of them seated around Mick's office table, the Corkman studied the few odd tea leaves floating on the surface of his steaming mug.

Speaking slowly, Michael said, "Lads, I've been thinking, is it possible that Arthur's death may help bring the war to an end and unite our divided cause?"

Without waiting for an answer, Mick continued. "At the moment I am a soldier, but I think I can promise that if those who are against us will, even now, come forward and accept the terms offered by the government, our differences can be composed.

"Look at the map: see where our troops are, what they have achieved, and where the armed forces of the other side have been driven. But, even so, it is not too late for de Valera and those who are with him to honour the passing of a great patriot by now achieving what that patriot has given his life for – a united Ireland, and Irish nation."[19]

"As fine and practical an offer as that is, Michael, I'm just afraid Lynch will see it as capitulation, even if his men don't have to surrender their arms," said Aran. "Nevertheless, it won't hurt to send Liam a note to that effect, but I'm not holding my breath."

The Big Fellow winced momentarily, and then nodded his agreement with the Gortman's sentiments.

❧

On the 16th, Michael Collins, Commander-in-Chief of the National Army, and General Richard Mulcahy, dressed in their dark-green military uniforms, marched behind Arthur Griffith's coffin as it made its way up Sackville Street to Glasnevin Cemetery. Behind the two generals, walking in three ranks, paraded the rest of the General Staff, several units of Irish Army troopers and Aran's little band of Flying Gaels.

Thousands crowded the streets to pay their last respects to Ireland's president and catch a glimpse of the Big Fellow. It was Michael's first public appearance in uniform and he seemed to tower above the heads of his fellow soldiers.

The following day, two short newspaper quotes about the funeral caught Aran's attention. P. S. O'Hegarty stated, "He [Arthur Griffith] forced England to take her right hand from Ireland's throat and her left hand out of Ireland's pocket."[20]

Further on in another article, Piaras Béaslaí said of Michael

---

19. Ibid., 321.
20. O'Hegarty, op. cit., 95.

Collins, "The people looked to him with confidence as the one man who could get the nation out of the morass into which it had sunk."[21]

❧

Sarah Anne and Áine had #5 Mespil Road spotless. They even decorated the sitting room with some colourful streamers and candles. Though it was mid-August, a cold breeze had turned the evening air chilly. Aran laid a small turf fire. Michael's stomach had calmed a bit so he could enjoy the meal the two women had prepared: a beautiful lamb roast, range-roasted potatoes, courgettes from Áine's garden and neeps in honour of Duncan's presence. This wonderful feast was topped off by buckets of tea, several bottles of whiskey and a delicious cherry trifle.

Due to space restrictions only the Nayler, Larry and Pat Grogan had joined Michael, the McCrackens and the O'Neills. After dinner several of the other Flying Gaels dropped by for a drink and a song. Gabriel pulled out his guitar and being blessed with the gift of 'the music' led the gathering in song. The patriotic words of Thomas Davis and Thomas Moore were among the favourites sung that evening.

By popular request, Aran retold the story surrounding the small metallic Easter-lily badges he'd had a local artist make prior to leaving New York in the spring of 1917.

"It was right here in this house that I presented the tokens to our little band of revolutionaries. It was my intent that they should serve as reminders of the ideals underpinning Easter Week, 1916. The little badges were also meant to symbolise our trusted friendship and commitment to the common cause that binds us together and to Ireland.

"There are three individuals here in this house tonight wearing theirs: Sarah Anne, Gay and myself. Three others, symbolic of the hard times this country is going through now, are elsewhere. Liam Mellowes is locked away in Mountjoy. Shadow and

---

21. Dwyer, op. cit., 321-322.

Danny Kelly are somewhere, supporting their IRA Executive. Finally, the seventh is back in Amerikay. I posted it to Turlough Molloy's family in Alexandria, Virginia after he was killed above Ballynagree up in the mountains of West Cork during the summer of 1920."

Pausing in their merriment to reflect on Aran's words, many said a prayer that the Civil War would soon be over.

After a few more songs and a last whiskey, the party broke up, but instead of leaving, Michael decided to sleep upstairs in the extra bed. Before Aran and he said goodnight, the two friends sat and watched the last flames of the turf fire burn themselves out.

Finally, they stood up, shook hands and embraced one another. The shared bond of love and mutual respect had never been stronger between the two men.

❧

Michael, Aran, Gay and their small military convoy left Portobello Barracks early on Sunday morning, 20 August. Prior to departing, the Big Fellow had a chance encounter with Joe Sweeney on the parade ground.

Once again, another of the Corkman's friends cautioned him not to go through with his plans to visit West Cork.

"Ah, Joe," Michael said, "nobody will shoot me in me own country."[22]

Saluting one another, the two soldiers parted with Michael turning his back on Dublin Town for the last time.

❧

---

22. According to Tim Pat Coogan in his book *Michael Collins*, "…[Michael] Collins set off on his last, ill-advised journey for a variety of reasons. He wanted to continue his tour of inspection, which was also a morale-boosting exercise, as he was the man who embodied the new State, particularly since Griffith had died. Possibly also he hoped to make some peace contacts with his native Corkonians. He certainly wanted to seize some Republican funds and he simply wanted to visit his native place. Clonakilty was calling and a glass at the Four Alls would taste better and have a more therapeutic effect than one anywhere else in Ireland." p. 400.

While the convoy headed west and south eventually reaching the Imperial Hotel in Cork City in the early morning hours of the 21st, Éamon de Valera was on a mission of his own, a peace mission.

At this stage of the Civil War, many in Ireland viewed the hostilities as a personal struggle between the Long Fellow and the Big Fellow. But the Chief knew better. Michael had won the war; now he wanted to win the peace.

Dev had been travelling the countryside, talking to as many influential people as possible, but nobody was listening.

This was the same man who'd refused to take part in the Treaty negotiations because he said his presence was needed in Dublin. At that time Dev maintained he was the one who could best rally the Irish people in their fight for their independence, from Dublin not London. He also said he was the best person to help smooth ruffled Republican feathers should a compromise agreement be returned for approval. He was the same man who'd resigned his political leadership position of authority and had walked out of the Dáil for the sake of maintaining Republican unity. Yes, Dev was the man who'd defied the will of the people with his inflammatory rhetoric and had marched them inexorably down the road toward Civil War. Now, the very people, for whom he'd given his all, had chosen to ignore him.

With their shrinking level of troops on the run, with no Republican government to champion their cause, with no press backing their patriotic stance, with many of its most strident members in jail or dead, with most of their once-held 'Munster Republic' now lost, with no suitable strategy for winning the war on the horizon, with its present-day leadership fragmented and with no open lines of communication at its disposal, de Valera knew his once idealistic hopes now lay in tatters.

In the eyes of Liam Lynch and Liam Deasy, the Long Fellow, the man who'd wilfully destabilised the Irish government during the Treaty debates and had driven the country to the doorstep of war, had lost all personal credibility in his recent quest for peace.

When Lynch learned of Dev's presence in his command area, he sent a warning to Deasy not to cooperate with him.

Deasy, in turn, told his men, "Dev's mission is to try and bring the war to an end. On no account are you to give him any encouragement as his arguments don't stand up."[23]

The Chief and Liam Deasy met at a farmhouse in Gurranereagh, West Cork on the evening of 21 August, only two miles, as the crow flies, from Béalnabláth. They talked long into the night. Dev's position was that the Republicans had made their protest in arms, as Pearse had in '16. Now, with no hope of winning the war, they should work out an honourable surrender and fight their next battle in the Dáil.

Deasy saw his point, but insisted that the IRA wouldn't agree to an unconditional cease-fire.

It was on the following morning, as de Valera and Deasy travelled through Béalnabláth, that they learned Michael Collins and his military convoy had recently passed by. Mick's party had stopped briefly, asking directions for Bandon.

Realising that the Big Fellow might return by the same road, Deasy ordered Tom Hales to organise a party and waylay the convoy.

Conflicting reports indicated that Dev tried to call off the ambush but to no avail. He was reminded by Hales that he'd no authority to countermand his or anyone else's orders. He was in Lynch's command area and was not included in Liam's chain-of-command.

Insulted and angry, Dev headed for Kilworth crossroads where he borrowed a horse and trap for the long, slow journey to Fermoy. Once there, he was taken by motor car to Fethard, County Tipperary. There he stayed the night with friends, only learning of Michael's death the following morning. According to eyewitnesses, they say he was 'furious and visibly upset' upon hearing the news.[24][25]

---

23. Ibid, 323.
24. Mackay, op. cit., 286.
25. Dwyer records in his book *Big Fellow, Long Fellow* that "…the IRA man who told de Valera next day was pleased at the news, but the Long Fellow displayed no satisfaction. 'It's come to a very bad pass when Irish men congratulate themselves on the shooting of a man like Michael Collins,' was his reputed reaction." p. 329.

18

*"I have no regrets, for the future of Ireland is
assured. We die for Ireland, for the Republic, for
that glorious cause that has been sanctified by the
blood of countless martyrs throughout the ages
– the cause of human liberty."*

Liam Mellowes

THURSDAY MORNING, 24 AUGUST 1922[1]

*A*fter a short lorry ride from Cork's Shanakiel Hospital, the
Commander-in-Chief's body was transported by steamship to
Dublin. Michael was then taken by military tender to St. Vincent's
Hospital at Stephen's Green. There the body was embalmed and
dressed in a new uniform. The sculptor Albert Power was dispatched to take Michael's death mask. His old friend and renowned
painter Sir John Lavery painted him there in repose.

Michael's body remained in the hospital's mortuary chapel
until the following morning. Aran, Gay and a detail of Flying
Gaels stood guard all that day and night. By some strange coincidence, it was in that same chapel and on the very same slab
that the Big Fellow's friend Harry Boland had lain only three
weeks earlier.

---

1. A note to the reader: At this point in the story, you might want to go back
& review or reread Chapters 1& 2. It may help bring your mind back to the
story's present moment.

On Friday morning, the C-in-C was moved to Dublin City Hall on Cork Hill for the public lying-in-state. There he remained until Sunday evening. Again, Aran, Gay, members of Mick's old 'Squad' and his intelligence corps took turns standing at attention as thousands of viewers filed past his open coffin.

Late on Sunday evening, Michael's body was removed to the Pro-Cathedral where he lay in stained glass and marbled silence. Aran, Sarah Anne, Gay and Áine never left his side that entire night.

On Monday morning, the 28th a Requiem Mass was said, followed by a stately, six-mile procession to Glasnevin. Michael's coffin was draped with the Irish tricolour and carried on a gun carriage drawn by six coal-black horses and a detail of mounted artillerymen.

As the procession moved up along Sackville Street, Michael's coffin was flanked on foot by Richard Mulcahy, the newly appointed Commander-in-Chief. Seven other generals including Emmet Dalton and Seán Mac Eoin accompanied him. Behind them walked all the members of the Provisional Government, many foreign dignitaries and a convoy of military vehicles laden with wreaths and floral tributes. The three-mile-long cortège was witnessed by over half a million mourners who reverently lined the streets of Dublin.[2]

Aran Roe O'Neill and Gabriel McCracken were a part of the honour guard at the Pro-Cathedral and at graveside. General Dick Mulcahy delivered the funeral oration.[3]

☘

Michael's sudden and unexpected death briefly destabilised an already insecure Provisional Government. On the other hand, Republican leaders viewed it as an opportunity not to be overlooked. Lynch ordered Deasy to increase military pressure on all Free State forces found to be in any IRA command areas.

2. Ibid., 300.

3. "Well over 2,000 feet of motion-picture film was shot covering this event, making it the most extensively covered funeral to take place in Ireland until recent times." Coogan & Morrison. *The Irish Civil War*. op. cit., 231.

In the long term though, as Aran and Gay were soon to find out, the death of the Big Fellow most likely lengthened the Civil War and certainly made it a bloodier, more vicious affair. Left to its own devices, the Provisional Government soon instituted a number of harsh measures, including government sanctioned executions, which only deepened and widened the divide between the pro- and anti-Treaty factions.

❧

Michael's death totally devastated Aran. It was as if some huge weight had been suddenly thrust upon him, overpowering him with grief. He became lethargic and subject to periods of depression interspersed with fits of anger. Sarah Anne was unable to console him and Gabriel couldn't seem to penetrate the wall of isolation Aran had erected around himself.

The Gortman's despondency had a devastating effect on both Sarah Anne and Gay. They wanted his support and understanding in their time of need as well. Aran disregarded their pain, concentrating solely on his selfish requirements.

Two days after the funeral, Aran did a runner. The Gortman mysteriously disappeared. Dressed in civilian attire, he finished eating breakfast, kissed Annie goodbye and said he was going for a walk.

When he hadn't returned by mid-afternoon, Sarah Anne was rightfully concerned. Gay said he'd just gone off alone to find himself and not to worry.

Three days later, just at tea time, Aran walked back in the front door. Annie rushed to greet him. Thankfully, the old sparkle was back in his eyes. He looked rested and refreshed.

"I've been so worried. Where were you?"

Kissing his wife and holding her tight, the Gortman didn't answer her query. All he said after a long pause was, "I love you so much, Sarah Anne. Sorry, I've been such an amadán. Don't ye worry though, I'm all right now."

Smelling the fresh, clean scent of the outdoors on his clothing and feeling the rough stubble of his three-day-old beard, Sarah

Anne just held him close, glad to have him home again in one piece.

Together they stood as one in the doorway for what seemed like ages.

Finally, Aran pushed back and drank in her beauty from head to toe.

"Are you all right?" he asked, "…and the baby too?"

As he spoke, Aran reached down and lovingly placed the palm of his open hand on Sarah Anne's swollen belly.

"Yes, we are *now*, but where were you?"

Aran answered with just a single word, "Shadow."

"Oh," she replied, "Shadow. Of course, I understand now. Is he well?"

"He's fine. I'll tell you all about it, but not right now."

❧

Prior to the first meeting of the 3rd Dáil Éireann or 'new Free State' Dáil, as some referred to it in the press, de Valera requested and received a safe-conduct pass to meet with Mulcahy in Dublin on 6 September. At their get-together they discussed the war's escalation and tried to agree on some way to end it.

The new C-in-C insisted on an anti-Treaty IRA surrender while Dev's only counter was an assurance that the 3rd Dáil would be a national assembly of coalition TDs based on the results of the Election Pact agreement he'd made with Michael. Neither man conceded a point to the other.

As one reporter commented after learning of the results of their meeting, "de Valera again became the hunted while Mulcahy returned to his role as hunter."[4]

Finally, with increased confidence in the military and Civic Guard's ability to manage security concerns in Dublin, the 3rd Dáil first convened on Saturday, 9 September. The anti-Treaty TDs were excluded. The small Labour Party, with its seventeen seats, became the assembly's only token opposition.

---

4. Neeson, op. cit., 265.

William Cosgrave, running unopposed, was elected president as well as assuming Michael's former role as Minister for Finance. Mulcahy retained both of his portfolios: C-in-C of the National Army and Minister for Defence. Eight other ministers were appointed, mirroring in large measure the Provisional cabinet Michael had selected back in January, but any spirit of conciliation that might have been reflective of a Collins-led government was gone. In its place arose a cruel unwillingness to entertain any compromise directed toward the Republican anti-Treatyites.

With the burgeoning power of the military overshadowing the influence of the embryonic government's political authority, again there was discussion in political circles of a military dictatorship being established in the Irish capital. This was not the first time for such rumours. When the Four Courts' buildings were occupied back in April, there was talk of a Republican military dictatorship being set up under the leadership of Rory O'Connor. This soldierly takeover had not only called attention to Michael's Provisional Government failings to control Irish internal affairs, but underscored the IRA's impatience with political rhetoric and its contempt for the democratic process.

Once again in September, 1922, the time seemed fertile for the military power brokers to trump the country's vulnerable political leadership base. As one reporter noted, "The potential for military dictatorship was present while the army remained the only expression of government power and authority in many areas of the country."[5]

Aran, among others, was quick to note that, thankfully, Richard Mulcahy seem disinclined to reach for that brass ring. Though cognisant of the need for the military to manage the war, the C-in-C felt certain he must remain subservient to Cosgrave and his cabinet.

In assuming the responsibilities of head of state, Cosgrave was initially handicapped. Besides commanding neither Griffith's subtle but worldly leadership skills nor Collins's forceful personality and esteemed standing in the eyes of many, he'd been thrust into the limelight based on a successful record as a local

---

5. Hopkinson, op. cit., 182.

Dublin political figure. His 1919 appointment to de Valera's cabinet as Minister for Home Affairs coupled with his support for Griffith and Collins in the run-up to and during the Treaty negotiations, finally helped push him into the forefront of pro-Treaty politics.

Though some would have thought it a disadvantage, his lack of military experience helped balance the new 3rd Dáil's administrative leadership. On the flip side, however, his general inexperience did allow the more dominant and aggressive personality of Kevin O'Higgins to surface.

Initially Minister for Economic Affairs in the 2nd Dáil, O'Higgins became Minister for Home Affairs in Cosgrave's first administration. At thirty years of age, Kevin was a formidable debater and a tough negotiator who held de Valera in contempt. O'Higgins soon gained the reputation of being the government's 'tough man' who once described himself as 'being walled in by hate.'[6]

Soon that feeling of being surrounded by hatred grew and intensified, as Ministers Mulcahy and O'Higgins sponsored and backed a number of measures destined to raise the level of Republican animosity and bitterness in Ireland.

Besides formally ratifying the new Free State's constitution as required by the Treaty, Cosgrave's new government was forced to deal with the increased level of violence that was raining havoc throughout the country.

Having lost the ability to wage a conventional war against the Free State Army, Lynch decided to step up attacks on pro-Treatyite troop positions. This quickly escalated into a vicious guerrilla war, especially in counties Cork and Kerry. As a result of this stepped-up campaign, pro-Treatyite forces experienced a sharp increase in battlefield casualties.

In an effort to gain control of this deteriorating military

---

6. On the back cover of Terence De Vere White's biography of Kevin O'Higgins, the author describes O'Higgins as an uncompromising character. He was someone who always spoke his mind & was viewed by others as the 'strong man' of Saorstát Éireann. He also was held responsible by many in Ireland for the IRA executions during the Civil War & for the reprisal death of his friend, Rory O'Connor. Terence De Vere White. *Kevin O'Higgins*. Dublin, 1986.

situation, Mulcahy asked the Dáil on 27 September to enact draconian 'special powers' legislation that he dubbed the Public Safety Bill. This request made it a criminal offence to facilitate or to participate in any attack against Free State military personnel. In addition, anyone found in possession of an unauthorised weapon or an explosive device would also be charged.

At the same time, Cosgrave introduced companion legislation that was supported with vitriolic enthusiasm by Minister O'Higgins. The Chairman's demand established military courts for the express purpose of trying those individuals who'd been found in violation of the Public Safety Bill. The penalty, if convicted, was death. Thus, the government, lacking any opposing voice of reason or compromise, made it illegal for anti-Treatyites to wage war against it. This quickly became a huge psychological weapon in the Free State government's favour.

Another grim reminder of the eroding situation surfaced on 10 October. On that date Ireland's Catholic bishops issued a joint pastoral officially endorsing the Provisional Government's ruthless position. To add insult to injury, anti-Treatyites now faced excommunication in addition to pending arrest and execution if found in possession of a gun or explosives. Furthermore, priests were instructed to refuse communion to Republican prisoners, though many of the clergy chose to risk excommunication themselves by personally ignoring the edict.

With the Free State government clamping down and denying the Republicans a voice in the Dáil, the decision to establish its own anti-Treaty government was championed by de Valera. It was his hope that by uniting both the political and military wings of the Republican movement their mutual interests might be served.

Republican prisoners in Mountjoy, led by Liam Mellowes, supported the decision to form an anti-Treaty provisional government. Though realising he'd be powerless to effect legislation and would be subservient to IRA leadership, Dev reluctantly accepted the presidency of this new Republican body.

So, on 25 October and backed by the disenfranchised anti-Treaty membership of the 2nd Dáil, a twelve-man Council of

State was chosen in Dublin. As one newspaper noted, "…it could do little more than issue statements on anti-Treaty policy from time to time."[7]

One of Michael and Aran's greatest fears was rapidly becoming reality. Men in unrestricted control of governmental power, while professing a love for Ireland and its rule of law, had suddenly taken possession of the country. The Gortman, reading the handwriting on the wall, feared that events would soon spiral out of control and anarchy would rule the land. Unfortunately, events would soon prove him right.

❧

Much to Aran's relief, General Mulcahy finally agreed to honour Michael's commitment to re-establishing the Flying Gaels. Both men hoped its presence in the southwest would take some of the current military pressure off the Free State government.

So, having delayed their departure from Dublin by over a month, Aran and Gay finally headed for County Tipperary in early October with their families in tow.

The men of the Flying Gaels planned to take up residence in Ardfinnan. Sarah Anne would return, at least until after the baby was born, to Peter and Niamh's Black Rose pub in Cahir. In what was an easy choice for the three McCrackens, Áine and Mary Margaret would move back into the rented cottage where they'd previously lived.

❧

In mid-October, however, the political and warring situation worsened. With the military courts scheduled to begin operating on the 15th, the short amnesty period that had been in effect prior to the implementation of the Public Safety Bill came to an end. Irregulars, who hadn't surrendered their arms, were now subject to arrest and execution.

---

7. Neeson, op. cit., 271.

❧

During that autumn and early winter, as the guerrilla war intensified, attempts to reach a peaceful settlement dwindled. Former comrades-in-arms held fewer and fewer clandestine meetings as the two armies began backing away from seeking common ground. By now, the position of both sides had hardened and there was little hope of reaching any meaningful accommodation.

The first appalling executions under the Public Safety Bill took place in Kilmainham Gaol on 17 November. Four men, James Fisher, Peter Cassidy, John Gaffney and Richard Twohig, had been arrested in Dublin after they were discovered carrying weapons. Tried and convicted, they were shot to death adjacent to Stonebreakers Yard, the walled enclosure where fourteen leaders of the 1916 Easter Rebellion were put to death by British authorities that May.

The next to be executed was Erskine Childers. Just after dawn on the 24th, this time within the confines of Beggars' Bush Barracks, the Englishman cum Irishman was gunned down on the same day as his secret trial before a military court was scheduled to meet. With the sun not yet up and being as it was too dark to see clearly, Childers and members of his firing squad chatted and smoked cigarettes while he nobly disclaimed harbouring any animosity toward them for what they were about to do. Finally, as the moment approached, Erskine joked to his executioners, "Take a step forward, boys, that way ye can't miss."

As Dev's personal representative at the London Treaty talks and the delegation's Chief Secretary, Childers had been arrested at his cousin Robert Barton's house in Annamoe, County Wicklow early in the morning of 10 November. He'd spent the night there while on his way back to Dublin prior to assuming the position of secretary to the newly reconstituted Republican government.

A raiding party of Free State soldiers arrested him as he tried to draw the small, black-handled .32 Spanish automatic pistol. It had been given to him two years earlier by none other than Michael Collins himself.[8] The handgun, being little more than

---

8. J. P. Duggan, "Poltergeist Pistol." *History Ireland*, 3. 3 (1995): 27-28.

a toy, was in no way a weapon of war. Later, Childers stated he'd no intention of firing it because 'ladies were present.'

※

Aran and Sarah Anne's long awaited moment finally arrived on 30 November. Aran had been staying at the Black Rose for the last week thinking the baby would be born any time. In fact, according to Annie's calculation, the child was already two weeks late, but Niamh kept reassuring her that the first child is often unpredictable, especially considering whom its father and uncle were.

Early on that Thursday morning, with a midwife present and Áine and Niamh hovering nearby, a new O'Neill screamed its way into the world. Its tiny reddened, wrinkled and shivering body proudly displayed a matted shock of black hair. The child was a boy.

With the baby's first cries announcing to the entire world he'd arrived, Aran Roe was at Sarah Anne's side. Her perspiration-streaked but smiling face told him his wife had survived the ordeal with flying colours. His assessment was almost immediately confirmed with her demand, "Somebody, let me see my child, I want to hold him."

Moments later, she was cradling the tiny bundle, now warmly wrapped in a blanket her mother had lovingly crocheted and posted to Ireland months before.

Annie looked over at her excited husband. "Here Aran, you hold the baby. He's yours as well as mine."

Taking the wee thing in his arms and beaming from ear to ear, he proudly announced, "Sure he weighs at least a half a stone and not an ounce less."

"All right you two," crowed Gay. "Congratulations and all that, but what's his name to be. No more secrets from us. We all want to know."

Aran glanced around the room at all the assembled eager faces. "Annie, would you like to have the honour or shall I?"

"I think it's the father's place to make that announcement," she said.

"Looking down at the babe in his arms, Aran said, "Welcome to this world, Patrick Michael O'Neill."

There immediately followed a chorus of 'ohs' and 'ahs.'

"Sure, he's the namesake for two great Irishmen, Patrick Henry Pearse and Michael Patrick Collins. May his fame and life, please God, far surpass the both of them," said Gabriel.

"Amen," came the answering response.

An hour later, with baby and mother sleeping and the others enjoying a celebratory breakfast, Gay suddenly declared, "Jaysus, the Nayler's going to be upset wit ye, Aran. Here, your son is born on Saint Andrew's Day and you dared to name him after an Irish holy man."

Still grinning like the proud father he was, the Irish Rebel answered confidently, "Sure, he'll get over it in time so."

❧

That same day, Liam Lynch responded to the Free State's execution policy by issuing his own 'Orders of Frightfulness.' He warned that any member of the Irish government who'd voted for the Public Safety Bill or was hostile toward any member of the anti-Treaty Army was subject to be summarily executed. Additionally, any former member of the British Army, who had joined the pro-Treaty Army after 6 December 1921, was also to be shot on sight.

❧

Three days later, while in Dublin on business, Aran received special permission to visit Liam Mellowes in Mountjoy. After delivering to his former superior and dear friend some packets of tea and sugar, several chocolate bars, a pot of Sarah Anne's homemade marmalade and some cigarettes, he conveyed messages of best wishes from Patrick Michael, Sarah Anne, Gabriel and Larry. Together they talked of prison life, of old times and hopes for the future.

As his time to leave grew nigh, the Gortman pulled a copy of the day's newspaper from his briefcase. The front page carried a further condemnation of Lynch's recent retaliatory order.

Aran pleaded with Liam to write Lynch and Deasy, begging them to reconsider. He also promised he'd speak with Cosgrave, Mulcahy and O'Higgins about rescinding their aggressive legislation.

Liam just shook his head. He said it was too late and that the bitterness would have to play itself out. But despite the current mood in the country, he was optimistic that some day soon peace and unity would come to Ireland.

As they stood facing one another just prior to Aran's departure, Liam reached inside his jacket and produced an envelope.

"Here, I want you to have this. A warder told me you were coming to visit me today. As I thought about your coming and the wonderful times Richard,[9] Danny,[10] you and I shared, I jotted down a few personal thoughts. I want you to have them. When you read what I've written, think of me and say a prayer…for the both of us and for Ireland."

With that, Liam handed Aran the envelope.

As they shook hands, Liam said, "Aran, Pearse would be proud of you and what you've done for Ireland. Always carry Éireann's banner high."

❧

Later, back in his hotel room, the Irish Rebel opened the envelope and read Liam's words, carefully written out on a single sheet of paper:

> Aran, I have no regrets, for the future of Ireland is assured. We die for Ireland, for the Republic, for the glorious cause that has been sanctified by the blood of countless martyrs throughout the ages – the cause of human liberty. The Republic stands for truth and honour, for all that is best and noblest in our race. By truth and honour, by principle and sacrifice alone will

---

9. Richard 'Shadow' Doyle
10. Danny Kelly

Ireland be free. That this is immutable – Ireland must tread the path our Redeemer trod. She may shrink – but her faltering feet will find the road again. For that road is plain and broad and straight; its signposts are unmistakable. [11]

❧

Back in Cahir with Sarah Anne and Patrick, Aran learned that on 7 December, Brigadier General Seán Hales, a member of the Provisional Government who'd voted for the Public Safety Bill and brother of anti-Treaty IRA leader Tom Hales, was assassinated by members of the 1st Dublin Brigade on a Dublin street corner just outside of Government Buildings. Standing beside him, also waiting to cross the thoroughfare, was Pádraig Ó Máille, the Deputy Speaker of the Dáil. Pádraig was seriously wounded in the attack but was likely to survive.

❧

Early the following morning, with barely an hour to prepare, Rory O'Connor, Dick Barrett, Joe McKelvey and Liam Mellowes were taken from their cells at Mountjoy Jail and executed outside in the prison yard. Besides being leaders of the Republican Executive, they were proud representatives, one from each of Ireland's four provinces: O'Connor – Leinster; Barrett – Munster; McKelvey – Ulster; Mellowes – Connacht.[12]

The message was clear…the blood on the shamrock now engulfed Éireann.

---

11. Words by Liam Mellowes in a letter to his American friends John & Eileen Hearn (Massachusetts, USA) written on the morning of his execution, 8 December 1922. They are reprinted here from a booklet entitled *Liam Mellows* by Éamonn Ó hEochaidh, publisher & date unknown.
12. Rory O'Connor, Dick Barrett, Joe McKelvey & Liam Mellowes were shot to death without trial by order of the Free State government on the morning of 8 December 1922 in Mountjoy Jail, Dublin.

PART IV

"'Tis blood on the shamrock..."

JANUARY, 1923 – APRIL, 1949

TAKE IT DOWN FROM THE MAST
Unknown

Take it down from the mast, Irish traitors,
It's the flag we Republicans claim;
It can never belong to Free Staters,
For you brought on it nothing but shame.

You have murdered our brave Liam and Rory,
You've slaughtered young Richard and Joe;
Your hands with their blood are all gory,
Fulfilling the work of the foe.

Why not leave it to those who are willing,
To uphold it in war and in peace;
To the men who intend to defend it,
Until England's tyrannies cease.

We'll stand by Enright and Larkin,
With Daly and Sullivan the bold;
And we'll break down the English connection,
And bring back the nation you've sold.

You sold out the six counties for your freedom,
When we have given you McCracken and Wolfe Tone;
And the Ulster men have fought for you in Dublin,
Now you watch as we fight on alone.

Take it down from the mast, Irish traitors,
It's the flag we Republicans claim;
It can never belong to Free Staters,
For you brought on it nothing but shame.

19

*"The way to freedom is a hard and bloody one.
I can only hope and pray that my death will be
a contributing factor towards the great end for
which so much suffering has been endured –
our independence."*

Joseph McKelvey

MONDAY EVENING, 1 JANUARY 1923

*A*ran Roe O'Neill sat staring into the turf fire. The rocker he occupied was well suited for reflective thinking. Its gentle motion might have lulled him to sleep under normal circumstances, but not tonight. His thoughts and emotions were working overtime, as they had been for the last month or more. Haunting images kept replaying themselves in his mind's eye.

Michael's body sprawled motionless on that sullied bit of West Cork road. He'd never forget praying for a miracle while his trembling, blood-stained hands supported his friend's head. The Big Fellow's stately funeral was nothing more than an upsetting blur. Exhausted from lack of sleep and emotionally drained, he'd poured every last drop of energy he had into those seven horrific days. In a personal way, they were his last gift of love and respect to the Big Fellow.

Gay stirred in his comfortable easy chair just a few feet away. His legs, stretched out before him, were crossed at the ankles. Soft bubbling sounds occasionally emanated from his mouth. The Irish-American's head was tipped slightly to one side while his chin rested on his chest. The warmth of the fire and the relaxing effects of the whiskey had done their work.

Sarah Anne had disappeared into the bedroom to nurse baby Patrick. Sure that was some time ago. He guessed they both must have fallen asleep. It had been a long day for the two of them.

Aran could hear Áine and Mary Margaret chattering away in the kitchen. The evening tea would be ready soon, as the wonderful aroma of freshly baked scones filled the entire cottage. The Gortman's stomach churned in anticipation.

Despite the constant reminders of the war and its tragedies, he'd enjoyed the day. New Year's Day Mass at the church Sarah Anne and he'd been married in. Next, with the pub closed until evening, the McCrackens and now the three O'Neills enjoyed a toast to the New Year followed an hour later by one of Aunt Niamh's wonderful roasted lamb feasts. With no children of their own, Peter and Niamh had embraced Sarah Ann, Áine, Gay, Larry and himself as if they were their very own. Now, with the addition of Mary Margaret and Patrick, the elder McCrackens thought of themselves as grandparents.

After the wash up, Aran and Annie had walked down past the castle and out along the river. Civil War hostilities in the area had been nonexistent for several months, but he never went anywhere without his two trusted handguns: the Colt .45 revolver and his 9mm Luger automatic. In addition to his side arms, Aran cradled Michael's Lee-Enfield that the Corkman had with him at Béalnabláth.

Within the week, the Flying Gaels would be back in the field. He expected increased Irregular activity after the recent lull. Christmas, New Year's plus a stretch of cold, wet December weather had kept both sides close to home.

Later in the afternoon, with some energy to burn, Aran and Uncle Peter spent an hour splitting wood. A customer had dropped off fifteen or twenty large pieces of oak wood as payment for a bar bill he'd recently run up.

Finally, with winter's early nightfall, Annie, Patrick and himself had driven over to Gay and Áine's to enjoy a quiet evening together.

Relighting his pipe and finishing the last of his glass, Aran's thoughts drifted again. Memories of Michael dominated his thinking as those of Pearse had after the Easter Rebellion. He knew their haunting persistence would fade in time, but this evening they were fresh and vibrant.

He was not alone in his feelings of grief over the death of the Corkman. The unforgettable events of the Béalnabláth tragedy had ripped though the hearts and minds of many, especially members of the National Army. Aran was certain that some of those vengeful sentiments were behind the four executions at Kilmainham on the 17th, the arrest and killing of Childers a week later and the inexcusable shootings of Liam Mellowes and the other three at Mountjoy last month.

Liam and his comrades' deaths were nothing more than government-sanctioned murder. No one could claim their death sentences, handed down without benefit of trial, were authorised under the Public Safety Bill. That had only become law in October. Liam and the other three Republicans had been arrested, imprisoned and had never once appeared before a magistrate during their entire *five-month* period of incarceration. Sure there'd been no retroactive clause built into the Public Safety Act to his knowledge.

In his heart of hearts, Aran knew the proud deaths of Liam, Rory, Joe and Dick were a loss Ireland could ill afford or forget. The future influence these men could have had on their budding new nation was incalculable.

Joe's final words, emblazed in Aran's memory, was a testament to the past and a hope for the future shared by so many: "The way to freedom is a hard and bloody one. I can only hope and pray that my death will be a contributing factor towards the great end for which so much suffering has been endured – our independence."[1]

---

1. Joseph McKelvey, an IRA Lieutenant-General, wrote these words inside Mountjoy Jail on the morning of his death, 8 December 1922.

❧

After the heinous attacks on Hales and Ó Máille, a special cabinet meeting had convened that very evening. Reportedly, Minister Mulcahy proposed the idea of retribution with O'Higgins being the last member of the government's executive convinced of its merit.

By some strange twist of fate, Kevin's vote had condemned Rory O'Connor to death. Today, Civil War divided the very same men that the War of Independence had so nobly bound together in common cause. Just fourteen months ago, Rory had served as Kevin's best man at his wedding.

Rocking slowly before the fire, the Irish Rebel thought: *If there are two things we Irish are good at, it's remembering our past and holding on to our grudges.*

Tom Barry was another case in point. Though Tom and Michael never had what one might call a close friendship, Aran knew they certainly respected one another. During the Tan War, Michael often redirected the acclaim he received back to those who warranted the full credit. Tom Barry, with his successful use of guerrilla tactics, was one of those who deserved such recognition. With the signing of the Treaty, however, the two found themselves in opposite camps.

Aran remembered first meeting Tom soon after his return to Ireland. Barry had begun training men to serve in flying columns. In fact, it had been Shadow and Tom who'd planned the training exercise in the Boggeraghs that he'd participated in back during the summer of '20. Most of the Flying Gaels and some Volunteers from several Cork brigades also had been involved.

A year later, Tom married during the Truce period just as Kevin had. Michael attended that ceremony and later showed Aran a photograph of the wedding party. There in the front row were Tom and his bride Leslie Price. But for some strange reason, sitting between the new couple, was de Valera. He'd often meant to ask Tom how that arrangement came to pass. Was Dev in the seat of honour by invitation or was the Chief an interloper, demanding to be the day's centre of attention? Picturing the photograph in his mind, Aran knew many of the persons in the snapshot, once great friends, were now fighting on opposite sides of the Civil War divide.

With the outbreak of fighting in Dublin, Tom had been arrested with the other IRA men occupying the Four Courts. Eventually, he ended up in Kilmainham Gaol. It was there, on 23 August, that he and the others learned of Michael's death in West Cork on the 22nd, one year to the day after Tom's marriage to Leslie.

A month later, in a newspaper interview, Tom reported what he'd witnessed when the tragic news concerning the Big Fellow reached the gaol. He was quoted as saying, "Word spread around quickly so that everybody knew. A questioning silence spread throughout the jail."[2]

After a brief personal reflection, Tom continued, "I recalled looking down shortly afterwards from the corridor above on the extraordinary picture of about a thousand kneeling Republican prisoners spontaneously reciting the Rosary aloud for the repose of the soul of the dead Michael Collins, Commander-in-Chief of the Free State forces."[3]

Aran vividly recalled that two weeks after Michael's funeral, Tom escaped while being transferred from Kilmainham to Gormanstown Internment Camp in County Meath. It turned out to be a stroke of good fortune in more ways than one.

Later, a Free State official stated, "Had Barry still been in jail [in December], we'd have chosen him instead of Frank Barrett as the Munster man to be shot on the 8th."

Again on the run, this time from his former comrades instead of the English, Tom resumed his position of leadership within the Republican Army's Executive. Working directly under the command of Liam Lynch, Tom used his knowledge and skills of guerrilla warfare to wreak havoc among the forces of the National Army.

With thoughts of 8 December running though his mind, Aran couldn't help but think of Liam Mellowes. With his death, Larkin had lost a great comrade while James Connolly must

---

2. Meda Ryan. *Tom Barry: IRA Freedom Fighter.* Douglas Village, Ireland, 2003, 179.
3. Ibid.

have shed tears of sorrow from his grave, God rest their mighty souls.

Mellowes had been a great disciple of those two men. With Liam's death, Ireland lost a proud socialist and staunch labourite who believed that in an emerging Irish Republic, finally free of British imperial interests, Ireland would see its people take ownership of their own land. At long last, the Irish could utilise their talents and the country's natural resources for the advancement of their own national interests.

That thought reminded Aran of one of Connolly's poignant sayings, one that Liam often repeated: "The cause of labour is the cause of Ireland; the cause of Ireland is the cause of labour."

❧

Later that night, after Sarah Anne, Patrick and he had returned from Gay and Áine's cottage to the Black Rose, Aran couldn't sleep. He kept replaying the events of the last few weeks over and over in his mind.

Death had deprived Michael of seeing a lifetime of struggling culminate in an historic milestone. On 6 December, one year to the date after the British and Irish plenipotentiaries had signed their historical but soon to become vitriolic document, the Provisional Government ceased to exist. In its place, Saorstát Éireann was born.[4] On that same day, William Cosgrave was re-elected President of the Dáil and Kevin O'Higgins Vice-President. The other seven members of the cabinet were also reappointed. Some celebrated the occasion, but to Aran, Gay and others, it

---

4. As part of the Anglo-Irish Treaty agreement, Cosgrave's cabinet recommended to the British authorities that Timothy 'Tim' Michael Healy be appointed Ireland's first Governor-General of Saorstát Éireann. PM Bonar Law forwarded the recommendation on to King George V, who approved it. Thus, on 6 December, 1922, Healy, who was married to an aunt of Kevin O'Higgins, became the first to hold that ceremonial position. As Governor-General, he was a representative to three separate bodies: the British King, the British Government & the Irish Government. His political skills & influential British contacts proved helpful to the inexperienced Irish government, but his later criticisms of de Valera & his new Fianna Fáil party played a hand in his 'retirement' from the post in 1927.

was a bittersweet moment. Though it was the dawning of a new Ireland that many had dreamt of, had spilt blood over and had given their lives for, they could find little reason for rejoicing under the present circumstances.

Then, compounding the murderous tragedies befalling Ireland, James Craig's Northern Irish Government exercised its right, under paragraphs eleven and twelve of Anglo-Irish Treaty, to opt out of the proposed all-Ireland Parliament. This was not an entirely unexpected move, but his next was. In an apparent attempt to rub salt in Free State wounds, Craig's government issued a statement saying they were refusing to appoint their representative to the three-person Boundary Commission, as prescribed by the Treaty. The faith that Arthur Griffith and Michael Collins had placed in that arrangement began to teeter and collapse.

❧

Aran and Sarah Anne's first wedding anniversary passed with little notice. All eyes were focused on the new child. Between Patrick Michael's birth, his christening, the tragic deaths in Dublin, Christmas, Aran's twenty-fourth birthday and the New Year, there was too much going on.

On the 28th, however, Aran did surprise Annie with an old cameo brooch he purchased in a Dublin antique shop on Nassau Street across from Trinity College. For him, Sarah Anne had a photograph taken of Patrick, his very first. Dressed in his christening gown, he was just ten days old. The picture, carefully framed in its leather holder, was very special. Patrick's bright eyes and smiling face had been perfectly captured. The Gortman was thrilled. Something to treasure for a lifetime, he said.

❧

On Wednesday, 3 January, Aran and Gabriel rode their bicycles the eight miles from Cahir to their HQ in Ardfinnan. The cold, wet weather had broken the day before and south Tipperary was bathed in unusually mild, spring-like weather.

Several days before, Shadow had sent word to the Black Rose that he wanted to arrange a meeting with the two of them on the 3rd at the pub in Tar Bridge. Late afternoon had been suggested, sometime between four and five o'clock.

❧

The old RIC barracks in Ardfinnan had been given a proper facelift. The Nayler, Pat and several of the others had done a great job of it. The slate roof was patched and the building freshly painted inside and out. They furnished it with sleeping accommodations for sixteen. Heavy metal doors, both front and back, coupled with specially reinforced, looped-shuttered windows provided an added measure of security. Besides the fully equipped kitchen on the ground floor, there was an office, a dining room and a small armoury. Two larger rooms on the first floor slept eight each. The roughed-out cellar had been rigged up with two holding cells.

Much to Aran's surprise and approval, the men had dug a crude but serviceable, fifty-yard, underground passageway from the cellar under the walled yard to a derelict house located directly behind the barracks. As the Nayler explained it to Aran and Gay, it just gave them another option in case of an attack.

A ten-foot-high wall topped with barbed wire surrounded the property. Set back from the main Ardfinnan-Clogheen road, the building faced the River Suir. Two large metal gates provided access to a small garden area large enough to park their two vehicles: a Lancia armoured car transport and a 1919 black Buick touring sedan.

The village itself was very small: a pub, a general store cum post office and a forge run by a massive blacksmith by the name of Thomas Creegan. The village folk travelled to Cahir for Sunday Mass, while the children attended a one-room schoolhouse located just down past the bridge.

From the end of October through to early December, the Flying Gaels had made several sweeps around Lismore and Fermoy. They'd routed out several nests of Irregulars. Shots had been exchanged without injury to either side, but two dozen men were arrested. Aran had issued strict orders not to shoot to kill unless their or one of their own comrades' lives was at stake. He knew that was risky, but he'd no desire to endorse indiscriminate killing. He'd seen enough of that over the years.

"Fire your weapons. Let the Republicans know we're here and we mean business. Aim over their heads, give them a chance to surrender or lay down their guns and run, but don't draw down on them unless they start shooting at you. Then it's every man for himself."

❧

The Gortman and his sidekick left their HQ at twenty past three for their thirty-minute bicycle ride to the crossroads at Tar Bridge for their meeting with Shadow. The little bridge itself was a handsomely constructed humped-back stone structure spanning the River Tar, which flowed to the east along the base of the Knockmealdown Mountains. The river, no more than a mountain stream at the bridge, emptied into the River Suir near the village of Newcastle to the east. Just fifty yards to the south of the bridge was a crossroads. To the right a narrow, dirt-surfaced road led to Clogheen. To the left, the road meandered away from the mountains toward Newcastle. Off to the northeast was the town of Clonmel.

Though the dirt track they were riding along was rough, there was a slight drop in elevation, making the going easier. The fine weather was holding and it was a lovely day to enjoy the countryside.

As they pedalled along, they speculated on the purpose of Shadow's meeting.

"Business or personal?" queried Gay.

"Probably a little of both, knowing Shadow," guessed Aran, "but it's my hope that either he's convinced Lynch to declare a truce or that Shadow's decided to proclaim his neutrality and turn himself in."

"You may be a wee bit optimistic, old stock," said Gabby.

"And why shouldn't I be, Gay? This bloody madness must come to an end...sometime."

"Ah, such a happy group we were just a year ago," lamented Gabriel. "Your wedding and the gala celebration afterwards back at the Black Rose...who could've foreseen the current state of things back then?"

"Sure, Gay, the storm clouds have been gathering for some time," answered Aran. "Everyone knew where the Long Hoor stood on the Treaty. We knew his Document #2 wouldn't fly in the face of British resistance. No one wanted to go back to the negotiating table and start over again. It was either make do with the Treaty as it was or face the threat of war with the Sassenach."

"What a feckin' choice that was! Either way we were destined to hold the short end of the stick."

"Sure it wasn't what we wanted," said Aran, "but we could've made a better job of it."

"Well, the way that Dev went about it, you'd have thought *we* were the Empire, not England. Sure all his posturing didn't frighten the British and it sure as hell didn't deter Mick from doing what he thought was the way out."

"No, it didn't stop Mick; a bullet at Béalnabláth did."

"This country will live to regret that day, ye mark me words."

"It already has, Gay. Just look at us. We should be home with our families earning an honest living, but no. Here we are out in the middle of this beautiful countryside doing our damnedest to kill, maim or imprison our own kind while our old comrades are trying to do the same to us. Sure, it makes no feckin' sense!"

The words were no sooner out of Aran's mouth than a shot rang out. A bullet ploughed into Gay's left shoulder, throwing him off balance and into the Gortman riding next to him.

The force of Gay's body slamming into Aran knocked him sideways. Both men and bicycles crashed to a stop in the middle of the dirt track.

With their legs caught in the twisted wreckage of the bikes' metal frames, both men were trapped...unable to free themselves. Gabriel's right arm was across his chest as he grabbed at his wound.

With Gay draped over Aran, the Irish Rebel's face was no more than six inches from the jagged hole in his friend's coat. The odour of blood oozing from between Gay's clutching fingers filled Aran's nostrils. All the while, Gabriel was doing his best to muffle his cries of pain.

With the smell of the dirt road and the sight of blood, Aran was instantly transported back to a similar track in West Cork. Thankfully, though, Gay wasn't dead, he was only wounded.

Blinking his eyes to regain focus, Aran knew they were sitting targets. But being on the ground and below the low hedges surrounding them, they were probably out of sight of their attacker, at least momentarily. The shot that had hit Gay sounded as if it was fired from a distance of several hundred yards. If they moved quickly, they might be able to find a more protected position, but sure time was wasting.

"Gay, let go of your shoulder and get off me. I'm all tangled up under you."

"Ah-h-h," said Gabriel, as he tried to move.

"Come on, Gay, push. We don't have much time."

With some of the weight off him, Aran freed his arms and rolled Gay over onto his back.

As he crawled out from under his friend's body, Aran felt a piece of sharp metal slice through his trousers and into his thigh.

Wincing at the pain, he carefully freed his legs by pushing against Gay's hip with his foot as he rolled off the mangled bicycles.

Grabbing Gay under the armpits and bending low, Aran began dragging him toward the opposite ditch.

"Oh-h-h," uttered Gay. "For God's sake, not that shoulder."

"All right then, get to your feet now. They may be on us any second. Here, put your good arm around my shoulder. I'll steady you."

With great effort, Gay dragged himself up on to his knees and then to his feet. Wobbling, he lunged out, grabbing Aran's jacket for support.

"There, I have you. Now, keep low and head for that hole in the hedge just there," ordered Aran, pointing with his free hand.

To an innocent bystander, they might have been mistaken for two drunken sots making their way toward the comfort of a gully alongside the road.

But there were no bystanders and they weren't drunk. Far from it, for they knew they were scrambling for their lives.

As they forced their way through the opening in the hedge, they found themselves in a small field. About forty yards straight ahead was a low stone wall.

"Gay, can ya make it?"

"What feckin' choice do I have?"

"None. So let's go, but remember, keep your bloody arse down."

"It's not me arse that's bloody, you eejit!"

"Jaysus, how do you do it? Making jokes at a time like this."

With Gay's good arm around Aran's shoulders, the two ran as best they could for the protection of the wall.

Ten yards from their goal they fell.

Almost panicking, they righted themselves and finished their charge like frightened rabbits…Aran on all fours; Gay doing his impression of a three-legged dog.

Once over the wall, they lay in tall grass, panting like two wolfhounds on a hot day.

After pausing a few seconds to catch their breath, Gabriel muttered, "For fuck sake, what was that all about? Who knew we were National Army in the first place? Sure as hell you couldn't tell from what we're wearing. You don't think Shadow had us ride into an ambush, do ya?"

"It crossed me mind, but only for a second. Shadow would never betray us."

"Well, what then? Just some trigger happy son-of-a-bitch having a go at two defenceless yokes?"

"I thought of that too, but somehow I doubt it."

"Hawkins and the Black Spots?"

"Those bastards know we're breathing down their necks. With Mick out of the way, that only leaves the three of us: Shadow, you and me."

"I just can't believe anyone could be so evil and so bloody devious as to be tracking us day and night."

"Shadow would be the first to disagree with you and I'd be the second. Now, enough of this bloody blathering. We're wasting time, Gay. Who ever it is, they could be on us at any second."

With the colour back in Gay's face and from the tone of his voice, Aran knew Gabriel would be all right.

"Gay, I want you to move over to the right. Put your back into that corner where the two walls come together. Between putting pressure on that wound and with your pistol handy, keep an eye out. I don't want anyone coming up on you from behind. Do you have any extra magazines?"

"Two, but where are ye going?"

"I'm going to work me way around to the south. Maybe I can surprise the fucker and even the score."

"Ah, shyte, he'll be long gone by now."

"For his sake, I hope so."

Keeping low, both men moved down to the right.

"Now, lean into the corner there and keep a sharp lookout. I should be back in fifteen minutes. Just so you don't decide to plug me by accident, I'll give you my best impression of a hooting owl as I approach."

Gabriel nodded. A moment later, the Irish Rebel was over the stone wall, working his way across the adjoining field.

Gay grimaced as he tried supporting his left arm on his knee. The sharp pain in his shoulder had subsided, leaving a burning sensation that radiated down his arm to the elbow and across his chest. By now the fingers of his left hand were numb, but most of the bleeding had stopped.

For fuck sake, he thought: *I guess I should consider myself lucky. A little higher and that bullet would have taken me head off.*

After a quick look around, he laid his pistol in his lap and tried pulling back his jacket to have a look at his wound.

I'm really lucky. The bullet must have missed the artery or there would be more blood. I'm guessing it either glanced off a bone or it's just a flesh wound. Either way, if it had gone straight through, it might have punctured a lung or my heart. Sure, Áine would have given me one hell of a scolding if it had.

The thought of Áine givin' out to him caused the Irish-American to smile, despite his pain.

Gay leaned his head back against the stone support and said a prayer, thanking God for minding him so.

❧

Five minutes passed, then ten. The only sounds Gabby could hear were the cries of some crows in the distance and the tinkling of a cow's bell.

Suddenly, the rural calm was broken by the sound of gunfire. Three, then a fourth pop from a pistol were soon followed by two sharp cracks from a Lee-Enfield rifle.

Lord save us, there's a bloody war going on out there and I'm damn near useless.

Awkwardly, Gay rolled over onto his knees and peered over the walls that formed his protective barrier.

Gabby reasoned to himself: *The handgun reports could have been Aran's, but he wasn't carrying a rifle.*

Glancing around behind him just to be sure his back was clear, Gabby turned and looked in the direction of the road.

The hedgerow blocked his field of vision.

Then, off to his right, in the direction of the Tar, came two more pistol shots.

Those pistol shots aren't too far away.

A minute later, Gay heard Aran's hooting coming from the direction of the dirt track.

He hooted back.

Glancing over his shoulder once more to make sure he was still alone, Gay turned his attention to the hedgerow, his pistol ready just in case.

A moment later, Aran, followed by another, crawled through the gap in the shrubbery.

Well, I'll be, it's Shadow! Where the hell did he come from?

Up on his feet, Gay slipped his pistol back in its holster. Being careful not lose his balance or fall, the Irish-American, swinging his leg up on top of the wall, boosted himself over the stone barrier with his good hand.

Walking carefully over the uneven surface of the field, he headed toward his two friends.

"Sure, you're a sight for sore eyes, Shadow, but where'd ya come from? At first, we thought it was *you* shooting at *us*."

"You old amadán. If it'd been so, you'd be toes up by now."

Coming together, Gabriel threw his good arm around the Limerick baker, embracing him.

"Bloody hell, Shadow, I can't tell you how good it is to see you. How ya keepin'? Do those rebels you've been seein' lately feed you enough?"

"Better care than you've been receiving, I can see…and no, I haven't missed a meal since I was in your company last."

"Ah, you *are* an old stick," grinned Gabriel, "and as for me shoulder, sure it's nothing. Just a nick."

"We'll see about that," said Aran. "I want to get you back to Ardfinnan as soon as possible and have Marty take a look at it. You just may have to walk to Dublin if it's not good news."

"The bloody hell I will," roared Gay, "now tell me, what's the count?"

"Three dead," answered the Irish Rebel.

❧

After only a short walk back toward Ardfinnan, the three encountered an obliging farmer who took them into the village in his wagon.

Aran sent four men in the Lancia back towards Tar Bridge to collect the bodies. He ordered his men to take them to Clonmel.

"Leave them with General Prout's detachment for identification and burial, if necessary."

❊

With Aran's leg gash and Gay's shoulder wound cleaned and dressed, the three adventurers were the centre of attention. With the Flying Gaels gathered around the fireplace, the queries and answers came flying fast and furiously.

Gay described his wounding and the smash-up then told of their scramble to safety.

Next, Aran picked up the threads of the story, "After I left Gay, I worked me way across several fields and was about to cross the road when I saw two men with rifles clambering over a wall right in front of me. On my command to halt, the two began raising their weapons."

"That was their mistake," interrupted the red-headed Duncan.

Acknowledging his comment with a smile and a nod, Aran continued, "Not wanting to wait for a verbal reply, I fired four rounds from my Luger, bring them both down."

"Were they dead?" asked Liam McCullers.

"Well, as I was moving over to see if they were or not, someone up ahead of me let fire. Two bullets danced off the roadway just to my right."

"Bloody sniper," muttered Neil Morrison.

"At that point, I dropped down, taking cover in the gully on the opposite side of the road."

"I guess so!" exclaimed Pat. "Who was it that was still after you?"

"Sure, I'm just getting to that bit now, Pat," answered Aran. "Not knowing who was still out there, I stayed down for several minutes. Suddenly, I heard someone coming in my direction from off to me right. Swinging around so as to have a clear shot, I couldn't believe my eyes. There was this old coot working his way up along the edge of a field, rifle in hand."

Breaking into Aran's story, the Limerick man said, "If I'd known you had everything under control, I'd have stayed back in the comfort of the pub in Tar Bridge. But sure, when I heard the gunfire, I became concerned. I thought you two might be on your way to met me, so I borrowed a rifle from the pub owner and headed up the road just in case you were in trouble."

"You're lucky Aran didn't plug ya," said Duncan. "Of course, some of those other yokes might have too."

Shadow only smiled. "He was too busy, nailing another of those blighters who was moving up behind me. The one I never saw coming," said Shadow. "Sure, maybe I am losing me touch."

"Well, who the hell were they?" asked Caoimhín.

"Apparently, they were friends of Hawkins," said the Gortman.

"What? How do you know that?" questioned Rory.

"That third murdering bastard lived long enough to answer a few questions," replied Shadow. "He said for the past four months, he'd been working for an Englishman named Palmerston who was on some kind of personal vendetta to avenge the death of his brother. Apparently, this Palmerston had been bragging that he'd killed Michael Collins last August and that Aran and Gay were next on the list.

"Before he died, he mumbled something about a fourth man with them today, along with the Limey."

"Do you think he was slaggin' you, Shadow?" asked Larry.

"I don't think so," answered Shadow. The grim look on the baker's face told everyone around the fire he was serious.

"Shadow, maybe you should tell them what you told me back in August after Michael's death."

The Limerick man nodded in Aran's direction. "You all remember the great sorrow we all felt after Mick's death. Unable to shake its effects, Aran decided to get away from Dublin. He sent word to me he was heading for my old safe-house outside of Limerick.

"We spent two days together there. We talked and renewed our friendship. I also told him I'd help with his Black Spot inquiry.

"You see, on the night Michael was shot, Aran, Gay and Emmet Dalton promised to do some checking around. It seemed odd that the Big Fellow was the only fatality in the twenty-minute or so fire fight. Was it accident, an unfortunate casualty of war or some kind of a staged execution? Emmet said he'd check with his contacts around Cork while Aran and Gay promised to make some inquiries about the make-up of the escort party. Remember, they'd put it together themselves back in Dublin."

Shadow paused to drink tea from his mug.

"Beside the strange coincidence that a brigade meeting had been scheduled for that same day at Murray's farmhouse up behind Long's Pub, de Valera had passed that way just after Mick's convoy had stopped, asking for directions to Bandon. Knowing the Big Fellow was in the area, some say Dev was hoping to meet up with him and talk peace. Disappointed he'd missed Michael and learning an ambush was being organised in case the convoy should return that way later in the day, the Chief supposedly said, 'What a pity I didn't meet him. It would be bad if anything happened to Collins; his place will be taken by weaker men.'[5]

"Emmet's inquiry netted little news. Besides the Republicans manning the roadblock, there were several other parties of IRA men in the area, all retreating westward after Emmet's occupation of Cork City. As you're well aware, these were tough, seasoned guerrilla fighters, heading back to the mountains of Cork and Kerry, no doubt to stage one last final stand on their home turf."

Interrupting his story, Shadow asked, "Any chance for a bit more tea, and a glass of something would go down nicely as well."

With his mug refilled and a whiskey on the table beside him, the fifty-plus-year-old baker resumed his story.

"I guess you wouldn't be surprised if some of those retreating men just happened along as the shooting began, would ya? Seeing as there was a National Army convoy stopped along the road, I'm sure they were only too happy to join up with their fellow Republicans…a chance to take out some of their disappointments and frustrations and all that.

"Well, that was just what Emmet surmised. Sure any one of

---

5. Mackay, op. cit., 286.

those Volunteers might have fired the fatal shot. There was no way of telling.

"Back in Dublin, your two here pored over the list of those Dublin men they'd assigned to the convoy. They could vouch for everyone with the exception of Palmerston. He was the only unknown quantity. Sure the fact he was English might have sent up a red flag, but if you remember rightly, there were a lot of English signing up for National Army duty back then."

Shadow looked over at Aran and said, "Why don't you tell them the rest?"

"There's not much more to say. Besides his nationality, Palmerston or Hawkins, if you please, did have coal-black eyes, but so do others that we all know.

"I contacted Sam in London and he said that he'd heard rumours Eddy Hawkins had resurfaced and was over here.

"I realise that's not much to go on. English, black eyes, possible family connection, drops in and out of sight, Mick's ordering the attack on Field-Marshall French's life in Dublin several years ago, Wilson's assassination tied in with the IRA, Palmerston only one hundred yards up the road from Michael when he went down and the final link: Palmerston's sudden disappearance after the convoy returned to Dublin on the 23rd."

"Sure, I know it's all circumstantial stuff," offered Gay, "but today's 'death-bed' confession just confirmed our suspicions. Palmerston is Black Eddy Hawkins and he's after the two of us...and maybe you too, Shadow."

"You know what he looks like. Shoot the bastard on sight...no questions asked," ordered Aran.

"I never did like or trust that Palmerston," said Pat. "From the day last June when he was assigned to Liam's company, I didn't like him. He was a loner; kept to himself all the time. I should've been more distrustful...listened more carefully to my gut."

"Ah, you can't blame yourself or Liam for that matter," said Chris. "The army was glad to take anyone with military experience last summer."

"Oh, I know it wasn't your fault, Pat," said Gabby. "Just the luck of the draw I guess. But I'm still kicking myself for approving that feckin' convoy request after Griffith died. If he hadn't been with us, Mick might still be alive."

"Sure and you don't know that, Gay," replied Aran. "Remember, we were taking fire from all directions that evening. To say he was the one who shot Michael is a pile of shyte, pure and simple."

"Maybe so, but he bloody well had his chance, didn't he?" said Gay.

"If he'd wanted to kill Mick, he'd of had a thousand chances to do it," said Marty, coming to Gay's defence.

"To assassinate Michael is one thing, but to do it and get away with it is another matter all together," snapped Gay.

"But you certainly have to give him credit for one thing, he was a devious son-of-a-bitch who was smart enough to worm his way into a spot where he might succeed," said Larry.

"…and a patient one at that he was," said Conor.

"…and clever enough to bring down his own little reign of terror on Aran, Gabby and Shadow," said Rory.

"Revenge can be a powerful elixir," remarked Frank O'Leary.

Jimmy Carroll stood up and threw a few more sods on the fire. Turning to face Gabriel, he said, "Won't you agree with me, Gay, I doubt if we'll ever really know who did shoot Michael, God rest his soul."

Silence suddenly descended on the room as everyone was momentarily absorbed in his own thoughts.

Breaking the reflective mood, Dónal O'Grady asked, "How do ye think he got hooked up with that Black Spot crowd in the first place?"

"I doubt if we'll ever know who first contacted whom, but sure it doesn't really matter much, does it? In any event, whether he was encouraged by that lot or used his own initiative, he apparently decided to toy with Mick, Gay, Shadow and myself before trying to kill us," said Aran.

"The bloody bastard," murmured the Nayler, "…and to think, I had him in me crosshairs in Athy over a year ago."

"Initially, Duncan, we were all in the dark," said the Gortman. "How were we to tie things to his brother's death back then? The hold- up in Athy was just his first warning. Sure, he was toying with us. Next the ambush at Brompton Oratory was another of his warnings. That was soon followed by the Holyhead mail-boat business."

"I'm thinking that was just another of his warnings or he'd have been onboard himself," added Aran.

"Who's to say he wasn't?" offered Gay. "But even if he wasn't, the slip of paper with the black spot on it was his way to let us know he was serious."

"Anyway," said Shadow, "according to Sam in London, Eddy seemed to drop out of sight about then. Maybe MI5 was teaching him a few tricks. But regardless, I'm betting he was back in Ireland last spring and meant to kill Aran at the rail station in Kildare. Lucky for the Rebel here, he missed."

"Jaysus, as I said, I should have listened to my feckin' instincts," swore Pat. "For all we know, he might be passing himself off as a Republican sympathiser."

"Well, whatever he's doing, I'm sure it hasn't been too difficult keeping track of our whereabouts, with the possible exception of you, Shadow," said Aran.

Shadow looked over at Aran and Gay and said, "You'll have to admit, you two have certainly made yourselves easy targets."

"…like today," said Gabriel, looking down at his shoulder.

"Exactly, like breadcrumbs in a fairytale," offered Shadow. "I guess that was Black Eddy or one of his minions firing at Aran as he retreated this afternoon. Just letting us know they're alive and well and they'll be back for another crack at it sooner or later."

"With three of his hirelings dead and himself on the run, that should give Eddy something to think about so," said Aran.

"Hopefully it should, but who knows what's going through his demented mind. One thing for sure, I'm guessing he knows we're finally on to him. If he's not careful, he'll be the one dead, not us," said the Limerick man.

☘

Aran and Larry drove Shadow back to the pub at Tar Bridge the following morning. His bicycle was still where he'd left it.

Despite Aran's persuasive words, Shadow still refused to join the Free State cause. Accept for his close friendships with the Rebel, Gay and Sarah Anne, the Limerick man felt no allegiance to the pro-Treaty side. That feeling was only magnified with Michael's death and Liam's execution. His loyalties lay with the Republic and the men who now still fought for it.

With Larry staying back in the motor car, the two men conversed privately outside the pub.

Making a final plea, Aran said, "Shadow, I wish you wouldn't go. Stay back with us. The fighting can't go on much longer. Your moderating influence could have an enormous impact on both sides. Soon, we'll be at peace. Then, as we did in Amerikay, we can pause and gaze at the vast heavens and the rich beauty of our holy land.

"Please God, don't begrudge what we don't have, but give thanks for the many blessings we do. The future lies before us. Don't let the past poison your dreams of a new tomorrow."

"I'm sorry, but I've no choice. I must go. Say hello to Sarah Anne and, again, congratulations on the birth of Patrick Michael. He's lucky to have such wonderful parents. Tell Annie, I'll call in when I can and you give the baby a kiss for me."

With that, Shadow pulled Aran to his breast and held him fast.

"Mind yourself, you Irish Rebel. I love you. Éireann go brách."

Releasing Aran, the baker turned and climbed on his bicycle.

"God bless, Larry," he called in the direction of the motor car.

"God bless you too, Aran."

With a wave of his hand, Shadow headed off down the road for Ballyporeen. There he was going to hook up with Liam Lynch and others of his staff. Having recently been promoted to IO of the 1st Southern Division, there was much work to be done. The IRA was putting together plans for a spring offensive, plus

Shadow wanted to alert Lynch of the possible presence of Eddy Hawkins.

※

The December Free State executions had sent a message. Except for the attack on Dáil member Seán McGarry on 10 December, no other TDs had been assailed or killed. Instead, family members of TDs became the targets. Kevin O'Higgin's father was murdered. William Cosgrave's home was burned and his uncle killed soon after.[6]

Despite the urgings of the National government to save Ireland's architectural heritage and preserve the art treasures they contained, Republican columns intensified their campaign of attacks and burnings against Unionist homes.

Next they accelerated their programme of disabling railroad lines and blowing up bridges. Rural areas of the country were cut off from population centres with the effect that farm products couldn't reach their markets and goods distribution in general was greatly handicapped.

It seemed that the Irregulars, unable to win a military victory, were hell-bent on taking out their revenge on the country's historical magnificence and its economic capability.

In addition to losing the military advantage, the Republicans faced the impossible task of holding captured prisoners as well as providing for their own needs. Unlike the Free State government which had set up large internment camps at the Curragh and Gormanstown to hold captured anti-Treaty prisoners, the Irregulars had no such luxury. In fact they had a difficult time feeding and clothing their own. This forced the Republicans to continue looting businesses, banks and post offices. These actions only further distanced them from the sympathies and support of the civilian population.

With the war dragging on and with its increasingly negative impact on transportation, communications and economics, politi-

6. Litton, op. cit., 113.

cal activity was hindered as well. Sinn Féin, the dominate political force in the land, slowly began to collapse as Treaty opposition took the form of military aggression instead of democratic inter-action. Both pro- and anti-Treatyites' mind-sets had hardened. Attitudes on both sides of the divide became even more embit-tered. The use of 'military necessity,' to echo the words of Minister Mulcahy, had become an excuse for murderous brutality.[7]

❧

The Flying Gaels were handed a major coup toward the middle of January.

Due to National Army forces holding all major population centres in Munster and with the increased frequency of motorised patrols, Irregulars wishing to move from one location to another were forced to travel by foot and at night. This coupled with the need to constantly be on the lookout for and having to dodge squads of Free Staters made for slow going.

On the evening of the 18 January, a young army lieutenant, stationed in Clonmel, was home visiting his family. Their hillside residence was in a remote part of the Galty Mountains.

The man had only just arrived into his parents' home when his father mentioned that some of 'the boys' were staying just down the road. He indicated that one of them was 'a prominent kind of fellow.'

During the Tan War, this part of Tipperary was well known for its hospitality toward Republicans on the run. But now, times had changed.

Upon learning of the nearby visitors, the officer motorcycled back into Cahir and on to Ardfinnan. He'd met Aran months earlier and the two respected one another. Knowing of the Flying Gaels' HQ, he made for their door straight away.

❧

At nightfall, the column left their Ardfinnan headquarters.

---

7. Edward Purdon. *The Civil War.* Cork, Ireland, 2000, 53.

Twelve were in the armoured Lancia transport with Aran, Gay, Pat and Marty in the Buick. Gabriel, with his arm still in a sling, was making rapid recovery. Luckily, his wound turned out to be a superficial one. With nothing broken and no nerve damage, he'd be as good as new in no time. Meantime, his good right hand allowed him to handle his Webley revolver without difficulty.

When they were within three miles of the lieutenant's neighbour's home, the Gaels dismounted. Leaving three men behind to guard the vehicles, the others spread out and carefully advanced on foot.

Ninety minutes later they had the house surrounded. Gay, the Nayler, Caoimhín, the two McDonalds, Jimmy Carroll and Frank O'Leary took the back of the building while Aran, Pat, Chris McKee, Larry, Rory and Marty covered the front. Aran decided to give it an hour after the lamps were extinguished. He'd hate to miss a late arrival or two.

Finally, at eleven o'clock, with the cold and damp beginning to take its toll, Aran gave his infamous 'hoot' and all parties advanced.

Their revolvers drawn, cocked and finding both doors unlocked, the men easily gained entrance to the residence. With the house plan clearly imprinted in his mind, Aran with Duncan and Pat slipped up the staircase. Opening the first door on the left, they saw the outlines of two men in a narrow bed.

With Rory on the stairs sheltering a lighted lamp, Aran shouted, "Hands up! You're surrounded."

Startled and obviously outnumbered, both men threw their hands in air crying, "Don't shoot. We surrender."

Rory's lamp now illuminated the room. Aran exclaimed in surprise, "Holy Mother of God, its Liam Deasy."

Minutes later, the home owner confirmed these were the only two in the house. "If you'd been here last night," he said, "you would've found two more in the next room."

The Flying Gaels disarmed their two captives and peacefully withdrew without a dish broken or a stick of furniture out of place.

They transported Commandant Deasy, O/C of the 1st Southern Division and one of Liam Lynch's most trusted senior staff members, and one of Deasy's junior officers to Cahir House which was the Free State's military HQ in the area. Aran turned over his prisoners to the commandant with a simple word of warning, "Keep a sharp lookout. They're great ones for escaping."[8] [9]

The rest of the Gaels travelled back to Ardfinnan for the night, while Gay and Aran decided they'd surprise their wives with unplanned visits.

❧

Situated on the upper village square, Cahir House, the residence of the Cahir Estate manager, was just across the street from the Black Rose. The pub was closed at this hour, but after walking around back, Aran saw the kitchen light on. Sarah Anne was up with the baby.

Though he often spent two or three nights a week in Cahir, Sarah Anne was thrilled to see him. After a warm welcoming embrace, Annie put Patrick back to bed and rejoined her husband for a cup of tea and the story of Deasy's arrest.

For being apart only three days, Annie was full of news herself. Beaming with delight, she proudly announced she'd located a place for them to live.

"It's just above the jewellers, halfway down Castle Street on the right."

Aran nodded. He knew the shop well.

"You'll just love it," she said. "You can see the castle from the sitting room window and the river out the back. It even has a room for Patrick Michael."

"What about us?" joked Aran.

"Oh, don't be silly. We'll have a bedroom all to ourselves, plus there's a comfortable parlour and a nice kitchen."

Aran smiled at her enthusiasm.

"And guess what," she exclaimed, "you can leave your night

---

8. Deasy, op. cit., 107-109.
9. Calton Younger. *Ireland's Civil War*. Glasgow, Scotland, 1990, 497-498.

bucket in Ardfinnan, there's a lovely new flush toilet in the bathroom.

"The place needs a bit of fixing up, but Áine and one of her brothers has promised to help. We should be able to move in by the end of February."

He was not surprised at Annie's news of finding them a place of their own to live. They'd been looking for something suitable in the village ever since they'd returned from Dublin. Aran, however, was flabbergasted with her next announcement.

Finished with his tea and more than ready for bed, Sarah Anne reached across the table and took Aran by the hand. With a smile on her face and with her fingers entwined in his, Annie said, "Aran, I've one other bit of news. We're going to have another baby, my love…a playmate for Patrick Michael sure."

"Oh Lord have mercy, Sarah Anne, are you sure?"

"As sure as I was about having Patrick. It looks like the end of September. Please God, this war will be over by then and we can settle down and live in peace for a change."

Overjoyed with her news, Aran stood up and walked over to where Sarah was sitting. Carefully, he pulled his wife up, gathered her in his arms and held her close.

Then, slowly he pulled back just far enough so their lips met. With tenderness and passion, the Gortman kissed his wife as if it were his first.

❧

Later, after they'd made love, Aran lay awake. He couldn't help but think how Sarah Anne had changed in the six years he'd known her. Once a free, adventurous spirit, she'd left her parents' home in Virginia to live in Ireland. Since then, Annie had matured. She was still the same tall, beautiful brunette with flashing blue eyes that he'd fallen in love with, but today her appeal was even greater. Besides Annie's intelligence and dedication to Ireland's independence, she'd become a devoted wife, a loving mother and wise companion whom Aran loved with all his heart. He couldn't imagine life without her.

Both Sarah Anne and Aran were maturing. Once a rebel like himself, Annie too saw the wisdom of Michael's willingness to compromise and seek political solutions to satisfy Ireland's thirst for independence. With their first child growing in her womb and her husband actively engaged in the National Army's struggle in support of the Treaty, Sarah had followed in his footsteps. When the Cumann na mBán voted to reject the Treaty, four hundred nineteen to sixty three on the 5th of February last,[10] Annie had resigned her short-lived membership.

Soon after the vote, the organisation split with the breakaway, pro-Treaty women founding Cumann na Saoirse in 1922.[11] Sarah Anne joined the new group but wasn't a very active member.

❧

The following morning, Aran visited Cahir House and learned that Liam had been transported to Clonmel where Major-General John T. Prout had his headquarters. Deasy would be tried there and, if convicted, would be executed shortly afterwards.

It was obvious to both Aran and Gay that the Republicans' cause was lost, but ridding the countryside of pockets of determined IRA men would be protracted and costly. Lives on both sides would be lost while the civilian population and the Irish economy would take a merciless pounding until peace could finally be firmly established.

In their journey down from the Galtys last night, Liam Deasy had confided to Aran that he was glad it was over for him. The senior Republican officer described a recent inspection tour of IRA units in County Cork and how depressed he was after seeing the dreadful conditions under which they were operating.

After that heart-rending visit, Deasy said, "I'd planned on talking with Lynch about initiating peace negotiations."

❧

---

10. Dorothy Macardle. *The Irish Republic.* Dublin, 1999, 658.
11. Alvin Jackson. *Ireland: 1798-1998.* Oxford, United Kingdom, 1999, 269.

News reached Ardfinnan on the 24th that Deasy had been court-marshalled and sentenced to death. At the last minute, though prepared to die, he changed his mind and accepted the Free State's offer of imprisonment if he'd issue an order proposing the IRA end its war.

Attached to the communiqué was a copy of Deasy's directive:

> "I [Commandant-General Liam Deasy] agree and I will aid in immediate and unconditional surrender of arms and men as required by General Mulcahy. In pursuance of this undertaking I am asked to appeal for a similar undertaking and acceptance from the following…[a list to prominent Republican leaders followed including Éamon de Valera, Liam Lynch, Tom Barry, Frank Aiken among others] and for the immediate and unconditional surrender of themselves after the issue by them of an order of surrender on the part of all those associated with them, together with their arms and equipment."[12]

Deasy's plea was flatly rejected by Lynch. He disagreed with his subordinate's thinking that "an honourable retreat would help to conserve Republican ideals, and that there was little point in fighting on."[13]

❧

The number of Irregulars executed by the new government had totalled fifty-five at the end of January. Additionally, the army had executed eight Free State soldiers for treason. But the butchery would only continue.

In an attempt to kill a particularly odious Free State officer who'd reportedly tortured IRA prisoners, Irregular forces planted a mine at Knocknagoshel south of Abbeyfeale in northeast County Kerry. The resulting blast killed five National Army soldiers, including three officers plus badly wounding another.

---

12. ounger, op. cit., 498.
13. Litton, op. cit., 118.

In retaliation, the area's Free State commander issued a directive that in the future IRA prisoners would be used to clear areas thought to be mined.

Underscoring the level of hatred that had blossomed, particularly in Kerry, early the following morning nine Republican captives were tied to a mine at Ballyseedy Cross. The resulting triggered explosion killed eight of them. Miraculously, one of the prisoners survived the blast, having been blown clear of the impact area. Later, he described the circumstances of the detonation and how a group of Staters raked the dead men with rifle fire.

Republican reports contradicted the published Free State accounts of the tragedy. The government claimed that the explosion was accidentally set off as prisoners were attempting to remove an explosive device.

One newspaper account of the Ballyseedy incident reported, "…back in Tralee, nine coffins were prepared; to the amazement of the Free State troops only eight bodies were available to fill them. At the funeral the [Free State] military coffins were broken into and smashed to pieces."[14]

The situation in Kerry continued to escalate. On 8 March, at Countess Bridge near Killarney, a Republican-set mine exploded, killing four Irregular prisoners-of-war who were 'supposedly' trying to defuse it.

On that same day, at Castlemaine north of Killorglin, a small group of lucky Republicans escaped when they were ordered to clear mines.

Again, on 12 March, at Cahirciveen on the Ring of Kerry, five more prisoners were killed trying to remove a mine. Afterwards, a group of Free State soldiers were overheard bragging about what had happened.

Several weeks later, Aran read that a military inquiry had been held. Its purpose was to investigate the four Kerry incidents. In its official report, the army denied there were reprisals. They pointed out that the regrettable Cahirciveen incident was the result of Republican mines having been laid as part of the IRA's attempt to capture the town.[15]

14. Hopkinson, op. cit., 241.
15. Ibid., 240-241.

❧

Out of a desperate and hopeful attempt to end the internecine conflict, the Flying Gaels welcomed General Prout's call to arms on 9 April. Reports had filtered down to his headquarters that General Liam Lynch and a group of senior Republican officers had been seen in the area immediately south of Clonmel. The best guess was that they might be planning to cross over the Knock-mealdown Mountains on their way back to the Fermoy area.

Prout organised a huge sweep, involving some one thousand men, in a concerted effort to capture the IRA leader.

As the Flying Gaels were perfectly situated not far from the foot of the Knockmealdown Mountains, the Major-General wanted them to cover the right flank of the advance.

With all the Gaels in house, Aran relayed the battle plan to his men. "At midday, Lynch was spotted by a scout just to the southwest of Clonmel, moving on foot in a southwesterly direction. It appears there are seven others in his immediate party. The Chief of Staff is likely being supported by a squad of men from the 6th Battalion of the 3rd Tipperary Brigade."[16]

Spreading out a detailed map on the dining table, Aran began circling specific locations as he spoke, "General Prout is guessing Lynch will move along this line, the Newcastle-Clogheen Road, just south of us here."

The Gortman pointed out the road by running his finger along the map's surface between the two villages.

"If I were Lynch, I'd plan on crossing the Knockmealdowns if cut off. Prout must think so too, as he's calling on men from Dungarvan, Youghal and Lismore to come up over the top of the mountains and seal off any avenue of escape to the south."

The heads crowded around the table all nodded their agreement.

"Jaysus wept," said Gay, "the old boy isn't pulling any punches, is he."

---

16. As was the custom, when a member or members of the IRA Executive passed through a particular command area, men from the appropriate brigade battalion provided cover & offered logistical support.

"From what Aran says, Prout sees this as a chance to end the fighting here and now," said the Nayler.

Tapping his forefinger on the map to refocus attention, the Irish Rebel continued, "Prout will direct his 2nd Southern forces south on a line from Clonmel to Ballymacarbry then begin a tooth-combing sweep to the west. A battalion from Mitchelstown will fan out and move due east. Our job will be to head south about halfway between Clogheen and Newcastle. We're to seal off any attempt by Lynch to turn north. If he does, we're to move in, forcing him back and up onto the shoulder of the mountain. Of course, if we've an opportunity, we're to engage and capture him if possible."

"How soon do we move?" asked Marty.

"We'll wait until seven. With the added daylight, we should be well positioned by eight. It'll mean a night out in the open, but that's nothing new to us. At least the weather is in our favour. It'll be dry and mild this evening, at least let's hope so."

"How are we going to split up?" asked Larry.

"Two groups of ten each. I'll take the left side and Gay will come along on the right. We'll draw names to see who goes with whom. Any queries?

"Good. We have over four hours to get ready. Check your weapons, pack your gear and get some rest. It'll no doubt be a long night."

❧

Unbeknownst to the Flying Gaels, Liam Lynch and his men slept within four miles of their bivouacked position. Men of the 6th Tipperary guarded the maze of little roads and dirt tracks that crisscrossed the area on the east, north and west. To the south rose the Knockmealdown Mountains. Posted as lookouts, the Tipperary men were ready to raise the alarm if any Staters were spotted. As for Lynch and his party, they'd broken up into three groups and had found billeting in friendly farmhouses in the immediate area.

At five in the morning, one of Lynch's scouts spotted a party of Free State soldiers approaching from the west. Moving in two files, they straddled the narrow dirt track down which they advanced, using the verge as their footpath.

Immediately, Lynch and his men were alerted. As prearranged, the eight congregated in the farmhouse closest the mountain incline. Accustomed to National Army troop movements of this kind, they weren't initially concerned.

Three hours later, two more scouts rushed into the farmhouse with news that another group of Staters had been seen approaching over the mountain to the east. Suddenly, their line of retreat was endangered.

Realising this was more than a one-off happenstance, the IRA men gathered their gear and headed off through a wooded glen. Safely on the other side, they began climbing the mountain. Except for the occasional stand of evergreens and outcroppings of granite, the Knockmealdowns offered scant protection from a pursuing enemy.

Their northeast to southwest path led the eight men across the very face of the mountain range.

☘

After spending as comfortable a night as possible, sleeping rough under a single blanket, Larry notified his brother he'd been in contact with a patrol of National Army soldiers approaching from the Mitchelstown area. They'd received reports that Prout's men were closing in from the east, and the Flying Gaels were to commence applying pressure along the Clogheen-Newcastle line and southward beyond the River Tar.

Gay sent word to Aran that they should be ready to advance in ten minutes.

Moving in teams of two, separated by approximately fifty yards, the Flying Gaels moved out. Each man was equipped with a rifle, one or two handguns and rations for two days. The Nayler, who along with Rory were the western-most duo, carried a Lewis gun on his shoulder.

Aran hadn't been surprised when Duncan appeared in full Scottish kit including a glengarry hat, cloak, kilt, sporran, sgian dubh and garter flashes. Some of the men codded the Nayler when he dressed so, but Aran always figured they were merely a bit jealous.

Positioned near the middle of his squad's advancing line, Aran and Marty struck a determined pose. With their Lee-Enfields at the ready and their bandoleers loaded with extra magazines of .303 shells, they were eager to see Lynch captured. The brutalities in Kerry turned everyone's stomach.

"Marty, this feckin' nonsense must come to an end and please God may it be today. Sure I hope Liam and his men live to tell their grandchildren all about it, but it's time their reign came to an end."

Marty answered in a one-word whisper, "Amen."

❧

Martin Richardson had been a great addition to the unit. His skill with a rifle was on a par with Aran's. Over the course of the last year, his strength and stamina had improved greatly. Despite the practical experience he had gained in caring for the wounded, Aran often wondered how he'd be happy knuckling down and spending all those long hours studying for his medical degree. But Marty constantly assured him that his determination to be a doctor was even greater now than it had been before he began playing 'soldier,' as he liked to call it.

The sun was well over the horizon when Aran motioned the Gaels to halt. They had crossed the only east-west road in the area some distance ago and had moved over ploughed farmland, through stands of heather, gorse, ferns and pine saplings. Thistle and blackberry bushes were clearly visible, lining the fields and the narrow boreens along which they'd passed. Overhead puffy, light-grey and white clouds seemed to hang in a bright blue sky. The chirping of unseen birds could be heard when the men occasionally paused to catch their breath.

Now, after climbing for over four miles, Aran signalled a ten-minute rest stop with the fingers of both hands. Men on both sides of him passed the message along to the next group of two and so on. Spreading the fingers of his right hand was often painful, especially in the morning. Today was no exception. Aran's hand was a constant living reminder of another Hawkins nightmare.

The sun shone its brilliance on the mountainside up ahead. Aran took out his field glasses, a treasured souvenir from his stay in Amerikay. He searched the desolate shoulder of the mountain looming up in front of him.

Just as he was prepared to lower the binoculars, a flash of metal brought him to full attention.

There, moving in a single line were six, no seven, no eight men, each about ten paces apart. They were travelling light. He could see they didn't have rifles but one man had a silver revolver in his hand. Its glint had announced the fleeing men, as they moved diagonally at a slow, measured pace up along the mountainside.

That must be Lynch's party, reasoned Aran. *We're too far away from them to be certain, but I'm guessing it's the Chief of Staff.* Raising his glasses to study the figures once more, Aran saw them pause and disappear from sight.

Must have dropped down into a dry creek bed or cavity on the mountainside...taking a blow I imagine.

Not wanting to delay another moment, Aran sent word down the line for Gay to join him.

Several minutes later, Gabriel, huffing and puffing, was at his side.

"Jaysus, old stock, you *are* getting up in your years. Too many pints and cigarettes, my friend?"

"Ah, bugger off. I'm grand just the way I am. What's up?"

"I just spotted them up there on the mountain. Eight men."

Aran handed Gabriel his field glasses. "Look there. Find that clump of white birch. Just above that and to the right you'll see three large granite boulders. Down and slightly to the left you'll see a low ridge of smaller rocks. They're down in some kind of a gully or depression...taking a breather I'm guessing."

After ten or fifteen seconds of moving the glasses over the rough terrain, Gay announced, "Got it. Wait, I see a head bobbing up and down. Now it's gone, but sure as hell I've them spotted too. Eight men you say."

"Aye. No rifles…just side arms. What you say we go get them. You swing slightly to the right…try to keep ahead of them. My squad will come up from the rear. That should keep them from doubling back."

The two friends paused and studied the other's face for a moment.

"Remember, Gay, keep your head up and your arse down."

"You too, Aran.

❧

Moving as quickly as possible over the rough ground, Aran and his men began making up the difference on the fleeing Irregulars. They were less than a mile ahead.

Indeed, the men up ahead had stopped to rest, but now they were on the move again. So intent were they on their upward climb, they'd failed to look behind them.

They're bloody eejits, thought Aran.

Despite the fact his men were closing in on Lynch and his party, the Gortman wasn't worried. *We're still out of range of the Republicans' side arms.*

Over to his right, Aran could see Gay and his men advancing. They'd broken away from Aran's right flank, but were closing, not as fast as his men were but they were definitely narrowing the distance all the same.

Even if the Gaels didn't catch them, they were driving the IRA men straight into the arms of Prout's troopers advancing up from the southern side of the mountain range.

Suddenly a shot rang out. It was off to Aran's left and just behind his line of men.

The Gortman turned to Marty and said, "For Christ sake, Marty, what's that?"

"Sure as hell I don't know. I doubt it was one of our men, but I must confess, I've been concentrating on that crowd up ahead and keeping my footing. Sorry, I haven't been lookin' around."

"Me either. Let's hold up a minute and just see what's going on."

Aran thought: *Bloody hell, I'm guilty of the same crime I just derided Lynch's men for.*

The Irregulars had heard the shot too. They'd stopped and were now looking back. Several were gathered around one man.

Again, Aran took out his glasses and studied the eight.

"Marty, that's Lynch up ahead all right. Looks like Frank Aiken's with him as well. Sure, there's Bill Quirke and Seán O'Meara. It also looks like Seán Hayes standing there behind Seán Hyde. Oh my God, Marty, Shadow's with them...and Danny Kelly's there too."

Aran turned and looked behind him.

"Sure, I don't see anyone back there. Are you certain one of ours didn't fire by mistake?"

"No, I can't be certain, Aran, but I doubt it. These men are all pros."

Looking back uphill, Aran could see Lynch and his men were now doing their best to run across the rough, rocky ground.

"Damn it, Marty, they're making a break for it. Let's take them alive if we can."

On his feet and two steps ahead of Marty, the Irish Rebel began to run, rifle in his left hand, his Colt .45 in his right.

He'd gone only twenty yards when more rifle fire erupted off to the left.

Suddenly, he heard Marty scream, "Aran, Aran, I'm hit. For fuck sake, Aran, I'm hit. It's me leg."

Turning, Aran saw Marty down, writhing on the ground.

Dropping to one knee, the Irish Rebel took a quick look behind him. All the Gortman could see was a puff of white smoke rising from beside a huge boulder, a remainder of some forgotten ice age.

A moment later, Aran's head was spinning. A bolt of white lightning flashed before his eyes.

He reached out and tried steadying himself, but the burning pain in his chest was too intense. He'd lost all feeling in his arms and legs. He thought: *If only the pain in my chest would stop...*

By the time Gay reached the spot where Aran and Marty lay, Marty was unconscious and Aran Roe O'Neill was dead.

20

*"During the 1930s de Valera systematically
dismantled the Treaty and thus proved
[Michael] Collins right in his assessment that
the 1921 agreement could be the stepping-stone
to the desired freedom."*

T. Ryle Dwyer

TUESDAY AFTERNOON, 10 APRIL 1923

Soon after the first shots were triggered, heavy firing erupted from all quarters. Bullets glanced off rocks while others buried themselves in the boggy ground.

Liam Lynch's party didn't know whether to hunker down and fight or risk running for it. Trapped in the open and with little natural cover for protection, they ran.

Though the distance between the hunted and the hunter was too great, the Republicans still fired their handguns. Then suddenly and for no explainable reason, the air fell silent. The eight men paused in their frantic scramble forward.

At that moment, a single rifle shot reverberated across the naked face of the mountain. A man screamed, "My God, I'm hit."

Liam Lynch, the IRA Chief of Staff and military leader of the Republican cause, was thrown backwards by the force of the bullet's impact. He fell to the ground, badly wounded. The projectile had pierced his body just above his left hip. Its exit hole was visible above his right hip.

Frank Aiken and Bill Quirke rushed to their chief. With no time to waste, they lifted him up and tried carrying him. After a couple of hundred yards, and in great pain, Lynch ordered that he be put down and for the others to leave him there.

"I'm finished," he said. "I'm dying. Perhaps they'll bandage me when they come up."[1]

Frank Aiken took Liam's papers, which he didn't want falling into Free State hands, and hurriedly stuffed his commander's automatic into his own pocket. Placing a coat over Lynch, they left him where he lay.[2]

❧

With their commanding officers still several hundred yards behind them, confusion reigned about what the Flying Gaels should do when they arrived at Lynch's side.

One member of the flying column thought the fallen man was de Valera. Pat said no he wasn't and turned to the downed man, "Who are you? What's your name?"

"I'm Liam Lynch, Chief of Staff of the Irish Republican Army. Get me a priest and doctor. I'm dying."[3]

Moments later, Duncan arrived on the scene and with Lynch's men now out of sight, he ordered Liam McCullers to apply a field dressing and for four other men to rig up a makeshift stretcher using a greatcoat and two rifles.

By now all the Gaels had gathered around the downed IRA leader except Aran, Marty, Gay and Larry.

---

1. Florence O'Donoghue. *No Other Law*. Dublin, 1986, 305.
2. "Later, Frank Aiken wrote, 'It would be impossible to describe our agony of mind in thus parting with our comrade and chief. Even in the excitement of the fight we knew how terrible was the blow that had fallen on the Nation and Army on being deprived of his leadership. His command that we should leave him would have been disobeyed, but that the papers we carried must be saved and brought through at any cost. All would be lost if they were captured.'" Ibid.
3. Ibid.

Concerned by their absence, the Nayler sent Caoimhín and Chris McKee back down to discover what was delaying them.

Four hundred yards from the spot where Lynch lay, they found the missing Gaels.

Quickly understanding the gravity of the tragedy before him, Caoimhín fired his Lee-Enfield three times into the air.

❧

The Flying Gaels carried Liam Lynch off the mountain to a public house in Newcastle. A priest and doctor were summoned. Duncan contacted General Prout's HQ in Clonmel, asking for a military doctor and ambulance. They arrived a little after three. After a hurried medical examination, General Lynch was rushed to Clonmel where he received the best of care. Tragically, though, Lynch died at eight forty-five that evening.

Prior to leaving Newcastle, Lynch gave Nick Robinson one of his fountain pens as a gift of appreciation, saying, "God bless you and the boys who carried me down the hill. Poor Ireland! All this is a pity. It never should have happened.

"When I die, tell my people I want to be buried with Fitzgerald of Fermoy."[4]

As one reporter covering the events surrounding Lynch's death wrote, "With every mark of honour and respect he was borne from St. Joseph's church, Clonmel to Mitchelstown on Thursday [12 April], and on Sunday [the 15th], despite the deep and bitter sundering of civil war, friend and foe gathered in an immense funeral cortege to follow his remains through Glanworth and Fermoy to Kilcrumper. There he was laid as he wished beside his friend and comrade, Michael Fitzgerald."[5]

One person, speaking at his funeral, said of Liam, "He enriched that conscious sense of nationhood which is the soul of Ireland."[6]

❧

---

4. Ibid., 306.
5. Ibid.
6. Ibid., 307.

Aran Roe O'Neill's body was also carried down the mountain. Instead of taking him to Newcastle, Gay, Larry and Pat Grogan drove him to Cahir in the Buick sedan.

Their first stop was at Gay's cottage. Gabby told Áine what had happened. Expectedly, she was devastated by the news. With tears running down her cheeks, she gathered up Mary Margaret in her arms and dashed across the road, leaving the child with a neighbour.

Returning, Áine approached the motor car with trepidation. She looked through the rear window at Aran's lifeless form and burst out crying again. Closing her eyes and crossing herself, Áine said a prayer for the safe repose of Aran's soul. Despite a strong desire to reach out and touch his cheek, she didn't. Instead, Áine climbed onto her husband's lap for the short journey into Cahir.

With Pat behind the wheel and Larry in the back cradling Aran, the four occupants dreaded what faced them.

❧

Pat parked in the laneway beside the Black Rose. Áine climbed out but let Gay walk ahead of her. She didn't want to be the one to break the news to those inside.

Sarah Anne, who'd been helping out in the pub for the last few weeks, was in the kitchen, finishing up the noontime meal wash up. Patrick Michael was asleep in a portable cot atop the family's kitchen table. Sarah Anne let out a shriek of pain when she saw Gay unexpectedly standing in the back doorway. His dirt and tear-streaked face told her something was terribly wrong before his trembling voice could find the words.

Wrapping her arms around her brother and with her head buried in his chest, she sobbed uncontrollably. Annie was only able to utter one word over and over, between her tears and moans, "No, no, no."

Gradually, her knees gave way. Her arms became limp and she collapsed to the floor. Gay knelt down beside her. With his arms around his sister's shoulders, he held her fast.

Áine, now in the kitchen, was on her knees too, beside Sarah Anne. Together, the three sobbed as if their hearts would break.

Moments later, alerted by the sound of the car in the laneway and the crying in the kitchen, Peter rushed into the room from the bar. Between shouts for Niamh and asking what happened, he suddenly understood.

"Where is he?" demanded Peter.

Gay looked up and motioned with his head.

Stepping around the trio huddled on the floor, Peter ran outside. There he met Pat.

"How could you let this happen?" he cried.

Pat couldn't answer, but took Uncle Peter by the arm and led him around to the open door of the Buick.

Upon seeing Aran in the back seat with Larry, he began crying too. With his shoulders heaving and his head bowed, Peter McCracken leaned against the car. If he hadn't, he would have collapsed.

Wiping away his tears and gathering himself, Uncle Peter softly said, "I think we should carry him inside."

He request fell on deaf ears.

Waiting patiently for a few moments, he again repeated his directive. "Pat, come…give me a hand."

Silently, the two carefully removed Aran's body from the back seat. Then, with Larry's help, the three men carried the Irish Rebel around to the pub's front door. Once inside, they placed Aran on one of the establishment's tables.

The handful of patrons at the bar stared in disbelief. Each had known Aran. Suddenly, the realisation of the moment struck home. Standing up, each man made the sign of the cross as he walked past Aran's body. They left without saying a word, but their eyes spoke volumes.

❧

The parish priest, Father Francis, was called to administer the last rites.

The local doctor, a good friend of the McCrackens, came and examined the body. He said that a single bullet had penetrated Aran's back and had exited his chest, probably nicking his heart. He wouldn't have known much pain and most likely had died almost instantly.

Soon several of Niamh's friends arrived. They removed Aran's blood-soaked clothing, washed his body and dressed him in a clean, freshly pressed National Army uniform.

Annie found Aran's Easter-lily badge back at their newly rented flat and with Gay's help, she pinned it on his tunic, just above his left breast pocket.

As the two looked down at him, so many loving memories rushed to mind; as many as the tears now cascading down their cheeks.

A coffin was brought in and Aran was placed inside it.

With the pub now closed for business, the family and a few close friends kept vigil over the body.

Sarah Anne finally stopped crying. Gathering herself, she stood by Aran looking down at his ashen face. At one point, she brought Patrick Michael in to see his father. Lowering the four-month-old infant down, the child reached out and touched his father's lips with his tiny fingers. Annie imagined he was saying goodbye.

Gay and Pat busied themselves making final arrangements.

A wake was planned at the pub for the following afternoon. Afterwards, Aran's body would be removed to St. Mary's Church for the overnight. On Thursday morning, a Mass would be said. Afterward, family, friends and the Flying Gaels would drive up to Dublin. A burial at Glasnevin was scheduled for six in the evening. Gay had made certain, Major Aran Roe O'Neill would be buried in a plot beside General Michael Collins. A newly designated area, reserved just for the dead of Óglaigh na hÉireann, would be his final resting place.

❧

Later that Tuesday afternoon, after the shock and pain of

Aran's death had begun to sink in, Gay sat down with the family and described the tragic events of the morning. Together, the families crowded around Peter and Niamh's kitchen table. Being close to one another in familiar surroundings was very comforting.

Gabriel told about the column receiving Prout's orders and the plan to pursue Liam Lynch and his party. Next, he detailed the Flying Gaels' overnight bivouac and their early morning advance up into the Knockmealdowns.

"We were grouped in pairs, about fifty yards apart, and advancing in a line up into the mountains. It was a moderate incline but the footing was rough...loose boggy soil, lots of rocks, furze, heather, granite outcroppings...you know what it's like. Aran and Marty were more or less in the middle of our formation while Larry and I were over on the right flank.

"During a pause in our climb, Aran finally spotted Lynch and his party through his field glasses. They were a bit less than a mile ahead of us. For some strange reason none of the Irregulars carried rifles, only side arms. Our lads were at a decided advantage. The Gaels could have cut them down easily but Aran wanted to take them alive, if at all possible.

"At that point, Aran sent word for me to join him and have a look with the binoculars as well. There were eight of them...Lynch and seven others. We didn't realise it at the time but Lynch was with Shadow, Danny Kelly, Frank Aiken, Seán Hyde and three others.

"After sharing a few words, Aran decided we should divide our advance. He'd take half and head straight for them, cutting off any possibility of retreat. I was to lead the others off to the right and up in an attempt to cut them off. It would be a classic pincher manoeuvre."

Stopping momentarily, Gay wiped his face with his handkerchief as more tears were involuntarily rolling down his cheeks. He then reached out and took Sarah Anne's hand.

"After I rejoined Larry, we all began moving once again, but so had Lynch's crowd.

"Just about that time, as I remember it, a shot rang out off to my left. I stopped to look around. None of our lads had a rifle to his shoulder. It was at that moment, I saw someone…really it was more like a shadow…moving behind a huge boulder to the left of our line and slightly behind it at a range of seven or eight hundred yards.

"At that point, I did a quick head count. All of our men were accounted for.

"Lynch's party had heard the shot too. They'd stopped and were looking around. Until that moment, I'm guessing that crowd had no idea we were trailing them, but I must confess I was guilty of the same misjudgement. Neither Larry nor I had been watching our backs. We were both so intent on what lay ahead of us.

"With the sound of the rifle shot, it seemed that all the Gaels froze for just a moment. Looking down our line, I could see Aran had his binoculars out again. Between looks, he was talking to Marty and pointing.

"Turning, I glanced up in Lynch's direction. The eight of them had paused too, but were suddenly were moving again, this time at a greatly accelerated pace."

Gabriel shifted his weight. Reaching out with his right arm, he put it around Sarah Anne's shoulders.

"I don't know what it was, but something made me glance back in Aran's direction. He was on the move too, running up the grade…rifle in one hand and his Colt in the other. Marty was running as well…maybe a stride or two behind and just off to Aran's left."

Pausing to blow his nose again, Gabby looked around the table. Everyone's eyes and noses were red. Each face looked puffy, all wearing the look of pending doom. All…all that is except for Father Francis. His hands were peacefully folded in his lap. His countenance reflected a sense of controlled serenity. Over the years, he'd been in the homes of many a grieving parishioner.

Gay gave Annie a hug, then returned to his account. "At that moment, another rifle crack rang out. Marty pitched forward, dropping his rifle and reaching out to Aran, hoping the Gortman would brace his fall. I heard him scream something, but couldn't make out the words.

"Before Marty fell, I was running back downhill behind our

advancing line, toward Aran's position. Some of the Gaels were still moving forward, but others had dropped to the ground confused. As per Aran's earlier instructions, our lads began firing in the air, over the Republicans' heads.

"With my eyes first on Marty, then on Aran and then on the boulder, I saw a man in brown greatcoat and cap, drop to one knee.

"By this time I was flying...running over unseen rocks and avoiding obstacles that I'd stumbled over minutes before. At that point, I remember shouting, 'Aran look out...on your left!' But he didn't hear me.

"Slowly, the shadowy figure raised his rifle to his shoulder and fired. Suddenly, everything seemed to move at half-speed. White smoke rose from the barrel-end of the stranger's rifle. Aran dropped his Lee-Enfield and grabbed at his chest. Thrown forward by the impact of the bullet to his back, he tried to keep his feet under him but couldn't. Instinctively, he thrust out a hand, trying to break his fall, but it was no use. Slowly, he crumpled to the ground before my eyes.

"I had no idea Larry was right on my heels. He said I cried out a warning but it was too late. By the time I reached Aran he was gone."

With that pronouncement, Annie, who'd been holding back her sobs, let out a cry of agony. Tears streamed down her face. She bent forward, burying her head in the cradle of her arms. Her shoulders shook uncontrollably.

Uncle Peter sat at the top of the table stone-faced, his arms folded; his chin on his chest.

Aunt Niamh, now on her feet, moved around the table and stood behind Sarah Anne's chair. Her comforting hands on Annie's back seemed to help. Gradually, Sarah stopped crying.

Áine reached out and took her friend's hand.

Abruptly, Larry and Peter stood up and disappeared into the front of the house. A minute later they returned with glasses and a bottle of whiskey.

Father Francis bowed his head. With a wisdom born of comforting hundreds of others in the face of death's tragedy, he said, "Blessed be God forever, and blessed be our friend, Aran.

His bravery in this time of war was boundless. Bless his family and friends gathered around this table, especially his wife Sarah Anne. May Your love and the love of Your Son comfort and keep them. Amen."

Gay wiped away more tears and poured himself a large drink. It was a scene nobody ever wished to relive.

❧

Fifteen minutes later, with everyone's pain numbed with the comfort of hot tea and Jameson, Gay concluded his story.

"From out of nowhere, one word flashed through my mind, *Hawkins*.

"I looked up and saw the ghostly figure fire two or three more rounds in the direction of Lynch's party.

"Then the next thing I knew, whoever it was had turned and was running downhill. The coat-tails of his greatcoat were flying out behind like the wings of some strange prehistoric bird.

"With Aran at my feet, I stood and raised my rifle. I'd a clear shot and didn't miss.

"The gobshyte sprawled face-first on the ground, landing among some long grasses. As I approached, his legs were still twitching while the fingers of his right hand were opening and closing, almost spasmodically so.

"Coming to a stop, I drew my revolver. A dark stain had etched an almost perfect circle on the back of the coat. The bullet hole left by my rifle shot was centred in the middle of it.

"Being sure both the assailant's hands were visible and empty, I grabbed his two ankles and rolled him over. It was Palmerston or Eddy Hawkins, if you will, all right. He was still alive. A look of pain mixed with horror coloured his face.

"The man's lips moved and I think he said, 'Help me,' but I couldn't be sure.

"Then, Father, I did something I'm ashamed to admit. I spit in his face.

"'Hawkins,'" I said, "'take a good look at this mug of mine. It's the last one you'll ever see in this world. This is the face of the man who killed your brother and now this makes me two for two. Whether or not you killed Michael Collins, doesn't much matter any more. You killed my friend, and now, I'm taking back yours in return. May you rot in hell.'

"Sure I wasn't certain what I was going to do next, but the Lord above must have read my mind. Hawkins's body suddenly tensed. His eyes opened wide then slowly closed. His head slumped to one side. He was dead."

"Jaysus, Mary and Joseph," uttered the priest, crossing himself. "May our Lord bless him as He once blessed Judas Iscariot after His Son's death."

No one else at the table said a word.

Gay got up and poured himself some more tea and refilled several other cups. Throwing back the rest of his whiskey, he began to pace back and forth across the kitchen floor.

"As for Marty, nothing too serious, thanks be to God. He probably took a bullet meant for Aran.

"Back up above on the mountain, Lynch was down. Our lads swore they hadn't fired a shot with the intent of hitting or killing any of the fleeing men. I believe them.

"I'm guessing Hawkins had hit him by chance. Maybe he was aiming at Shadow, but at that range it would've been difficult to isolate just one man out of the eight. I remember seeing Hawkins fire several other shots before I nailed him.

"With Lynch's men disappearing into a wooded area and Caoimhín firing his distress call, most of the boys hurried to our aid. Eventually, McCullers patched up Marty. I organised three more details to carry Aran, Marty and the bollocks off the mountainside. The Nayler and four others had Lynch with them.

"Marty and Lynch were taken first to Newcastle and then on to Clonmel. Larry, Pat and I came straight here with Aran. I've dispatched Caoimhín Donleavy, Rory Sheehan and Sonny Lucey to drive to Gort. They'll break the news to Aran's family. If you're wondering about Hawkins, right now he's in the back of the Lancia. I'll take care of his body tomorrow sure."

❧

On Wednesday morning, several of the Flying Gaels made numerous telephone calls, notifying friends and leaving messages for former comrades telling of Aran's death.

While that was going on, Gay, Larry, Pat, Duncan and Rory drove Hawkins's tarpaulin-covered body up into the Galty Mountains. Like his brother before him, he was buried in an unmarked boggy grave.

That afternoon, Aran was waked by family and local village friends and acquaintances. At five o'clock, just prior to his removal to the church, Shadow and Danny Kelly arrived into the Black Rose. More tears and heartbreak followed.

❧

Sarah Anne, now three months pregnant and exhausted from the ordeal, decided to spend the night at the Black Rose instead of going home alone to the new flat above the jeweller's. She'd hardly been absent from her husband's side over the past day and a half.

Gay, Larry, Shadow, Pat, Danny and a patched-up Marty Richardson, now on crutches, acted as his honour guard. They took turns the night with their dear friend in St. Mary's Church.

❧

Sun and blue sky greeted the crowd gathering at St. Mary's on Thursday morning. Locals said it was the largest funeral they'd ever remembered in Cahir. Besides the Gortman's parents, grandfather, two sisters and four of his six brothers, all of the Flying Gaels were present. Marty, with his leg in a cast from the bullet's bone fracture, stood leaning against the open door of the church. He introduced himself and spoke with many of the people as they streamed inside. He'd been told by the doctor in Clonmel that there'd been some nerve damage, but with any luck, he should make a satisfactory recovery.

Liam Tobin and Tom Cullen arrived an hour early, driving down from Dublin with General Richard Mulcahy as their passenger. They informed Gay that William Cosgrave and Kevin O'Higgins would be at Glasnevin when they arrived for the burial later that afternoon.

Of course Shadow and Danny had special seats near the altar. What war had divided, death now was reuniting.

A small convoy of troopers from the disbanded 2nd Battalion of the Dublin Guards was also on hand.

The Naylor had arranged with a neighbour for his father to come. In the same motor car the two brought along Rory's three sisters. Mary and little Annie O'Mahony were accompanied by their older sister Hannah. Unfortunately, Gran was in ill-health and couldn't make the journey.

Much to everyone's surprise Tom Barry made a last minute appearance. Though he was still a wanted man, no one made any hostile move to arrest him or his four travelling companions.

With the addition of some local dignitaries, politicians and village folk the church was full to overflowing.

Peter and Niamh invited the out-of-town mourners back to the Black Rose for an early lunch of sandwiches and drinks after the Mass.

At half eleven, with Aran's flag-draped coffin in the hearse, all those going to the burial left for Dublin. The polished wooden casket was bedecked with a blanket of yellow roses. Several bouquets of white lilies with assorted greens along with a special arrangement of wild flowers had been placed next to the Gort-man for this his last journey on earth.

The black hearse, followed closely by the Buick sedan with Gay, Áine, Larry and Sarah Anne inside, headed out of Cahir for Dublin. Sixteen other vehicles with family, friends and comrades trailed along behind.

❧

Riding in the backseat of the Buick, Sarah Anne felt so lost and alone. Sure she knew she could count on Gay and Áine for comfort and support. Of course, Uncle Peter and Aunt Niamh would be there for her too. They'd been like a second family to her for years now. But so much of her world had revolved around

Aran and his work. Now there was a huge void. With one child to care for and another on the way, there'd be the worry of expenses and how she'd manage after everyone else became caught up in their own lives again.

As the wife of a National Army officer, she'd receive a monthly allowance, but would that be enough to support the three of them? She didn't know.

Gay had told her not to worry, but that was easier said than done. Larry had already been hinting about returning to Virginia. Gay said there was no question about his family staying in Ireland. This was his home, now and forever. Besides, the war wasn't over, at least not yet. With the Republicans not having time to digest what the effects of Lynch's death might have on their cause, sure there was always the chance things might be hotting up again soon.

Marty, though he said it was most premature, thought he might resign his commission and head back to Boston. A place at Harvard Medical School was waiting for him that autumn. The future of the Flying Gaels was up in the air too. Her brother Gabriel was the likely candidate to succeed Aran, if in fact Mulcahy decided the group should stay together.

One factor that might convince the Minister to keep the flying column intact was the fear of Republican revenge. As with Michael's death, the Irregulars feared the Free Staters might retaliate and in a way they did. The passing of the Public Safety Bill was a form of retaliation just as Lynch's Orders of Frightfulness were his way of answering back. Now, with Liam Lynch dead, seemingly at the hands of the government, the IRA might up the ante. On the other hand, the Republicans just might fold their cards and go home.

Shadow had said there was a job for Gay and Larry if they chose to move to Limerick. His bakery business continued to flourish and with his advancing years, he wanted to hire a general manager. There was even the possibility that a top position at the mill in Cahir might open up soon as well.

By some quirk of fate, Áine and Annie had been talking about opening a flower shop in the village. By sheer coincidence, just a month ago, several people in Cahir had approached them about doing just that.

All of those thoughts flashed through Sarah Anne's head. But the one thought of having to spend the rest of her life without Aran Roe O'Neill was too overwhelming. Its crushing impact blotted out all the goodness she could ever contemplate. Though her eyes were closed, her tears of grief found their way out.

All she could picture was Aran, lying dead on the side of the Knockmealdowns. Gay had told her that when the Gaels were about to lift him onto their makeshift stretcher for the journey downhill, he noticed that Aran had fallen on a carpet of vivid blue spring gentian. A tiny white wild flower, that he didn't recognise, blanketed the ground there as well.

Despite the tragedy of Aran's death, the mountainside was beautiful, overlooking the River Suir valley as it did. When Gay asked Annie if she'd like to visit the spot some day, she closed her eyes and slowly nodded yes.

❧

As the hearse and parade of cars turned off the Finglas Road, through the main gates into Glasnevin Cemetery, they were met by a squad of National Army soldiers.

Silently, the mourners left their motor cars and gathered around the hearse. As the last persons approached, out from the caretaker's cottage stepped the president and vice-president of Saorstát Éireann. Sarah Anne knew it was the same cottage Aran had spent a short time in while on the run following Pearse and Connolly's surrender to General Lowe in the spring of '16. Aran had pointed it out to her on the day Arthur Griffith was buried.

With sombre expression on their faces, the two men walked forward and offered their condolences to Sarah Anne, Aran's family and the McCrackens.

Marty's parents, his grandmother and sister were waiting too. Additionally, Mrs. Pearse and one of her daughters, Margaret, had made a special effort to come.

Off to one side, there was an elderly couple Annie didn't recognised.

Seeing Sarah Anne looking in their direction, the two strangers approached and asked if she was Aran's wife. After acknowledging she was, they introduced themselves as Thomas and Anna Coogan. They offered her their condolences and explained who they were. Anna said, "Aran spent a night with us after the Easter-Week troubles."

Nodding, Thomas asked, almost in a whisper, "I'd given him my new Colt revolver back then. What ever became of it?"

"Oh my God," said Annie. "He carried it with him all these years. In fact, it was in his hand when he was killed. My husband's spoken of you two often and prised that revolver. I know it saved his life on many occasions. My brother, Gabriel over there, has it now. Thank you both for coming and remembering him."

"No, our thanks must be extended to you. It's because of the courage shown by men like Aran that Ireland's self-respect has been restored. Nineteen sixteen reawakened our very soul. Ireland's independence isn't far off."

With the soldiers at attention and the mourners grouped around, the casket containing Aran's body was removed from the hearse.

Shadow, Gay, Larry, Danny, Pat and Aran's father stepped forward. They lifted the coffin onto their shoulders, and following the honour guard, walked the short distance to his grave. Immediately to the right of the Gortman's burial place was Michael Collins's grave. Several bouquets of fresh flowers decorated the grass around the simple cross that marked the grave of the Big Fellow.

With the coffin resting on two wooden planks atop the earth's opening, Father Francis led the assembled in prayer. He then blessed Aran once again with Holy water and incense. The casket was raised, the supports removed and slowly it was lowered into the depths of the cool Irish earth. Shadow stepped forward and said a few words. Moments later, a rifle salute broke the prayerful silence.

The ceremony was over.

Many in attendance lingered to pay their final respects. As they left, handfuls of earth and flowers were thrown down into the grave.

Those not returning home were invited to spend the night at the Clarence Hotel on the quays. A special dinner had been arranged for half eight that evening.

The last to leave the graveside were the five McCrackens and Sarah Anne. With their tears and prayers bidding Aran goodbye, they turned and walked away, leaving the Irish Rebel to sleep peacefully among the heroes and the ordinary of Ireland's dead.

❧

The IRA Army Executive met on 20 April. They elected Frank Aiken as Chief of Staff to replace the fallen Liam Lynch. Declaring an end to hostilities was discussed, but no agreement could be reached.

The following day, de Valera issued a statement to the Free State government, outlining the terms upon which a negotiated settlement might be reached.

Cosgrave's Cabinet rejected the offer out of hand. The terms were too one-sided and in direct violation of the Treaty. They included the removal of the oath of allegiance to the crown, all IRA property was to be returned and its funding restored. In addition, buildings must be made available so the IRA could safely store its weapons, under seal of course. O'Higgins stated, "This is not going to be a draw, with a replay in the autumn."[7]

On 24 April, beaten, disorganised and dispirited, Aiken issued an order for the men of the Republic to cease fire, dump arms and retire from the field. Dev issued his own set of orders: "Military victory must be allowed to rest for the moment with those who have destroyed the Republic.... You have saved the

---

7. Litton, op. cit., 122.

nation's honour, preserved the sacred national tradition, and kept open the road of independence."[8] [9]

For the most part, the order to 'go to ground' was obeyed, except for a few pockets of continued resistance in more remote areas. Despite this, however, National Army forces continued to search for weapons and make arrests well into the summer. Fifteen thousand Republicans were already being held in jails or internment camps when the cease-fire was declared. Many more were added to this total in the months following the official cessation of hostilities.

At the war's end, if one could call it an end, seventy-seven Republican prisoners had been executed by their fellow Irish. Forever more, the number '77' serves as a mark of Cain, indelibly burned into the hearts and minds of many in Ireland.[10]

There are no reliable figures accounting for Ireland's Civil War dead and wounded. General Mulcahy was quoted as saying 'around 540 pro-Treaty troops were killed between the Treaty's signing and the war's end.' Official Government figures peg the number of army deaths at eight hundred between January, 1922 and April, 1924. As for Republican deaths, no records exist. Most likely, though, they were in excess of Free State casualties. Many civilians also died or were wounded, but the total number is unknown. One thing is clear, however, the number of Irish killed during the ten-month Civil War certainly exceeded the Irish fatalities from the earlier thirty-month War of Independence.[11]

The conflict's effect on the Irish economy was horrendous. One report states: "The war...imposed a major burden on the new government. It has been estimated that the material dam-

---

8. Ibid.

9. As part of his message to his fellow Republicans, whom he referred to as 'Soldiers of the Republic, Legion of the Rearguard', de Valera assured them their sacrifices hadn't been in vain. He noted that though today's Irish people were tired of war & its unwelcome consequences, they would soon forgive & forget. At some future time, they would again rally around the standard. "When they are ready," he wrote, "you will be, and your place will be again as of old with the vanguard." Kee, op. cit., 174.

10. Sixteen Irishmen were executed by the British authorities after the 1916 Easter Rebellion. Twenty-four more were executed by Britain during the Anglo-Irish War of Independence, 1919-1921.

11. Hopkinson, op. cit., 272-273.

age involved amounted to more the £30 million and that it cost around £17 million to finance the war. Property damage easily exceeded that of the Anglo- Irish War [1919-1921]."[12]

❦

With a general election scheduled for 27 August, it was de Valera's hope that a strong showing by people sympathetic to the Republicans' plight would begin to tip the balance of power back in his favour.

Though still a wanted man, Dev campaigned over the summer. He tried consolidating his power base and rallying his impotent Republican government.

An insight into his political thinking at the time can be found in one of his statements: "The more progress we make at the coming elections, the more certain will be our victory at the subsequent elections. The elections give an opportunity for explaining our position and reaching the people, which I think should be availed of."[13]

His party's weakness, however, was only magnified by its refusal to recognise the Free State government and, if elected, candidates pledged to abstain from taking their seats. Thus, without representation, his party would be powerless.

While speaking at a meeting in Ennis on 15 August, Éamon de Valera was arrested and imprisoned without trial as a danger to 'public safety.'

In a bit of biting satire, one historian noted, "...[de Valera] was captured just in time to escape oblivion. He might have faded out in ridicule, had the government treated him 'as a political curiosity', because there were deep divisions in the Republican ranks over his role in calling off the Civil War."[14]

Speaking for the government, O'Higgins said, "Through him, and at his instigation, a number of young blackguards had

12. Ibid., 273.
13. Litton, op. cit., 123-124.
14. Dwyer, op. cit., 334.

robbed banks, blown up bridges, and wrecked railways, and that in the name of an Irish Republic."[15]

Surprisingly, pro-Treaty Sinn Féin which had officially changed its name in March, 1923 to Cumann na nGaedheal didn't do as well as expected. They scored only sixty-four seats to the former anti-Treatyite Republicans, now just calling themselves Republicans, forty-four. The Labour Party won fourteen seats, a loss of three TDs from the last election.

Many pundits pointed to the government's harsh and vindictive treatment of prisoners as the reason many people rejected their party at the polls. This Free State policy had pushed Ireland to the brink of becoming an immoral, physical slaughterhouse.

On 19 September 1923, the newly elected 4th Dáil assembled at Leinster House in Dublin. William Cosgrave was re-elected President and an Executive Council of the Irish Free State was appointed.

❧

The last of the war's Republican prisoners, many untried and never convicted of a crime, were finally released in July, 1924 after Éamon de Valera, the last prisoner being held in Kilmainham Gaol, was given his freedom. A general amnesty was declared by the Free State government on 8 November 1924.

❧

While the Civil War had raged in the twenty-six counties, the Northern Irish government consolidated its power and clamped down on IRA activists and nationalist sympathisers. Craig met with little resistance in doing so.

The Boundary Commission, one of the compelling reasons the Irish delegation signed the Treaty in December, 1921, finally met in 1924, two years after its intended meeting date. Craig reiterated his refusal to nominate a NI representative. So the

---

15. Ibid.

British Government, acting in his stead, selected J. R. Fisher, a Unionist and personal friend of Craig's, to serve on Northern Ireland's behalf. Eoin MacNeill represented Saorstát Éireann and the Honourable Mr. Justice Richard Feetham, the official British commissioner, acted as London's representative and committee chairman.

The three met off and on for a year. Finally, in November 1925, a newspaper leak revealed virtually no changes in the border between North and South except for a small bit of County Donegal that was to be ceded to the Belfast government.

The official findings of the Commission were never released. Northern Nationalists had been betrayed.

Instead of pressing the point, Dublin struck a deal with London. The British would waive the findings of the Commission in return for voiding some of Ireland's financial obligations owed London as per the Treaty.

Irish Republicans, on both sides of the border, felt as their ancestors must have when England reneged on her 1691 Treaty of Limerick.

❧

In January, 1926, with de Valera again serving as president of Republican Sinn Féin, he tried to enter the Dáil and take his rightfully elected seat. His party forbade him doing so, stating their abstention from the Dáil was a matter of principle.

Thus, in March of that year, he resigned his presidency and formed his own political party which he called Fianna Fáil.[16] Little did he realise it at the time, but this party would become one of his most enduring accomplishments.

On 9 June 1927, a national election was held in the twenty-six counties to elect members to the 5th Dáil Éireann. It was the first election contested with Fianna Fáil in the running. They did surprisingly well, taking forty-four seats to Cumann

16. Fianna Fáil (Warriors or Soldiers of Destiny) was founded on 23 March 1926 & was destined to become Ireland's largest & most powerful political party. Its origins can be traced back to the 1920s with its links to the anti-Treaty/Sinn Féin movement, its ties with Éamon de Valera & the Republican IRA secessionists.

na nGaedheal's forty-seven. The other sixty-two seats were won by smaller political parties and independents. Cosgrave lost his ruling majority and his government fell in September. Dev's new party had taken most of the support and membership from the abstentionist anti-Treaty/Republican Sinn Féin party and claimed them for itself.

That summer Dev put Michael Collins's boast that the oath of allegiance was a meaningless gesture to the test. At the first meeting of the new assembly, held on 11 August 1927, Dev entered the Dáil. He signed his name in the roll book and stated he'd no intention of taking any oath to an English crown. With himself and his colleagues' names duly signed in the Dáil's register, the Fianna Fáil TDs simply walked into the assembly hall and took their elected seats. There were no objections lodged by the opposing parties.

As one person remarked at the time, "What if he'd done that in 1922, would there have been any need for a Civil War?" Many agreed there wouldn't have been.

❧

The bitter residue of Civil War erupted again that summer. On Sunday, 10 July 1927, while on his way to twelve-o'clock Mass, Kevin O'Higgins was gunned down by three men. He died several hours later. The culprits were never caught.

Though best remembered for his harsh Civil War policies, the Dáil's Executive Council Vice-President, Minister for External Affairs and Minister for Justice, O'Higgins in recent years had developed a policy of a free and undivided Ireland within the British Commonwealth based on the equality of Commonwealth member nations.

Still remembered as a Collins man, most in Ireland knew which side of the political divide his assassins represented.

❧

Because of Cosgrave's teetering political position, new elections were called for on 15 September that year. The Cumann na nGaedheal party did manage to win a slight majority over Fianna Fáil, but it was only able to form a ruling coalition government with the help of the Farmer's Party and other independent TDs.

The handwriting was on the wall, however. De Valera's political power and acumen were on the ascendancy. Cosgrave's was on the decline.

In 1932, backed by an election programme designed to appeal to a wide section of the electorate while at the same time downplaying its Republican heritage, Fianna Fáil swept into office, ousting Cumann na nGaedheal.[17]

People wondered if democracy had truly taken root in Ireland. If defeated at the polls, would Cosgrave's backers, 'winners' of the Civil War, hand over the reins of governmental power to de Valera's party, whose members had largely precipitated but 'lost' the war?

Thankfully, the election was peaceful, and yes, the Irish Free State did see its first change of government since its inception. No political coup d'état materialised.

In tribute to William Cosgrave, one journalist wrote, "He proved a conservative and stoical politician – a safe pair of hands who patiently created the new Free State out of its revolutionary disarray, giving it an honourable if unadventurous character and prepared it for its maturity as a nation state."[18] [19]

---

17. On 3 September 1933, Cumann na nGaedheal joined forces with the Centre Party & the Army Comrades Association to form a new Irish political party called Fine Gael (Family of the Irish). Though Fine Gael was to become one of Ireland's two dominant political parties, it origins are forever tied to the early 1920s & its links with the pro-Treaty/Sinn Féin party championed by Arthur Griffith & Michael Collins.

18. Purdon, op. cit., 46.

19. A major criticism of Cosgrave's administration was their inability to view the Treaty as a means to an end instead of an end in itself. Rather than working the agreement to obtain an even greater degree of Irish independence, his government tended to concentrate on implementing the specific terms of the Treaty & not going beyond or stretching its limits. This was exactly what Michael Collins *didn't* want to have happen. He envisioned the Treaty as a way of winning a greater measure of freedom as per his 'stepping-stone' theory.

With the reins of power back in his hands, as he always thought they should be, Dev set about dismantling the Treaty. In April, 1933, the Chief said he would, "…not willingly assent 'to any form of symbol' incongruous with the country's status as a sovereign nation."[20]

Dev went on to say at that same Arbour Hill Cemetery[21] gathering, "Let us remove these forms one by one so that this State that we control may be a Republic in fact and that, when the time comes, the proclaiming of the Republic may involve no more than a ceremony, the formal confirmation of a status already attained."[22]

The oath of allegiance was abolished in 1933. The termination of farm annuities to the British Exchequer was another welcomed move. The powers of the Governor-General were reduced and the right of appeal to the British Privy Council was eliminated.

Finally, in 1937, the Irish constitution that Collins had crafted in 1922 was rewritten and approved of by the people. Officially Saorstát Éireann became Éire or Ireland and Éamon de Valera became the country's first Taoiseach or Prime Minister.

Additionally, the office of the Governor-General was abolished and replaced by a ceremonial head of state or president. Douglas Hyde, the Irish scholar and first president of the Gaelic League, initially established in 1893, became Ireland's first President a year later. Also, 1938 saw another element of the Anglo-Irish agreement reversed. The contentious Treaty-port issue was finally resolved with the twenty-six county government retaking control of three of the four contentious Irish seaports.[23]

---

20. Dwyer, op. cit., 338.
21. Arbour Hill is a small, former British Army cemetery near Phoenix Park which contains the mass-grave burial plot of fourteen of the sixteen executed, 1916 Easter Rebellion leaders including Patrick & Willie Pearse, James Connolly, Thomas Clarke, Thomas MacDonagh, Joseph Mary Plunkett, Edward Daly, Michael O'Hanrahan, John MacBride, Éamonn Ceannt, Seán Heuston, Con Colbert, Michael Mallin & Sean MacDiarmada.
22. Ibid.
23. The dockyard ports at Berehaven & Queenstown [today Cobh], both in Co. Cork, plus the one at Lough Swilly harbour, Co. Donegal, were returned to Irish control. The fourth Treaty port in Belfast Lough reminded in British hands as it was situated in Northern Ireland.

De Valera's dream of Ireland becoming a Republic was on the brink of becoming reality…but, alas, a divided one, for during Dev's watch the border remained unchanged.

As one historian stated, "During the 1930s, de Valera systematically dismantled the Treaty and thus proved that Collins was right in his assessment that the 1921 agreement could be the stepping-stone to the desired freedom. On coming to power in 1932, de Valera admitted he had underestimated the real significance of the Treaty."[24]

❧

With all the changes the Long Fellow nursed Ireland through, the one area in which he remained steadfast was his attitude toward his political rival, Michael Collins. He continually downplayed Michael's contributions to Ireland, his political significance and the high esteem in which many continued to hold Collins.

No better example of his spiteful attitude toward the Big Fellow can be found than in his refusal to permit a monument to be erected on Michael's grave site.[25] Finally, in 1939, after more than four years of bloody-minded obstinacy, an eleven-and-a-half-foot-tall Celtic Cross was placed over Mick's grave, but the Long Hoor had to approve everything: the cross was to made of limestone not marble; the cost was not to exceed £300; there could be no public subscription to defer its expense; there could be no advance publicity regarding its design, cost or installation; the inscription on the front had to be in Irish with wording approved by himself; the inscription on the back had to include 'M. Collins erected by his brothers and sisters'; and no member of

---

24. Ibid., 337.
25. The dispute over the marker was much more involved than its mere size, though that was a definite issue. The Collins's plot is eight feet by four feet. The proposed base of the monument was four feet, six inches. Thus, three inches on either side would project outward on to the bordering pathways. Finally, the encroachment was approved of considering the likelihood that the pathways would never be used as a burial ground. Coogan. *Michael Collins.* op. cit., 429.

the family could be present at its installation with the exception of Michael's brother Johnny.[26]

Fearing that others might later accuse him of being small-minded, Dev signed the monument's order of approval E. de Valera, Acting Minister for Finance instead of Taoiseach. Obviously, he was embarrassed that other world leaders might accuse him of pettiness when it was learned that the Irish Prime Minister himself had become embroiled in such absurd theatre.[27]

❧

In 1948, an election for the 13th Dáil was held. Fianna Fáil lost to a coalition (inter-party) government. A relatively unknown politician, John Costello, become Taoiseach.

During that year, Ireland adopted new legislation abolishing the External Relations Act which had been written into the revised 1937 constitution. This allowed Ireland to break the last governmental tie formally connecting it with Britain.

On 7 September 1948, Costello declared the Irish state to be a Republic. Seven months later, the twelve-year existence of Éire ended and the Republic of Ireland was officially established. The date of that historic occasion was Easter Monday, 18 April 1949; thirty-three years after Patrick Henry Pearse, James Connolly and Aran Roe O'Neill marched out.

---

26. Besides Johnny Collins, there was a priest, an altar boy and the head grave digger…no one else!

27. Toward the end of de Valera's life, he said, "It's my considered opinion that in the fullness of time, history will record the greatness of Collins and it will be recorded at my expense." Ibid., 432.

21

"Oh, the cold winds from the mountains are calling soft to me,
The smell of scented heather brings bitter memory.
The wild and lonely eagle up in the summer sky,
Flies high o'er Tipperary where my young love died."

Adapted from the song lyrics "Shanagolden"
by Seán McCarthy

HOLY SATURDAY AFTERNOON, 16 APRIL 1949

With the coming of evening, the sunny brightness and spring warmth of Holy Saturday afternoon slowly faded. The brilliance of day gradually dissolved into muted shades of diffused light.

An ebb tide of chilliness enveloped the old cemetery. Silently, like fingers unfolding in the grass, dark shadows crept out from weathered tombstones. Stately elm, oak, beech and chestnut trees, still busy shaking the spring newness from their green leaves, swayed gently with each gust of air.

A light wind had sprung up, blowing in from Dublin Bay. The scented sea breeze smelled salty sweet and was punctuated by the doleful cries of wheeling, snow-white gulls.

Small knots of people and the occasional solitary figure seemed reluctant to conclude their goodbyes to death-silenced loved ones. Gradually, though, the assembled mourners wended their way toward the Finglas Road entrance of Glasnevin Cemetery.

Before they exited, though, many momentarily paused and blessed themselves before Daniel O'Connell's tomb or the grave of Charles Stewart Parnell. Others stopped and paid tribute to the scores of Republicans, buried in their own special plot. These dead were some of the Irish who'd fought and sacrificed for their nation's freedom.

Softly, somewhere in the distance, a church bell struck five o'clock. Its ringing acted like a magnet, calling the visitors away from Glasnevin and back to their homes, to an Easter Vigil or to some other much-anticipated weekend celebration. Tomorrow was Easter Sunday. On the following day, Easter Monday, the Irish Republic would be officially recognised.

Martin Richardson, the first of the three to arrive, walked into the cemetery against the tide of those leaving. The fifty-two-year-old bachelor and doctor drove across country to be in Dublin this weekend.

After finishing his medical degree at Harvard University, he'd completed a hospital internship in Amerikay. Then, after practicing medicine in Boston for some years, he returned to live in Ireland twelve years ago. Today, he had a busy practice in Galway.

Waiting among the silent tombstones for the other two to arrive, he was reminded of his beloved, ninety-year-old grandmother, Nanna, who'd died in her sleep back in the summer of '25. Because of the distance involved and the expense, he hadn't come home for her funeral.

Sixteen years later, his father died. Tragically, while attending a legal conference in Belfast, his hotel was bombed by German aircraft in May, 1941. On the 15th, the Luftwaffe dropped thousands of incendiaries on the city. His father was one of one hundred fifty people killed. Many more were seriously wounded or burned.

Today, his mother still lived in their modest family home on Carlingford Road. His sister, Mary Elizabeth, and her husband Malachy shared the house with her.

Often described as good-looking, maybe even distinguished, Marty's grey eyes still twinkled, whether he was with friends or a patient. His surgery in Galway was in constant demand. There was normally a waiting list of people trying to see him.

Despite all his medical successes, the past was always with him. He walked with a pronounced limp. Hawkins's bullet had torn through his left thigh, fracturing his femur. The residue of that day in the Knockmealdown Mountains continually nagged at him.

Gabriel McCracken was the next to arrive. He joined Marty on the old wooden bench just down the path from Aran's and Michael's graves. Gay, a successful businessman, was now a noted Irish senator.

After giving Shadow's offer of work some thought, he and his family moved to Limerick in the autumn of '23. Quickly, he'd become general manager of the Doyle Bakery 'empire,' as he liked to call it. Despite the economic slow-down of the 1930s, the business flourished. Today, the bakery had expanded and supplied bread and baked goods to retail establishments throughout Ireland.

With the death of their father in 1931, Larry left Ireland and returned to the McCracken family farm in America.

As for his political career, Gabby was first elected to Seanad Éireann in 1944, as an independent. Currently, he was serving his second term in Ireland's legislative upper body.

While living in Limerick, Áine and he had two more children, a son, Aran, and a second daughter, Deirdre. Today, their first-born, Mary Margaret, was twenty-eight and more beautiful than ever, according to her proud father. She's currently completing a law degree at UCD and living in Ballsbridge, a Dublin suburb, with her two roommates.

As the two old friends sat in reflective silence, Gay pulled out a packet of cigarettes and offered one to Marty. Both men tamped the end of their fags on the bench before Gay struck a match and lit them.

Though Gabriel, now sixty-three, was still taller than most Irishmen, time and gravity tugged at him. There was a distinct roundness to his upper back which he constantly tried to correct by squeezing his shoulder blades together and throwing his chest out. His once short-cut hair was now almost completely white. Long silver locks curled around behind his ears and touched the top of his coat collar. Still a handsome man, age had taken its toll in other ways. Thanks to cigarettes, tea and stout, his teeth had lost their whiteness. Once the light-hearted conversationalist, he'd grown more thoughtful and quiet in his older age. Today, his soft confident voice echoed a lifetime of experience and, like his father before him, his discerning opinions were often sought by others.

At twenty past five, Richard 'Shadow' Doyle appeared at the top of the footpath. Waving to his old comrades, he hurried forward to meet them.

Shadow, the elder statesman of the troika, was sixty-seven or was it sixty-eight? He claimed to have lost track somewhere along the way. Aran's mentor, Gay's friend and Marty's success story, Shadow shook each man's hand and joined them on the bench. He'd never remarried.

On this pleasant spring evening, the three men spent a few minutes making small talk and catching up on the latest news.

Several weeks after Aran's funeral, Shadow was arrested and, luckily, spent only two months in a Limerick jail. A kindly warder, out of respect for who he was and by virtue of his having to care for three young daughters, released him. Through some political chicanery, Richard Mulcahy issued him a full pardon.

With the war over, he returned to the family bakery in Limerick and reaped the benefits of working with Gay.

All three of Shadow's daughters now were married. Today, they'd families of their own. Between visiting them and Sarah Anne, Gay's new nickname for him was 'travelling man.'

As one of his ways of dealing with Aran's death, Shadow became a second father to Patrick Michael. During the lad's growing-up years, the two would go off for days, sometimes even weeks at a time. They'd fish, hike, camp and live in the outdoors. After one unusually long outing among the mountains of Connemara, Gay accused Shadow of trying to relive the time the Irish Rebel and he had spent in the Appalachians during the winter of 1916–1917. When pressed about it, Shadow just smiled and said nothing.

Now stooped and with just a fringe of white hair ringing the back of his head, the Limerick man read stories to his grandchildren and painted. He'd discovered his artistic talent quite by accident. Having bought some water-colours as a gift for Patrick, the two had tried them out. Lo and behold, as if by magic, each picture Shadow finished seemed to come to life. Without benefit of a single lesson, he'd become a celebrity. Galleries in Limerick, Cork, Dublin and Belfast clamoured for his work.

Though in recent years he'd spent less time at his easel, he still maintained it helped him connect with Ireland's past. It was his wish that others might learn to appreciate and understand their country's beauty, history and its struggles through his art. Just two months ago, Shadow and Irish artist Seán Keating had done a show together in their native hometown of Limerick.

As for Marty's success story, five years ago he'd saved Shadow's life. Unexpectedly, a persistent head cold had moved to his chest. Four days later, the illness turned into pneumonia. With a raging fever and his body racked with pain, Sarah Anne rushed Shadow to Galway and his friend's surgery. After two weeks in hospital and two more as a patient in Marty's home, the baker recovered. He was lucky. Many seldom survive such a serious sickness. Thankful to be alive, the Limerick man never let Marty forget he'd saved his life. Whenever Shadow praised his friend's medical acumen, the American-trained doctor just smiled, held up a hand and said, "What are friends for?"

With their legs aching to move, the three men rose and walked some of the paths that zigzagged their way through the cemetery.

When together, they usually didn't talk of the 'old days,' but it was constantly on their minds. Their fight for freedom, the times they spent with Mick Collins, Liam Mellowes, Arthur Griffith, Dick Mulcahy, Tom Barry, just to name a few, were indelibly etched in their minds. Of course, the memories of Aran were there as well. That young, fearless warrior who'd gradually matured, becoming a seasoned veteran…a man of high ideals bound by the sinuous bonds of love and loyalty.

❧

Back at Aran's and Michael's graves, the three spent several more moments in prayerful reflection.

"I wish Aran could've lived to see Monday come. The fulfilment of a dream, his dream," said Marty. "We *all* miss you so, Aran Roe O'Neill."

"Sure, and it would have been wonderful to see the both of them, Mick and Aran, at the head of the parade," said Gay. "Sadly, it was Michael's determined efforts to save Ireland from Civil War that were eventually overwhelmed by the Long Hoor's willingness to do nothing…and now the man has the balls to say he's proven the Big Fellow right. It just makes me sick to think about it."

"Gay, I won't argue with you. It was a tragic time, but as long as Marty's putting Aran and Mick at the head of the parade, I think Griffith and Pearse should be there too," said Shadow.

"Sure wasn't it Arthur's Sinn Féin and his insistence on an Irish Ireland coupled with Pat's Easter Rebellion that awoke the nation's consciousness? Together, those two paved the way for our independence."

"Yes, they did, Shadow, and while we're at it, please God, don't forget the millions of brave Irishman and women that went before them," said Marty.

"…and those that went after," added Gay.

❧

Sarah Anne came to Dublin for the Easter Monday ceremony too. Now fifty-three, she'd brought her two children with her. Patrick Michael was twenty-six. Seeing him walk into a room, you'd swear it was Aran. He was the mirror image of his father. With the Gortman's tragic, early death, he'd never known his father, but he'd heard the stories. As a recent graduate of UCG, Patrick Michael was embarking on a fledgling political career under the tutelage of another Irish rebel's son, Seán McBride.

Sitting with her mother and brother in the lounge of the

Clarence Hotel was Fiona Aisling O'Neill, who'd been born on 27 September 1923. It was clear the young woman certainly favoured her mother. Tall, brunette, with flashing blue eyes, she was her brother's junior by only ten months.

Fiona had taken over the running of her mother's flower shop in Cahir six years ago. Bright, intelligent and very attractive, she'd all the lads in town after her just as her mother had when she'd first come to Ireland.

...and as for Sarah Anne, the sadness of her life had been brightened by the love of two wonderful children. With Uncle Peter and Aunt Niamh's encouragement and Shadow's generous financial backing, she'd opened a flower shop in Cahir after Aran's death. When Gay and Áine decided to live in Limerick, Annie moved out of her flat and into their wonderful cottage.

After Aran's death, she began keeping a journal. It was her way of helping to cope with her loss. One book became two. Two became four and so on.

In reading bits and pieces to friends, they all encouraged her to write more. "Try putting your thoughts into story form," they said. "Submit them to a publisher," suggested Áine, "people would love reading your words."

Sure to make a long story short, in 1927, Annie submitted a piece called "Oh, the Cold Winds from the Mountains." Surprisingly, her offering was accepted and published. It proved to be a great success, winning the Best Short Story of the Year Award sponsored by a leading Irish newspaper.

More writing successes followed. Today, Sarah Anne O'Neill was one of Ireland's favourite novelists. Her books were in constant demand. On Monday, as part of Dublin's Irish independence celebration, her seventh novel was being launched at Eason's bookshop in O'Connell Street, only a few steps from the GPO where it all began back in 1916. Entitled *The Irish Rebel*, it was the story of a young man and woman who fell in love against the backdrop of the war and rebellion.

EPILOGUE:

"Life springs from death;
and from the graves of patriot men and
women spring living nations."

Patrick Henry Pearse

OH, SPEAK THEIR NAMES
by Ben O'Hickey

Oh speak of them in tender tones, and drop a tender tear,
For those who left their happy homes, without a thought of fear.
For those who fought our land to free,
Yes those who fought and bled!
Oh speak their names in tender tones,
The martyred Irish dead.

Yes, sing their praises night and day,
And keep their memories green,
No braver, nobler men than these the world has ever seen,
They gave their lives to save our land,
In history write it red.
Oh speak their names in tender tones,
The martyred Irish dead.

22

"Oh those who died for liberty,
Have heard the eagle scream.
All the ones who died for liberty,
Have died but for a dream."

Liam Weldon

EASTER MONDAY, 10 APRIL 1966

*I*n 1966, as part of the fiftieth anniversary of the 1916 Easter Rebellion, one of Dublin's most brilliant and talented balladeers, Liam Weldon, penned some lyrics and put them to music as part of that celebration.

In remembering Ireland's 20th-century watershed Rebellion and its ensuing War of Independence, many were seduced by the wealth of inspiring words and glowing references to the lofty ideals of the past.

But in spite of all the tributes, Liam Weldon remembered the many promises politicians had made and had broken since those heroic events occurred. He recalled the bitter recriminations showered upon those who'd fallen victim of Civil War differences in the 1920s and beyond. These were people who'd been denied work, threatened by yobs and forced to leave their own country.

Liam Weldon, a community leader and social activist, knew

513

his was an unpopular voice, focusing on the country's shortcomings instead of simply applauding its successes. This was a man from the Liberties who knew first-hand the economic, political and social maladies that had infected Ireland over the past forty years...much of it springing from the diabolical alienations born during Ireland's Civil War.

Liam Weldon was a man not afraid to question Ireland's evolving independence, especially as it affected the marginalised, the disenfranchised, the ignored and the forgotten. He hated waste and wanted to challenge the complacency of middle class stagnation. His strong words were clear and unmistakable. They called to the nation's leaders to recognise that all was not right and that a reassessment of present-day directions was needed.

❧

DARK HORSE ON THE WIND
by Liam Weldon

Oh those who died for liberty,
Have heard the eagle scream.
All the ones who died for liberty,
Have died but for a dream.
Oh rise, rise, rise, Dark Horse on the wind,
For in no nation on the earth,
More broken hearts you'll find.

The flames leaped high, reached to the sky,
Till they seared a nation's soul.
In the ashes of our broken dreams,
We've lost sight of our goal.
O rise, rise, rise, Dark Horse on the wind,
And help our hearts seek Róisín,
Our soul again to find.

Now charlatans wear dead men's shoes,
Aye and rattle dead men's bones.
Ere the dust has settled on their tombs,
They've sold the very stones.
O rise, rise, rise, Dark Horse on the wind,
For in no nation on the earth,
More Pharisees you'll find.

In grief and hate our motherland
Her dragon's teeth has sown.
Now the warriors spring from the earth,
To maim and kill their own.
O rise, rise, rise, Dark Horse on the wind,
For the one-eyed Balor still reigns king,
In our nation of the blind.

GLOSSARY

'16: the Easter Rebellion, 1916

'47: Black '47 (1847); the Great Famine, 1845–1850

'98: the Rebellion of 1798, the Year of Liberty

1881 Land Bill: Irish land reform bill passed by British House of Commons

Áine: (pron: OWN-ya) Ann/Anne

Amadán: fool

Amerikay: America

Angelus: (Angelus domini – the Angel of the Lord) a devotional exercise said by Catholics commemorating the Incarnation at 6 am, 12 noon and 6 pm daily

Anti-Treaty [IRA]: Irishmen and women (& members of the IRA) who opposed the Treaty. They were commonly known as Republicans, anti-Treatyites or anti- Treaty (IRA). The men who retained their earlier Volunteer status or now enlisted in the anti-Treaty military (unpaid) were nicknamed 'Irregulars' or simply 'bands.'

Ard Fheis: (pron: Are-desh) a (political) convention

Aisling: (pron: ASH-ling) vision or dream

*Asgard***:** Erskine Childers's yacht used to import arms into Ireland, 26 July 1914

Auxie: an abbreviation for the Police Auxiliary Cadet Division of the RIC. They were former British officers recruited and sent to Ireland to reinforce the 'King's writ.' Paid £1/day, with their 'licence to kill' attitude, they were even more vicious than the Tans. Arriving in mid-summer 1920, there were over 500 Auxies in southern Ireland by that autumn & about 2,000 by summer, 1921.

Banshee: a female spirit whose wailing cries warn of pending death; 'the white angel of death'

Béalnabláth: (pron: Bale-nu-blaw) translated by some as meaning the 'Mouth of the Flowers.' It was in this narrow ravine or valley in rural West Cork that Michael Collins was killed on 22 August 1922.

Beggars' Bush Barracks: built in 1827 for quartering British infantry soldiers stationed in Dublin. The name Beggars' Bush is much older, however. It refers to a 17th- or 18th-century area of then rural, undeveloped land about three miles from Dublin Town's centre. It was covered in trees, bushes and undergrowth and was an area where beggars often congregated.

Bewley's: Bewley's Oriental Cafés, noted for their teas, coffees, breakfasts, etc.; a Dublin tradition since 1840

Black & Tans: former enlisted British soldiers recruited and sent to Ireland to reinforce units of the Royal Irish Constabulary. Paid ten shillings/day, they were infamous for their brutal reprisals, particularly upon the Irish civilian population. First arriving in early 1920, their ranks rose to over 1,000 by late summer. Their nickname originated from their mismatched bottle-green (RIC) and khaki (British Army) uniforms. From a distance, they appeared to be dressed in black and tan apparel. By some strange coincidence, along the Tipperary-Limerick border, there were several famous packs of hunting dogs with similar two-tone coloured coats also nicknamed 'Black & Tans.' By summer, 1921, their numbers had swollen to approximately 9,000.

Blackguard: a villain

Blighter: a contemptible or annoying person

Bloody Sunday: 21 November 1920; Michael Collins's men, in a surprise attack, killed fourteen British intelligence agents in their living quarters. Later that day, the Auxies killed thirteen and wounded sixty innocent persons who were watching a Gaelic football match at Croke Park in Dublin.

Bollocks: the testicles or an exclamation of contempt, e.g., nonsense, rubbish, etc.

Bodhran: (pron: BOW-ron) a round, single-headed, hand-held drum covered in animal skin, usually goat. It is played with the hand or a single wooden beater called a cipín (pron: kip-peen) or little stick. The instrument evolved from the tambourine and resembles a tray used on Irish farms to separate chaff and grain.

Bog-trotter/Bogman: a country hick or simpleton

Bonnet: the hood of a motor car

Boot: the trunk of a motor car

Boreen: a narrow country lane

Broadstone: a Dublin Railway Station north of the River Liffey (today no longer in existence)

Bugger about with: mess about; mislead

Bugger off: go away

Bunch of Grapes: an historic London pub on Brompton Road in Knightsbridge

Buttie: a sandwich

C-in-C: abbreviation for Commander-in-Chief

Caffler: a layabout

Cailín: a colleen; a girl

Castle, the: Dublin Castle; seat of British civil authority in Ireland since the 16th century

Cathal: (pron: CAW-hull) Charles

Ceann Comhairle: (pron: cam COR-la) the speaker or leader of the Irish parliament or assembly

Chancel: part of a church located near the alter; usually reserved for the clergy and the choir; often separated from the nave by steps or a screen

CID: abbreviation for Criminal Investigation Department; it was headquartered in Oriel House, St. Stephen's Green, Dublin; later it was coupled with the DMP and, finally with the Ireland's national police force, Garda Síochána na hÉireann (Guardians of the Peace of Ireland), in 1925

Civic Guard: an armed, civilian police force founded in February, 1922, replacing the disbanded RIC. Its responsibility was to maintain law and order in the twenty-six counties excluding Dublin. Dublin Town was still under the authority of the DMP until 1925. Michael Staines was its first commissioner.

Clan na Gael [Family of Gaels]: an Irish nationalist organisation founded in New York City in 1867. In the 20th century, it helped equip the Irish Volunteers (1913) and supported the 1916 Easter Rebellion

Clann na Poblachta [Family of the Republic]: (pron: PUB-la-ca) a political party founded by Seán McBride in 1946; it appealed to disillusioned young urban voters and Republicans who'd lost hope of achieving anything through violence.

Clarence Hotel, the: a hotel opened in the 1850s & located on Wellington Quay, Dublin

Claymore: a Scottish two-edged broadsword

Coddin': to joke with; to fool; to play a trick on someone in a good natured way

Copper-fasten: make more secure; firmly fasten

Coppers: policemen

Connacht: one of Ireland's four provinces composed of 5 western counties

Corn: any cereal crop before or after harvest, e.g., wheat, oats, barley, rye, etc.

COS: abbreviation for Chief of Staff

Cot: a child's bed often with high sides

Courgette: zucchini

Craic: (pron: crack) a good time; fun

Cronje hat: a broad brimmed hat worn by the Irish Volunteers; often the left brim was pinned to the crown; named for General Piet Arnoldus Cronje (1840–1911), leader of the South African Republican military forces, Anglo-Boer War, 1899–1902

Crossley tender: a lorry, usually fitted with benches behind the cab, often used for transporting military troops; a military transport vehicle or tender

Cumann na mBán [Society of Women]: established in 1914 as an auxiliary corps of the Irish Volunteers. It played a largely supportive role during the 1916 Easter Rebellion but displayed a more active military presence in the War of Independence and Irish Civil War.

Cumann na nGaedheal[1] [Party/League/Society of the Irish]: the name of two distinct Irish political organisations or parties. The first Cumann na nGaedheal was formed in 1900 by Arthur Griffith as an umbrella group of small anti- English organisations. Its aim was the total de-Anglicisation of Ireland with an emphasis on Irish culture, Irish economic protectionism and the development of an Irish foreign policy. They lobbied the IPP to abstain from Westminster in 1902 and protested the visit of King Edward VII to Ireland in July, 1903. It became part of Sinn Féin in 1907 and had no link to the political party of the same name founded by William Cosgrave in 1923.

Cumann na nGaedheal[2]: an Irish political party founded by William Cosgrave in March, 1923 with its origins springing from the pro-Treaty wing of Sinn Féin. With Cosgrave as its only leader, it played an important role in formation and consolidation of the new Irish Free State (Saorstát Éireann). It was the 'victorious' Irish Civil War party. Notable accomplishments include the establishment of the Garda Síochána na hÉireann (1923), the Electricity Supply Board (ESB) (1927), the Shannon hydro-electric scheme (1924) and Agricultural Credit Corporation (1927). Its greatest international successes were implementing the terms of the Anglo-Irish Treaty (1921) and partnership in drafting the Statute of Westminster (1931) which put the parliaments of the Commonwealth's dominions on a par with the Imperial Parliament in Westminster. The party lost power in 1932 and was absorbed by Fine Gael at its founding in 1933.

Cumann na Poblachta [League/Society of the Republic]: (pron: PUB-la-ca) a short- lived, anti-Treaty, political party founded by Éamon de Valera in mid-March, 1922

Cumann na Saoirse [Society of Freedom]: established by pro-Treaty women in February, 1922 who'd broken away from anti-Treaty Cumann na mBán women

Curragh, the: a large, flat, open plain in Co. Kildare famous for its horse racing and horse stables; since the end of the 1600s, the 'Curragh Camp' was used as a British military campsite, training ground and barracks for up to 10,000 soldiers; with the departure of British troops from Ireland in 1922, it was taken over by the new Free State government as an military training facility; it was also used as an anti-Treaty IRA prisoner-of-war camp, 1922–1924

Dáil Éireann: the Irish (Republican) parliament or assembly

DMP: abbreviation for Dublin Metropolitan Police

Dodgy: cunning; artful; tricky

Donkey's years: a long time

Draper: a retailer of textile fabrics

Dray: a low horse-drawn cart, usually without sides for hauling heavy loads

Dungannon Clubs: social, cultural, temperance clubs with a political agenda; a series of clubs design to appeal, at least initially, to Ulster nationalists, many of whom were IRB members, first established in Belfast, 1905. The clubs' founders wished to evoke the memories of the Dungannon (Co. Tyrone) Convention of 1782 and the subsequent winning of Irish legislative independence via Henry Grattan's Patriot Parliament in College Green, Dublin. Loosely tied to the Sinn Féin movement, it went a step further, boldly declaring its aim was the establishment of an Irish Republic.

Éire: Ireland

Éireann: (pron: AIR-inn) Ireland

Éireann go brách: Ireland forever

Eejit: idiot

Eoin: John

Executive forces, the: another name for the IRA anti-Treaty Army; the name was taken from the sixteen-man army Executive chosen at the 26 March 1922 Army Convention. On 9 April, a new Constitution was cobbled together, outlining the goals of the breakaway army under the leadership of its COS, Liam Lynch. Joining him on the Executive (Cabinet) were Frank Barrett, Stan Dardise, Liam Deasy, Tom Hales, Tom Maguire, Joe McKelvey, Liam Mellowes, Seán Moylan, Joe O'Connor, Rory O'Connor, Peadar O'Donnell, Florrie O'Donoghue, Seán O'Hegarty, Ernie O'Malley & Séamus Robinson. The Executive's proposals failed to gain unanimity within its own ranks and were ignored by the PG. Liam Lynch still held out hope that the new Free State constitution Collins was overseeing would satisfy Republican demands.

Farrier: a blacksmith who also looks after horses

Fecken': thoughtless; ineffective; irresponsible

Feckin': fucking

Feckless: thoughtless; ineffective; irresponsible

Fenian: Specifically, a member of the Fenian Brotherhood founded in the United States (1858) whose stated purpose was freeing Ireland from British rule. Collectively, any Irish Republican seeing the overthrow of British rule in Ireland and closely associated with the IRB

Fianna Fáil [Warriors/Soldiers of Destiny]: Irish political party founded 23 March 1926 by Éamon de Valera after he broke away from Sinn Féin two months earlier. It historic ties lie with the anti-Treaty/Republican IRA wing of Sinn Féin. Today, it is Ireland's largest and most politically powerful party.

Fine Gael [Family of the Irish]: Irish political party founded 3 September 1933 from the consolidation of Cumann na nGaedheal, the Centre Party and the Army Comrades Association. It historical ties lie with the pro-Treaty wing of Sinn Féin and was closely associated with the politics of Arthur Griffith and Michael Collins. Today, it is Ireland's second largest political party.

Fíona: (pron: FEE-ona) fair

Flags: flagstones

Flashes: (Scottish) coloured patches of cloth attached to a garter worn at the top of leg stockings

Flying column, a: a military force capable of rapid movement and independent operation. Michael Collins used this tactical idea to great advantage during the Anglo-Irish War of Independence. Usually composed of 15-20 men dressed in civilian attire, a column would attack, engage the enemy and withdraw quickly. Fighting on familiar ground, they had a distinct advantage over British Army units who employed more traditional battlefield techniques. General Tom Barry was famous for his training and use of flying columns in Co. Cork.

Flying Gaels: an imaginary flying column founded in 1919–1920 by Michael Collins, Liam Mellowes, Richard 'Shadow' Doyle and Aran Roe O'Neill; played an active role in Anglo-Irish War of Independence and the Irish Civil War

Footpath: sidewalk

Foolscap: writing paper named for the imprinted watermark revealing a fool's cap

Foreigner, the: the English; the Sassenach; the Stranger

Fry, a: a large Irish breakfast consisting of eggs, rashers, sausage, black and/or white pudding, tomato, bread and butter (jam is optional)

Furze: gorse; a thorny bush with small yellow flowers

GAA: abbreviation for Gaelic Athletic Association; founded in the Hayes Hotel, Thurles, Co. Tipperary in 1884

Gaelic League: founded in Dublin in 1893 to promote the Irish language and culture

Gaffer: an old fellow; a boss or foreman

Gaiters/Puttees: leather or cloth lower-leg coverings usually worn by military personnel

Gaol: (pron: jail) jail

Garda Síochána na hÉireann [Guardians of the Peace of Ireland]: founded in 1923, it replaced the Civic Guards. Today, it remains Ireland's national unarmed police force.

Gearóid: Garrett; Gareth

GHQ: abbreviation for general headquarters

Glengarry hat: a brimless Scottish hat with a cleft down the centre and usually with two ribbons hanging down at the back

GOC: abbreviation for general officer commanding

GPO: abbreviation for Dublin's main General Post Office

Hectare: a measure of land equal to about 2.5 acres

Hipped roof: a roof with sides and ends inclined at an angle

Holyhead: a northwest Welsh harbour on Holy Island in the Irish Sea

Hood: re: motor car – convertible top or open roof

Hoor: whore

Hoor's melt: a vulgar reference to a woman's genitalia

HQ: abbreviation for headquarters

Invincibles, the: a short-lived IRB splinter group that murdered two British officials in Dublin in 1882; five of the six assassins were hanged in Kilmainham Gaol

IO: abbreviation for intelligence officer

IPP: abbreviation for Irish Parliamentary Party (the dominant Irish political party of the late 1800s & early 1900s)

IRA: abbreviation for the Irish Republican Army, first established in Ireland in 1916 and briefly in Canada in 1865

IRB: abbreviation for the Irish Republican Brotherhood, founded in 1858 and closely associated with the Fenian Brotherhood in the United States

Irish Constabulary: the Irish police force prior to 1867

Ironmongery: a hardware store

Is toil: in favour of; for

IV: abbreviation for Irish Volunteers, founded in Dublin on 25 November 1913

Jackeen: name for a Dubliner by a non-Dubliner. As Dublin was always the most 'English' of Irish towns, the term was coined as a derisive reference to one's 'possible' national loyalty. Jack refers to Union Jack, the British flag; the suffix 'een' stands for 'little' in Irish; thus, the word literally means 'little Jack.'

Jameson: an Irish whiskey

Jaysus: Jesus

Jumper: a sweater

Kingsbridge: a Dublin Rail Station (today Heuston Rail Station is located along River Liffey at the western end of town)

Kingstown: a harbour on the Irish Sea, Co. Dublin (today the seaport of Dun Laoghaire, pron: DUN-gary)

Land League, the: the National Land League of Mayo was founded in 1879 by Michael Davitt. Two months later, it was expanded to form the Irish National Land League. Its objectives were to reduce landlord rents and champion peasant land ownership. Two years later, with its leadership in jail, it was proscribed and the movement soon collapsed. Much of its membership became part of the Irish National League, a political movement targeting widespread reform in Ireland.

Larne: a seaport on Belfast Lough, Co. Antrim

Leinster: one of Ireland's four provinces composed of 12 counties

Liam: William

Liberties, the: an economically-deprived urban ghetto on the south-side of central Dublin

Lifted: kidnapped

Looped windows: a narrow, vertical slot in a door, wall or window designed for emitting light as well as for looking or shooting through

Lorry: a military tender; a motor-driven truck

MI5: abbreviation for Military Intelligence Section 5; the British Secret Service responsible for safeguarding homeland security founded in 1909

Míceal: Michael

Military tender: a lorry or a motor-driven truck

Mountjoy Jail: Dublin's largest prison

MP: abbreviation for a member of parliament; legislative member of the British House of Commons

Mufti: civilian attire; clothing worn by someone who also wears a (military) uniform

Munster: one of Ireland's four provinces composed of 6 counties

Namby-pamby: lacking vigour or drive; weak

Nancy (as in nancy boy): an effeminate man

NCO: abbreviation for non-commissioned officer

Neep: the Scottish name for turnip

NI: abbreviation for Northern Ireland

Ni toil: not in favour of; against

Night bucket: a chamber pot

O/C: abbreviation for officer commanding

Óglaigh na hÉireann: (pron: O-gla na air-en) the Irish Volunteers

Old stick/old stock: an affable label/nickname for a friend

Orangeman: a member of the Orange Order (1795); usually Protestant with pro- unionist/loyalist sympathies holding anti-Catholic, anti-Nationalist/ Republican sentiments

Over the moon: extremely happy; delighted

Pádraic/Pádraig: Patrick

Paddy's, a: an Irish whiskey

Peadar: Peter

Peckish: hungry

Peeler: slang for policeman; nicknamed after British Prime Minister Sir Robert Peel who reorganised the Irish Constabulary in 1836

Petrol: gasoline

PG: abbreviation for the Provisional Government

PGI Committee: the Provisional Government of Ireland Committee was established under the authority of the Anglo-Irish Treaty. Britain's headman was Winston Churchill while Michael Collins was Ireland's chairman. The Committee oversaw the day-to-day issues of Ireland's Treaty compliance.

Phoenix Park: a park in the western suburbs of Dublin Town; the largest enclosed urban park (1,752 acres) in Europe

Piaras: (pron: PEER-as) Peter

Pince-nez glasses: eye glasses with a nose clip instead of earpieces

Pinny: an apron, usually with a bib

Pitch: a sport playing field

Plenary session: a meeting attended by all members

Plenipotentiary power: having full, independent power of action; absolute power

PM: abbreviation for prime minister

Press: a large (often partly shelved) cupboard or armoire/wardrobe for hanging and storing items/clothes

Priomh Aire: prime minister/first minister

Pro-Treaty (IRA): Irishmen and women (& members of the IRA) who supported the Treaty. They were commonly referred to as 'Free Staters,' 'Staters,' pro- Treatyites or pro-Treaty (IRA). The men joining the military (paid) were part of the Provisional National Army, National Army or Irish Army.

Pub: a public house

Puck goat: a billy-goat, enthroned on a chair in Killorglin town square (Co. Kerry) as part of a large fair held each August

Quay: (pron: key) a ship's dock or wharf

Queenstown: a harbour southeast of Cork City, Co. Cork (today Cobh, pron: cove)

Quisling: a collaborator or fifth-columnist; a traitor

Range/cooker: a stove

Rashers: thinly sliced bacon or ham

RIC: abbreviation for the Royal Irish Constabulary, Ireland's police service from 1822–1922; the title 'Royal' was added after the Rebellion of 1867

Rota: a roster

Rozzer: slang for a policeman

RUC: abbreviation for the Royal Ulster Constabulary, Northern Ireland's police service founded in 1922 as a result of the Anglo-Irish Treaty, 1921

Saorstát Éireann: Irish Free State

Sassenach: originally a Scot-Gaelic word (Sasunnach) meaning Saxon. In Ireland, it became a nickname for the English occupier; the Stranger; the Foreigner

Scraw: a thin layer of grassy turf that covers a roof's wooden frame and is positioned directly under the roof's outer thatch covering.

Seamus: James

Seán: John

Seanad Éireann: Ireland's senate

Serviette: a napkin

Sgian dubh: (pron: Skeen doo) a Scottish knife or dagger tucked in the top of a near- knee-length stocking. Dubh means black which usually refers to the colour of the handle or possibly the fact that the weapon is a secreted or hidden one.

Shillings: 20 shillings = 1 Irish punt (pound)

Shoneen: a traitor or collaborator

Shyte: shit

Side car/jaunting car: a light, two-wheeled, horse-drawn vehicle

Slag: to tease or make fun of, usually in a kindly way

Slán: farewell

Slán leat: (pron: slawn-let) goodbye

Slanging: to use abusive language

Slanging match: a prolonged exchange of insults

Slieve na mBán: Irish for Mountain of Women and the nickname of the Rolls Royce 'Whippet' armoured car used as part of Michael Collins's military convoy on his fateful journey to West Cork at the end of August, 1922; a mountainous peak in Co. Tipperary

Sliotar: a hurly ball used for playing hurling

Snaps: photographic pictures

Snug: a panelled or partitioned booth, usually in a public house

Sod[1]: a piece of dried peat/turf used for fuel

Sod[2]: an unpleasant or awkward person/thing (often considered a taboo word)

Sods of turf: cut and dried pieces of peat used for fuel

Soft day: a damp, drizzly, wet day

Sopper: another name for a strawboy

South Dublin Union: a workhouse or public institution where the destitute receive food and lodging in return for work

Spanner: a wrench

Sporran: a leather or a fur covered Scottish pouch usually worn in front of the kilt

'The Squad' or Twelve Apostles: first a volunteer then later a paid 'hit squad' organised by Michael Collins in 1919 to intimidate and/or murder spies and assassins in Ireland (Dublin) who were in the employ of the British government

Stone: a unit of weight = fourteen pounds

Stoat: a flesh-eating member of the weasel family

Stranger, the: the English, the Sassenach; the Foreigner

Strawboy: usually neighbourhood boys/young men who dress up in old (women's) clothing & who blacken their faces or wear long straw masks; they appeared, uninvited, at wakes, weddings or special occasions; they often sing, dance, recite poetry or play music in return for drink or money; its considered bad luck to turn them away

Súgán chairs: (pron: SUE-gone) woven rope or reed bottom and backed chairs

Ta: thank you

Tan War, the: the Anglo-Irish or Irish War of Independence (1919–1921)

Tans: the Black & Tans

Taoiseach: chief/ruler/prime minister

TD: Teachta Dála, legislative member of Irish assembly, Dáil Éireann

Tea: a cooked evening meal or supper (as in 'he had his tea…')

Thatch: a roof covering of straw or any variety of dried grasses

Tiles, as in a day/night on the tiles: a day/night of drinking in a pub often spent standing at the bar

To put on the long finger: to put off or delay taking any action

Toadying: an obsequious hanger-on; fawning

Tory: a member of the British Conservative political party

Townland: a land division of varying extent; the smallest geographical unit of land usage in Ireland. Smaller than a parish or county, a townland can vary in size from as small as half an acre to more than 7,000 acres. Size often depends on fertility of the soil. The more fertile the land is, the smaller the townland size and vise versa.

Trap: a light, two-wheeled, horse-drawn carriage

Trifle, a: a dessert; a confection of sponge cake with custard, jelly, fruit, cream, etc.

Trucileers: a contemptuous nickname given to some new members of the National Army who'd enlisted after the Truce was declared in July, 1921. Though many had never fired a shot for Ireland during the War of Independence, they were pleased to be linked with those who had.

UCD: abbreviation for University College Dublin

UCG: abbreviation for University College Galway (today NUI Galway: National University of Ireland, Galway)

Uilleann pipes: (pron: ILL-awn) uillinn, the Irish word for elbow, is a bellows-blown Irish instrument (double-octave range) using the elbow to power the bag instead of being mouth-blown as is characteristic of the Scottish bagpipes (single-octave range).

Ulster: one of Ireland's four provinces composed of 9 counties

USC: abbreviation for the Ulster Special Constabulary founded on 1 November 1920

UVF: abbreviation for the Ulster Volunteer Force founded in late 1912-early 1913

Vaughan's Hotel: an inexpensive Dublin hotel on Rutland Square (today no longer in existence but the building still stands, #29 Parnell Square)

Verge: a grass edging along the side of a road

Warder: a prison officer/a guard

Whitehall: a street in London on which many British government offices are located.

Windscreen: a windshield of a motor car

Woodbines: cigarettes manufactured in Belfast

Yobs: louts, thugs

Yoke: an unspecified thing that defies description; sometimes used in a derogatory way when referring to a person: "He's a strange yoke."

SELECTED
BIBLIOGRAPHY

Augusteijn, Joost, ed. *The Irish Revolution 1913–1923*. Houndmills, Basingstoke, Hampshire, United Kingdom: Palgrave, 2002.

Barry, Tom. *Guerilla Days In Ireland*. Dublin: Anvil Books Limited, 1989.

Bell, J. Bowyer. *The Gun in Politics: An Analysis of Irish Political Conflict, 1916–1986*. New Brunswick, NJ: Transaction Publishers, 1991.

Bennett, Richard. *The Black and Tans: The British Special Police in Ireland*. New York: Barnes & Noble Books, 1995.

Boylan, Henry. *A Dictionary of Irish Biography*. Niwot, CO: Roberts Rinehart Publishers, 1998.

Collins, Michael. *The Path to Freedom: Articles and Speeches by Michael Collins*. Dublin: Mercier Press, 1995.

Coogan, Tim Pat. *Michael Collins*. London: Arrow Books Limited, 1991.

Coogan, Tim Pat. *De Valera: Long Fellow, Long Shadow*. London: Hutchinson, 1993.

Coogan, Tim Pat. *The IRA: A History*. Niwot, CO: Roberts Rinehart Publishers, 1993.

Coogan, Tim Pat and George Morrison. *The Irish Civil War*. Boulder, CO: Roberts Rinehart Publishers, 1998.

Cooke, Pat. *Scéal Scoil Éanna: The Story of an Educational Adventure*. Dublin: Office of Public Works, 1986.

Curtis, Liz. *The Cause of Ireland: From the United Irishmen to Partition*. Belfast: Beyond the Pale Publications, 1994.

Davis, Richard. *Arthur Griffith and Non-Violent Sinn Féin*. Dublin: Anvil Books, 1974.

Deasy, Liam. *Brother Against Brother*. Cork, Ireland: Mercier Press, 1998.

Doherty, Gabriel and Dermot Keogh. *De Valera's Ireland.* Douglas Village, Cork, Ireland: Mercier Press, 2003.

Donnelly, Mary. *The Last Post: Glasnevin Cemetery.* Dublin: National Graves Association, 1994.

Doyle, Roddy. *A Star Called Henry.* New York: Viking, 1999.*

Durney, James. *The Volunteer: Uniforms, Weapons and History of the Irish Republican Army 1913–1997.* Naas, Ireland: Gaul House, 2004.

Dwyer, T. Ryle. *Michael Collins and the Treaty: His Differences with De Valera.* Dublin: The Mercier Press, 1988.

Dwyer, T. Ryle. *Big Fellow, Long Fellow: A Joint Biography of Collins & de Valera.* New York: St. Martin's Press, 1998.

Dwyer, T. Ryle. *The Squad and the Intelligence Operations of Michael Collins.* Douglas Village, Cork, Ireland: Mercier Press, 2005.

Elliott, Marianne. *The Catholics of Ulster: A History.* New York: Basic Books, 2001.

Farry, Michael. *The Aftermath of Revolution: Sligo 1921–1923.* Dublin: University College Dublin Press, 2000.

Feehan, John M. *The Shooting of Michael Collins.* Cork, Ireland: Royal Carbery Books, 1991.

Feeney, Brian. *Sinn Féin: A Hundred Turbulent Years.* Madison, WI: The University of Wisconsin Press, 2002.

Flanagan, Thomas. *The End of the Hunt.* New York: Dutton, 1994.*

Forester, Margery. *Michael Collins.* Dublin: Gill and Macmillan, 1971.

Garvin, Tom. *1922: The Birth of Irish Democracy.* Dublin: Gill & Macmillan, Ltd., 1996.

Golway, Terry. *For the Cause of Liberty: A Thousand Years of Ireland's Heroes.* New York: St. Martin's Press, 1998.

Greaves, C. Desmond. *Liam Mellows and the Irish Revolution.* London: Lawrence and Wishart, 1987.

Griffith, Kenneth and Timothy O'Grady. *Ireland's Unfinished Revolution: An Oral History.* Boulder, CO: Roberts Rinehart Publishers, 1998.

Hart, Peter. *The I.R.A. & Its Enemies: Violence and Community in Cork 1916–1923.* Oxford, United Kingdom: Oxford University Press, 1999.

Hart, Peter. *The I.R.A. at War 1916–1923*. Oxford, United Kingdom: Oxford University Press, 2003.

Hart, Peter. *Mick: The Real Michael Collins*. New York: Viking Penguin, 2006.

Hopkinson, Michael. *Green Against Green: A History of the Irish Civil War*. Dublin: Gill and Macmillan, 1988.

Jackson, Alvin. *Ireland: 1798–1998*. Oxford, United Kingdom: Blackwell Publishers Ltd., 1999.

Jordan, Neil. *Michael Collins: Film Script and Journal*. London: Vintage, 1996.

Kee, Robert. *The Green Flag: Volume Three: Ourselves Alone*. London: Penguin Books, 1989.

Kostick, Conor. *Revolution in Ireland: Popular Militancy 1917 to 1923*. London: Pluto Press, 1996.

Lalor, Brian, general ed. *The Encyclopaedia of Ireland*. Dublin: Gill & Macmillan, 2003

Liam, Cathal. *Consumed In Freedom's Flame: A Novel of Ireland's Struggle for Freedom 1916–1921*. Cincinnati, OH: St. Pádraic Press, 2001.*

Litton, Helen. *The Irish Civil War: An Illustrated History*. Dublin: Wolfhound Press Ltd., 1995.

Llywelyn, Morgan. *1921*. New York: Forge, 2001.*

Macardle, Dorothy. *Tragedies of Kerry 1922–1923*. Dublin: Irish Freedom Press, 1998.

Macardle, Dorothy. *The Irish Republic*. Dublin: Wolfhound Press, 1999.

MacAtasney, Gerard. *Seán MacDiarmada: The Mind of the Revolution*. Nure, Manorhamilton, Co. Leitrim, Ireland: Drumlin Publications, 2004.

Mackay, James. *Michael Collins: A Life*. Edinburgh: Mainstream Publishing Company, 1996.

Macken, Walter. *The Scorching Wind*. London: Pan Books, LTD., 1988.*

Martin, David. *The Road To Ballyshannon: A Searing Novel of Twentieth-Century Ireland*. New York: St. Martin's Press, 1981.*

McGee, Owen. *The IRB: The Irish Republican Brotherhood from the Land League to Sinn Féin*. Dublin: Four Courts Press, 2005.

McRedmond, Louis, ed. *Ireland The Revolutionary Years: Photographs from the Cashman Collection, Ireland 1910–30.* Dublin: Gill and Macmillan & Radio Telefís Éireann, 1992.

Morrogh, Michael MacCarthy. *The Irish Century: A Photographic History of the Last Hundred Years.* Niwot, CO: Roberts Rinehart Publishers, 1998.

Moylan, Seán. *Seán Moylan: In His Own Words.* Aubane, Millstreet, Co. Cork, Ireland: Aubane Historical Society, Undated.

Neeson, Eoin. *The Civil War 1922–23.* Dublin: Poolbeg Press Ltd., 1995.

Nelson, Justin. *Michael Collins: The Final Days.* Dublin: Justin Nelson Productions Ltd., 1997.

Ó Broin, Eoin. *Michael Collins.* Dublin: Gill & Macmillan, 1980.

Ó Broin, León, ed. *In Great Haste: The Letters of Michael Collins and Kitty Kiernan.* Dublin: Gill & Macmillan, Ltd., 1996.

O'Casey, Seán. *Three Dublin Plays: The Shadow of a Gunman, Juno and the Paycock & The Plough and the Stars.* London: Faber & Faber Ltd., 2000.*

O'Connor, Frank. *An Only Child.* Boston: G. K. Hall & Co., 1985.

O'Connor, Ulick. *Michael Collins and the Troubles: The Struggle for Irish Freedom 1912–1922.* Edinburgh: Mainstream Publishing Company, 2001.

O'Donoghue, Florence. *No Other Law.* Dublin: Anvil Books, 1986.

O'Dwyer, Martin. *A Pictorial History of Tipperary 1916–1923.* Cashel, Co. Tipperary, Ireland: The Folk Village, 2004.

O'Farrell, Pádraic. *Seán Mac Eoin: The Blacksmith of Ballinalee.* Mullingar, Ireland: Uisneach Press, 1993.

O'Farrell, Pádraic. *Who's Who in the Irish War of Independence and Civil War.* Dublin: The Lilliput Press, 1997.

O'Flaherty, Liam. *The Informer.* New York: A Harvest Book, Harcourt, Inc., 1980.*

Ó Gadhra, Nollaig. *Civil War in Connacht 1922–1923.* Cork, Ireland: Mercier Press, 1999.

O'Hegarty, P. S. *The Victory of Sinn Féin.* Dublin: University College Dublin Press, 1998.

O'Keeffe, Jane O'Hea and recordings by Maurice O'Keeffe. *Recol-*

lections of 1916 and Its Aftermath: Echoes From History. Tralee, Ireland: 2005.

O'Malley, Ernie. The Singing Flame. Dublin: Anvil Books, 1992.

Osborne, Chrissy. Michael Collins Himself. Douglas Village, Cork, Ireland: Mercier Press, 2003.

O'Toole, Fintan. The Irish Times Book of the Century. Dublin: Gill & Macmillan Ltd., 1999.

Pakenham, Frank. Peace By Ordeal: The Negotiation of the Anglo-Irish Treaty. London: Pimlico, 1992.

Purdon, Edward. The Civil War 1922–1923. Cork, Ireland: Mercier Press, 2000.

Ryan, Desmond. Michael Collins. Dublin: Anvil Books, 1994.

Ryan, Louise and Margaret Ward, eds. Irish Women and Nationalism: Soldiers, New Women and Wicked Hags. Dublin: Irish Academic Press, 2004.

Ryan, Meda. The Day Michael Collins Was Shot. Dublin: Poolbeg Press Ltd., 1989.

Ryan, Meda. Tom Barry: IRA Freedom Fighter. Douglas Village, Cork, Ireland: Mercier Press, 2003.

Ryan, Meda. The Real Chief Liam Lynch. Douglas Village, Cork, Ireland: Mercier Press, 2005.

Sexton, Seán. Ireland: Photographs 1840–1930. London: Laurence King Publishing, 1994.

Taylor, Rex. Michael Collins. London, Four Square, 1958.

Travers, Pauric. Éamon De Valera. Dublin: Historical Association of Ireland, 1994.

Twohig, Patrick J. The Dark Secret of Béalnabláth. Ballincollig, Ireland: Tower Books, 1991.

Ward, Margaret, ed. In Their Own Voice: Women and Irish Nationalism. Crosses Green, Cork, Ireland: Attic Press Ltd., 2001.

White, Terence De Vere. Kevin O'Higgins. Dublin: Anvil Books Limited, 1966.

White, Gerry and Brendan O'Shea. Irish Volunteer Soldier 1913–1923. Northants, United Kingdom: Osprey Publishing, 2003.

Younger, Calton. Ireland's Civil War. Glasgow, Scotland: Fontana Press, 1990.

* Historical Fiction

ABOUT THE AUTHOR

CATHAL LIAM has authored two previous books on Ireland. *Consumed In Freedom's Flame: A Novel of Ireland's Struggle for Freedom 1916–1921*, first published in 2001, earned *ForeWord Magazine's* Book of the Year bronze medal for historical fiction. His *Forever Green: Ireland Now & Again* received the 2003 Book of the Year honourable mention award for travel essays, also from *ForeWord Magazine*. He currently lives in Cincinnati, Ohio with his wife, Mary Ann.

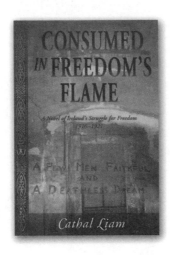

"The Irish have always had more history than they knew what to do with. Essayist and poet Cathal Liam has joined such fiction writers as Morgan Llewelyn and Liam O'Flaherty by assembling a comprehensive and intelligent piece of historical fiction for the general reader as well as those who can recite *'The Bold Fenian Men'* at a moment's notice. One does not have to read too far into the narrative to know that Liam understands how to capture an era filled with colorful and tragic men and women. As a result, *'Freedom's Flame'* is as compelling as the events it recounts."
—Rob Stout, *The Patriot Ledger* (Quincy, MA)

2001 Bronze Medal Winner for historical fiction, *ForeWord Magazine*

Another Irish offering from St. Pádraic Press

Forever Green:
Ireland Now & Again

by Cathal Liam

    This collection of writings by author Cathal Liam melds a rich stew of imaginative stories, political commentary and original poems. His affirmations and remembrances portray a changing Ireland in the twentieth century. From the bookend events of the 1916 Easter Rebellion to the 1998 Good Friday Peace Accord, Ireland's people, politics and culture have been in flux. Incontrovertibly Irish in tone and intent, this book recalls an Ireland of yesterday while critically probing the political machinations of today.

"Cathal Liam is an entertaining writer who moves from political commentary to poetry to storytelling and back again, all in the same book! This is a wonderful rollicking and passionate journey through the soul of Ireland and Irish-America."
—Terry Golway, author of *Irish Rebel: John Devoy and America's Fight for Ireland's Freedom; For The Cause of Liberty: A Thousand Years of Ireland's Heroes; So Others Might live: A History of New York's Bravest the FDNY from 1700 to the Present*

"With his deft prose and his deep knowledge of Ireland then and now Cathal Liam has captured the evolving face of 20th-century Irish politics, history and culture, as well as the isle's collective persona. His ability to relate the past to the present in *Forever Green: Ireland Now & Again* makes this book a must for anyone interested in not only Ireland's past and present, but also its future. An engrossing and entertaining work."
—Peter F. Stevens, Editor of *The Boston Irish Reporter* and author of *The Voyage Of The Catalpa: A Perilous Journey and Six Irish Rebels' Escape to Freedom*

2003 Honorable Mention Winner
for Travel Essays, *ForeWord Magazine*